BEDDING HIS VIRGIN MISTRESS

CHAPTER ONE

CARLY glanced discreetly at the small mixed party she was minding in her role as partner in one of the country's most prestigious and exclusive event-organising businesses, and wondered how long it would be before she could leave. The event was a fortieth birthday party for a banker and he'd chosen to have it at *the* London Nightclub CoralPink. It would not have been the venue she would have chosen but in a business where ultimately the customer was always right that was not her decision to make.

Already, though, she could see that their client's wife was beginning to look less than pleased at the amount of attention her husband was giving the upmarket eye candy on view. There were already half a dozen empty bottles of Cristal champagne on their table, and another of the men was chatting up a girl who had been walking past, inviting her to join them. Male libidos and wifely tempers were both beginning to rise ominously in the club's hormone-drenched heat, Carly realised dispiritedly.

She had balked at this assignment all along, knowing it wasn't her cup of tea. She preferred the kind of event she had supervised over the weekend—a jolly surprise eightieth birthday party held for a sharp-witted grandmother by her large family. It had taken some delicate finessing of finances on Carly's part to ensure that everything they had wanted was achievable within their modest budget, and she had been justifiably proud of the end result.

Mike Lucas's wife was going to explode in a minute if he didn't stop flirting with the young girl he had grabbed. Carly swiftly got up and made her way towards him, intent on defusing the situation before it got out of hand.

Ricardo didn't know why the hell he had allowed himself to be persuaded to come here. His appetite for the proposed business deal that had brought him here had already soured. The whole set-up was everything he loathed, and could best be summed up as rich, immoral men being pursued by greedy, amoral women, he decided cynically.

His attention was caught by the occupants of a table several feet away. A group of forty-something men, paunchy and sweating from a combination of the club's heat and the effect of the skimpily dressed young women thronging the room. Their wives and partners might be younger than they, but they were nowhere near as young as the girls the men were watching—apart from one. She was younger than the rest but still a woman and not a girl, and as Ricardo watched her she got up from her seat and walked round to the other side the table, where one of the men had started to paw a giggling leggy brunette for whom he had just ordered a bottle of champagne.

'Mike.' Carly smiled as she leaned towards him, strategically placing herself between him and the unknown girl.

'Hello, sexy. Want some champagne?'

Mike Lucas made a grab for her, pulling her down onto his knee and putting his hand on her breast.

Immediately Carly froze, warning anger zigzagging through the glance she gave him, but Mike was too drunk to notice. Still grinning, he pulled the other girl towards him as well. Unlike Carly, she made it plain that she was enjoying the attention.

'Look what I've got,' Mike called out to his friends, one hand on Carly's breast and the other on the other girl's. He jiggled them inexpertly and boasted drunkenly, 'Hey, what about this for a threesome, guys?'

Ricardo's hooded gaze monitored the small unsavoury scene. The sight of women selling their bodies was nothing new to him. He had grown up in the slums of Naples, and these women—these spoiled, pampered, lazy society women, with their designer clothes and their Cartier jewellery—were, as far as he was concerned, far more to be despised than the prostitutes of the Naples alleys.

He pushed back his chair and stood up, throwing a pile of banknotes down onto the table. The man who had invited him to the club was talking to someone at the bar, but Ricardo did not bother to go over and take any formal leave of him before quitting the club.

As a billionaire he had no need to observe the niceties that governed the behaviour of other, less wealthy men.

Ricardo studied the newspapers the most senior of his quartet of male PAs had left on his desk for him. He read them as he drank the second of his ritual two cups of thick, strong black coffee. Some tastes could be acquired, but others could never totally be destroyed or denied. He frowned, a look that was a formidable blend of anger and pride forking like lightning in the almost basalt darkness of his eyes.

He was not a prettily handsome man, but he was a man who commanded and indeed demanded the visual attention of others—especially women, who were aware immediately of the aura of raw, challenging male sexuality he exuded.

He reached for the first newspaper, flicking dismissively and contemptuously through its pages until he found what he wanted. A smile, in reality no more than cynically bared white teeth against the warmth of the skin tone that proclaimed his Italian heritage, curled his mouth without reaching his eyes as he glanced swiftly down the newspaper's much trumpeted, newly revised 'Rich List'.

He didn't have to look very far to find his own name. Indeed he could count on the fingers of one hand the names that came above his.

Ricardo Salvatore, billionaire. Estimated fortune… Ricardo gave a short, grim laugh as he looked at a figure that fell well short of his actual wealth.

Beneath his name there were also a couple of lines describing him truthfully as single and thirty-two years old, and untruthfully as having founded his fortune on an inheritance from his uncle. A further line offered the information that, in recognition of his charitable donations to a variety of good causes, it was rumoured that Ricardo Salvatore was to be given a knighthood.

Now Ricardo did smile.

A knighthood! Not a bad achievement for someone who had been orphaned by the deaths of his young Italian mother and British father in a rail accident, and who, because of that, had ended up growing up virtually alone in the worst of Naples' slums. It had been a tough and sometimes brutal way to grow up, but occasionally Ricardo felt that he had more respect and admiration for the companions of his youth than he did for the people he now mixed with.

Family ties and close friendships were not things that had ever formed a part of the fabric of his life, but he did not feel their absence. In fact, he actively liked his solitariness, and his corresponding freedom from other people's demands. He had learned young how to survive—by listening and observing—and how to make his own rules for the way he lived his life. He drew his strength from what existed within him rather than what other people thought of him. He had been just eighteen, fiercely competitive and ambitious, when he had gambled for and won the money that had enabled him to buy his first container ship.

He dropped the newspaper onto his desk, picked up the file adjacent to it marked 'Potential Acquisitions' and started to speed-read through its contents. Ricardo was always on the look out for promising new acquisitions to add to his portfolio, and Prêt a Party would fit into it very neatly.

The first time he had heard of the organisation had been when a business acquaintance had mentioned it in passing, commenting that he was a family friend of its young owner. In fact, knowing Marcus Canning as he did, he was rather surprised that a man as financially astute as Marcus hadn't seen the potential of the business for himself.

He gave a small shrug. Marcus's reasons for not acting on the potential of Prêt a Party were of relatively little interest to him. By nature Ricardo was a hunter, and, like all hunters, he enjoyed the adrenalin-boosting thrill of the chase almost as much as he enjoyed the ultimate and inevitable kill at the end of it.

Prêt a Party might only represent a small

'kill,' but Ricardo's preparations for the chase would still be carefully planned.

The normal avenue of obtaining detailed industry reports was not one he favoured; for one thing it tended to alert every other hunter to his interest, and for another he preferred his own methods and his own instincts.

The first thing he wanted to do was find out a good deal more about how the business worked—how efficient it was, how profitable it was, and how vulnerable to a takeover that would be profitable to him. The best person to tell him that was, of course, the owner, Lucy Blayne, but she was hardly likely to equip a potential and predatory buyer with such information. Which was why he had decided to pose as a potential client. The kind of fussy client who wanted to know every single in and out of how things worked and how his commission would be handled before he gave it. The kind of client who insisted on seeing Prêt a Party's organisational capabilities at first hand.

Of course in order to have these 'eccentricities' catered for, he in turn would have to dangle a very large and very juicy carrot in front of Lucy Blayne.

And that was exactly what he was going to do.

'Carly! Thank God you're back! It's absolute chaos here!'

Walking into Prêt a Party's smart but chaotic office in Sloane Street, one of the most upmarket areas of London, Carly acknowledged ruefully that things must indeed be chaotic for her once schoolfriend and now employer—kind-hearted and sweet-natured Lucy Blayne—to be in too much of a rush to ask Carly how things had gone last night.

One pretty but terrified-looking young girl who was new was rushing around trying to cope with the non-stop ringing of the telephone, whilst a couple more, who weren't new, were earnestly reassuring clients that, yes, everything was in hand for their big event.

'We're just sooo amazingly busy—that launch party we did for you-know-who, the It Girl of the moment's new jewellery range, got a mensh in *Vogue*. Nick's bringing us in so much new business,' Lucy enthused.

Carly said nothing. She had done her best not to let Lucy see how much she disliked Nick, and of course there was no way she could tell her friend why. Lucy was deeply in love with her new husband, and Carly knew how much it would hurt her to learn that Nick had actually come on to Carly herself within days of Lucy introducing him into the business.

'Oh!' The pretty young girl looked shocked and almost dropped the telephone receiver.

'It's the Duke of Ryle,' she told Lucy theatrically, in a cut-glass upper-class English voice. 'And he wants to speak to you.'

Lucy rolled her eyes. 'Don't disappear, there's something important I need to discuss with you,' she told Carly quickly, before saying cheerfully, 'Uncle Charles—how lovely. How is Aunt Jane?'

Smiling reassuringly at the flustered and flushed-faced young girl, Carly edged her way past the overflowing desks in the outer office and into her small private office, exhaling in relief as she stepped into her own circle of peace.

A note on her desk caught her eye and she grinned as she read it.

BEWARE—Lucy is in major panic mode—Jules

The three of them—Lucy, Julia and Carly—herself, had been at school together, and Carly knew that Jules, like her, had been extremely dubious at first when Lucy had told them she intended to set up an event organisation company.

But Lucy could be very persuasive when she wanted to be, and since—as Jules had pointed out—neither of them had any other job to go to, and Lucy, thanks to her large trust fund, could afford to both set up the business and pay them a respectable salary, they simply could not refuse.

Now, three years later and much to her own astonishment, Carly had been forced to admit that Lucy's business was beginning to look as though it had the potential to become a really big success. Just so long as she continued to insist that they kept a firm grip both on reality and their costings.

'Come back!'

'Jules!'

'So, how did last night go?'

Carly grimaced expressively. 'Well, let's just say that the tabloid journalist who snapped Mike Lucas with one hand down the front of the Honourable Seraphina Ordley's Matthew Williamson frock and the other gripping my far less worthy, five-year-old second-hand Armani silk-clad breast will by now have realised his mistake. "Thou shalt not photograph the niece of one's rag's major shareholder in a pose more suited to a failed contestant from *Big Brother*".'

'Ordley?' Jules mused. 'So she's a Harlowe, then.' As she was an earl's granddaughter, Julia knew *Burke's Peerage* inside out. 'It has been said that the Harlowes' motto should be "As in name, so in action". It's a Charles II title,' Jules explained. 'He handed them out like sweets to his cast-off mistresses. You aren't smiling,' she accused Carly.

'Neither would you be if you had been there last night.'

'Oh. As bad as that, was it?'

When Carly made no verbal response, but instead simply looked at her, Jules grinned. 'Okay, okay, I apologise. I should have been the one to go with them, I know, and I backed out and left you to do it for me… Did he really grab your boob, Carly? What did you do?'

'I reminded myself that the evening was making us a profit of £6,000.'

'Ah.'

'And then I dropped a full bottle of Cristal on his balls.'

'Oh!'

'It wasn't funny, Jules,' she protested, when her friend started to laugh. 'I love Lucy to bits and most of the time I'm grateful to her for including me in her plans—like when she decided to set up this business. But when it comes to events like last night's…'

'It was one of Nick's, wasn't it?'

'Yes,' Carly agreed tersely.

'And the weekend—did you manage to get time to see…them?'

Carly frowned. The three of them were so close that there were no secrets between them, but even so the habit of loyalty was ingrained deeply within her.

Jules—or the Honourable Julia Fellowes, to give her her correct title—touched her gently on the arm, and Carly shook away her own reticence.

'It was dreadful,' she told her simply. 'Even now I don't think they've really taken it in. I felt so so sorry for them. They've lost so much—the estate and everything that went with it—and the prestige living there gave them was very important to them. And now this.'

'Well, at least thanks to you they've got a roof over their heads.'

'The Dower House.' Carly pulled a face. 'They hate living there.'

'What? When I think of how you've beggared yourself to get a mortgage and buy it from the estate for them—oh, honestly, Carly.'

'I might not be able to afford a designer lifestyle, but I've hardly beggared myself. Thanks to you I'm living rent-free in one of the poshest parts of London. I've got a job I love, all the travel I could possibly want…'

She had balked initially at Jules's generous offer that the three of them should share her flat—the three of them being Jules, Carly, and Jules's notorious 'I'm having a bad day and I need to shop' habit. Other people ate chocolate, or rowed with their mother; Jules bought shoes.

But who was she to mock other people's security blanket habits? Ever since she could remember she had saved: pennies, and then her allowance…comfort money. Not that it was bringing her much comfort now. Thanks to the needs of her adopted parents, her bank account was permanently empty.

'…and a weight round your neck that no one should have,' she heard Jules telling her protectively.

Ignoring her comment, Carly said, 'I wish I could have stayed for a bit longer. I felt guilty leaving them.'

'*You* felt guilty? That's crazy. Carly, you don't owe them anything. When I think of what they did to you!'

'You mean like giving me a first-class education?' Carly offered her quietly.

It was at times like this that she recognised the huge gap that existed between herself and the other two. Despite their shared education, they had been born worlds apart.

'You've had to pay for it,' Julia told her protectively.

Carly made no response. After all it was true—but not in the way that Julia had meant. The payment she found unbearable was the knowledge that she was destined always to be an outsider, someone who did not quite fit in—anywhere.

Julia gave her another hug.

Pretty, brunette Julia, and gentle, tender-hearted blonde Lucy—Carly had envied them both, just as she had envied all the other girls at school: girls who knew beyond any kind of doubt that they were taking their rightful place in their own world. Unlike her. She had known she had no right to be there in that alien, wealthy environment. Everything about her had screamed out that she did not and could not fit in. She had felt so out of place—a fraud, a pauper, a charity case, someone whose life had been bought! And, of course, very quickly everyone had known just why she had come to be there.

'Sometimes I wonder what on earth I'm doing in this business.' Lucy exhaled as she came to join them.

'Only sometimes?' Carly teased her.

Lucy grinned.

'We've got a major client scenario about to take place. Nick is on his way over with him right now.'

Carly looked away discreetly as she saw a small shadow touch Julia's eyes. It had been Julia who had introduced Nick to Lucy, and sometimes Carly wondered if Nick, with his flashy pseudo-charm which she found so unappealing, hadn't perhaps made Julia as vulnerable to him as Lucy had been. Was she being overly cynical in worrying that Nick had married Lucy more for her trust fund and her family's social position and wealth than because he had genuinely fallen in love with her? For Lucy's sake she hoped it was the latter, but it had all happened so quickly—too quickly, Carly felt. And now here was Nick, a man she didn't like or trust, taking a very prominent role in the business.

'How major?' Carly asked.

'Jules, call over one of the girls, will you?' Lucy begged. 'I'm dying for an espresso! Absolutely huge. Apparently he knows Marcus—and you can imagine how I feel about that!'

Marcus Canning was Lucy's *bête noir*: a family friend who was also one of her trustees and who, against Lucy's wishes, had insisted on being kept fully informed of every aspect of the business before he would agree to Lucy investing her trust fund money in it. Personally, Carly thought that Marcus Canning, with his well-known reputation for astute financial dealings, was a good person for them to have on board, and she had felt both proud and pleased when he had praised her at their last financial meeting for the way she was running the administrative and financial side of the business.

'And, of course, if he does commission us then we're going to make a bomb!' she heard Lucy announcing enthusiastically.

'Who is he, and what does he want?' Julia chimed in.

'He's Ricardo Salvatore. He's mega-wealthy, and his story is real rags to riches stuff. There was an article in one of the Sunday supplements about him a couple of months ago. He grew up in Naples and he was orphaned very young. But he ran away from the orphanage when he was ten years old and ran wild with a group of children who existed by stealing and begging, generally blagging a living. He's a billionaire now, and he owns—amongst other things—three top-of-the-market exclusive luxury cruise liners. What he wants is for us to organise private parties and that kind of thing for people on these cruises at several villa venues throughout the world. He also owns the villas—and in one case the island it's on.

'He rang earlier, at a very bad moment. In fact, while we were still in bed at home.' She pulled a face and then giggled. 'Poor Nick was…well… Anyway, Nick's just phoned to warn me that they're on their way over here. Ricardo's told him that before he makes a decision he wants to observe a variety of our already planned events, as a sort of unofficial extra guest.'

'What? You're going to let him gatecrash other people's parties?' Carly demanded, shocked. 'Are you sure that's wise?'

'I can't imagine many of our clients would refuse to have a billionaire as an extra guest!' Lucy told her defensively. 'Anyway, Nick has already told him it's okay, and the thing is, Carly, it makes sense if you are the one to accompany him.'

'Me?'

'One of us has to go with him,' Lucy pointed out. 'And besides…' She bit her lip. 'Look, don't take this the wrong way, but I think you'd have more in common with him than either of us, and he'll feel more comfortable with you…'

It took Carly several seconds to catch on, and when she did she her face burned.

'I see.' She knew her voice was tense and edgy but she couldn't help herself. 'So what you're saying is that he's a self-made man, not out of the top drawer and not—'

'Oh, rats. I knew you'd take it the wrong way.' Lucy groaned. 'Yes, he *is* a self-made man, Carly—and a billionaire self-made man at that—but that wasn't what I meant! It isn't anything to do with class! I want *you* to escort and accompany him because I know you'll make a better impression on him than anyone else. Apparently he likes all that stuff you like—reading, museums, galleries. And it is desperately important that we do make a good him impression on him and secure his business.' She paused, and then told them both, 'I didn't want to tell you about this, but the truth is that things haven't being going as well as they were. We had that warehouse fire earlier in the year, which destroyed loads of our stuff…'

'But we were insured!' Carly protested.

Lucy shook her head.

'No, we weren't. Nick felt that the quotes you'd got were too high, and he asked me to hold off paying the premium until he'd checked out some other insurers,' she told her unhappily. 'I thought Nick had gone ahead and insured us with new insurers, but I'd got it wrong, and of course, unfortunately, the existing insurance lapsed.'

Carly frowned. Lucy looked and sounded strained and uncomfortable. She couldn't help wondering if Lucy was trying to protect Nick by taking the blame for his negligence.

She ought to be grateful to this as yet unknown potential client for giving her the opportunity to escape—if only for a while—from her growing discomfort about the way Nick was using the business's bank account as though it were his own private account. Since Lucy had made it clear that Nick was to have *carte blanche* to withdraw money from the account whenever he liked, there was no legitimate objection she could make. Nick had shrugged aside her concern about their growing overdraft by telling her that the deficit would be made good from Lucy's trust fund, but to Carly it seemed shockingly unbusinesslike to waste money paying interest on an overdraft.

'They'll be here in a few minutes. God, I hope we get his business.' Lucy yawned. 'I am sooo tired—and we've got dinner with the folks tonight. How about you? Have you got anything on?'

'Only my writing class,' Carly answered.

'I don't know why you're still going to that,' Julia told her ruefully.

Originally they had decided to attend the writing group together, at Julia's suggestion—mainly, Carly suspected, because Julia had been dating an up-and-coming literary novelist. But after a couple of weeks the romance had faded, and Julia had taken a period of extended leave to visit her sister in Australia, leaving Carly to attend the weekly meetings on her own.

'Mmm…'

'Well, it won't hurt to miss one class, surely? Unless, of course, it's Miss Pope's turn to read one of her poems?' Julia giggled.

Carly tried and failed to give her a quelling look.

'They are pretty awful,' she agreed, joining in her laughter.

'What project has the Professor given you all to write about this time?' Julia gave a small shudder. 'It's not litter again, is it?'

'No,' Carly confirmed carefully, 'it isn't litter. Actually it's fantasy sex!'

It was amazing what the word *sex* could do, she reflected ruefully as both her friends turned to stare at her.

'Fantasy sex?' Lucy demanded. 'What, you mean like…imagining sex with a fantasy man?' She started to laugh. 'Why?'

'Professor Elseworth wants us to stretch our imagination and take it into a new dimension.'

'Right now, any kind of sex is a fantasy for me,' Julia remarked gloomily, before adding, 'But I can't imagine *you* writing about fantasy sex, Carly. I mean, you don't actually do it at all, do you?'

Carly bared her teeth in a ferociously fake smile.

'No, I don't. And I won't until I find someone worth doing it with!'

'Well, okay—I mean, I don't have a problem with that—but how on earth are you going to write about fantasy sex when…?'

Carly gave her a withering look.

'I'm going to use my imagination. That is the whole point of the exercise,' she told her with awesome dignity.

'Rather you than me!'

'No talking about sex during working hours,' Lucy began mock primly, and then stopped as, to Carly's relief, their newest recruit arrived with Lucy's espresso.

In all honesty she would be only too happy to have an excuse to miss out on her writing class and its assignment. She certainly didn't want to write about fantasy sex—or indeed sex of any kind. She knew there was a barrier between her and the potential enjoyment of her sexuality. But how could she ever give herself freely and openly, to a man and to love, when she could never imagine being able to reveal her emotional scars to him? How could there be true intimacy when she herself was so afraid of it? So afraid of being judged and then rejected? Didn't events such as the one she had attended last night confirm all that she had always thought and feared? Giving yourself in and with love to another human being meant giving yourself over to being judged as not good enough, not acceptable, not worthy, and ultimately to rejection. And she had learned very young just how much that hurt.

Her game plan for her life involved focusing on emotional and financial security: building her career, enjoying the company of her friends, ultimately travelling—if she could afford to do so—but always ensuring that she never made the mistake of falling in love.

She had decided that she was only going to have a sexual relationship if she met a man she wanted physically with intense passion and hunger—a man with whom she knew she could share the heights of physical pleasure in a relationship that carried no health risks. A serial male sexual predator was not an option. And at the same time she would also have to feel one hundred per cent confident that she would never be at risk of becoming emotionally involved with him. Add to that the fact that she wasn't even actively looking for this paragon, and it seemed a pretty foregone conclusion that she was likely to remain a virgin indefinitely.

Not that the prospect bothered her.

CHAPTER TWO

'AND you're sure my requirements won't be a problem for you, Nick? I know you don't have a large staff,' Ricardo said blandly.

'Absolutely not. Lucy said that Carly jumped at the chance. In fact she begged for it.' Nick laughed. 'And I don't suppose anyone can blame her. After all, when you've been used to the best of everything all your life and suddenly it isn't available any more, and you're a decent-looking woman, I suppose you're bound to look forward to spending time with a rich man.'

'She's looking for a rich husband?'

Nick grinned.

'Who said anything about marriage? Anyway, come up to the office and I can introduce you to her.'

'I think you said earlier that she is your wife's partner?'

'Employee. The three of them—Lucy, Julia and Carly—were at school together. Neither Julia nor Carly have put any money into the business, though.'

'So financially the partnership is—'

'Just me and Lucy,' Nick informed him.

'Carly normally does all the financial and administrative stuff, but to be honest I don't think she's up to the job. You'd be doing me a favour by taking her off my hands for a week or two, so that I can get the financial side of things sorted out properly. Lucy's a loyal little soul, and devoted to her friends—you know the type, all breeding and no brains.' He shrugged. 'I don't want to say too much to her. Anyway, having Carly with you won't be too much of a hardship—she's a good-looker, and obliging too, if you know what I mean—especially if you treat her generously. Like I said, Carly has her head screwed on.'

'Are you speaking from personal experience?' Ricardo asked him dryly.

'What? Hell, no. I'm a married man. But let's just say she let me know that it was available if I wanted it,' Nick boasted.

He was well aware that Carly didn't like him, and it amused him to think of what he was setting her up for. Discrediting her wouldn't do him any harm in other ways either, he congratulated himself. For one thing she wouldn't be able to go tittle-tattling to Lucy.

'Carly is very good at getting other people to pay her bills for her—as both Lucy and Julia already know. She's even managed to blag a rent-free room in Julia's flat. If she can't find a rich man to finance her, then the lifestyle that working for Prêt a Party gives her is the next best thing. All that first-class travel and accommodation provided by the clients, plus getting to mingle with their guests.' He winked at Ricardo. 'Ideal for her type of woman. Once I've introduced you, I'll get her to go through the list of our upcoming events with you so that you can cherry pick the ones you want to attend.'

'Excellent.' Inwardly, Ricardo decided that Nick sounded more like a pimp than a businessman. Or in this business did the two go hand in hand?

They had reached Prêt a Party's office, and Nick pushed open the door for him.

'Ah, there's Carly,' he announced. 'I'll call her over.'

There was no way she could pretend not to be aware of Nick's summons, Carly had to acknowledge reluctantly, and she walked towards him. She was wearing her normal office uniform of jeans and a tee shirt—the jeans snugly encased the slender length of her legs but irritatingly, the tee shirt skimming the curves of her breasts had pulled free of the low waistband of her jeans. It was a familiar hazard when one was almost five foot ten tall, give or take one eighth of an inch, and it exposed the flat golden flesh of her taut stomach. Whenever she could, Carly ran—mostly on her own, but sometimes with a group of fellow amateur runners—and her body had a sensuous grace of which she herself was totally unaware.

Long thick hair, honey-brown, with natural highlights, swung past her shoulders as she walked calmly towards Nick—and then missed a step as she saw the man standing to one side of him.

If she were in the market for a man—sex-wise, that was, because she would not want one for any other reason—then this was definitely a man she would want. She could feel the power of his sexuality from here; she could breathe it in almost. And it was very heady stuff. Far more potent than any champagne, she thought dizzily.

A vulnerable woman—which, of course, she was not—would find it almost impossible to resist such a man. He was a living, breathing lure for the whole female sex. Except for her. She had exempted herself from such dangers.

Ricardo frowned in immediate recognition as he watched her walking towards them and coldly came to two very separate decisions.

The first was that he intended to have her in his bed, and the second was that she embodied everything he most disliked about her class and type.

She was stunningly beautiful and irritatingly confident. And he already knew from listening to Nick that she was a woman who judged a man by his wallet and how much she could extract from it. A gold-digger, in other words.

'Hello, gorgeous. Let me introduce you to Ricardo—oh, and by the way, Mike Lucas rang me to tell me how much he enjoyed your company last night,' Nick told Carly, as he put his arm round her shoulders and drew her close to his side.

Pulling herself free, Carly extended her hand to Ricardo and smiled at him with genuine pleasure. After all, he was going to be releasing her from the unpleasantness of Nick's unwanted company.

Well, she certainly didn't believe in wasting any time, Ricardo thought cynically as he took the hand Carly had extended and shook it firmly.

'Ricardo wants to have a look at our upcoming events so that he can decide which ones he wants to attend. You can use my office, Carly,' Nick told her benignly.

His office? Carly had to look away. 'His office', as he called it had, until he had come onto the scene, been her office. In fact it still was her office, she reflected, since she was the only one who did any work in it. Nick's only appearances in it were when he came in to ask her to countersign another cheque.

Carly smiled as she led the way to the small sectioned-off cubicle where she worked. Ricardo had lost count of the number of women who had smiled at him the way Carly was doing right now—with warmth and promise—especially women of Carly's type. Upmarket, privately educated pampered women, contemptuous of the very idea of supporting themselves, whose goal in life was to find a man to financially underwrite their desired lifestyle.

His gaze narrowed. Female predators were a familiar risk to any man to whom the press attached the label 'wealthy'; he had discovered that a long time ago. He had been twenty-two and merely a millionaire the first time he had encountered the type of well-bred young woman who believed that a man like him—a self-made man who had come up from nothing—would be delighted to spend lavishly on her in exchange for the social cachet of being connected with her.

She had been the sister of the thrusting young entrepreneur with whom he'd had business dealings. Initially he had thought he must be mistaken, and that she couldn't possibly be coming on to him as openly as she'd seemed to be. He had indeed been naïve. There had been an expensive lunch to which she had invited herself, he remembered, and an even more expensive afternoon's shopping, when she had pointed out to him the Rolex watch she wanted. Like a besotted fool he had gone back to the shop and bought it for her the moment she had left him to return to her brother. He had then, even more besottedly, booked himself out of his hotel room and into a huge suite, had ordered a magnum of champagne and the most luxurious meal he could think of, and then wasted more time than he cared to think about dreaming of the pleasure that lay in store for them both. He would make love to her as she had never been made love to her before, and then, in the morning, he would kiss her awake and surprise her with the watch…

He had very quickly been brought back to earth when, instead of relishing his tender caresses, the object of his adoration had told him peevishly to 'hurry up', and then pouted and sulked until he produced her watch. The final blow to his pride, though, had been unwittingly delivered by her brother, who had informed him that his sister was as good as engaged to an extremely wealthy older man. Fortunately, although his illusions had been shattered, his heart had been left intact, and the whole experience had taught him what he considered to be a valuable lesson: the only difference between spoilt, pampered society women and the prostitutes of Naples was that the prostitutes had no option other than to sell themselves if they wanted to feed their children.

He had yet to meet a woman whose desire for him did not go hand in hand with her desire for his money, no matter how much she might initially deny it. Indeed, if he hadn't been so fastidious he knew that he would have found it cheaper to hire the services of a professional than to satisfy the financial demands of the society women who had shared his bed. The discovery that the last one to do so had been contemplating being unfaithful to him with an elderly billionaire old enough to be her grandfather had confirmed his cynical belief that no woman was too beautiful or too well born to be above using her 'assets' to secure financial security.

He would take Carly to bed and he would ensure that both of them enjoyed the experience, and that would be that. Why shouldn't he take advantage of what she was? She was a beautiful woman, and it was a very long time since he had last had sex, but her social standing cut no ice with him, and nor was he impressed by it—quite the opposite, in fact.

'Here's a list of our upcoming events and their venues,' Carly announced a little breathlessly, after she had printed it off from the computer.

She hadn't expected to be so acutely aware of Ricardo's powerful and sensually invasive sexual aura. She wasn't used to this kind of man, and there was an unfamiliar flutter in her stomach and a hyped-up sensation of excitement in her head. She felt both excited and apprehensive, as though somehow her whole body had moved up into a higher gear, a more intense state of awareness. It was simply her hormones responding to his hormones, she told herself prosaically. Her office was way too small for the two of them.

Out of the corner of her eye she saw that he was removing his suit jacket, and she discovered that she was sucking in an unsteady breath of reluctant female appreciation. Beneath the fine cotton of his shirt she could see the muscular hardness of his body. She had recently read an article in a magazine about the new fashion for men to wax their chest hair. He obviously didn't subscribe to it.

The author of the article had propounded the theory that women found the abrasion of male body hair unwelcome against their own flesh. Carly's tongue-tip touched her lips. A fine mist of sensual heat had broken out on her skin. Beneath her tee shirt her bra-covered breasts suddenly ached, her nipples pushing against the restraining fabric.

How could she be having such intensely sexual thoughts about a man she had only just met? It must be because she had been talking about sex to Lucy and Jules. Yes, that was it; her mind was obviously more focused on sex than usual.

He was still studying the list she had given him, plainly oblivious to what she was experiencing, and of course she was glad about that—wasn't she? After all, she had never been the kind of woman who felt piqued because a man didn't show any interest in her.

Because until now she had not met the right kind of man?

'Perhaps if you were to tell me what kind of event you are thinking of having I might be able to pick out the best events for you to attend,' she suggested hastily.

'I haven't made up my mind as yet.'

Carly looked blankly at him. She had naturally assumed that, like their existing clients, he must have a specific event in mind.

Ricardo permitted himself a small cynical smile. If his plans went ahead as he expected, the first event Prêt a Party would be organising for him would be a party to celebrate his acquisition. But of course he wasn't going to tell Carly that. She, he had already decided, would be one of the first surplus-to-requirements 'assets' of the business to be offloaded.

'I understand you are responsible for the administration and accounts of the business?'

'Er, yes…'

'You must be very well organised if you can carry out those duties and still have time to accompany clients to their events.'

'I don't normally. That is, I stand in for the others sometimes.'

She was making it sound as though she had to be coerced into doing so, Ricardo thought cynically. Of course he knew better.

'Carly, your mother's telephoned. She wants you to ring her—Oh, I'm sorry.' The young girl who had burst into the office came to an abrupt halt, her face pink, as she realised that Carly wasn't on her own.

'It's all right, Izzie, I'll ring her later. Thank you.' But as she thanked the younger girl Carly's heart was sinking beneath her professional smile. She already knew what her adoptive mother would want. More money.

Carly did her best, but the truth was that the woman had no real understanding of how to manage money. The fortune her adoptive father had once had was gone, swallowed up in lavish living and unwise investments. A stroke had made it impossible for him to do any kind of work, and so Carly found herself in the position of having to support them as best she could. But it wasn't easy. Her adoptive mother ran up bills and then wept because she couldn't pay them—like a small child rather than an adult. Their anguished unhappiness and despair made her feel so guilty—especially when…

She was so lucky to have friends like Lucy and Jules, Carly reflected emotionally. She might get on reasonably well with her adopted parents now, but that had not always been the case. Without Lucy and Jules what might she have done to escape from the misery and the wretchedness that had been her own childhood? Taken her own life? She had certainly thought about it.

Where had she gone? Ricardo wondered curiously, watching anxiety momentarily shadow her eyes before she blinked it away. He cleared his throat.

'Right. Here are the events I wish to attend.'

Pushing back her private thoughts, Carly leaned over the desk to study the list he had tossed towards her.

He had selected three events: a private party in St Tropez on board a newly acquired private yacht, to celebrate its acquisition; a media event in the Hamptons to launch a new glossy magazine, to which old money, new names and anyone who was anyone in the fashion world had been invited and a world-famous senior rock star's birthday bash at his French château.

Carly started to frown.

'What's wrong?'

'The St Tropez yacht party is next weekend, and only four days before the Hamptons do. It might be difficult co-ordinating flights and all the other travel arrangements.'

She kept a tight rein on expenses—or at least she had done until Nick had started to interfere. They always booked cheap, no frills flights to overseas events if they weren't being flown out by the clients.

Ricardo raised an eyebrow.

'That won't be a problem. We'll be using my private jet.' He gave a dismissive shrug of those powerful shoulders. 'One of my PAs can sort out all the details. Oh, and they'll need your passport, ASAP. I understand from Nick that your normal practice is to be *in situ* a day ahead of the actual event. That suits me, because that way I shall be able to see how things are organised.'

Too right he would, Ricardo decided.

He was standing up, and Carly followed suit. He was so tall—so big! She was suddenly aware of her reluctance to go through the doorway, because it would bring her too close to him. Too close to him? Get a grip, she mentally advised herself unsympathetically.

'My PA will be in touch with you regarding flight times.'

She walked determinedly towards the door. She was almost level with him now. In another few seconds she would be through the door and safe. Safe? From what? Him pouncing on her? No way would he do that, she told herself scornfully.

And then she made the mistake of looking up at him.

It was like stepping through a door into a previously unknown world.

Her heart whipped round inside her chest like a spinning barrel. Against her will her head turned, her lips parting as her gaze fastened on his mouth. His top lip was well shaped and firmly cut, his teeth white and just slightly uneven, and his bottom lip…

His bottom lip. A smoky sensuality darkened her normally crystal-clear grey eyes as she fed visually on the promise of its fullness. How would it feel to catch that fullness between her own lips? To nibble at it with small biting kisses, to…

'A word of warning—' Ricardo began.

She could feel guilty colour staining her skin as her mind grappled with inexplicable thoughts.

'It is imperative that full confidentiality as to the purpose of my attendance at these occasions is maintained at all times.'

He was cautioning her about the events—that was all! Carly exhaled in shaky relief.

'Yes—yes, of course,' she agreed quickly, as she finally made it through the doorway on legs that had developed a very suspicious weakness.

But she was unnervingly aware of him behind her.

'And one more thing.'

'Yes?' she offered politely, automatically turning round to face him.

'The next time you look at my mouth like that…' he said softly, with a mocking smile.

'Like what? I didn't look at it like anything!' Carly knew that her face was burning with guilt, but she had to defend herself.

'Liar. You looked at it, at *me*, as though you couldn't wait to feel it against your own. As though there was nothing you wanted more than for me to push you up against that door-frame and take you right here and now. As though you could already feel my hands on your skin, touching you intimately, and you were loving it. As though—'

'No!' Carly denied fiercely. And her denial was the truth—she hadn't got as far as thinking anything so intimate as that!

To her relief she could see Lucy hurrying towards them to introduce herself to him.

It was over an hour since Ricardo had gone, and Carly was still thinking about him. But a woman would surely have to be totally devoid of any kind of hormones to remain unaware of Ricardo as a fully functioning man.

And that was her sole excuse, was it? She pushed back her keyboard and stood up. She was shaking slightly. Her face was burning and her body ached. She felt shocked. Guilty. Horrified, in fact, by the door she had unwittingly opened in her own head, and—even worse—was uncomfortably aware that she was physically aroused. Physically, but of course not emotionally—that was impossible. After all, she had sworn never to fall in love, hadn't she? Never to fall in love; never to give herself emotionally to anyone; never to risk the emotional security she had given to herself.

She started to pace the small office. Her childhood had taught her all there was to know about the pain that came with being emotionally rejected. She had fought hard to give herself the protective air of calm self-confidence she projected to others, and for the right to claim their respect. The pathetic, needy child she had once been, desperate for approval and love, had been totally banished, and that was the way Carly intended it to stay.

So why was she thinking like this? No one was threatening her self-reliance, after all—least of all Ricardo Salvatore, who probably had the same loathing of emotional bondage as she did herself, if for very different reasons.

CHAPTER THREE

CARLY checked her watch—Lucy had given both Carly and Jules smart Cartier Tank Francaise watches for Christmas in the first year the business had made a profit—and then bent down and grabbed the handle of her case.

The car Ricardo Salvatore was sending to pick her up was due to arrive in exactly two minutes' time. It was time for her to leave.

She heaved her suitcase off the floor, grimacing a little ruefully as she did so, remembering how Lucy had burst into the office the previous Thursday morning announcing, 'Oh, my God, Carly—I've just realised! There won't be anything in the Wardrobe that will fit you!'

The 'Wardrobe' was a standing joke between them all, and was in actual fact a small room in Lucy's parents' London home which housed the glamorous outfits Lucy and Jules, who were very much the same height and build, wore when they were 'on duty' at events.

The clothes—all designer models—were second hand, surreptitiously trawled from a variety of sources, and the subject of amused speculation between them.

'Just look at this!' Lucy had marvelled after their last expedition, as she held up what looked like a sequin-covered handkerchief with halter neck straps. 'Who on earth would buy this?'

'You did,' Carly had pointed out, laughing.

'Yes, but *I* only paid fifty pounds for it—it cost over a thousand brand-new.'

'It's very sexy,' Jules had pronounced.

'It's repulsive,' Carly had criticised. 'Vulgar and tarty.'

'Mmm... Well, Nick spotted it.'

But the Wardrobe contained nothing that would fit Carly, and so, that Thursday, Lucy had announced firmly, 'Come on, Carly. We've got to go out on a trawl!'

Carly had tried to protest and resist, but Jules and Lucy had been insistent.

The result of their foray into the second-hand shops and market stalls of Lucy's favourite haunts—which had emptied the clothes budget Carly had so carefully worked out—had been collected from the dry cleaners this morning and were now packed in Carly's case, along with her own clothes.

Mentally Carly reviewed them—a white silk trouser suit which Lucy had cooed over, enraptured, pronouncing, 'Oh, this is so retro—Seventies rock wife! And you've got the boobs for it, Carly.'

Maybe she had, but she certainly wouldn't be wearing the jacket over bare skin and half open! There were also a couple of evening dresses, both of which were potentially so revealing that Carly had already decided she would be wearing a silk jacket over them.

She hadn't been very keen on the designer swimsuit Lucy had found either. It was cut away in so many places that Carly feared it threatened to reveal more of her than the skimpiest of bikinis, but at least it had matching culotte pants and a jacket.

Her own classic casuals—the simple linen separates she favoured for summer and some up-to-the-minute accessories they had found in the likes of Zara—had all passed Lucy's inspection and been declared perfect for the events she would be attending.

Dragging her suitcase behind her, Carly pushed open the door onto the street and stepped out into the late-morning sunshine.

Ricardo watched her from his vantage point in the back seat of the limo, as the driver moved the car out of the parking bay he had found further up the street.

Oh, yes, she was a typical example of her upmarket, 'no expense spared but someone else pays' lifestyle, Ricardo decided cynically as he watched her. Immaculate white tee shirt, perfectly fitting blue jeans, long shiny hair, minimal make-up, sunglasses, discreetly 'good' watch, penny loafers. The too-thin girl in designer clutter who was tottering past her on spindly heels, clutching a weird-looking handbag, couldn't hold a candle to her. Because Carly had *class*.

What would she be like in bed?

He didn't intend to let too much time elapse before he found out.

He thought of another society woman from his youth, one whom he had met when he was growing cynical but not yet completely hardened. Initially he had thought her pretty, but she hadn't looked very pretty at all when he had flatly refused to meet her escalating demands—especially when he'd discovered they included a wedding ring in exchange for the supposed benefit of marrying into a higher social bracket. He'd told her that he preferred an honest whore.

Women like her, like Carly, might not openly demand money in return for sex, but what they were looking for was the richest and highest status man they could find—their bodies in exchange for his name.

It was a trade-off that nauseated him, as did those who participated in it.

He had no illusions about women or sex. He had lived too long and seen too much for that. His wealth could buy him any woman he wanted, and that included Carly. She had made *that* plain enough already, with the way she had looked at his mouth.

She hadn't even tried to be subtle about it! She had stared openly and brazenly at him. If they hadn't been in her office it would have been an open invitation to him to push her tee shirt out of the way and free her breasts to spill into his hands so that he could accept their flaunting invitation.

It had told him that he could have yanked down her jeans and explored and enjoyed her and she would not have said a single word in denial.

And then in the morning she would no doubt expect to receive her payment—a piece of jewellery, a telephone call from an exclusive shop inviting her to choose herself something expensive…

That was the way things were done in her world.

He was wasting too much time on her, he warned himself. His primary reason for what he was doing was the potential acquisition of Prêt a Party, not the inevitable sexual acquisition of Carly Carlisle who, although she did not know it yet, would be one of the first in line to lose her job.

Carly frowned as the large, elegant steel-grey car drew up alongside her.

A limo, Lucy had said, and she had pictured a huge, shiny black ostentatious vehicle, not something so supremely understated. But the rear door was opening and Ricardo was getting out.

'Is this all your luggage?'

She gaped at him as he reached for her case, and then looked uncertainly towards the chauffeur.

'Charles is driving. I am perfectly capable of picking up a case,' Ricardo told her dryly, following her uncertain look.

'The...my case is heavy,' she told him, but he ignored her, picked it up and put it in to the boot of the car as if it was as light as a feather pillow.

He was wearing a black tee shirt and a pair of tan-coloured casual trousers, and the muscles in his arms were hardening as he lifted her case. He looked more like a man who worked outdoors than one who sat at a desk, she acknowledged, unwilling to admit to the response that the sight of him was eliciting from her own body.

After what had happened when she had given her imagination its head, she was now keeping it on a controlling diet of bread and water, and that meant no thinking about the effect Ricardo could have on her! So he had a good enough body to carry off the macho male thing—so what? she told herself dispassionately.

But the sight of his black-clad back, bent over the open boot, suddenly transformed by her rebellious thoughts into a totally naked back bent over her equally naked body, evoked such a powerful sensual image that she felt as though she were transfixed to the spot.

So it was true. You *could* go weak at the knees, Carly reflected several minutes later as she sat primly straight in the back seat of the powerful car, dizzily aware that her private thoughts were anything but prim. All those enforced deportment classes at school had definitely left her with an automatic 'sit up straight' reflex.

She was accomplished, Ricardo admitted to himself. That cool, remote pose she had adopted, that said *Pursue me* would certainly work with most men. Unfortunately for her, he was not most men. He opened his briefcase and extracted some papers.

As soon as they were free of the city traffic the powerful car picked up speed. Carly was pleased that Ricardo was engrossed in his work, because that left her free to think about hers, instead of having to make polite conversation with him.

Since their clients were using their own yacht as the venue for their party there was no construction work in the shape of marquees on the like for her to oversee. The client's chef and kitchen staff were being augmented by a chef from the upmarket caterers she had sourced. They were already on the yacht. Menus had been agreed, floral arrangements decided on—she would be meeting with the florists, who had also been flown in from London.

The arrival and deployment of the hostess's hairdresser, make-up artist, and a dresser from the couture house she favoured were also

Carly's responsibility, plus a hundred or more other small but vitally important arrangements.

She had an inch-thick pile of assorted coloured and coded lists in her briefcase, most of which she had actually memorised.

'You're so much better at this than me,' Lucy had told her ruefully before she left.

Carly had smiled, but she knew that it was true.

Carly shifted her body against the leather upholstery. It was ridiculous that she should be so acutely conscious of Ricardo's presence in the car with her—and even more ridiculous that she should be so acutely aware of the impact he was having on her physically. So much for the 'bread and water' regime, then!

The grand slam of his raw sensuality had sliced through her defences, leaving an alarming trail of female awareness in its wake. Her jeans, normally a comfortable easy fit, suddenly seemed to be uncomfortably tight, clinging to her flesh in a way she could only mentally describe as erotic, as though somehow she were being caressed by the lean, powerful male hands she couldn't resist looking towards.

She could feel the heat expanding inside her, dangerous little languorous curls of it thrusting against her sensitive flesh. She crossed her legs and then uncrossed them. Her arm accidentally brushed against her own breast and immediately she was aware of the hot pulsing of her nipples.

This was *crazy*. It felt as though somehow or other an unfamiliar and certainly unwanted very sexual alter ego had been released inside her. And, what was more, it seemed to be attempting to take her over! Or had it always been there and it had simply taken meeting Ricardo Salvatore to make her aware of it, just as her own senses were making her aware of him?

This was definitely crazy.

She realised with relief that they had reached the airport. The car slowed down and turned into an entrance marked 'Strictly Private'.

A uniformed customs officer stepped out of a nearby office and came over to the car.

'Your passport, please,' Ricardo demanded, turning to Carly.

Foolishly, she had not been ready for this formality, and it took her several seconds to open her bag, find her passport, and then hand it over to Ricardo.

As he took it from her, her open bag slipped from her hand, showering the immaculate leather and the car's floor with coins, her lipstick, her purse and several other small personal items.

Her face hot, she undid her seatbelt and tried to pick them up as fast as she could, but the lipstick rolled away out of her reach with the movement of the car as the driver set it in motion again.

To her dismay the lipstick had rolled along the leather and come to rest right next to Ricardo's thigh.

She couldn't retrieve it without touching him.

She moistened her lips with the tip of her tongue.

'Could I have my lipstick, please? It's... You're sitting on it,' she told Ricardo.

'What?'

The look he gave her was totally male and uncomprehending.

'My lipstick!' Carly repeated. 'It fell out of my bag and now it's...'

She looked meaningfully at the leather seat, somehow managing at the same time to keep her gaze off his thigh.

His sigh was definitely exasperated as he reached down and picked up the small slim tube.

It was a relief to release her own pent-up breath as he handed the lipstick to her. She reached out for it, too focused on what she was doing to be aware of a deep pothole in the tarmac, which the driver couldn't avoid because of an oncoming vehicle.

The violent movement of the car flung her bodily against Ricardo, sending her slamming into his side. The air was driven out of her lungs by the force of the impact, leaving her half lying against him, her face buried in his tee shirt, her hand ignominiously clutching at his arm.

A shock of unfamiliar sensation hit her all at once, like a hail of sharp-pointed arrows. His personal man-scent, the texture of his tee shirt, the hardness of his chest beneath her cheek, the softness of something that she realised must be his body hair. The slow, heavy thud of his heartbeat…

Somewhere inside her head unwanted images were forming. A man—Ricardo—carrying her in his arms, his torso bare, his flesh warm beneath her fingertips. She could feel the heat of her own desire for him. Her fingers tightened automatically on his arm, her nails digging into his flesh.

Abruptly Carly snapped back to reality, and to the humiliating awareness of what she was doing. Her face burning, she released Ricardo's arm and pulled away for him, refusing to look at him.

As she retreated to her side of the car Ricardo shifted his own position and turned away from her, to conceal the telltale thick ridge of flesh pressing against the fabric of his trousers.

He was beginning to realise that he had badly underestimated the effect Carly was going to have on him. It was one thing for him to acknowledge to himself that he was happy to have sex with her, but it was quite another to have to admit that his desire for her was far more urgent than he had planned for—and, even worse, that it was threatening to overwhelm his self-control. He simply did not want this fierce, thrusting surge of need, this urgent, compelling hunger to take hold of her and fill himself with the scent and the feel of her; the taste of her, to fill her *with* himself and to…

The ache in his body was intensifying instead of fading, and he had to resort to the subterfuge of opening his newspaper and busying himself re-reading it in order to conceal that fact.

'Thank you, Charles.'

Carly had no time to do more than smile her own gratitude at Ricardo's chauffeur before a smartly uniformed flight steward was escorting her up the steps to the waiting private jet, whilst Ricardo paused to speak with its captain—*his* captain, Carly realised.

She had often heard Lucy marvelling about the luxury of travelling in the private jets owned by some of their more wealthy clients, but this would be the first time she had experienced it for herself.

The interior of the jet had more resemblance to a modern apartment than to any aeroplane Carly had flown in. A colour scheme of off-white and cool grey set off the black leather upholstery of the sofas, and the steward discreetly indicated to her that both a bedroom and a separate shower room lay to the rear of the sitting area.

'The galley is behind the cockpit, and there is another lavatory there as well—' He broke off from his explanations, to say formally, 'Good morning, sir.'

Carly turned round to see Ricardo standing in the open doorway.

'Morning, Eddie. How are Sally and the new baby?'

There was a genuine warmth in his voice that touched a painful nerve within Carly's heart.

'They're both fine. Sally was over the moon that you flew her folks here for the birth. She was resigned to them not being able to be there.'

Ricardo shrugged, and changed the subject. 'Phil says that we're going to have a good flight, both to Nice and on to New York.' He turned to Carly. 'I've got some work I need to attend to, but feel free to ask Eddie for anything you need.'

'If you would like to sit down here, madam, until we've taken off?' Eddie suggested politely to her, indicating a space on one of the sofas.

Obediently, Carly went and sat down.

'Perhaps I could get you a glass of champagne?' the steward said, once he had shown Carly how to use her seatbelt, and explained to her how to access the power and telephone lines for her laptop should she wish to use it. 'We've got a very nice Cristal.'

Carly couldn't help it. She gave a small shudder. 'Water will be fine,' she told him emphatically.

From his own seat at a desk on the other side of the cabin, Ricardo frowned. Why had she refused champagne? She certainly hadn't been having any qualms about drinking it the night he had seen her in CoralPink.

Thanking Eddie for her water, Carly unzipped her own laptop. Ricardo wasn't the only one who had work to do. Five minutes later, as the jet taxied down the runway, Carly was deeply engrossed in reading her e-mails—but not so deeply that she wasn't acutely aware of Ricardo's presence.

She couldn't forget the disturbing effect those fleeting seconds of physical intimacy in the car had had on her. Her stomach muscles clenched immediately, as though in rejection of the response she had felt, her mouth going dry.

Eddie had said the jet had a fully equipped bedroom… The ache inside her sharpened and tightened and then started to spread.

The jet lifted off the tarmac and Carly held her breath, willing herself not to think about Ricardo.

* * *

'I'd like to ask you a few questions about certain aspects of the way Prêt a Party's business works.'

Dutifully Carly put aside the list she was studying. Ricardo was, after all, a potential client.

'Were I to commission Prêt a Party to organise an event for me, who would be responsible for establishing the cost of everything involved?'

'I would,' Carly answered him promptly.

'And would you do that by sourcing suppliers yourself? Or does someone else—Lucy, for instance—source suppliers?'

'Normally I would source them. We've been in business for long enough now to have established a core of suppliers we use on a regular basis. However, sometimes a client will specify that they want to use a specific caterer, or florist, or musician. When that happens we either negotiate with them on the client's behalf or, if the client prefers, they negotiate with them themselves. If they opt to do that then we ask that the clients also make themselves responsible for paying the supplier's bill.

When we're in charge of suppliers' estimates and invoices we know exactly what their charges will be—that isn't always the case if the client has commissioned a supplier.'

'Presumably you obtain good discounts from your regular suppliers?'

'Of course, and we pass them on to our clients via our costings for their events. But discount isn't the main criteria we apply when selecting suppliers. Quality, reliability, exclusivity are often more important to our clients than cut-price deals.'

'What do you do when potential suppliers offer to make it worth your while to select them?'

Carly couldn't look at him, and she could feel her face starting to burn. Since Nick had joined the business she had received several such approaches from suppliers, who had insisted that Nick had promised them work. Nick himself had tried to pressure her into using them, but Carly had refused to do so. She knew that Lucy would never have authorised such dishonest business practices, but she hadn't felt able to tell her friend what her husband was doing because she didn't want to hurt her. And she certainly couldn't tell Ricardo—a potential client—about them.

'We…I…I make it plain to them that that we don't take bribes and that they are wasting their time,' she hedged, uncomfortably aware that she was not being totally honest.

Ricardo looked at her, but she was refusing to look back at him, her body language reflecting both her guilt and the lie she had just told him.

Backhanders from suppliers would add a very sizeable 'bonus' to Carly's salary, Ricardo thought grimly.

It surprised him that she wasn't making more use of the fact that they were alone and in the intimate surroundings of the jet in order to let him know that she was available. And did that disappoint him? He shrugged the thought aside. Hardly. He had simply assumed that she would want to showcase her skills for his benefit.

He recognised the discreet little come-ons that women like her were so adept at giving, such as leaning close to him whilst pretending to show him something, so that he could breathe in her perfume—which he had not as yet been able to identify other than to be aware that it suited her. A good quality signature perfume? Custom blended? Expensive! Blended exclusively for her? *Very* expensive! By one of the top three perfumiers? Very expensive—and paid for by a very rich and very doting man!

At least she had not had a boob job. He had been aware of that the moment she'd fallen against him. But she was wearing a bra, a plain, seamless, no-nonsense tee shirt bra. Unusual for a woman out to snare a man, surely? And unnecessary, in view of the excellence of the shape and firmness Mother Nature had generously given her.

Had she leaned over him now, he would have lifted his hand to caress her breast and even, had he felt so inclined, pushed aside her tee shirt and bra and explored the shape and texture of her naked breast, both with his fingers and his lips.

He found himself wondering idly if her grooming regime went as far as a Brazilian wax. He personally wasn't enamoured of the look, although he knew of men who insisted not just on a Brazilian but that their lovers go for the full Hollywood 'everything-off' wax. He personally preferred something a bit more natural, a bit more sensual. And she had such thick, luxuriant, clean and shiny hair—the kind that made him want to reach out and touch it. He moved uncomfortably as he tried to change the direction of his thoughts.

'We'll be landing in a few minutes.'

Carly smiled at the steward and put away her papers. She would be rather glad to get off the plane, although not because she was afraid of flying—at least not in the non-sexual sense. There she was again! Thinking about sex.

And all because… Because what? Because secretly she wanted to have sex with Ricardo? Chance would be a fine thing, she mocked herself. But if she were to be given the chance…

The first thing Carly noticed as they came out of the airport was the small group of beggars—children, not adults—clustered pathetically together whilst people ignored them. Thin and dirty, wearing shabby torn clothes, they stood out amongst the seething mass of people to-ing and fro-ing, and yet everyone was acting as though they simply did not exist. The smallest of them was barely old enough to walk.

Ricardo had gone to collect his valet parked rental car, telling her to wait where she was.

She had noticed a sandwich shop on her way out of the airport, and now, impetuously, she came to a swift decision. Wasn't the golden rule to give food rather than money because money might be taken from them? Dragging her case behind her, she hurried back to the sandwich bar.

The children watched her approach without interest. Their pinched faces and emotionally dead eyes wrenched at her heart. When she handed them the food, small claw-like hands snatched it from her.

'Euros,' the older children demanded sullenly, but she shook her head.

She could see people looking disapprovingly at her, no doubt thinking she was encouraging them to beg.

Her mobile was ringing. Carly felt a familiar sense of anxiety and despair twist her stomach when she saw that the caller was her adoptive mother—she could never think of her as anything other than that, and she was, she knew, bound to her adoptive parents by guilt and duty rather than love. Guilt because she did not love them, and because she was alive whilst their own flesh and blood daughter was dead.

Fenella had made her life a misery when they were growing up together, and her death from a drugs overdose had not been the shock to her that it had been to her parents—how could it, in view of the number of times Fenella had turned up at her flat either to beg or harangue her into giving her money to fund her habit? And of course when they were growing up Fenella had been the loved and valued one, whilst she… Automatically she clamped down on her thoughts. She was an adult now, not a child.

It took her several minutes to find out what was wrong. Her adoptive parents had run up a bill of several thousand pounds for which they were past the stage of final demands and warnings and which they could not now repay. How could they have spent so much? Carly felt slightly sick. She did some mental arithmetic and heaved a small sigh of relief. She had just about enough in her own accounts to cover it.

'Don't worry—I'll sort everything out,' she promised, fighting not to feel upset at the thought of such a large sum of money—to her—being wasted. Ending the call, she turned towards her case, her eyes widening as she stared in disbelief at the empty space where it should have been.

Carly was trying desperately not to give in to her panic as she saw Ricardo striding imperiously towards her.

'The car's this way.'

Somehow or other he had relieved her of both her laptop and her hand luggage.

'Where's your case?'

Her mouth went dry with panic.

'I…er… It's gone,' she told him uncomfortably, well aware that she probably only had herself to blame, and that her act of charity had badly backfired on her.

'Gone?'

'Yes. I think someone must have stolen it.'

Ricardo absorbed her none too subtle message cynically. Managing to 'lose' her luggage was certainly a dramatic start to setting him up to replenish her wardrobe. What *had* she done with it? Put it in a left luggage locker?

'So now you don't have any clothes to wear?' he offered helpfully. He would play along with her for now, if only to see her *modus operandi* in action.

Carly exhaled shakily, relieved that he was taking it so well.

'No—nothing apart from what I'm wearing.' And, thanks to that desperate phone call she had just received, she wouldn't be able to afford to replace what she had lost either, she realised with growing dismay.

'Annoying, I know. But at least you'll be able to claim on your insurance policy later,' he told her dispassionately, and then watched her. He had to admit that she was very good—that small indrawn breath, that tiny betraying flicker of her eyelashes, which demanded a response. 'You are insured, I trust?'

'I do have insurance,' Carly agreed.

But it was not the kind of insurance that would enable her to replace her carefully chosen designer wardrobe, she realised dispiritedly.

'So there isn't any problem, is there?' Ricardo offered smoothly. 'After all, you are in one of the best places in the world for female retail therapy, aren't you?'

'I'm sure it's certainly one of the most expensive,' Carly agreed wryly.

'I'd better find a police station and report it, I suppose.'

Ricardo listened appreciatively. She was *very* good.

'I doubt that would do any good. You can report it by phone later from the villa, if you wish.'

He was impatient to leave and she was holding him up, Carly realised at his crisp words. And he was a potential client.

So what did she do now? She couldn't keep her promise to her adoptive parents, to whom she needed to transfer the money quickly, *and* replenish her wardrobe. None of her small 'for her old age' investments could be realised quickly, and she was loath to put a further charge on the business by asking Lucy for money to replace clothes *she* was responsible for losing—especially since they had emptied the budget and cash flow was problematic.

This was not a good time to remember the lecture she had delivered to both Jules and Lucy about how they should follow her example and refuse to possess any credit cards.

She had a few hundred euros in cash—petty cash and personal spending money—probably about enough to buy herself some new knickers, she acknowledged derisively.

Which meant…

What? It was a Saturday; her bank would be closed. Attempting to arrange a temporary bank loan here, with her limited French? Not a good idea. Ringing Jules, explaining what had happened and asking her for a temporary loan? Better—if Jules was even there. But Jules would probably tell Lucy, and then Lucy would insist on sending her money from the business. Asking someone else if they could help her out? Like who? One of their contractors? Or… She looked uncertainly at Ricardo as she followed him to the car.

There was nothing she hated more than being beholden to someone, accepting a benefit she could neither repay nor return. It went against everything she believed in to ask anyone to even lend her money—and were the money for her own personal spending she would have starved rather than consider it. But it wasn't. It would just be temporary. And she had a duty to the business that surely overrode her own pride?

As they reached the car Ricardo looked at Carly. It was obvious to him that she was expecting him to do the gentlemanly thing and offer to replace her lost clothing. Poor girl—how on earth could she be expected to manage with just the contents of her hand luggage and the clothes she stood up in? She couldn't—and, since effectively she was here at least in part for his benefit, naturally he, as a very wealthy man should offer to provide her with a suitable new wardrobe.

And when he didn't respond as she obviously wanted him to, what, he mused, would be her next move?

Did St Tropez have second-hand clothes shops? Charity shops? Carly wondered worriedly as she thanked Ricardo when he politely held open the passenger door of the car for her. Surely it must. French women were known to be shrewd in such matters.

'Something wrong?' Ricardo asked her smoothly.

She was very tempted to admit just how much was wrong—although she doubted he would share her dismay at the thought of a £4,000 bill, she thought ruefully. She opted for discretion instead, and told him lightly, 'I didn't realise you'd be driving yourself. I was expecting a chauffeur-driven car.'

Of course she was. Women like her did.

'Even billionaires sometimes like to economise,' he told her dryly, before adding, more truthfully, 'I like driving, and I grew up in Naples. If you can drive there and live, you can drive anywhere.'

The car was plain and solidly built, but—blissfully—the air-conditioning was wonderfully effective.

They were stationary in a queue of traffic, and at the side of the road a young man was offering a stunningly pretty girl a peach. As Carly looked on, the girl, oblivious to everything and everyone other than the young man, leaned forward and cupped her hand round his. Then, without taking her gaze from his, she took a bite out of the ripe fruit whilst its juice ran from it onto their interlocked hands.

The small tableau was so intensely sensual and intimate that Carly immediately looked away—and found she was looking right into Ricardo's eyes.

Could he see in hers that she had watched the young couple, wondering how it would feel if *he* had been the one offering the peach to her? If its juice had run on *her* bare skin, would he have bent his head to savour its path with his tongue? Would he have…?

She started to tremble violently, small beads of sweat breaking out on her skin, and her body was suddenly thrown forward against her seatbelt as Ricardo depressed the accelerator savagely, causing the car to shoot forward.

What the hell was the matter with him? Ricardo berated himself silently. No way was he dumb enough to fall for something so obvious as the tired old come-on Carly had just tried out on him. *Look at my lips, watch my tongue, imagine…*

It was those damned eyes of hers that did it! How the hell did she manage to get them to turn so smoky and lustrous with desire on demand like that?

Hell—insanely, for a second, she'd almost had him persuaded that the sight of those two kids with their peach had made her ache for him as if he was the only man on earth. Not that his body needed much persuading. It was all too eager to believe she wanted him.

CHAPTER FOUR

'WHERE exactly are we staying?' Carly asked Ricardo, hoping that it would be within easy walking distance of the town and the harbour. She would need easy access to both from early tomorrow morning, so that she could liaise properly with their contractors and get to the bank, as she had promised her parents, plus somehow find time to replenish her wardrobe.

'Villa Mimosa,' Ricardo answered her. 'It's outside St Tropez itself, up in the hills overlooking the sea. I'm not a particular fan of over-hyped, supposedly *in* places. Invariably, every minor celebrity that TV and magazines have ever created flock to them for maximum publicity exposure, destroying whatever charm the place may once have had. I like my privacy, and personally I prefer quality to quantity every time.'

'Oh, yes. Me too,' Carly agreed immediately. 'But I do need to be able to get into St Tropez quickly and easily.'

'Ah, you're thinking about replacing your missing clothes,' Ricardo said affably.

Carly couldn't help laughing. 'That, yes—but I was thinking more of liaising with our contractors.'

'Mmm. I thought the purpose of this trip was for you to liaise with me,' Ricardo told her softly.

Damn and double damn. He cursed himself mentally as he saw Carly absorbing the subtle flirtatiousness of his remark. Why the hell had he done that? Why hadn't he waited and let her come on to him? Now she knew he was receptive to her!

Ricardo had just flirted with her! A heady mixture of pleasure and excitement danced along her veins. Careful, she warned herself. Remember you don't want to get into a situation you can't afford. On the other hand, there was such a thing as being too cautious. After all, her common sense told her that a man like Ricardo would not be interested in anything more than the very briefest kind of relationship—a 'no commitment of any kind' type of relationship. The perfect kind of relationship, surely, for a woman like her, who did not want to fall in love but who secretly—even if this was the first time she had admitted it to herself—wondered what it would be like to have sex with a man all her instincts told her would be a once-in-a-lifetime lover. Why shouldn't she live a little recklessly for once?

'Well, I certainly want to do my best to please you.'

Carly could scarcely believe such words had come from her own lips. Words that, no matter how demurely she had spoken them, could surely only convey to Ricardo a very provocative message.

Ricardo turned his head to look at her. That was more like it!

The look in those dark eyes was quite unmistakable, Carly recognised, as her heart missed a beat and sweet, hot, sensual arousal poured through her body like warm honey.

'We're here.'

'What? Oh. Yes.'

She had actually blushed, Ricardo marvelled as he stopped the car. And her nipples were standing out beneath the fabric of her tee shirt in flagrant sexual arousal.

Ridiculously, suddenly he was as hot for her as though he were a mere youth and this was his first time.

She might as well ask for his help and get it out of the way now, Carly decided. Because once they got inside…

Once they got inside *what*? Once they got inside she hoped he would take her to bed?

Her thoughts were leaving her torn between shock and delight. And urgency! Suddenly she wanted very much to get the matter of her need for a short-term loan and her discomfort about mentioning it to him out of the way.

So that she could be free to encourage him to flirt with her and ultimately—maybe—take her to bed without it hanging over her?

The unfamiliar recklessness of her own thoughts took some getting used to. But she wasn't tempted to abandon them, was she?

So first things first, and then…

She cleared her throat and took a deep breath.

'Ricardo… I…er…'

The husky little catch in her voice was very effective, Ricardo thought, as he waited for her to continue.

'I feel very uncomfortable about this, but…'

'Yes?' he encouraged when she pretended to falter. After all, he reasoned cynically, the sooner he could get this farce over with, the sooner he could satisfy the itch to possess her that had now become an almighty, savage, unignorable ache.

Carly took heart from the kindness in Ricardo's patient encouragement.

'I need to replace some of the things that were in my suitcase. I don't want to worry Lucy—it's my job to deal with the accounts, after all—and… And I know this is…' Her face had started to burn. 'I was wondering if I could ask you to lend me some money—just temporarily, of course.'

Why had she ever thought this was a good idea? Carly wondered, feeling acutely embarrassed. Just listening to herself as she stumbled over her words made her go cold with horror at what she was doing. And if *she* found her request unacceptable, then what on earth must Ricardo be thinking?

'I feel dreadful about this,' she admitted honestly, 'but I can't think of what else I can do.'

Really? Didn't she possess a bank account of her own? A credit card? A debit card? The ability to walk into a bank?

'It would just be a loan. I would pay you back, of course…'

Indeed she would—and with interest.

Several different potential responses presented themselves to him, but in the end he decided that, since Carly was so patently thick-skinned, he might as well go for the oldest and least believable of all of them.

So he smiled at her, and then he took hold of her hand and patted it. And then he told her smoothly, 'I shall be delighted to help you. How much do you think you will need?'

She was gazing at him starry-eyed, her face slightly flushed, her lips slightly parted, as though she could hardly believe her good fortune.

Such a heroic effort deserved a generous reward, Ricardo decided cynically.

'Wait! I've had a better idea.' But she, of course, had no doubt already had the same idea before him. 'Why don't we go into St Tropez together tomorrow and you can choose whatever you think you may need?'

For some reason she didn't look as delighted as Ricardo had expected.

Ricardo had made her a wonderful offer, but she was not sure it was one she felt comfortable with, Carly reflected, as she thanked him.

'That's very generous of you.'

'I'm delighted to be able to help,' Ricardo assured her, before adding, 'Come on, let's go inside.'

Carly was used to staying in beautiful and magnificent properties, but the Villa Mimosa was truly breathtaking. Its setting alone—tucked into a hillside, overlooking the Mediterranean—provided a view that must surely always catch at the heart.

From the balcony of her bedroom she could look out over immaculate gardens and across a miraculous infinity pool to the horizon, and although it was a couple of hours now since they had arrived at the villa she still kept going to the balcony and gazing at the view.

The middle-aged Frenchwoman who had welcomed them had explained that she was the maid but that she did not live in. Cathy must have looked rather surprised at that, she realised, because after she had left them Ricardo had explained to her that he preferred to have his own personal staff on hand or do without.

'My own people know how I like things done, and they know too that I like my privacy. It's mid-afternoon now, and I have some business matters to attend to,' he had told her, 'so why don't we agree to meet up on the terrace at, say, six? My choice would be for us to eat in,' he had added suavely. 'I can arrange to have something delivered.'

Carly had felt her heart miss a couple of beats at the potential implications of dining alone with him.

'That sounds perfect,' she had answered, and then worried when she had seen the gleam in his eyes that she had sounded naïvely over-enthusiastic.

Six o'clock, he had said. And it was five now. She might not have anything to change in to, but she certainly intended to shower and tidy herself up.

Half an hour later, showered and still wearing the thick towelling robe she had found hanging up in the bathroom, she was just brushing her hair when she heard a soft tap on her bedroom door. It opened and Ricardo walked in, carrying two well filled champagne glasses.

'I've mixed you a Bellini. I hope you like them.'

'Oh, yes. Yes, I do,' she agreed.

Unlike her, he was fully dressed, in dark linen trousers and a white linen shirt, his bare brown feet thrust into soft plain leather sandals.

He came over to where she was sitting and put one glass down on the glass-topped dressing table, then held the other out to her.

'Try it first,' he urged her.

Sipping from a glass whilst he held it surely shouldn't be such a sensually intimate experience, should it? And why couldn't she stop looking at the long brown fingers curled round the stem of the glass? She tried to focus on something else, but discovered that the only other thing to focus on was his body, and that the place where the line of his trousers was broken by a telltale bulge was exactly on her eye line. And, what was worse, she couldn't seem to stop herself from gazing appreciatively at it.

'It's lovely,' she assured him hurriedly, taking a sip and then turning away. 'I hadn't realised that was the time. I'd better hurry up and get dressed.'

He gave a small shrug.

'You might as well stay as you are. I hope you like lobster by the way.'

'I love it,' she told him truthfully.

'And I also hope that the gourmet meals-on-wheels outfit who brought the food are as good they are supposed to be. I thought we'd eat outside on the terrace.'

He was obviously expecting her to go with him, Carly realised. A bathrobe wouldn't normally have been her first choice of dinner outfit, but on this occasion it seemed she had no alternative.

'I really am grateful to you for being so kind about the money,' she told him.

'Good. Maybe later you might find a way of showing me how much, mmm?'

Ricardo watched cynically as somehow or other she managed to summon a look of shocked bemusement quickly followed by hot excitement into the smoky darkness of her eyes. But his cynicism wasn't stopping him from wanting her, was it? he reminded himself. In fact he had spent the last three hours thinking about very little other than satisfying that want. Which was why, in the end, he had given in to it and gone to her room.

Was Ricardo saying what she thought he was saying? Carly wondered dizzily. Or was she letting her own erotic imagination run away with her?

At least Lucy and Jules would be pleased to learn she was about to abandon her virgin status. Abandon…it was such an emotive word, such a sensual word. And, recklessly, she was already eager to abandon herself to the physical pleasure of Ricardo's possession.

'Or would you prefer to make a start now?'

Carly's eyes widened as he came to within a few inches of her and bent his head toward hers, his hand resting lightly on the side of her face.

She had never been kissed like this before. There was no physical contact other than that of their lips and his fingers lightly caressing her face. His mouth moved more fiercely on hers and Carly responded instinctively, moving closer to him, leaning into him as his tongue drove deeper into the soft recesses of her mouth to take possession of it.

She started to raise her arms, wanting to hold him, but to her confusion he stopped her, gripping her shoulders and releasing her mouth to step back from her.

Whilst she looked up at him in confusion he untied the belt of her robe and then pushed it off her shoulders in one swift easy movement that left her totally naked in front of him. Her only covering was the hot wave of colour that beat up under her skin. His gaze dropped to her body with the swift descent of an eagle to its prey. It stalked slowly over creamy slender shoulders, down to ripely rounded breasts, softly heavy with sensual promise, silky pale skin contrasting with the darker aureoles from which her rose nipples thrust so eagerly.

Her ribcage curved into a narrow waist, below which her hips flared out again, and her legs were, as he had already known they would be, unbelievably long and perfectly shaped. A soft cap of downy dark curls formed a neat little triangle just above the delicately shaped outer lips of her sex, curled protectively over it.

A dozen—no, a hundred different sensations and desires struck him, which in the end were only one need, one desire, and that the most ancient and powerful of all male needs and desires.

His gaze was fixed on her as though her body was a visual magnet from which he could not look away.

He wanted her. He wanted her right here and right now. He wanted her as he had never wanted any woman before. His own flesh was so immediately and intensely aroused that it was almost painful.

He wanted to take her quickly, fiercely, hotly plunging his flesh within hers and filling her, as though in taking her he would somehow drive out his own need for her.

And yet at the same time he wanted to savour the experience of having her, to relish it and wait for it.

Carly felt like a…a houri in front of a sultan—aware of her own nakedness before him and in some weird way actually physically excited by the fact that he was seeing her like that. Because she knew that he desired her, and his desire for her gave her power over him? The telltale bulge had now become a definite and openly defined ridge of flesh she badly wanted to reach out to and caress. Carly touched her tongue-tip to her lips.

No man had looked at her in the way Ricardo just had. With such a blazing heat of desire that she could have sworn she'd actually felt its burn against her skin.

But then no man had ever seen her like this—stripped bare, vulnerable, the whole of herself revealed.

She could feel a small, excited pulse beating inside her body.

Ricardo was picking up her Bellini and handing it to her. Uncertainly she took it from him. 'You have a beautiful body,' he told her emotionlessly. 'I'm tempted to tell you to stay like this, so that I can continue to have the pleasure of looking at it, but I'm not sure my self-control could go the distance.'

He bent down to pick up her robe and handed it to her.

When she learned forward to take it from him, he lowered his head and took one taut nipple into his mouth. Could those fierce pangs she felt deep inside her body really be caused by the fierce tugging of his mouth on her nipple? She heard herself moan and was afraid she might collapse. Her legs felt so weak. And yet when his mouth was no longer there she ached for its return, she realised, as he pulled her robe back on for her as unceremoniously and as swiftly as he had removed it.

'More wine?'

Should she? Carly stared into her empty glass. 'No. No more,' she told him firmly, aware of how quickly what she had already had to drink had gone to her head.

It had been heaven eating out here on the secluded patio. The night air was soft and scented, the smallest of warm breezes was caressing her skin, and the moon was a fat yellow disc up above them.

She gave a small sensual shiver, acknowledging that the memory of those few minutes in her bedroom had left a very erotic imprint on her body.

'More lobster?'

Carly shook her head.

'No?' Ricardo questioned softly. 'You're satisfied, then, in every single way?'

He reached across the table and took hold of her hand, caressing it lightly.

How on earth could Ricardo touching her hand cause her throat to constrict? Carly wondered helplessly as she gazed at him, unable to speak.

She was extremely clever, Ricardo acknowledged. She obviously knew from past experience that men liked to do their own hunting. She had let him know she was available, and now she was sitting back and letting him set the pace.

He released her hand and stood up. Carly looked up uncertainly. Ricardo smiled back at her and held out his hand. A little breathlessly, she pushed back her chair and stood up herself. Holding her hand, he drew her towards the low wall that separated the terrace from the rest of the garden.

'Wait,' Carly protested, just before they reached it.

He watched her as she wriggled swiftly out of the robe. She had been aching to do it all through the meal, unable to stop thinking about how she had felt and how he had looked at her earlier on. She had never previously given any thought to her own nakedness in terms of its erotic appeal, but now she was acutely aware of the warm touch of the night air on her skin, and the gloriously wanton feeling that knowing Ricardo couldn't stop looking at her was giving her.

Ricardo felt as though the air was being ripped out of his lungs, whilst at the same time the darkest kind of male pleasure was exploding inside him.

He took hold of her, imprisoning her between his own body and a thick mass of geraniums tumbling over the wall, his hands at the curve of her waist, his mouth fastening on hers.

Carly melted into him, her lips parting eagerly in invitation, her arms winding round his neck. His tongue, deliberately pointed and hard, thrust against her own, its stabbing movement making her moan and shake with pleasure. She wanted him to give her more of it, to fill the hot, wet cavity he was pleasuring until she could take no more of him.

She whimpered in pleasure and arched her body into his, removing one hand from his neck to unfasten his shirt buttons.

She was just as he had known she would be! Just like every other woman who had looked at him and seen an easy future for herself, Ricardo told himself. But his hands were still sliding up over her ribcage to mould the warm weight of her breasts; his fingers were seeking the eager hardness of nipples as swollen and firm as small thimbles.

She moaned against his tongue as he played with them, caressing and rubbing them, and her own fingers struggled with his zip before she finally managed to slide it down.

He had expected her immediately to touch him intimately, but instead she moved closer to him, rubbing herself sensuously against him with a soft sound of pleasure.

Her height meant that she fitted him as perfectly as though they had been made for one another. He released her breasts and allowed her to rub their sensitive tips against his flesh, his hands supporting her back and then massaging it, shaping her spine and going lower, to cup the rounded curves of her buttocks, hold the bones of her hips. His hand slipped lower, his fingers finding the cleft between her legs. He might not be able to see the ripe readiness of her desire-swollen lips, but he could feel it.

His fingers dipped seductively into the wetness of her sex.

She made a sound deep in her throat and moved eagerly against him, the movement of her body against him in time with the thrust of his tongue within the soft, dark cave of her mouth.

His body was straining against her, and the moment he moved she looked down, her gaze fastening on the swollen, darkly veined head of his sex.

His fingers stroked the length of her wetness, caressing her more intimately with each stroke until she felt hot and open, her eager moans inviting him to plunge deeper. Her fingertips were just skimming the hard outline of his penis, almost as though she was afraid to touch it. Or was she simply enjoying tormenting him because she knew how much he wanted her?

Perhaps he should punish her a little for doing that to him?

Punish her and please himself, he thought hotly, as his fingertip massaged the slick wetness of her clitoris and he felt her whole body jump and then shudder wantonly.

Her fingers were circling him, holding him, exploring him, her touch cool against his own heat.

He had to have her.

Carly made a small mewling sound of pleasure deep in her throat and reached out for him, cupping his face with her hands and pressing her mouth passionately against his. All she wanted—all she would want for the rest of her life—was this, and him.

Abruptly she pulled back from him.

Her heart was thudding unevenly with the shock of her thoughts and feelings. Her emotional thoughts, and her equally emotional feelings. She felt sick and shaky as reaction set in and she recognised her own danger. How had this happened? How had she gone from wanting to have sex with to him to wanting *him*?

'What's wrong?'

She was too engrossed in her own thoughts to hear the sharp warning of male frustration in Ricardo's voice.

'I'm sorry… I…I don't think this is a good idea…'

Ricardo could taste the raw savagery of his own furious disbelief. How could he have been such a fool as to let her play him so cleverly? To let her arouse him to the point where nothing mattered more than him having her?

'So what would make it a good idea?' Ricardo demanded bitingly, gripping her arms and swinging her round so hard that she almost stumbled. 'Or should I say how much would make it a good idea? Five thousand? Ten? *Carte blanche* on a credit card?'

Carly stared at him in bewildered shock.

'And you can cut that out,' Ricardo told her. 'I've known what you are from the start. Nick Blayne made it plain enough—not that he needed to. It was obvious what you were from the night I saw you in that damned club, letting someone else's husband paw you.'

A slow, achingly painful form of semi-numbness was creeping up over her body, paralysing her ability to move.

'Well? Come on—answer me. Obviously the promise of a ''loan'' wasn't enough. So what else are you after? A new designer wardrobe? A Cartier diamond? Nick told me that you were good at recognising how to get the maximum amount of financial benefit out of a relationship.'

Belated anger seared through her. 'I'm certainly good at recognising what he's doing to the business—and ultimately to Lucy,' Carly told him hotly. Humiliation was scorching her skin as she absorbed what Ricardo had said to her—what he had said *about* her.

'Well?' Ricardo demanded again, ignoring her furious outburst. 'How much?'

'Nothing,' Carly told him proudly. 'You could have had me for nothing, Ricardo. For no other reason than that I wanted you, for nothing other than the benefit to me of having sex with you.'

'What?' He gave her a derisively cynical look. 'We both know that that's a lie, and it's not even a good one. You are the one who called a halt.'

Yes, she had. But not for the reasons he was so insultingly suggesting. And she certainly couldn't tell him now why she had wanted to stop.

'You are so wrong about me. I would never—have never—' She stopped as she saw the contemptuous look in his eyes.

'What about the money you asked me for?'

The money she had wanted to borrow from him? Of course—in his eyes that had damned her.

'You don't understand—that *was* just a loan. I *will* pay you back,' she told him quietly.

Ricardo was in no mood to be placated.

'Oh, I think I do understand. Let's see. You pretend to lose your suitcase, then you come on to me, expecting that I will take the bait. Then when I do you immediately back off, thinking that I'm going to ache so damned much for you I'll do anything to have you. How complicated to understand is that?' His mouth twisted in open contempt.

She had thought she knew what it was like to have her pride ripped from her, leaving her exposed to people's contempt, but she had been wrong, she recognised through the blur of her shocked, anguished, furious humiliation.

But what was even worse was that she now knew exactly what he had really been thinking about her.

Automatically she tried to defend herself, protesting emotionally, 'You're wrong!'

But he stopped her immediately, challenging her. 'About what? You coming on to me?' He shook his head. 'I don't think so. Not that you didn't get something out of it yourself, so don't bother trying to pretend you didn't. No woman gets as hot and wet as you did and—'

It was too much. Carly reacted immediately and instinctively, her pride driving her to react in a way that was pure, instinctive, emotionally wounded female.

She raised her hand, but before she could do any more Ricardo was gripping her wrist in a bruisingly painful hold.

'If you want to fight dirty that's fine,' he told her softly. 'But remember I grew up on the streets. If you hit me, then I promise you I shall retaliate in kind.'

When he saw her face he laughed. 'No, I don't hit women. But there are other ways of administering punishment!'

'You are a barbarian!' Carly whispered shakily. 'And you have no right… You are totally wrong!' Tears of reaction were stinging her eyes now, but no way was she going to let him see that. 'I only asked to borrow the money because I didn't want to worry Lucy.'

'Yes, of course. Blame someone else. Women like you are very good at that.'

Carly had had enough. 'You don't know the first thing about a woman like me!'

'On the contrary, I know a very great deal.' Ricardo stopped her sharply. 'I know, for instance, that you are the product of generations of so-called good breeding, that your parents are wealthy and well connected, but that you yourself do not have any independent means. You also went to one of the country's top schools. In short, you believe you have an automatic right to the very best of everything and an even more deeply ingrained belief that because of what you are you are superior to those people who have not had your advantages. You expect to be granted a first-class passage through life, preferably paid for by someone else. You are a taker, a user—a gold-digger.'

Something—a bubble of either pain or hysterical laughter—was tightening her chest and then her throat.

'And I know that *you* are a prejudiced, ill-informed misogynist. And—as I've already said—you know nothing about me,' she told him shakily, before turning on her heel and walking away from him.

Alone in the safety of her room she gave in to the tremors of aftershock racking her body, holding onto the back of a chair to steady herself. One day—maybe—she would look back on this, on *him*, and what he had said to her, with irony and perhaps even amusement. Because he was so breathtakingly, hugely wrong about her.

But for now… For now she would be grateful to him for showing her how easily she could have slipped into the emotional danger she had always feared and for going on to destroy every single tendril of those tentative feelings. At least now she was safe from feeling anything for him other than furious outrage.

Were it possible for her to do so, she would leave the villa immediately. But she had Lucy and the business to think of, and Carly had been taught from a very young age to carry a dual burden of gratitude and responsibility.

She would have to stay, and she would have to remember why she was here and why he was here, and behave towards him with all the professional courtesy she could muster.

For the rest, she would rather go naked than ask him for so much as a rag to cover her—would rather starve than accept a crust from his table, rather die than let him see how very much he had hurt her and in how many different ways.

'I know what you are,' he had said.

But the truth was he did not know her at all.

The truth was… The truth was a secret, and so painful that she could not bear to share it with anyone.

CHAPTER FIVE

CARLY stood on the harbourside, her eyes shaded by dark glasses, as she and the chefs ticked off the items being delivered.

It was eleven o'clock in the morning and she had been up since half past five. Luckily she had managed to persuade a taxi driver to pick her up from the villa, despite the earliness of the hour, initially to go to the flower market with the florist, Jeff, and his team to ensure that the freshest and most perfect blooms were purchased for the party, and then to accompany the two chefs when they bought the fresh produce they needed.

She was trying very hard not to keep looking at the strip of pale flesh where her Cartier watch had been. She had loved it so much—not because of its monetary value but because of what it represented. The owner of the small shop she had found tucked down a narrow alley had expressed neither curiosity nor surprise when she had handed over her watch in return for a wad of euros and a pawn ticket. Once she got home she intended to speak with her bank and arrange to either take out a loan or realise some of her assets so that she could both buy it back and give herself a small cash reserve. She hated the idea of being in debt, but there was nothing else she could do.

As soon as she could snatch an hour she intended to replace the lost clothes as best she could. Which wasn't going to be easy. True, she had seen a wide variety of trendy shops and boutiques on her way to and from the market, but the clothes at the cheaper end of the market were really only suitable for the very young, whilst those she would have considered suitable were way, way out of her price range.

Luckily, on her way back from the flower market she had spotted a stall selling casual holiday wear and had been able to buy a pair of three-quarter capri pants and a couple of tee shirts. Buying new underwear had proved a little more difficult, but eventually she had found the small shop she had been recommended to try, tucked down a side street off Rue Georges, and had been able to buy a pack of plain white briefs and a simple flesh-coloured bra.

Behind them the harbour was filled with the huge white luxury yachts of wealthy visitors, but the yacht belonging to Prêt a Party's client surely had to be the most expensive and glamorous looking of all.

Carly had been given a tour of it earlier by Mariella D'Argent's PA, Sarah, who had also generously offered Carly the use of her own small cabin to change in, and had then insisted on taking her travel-worn clothes to the yacht's laundry, promising that Carly would have them back before evening.

'It's a pity we aren't the same size, otherwise I could have loaned you something,' she had commiserated when Carly had told her what had happened with her luggage. 'Mariella is, though,' she had added thoughtfully. 'Okay, she may be a bit taller…'

'And at least two sizes thinner,' Carly had tacked on, laughing.

Mariella D'Argent, their client, had been one of the fashion world's best known and best paid top models before her marriage to her financier husband, and even now, at close to forty, she was still an exceptionally stunning and beautiful woman. And an even more exceptionally spoiled one, Carly had decided, after listening politely to her fretful demands.

'Mmm, and guess how she stays that way.' Sarah had grimaced. 'I swear to heaven one of these days she's going to get it wrong—sniff Botox up the new nose her surgeon has had to construct for her and inject cocaine into her wrinkles. And then, of course, there's always the danger that she might take his Viagra whilst he takes her Prozac—or at least there would be if they still shared a bed.'

Carly had tried not to laugh.

'Anyway, what about one of those fab silky floaty cotton kaftans that are all the rage? A short one, worn over some slinky cream or white pants, and perhaps a stunning belt—that would look terrific. Or a sarong tied round them, perhaps? That's a very cool look now,' Sarah had suggested helpfully.

Carly had nodded her head and smiled, even whilst knowing that the type of oh, so casual but oh, so expensive items Sarah was referring to were completely outside her budget. She had seen the kaftans Sarah had described on her way down to the harbour this morning. Gorgeous, silky fine floaty wisps of cotton, with wonderful embroidery and a price tag of well over a whole month's salary!

The party was due to start at ten o'clock in the evening, prior to which the D'Argents were holding a 'small' dinner party for fifty of their guests onshore.

'So, what do you think of this?'

Dutifully Carly gave her attention to the clever arrangement of greenery and mirrors the florist had used to create a magical effect, making the small reception area appear far larger than it actually was.

'Very impressive, Jeff,' she told him truthfully.

Their own construction crew were speedily finishing erecting a framework for the tenting fabric, which was cream with a design on it in black to complement Mariella D'Argent's theme for the evening: cream, black and grey.

Currently a redhead, she, of course, would look stunning in any combination of such colours!

Looking at the fabric, Carly thought briefly of persuading the man in charge of the construction crew to give her a piece. Wrapped around plain black trousers it would look stunning—but perhaps just a bit too obvious? On the other hand, wearing it, she should be able to melt into her surroundings!

A rueful, mischievous smile illuminated her face—and that was how Ricardo saw her as he drove into the harbour area.

He had thought at first when he got up that she was still sleeping, and it had been nearly midday when he had finally decided to go and check on her.

The discovery that she had left the villa without him knowing had caused him a quixotic mix of emotions, the most dangerous and unwanted of which had been a shaft of pure male possessiveness and jealousy.

Because she had aroused him? She was far from the first woman to have done that, and he certainly hadn't felt possessive about any of the others!

Deep down inside himself Ricardo was aware of the insistent and powerful effect she had on his emotions. She made him feel incredibly, furiously, savagely angry, for one thing. For another, she was making him spend far too much time thinking about her.

He was still several yards away from her when Carly suddenly became aware of his presence, alerted to it by a sudden tingling physical awareness that had her turning round apprehensively.

Dressed in natural-coloured linen trousers and a white linen shirt, dark glasses shielding his eyes from the brilliant glare of the sun, he looked utterly at home against the moneyed backdrop of St. Tropez, and Carly was not surprised to see several women stop to look appreciatively at him as he strode towards her.

'How did you get down here?'

The peremptory demand was curt and to the point.

'I called a cab.'

He was frowning.

'You could have asked me to drive you.'

She gave him a bitterly angry look and started to turn away from him without responding.

Immediately he placed a restraining hand on her arm.

'I said—'

'I heard what you said.' Carly stopped him. 'And for your information I would have walked here—barefoot, if necessary—rather than ask you for help.'

A cautionary inner voice tried to remind her that she had decided to behave towards him with cool professionalism.

'The wounded pride effect won't cut any ice with me, Carly,' he told her. 'I see you've managed to acquire a change of clothes,' he added dryly.

No way was she going to tell him that the cost of the taxi plus these clothes had taken all but a few of her small store of euros, and that without the money she had got from pawning her watch right now she would have had less than the cost of a cup of coffee and a sandwich in her bag. She pulled away from him instead.

A small commotion on the yacht's walkway had her turning round to watch Mariella D'Argent, flanked by sundry members of her personal staff, walking towards them.

The ex-model looked stunning. She was wearing close-fitting Capri pants low on the hips to reveal an enviably taut flat stomach and hipbones. A contrasting halter-necked top skimmed the perfect, if somewhat suspiciously unmoving shape of her breasts, which were obviously bare beneath it. A large straw hat and a pair of huge dark sunglasses shielded her face from the sunlight, and on her feet she was wearing a pair of impossibly flimsy high-heeled sandals.

She ignored Carly, smiling warmly at Ricardo instead and exclaiming excitedly, 'Ricardo, darling—how wonderful. I didn't know you were in St Tropez. You must join us tonight. We're having a small party to launch the new yacht.'

Carly watched as Ricardo smiled his acceptance without saying that he had already intended to be present.

'And you must come to the dinner we're having first—just a select few of us.'

Behind Mariella's back Sarah caught Carly's eye and pulled a face.

'What are you doing now?' Mariella was asking. 'We're all on our way to Nikki Beach. Why don't you come with us?'

'I don't think so, Mariella,' Carly heard Ricardo reply firmly. 'I'm afraid I've outgrown the appeal of paying a hugely inflated sum of money to buy a bottle of champagne to spray all over some so-called model's equally hugely inflated chest.'

Mariella gave a small trill of laughter—which was quite an impressive feat, since not a single muscle in her face moved as she did so, Carly reflected, then pulled herself up mentally for being a bitch.

'That won't please her,' Sarah muttered to Carly as she came to stand next to her. 'And she's already in a strop because *Hello!* magazine has pulled out of giving the party a double-page spread. It's doing one on some film star's new nursery instead. Who's the hunk, by the way?' she whispered, looking at Ricardo.

'A potential new client,' Carly answered her. 'He wants to see the way we work.'

'Mmm, well, he's certainly brightened Mariella's day for her. What's the betting she's already planning how to lure him down to her stateroom and which Agent Provocateur underwear she's going to be wearing when she does?'

'I don't think she'll have to try very hard,' Carly answered lightly. 'They seem very much two of a kind.'

So why was she suffering such a wrenching pain at the thought of them together?

It was physical frustration, that was all, she reassured herself as she continued to ignore Ricardo, keeping her back turned towards him. Because after the pang of longing that had come through her when she had seen him striding towards her she didn't trust herself to be able to look directly at him.

From the table where he was sitting at a café opposite the harbour, Ricardo had an uninterrupted view of the D'Argents' yacht and the activity around it being orchestrated by Carly.

It was true that last night he had been too enraged and frustrated to think analytically about the way she was likely to react to his denunciation of her, and it was also true that, had he done so, it certainly wouldn't have occurred to him that she would retreat behind a screen of icy politeness and professionalism. On the one hand meticulously making sure that he was provided with ample opportunity to witness every aspect of the preparations for the upcoming event and ask whatever questions he wished, and yet on the other managing to convey to him very clearly that she loathed and resented every second she had to spend in his company.

As a portrayal of an affronted woman whose morals were beyond reproach it was very impressive, he admitted. Unfortunately for her, though, he knew she was no such thing. So she was wasting her time.

It was irritating that Prêt a Party's financial year-end meant that the only figures available for his inspection were virtually a year out of date. He had given instructions that he wanted more up to date financial information, but that, of course, would take time as it would have to be acquired discreetly. He certainly did not want anyone else alerted to the fact that he was considering it as an acquisition.

He picked up the local newspaper a previous occupant of the table had left and opened it. Italian was his first language, but he was fluent in several others, including French. He was idly flicking through the pages when a sentimentally captioned photograph on one of them caught his eye. Frowning, he studied it in disbelief.

An 'angel of mercy', the paper fancifully described a young woman holding out sandwiches to a group of beggar children. The photo accompanied a piece on the best ways to help street children, and the woman was quite definitely Carly, even if she had been photographed with her back to the camera. He also recognised the airport location, and the suitcase on the ground behind her—although not the outstretched male hand that was just in the shot, grasping it.

He closed the paper, his mouth grim.

Okay, so maybe—just maybe—her suitcase had genuinely been stolen. As for her act of charity… He hadn't missed the way she had reached out to the smallest and weakest of the children, making sure that he received his fair share of the food she was handing out. As a boy he had had first-hand experience of what it was like to have to beg for food.

A large limousine drew up in front of Carly and several people got out and started to walk towards her. One of them she recognised as the current 'in' classical violinist who had been hired to play as the guests came on board.

Immediately she went to greet him and introduce herself to him and his entourage. The violinist, unlike the catering staff and the florist, had been invited to mingle with the guests later in the evening, and had been given a room in a St Tropez luxurious boutique hotel, paid for by the D'Argents.

Naturally he wanted to know where he would be playing, and dutifully Carly set about answering his manager's questions.

Inside she was still feeling sick with shock and misery over Ricardo's accusations, but she was here to do a job, not indulge her own feelings. And besides, she had a long history of having to hide what she was feeling and the pain and humiliation others had inflicted on her.

Her adoptive parents might turn to her for financial assistance, but it had been their own daughter to whom they had given their love, not Carly.

Ricardo got up and came towards Carly.

'I'm going back to the villa shortly. Presumably you will wish to go back yourself at some stage, in order to get ready for this evening. Should you want a lift—'

'I don't,' Carly told him curtly, without looking up from checking one of the invoices in front of her.

'Cut out the hard-done-by act, Carly,' Ricardo snapped, equally curtly. 'I'm not taken in by it.'

'I don't wish to discuss it.'

'You thought you'd fooled me and you don't like the fact that I caught you out.'

'No. What I don't like is the fact that I was stupid enough to think there was anything remotely desirable about you.'

'But you did desire me, didn't you?'

'You must excuse me, Mr Salvatore. I've got work to do.'

She didn't turn to watch him as he walked away from her, but nevertheless she knew immediately when he had gone.

'How's it going?'

Carly gave Sarah, the PA, a slightly harassed smile.

'Okay! So far there's only been one major fall-out between the chefs.'

Sarah laughed. 'You're lucky,' she announced, 'You can add a zero to that so far as the D'Argent's are concerned. Not that *they* fall out so much as *she* falls out with *him*! Did you manage to find something to wear for later?'

Carly shook her head. 'I haven't had time,' she told her truthfully.

'Would these be any use, then?' Sarah asked her, pointing to the overstuffed bin liner she had just put down.

'It's some stuff Mariella told me to get rid of ages ago. Look at this—it would be perfect for you for tonight,' she announced, whipping a mass of silk black fabric out of the top of the bin liner. 'It's a sort of top and palazzo pants thing, all in one.'

The fine silk floated mouthwateringly through Carly's fingers. 'Are you sure that Mariella won't mind?' she asked Sarah worriedly.

'I doubt she'll even notice. Not once she hits the champagne and cocaine,' Sarah answered bluntly.

'It's very sheer…' Carly hesitated.

'You can wear a body underneath it—although Mariella didn't. Oh, and you'll need a pair of high heels—you should be able to pick something up at the market whilst they're having dinner. And if you can't get away you can use my cabin to shower and get changed in.'

Carly gave her a grateful look of relief. 'I was wondering how one earth I was going to manage to make time for that,' she admitted. 'I daren't leave the chefs alone together for too long, and I've promised Jeff I'll make sure no one touches his box trees!'

Sarah laughed and shook her head. 'When is my prince going to come and take me away from all this?' She sighed.

CHAPTER SIX

'HERE they come...'

Carly gave Sarah a slightly distracted smile as they both watched the long line of limousines queuing up to disgorge the D'Argents' guests.

Carly had changed into the black outfit Sarah had given her, and was self-consciously aware of how very suggestively revealing it was. Not even the flesh-coloured body she was wearing beneath it could totally offset the effect of the layers of sheer black fabric floating around her body, revealing with every movement the sensual gleam of her skin beneath the silk.

If she had had something else to wear she would have done so. Sarah had intended to be kind, Carly knew, but no way was this outfit, with its tight-fitting top and hip-hugging palazzo pants bottom, suitable as discreet 'work wear'. But the other outfits had been just as bad.

Already as people approached the gangway they were looking at her—especially the men, some of whom were giving her openly lascivious glances.

Two over-chunky and businesslike dinner-suited bouncer types were checking the invitations before allowing guests to step forward into the open-fronted enclosure, where uniformed staff were waiting to offer welcome glasses of champagne cocktail. The glasses were arranged on white trays, whilst the cocktails were a steel-grey colour.

'What on earth is in them?' Carly had whispered to their own *maître d'*.

'Champagne, liqueur and colouring,' he had told her dryly. 'Mariella D'Argent was insistent that they had to be grey!'

Prior to the D'Argents' return Carly had made a swift inspection of the yacht's receptions areas, to check that everything was as it should be. Privately she felt that the glass floor over thousands of small white lights was a bit OTT, but she had been assured that it was nothing compared with what some people asked for.

The violinist had begun to play, the dinner guests had returned, and Mariella had gone to her suite to get changed into her specially commissioned outfit.

A posse of older men and their too-young arm candy were arriving, the girls all wearing similar teeny-weenie, heavily embroidered clinging dresses and tottering on too-high heels. They were all obviously bleached blondes. Carly suppressed a small sigh.

More guests were arriving, and Carly recognised amongst them some very A-list celebrities—a famous actress, the daughter of a pop icon, a couple of ex-models—all of them accompanied by good-looking men.

But Ricardo hadn't arrived as yet. Not that she was looking for him!

'I'd better go in and be on hand, just in case Mariella wants me for anything,' Sarah whispered to her.

Nodding her head, Carly continued to keep a discreet watch on the arrivals.

'We're going to run short of cocktails any minute,' the *maître d'* muttered warningly.

It took over an hour for all the guests to arrive, by which time Carly was downstairs in the main salon, keeping an eye on the proceedings there and trying to avoid getting too close to Mariella—just in case she should object to Carly wearing her discarded outfit!

Drugs were being passed round openly, and the sound of laughter was growing louder as they began to take effect.

Already some of the guests had started to behave recklessly. A well-known media mogul had grabbed a girl almost in front of Carly and now proceeded to caress her intimately whilst the girl herself encouraged him.

This was just not a lifestyle with which she felt comfortable, Carly reflected with revulsion. She couldn't understand how anyone could find any pleasure in something that ultimately was so very destructive. Drugs were anathema to her. Her eyes shadowed as she remembered how she had seen the misery that they could cause.

She felt a tug on her arm and turned to see one of the older men leering at her. She'd realised from overhearing them talking earlier that they were Russian.

'You come with me,' he demanded drunkenly.

'I'm sorry, I'm not a guest. I'm working,' Carly told him politely, trying to disengage herself.

'Good, then you work for me…in bed,' he responded coarsely. 'I pay you good, eh?'

Carly felt nauseated. Was that how all men saw women—as someone, *something* they could buy? A commodity they could use? Or did she attract that type because somehow instinctively they could sense what she had come from?

Trash! She winced as though she had been knifed, hearing again the contemptuous word that had been thrown at her so often during her childhood.

'You are trash, do you know that? Garbage. In fact, that's where they found you—lying in the rubbish, unwanted—and that's where you should have stayed.'

Abruptly she realised that she could feel the man's hot breath on her bare skin.

She turned to demand that he release her, and then tensed. Ricardo was standing on the other side of the salon, watching her.

He knew what she was, Ricardo reminded himself savagely, so why did the sight of Carly allowing another man to hold her arm so intimately fill him with jealousy instead of contempt? And why the hell was he now pushing his way through the crowd milling through the salon, in the wake of the D'Argents, in order to get to her? After all, he had already seen the proprietorial way her male companion had reached for her. And what was driving him through the crowd certainly wasn't rooted in some kind of male solidarity, or an altruistic desire to warn her latest victim of just what she was, was it? He derided himself cynically. The truth was, he preferred not to analyse just what the sight of another man holding on to her was doing to him—or why.

Instead he channelled his anger into deciding that her escort's taste in clothes—for obviously he must have bought her the abomination she was wearing—was about as good as Carly's was in men. The pair of them deserved one another, and Carly deserved everything she would get from selling herself to a man who might just as well have had what he was tattooed across his forehead.

But Carly wasn't here to have a relationship with another man, and he intended to remind her in no uncertain terms that *he* was supposed to be her prime concern. How dared she reject him and then let that overweight, sweaty nobody put his greasy hands all over her? Where was her pride? Her self-respect? Didn't it ever occur to her that she was intelligent enough to earn her own living and support herself, instead of debasing herself by offering herself to any man who would give her the price of a few designer rags?

'You! Here!'

Carly stared at the man who had spoken to her so arrogantly as he approached, and then realised that he was with the man who was holding her.

'How much do you want?'

He was already opening his wallet and starting to remove money from it.

Another man had joined the other two, taller and leaner, and with an unmistakable air of authority about him. He spoke sharply to them, and to Carly's relief she was immediately released.

'I apologise for my countrymen—I hope you will not condemn all Russian men as unmannerly oafs because of them?'

He was charming, and very good-looking, Carly acknowledged.

'Of course not,' she assured him.

'You are here alone?'

Someone pushed past and he reached out a protective arm to shield her. Unexpectedly Carly suddenly felt very femininely weak and vulnerable. She wasn't used to men behaving protectively towards her.

'I'm with the event planning organisation,' she explained.

'Ah, so you are responsible for this magnificent party we are enjoying?'

He was flattering as well as charming, Carly recognised.

'In part,' she agreed.

'And you are staying here, on board the yacht?'

'No, I'm—' Carly broke off as she saw both Sarah and the *maître d'* edging towards her. 'Please excuse me,' she apologised to him. 'But I must get back to work.'

'Mmm, I see Igor was chatting you up. Mariella won't like that,' Sarah warned Carly, when she joined her, having dealt with the *maître d'*. 'She's already got him marked down as husband number four. Mind you, she'll have her work cut out, because she certainly isn't the only woman who's hoping for a legal right to his billions. God, I hate these dos,' Sarah complained. 'Sometimes I wonder why the hell I don't just give in my notice and go home.'

'Why don't you?' Carly asked her

'Let's just say there's a man there who I can't have,' Sarah told her bleakly. 'I need another drink. I'll be back in a minute…'

Carly was standing with her back to him, watching Sarah hurry away from her, when Ricardo finally managed to reach her.

'Lost your new admirer?'

Carly stiffened, and then turned round reluctantly to face him.

Before she could defend herself, he continued savagely, 'What the hell possessed you to let him buy you that? You look like a tart,' he told her mercilessly. 'Or was that the idea? It certainly looked as though he was doing a brisk business in selling you on to his friends.'

Carly's face burned. 'You are despicable,' she told him. 'And for your information—'

'Ricardo, darling—there you are!'

Although she was delighted to have Ricardo's attention removed from her, Carly couldn't help wishing that the woman claiming it was not Mariella—especially when she saw the way Mariella was staring at her outfit.

Fortunately, though, before she could say anything Sarah returned. Equally fortunately, she immediately realised what was happening and adroitly came to Carly's rescue, exclaiming, 'Mariella! Carly hasn't been able to stop singing your praises for being so kind to her and saving her so much embarrassment. I told her that it is typical of you to be so generous, and that you'd understand immediately how she felt about having her suitcase stolen. I knew you wouldn't mind if I let her borrow those old things you told me to put to one side for the charity shop. Remember? You said they were too big for you…'

Was it the weight of false sentiment and sugar in Sarah's paean of praise that miraculously squashed the hostility in Mariella's gaze? Carly wondered cynically. Suddenly she became all gracious smiles.

'Of course. I love helping other people—everyone knows that. Although I must say you are rather too big to fit into my things, my dear. Of course I am very slim,' she added smugly, before ignoring Carly to turn to Ricardo and say prettily, 'Ricardo, why don't I introduce you to a few more people…?'

As Mariella drew Ricardo away Sarah exhaled and apologised to Carly.

'I hope you didn't mind me saying that—only she looked as though she was about to create a bit of a scene…'

'No, I didn't mind at all,' Carly assured her truthfully. But she would have loved to see

Ricardo's face if Mariella had claimed ownership of her outfit when he had been in the middle of insulting it. Although he hadn't merely insulted the outfit, had he? He'd insulted her as well.

She didn't care what he thought about her, Carly assured herself. After all, she knew the truth and she knew that he was wrong. At least this way, even if she couldn't deny or ignore the physical, sexual effect he had on her, she knew she would be safe from any risk of becoming emotionally attracted to him.

Not, of course, that she *had* been in any danger of that.

It seemed as if the evening was never going to end, Carly thought wearily. The last of the guests had finally gone, but she and the others were still cleaning up.

'Look, why don't you go? There's nothing more for you to do here,' Jeff the florist said in a kind voice.

'It's my responsibility to stay until everything is packed up,' Carly told him.

'You don't think that anyone else would stay around this long, do you?' He grinned at her and shook his head. 'We're perfectly capable of sorting what's left, and besides…' He was looking past her and she turned her head to see what he was looking at.

Her heart gave a sudden heavy thud as the door of the car which had drawn up a few yards away opened and Ricardo got out.

The last time she'd seen him he had been deep in conversation with a stunning redhead whom she was sure she had heard murmuring something about going back to her hotel suite with her. So what was he doing back here now?

Why should the fact that he was striding so purposefully towards her make her legs and her will-power quiver with weakness? He had insulted her in the most offensive way possible, and yet here she was letting his sexuality and, even worse, her own reaction to it, get to her.

Maybe she should adopt a different and more modern attitude. After all, she had heard plenty of women say openly and unashamedly that they were up for having sex with a man without wanting or needing any kind of emotional connection with him. Surely that kind of relationship was exactly what would suit her best?

'It's gone three a.m. and we leave for New York in the morning,' he told her curtly.

'You go, Carly,' Jeff repeated. 'We can easily finish up here now.'

It seemed that she didn't have any choice. Turning aside, Carly went to retrieve the canvas hold-all she had bought earlier to hold her modest new purchases.

She watched with a certain sense of grim satisfaction as Ricardo frowned and took it from her.

'Before you say anything,' she warned him coolly, when they were out of Jeff's hearing, 'I didn't have to sell my body to buy either the bag or its contents. What happened to the redhead, by the way?' she asked unkindly as they walked back to the car. The fact that Ricardo was a potential client had been overwhelmed by her still smarting pride. 'Didn't she come up to your expectations—or was it you who didn't come up to hers?'

'Neither. She left with the man with whom she arrived—and even if she hadn't *I* don't take those kinds of risks with my health,' Ricardo answered pointedly.

He was opening the car door for her, but Carly paused to turn round and demand angrily, 'Meaning what? That I do? Isn't the discovery that you've already made one offensive and insulting error of judgement about me enough?'

Without waiting for his response she got into the car, ignoring him as she reached for the seatbelt, and continuing to ignore him when he walked round the car, climbed into the driver's seat and started the car engine.

They reached the villa. Carly opened the car door and got out without waiting for Ricardo to help her.

The pink-washed building was bathed in a soft rose glow from the artfully placed nightscape lighting, which illuminated both the villa and its gardens. Rose-pink—the colour of romance. A small, painful smile twisted her lips.

'Carly.'

She stopped walking and turned to look as Ricardo caught up with her.

'Why didn't you tell me that the outfit you were wearing belonged to Mariella?'

'Perhaps I didn't want to spoil your fun. You were obviously enjoying thinking the worst of me,' she answered sharply.

'You can't blame me for making entirely logical assumptions. You're a woman in her twenties with a career, therefore logically you must have a bank account. Having a bank account means that you have access to credit cards, bank loans, a wide variety of different ways of borrowing money in an emergency—as this—' he indicated the bag he was now carrying '—proves. And yet you chose to ask me for a loan.'

'Logical assumptions? You've already as good as admitted that the assumptions you've made about me, far from being logical, are based entirely on your own preconceived ideas and personal hang-ups. The truth is that you know nothing whatsoever about my life or my circumstances. If the women you mix with are the type who are happy to exchange sex for a few gaudy trinkets and a wardrobe of designer clothes, then I'm afraid that so far as I'm concerned it says just as much about your judgement and morals as it does about theirs.'

'Really? Well, *my* judgement told me that you were more than ready to have sex with me until you found out that sex was all you would be getting. Miraculously, now that you know that, suddenly you have all the money you need to replace your stolen clothes. Oh, and a word of warning. That gang are notorious for wanting value for their money. They'll pass you round from hand to hand and have all they want of you. You may not find it worth the pay.'

No one had ever made her feel so furiously angry. She was so angry, in fact, that for once she forgot her normal caution and instead burst out, 'You are so wrong. The only reason I was ready to have sex with you was because I wanted you—but, luckily for me, I wanted to retain my self-respect more. And as for my bank account and my new clothes—I asked you for a loan because I have had to empty my bank account to…to make my parents a…a loan. I do not own a credit card, since I disapprove of their punitively high rates of interest, and there wasn't time for me to realise any of my assets.'

Ricardo frowned. Surely no one could manufacture the level of fury Carly was showing? But he wasn't simply going to give in.

'But obviously somehow you managed to find some money?'

'Yes, but not by selling my body, as you so obviously would like to think.'

'No? How, then?' The cynical disbelief in his voice infuriated her.

'If you must know—not that it is any of your business—I pawned my watch,' she told him flatly.

Ricardo discovered that a sensation akin to the slow, measured drip of ice being fed straight into his bloodstream was creeping up over him—a mental awareness that somehow he had got something very important spectacularly wrong.

He couldn't remember the last time anyone had wrongfooted him, and the knowledge that it should be Carly who had done so sparked off inside him a very dangerous cocktail of emotions. He looked down at her bare wrist and then back at her face.

'You said your parents needed a loan? Surely you could—'

'I don't want to talk about it.' Carly cut him off quickly.

Ricardo frowned. Surely the kind of woman he had assumed her to be would have been only too eager to make much of the glow of virtue accruing to her from such selflessness. But Carly was turning away from him, quite plainly agitated and anxious to change the subject.

Why? Ricardo wondered. What on earth could there be about something as generous as lending money to one's parents to spark off the hostility and fear he could see so plainly in her eyes?

She was starting to walk away from him. He looked down at her wrist again, and then back at her face.

He had always trusted his instincts, and right now those instincts were insisting that Carly had been telling him the truth. Therefore he was guilty of seriously misjudging her. And his body was telling him that, no matter what she was or what she had done or not done, he wanted her.

He strode towards her, catching hold of her arm.

Immediately her whole body tensed, and she demanded fiercely, 'Let go of me.'

'Not yet. You aren't the only one who takes their moral responsibilities seriously. I obviously owe you an apology.'

Ricardo was actually apologising to her? He certainly needed to, she reminded herself angrily. And she needed to apologise to herself, for being so stupid as to actually still want him.

'Yes, you do,' she agreed coolly. 'But I don't want it.'

She watched his stunned disbelief give way to male anger.

'No? But you do want me, don't you?' he taunted softly.

'No,' she began, but it was already too late. He pulled her hard against him and bent his head to take her mouth in a savagely intimate kiss before she could object. And, of course, the moment his mouth touched hers, her own helpless response betrayed her. She tried to pull away but he held on to her, and her eyes widened as she saw in his eyes the same hunger she knew was in her own.

She made a small helpless sound of denial and need, and then she gave in. His mouth moved urgently on hers and her lips parted eagerly, greedily for its possession, her nails digging into the hard muscles of his arms as her need roared through her.

It was last night all over again—only this time they were impeded by two sets of clothes. She had changed back into her own things before supervising the clearing up after the party. Now she was being driven wild by her longing to be as naked and open to him now as she had been the previous evening.

Her fingers clenched spasmodically on his arm, her body gripped by savage shudders of dark pleasure.

She wanted his hands on her breasts, on *all* of her—his fingers finding her, touching her as they had done last night. Just wanting him to touch her in that way made her go hot and limp with the desire she could feel pulsing inside her. She wanted him there…there—deep, deep inside her, thrusting hard and fast against the possessive hold of her muscles, taking her, satisfying her quickly and mercilessly.

She could feel the open heat of his mouth against her throat as he tipped her back over his arm, moonlight gleaming whitely on her skin as he tugged off her top to reveal her breast, darkly crowned in the night light.

His thumb-tip rubbed against the deep dark pink of her nipple and she cried out—a sharp, agonised sound of primitive female mating hunger.

She wanted him to take her now, here. As quickly and completely, as fiercely and thoroughly as a panting she-creature on heat. She wanted him to fill her, flood her with his own release, and to go on doing so until she was sated and complete.

She reached for the hardness she knew was waiting for her, running her fingers over and over the jutting ridge of his erection, quivering with anticipation. The head would be swollen and hot, the body thick and darkly veined, the flesh tightly drawn over the hard muscle, but still fluid and slick when she touched it.

In her imagination she could already feel the first rub of that engorged head between the lips of her sex, and then against the sensitive pleasure-pulse of her clitoris over and over again, faster and faster, until she was wet and hot with her pleasure. Until she could endure no more and Ricardo finally plunged deep inside her.

As though she had cried her desire out loud to him, she felt Ricardo tugging at her clothes, his hands hard and firm against her naked skin. His mouth found her nipple and drew fiercely on it. She cried out again in a mewling sound of intense arousal.

His mouth returned to hers. She felt as though she had been starving for it, for him, as though she had been waiting all their life to be with him. She felt…

Immediately she tensed, pushing him away, her voice tight with rejection and self-loathing as she told him fiercely, 'I don't want this.'

'Yes, you do. You want this and you want me, and you can't deny it!' Ricardo challenged her whilst he fought to control his breathing. And to rationalise what had happened—if he could rationalise it. It was something he had had no intention of allowing to happen at all. But from the moment he had touched her he had been out of control, unable to stop what was happening to him.

Carly drew in a deep, shaky breath.

'We mustn't.'

'We must not what?' Ricardo demanded. 'We must not want one another?'

Carly turned her head away from him and shook it in bewilderment. 'This can't happen again,' she told him quickly.

Baffled and frustrated, Ricardo reluctantly let her go. She wanted him, and he certainly damned well wanted her, so why was she behaving like this? One thing he did know was that he was determined that he would have her, sooner or later—and he would prefer it to be sooner.

Thank heavens Ricardo hadn't followed her to her room. Because if he had she knew that she would not have been able to resist him. And she had to resist him, because she wanted him far more than it was safe for her to do.

Why, though, did she feel like this about him? Why did she want him when she had never wanted any of the other men she had met?

Was it because subconsciously she knew he was different from them? Because the most intimate part of her recognised that, at some primal level, she felt a deep-rooted kinship with him?

Because, like him, she too had known and suffered childhood poverty and the withdrawal, the denial of the love and nurturing, the protection every child should be given as of right?

The wretched squalor and unhappiness of her own early childhood had marked her for ever, as she knew his must have marked him.

Not even Julia and Lucy, who thought they knew everything about her, knew the full truth of the beginning of her life—how she had been found dressed in rags, abandoned in the street beside some rubbish, her pitiful cries alerting a loitering tramp to her existence.

She had been a piece of unwanted humanity, left there to die. Unwanted and unloved, even by her own birth mother. No wonder, then, that her adopted mother had never been able to love her either.

CHAPTER SEVEN

'YOU mentioned last night that you didn't have any money in your bank account because you'd had to help your parents?'

Carly almost dropped the glass of water she had been drinking. A little unsteadily, she put it down. They had boarded Ricardo's jet several hours later than Ricardo had originally planned, although he had not give her any reason for the delay, and would soon be landing at JFK airport for their onward journey to the Hamptons.

She looked out of the window, telling herself that it was pointless now to berate herself for letting anger lead her into admitting that she had needed to help them.

'I...I shouldn't have said that,' she admitted uncomfortably. 'And I wouldn't have done if you hadn't made me so angry.'

'I misjudged you, and I've apologised for that. A man in my position becomes very cynical about other people's motives. Why did you have to give your parents money? Are you an only child?'

'I…I had a sister…'

Her mouth had gone dry, and she wanted desperately to bring their conversation to an end.

'Had?' Ricardo questioned, as she had known he would.

'Yes. She… Fenella died a…a few months ago,' she told him reluctantly.

Ricardo could almost feel her resistance to his questions as he registered her words and felt the shock of them, plus his own shock that she should be so composed.

'I'm sorry. That must have been dreadful for you.'

Carly looked at him.

'Fenella and I weren't really related. I…her parents adopted me when I was very young. They adored her, and they were naturally devastated by her death,' she told him in a guarded voice.

'But you weren't?' Ricardo guessed.

'We were very different. Fenella naturally was always the favoured child. Adoption doesn't always work out the way people hope it will.'

Carly looked away from him. It was obvious that she was withholding something from him, *withdrawing* herself from him, in fact—as though she didn't want to let him into the personal side of her life. To his own astonishment he discovered that he didn't like the fact that she was reluctant to talk openly about herself to him. What was it about her that caused him to have this compulsion to learn more? And was it more, or was it *everything* there was to learn?

His curiosity was merely that of a potential employer, he assured himself.

'What do you mean, adoption doesn't always work? Didn't it work for you? Weren't you happy with your adoptive parents?'

'Why are you asking me so many questions?'

Ricardo could almost feel her anxiety and panic.

'Perhaps because I want to know more about you.'

On the face of it he already knew all he needed to know. But it was what was beneath the surface that was arousing his curiosity. She was concealing something from him, something that changed her from a self-confident woman into someone who was far more vulnerable—and also very determined to deny that vulnerability. He had a fiercely honed instinct about such things, and he knew he wasn't wrong. So what was it? He intended to find out. But what would it take to break down her barriers?

He looked at her and watched in satisfaction as, under his deliberate scrutiny, the colour seeped up under her skin.

'You haven't answered my question,' he reminded her.

'No, I wasn't happy.' The terseness in her voice warned him that she didn't like his probing.

'What about your natural parents?'

Ricardo could see immediately that his question had had a very dramatic effect on her.

Her face lost its colour and he could hear her audibly indrawn breath. He expected her to refuse to answer, but instead she spoke fiercely.

'My mother was probably a drug addict, who died in a house fire along with two other young women. No one knew who my father might have been. I was left to die amongst the rubbish outside a hospital. A tramp found me. I was only a few weeks old. I was ten years old and in foster care when Fenella's parents decided they wanted to adopt a sister for her, because they were concerned that she might be lonely.'

Ricardo was frowning.

'They adopted you for their daughter?'

'Yes. I imagine they felt I'd be easier to house-train than a puppy and less expensive to keep than a pony,' Carly told him lightly. 'Unfortunately, though, it didn't work out. Fenella, quite naturally, hated having to share her parents and her toys with an unwanted sibling, and demanded that her parents send me back. I think they wanted to, but of course it was too late. I wasn't allowed to touch anything of Fenella's, or even to eat in the same room with her at first. But then we were both sent to boarding school. That's when I met Jules and Lucy. Somehow or other my…my history, and the fact that I wasn't really Fenella's sister, became public knowledge.'

'You mean she told everyone?' Ricardo asked bluntly.

'She was a year older than me, so she'd already made her own circle of friends at the school before I went there. She was a very popular girl—she could be charming when she wanted to be—and I very quickly became ostracised.'

'You were bullied, you mean?'

'I was different and I didn't fit in,' Carly continued without answering him. 'But luckily for me, Jules and Lucy came to my rescue and gave me their friendship. Without that and them…' The shadows in her eyes caused Ricardo to experience a sudden fierce surge of protectiveness towards her, and anger towards those who had so obviously tormented her.

'What happened to Fenella?'

Carly shook her head. It disturbed her to realise how much she had told him about herself.

She wasn't going to tell him any more, Ricardo recognised, as he watched her turn away from him to focus on her laptop.

Carly frowned as she tried to study the figures on the company's bank statements on her screen. Answering Ricardo's questions had brought back so many painful memories.

She had truly believed when she had been adopted that she was going to be loved by her new parents and sister, and she had given them her own love unstintingly. It had confused her at first when she had been rebuffed, but then she had seen her adoptive mother hugging Fenella, fussing over her, and she had begun to realise that there was a huge difference between the way Fenella was given her parents' love and approval, and the way she was refused it.

She had tried to make herself as like Fenella as possible, mirroring the other girl's behaviour as closely as she could, assuming that this would gain her adoptive parents' approval. Instead it had simply made Fenella hate her even more. Now, as an adult, she could not entirely blame them. Fenella had been their child, after all. But her experience with her adoptive parents had taught her the danger of giving her love to anyone.

The figures in front of her blurred, and she had to blink fiercely in order to be able to concentrate on them.

Suddenly, when she saw them properly, she frowned, firmly putting her own problems to one side as she stared in shocked anxiety at the unfamiliarly large cheques that had gone through the account, almost completely emptying it of cash.

It was unthinkable that this should have happened. She prided herself on keeping a mental running total of what was going in and out of the account, and according to her own mental reckoning they should have been several hundred thousand pounds in credit. In fact, they *needed* to be several hundred thousand pounds in credit to meet the bills their suppliers would be presenting at the end of the month, and to leave sufficient working capital to carry them until they received payment from other clients.

So what were these cheques for? She couldn't remember signing them. A cold trickle of anxiety mixed with instinct iced down her spine. Her heart started to beat uncomfortably heavily. She needed to see those cheques.

Carly had quickly become totally engrossed in her work. Too quickly, Ricardo thought. Did she use it to block out emotional issues she found it difficult to handle? She had not said so, but he imagined that she must have suffered severe emotional trauma during her childhood.

That he should even have such a concern, never mind actively feel protective of her because of it, was such alien emotional territory to him that it took several seconds to recognise his own danger. Once he had done so he reminded himself firmly that that had been then and this was now, and now he wanted her in his bed.

Carly ordered photocopies of the cheques. Until they came she wouldn't be able to do anything else.

'Carly!'

She acknowledged Ricardo with a wary look.

'I hope you ached as much for me last night as I did for you.'

She could feel her face starting to burn.

'I'd really rather not talk about it. I've already said that I don't want to…to go there.'

Her voice was calm, but he could see that her hand was trembling.

He gave a small shrug.

'Why not? Why should we deny ourselves something it's obvious we both want? Sexually there's a chemistry between us that maybe neither of us would have wanted, given free choice, but I don't see any point in trying to pretend that it doesn't exist. And, given that it does exist, perhaps it would be better for both of us if we enjoyed it instead of trying to ignore or reject it. That way at least we could get our sexual hunger for one another out of our systems.'

Our sexual hunger. Three simple words. But they had the power to change her life for ever. Had Adam felt what she was feeling now when Eve had handed him the apple and announced, 'Here, take a bite?' Had he thought then, just as she was thinking now, of all that he would be denying himself if he refused? If she had sex with Ricardo it wouldn't change the world, but it would change her. Was she brave enough to accept that? Or would she rather spend the rest of her life wishing and wondering?

'I don't want to have an affair with you,' she answered him. An affair would involve falling in love, putting herself in a situation where ultimately she would be rejected in favour of someone else. Every emotional experience she'd ever had had taught her that. In her foster homes, with her adoptive parents, and then at school. Even with her closest friends, Lucy and Jules, she was aware that they shared an extra special bond of birth and upbringing which excluded her.

'But you do want to have sex with me,' Ricardo guessed.

Her face was burning, but she managed to hold his gaze.

'I…I think so.'

The look he gave her was pure male power.

'Are you asking me to make the decision for you?'

'What would be the point? I'm sure a man with your experience could find someone else who wouldn't need to have a decision made for them.'

'I'm sure I could,' Ricardo agreed dryly. 'However, they would not be you, and it is you I want. But, since we're on the subject of relationships, how many relationships *have* there been for you?'

He had caught her unprepared, slipping the question under her guard.

'Er… I don't… I can't really remember,' she told him untruthfully. 'And besides, it isn't really any of your business, is it?'

'It would be if we slept together,' Ricardo told her.

How could she tell him the truth?

How could she say that he was different—special—that she had never felt the way she did about him with anyone else, and that that alone was enough to make her feel threatened and afraid? And if she couldn't tell him that, then how could she tell him that she had never done with anyone else what she so much wanted to do with him?

'What time do you think we will arrive at the Hamptons?' she asked instead.

The look he gave her made her feel as though he had set a match to her will-power and it was curling up into nothing inside her.

'We'll be there in plenty of time. We'll stay over in my New York apartment tonight and fly out tomorrow.'

'Wouldn't it make more sense to go straight there?'

'Not really. You're looking and sounding very agitated, Carly. Why?'

'No reason. I mean, I'm not. Why should I be?'

'Perhaps you don't feel you can trust yourself to be alone with me?' Ricardo suggested softly.

Carly had had enough.

'It isn't a matter of that! I just don't think we should put ourselves in a position where—'

'Where what? Where you might be tempted to offer yourself to me and I might accept? Is that what you mean?'

'No! At least…' That was exactly what she had meant, she admitted to herself. Only in her mental scenario it had been Ricardo offering himself to her, not the other way around.

Something about the way he had phrased his statement touched a raw nerve. 'I don't like what you're implying,' she told him frankly. 'I appreciate that lots of women probably come on to you because...'

'Because I'm very rich?' he suggested smoothly, picking up her dropped sentence.

His voice might sound smooth, but beneath it he was angry, Carly recognised. He might not feel concerned about her sensitivities, but he obviously did not like her treading on his own!

'I wasn't going to say that.'

'Liar!' Ricardo told her, adding coolly,

'Besides, there are always several components to sexual desire, surely? For instance there are those which relate to our senses—sight, scent, taste...touch...'

Carly could feel herself beginning to respond to each word that rolled off his tongue.

Yes, the sight of him aroused her, and his scent certainly did, and as for his taste... She pulled in her stomach muscles to try and control the ache spreading through her. And touch… She pulled them in tighter, but it was already too late to halt what she was feeling. And, yes, the sound of his voice as well…

'And then there are those that relate to personality, status…lifestyle. For instance—' He broke off as the steward emerged from the crew's quarters and came towards them.

Carly could feel herself shaking slightly inside—the sensual effect on her body from just listening to him.

'We'll be landing in half an hour. Would you like another drink before we do? Or something to eat?'

Carly shook her head, unable to trust herself to speak. Ricardo had dragged from her confidences and admissions she would normally never have made to anyone, and right now emotional reaction was beginning to set in—much the same way as physical reaction would have set in if she had just had a tooth pulled without anaesthetic. She felt slightly sick, more than slightly shaky, and very much in shock.

Perhaps Ricardo was right, and the only way to overcome her physical ache for him was to satisfy it instead of trying to avoid it.

Ricardo watched her, shielding his scrutiny with a pretended concentration on his own papers. Over and over again she broke out of the stereotyped image he wanted to impose on her. No other woman had shown him—given him—*shared* with him—such an intensity of sexual desire. And no other woman had ever aroused him to such a point of compelling compulsive hunger either.

They were coming in to land, the jet descending through the thin cloud-cover.

Carly packed away her papers and fastened her seatbelt. She had always been the sort of person who took every precaution she could to protect herself. But she had not been able to protect herself from what was happening to her now—and wasn't it true that a part of her didn't want to be protected from it?

'Ah, Rafael, there you are…this is Ms Carlisle.'

The young Mexican gave Carly a grave smile.

'Carly, please,' she corrected Ricardo as she shook Rafael's hand.

'Rafael and his wife Dolores run my New York apartment. How is Dolores, Rafael?'

'She is very well, and she said to tell you that she is making a special meal for you tonight. It is Italian. She also said to tell you that the orphanage is very happy and the children think you should be called Saint Salvatore.'

Saint Salvatore? Carly questioned mentally, watching the way Ricardo frowned.

'You want me to fly the chopper to the apartment block?' Rafael asked.

Ricardo shook his head.

'No, I'll fly it myself.'

Ricardo had a pilot's licence? Carly tried not to look either awed or impressed as Rafael urged her to climb on board the golf-buggy-type vehicle he had waiting for them.

She'd never flown in a helicopter before, and she acknowledged that she felt slightly daunted at the prospect of doing so. But she had no intention of saying so to Ricardo.

'I'll go and fetch the luggage,' Rafael announced, once he had helped Carly out of the buggy.

'We'll use the chopper tomorrow to get to the Hamptons,' Ricardo said as he guided Carly towards it. 'It will be much quicker and easier. You will have an excellent overview of New York City if you sit beside me. Technically Rafael should take that seat, since he is my co-pilot, but—'

'Oh, then he must sit there,' Carly insisted quickly.

'You sound apprehensive. Don't you trust me?'

'I…'

'I can assure you, I take a keen interest in my own continued existence!'

Ricardo had been right about the view of New York, Carly acknowledged, and she held her breath instinctively as he flew them between two huge tower blocks.

Via the headphones she was wearing she could hear his running commentary on the city below them—the straight lines of the modern streets, and then the curve in Broadway where the new merged with the old.

'That's Wall Street down there,' Ricardo told her, and she looked, bemused to see how quaintly narrow and small it seemed. He turned the helicopter and announced, 'We'll be flying over Central Park soon. My apartment's way up on the east side.'

The streets on either side of the park were lined with what looked like nineteenth-century buildings, and Carly held her breath as Ricardo headed for one of them, not releasing it until she saw the helicopter landing area marked out on its roof.

'You don't leave the helicopter here, do you?' Carly asked once he had helped her out.

Ricardo shook his head. 'No. Rafael will fly it back to the airport and then drive back. I dare say he will take Dolores with him, and they will call on their family on the way back.'

He was obviously a fair and well-liked employer, Carly reflected as he guided her towards the building and in through a doorway to a small foyer and lift. Once they were inside Ricardo punched a code into the panel and the doors closed, enclosing them in what—for Carly—was a far too intimate bubble of seclusion. Immediately the thought filled her mind that if he should turn to her now and take her in his arms she would not want to resist him.

'Don't look at me like that,' Ricardo warned her softly, so easily and immediately reading her thoughts that she could only gape at him. 'I can't—not in here. That's a camera up there,' he told her, pointing upwards towards the ceiling.

The lift stopped silently and smoothly and the doors opened onto another foyer. It was a large, coolly spacious one this time, with only one door opening off it, its walls painted a flat matt cream to highlight the paintings hanging on them.

'Lucien Freud?' Carly questioned, recognising the style immediately.

'Yes. His work has a raw feel to it that I like.'

The posed nudes *were* compelling, Carly admitted.

The foyer's single door opened and Ricardo stood back to allow her to precede him.

He had excellent manners, and they seemed to be a natural part of him rather than something carefully learned. But from the brief description she'd had of his early life she doubted if standing back to allow others to precede him was something he'd learned on the streets of Naples.

A small, dark-haired woman with twinkling eyes was standing in the inner hallway, waiting for them.

'Ah, Dolores. You got my message about Ms Carlisle?'

'Yes, and I have prepared a guest suite for her. You had a good journey, I hope, Ms Carlisle?'

'Yes, indeed—and do please call me Carly.'

'You go with Dolores; she will show you to your suite,' Ricardo told Carly, before continuing, 'What time is dinner planned for, Dolores?'

'Eight-thirty, if that is okay with you? And Rafael—he said that you will want an early lunch tomorrow, before you fly to the Hamptons?'

'Yes, that's right. I'd better warn you that Ms Carlisle may not make it to the dinner table tonight. It may be three in the afternoon here, but for her it's eight in the evening.'

'Oh, my goodness! You would perhaps like something to eat now, then?' Dolores asked Carly.

'No, I'm fine,' Carly assured her.

She would have to make contact with the New York agency who were sharing the organisation of the Hamptons event with them, and she had hoped to have time to fit in a bit of sightseeing. She was also planning to ask Dolores if she could recommend somewhere Carly might find clothes that would be within her budget. Jeans might be the universal uniform, acceptable everywhere, but she could hardly turn up at the glitzy events she was overseeing wearing them. And unfortunately Mariella's cast-offs—designer label or not—were simply not the kind of clothes she would ever feel comfortable wearing.

'So, you will sleep here, in this guest suite, and you will have a lovely view over the park. Come and see, please.'

Dutifully Carly followed Dolores through the door she had just opened.

The room she walked into was huge, its windows, as Dolores had stated, overlooking the greenery of the park.

'Here there is a desk, and you can plug in your computer,' Dolores told her.

Carly nodded her head.

'And here there is a television.' She folded back what Carly had assumed was wall panelling to reveal a large flatscreen TV hidden behind it, along with shelves of DVDs and books. 'See—the TV, it pulls out so you can watch it from your bed,' Dolores told Carly, proudly displaying this extra function. 'The dressing room and your bathroom are through here. Mr Salvatore, he have everything ripped out when he moved in here, and it's all new. Even in our rooms as well.'

The dressing room was lined with mirror-fronted wardrobes and contained a small sofa, whilst the bathroom was almost a luxury mini-spa. Carly was unable to stop herself from comparing it with the rather more basic bathroom in the flat she shared with Jules.

'It's all wonderful,' she told Dolores truthfully.

'Yes. Mr Salvatore, he is a very good man. Very kind—especially to the children. When he hear that there is an orphanage in our old home town that has no money, he goes there to see it and then he writes one big cheque!' Dolores beamed.

Carly phoned Lucy and then the New York event organiser who was co-running the event. Everything seemed to be in hand, she thought as she stifled a yawn.

The bed looked very tempting, and she *was* tired. Perhaps an hour's sleep might do her good. It was only five o'clock New York time—more than three hours yet before dinner.

She was too tired to shower, and so, after removing her shoes and folding back the bedspread, she simply lay on top of the bed. Sleep claimed her the moment she closed her eyes.

CHAPTER EIGHT

IT WAS the small sound of a door clicking closed that woke her. At first she struggled to remember exactly where she was, reluctant to be dragged out of her sleeping fantasy of lying naked in Ricardo's arms whist he caressed her.

She sat up and then swung her feet onto the floor, all too aware of the pulsing ache in her lower body. She could hear someone moving about in the dressing room.

Ricardo? Her heart bumped against her ribs, excitement spiked with anticipation heating her body. If it was—if he wasn't going to give her the chance to say that she wanted him but intended instead to simply overwhelm her with the reality of her desire for him—there was no way she was going to be able to reject him, she admitted to herself, and she hurried across the room, pushing open the dressing room door.

Dolores was just closing one of the wardrobe doors. She turned towards Carly with a warm smile.

The deep-rooted sensual ache she had begun to learn to live with turned into a fierce pang of anguished need. How could just a few hours in his company have turned her body into this sexually eager collection of erotically aroused nerve endings and hotly responsive flesh? Her whole body ached, hungering for his touch and his possession. It was being consumed by a fever of longing and arousal. Virtually all she could think about was how long she would have to wait. The question driving her thoughts now wasn't 'if' but 'when'.

'I have hung everything up for you, so that they don't get too crushed. I can pack them again before you leave tomorrow. So you have any laundry you want me to do?'

Everything? What *everything*? What did Dolores mean?

There was an unfamiliar case on the dressing room floor—a Louis Vuitton case, Carly realised with horrified fascination—and a matching vanity case placed right next to it. And there was a mound of neatly folded tissue paper on the pretty daybed-cum-sofa, and some shoe boxes placed beneath it.

'Dolores, I think there must be some mistake,' she began faintly. 'Those cases aren't mine.'

Dolores looked confused.

'But, yes, they are. Rafael fetched them from the jet himself. Just as Mr Salvatore instructed him to do. So that they will not be lost.'

A horrible sense of disbelief mixed with anger was filling Carly. Unsteadily she went over to the nearest wardrobe and pulled back the door.

The clothes hanging in it were totally unfamiliar. She lifted down one of the skirts and checked the label, her hands trembling.

It was certainly her size, *and* her colour.

She put the skirt back and went over the sofa, kneeling on the floor as she opened one of the shoeboxes.

The delicate strappy sandals inside were her size too.

'There is something wrong?' Dolores asked her worriedly

Carly replaced the sandal in its box and stood up. 'No, Dolores. Everything is fine,' she told her.

But of course she was lying.

She went slowly through all the clothes hanging in the wardrobes. Expensive, elegant, beautiful designer clothes, in wonderful fabrics and a palette of her favourite colours: creams, chocolate-browns, black. She touched the fringed hem of a jacket in Chanel's signature pastel tweed—warm cream threaded with tiny silky strands of brilliant jewel colours. She had seen exactly the same jacket in Chanel's Sloane Street store and had stood mutely gazing at it, almost transfixed by its beauty. It would go perfectly with the toning heavy silk satin trousers hanging next to it. She knew exactly how much the jacket would have cost because she had been foolish enough to go into the store and ask. More than she would ever spend on clothes in a whole year, never mind on one single item. She stepped back from the wardrobe and closed the door firmly.

Did he really think she would allow him to do this to her? After what he had said to her? After what he had thought of her? Oh, yes, he had claimed it was a mistake and he had apologised, but…

Inside her head, from another lifetime, she could hear a flustered nervous voice insisting, 'Say thank you to the nice lady for the lovely clothes she's bought for you, Carly. Aren't you a lucky, lucky girl? And such a very pretty dress. I'm sure she'll be ever so grateful once she realises how lucky she is…won't you, Carly?'

Grateful? She had sworn on her eighteenth birthday that never, ever again was she going to have to be grateful for someone else's charity. That she would support herself, by herself, and that was exactly what she had done.

She had financed her own way through university via a variety of low-paid, physically hard jobs—bar work, cleaning, working as a nursing aide in an old people's home—determinedly ignoring the allowance being paid into her bank account. The first thing she had done when her adoptive parents had broken the news to her of their financial ruin had been to give that money back to them.

'Dolores, I need to speak with Ricardo. Can you tell me where I will find him, please?'

'He is in his office. But he does not like to be disturbed when he is in there.'

He didn't like being disturbed? Well, he was about to discover that neither did she. And what he had done *had* disturbed her. It had disturbed her…and it had infuriated her—a very great deal!

Dolores didn't want to give her directions for the office, but Carly insisted. She knocked briefly on the door and then, without waiting, turned the handle and went in.

Ricardo was seated behind a desk on the opposite side of the room from the door. The evening sun light coming in from the two high windows behind dazzled her whilst leaving his face cloaked in shadow.

'Dolores has filled the wardrobes in my room with clothes which she believes are mine.'

'Ah. Yes, I'm glad you reminded me; I had almost forgotten. I've spoken to the manager at Barneys and arranged a temporary account there for you so that you can get something suitable for the French do. I didn't want to risk picking out something myself. You'll have time to go over there tomorrow morning. It's right behind the Pierre Hotel—'

'No!' Carly stopped him angrily.

'No what?' Ricardo demanded, pushing back his chair and standing up.

Carly had to take a steadying breath. Every sinuous movement of his body reminded her of how it had felt against her own, of how much she wanted it, ached for it, longed for it.

Ricardo had changed his own clothes at some stage, and was wearing a tee shirt and a pair of jeans. Some men could wear jeans and some could not. Ricardo was quite definitely one of the ones who could. Longing shot through her—pure, wanton, female liquid need.

'No. I won't wear clothes that you have paid for.'

'Why not?' he demanded. 'You eat food bought with my money, sleep in a bed paid for with it. Why should you refuse to wear clothes it has bought?'

'You know why. You accused me yourself of trying to force you to—'

'I was wrong about that and I apologised.'

His voice was terse, and Carly could see he did not like being reminded that he had been at fault.

'Yes, I know that,' Carly agreed reluctantly 'But—'

'But what? You object to the colours I chose? The styles?'

'*You* chose?' she breathed in disbelief. 'How could you have done that? You couldn't possibly have had time!'

He gave a small shrug.

'I made time.'

'How?' Carly challenged him.

'I went into St Tropez this morning, before we left.'

Carly stared at him. Was he making it up…making fun of her, perhaps?

'How did you know my size?'

'I'm a man,' he told her dryly. 'I've touched your body. Held it close to my own. You have full breasts, but a very narrow ribcage. I can span your waist with my hands, your hips curve as woman's hips should do—shall I continue?'

'No,' Carly told him in a choked voice. 'I won't wear them,' she added in the next breath. 'I won't take charity.'

'Charity!' Ricardo frowned, sharply aware of the anguish in her voice, and wondering about her use of the word *charity*. 'And I will not take a woman out with me who has nothing to wear other than a pair of jeans!'

'You are not taking me out with you. I am here to work.'

'Maybe, but it is not out of the question that we could be photographed together by someone who does not know the real situation.'

'You're a snob,' Carly accused him wildly.

'No. I am a realist! I believed that you were entirely professional in your attitude towards your work, but it seems that I was wrong.'

'What do you mean?'

'I should have thought it was obvious. Were you the professional I believed you to be you would accept the necessity of dressing suitably for your role instead of behaving like an outraged virgin. Especially since we both know that is something you most definitely are *not*!'

He might think he knew that, but she knew something very different indeed, Carly reflected. 'And that is the only reason you bought the clothes?'

'What other reason could there be?' he challenged her.

'You've already made it clear to me that you think sex is something you can buy,' she pointed out. 'But I won't and can't be bought, Ricardo.'

He was very angry, she recognised, his pride no doubt stinging in much the same way as hers had when she had opened those wardrobe doors. Good!

'You're making a mountain out of a molehill. I have simply provided you with the kind of clothes I expect the women I am seen with in public to wear. That is all. Had you not had your case stolen it would not have been necessary, but it was and it is. If it makes you feel any better, then perhaps you should think of the clothes merely as being on loan to you, to wear as a necessary uniform. As for paying for sex—I think I am capable of recognising when a woman wants me, Carly.'

There was nothing she could say to that.

'It's almost dinnertime. I hope you are hungry. Dolores is very proud of her cooking,' he announced coolly, changing the subject.

Carly looked down at her jeans.

'I'm really not hungry.'

Not for food, perhaps—but for him? Ah, that was a different story. She was hungry for him—starving for him, in fact. Starving for the feel and the scent of him, for the taste of him, the reality of him. She could feel her body aching heavily with the weight of that hunger.

A sense of desolation and pain filled her. She hadn't asked to feel like this. She didn't want to feel like this. Not for any man, and least of all for a man such as this one.

Ricardo studied her downbent head. She looked tired, somehow vulnerable, and he could feel a reluctant and unwanted compassion—a desire to protect her—stirring inside him.

His only interest in her—aside from the fact that he wanted her like hell—was because of her role in Prêt a Party, Ricardo reminded himself fiercely. Emotional entanglements and complications just weren't something he had any intention of factoring into his life. He was prepared to accept that one day he might want a child—a son, an *heir*—but when that day came he intended to satisfy that need not via marriage, with all its potential financial risks, but instead by paying a carefully selected woman to have a child for him and then to hand over all rights to it to him. With modern medical procedures he wouldn't even need to meet her.

'If you wish, I am sure Dolores will be happy to serve you dinner in your room,' he told her brusquely.

Carly veiled her eyes with her lashes, not wanting him to see what she was feeling.

If last night she had not stopped him, tonight—this night—they would have been together, and food would have been the last thing on either of their minds. It could still happen. All she had to do was go to him and touch him, show him, give way to what she was feeling. Other women had no qualms about showing men that they wanted them, so why should she?

She gave a small shiver, already knowing the answer to her own question.

CHAPTER NINE

SHE was used to the motion of the helicopter now, and did not feel as apprehensive as she had done before. They had already left New York behind them. The traffic on the highway beneath them looked like a child's toys.

She was alone with Ricardo in the helicopter this time, but he wasn't giving her a running commentary on their surroundings as he had done before. She told herself that she was glad of his businesslike attitude towards her, and the distance it had put between them.

Had he come to any decision yet as to whether or not he intended to use Prêt a Party's services? If so, she hoped that he had decided in their favour. They certainly needed the business.

She had received the e-mailed copies of the cheques she had requested and her inspection of them had confirmed what she'd already suspected. All the cheques bore—as legally they had to, according to the terms of the business—two signatures. Her own and Nick's. Only she knew that she had not signed the cheques herself. Which meant that someone had forged her signature. Someone? It could only have been Nick. Lucy was the only other person beside herself who had keys for the cupboard in which she kept the chequebooks.

Even without checking her forward costings for the year Carly knew that, because of the huge amount Nick had withdrawn from the business, by the time they reached their year-end they would be showing a loss of nearly half a million pounds.

The terms of their bank account were that Lucy would personally make up any overdraft from her trust fund. They had been in business for three years so far, and Carly had taken great pride in the fact that she had managed the financial affairs of the company so well that the bank had not had to invoke this condition. Until now.

Half a million pounds. She had no idea how much money there was in Lucy's trust fund, but she suspected that Nick would know. And she suspected too that he had made a deliberate and cold-blooded decision to help himself to money from it via the business, because he knew that Marcus would never agree to hand so much money over to him.

But understanding the situation was one thing. Knowing what to do about it was another. By rights she should tell Lucy what she had discovered, because she was sure that the *carte blanche* Lucy had given Nick to draw money from the business did not include forging Carly's signature in order to get even more. But Nick was Lucy's husband. Lucy would be bound to feel humiliated and hurt if Carly told her that he had been stealing from her. And what if Lucy refused to believe her and Nick insisted that he had not signed Carly's name? Would it be better if she got in touch with Marcus and alerted him to what was happening? Carly felt torn between her loyalty to Lucy and her fear for her.

Mentally shelving the problem, she focused instead on more immediate issues. She had spoken to her opposite number at the New York event organisers earlier, and she had assured Carly that everything was going according to plan.

'It looked like there was going to be a problem with the caterers at one stage. The magazine told us they wanted only colour-co-ordinated vegan food, in their house colours, but then they rang up saying that they'd heard that a certain glossy magazine editor only ate Beluga caviar and they had to have some.'

Carly had sympathised with her. Everyone knew how that particular British editor dictated and directed what was 'in' in certain important New York fashion circles. Just having her attend the event would be a major achievement. Of course she'd agreed gravely with her counterpart—it was essential that the caviar was provided, even though it meant breaking the colour-co-ordinated theme.

'We're serving champagne cocktails on arrival—peach and rhubarb with pepper. We're using this new chef who's into mixing together different textures and tastes. He's very *avant garde*. Virginia wants everything exclusive but statement-making simple. That's why she's chosen the Hamptons as the venue.'

Carly had continued to listen sympathetically.

Only the very richest of the rich could afford to live the 'simple' life Hamptons-style. She had read up on the area and knew that it was the preserve of those with old money—or at least it had been, until the media and fashion set had discovered it.

The magazine had been insistent that they wanted a very stylish and upmarket event—which was, Carly suspected, why they had been commissioned.

Lucy might not be the type to boast that her great-grandfather had been a duke, but the fact remained that she was very well connected socially.

'We've got the silverware on loan from Cristoffle, and the stemware is Baccarat—but very plain, of course.'

'Of course,' Carly had agreed, mentally praying that everything was well insured.

She had thought she knew what luxury was, but she had been wrong, she now admitted. As her visit to Barneys this morning had shown her. The exclusive store far surpassed anything she had ever seen, and had made her wonder who on earth could afford to shop there.

An elegant sales assistant had offered to help her, and Carly had suffered being shown a variety of stunning but impossibly expensive gowns—they could not be called anything else—before finally escaping by announcing that she had run out of time.

Any one of the dresses she had been shown would have been perfect for the French château birthday ball, but one in particular had stood out from the rest—a column of palest green silk, layer after delicately fine layer of it, the fabric floating magically with every movement of the air.

Carly had hardly dared to try it on, but the sales assistant had insisted and she had had no option other than to give way.

'It is perfect for you,' she had told Carly, and Carly had mentally agreed with her. But she had shaken her head and taken it off.

The Hamptons event was due to commence at four in the afternoon and go on until eight in the evening. A private house had been hired for the occasion, with large lawns and its own beach, and Carly had dressed—she hoped—appropriately—both for the occasion and the fact that she was part of the 'hired help', plus the fact that she was representing Lucy.

To do so she had had to give in and wear one of the outfits Ricardo had paid for. A pair of plain white Chloe linen pants teamed with an almost but not quite off the shoulder knit in navy and white. She had teamed the trousers with simple but oh, so expensive beige leather flats, and in order to accommodate all the paperwork she had to carry around with her she had splashed out this morning in New York before leaving and bought herself a large and stylish dark red straw bag—not from Barneys, where she had sighed over the unbelievable display of bags, but from a regular department store, and a marked-down sale item at that.

A couple of 'of the moment' trendy Perspex bangles, her own small gold earrings, and her good (although several years old) Oliver Peoples sunglasses completed her outfit.

She had been curious to see what Ricardo would wear. She had heard that there was an unofficial casual 'uniform' for visitors to the island—a variation on the traditional faded red jeans which had become a Hamptons visitors trademark—and had been unexpectedly touched and impressed to see that he was wearing classic Italian casual—almost as though he wanted to underline his own nationality. It was a mix of white and beige in cotton and linen, and he managed to wear it without looking either crumpled or over-groomed—which was quite an achievement.

Bare brown feet thrust into soft leather open shoes were a raw and masculine touch that certainly made her very much aware of the fact that he was dangerously male—and very much aware of him as well, she admitted, as she ignored the temptation to turn her head and look at him.

The more time she spent with him, the more she was being forced to accept how much he aroused her physically.

Even now, just sitting here beside him in silence, she could feel the tormenting ache of her own need growing stronger with every pulse of her body.

She was out of her depth. Why didn't she admit it? If he were to turn to her now and tell her that tonight he wanted to take her to bed and make love to her until morning there was no way she would refuse.

And why should she? She could go through the rest of her life without ever again meeting a man who could make her feel like this.

And sex without love was surely like… Like what? Like whisky without water? Undiminished? Its strength and flavour heightened by the fact that it was not touched by anything else? Why shouldn't sex be like that? Why shouldn't it? Why couldn't it be a pure, intense, once-in-a-lifetime experience just as it was?

What she had to ask herself was, if she didn't have sex with Ricardo, in later years would she praise herself or would she berate herself? Would she feel that she had gained or lost? Would she yearn to have the opportunity back again or…?

What was she trying to do? Persuade herself into bed with him? Wasn't that Ricardo's role? Nothing about him suggested to her that he was the kind of man who wasn't capable of going in all-out pursuit of anything and everything he wanted, be it a woman or a business. Ricardo played to win. If he truly wanted her he would be the one doing the persuading—and he would surely have persuaded her into his bed by now! As if she actually needed persuading, she admitted wryly.

But why did she want him so much? It definitely wasn't because of his money! And equally definitely it wasn't because of love. Loving someone meant risking being hurt.

So it was the man himself, then? The tightening sensation within her own body told her she had found the truth.

All these years of believing she wasn't interested in sex—she had told herself that nothing would ever induce her to adopt the casual attitude towards sex of so many women she knew, which she found repugnant—had been washed away by the ferocity of her own desire, like a dam bursting its banks to flood a hitherto dried-out gully.

She had a terrible and terrifying urge to turn to Ricardo and ask him to turn the helicopter around. To take her back to New York and his apartment, his bed, so that she could discover for herself which was the more powerfully sensual and erotic—her fantasies or Ricardo's reality.

When had the balance, the scales themselves tipped? Ricardo wondered savagely as he tried to fight against the message his body's fierce hunger was sending him.

When had his hunger for Carly started to occupy his thoughts more than acquiring Prêt a Party? When had he somehow given way and abandoned the rule he'd thought he had set in stone never to allow himself to want any woman so much that the wanting overpowered him?

He didn't know! What he did know, though, was that he had looked at her earlier, when she had walked towards him in his apartment, and had had to fight against the madness of an overwhelming need to take hold of her and kiss her until he could feel in her the same passionate response he had felt in her before—until her body was pliant and eagerly, erotically desirous of his touch, and her breathing was signalling an arousal that matched his own.

They had almost reached their destination; he could see the helipad up ahead of him. It was too late to turn back now.

East Hampton. New money and lots of it—or at least that was what she had read, Carly thought as a uniformed hunk, wearing eye-wateringly canary-yellow cut-offs and a bright blue logoed polo shirt—all muscles and too-white teeth—tenderly handed her down from the helicopter. What was it about such movie-perfect men that was so antiseptic and unsexy? Carly mused as she was asked for her name. And was it her imagination or did the bright smile fade just a little once its owner realised she was here as part of the workforce?

To the side of her, though, Ricardo was being greeted almost effusively by a stunningly pretty girl also wearing a greeter's uniform.

So this was corporate entertaining New York style! Certainly everything was well organised, very slick and professional—right down to the small packs they were being handed which she already knew included a map of the layout of the house and its gardens, a timetable of the afternoon's events, and a ticketed voucher so that guests could collect their goodie bags as they left—no cluttering the tables or, even worse, disgruntled guests leaving rejected and unwanted gifts behind them.

Ricardo was certainly receiving the *de luxe* treatment, Carly decided, as a further glance in his direction informed her that his greeter was still making him the focus of her attention whilst her own had mysteriously disappeared. He was nursing a half-empty glass of red wine, glancing away from his companion to stare down into its depths.

If Ricardo were a glass of full-bodied, richly flavoured red wine, Carly thought fancifully, she would want to drink deeply of him, not sip delicately at him. She would want to roll the glorious velvety texture of him around her tongue before allowing him to turn the whole of her body to liquid pleasure. She would want to breathe in the richness of him and savour his unique musky flavour. She would want to fill her senses with the richness of him and then…

Hot-faced, Carly struggled to call her thoughts to order. Ricardo wasn't a wine, he was a man. And just seeing the way he was smiling back at the girl who was so obviously flirting with him filled Carly with a fierce, painful surge of jealousy.

She was here to work, she reminded herself starkly, and she turned her back on Ricardo and made her way towards the main hospitality area.

They were, of course, virtually the first arrivals, and Carly wanted to check in with both the New York event organiser and the clients to make sure that everything was going to plan. Waiters and waitresses—their uniforms comprising retro Hawaiian-style shirts with a brilliantly patterned design made up of front covers of the magazine—were already circulating with trays of drinks, presumably serving the clients themselves.

When Carly reached the main pavilion a security guard on the door stopped her, and she showed him both her pass and her identity badge. Once inside, she found the magazine's PR team and Luella Klein, her opposite number from the New York event organiser, standing together, engaged in conversation.

'*Lurve* the shirts those guys out there are wearing!' Luella announced dramatically as soon as the introductions were over.

'That was Jules's idea.' Carly smiled.

'Yeah, great—and cool, too. We've had the goodie bags made out of the same fabric!'

Carly nodded her head. Using the magazine's past covers as a basis for the design theme of the event had been the result of a brainstorming session held between Lucy, Jules and herself when they had first been approached to pitch for this event.

Getting a canapé menu organised that would translate into plates of food put together in the magazine's house colours had proved to be a major headache, though, with several chefs refusing the commission before Carly had had the bright idea of getting one of the top catering colleges to take it on as a showcase for the talents of their students.

She was just keeping her fingers crossed that the results would be as impressive as the sample plates they had seen photographs of earlier in the year.

'And it may sound kinda silly, but I've always had a thing about Italian men—'

'I'm sorry—I have to go.'

The young woman, who had spent the best part of the last fifteen minutes congratulating herself on having got Ricardo's exclusive attention, just about managed not to stamp her expensive heel down into the turf as he cut through her breathless words and started to walk away. Her chagrin gave way to resentment as she saw that he had left her to go to someone else—a woman who was standing with a group of caterers, of all things. Grudgingly she acknowledged that the white linen trousers her competitor was wearing did do full justice to legs that, as the male sex would have it, went all the way up to her armpits.

Carly smiled her thanks at the team leaders of the hired catering staff. It was nearly nine in the evening and most of the guests had left. Most, but not all. Not, for instance, the baby blonde whom she had seen clinging fragilely to Ricardo's arm earlier in the afternoon, whilst she had been talking to a trio of famous British fashionista sisters whom she knew, in a roundabout sort of way, via mutual contacts in London.

The clients had just told her how pleased they were with the event, and her New York opposite number had said that she knew her agency would want to do business with Prêt a Party again.

All in all, a successful event. A successful event but not, so far she was concerned, a personally successful or mood-enhancing few hours. But then she was not here for her own benefit, was she? Carly reminded herself, as she dismissed the waiting staff and wondered how long it would be before she could reasonably suggest to Ricardo that they leave.

Two men—executives from a big New York PR agency to whom she had been introduced earlier—were approaching her. She forced her lips to widen in what she hoped looked like a genuine professional smile.

'Good event,' one of them told her approvingly. 'Harvey thought it was real neat—didn't you, Harv?'

'Yeah,' the second one agreed. 'Real neat!'

Ricardo increased the pace of his stride. Every time he gave in to his need to look for her Carly was surrounded by other men. And he didn't like it. He didn't like it one little bit!

'Sorry to break up the party,' he announced untruthfully now, as he reached the trio.

Immediately the two men fell back, leaving an empty space at Carly's side, which Ricardo promptly filled. As he did so he deliberately stood so that he was blocking out the other men—and anyone else who might have wanted to approach Carly.

'Have you seen everything you want to see?' Carly asked him brightly. All afternoon she had been reminding herself that she was supposed to be making sure that Ricardo was so impressed with Prêt a Party's skills that he offered them a contract.

Ricardo was tempted to tell her bluntly and in explicit detail that *she* was what he most wanted to see—preferably lying naked on his bed, with that look in her eyes that said she wanted him like crazy.

Instead he nodded his head tersely and asked, 'How soon can you be ready to leave?'

Her New York counterpart had already assured her that there was no need for her to stay, and she had spoken with the clients.

'I'm ready now.'

'Fine. Let's go, then.'

Carly didn't really want to move. Ricardo was standing right next to her, and if she turned towards him now they would be standing body to body…like lovers…

'What's wrong? Missing the attention of your new friends? Want me to call them back?'

Instead of turning towards him, Carly took a step back.

'No, I don't,' she told him quietly. 'And as for what's wrong—I was just wishing that I didn't ache so much for you to take me to bed!'

She turned away from him and started to walk towards the helipad, trembling inside from the shock of actually having told him what she was thinking and how she felt. Her face and body both felt equally hot, but for very different reasons. Her face was burning because of her embarrassment, but her body was burning because what she had said to him was the truth.

Ricardo caught up with her before she had taken more than three steps, his hand on her arm halting her progress until he could stand four-square in front of her.

'Is that an admission or is it an invitation?' he asked silkily.

Carly forced herself to look up at him, and to hold his gaze as she responded calmly, 'Both!'

Ricardo couldn't even remember how many women had propositioned him over the years, never mind count them, but none of them had ever spoken to him like this—simply and directly, admitting and owning their need for him.

'That's quite a change of heart! Why?'

'I suddenly realised how much I would regret it if I went to my grave without knowing you.'

'*Knowing* me?'

His voice was cynically mocking as he moved aside so that they could continue to walk together to the helipad.

'Without having sex with you,' Carly corrected herself steadily. 'Obviously it goes without saying that it *is* only sex that we both want.'

'Less than twenty-four hours ago you were outraged because I'd paid for your clothes. Now you're offering to have sex with me?'

'I was furious because I felt what you'd done implied that I could be bought. Choosing freely to have sex with you is completely different.'

'Indeed. Didn't it occur to you that I might feel equally insulted by your suggestion that I would want a woman I had to bribe into bed with me?' he challenged her.

They had almost reached the helipad.

She had spoken to him, touched a deeply secret part of him, as no other woman had ever done, and instinctively he felt wary of his own emotional response to that. At the same time he also felt challenged by the fact that she was so obviously determined not to allow herself to become emotionally involved with him. A woman who wanted to give herself freely to him physically whilst refusing to become emotionally involved? Shouldn't that knowledge delight him instead of irking him? he taunted himself derisively. He certainly wasn't going to refuse her, was he?

Carly wondered what he was thinking. Was Ricardo shocked by what she had said? Turned off by it? Indifferent to it? Should she have been less direct, and instead created an artificial opportunity for him to come on to her if he wanted to do so?

Ricardo had gone to speak to the ground staff brought in to take care of the helicopters lined up away from the helipad. She could feel her stomach muscles clench as he walked back to her.

'I was watching you earlier on today,' he told her softly. 'Imagining just what it would be like to have those long legs of yours wrapped tightly around me whilst I took you. How do you like it best? Tell me!'

Shocked pleasure rushed through her, hot, sweet and intoxicating. A dizzying, breathtaking sensation of open and responsive arousal.

Ricardo watched her, acknowledging that the look of dazzled, dazed anticipation in her eyes was doing more to arouse him than he would have thought possible.

'Time to go,' he said, nodding in the direction of the waiting helicopter.

'You've been very quiet. Second thoughts?' Ricardo challenged Carly as he piloted them towards the landing pad of his New York building.

'About what? Telling you that I want you? Or the fact that I do want you?'

Did she realise how the musical sound of her voice could play on a man's desire, heightening it and arousing him? Ricardo wondered as he looked directly at her.

'Either.'

Carly shook her head. She had spent most of the flight surreptitiously sneaking glances at

Ricardo and then imagining herself touching him, learning him, allowing the fantasy that she hoped would soon become a reality to guide and slightly shock her thoughts. She'd touch first with her fingertips, tracing the bones that shaped him, and then with her hands as she absorbed the strength of his muscles and the taut smoothness of his flesh. And then finally with her lips and her tongue, as she explored every delicate hollow and plane of him.

The heat that constantly beat through her body was roaring now, pulse-points of urgency throbbing not just between her legs and in her breasts but everywhere—her fingertips, her toes, her lips—everywhere…

'I've said more than I should,' she admitted huskily.

'Yes,' Ricardo acknowledged coolly. 'You have. Haven't the other men in your life preferred to do their own hunting and their own propositioning?'

There was a small jolt as the helicopter hit the ground.

She waited silently for Ricardo to climb out and then come round to help her. Above them, stars glittered in the darkness of the night sky, but it was impossible for them to compete with the brilliance and colour of the New York skyline.

His hands on her body felt hard but remote. Rejecting? Had she got it wrong? Had she misunderstood? Had he merely been pretending before that he wanted her?

He had set her free, and she had no option other than to walk ahead of him to the lift foyer door.

Ricardo followed her and activated the lift. Within seconds they were stepping out of it into his own private entrance foyer, and within seconds of that he was opening the door to his apartment.

'Dolores and Rafael are away for a family event,' he told her.

Carly nodded her head. Disappointment was a cold, sick, leaden lump weighing down her body. It struck her how ironic it was. Had someone previously suggested to her that she would find herself in this kind of situation, the feelings she would have expected would have been shame and humiliation, rather than the gut-wrenching sense of disappointment she actually did have.

All those years of silently, determinedly telling herself she had a right to her pride had obviously not made as big an impression on her psyche as she had believed.

They were in the large square hallway. It was nearly eleven o'clock. She turned away from Ricardo, intending to make her way to her suite and the sleepless night she suspected lay ahead of her.

'This way.'

His fingers closed round her bare forearm and immediately her flesh reacted in a burst of over-sensitivity and raised goosebumps.

This corridor was unfamiliar, its walls hung with what she suspected must be priceless pieces of modern art. At the end of it was a pair of double doors. Ricardo opened one of them without releasing her.

Silently she walked through it into the darkness that lay beyond. Ricardo let her go, and she heard the quiet snap of the door closing.

She could feel him standing behind her, and waited for him to switch on the lights, but instead he turned her round, his hands gripping her upper arms.

CHAPTER TEN

'NOW. *Now* you can tell me that you want me.'

His voice was a raw sound of out-of-control male need.

A thrill of shocked delight exploded inside her. She could feel herself shaking with excitement as he pulled her into his own body and took her mouth with explicit sexual hunger.

Her response to him rolled over her like an eighty-foot wave, swamping her, picking her up and taking her bodily. She had no defence against it, nor did she want one.

His tongue, seeking and demanding, thrust hotly between her lips without any preliminaries. Her small sob of pleasure was submerged beneath his own sounds of overriding need. His hands were on her body, tugging down her top, pushing aside her bra.

Carly moaned as his hands grazed her nipples, and then moaned again more sharply when he took one between his thumb and forefinger and began to tease it into hard, tight, aching need. Without knowing she was doing it Carly ground her hips against him, mimicking the hard thrust of his tongue between her lips.

'Don't,' he cautioned her thickly. 'Do you want me to completely lose control and take you here?'

Getting her back here without touching her had strained his self control to its limits. And now…

'Yes,' Carly told him quickly, feeling the words catch against her throat. 'I want you to take me, wherever and whenever you want—but most of all I want you to do it *now*. Now! Ricardo, now!'

Did she realise that she had just destroyed the last shreds of his control, what her hungry, half-moaned words were doing to him?

'Now?' he repeated.

His eyes, accustomed to the darkness, showed him the pale glimmer of her breasts. He stroked his forefinger round one nipple and watched her whole body surge with pleasure.

He could feel the muscles locking in his throat. He bent his head and took the tight sexual flowering of her desire for him into his mouth, savouring the sensation of the smooth swell of her breast before running his tongue over her nipple, all the time trying to hold onto his sanity, to stop himself from pushing her up against the wall and tearing the clothes off her so that he could have the pleasure of sinking as deep inside her as he could get.

Carly could hear someone start to moan, but it took her several seconds to recognise that she was the one making the noise. She felt as though she were on a long slide, unable to stop herself from plunging into her own pleasure. Not wanting to stop herself.

Reluctantly Ricardo released her nipple, his fingers immediately returning to enjoy its arousal.

'How do you want it?' he demanded softly. 'Do you have a favourite position? Do you want to take care of the condom issue or shall I?'

Carly looked at him and took a deep breath. 'I think this is when I should tell that I don't have very much previous experience,' she announced carefully.

'What?'

She couldn't tell whether the harshness in his voice came from anger or disbelief.

'What does that mean?'

Carly swallowed, and then said in a small voice,

'Actually, I'm afraid it means that I haven't… There hasn't… I'm still a virgin.'

'*What?* You're joking, right?

Carly shook her head.

He released her abruptly and stood back from her, looking at her for what felt like for ever.

'I can't think of one single reason why the hell you would be a virgin.'

'Actually, there are several,' Carly responded with dignity. 'For one thing… Well, I don't suppose the opportunity has been there at the right time or with the right man,' she hedged.

Her revelation was the last thing Ricardo had expected. If she had kept to her virgin purity until now why was she, to put it crudely, offering it to him on a plate? Did she think he would feel some sort of moral responsibility towards her? Was that it? Was she setting some sort of trap for him? Would she try to use emotional blackmail to turn mere physical intimacy into something more?

If he had any sense he would send her back to her own room, right now, but somehow, in some way, a part of him was actually responding to what she had told him with a primitive surge of male possessiveness. It actively *liked* the thought of the sexual exclusivity of being her first lover, of knowing that the sensuality he would imprint on her would remain with her throughout her life, that if the experience he gave her was truly pleasurable then she would treasure it all her life. And she would not be comparing him to anyone else. Was he really that vain? That insecure? Ricardo grimaced to himself, knowing that he wasn't.

'You damn sure don't act like a virgin,' he told her grimly.

Probably because when she was around him she didn't think that she was. Mentally, in the privacy of her own thoughts, the intimacy she had with him had gone well beyond the bounds of virginity.

'Perhaps I shouldn't have told you?' Carly offered.

Ricardo looked at her with incredulity.

'Don't you think it would have been obvious? Especially given the kind of intimacy I'd planned to—'

He saw the excitement begin to burn in her eyes and he cursed himself for the way his body immediately responded to it.

'Are you sure this is what you want? An affair that—?'

Carly stopped him. 'I don't want an affair. I just want to have sex with you.'

'Just sex?' Ricardo questioned, not sure that he believed her.

'Yes. But of course if you'd rather not…' she added lightly.

No one gave that kind of challenge to Ricardo.

'You'll cry ''enough'' before I do,' he told her against her mouth.

He was barely brushing her lips with his own, a feather-light touch that, as Carly quickly discovered, made her hunger for more. Her own lips clung to his, willing him to part them with his tongue as he had done before, and a shudder of visible pleasure gripped her body when finally he did so, thrusting the seeking point of his tongue deep and hard within the warm softness of her mouth.

His hand cupped the back of her head and his tongue plunged deeper, twining with her own. She could feel the heavy slam of her heart as it banged against her ribs—or was it his?

He was holding her right up against him, so close that she could feel his erection. And she wanted to feel it. And not just to feel it—she wanted to see it, touch it…experience it deep inside her.

She felt weak and dizzy with arousal, her whole body shuddering with pleasure when Ricardo cupped her breast and then slowly circled his fingertip around her nipple. Lazy delicate circles that were driving her insane. She sucked in a deep breath and felt the corresponding tightening low down in her body. Unable to stop herself, she reached out and touched the hard ridge of male flesh, mimicking Ricardo's caress as she circled the head of it with her fingertip and then traced its whole shape through the fabric of his clothes. It felt thick and strong. Her fingers trembled and so did her body.

To her shock Ricardo immediately released her. She stared up at him through the darkness.

'I need a shower,' he told her thickly, 'and you are going to share it with me.'

He had taken hold of her hand. She could break free of him if she wanted to, but she knew that she didn't.

He guided her through the darkness past the shape of a huge bed and then into a dressing room, switching on the light as he did so.

'It's a wet room,' he told her. 'So we undress in here.'

Undress. Her mouth went dry. But Ricardo had turned away from her and was already stripping off his clothes.

Mesmerised, Carly watched him, her curiosity followed by an awe that darkened her eyes so that when Ricardo looked at her he could see arousal shimmering in them, just as she could see his arousal, straining tautly from its thick mat of dark springy curls.

Her legs had suddenly gone weak.

Her fingers trembling, she started to tug off her own clothes, hesitating only when she got down to the silky sheer thong that barely concealed her sex.

Ricardo had turned away from her and was walking towards the door to the wet room. Carly took a deep breath and then followed him.

Ricardo touched a button, and immediately lusciously warm water sprang from hidden jets, soaking her.

'Do you really need this?' Ricardo was standing in front of her, hooking one lean finger under the narrow strap of her thong whilst the pad of his thumb stroked sensuously against her bare skin. Thrills of pleasure skittered over her.

He leaned forward and stroked his tongue-tip over her lips. Carly exhaled in a voluptuous sigh and closed her eyes, moving closer to him. The soft stroking touch of his fingertip traced the edge of her thong very slowly, and then traced it again.

'Mmm…'

She could feel the heat building up between her legs.

Ricardo's fingertip was tracing down the side of her thong. She could feel herself starting to shudder.

His hand moved back, easing her thong down…out of his way. Her legs had gone so weak she could barely stand to step out of it.

Half dazed, she started to soap herself, tensing when Ricardo took hold of her hands and told her softly, 'That's my job—and my pleasure.'

The silky suds made his hands glide sensuously over her flesh: her breasts, exquisitely sensitive now to his touch, her belly, where the spread of his fingers caused the heat inside her to turn her liquid with longing, her behind, which he soaped with a long slow movement that left one hand resting on the back of her thigh whilst the fingers of the other stroked between her legs, and then right up along the wet cleft between the swollen lips of her sex.

Helplessly Carly leaned into his caress, her body clenching on shudders of arousal. Driven by age-old instinct, she reached out and enclosed him with her hand, eagerly caressing the full length of him, and then released him again so that she could explore the swollen head of his erection. Now he was the one doing the shuddering, then subjecting them both to a sudden swift pounding of more water jets to rinse their bodies free of suds.

She had always believed that she was far too tall and heavy for any man to ever be able to pick her up bodily, but now, for a second time, Ricardo was proving her wrong, Carly thought, as Ricardo finished towelling her dry and then lifted her into his arms.

The bedroom was now bathed in soft lamplight, and the bedlinen was cool beneath her skin as Ricardo laid her on the bed and then bent his head towards her own.

'Still want this?' he whispered against her lips.

'Yes,' Carly whispered back. 'Do you?'

For the first time since she had known him she saw genuine humour in his eyes.

'My arousal and desire are quite plainly evident.'

'So are mine—to me,' Carly told him huskily.

His hand cupped her breast. 'You mean this—here?' he murmured, his thumb stroking lightly against her nipple. 'Or this—here?' His knowing stroke the full length of her sex made her moan with pleasure. Her arousal-swollen flesh housed a million nerve endings that were pleasure points, and it seemed to Carly that Ricardo's caress lingered over each one of them. And then he stroked her clitoris, rhythmically and deliberately.

Immediately her body arched in supplication, her gaze fixed on his. How could she ever have thought his eyes were cold? They burned now with dark fire.

His hand moved away. He kissed the side of her throat and then her collarbone, sliding his free hand into her hair and cradling the back of her head. Already she was anticipating—longing for the feel of his mouth against her.

Her throat tightened, shudders of pleasure running through her as his tongue-tip traced a lazy line down to her breasts and circled each nipple. A soft breath of longing bubbled in her throat. His lips closed over one nipple, his tongue working it. She gasped breathlessly, reaching out to hold his head against her body, her fingers locking into his hair as she arched up against him, unable to stop herself from wanting the wild surges of pleasure his mouth and fingers were creating inside her.

Of their own volition her legs fell open, her muscles contracting as she felt the warmth of Ricardo's hand skimming her body and then coming to rest against the small curls covering her sex.

Heat ran through her to gather beneath his hand. A pulse of need was beating where he touched her.

She had believed that she knew desire, but all she had known was its shadow. This, its reality, was overpowering, overwhelming her.

She felt Ricardo's thumb probing the cleft below the soft curls. A pleading, mewling sound broke from her lips and she lifted her body towards him.

The dark fire in his eyes burned even more hotly. But not as hot as the fire burning inside her.

Wild tremors seized her and she whimpered in helpless arousal as he parted the outer lips of her sex and then started to caress her.

The white heat of ravening need filled her, her head falling back against the pillows. Her hips writhed frantically against the movement of his fingertip as he rubbed it the full length of her, lingering deliberately on the hard swell of her clitoris.

No woman had ever abandoned herself, given herself to him and his pleasuring of her like this, Ricardo acknowledged. He didn't know how much longer he could keep his own arousal under control.

She felt hot and wet, the swollen lips beneath his fingers opening to him of their own volition to offer him the gift of her sex.

A wild surge of longing engulfed him. It wasn't enough that he could feel her; he wanted to see her as well.

Carly cried out in protest as she felt Ricardo move, but his hand was still resting reassuringly on the mound of her sex and his body was still openly aroused. Her eyes, though, still asked an anxious question, and as he sat up Ricardo answered it for her, telling her rawly, 'I want to see you. I want to watch your sex flush with pleasure and lie open and eager for my touch.'

Wild thoughts of urging him, begging him not to, fled, as she felt him caressing her again. But this time... This time, as her head dropped back and her body was gripped by intense surges of pleasure, she could feel him caressing her lips apart, exposing her swollen, glistening secret inner flesh to his gaze and his touch. Just the pressure of his fingertip against her clitoris made her cry out in frantic arousal. He bent his head and his tongue stroked along her silken folds. All the way along them, Carly recognised on a shudder of fierce delight, as the hard-pointed tip of his tongue probed and stroked into life sensations she had never imagined existing.

He couldn't hold out much longer, Ricardo realised, as he felt his body throb in reaction to the pleasure of tasting her and arousing her. He drove the tip of his tongue into her moist opening and heard her moan of pleasure He stroked her clitoris with quick rhythmic strokes of his tongue and eased a finger slowly into her.

Immediately her muscles closed round it, holding it, and his body responded with a savage thrust of male urgency.

He could feel his heart thudding, sweat beading his forehead, but he made himself go slowly. One finger, and then two, waiting for her body to accommodate him and then respond as he caressed her.

She was moving urgently against him now, her body aroused and eager as she thrust against him and moaned.

Frantically Carly reached out and touched Ricardo's body, her fingers closing round him, moving over him. He felt so hot and slick, the foreskin moving easily and fluidly over the swollen head of his erection. Her body tightened, and excitement locked the air into her lungs in expectation.

Still caressing her, Ricardo pulled her beneath him, easing himself slowly into her, his muscles aching with the punishing pressure he was exerting over them as he refused to give in to their demand for him to thrust deeply and fully.

Her muscles closed round him, making him shudder with violent need. He thrust deeper, and then deeper still, whilst Carly dug her nails into his shoulder—not in pain, but in urgent female need to have more of him. Unable to stop herself, she gave voice to that need, the words tumbling huskily from her lips as she pleaded frantically, 'More… Ricardo. Deeper…' matching her pleas to the eager movement of her body against his.

'Like this? How much more? This much?'

She gasped into his thrust, driven by her own need to make him fill her and take her higher.

'Mmm. Yes. More…deeper…again.'

Her frantic litany of pleas and praise fell against Ricardo's senses like a song sung in sensual counterpart to their mingled breathing, underscored by the rise and fall of its urgency and satisfaction, whilst her body's response to him blew apart his intention of remaining in control.

His own need to go deeper, harder, to know and possess all of her, overwhelmed him. His increasingly powerful thrusts took them both higher, and his own satisfaction was matched by the eager rhythmic movement of Carly's hips, and the sounds of her rising pleasure. She clung to him, kissing his throat and his shoulder, then raking his arm with her nails in a sudden ecstasy of physical delight as he drove them both closer to the edge.

It was too much for his self-control. The muscles in his neck corded as he fought to delay his own climax, but it was too late. His body was already claiming its final mindless driving surge of release.

Carly called out a jumble of helpless words of feverish pleasure as Ricardo's fierce pulsing thrusts of completion carried her with him over the edge of pleasure, her body suddenly contorting in a burst of rhythmic climactic contractions of release.

It was over.

Very carefully, Ricardo rolled Carly over onto her side and held her against him.

Carly lay there, trying to steady her breathing, her body still trembling with reaction. Tears blurred her vision, although she had no idea why she should want to cry. The pleasure had been so very much more than she had imagined.

Ricardo was lying facing her, his arm resting heavily but oh, so sweetly over her, holding her close to him.

'Are you okay?'

'I think so,' she answered shakily. 'I'm still trying to come back down to earth. I hadn't realised it would be so…' She stopped.

'So what?' Ricardo probed.

'So…so intense. Not when you…when we don't…when this isn't about loving one another,' she finally managed to say.

She felt Ricardo moving, but before she could say anything he was holding her tightly in his arms and kissing her. Slowly and gently and…oh, so very sweetly.

It was six o'clock and the park was quiet. Ricardo had left Carly sleeping, easing himself away from her body and taking care not to wake her.

He had woken a dozen times during the night, silently listening to her breathing, watching her, and whilst he was doing so he had relived the intimacy they had shared, trying to analyse his own reaction to it.

He had had sex before, after all, and he had had good sex before. But never, ever anything that had come anywhere near to making him feel the way he had felt with Carly.

Her use of the word 'intense' had mirrored his own feelings.

Why, though? Why should her body, her flesh, her need be so very different? Not because she had been a virgin? No, definitely not because of that!

The second time they had made love, in the early hours of the morning, had to him been an even more intense experience than the first time. And Carly had made it plain to him that she had no regrets. Her virginity had been something he'd had to take account of in possessing her, yes, but it had not been the cause of that difference.

So what was it about her that lingered so strongly that he had needed to keep waking up to check that she was still there?

What was it about her that made his whole body compress with possessiveness at the thought of losing her?

Was it the intensity of the intimacy they had shared? The fact that, for some unfathomable reason, something in her humbled and softened something in him? He didn't know. But he did know that, whatever it was, it had somehow caused an abrupt turnaround inside his head, and that instead of mentally working out how fast he could get away from her and get on with the really exciting things in his life—like another business acquisition—he was actually wondering how he could prolong their time together.

He looked at his watch. Soon she would be waking up. And he wanted to be there when she did.

* * *

'Carly?'

Reluctantly she opened her eyes.

She had woken up an hour earlier, wondering where Ricardo had gone, and then, after showering and brushing her teeth, she had come back to bed and promptly fallen deeply asleep again.

Ricardo was sitting on the side of the bed next to her, and what was more he was fully dressed.

She struggled to sit up, and then realised self-consciously that she was naked.

'We need to leave for France this afternoon,' Ricardo reminded her.

'Oh, yes, of course. I—'

She gave a shallow gasp as Ricardo leaned forward and covered her mouth with his own. Automatically she clung to his shoulders, and then wrapped her arms around his neck when she felt his tongue demanding possession of her mouth. Already her body felt sweetly heavy with longing for him, drawn to him like a moth to a flame.

He lifted his mouth from hers and she stretched sensuously, watching the heat burn in his gaze as it feasted on her, relishing the hot glitter. His hand cupped her shoulder and then stroked slowly over her, ignoring the urgent, desiring peaking of her nipples and coming to rest on her hip, his thumb moving lazily over the indent of her belly. Feathery, frustrating little touches that had her arching up to him in silent demand.

'Undress me!'

The command sounded thick and slightly unsteady, rather like her own fingers as they curled round the hem of his tee shirt and then trembled wildly the minute they came into contact with the hard-muscled heat of his skin.

Her task might have been easier if Ricardo hadn't tormented her, occupying himself by kissing her and caressing her whilst she was trying to complete it, Carly decided, but she finally tugged off his tee shirt, to be rewarded with the hot fierce suckle of his mouth on her breast.

Sensation pierced her, sweet and shocking and achingly erotic, and the stroke of his tongue and the deliberate, delicate rasp of his teeth made her moan and beg for more.

In the end he had to finish undressing himself, shedding his clothes with unsteady urgency and then taking hold of Carly and lifting her to straddle his prone body.

He watched as her eyes widened, and kept on watching whilst he stroked his fingertip through her wetness.

She cried out immediately, her body tensing. Ricardo reached up and laved first one and then the other nipple with his tongue, feral male arousal gripping him as the morning sun highlighted for him the swollen wet crests. He found the sensitive heat of her clitoris and rubbed his fingertip rhythmically over it.

Carly arched tightly against his touch, her eagerness for him darkening her eyes as she reached for him and positioned herself over him, slowly sinking down on him, taking him into her.

Ricardo kept still, hardly daring to breathe, hardly able to endure the pleasure of the sensation of her body opening to him, her muscles slowly claiming him.

Experimentally Carly moved her body, gasping in shocked delight as she felt her own pleasure. She moved again, eagerly and demandingly. Exhaling, Ricardo responded to her need, grasping her hips as she took control, letting her take as much of him as she wanted, and then groaning in raw heat as she demanded more.

She came quickly, almost violently, just before Ricardo, in a series of intense spasms that left her too weak to even move. It was left to Ricardo to lift her from him and then hold her sweat-slick trembling body against his own, his arms wrapped securely around her.

CHAPTER ELEVEN

'I SHOULD really stay at the château, so that I can be on hand in case anything goes wrong.'

They had arrived in France two hours ago, and now Carly was seated next to Ricardo in the large Mercedes hire car that had been waiting for him at the airport. He had just informed her that he wanted her to stay with him at the house he was renting instead of at the château where the party was to be held.

'If anything does go wrong you can be there within minutes,' he told her.

She knew that he was right, and she knew too that she wanted to be with him. How, in such a short space of time, could she have become so physically addicted to him that she could hardly bear not to be close to him?

'How are you feeling? Are you okay?'

Both his question and the almost tender note in his voice startled her.

'I'm—I'm fine. I can't believe I didn't realise before how…how compulsive sex can be.'

Ricardo started to frown. Her answer wasn't the one he had been expecting. Or the one he had wanted?

'It wasn't just sex for you, though, was it?' he challenged her.

Carly couldn't look at him. Prickles of warning were burning their way into her head, triggering her defences.

'Why do you say that?'

'A woman doesn't get to your age still a virgin unless she's either too traumatised to want sex or she's waiting to feel as drawn to a partner emotionally as she is sexually.'

'No, that isn't true. The reason I haven't had sex before now is because I *haven't* wanted any emotional involvement, not because I have.'

Ricardo could hear the panic in her voice. No matter how old-fashioned it might be, every instinct he possessed told him that she had to have very deep emotional feelings for him to have responded the way she had. His male logic couldn't accept that, given her virginity, it could be any other way.

'Human beings are allowed to have emotions, you know,' he told her wryly. 'But my guess is that you are afraid of emotional vulnerability because of what you experienced as a child. Your adoptive parents rejected you, gave their love to their own daughter whilst withholding it from you.'

Carly was too intelligent to try and deny what he was saying.

'I may have been an emotionally needy child, but I have no intention of allowing myself to become an emotionally needy woman.'

'There's a huge difference between being emotionally needy and loving someone.'

'Maybe. Or maybe, just as some people are genetically disposed to be more vulnerable to drug addiction, some people might be genetically disposed to emotional vulnerability. I prefer not to put my own resistance to the test.'

'How did your adopted sister die?'

His question caught her off guard.

'She…she was a drug addict. She died from an overdose of heroin. She started using drugs when we were at school. She was a year above me, and in a different crowd. I… It never appealed to me. I told you that my mother was one of three young women who died in a house fire. They were probably all drug addicts. I never… I couldn't… I know that, deep down inside, my adoptive parents blamed me for her addiction. My adoptive mother admitted as much. She said that she felt by bringing me into their lives they had brought in the evil of drug addiction.'

'Rubbish,' Ricardo announced briskly. 'It strikes me that they were looking for someone to blame and picked on you.'

'Maybe, but I still feel guilty. They loved her, not me, and now she's dead. All they've got left is me. I've tried to do what I can to help them, to repay them for everything they've given me.'

'Everything they've given you? Such as what?'

'A chance to live a normal life. My education. Without them I could have ended up making a living selling myself on the street, like my mother probably did.'

'No,' Ricardo told her firmly. 'No, you would never have done that. Somehow you would have found a way to set yourself free.'

Carly could feel emotional tears prickling her eyes. Emotional tears?

'I want you, Carly, and not just physically. You touch my emotions and delight my senses. When you aren't with me, I want you to be. You've become integral to my pleasure in life—to my happiness, if you like. I want to explore with you what's happening to us. I trust you enough to tell you that, and to tell you too that emotionally I am vulnerable to you. Is it really so hard for you to do the same?'

'I don't know what to say,' she admitted shakily.

'Then don't say anything,' Ricardo told her. 'Just allow yourself to feel instead. And when we're together you *do* feel, don't you, Carly?'

'I…I know that when we have sex it gives me a lot of pleasure.'

She answered him primly, but prim was the very opposite of what she felt. Just talking with him like this had made her body begin to pulse with sensual need. It seemed a lifetime since they had last had sex, though in fact it was less than twenty-four hours. Already she was longing for the opportunity to spend more time with him in intimate privacy. Her legs were weak, and she had to make a small denying movement in her seat to clamp down on the sensation pulsing inside her.

She could feel Ricardo looking at her. She turned her head and looked back at him. He knew! Somehow he knew what she was feeling. The car was an automatic, and he reached for her hand, placing it against his own body.

It wasn't the answer he wanted, but it would do—for now. If her sexual response to him was her area of vulnerability, then he would have to use that to try and break down her emotional barriers.

Ricardo was hard!

Carly tried to swallow, and for one wanton shocking moment she actually found herself wishing she were the kind of woman who felt comfortable abandoning her underwear, and that only the lightness of a thin summer skirt, instead of jeans and beneath them her thong, separated her from Ricardo's intimate touch.

'Don't,' she heard Ricardo growl thickly. 'Otherwise I'll have to stop. And the back of a car just doesn't have room for what I want to do with you right now…'

'What do you want to do?' Carly encouraged him huskily.

She felt his momentary hesitation mingling with her own shock that she could be so enticing.

'I want to spread you out in front of me, your body naked and eager…just like it was that first time. I want to start at your toes, touching every inch of you, tasting every inch of you. I want to bring you to orgasm with my hand and my mouth, and watch you take your pleasure from me…'

Carly let out a soft beseeching moan. 'Stop it,' she begged. 'I can't—'

'Wait?' he demanded softly. 'Do you think it's any different for me?'

Emotionless sex! Ricardo knew perfectly well that he was brooding too much and too betrayingly over Carly's attitude. She had no idea just what emotionless sex actually was, he told himself fiercely. She had already admitted to him that she was simply trying to protect herself from being hurt, as she had been hurt as a child. And because of that she was refusing to admit that her emotions were as dangerously involved with him as his were with her. After all, she had given herself to him totally and completely as his, and he had claimed her in exactly that same way.

The figures he had been working on for making a bid for Prêt a Party were in front of him on the table of the small café where they had stopped for drink. He glanced uncaringly at them whilst he waited for Carly to return from the lavatory. He no longer cared how profitable it was, or indeed whether or not he acquired it. In fact the only acquisition he was really interested in right now was the total and exclusive right to Carly herself—preferably by way of an unbreakable and permanent legally binding document.

Where was she? His muscles tensed, and then started to relax as he saw her hurrying towards him. Two men at another table were also looking at her, and immediately he wanted to get up, lay claim to her.

'We need to stop at a chemist,' he told her as he signalled for their bill. When she looked at him in concern, he explained succinctly, 'Condoms.'

'Oh!' Carly could feel her face going pink.

'Not that I think there's any risk to either of us from a health issue point of view, but I assume you aren't protected from pregnancy?'

'Yes. I mean, no. I mean, no—I'm not protected,' Carly confirmed guiltily. How could she have overlooked something as basic and important as that?

The château owned by a famous rock star and his stunningly attractive American wife was in the Loire valley, home to some of France's famous wine-growing districts. Carly had seen photographs of the château in a magazine article about the star and his family, and she knew that his well-born wife had scoured Europe's antique dealers and employed the very best craftsmen in order to restore the building and turn it into a modern home. A mirrored ballroom similar to that at Versailles was the showpiece of the restoration work, along with the gardens.

This event was by far the largest of the three they had attended. Just about everyone who was anyone had been invited. Five hundred celebrity guests in all, mainly from the world of rock music, films, the upper classes and fashion.

In addition to a six-course dinner, the menu for which had been organised by one of the world's leading chefs, and the regulation post-dinner dancing, the rock star's wife had chosen to have magicians moving amongst the tables, performing a variety of tricks. Cream, gold and black were the colours she had chosen, insisting that the flowers used for table decoration must not have any scent as she wanted to have the huge marquee scented only by the special candles she had ordered in her favourite room fragrance.

The marquee itself was to be black, ornamented with cream and gold, the dining chairs were cream with black rope ties, and the floor a dazzling gold that looked like crushed tissue paper beneath glass.

The house Ricardo had rented was in a small picturesque town a few kilometres away from the château on the bank of the River Loire, a tall, narrow honey-coloured stone building wedged in amongst its fellows on a dim, narrow, winding cobbled street, with its own private courtyard at the rear and a balcony on the second floor which overlooked the Loire itself.

It came complete with Madame Bouton, who was waiting to introduce herself and the house to them, explaining that she would come every morning to clean, and that she was willing to buy them whatever food they might require.

'What's that look for?' Ricardo demanded as soon as Madame had gone.

'I'm just so hungry for you,' Carly told him simply.

A sensation like a giant fist striking his chest hit him with a combination of unfamiliar emotions spiked with warnings. And then he looked into her eyes, at her mouth…

They didn't make it out of the kitchen. They didn't even make it out of their clothes. The sex was hot and immediate. Ricardo's hands cupped the bare cheeks of her bottom as he lifted her onto the table, and Carly wrapped her legs tightly round him.

She had been waiting for this and for him all day—thinking, fantasising about him, longing for him—and just the sensation of his mouth against her naked breast as he pushed aside her clothes took her to such a pitch of excitement that she thought she might actually orgasm there and then.

But, as she quickly discovered, she had more things to learn from Ricardo about the pleasure of sex. A lot more!

When he had delayed both their climaxes to the point where Carly was ready to scream with frustration, he finally complied with her urgent demands, and the intensity of orgasm that followed left her lying limply against him whilst her body shook with tremors of sensual aftershock.

Wearing her cropped jeans, a tee shirt, and a hat to protect her head from the heat of the sun, Carly stood listening to their clients as the three of them discussed the event.

'I really like the interior of the marquee, but I'm not sure now about the flowers. I think I want to change them,' Angelina Forrester informed her. 'I love the drama of having black. Perhaps if we changed things so that the tablecloths are just barely cream and the flowers black…you know, very heavy and oriental-looking. Sort of passionate and dangerous!'

Carly's heart began to sink as she recalled the trouble and the expense they had gone to in order to comply with Angelina's initial demand for scent-free blooms.

'Bloody hell, Angelina, does it matter what colour the bloody flowers are?'

The Famous Rock Star looked and sounded angrily impatient, and Carly could see the pink tinge of temper creeping up his wife's perfect complexion.

'Perhaps if we added one or two dramatic dark flowers to the table decorations?' Carly suggested calmingly, mentally deciding that if Angelina agreed to her suggestion the extra flowers would have to be artificial—or sprayed. No way was there time to source black-petalled flowers for tomorrow night! She would need to speak to the florist as well…

'Well… I'd have to see what you mean…' Angelina hesitated.

The Famous Rock Star swore crudely. 'All this because you've changed your mind about your bloody dress!'

The pink tinge had become distinctly darker.

Discreetly Carly excused herself, explaining that she needed to speak with the hired entertainers.

Arms folded over his black-clad chest, his long chino-covered legs stretched out in front of him, Ricardo propped himself up against a nearby wall and watched her.

She had good people-managing skills, and she was able to establish a genuine rapport with those she worked with. She treated them well, and with respect, and they in turn were obviously prepared to listen to what she had to say. But he didn't want her as an employee. He wanted her as a woman. He wanted her exclusively and permanently as his woman. He had, he admitted, fallen deeply and completely in love with her.

He heard a burst of laughter from the mainly male group surrounding her and immediately his muscles contracted on a primitive surge of male jealousy.

He was halfway towards her before Carly became aware of his presence, alerted to the fact that something was happening by the sudden silence from those around her.

She turned round and saw Ricardo striding towards her, and her heart turned over inside her chest with need, her whole body going boneless with the pleasure of just looking at him.

'I thought you might be ready for some lunch.'

'Yes, I am. I think there's a sort of workers' canteen affair set up somewhere.'

Ricardo shook his head and then took hold of her arm, deliberately drawing her away from the others.

'No. Not here. I was thinking of somewhere more…private.'

She knew he could feel the betraying leap

of her pulse because his thumb was resting on her wrist.

'Yes!' she told him unsteadily. 'Yes.'

Their clothes lay abandoned on the bedroom floor—Ricardo's tee shirt and her top, his chinos and her cut-offs, the smooth plain Calvins in which he could have posed as effectively and even more erotically than any male model—or so at least Carly considered—her bra, and finally the tiny side-bow-tied silky thong he had given her only yesterday. A gift for her that he would ensure brought pleasure to them both, he had told her seductively.

They lay skin to skin, Ricardo's hands slowly shaping her whilst she lay in the luxurious sensual aftermath of their earlier urgent coupling.

'You're quiet,' Ricardo murmured.

'I'm just thinking about how perfect this is and how happy I am,' Carly admitted.

Ricardo looked at her, and then cupped her face and kissed her.

'So you're ready to accept that we do have something special, that it isn't just sex, then?' he said softly.

He reached for her hand and twined his fingers through hers, holding it—and her—safely. She had fought so hard to deny what she felt, but today, lying here in the sun with him, she knew that she couldn't deny her love any longer.

'I... Ricardo, I...I do feel emotionally connected to you.'

'"Emotionally connected"?' Ricardo queried, shaking his head as he continued tenderly, 'Is the word "love" really so very hard to say? Or are you waiting for me to say it first?'

Without waiting for her to reply he kissed her gently, saying, 'I—love—you—Carly,' spacing out the words between kisses.

There could be no greater happiness than this—no greater sense of belonging, no deeper trust or awareness of being loved, Carly decided as she let him walk into her heart.

'Ricardo, we ought to get dressed.'

'Why?'

'I'm supposed to be working,' she reminded him, trying to sound as though she meant it.

'Mmm...'

Ricardo had slid his hand into her hair and was kissing the sensitive little spot just beneath her ear. But it was too late. Her own reminder to herself that she should be working had made her uncomfortably aware that she still had not dealt with the problem of Nick forging her signature.

'What's wrong?'

'Nothing's wrong. What makes you think that there is?'

'You're anxious and tense, and you're avoiding eye contact with me,' Ricardo told her wryly. 'So much for me hoping that you'd finally let me in past the barricades.'

'No, it isn't anything to do with that,' Carly assured him.

'Then what is it to do with?'

He had caught her neatly with that one. There was no point in her trying to pretend now that she wasn't worrying about anything.

'It's… It's something that doesn't only concern *me*, Ricardo.'

'The business?' he guessed.

Carly nodded her head.

'You're a potential client, and…'

He reached for her and looked into her eyes. 'I thought we'd gone way beyond that. What we have means that our personal bond with one another comes way, way before our loyalties to anything or anyone else. Surely you know that you can trust me?'

'Yes.'

'So what's the problem?'

Hesitantly, she started to explain.

'You mean to say that he's forged your signature so that he can steal from his own wife?' he said incredulously.

'I don't know that, but it does look that way. I'm just so worried about what I should do. If I tell Lucy she's going to be so hurt, and she may not even believe me. I've been in touch with the bank and told them that no cheques are to be allowed through the account for the time being, so at least that should stop him from drawing any more.'

'How much has he taken?'

'A lot. In fact so much that the company just won't be viable by year-end unless Lucy makes up the shortfall from her trust fund.'

'So as of now the business is a sitting duck for any lurking predator?'

'Well, yes, I suppose it is. Although I hadn't thought of it in that way,' Carly admitted. 'My concern has been for Lucy and how this is going to affect her.'

'Well, you've done as much as you can do for the moment. If I were you I'd simply put it out of your mind until we get back to London.'

Strange how that one small word 'we' could mean so very much, Carly thought, as Ricardo drew her back down into his arms.

Ricardo felt the tight coiling of his own stomach muscles as Carly's nipple responded to the slow stroke of his thumb-pad. He could already see the betraying tightening of the muscles in her belly, and the now familiar way in which that threw into relief the mound of her sex.

Carly closed her eyes and gave in to what she was feeling, hoarding the pleasure to her like a child trying to hold a rainbow. She raised her head and kissed the column of Ricardo's throat, running the tip of her tongue along it, right up to his ear, then slowly and luxuriously exploring the hard whorls of flesh.

They had already made love once, but once wasn't going to be enough. She whispered to Ricardo what she wanted, her voice blurred with pleasure and longing, her body shuddering with expectation. The moment he placed his hand on her mound she spread her legs in eager anticipation and invitation, then murmured her appreciation when Ricardo parted the still-swollen lips of her sex with his fingers and started to caress her.

'What about this?' he asked thickly, rolling her over on top of him and holding her just off his own body, his mouth at the juncture of her thighs.

Carly's heart thumped excitedly against her ribs. She had wondered...been tempted...but hadn't liked to suggest such intimacy.

But now, with him holding her arched over him, his fingers exploring her wetness and then holding her open, so that his tongue could sweep the full length of her eager arousal, she could only shudder in mindless, wanton pleasure. His tongue pressed against her clitoris, caressing it into swollen heat, whilst his fingers stroked into her, finding a new pleasure spot she hadn't known existed.

Unable to stop herself she reached for him, circling the head with her own tongue, whilst her fingers worked busily on the shaft. Daringly, the fingers of her free hand moved a little lower.

She heard him groan, his whole body stiffening, and his response increased her own arousal. She could feel him lapping fiercely at her, the intimate stroke of his fingers bringing her so quickly to orgasm that she cried out in the immediacy and intensity of it.

Her body was still tingling, still quivering intensely, when he turned her over and entered her.

Immediately her muscles fastened around him, the small shallow ripples growing into violent shuddering contractions of almost unbearable pleasure.

'I love you so much,' Carly whispered, as she lay held fast in Ricardo's arms. 'I never, ever thought I could feel like this. So loved and loving, and so very, very happy.'

CHAPTER TWELVE

A SMALL tender smile curled Carly's mouth as she let herself into the house. It was lunchtime, and with the birthday ball taking place in a few hours' time by rights she should have been at the château, just in case she was needed, but instead she had given in to Ricardo's whispered suggestion that they snatch a couple of hours alone together.

Ricardo had dropped her off outside before going to park the car, promising her that he wouldn't be very long.

Any time spent apart from him right now was far, far too long, she reflected as she put the fresh bread they had stopped off to buy on the kitchen table and then, unable to stop herself, walked into the room Ricardo was using to work in.

What was it about loving someone that caused this compulsion to share their personal space, even when they weren't in it? She had become so sensitive to everything about him that she was sure she could actually feel his body warmth in the air. Half laughing at herself for her foolishness, she paused to smooth her fingers over the chair in which he normally sat. There were some papers on the desk. She glanced absently at them, and then more hungrily as she saw his handwriting.

And then, as she realised what she was looking at, she stiffened, picking up the papers so that she could study them more closely whilst her heart thudded out an uneven, anguished death knell to her love.

Ricardo frowned as the empty silence of the house surrounded him.

Carly heard him call her name, and then come down the hallway, but she waited until he had walked into the small room before she confronted him. The papers were still in her hand, and she held on to them as she might have done a shield as she accused him bitterly, 'You lied about wanting to give Prêt a Party your business. You don't want to give us anything. You want to take us over.'

'I was considering it, yes,' Ricardo agreed levelly.

'You used me! You deliberately tricked me with all those questions you asked!' Her voice was strained and accusatory, her eyes huge in the pale shape of her face.

'The only questions I asked you were exactly the same ones I, or anyone else, would have asked if they had been intending to give Prêt a Party their business.'

'You pretended to want me…to love me…because—'

'No! Carly, no—you mustn't think that.' As he stepped towards her she moved back from him. 'Yes, I had originally planned to find out from you as much as I could about the way the business is run—that's simple defensive business practice—but—'

'You accused me of being a gold-digger. But what you are, Ricardo, is far, far worse. You used me. You let me believe that you cared about me, that you loved me, when all the time what you really wanted was the business.'

'Carly, that is not true. My potential acquisition of Prêt a Party and my love for you are two completely separate issues. Yes, originally I did think I might get an insight into any vulnerabilities the business might have through you, but I promise you that was the last thing on my mind when we became lovers. In fact because of that—because of *us*—I—'

'I don't believe you.' Carly cut him off flatly. 'I thought I could trust you. Otherwise I would never have told you what I did about Lucy and Nick. I've made it all so easy for you, haven't I? Because of my stupidity Lucy will lose the company. All the time I was letting myself believe that you were genuine, that you cared about me, what you really wanted was Prêt a Party.'

'It isn't like that. When you confided in me you were confiding in me as your lover, and I can assure you *can* trust me—'

'Trust you? Carly interrupted him furiously. 'What with? You've taken all the trust I had, Ricardo, and you've destroyed it. You knew how hard it was for me to allow myself to admit that I loved you—but you didn't care what you were doing to me, did you? Not so long as it got you what you wanted. And you wanted me vulnerable to you, didn't you? The only thing that matters to you is making your next billion, nothing else and no one else. I hate you for what you've done to me, and I hate you even more for what you're going to do to Lucy.'

'Carly, you've got it all wrong. I *did* think about acquiring Prêt a Party, but once I'd met you the only acquisition I cared about was the acquisition of your love.'

Her muscles ached from the tension inside her body, and even though she knew he was lying to her, incredibly she actually wanted to believe him. No wonder she had been so afraid of love if this was what it did to her. How could she still ache for him, knowing what she did?

'You're lying, Ricardo,' she told him. 'If you weren't planning to go ahead with the acquisition why were the papers on your desk?

'I was considering the best way to stop you worrying about Lucy and her trust fund,' he told her quietly.

Carly gave him a mirthless smile. 'Of course. And no doubt you'd decided that the best way was for you to acquire the business. You may have taken me for a fool, Ricardo, but that doesn't mean I intend to go on being one.'

'You're getting this all wrong. I can see that right now you're too upset to listen to reason—'

'Reason? More lies, you mean! I trusted you, and you betrayed that trust!' Carly could feel the anguish of her pain leaking into her voice, betraying to him how badly he had hurt her and how much she loved him.

'Trust works both ways, Carly. I could say to you that I trusted *you*, to have faith in me and my love for you. Those papers were on my desk because I was trying to come up with a way of helping Lucy without benefiting that wretched husband of hers, and the reason I was doing that was because of you. Because I love you, and I knew how upset and worried you were.'

Carly stared at him in disbelief.

'You can't really expect me to believe that,' she told him contemptuously.

'Why not? It's the truth. And if you loved me you would trust me and accept it as such.'

Tears were burning the backs of her eyes and her throat had gone tight with pain. This was the worst kind of emotional blackmail and cold-blooded cynicism, and she wasn't going to fall for it a second time.

'Then obviously I don't love you,' she told him, too brightly. 'Because I don't trust you and I don't accept it. Why should any woman accept anything a man tells her? Look at the way Nick is cheating Lucy. It's over, Ricardo, and it would have been better for me if it had never started in the first place.'

Carly stared bleakly into the mirror. She hated the fact that the only suitable outfit she had to wear for the party was a dress that came from Barneys, which Ricardo had paid for. Well, after tonight he could keep it—and everything else as well.

Including her heart?

She was perilously close to losing control, she warned herself, and no way could she afford to do that. She still had a job to do, after all.

It had been a very long day. Fortunately she had finally managed to get Angelina's approval for the flowers, even if the florist had initially been furious at the change of plan.

Guests who had arrived early and were staying locally had started to appear at the château, wanting to look at the marquee and demanding to see the seating plan.

Privately Carly felt that Angelina, or one at least one of her PAs, should have been on hand to deal with them, but it seemed that several other members of the Famous Rock Star's original band had already arrived, with their entourages, and this had led to an impromptu pre-party party taking place.

'I bet it's all sex, drugs and rock and roll up there,' one of the entertainers had said to Carly dryly, nodding his head in the direction of the château.

Discreetly, Carly had not made any response. But she did know that some seriously businesslike heavies had been hired by the celeb magazine with exclusive rights to reporting the event to protect the guests and the event from any unwanted intrusion by rival members of the press.

Outwardly she was conducting herself professionally and calmly; inwardly she was in emotional turmoil.

Ricardo had lied to her and deceived her, used her, and yet unbelievably, despite all that, and despite what she knew she had to do for the sake of her own self-respect, she still ached for him. Given the choice, if she could have turned back time and not seen those damning papers she knew she would have chosen to do so. How could she still love him? She didn't know how she could; she just knew that she did.

She had removed her things to a spare bedroom, and would have moved out of the house itself if it had been practical to do so. As it was, she was going to have to travel to the château with Ricardo, because it had proved impossible to book a taxi. She didn't know how she was going to endure it, but somehow she must.

And she hadn't even thought properly yet about what she was going to say to Lucy.

Ricardo was waiting for Carly to come downstairs. Did she have any idea how he felt about what she had said to him? Did she really think all the vulnerability and pain was on her side? It tore him apart to think that he had hurt her in any kind of way, and he cursed the fact that he had left those papers on his desk. He also cursed the fact that she had stubbornly refused to accept his explanation.

He heard a door open upstairs and watched as Carly came down the stairs towards him. She looked so beautiful that the sight of her threatened to close his throat. Carly's face was pale and set, and she looked very much as though she had been crying. He wanted to go to her, take her in his arms and never let her go, but he knew if he did she would reject him.

The guests had finished eating, and the magicians had cleverly kept them entertained whilst the tables were cleared. Any minute now the dancing would start.

Carly's head ached, and she longed for the evening to be over. She couldn't bear to look at Ricardo. They were seated at a small table tucked away next to the entrance used by the waiting staff. She would not be able to dance, of course; she wasn't here as a guest. Not that she wanted to risk dancing with Ricardo—not in her present vulnerable state.

Her feelings were just the last dying throes of her love for him, she tried to reassure herself. She was only feeling like this because she knew that after tonight she would never see him again. She was going to miss having sex with him, that was all.

She got up and told Ricardo stiffly, 'I'd better go and check that the bar staff have everything they need.'

He inclined his head in acknowledgement, but didn't make any response. She delayed going back for as long as she could, hoping that when she returned to the table Ricardo might have gone, and yet as she approached the first thing she did was look anxiously for his familiar dark head, as though she dreaded him not being there rather than the opposite. How was she going to get through the rest of her life without him, lying alone in her bed at night longing for him?

'The fireworks are about to start,' Ricardo warned her before she could sit down.

As a special finale to the evening a firework display had been choreographed and timed to go with music from the Famous Rock Star's biggest hit, and to judge from the enthusiastic reception the display received from the assembled guests it had been well worth the time spent on its organisation.

Carly, though, watched the display through a haze of tears, standing stiffly at Ricardo's side, aching to reach out and touch him, but refusing to allow herself to do so.

Despite what he had done she still loved him, and because of that she was hurting herself just as much as he had hurt her.

It was almost four o'clock in the morning before she was finally able to leave. She wasn't returning to the house she had shared with Ricardo though; she had arranged with one of their suppliers to return direct with them to Paris, and from there she intended to fly home. She had her passport with her, and her clothes—her *own* clothes, paid for with her *own* money—were already stowed in the supplier's four-wheel drive.

A cowardly way to leave, perhaps, but she didn't trust herself to spend another night with him. She had some pride left still, she told herself fiercely, even if he had taken everything else from her.

CHAPTER THIRTEEN

SHE had been back in London for three days now, and still hadn't been able to persuade herself to go into the office. Officially at least, so far as Lucy was concerned, she was taking a few days' leave. The reality was that she had felt too sick with loss and misery to do anything other than retreat into herself and stay in her bedroom. Fortunately Jules was away, so she had the flat to herself, but today she had to go out—because today she had an appointment to see Marcus.

No matter how much she was suffering because of Ricardo's deceit and betrayal, she reminded herself that she still owed a duty to Lucy, both as a friend and an employee, and so she had screwed up her courage and got in touch with Marcus to tell him she had some concerns about the financial affairs of the business that she did not at this stage want to discuss with Lucy. Fortunately she'd had his e-mail address, and virtually immediately he had e-mailed her back to ask her to go and see him.

The first thing she noticed when she abandoned the comfort of her 'at home' joggers and top was how loosely her jeans fitted her. It was true that she had not felt much like eating, but the sight of her pale, drawn face and grief-shadowed eyes when she looked at herself in the mirror told her that it wasn't just lack of food that was responsible for her altered appearance. But there was nothing she could take to alleviate the devastating effect of lack of Ricardo, was there? At least only she knew how humiliatingly she longed for him, despite what he had done.

Love knew no sense of moral outrage, as she had now discovered. And, equally, once it had been given life it could not be easily destroyed. She had tried focusing on all the reasons she should not love Ricardo, but rebelliously her thoughts had lingered longingly instead on the happiness she had felt before she had discovered the truth. It might have been a false happiness, but her heart would not let go of it. Her heart longed and yearned to be back in that place of happiness, just as her body yearned to be back in Ricardo's embrace.

She took a taxi to the address Marcus had given her, and was surprised to discover that she had been set down not outside an office building, but outside an elegant house just off one of London's private garden squares.

Even more surprisingly it was Marcus himself who opened the door for her and showed her in to the comfort of a book-lined library-cum-study.

'You must think it rather odd that I've got in touch with you privately,' Carly began awkwardly, having refused his offer of a cup of coffee. She was so on edge that for once she did not feel the need for her regular caffeine fix.

'Not at all,' Marcus reassured her. 'In fact…' He paused, and then looked thoughtfully at her.

'I think I have a fair idea of why you want to see me, Carly.'

'You do?'

'Ricardo has been in touch with me. He told me that you would probably wish to talk to me.'

Carly could feel her face burning with the heat of her emotions.

She couldn't understand why Ricardo should have been in touch with Marcus, but just hearing Marcus say his name made her long for him so much she could hardly think, never mind speak. But of course she had to. She took a deep breath to steady herself, and began.

'Marcus, Ricardo is planning to acquire Prêt a Party, and I'm afraid I may have made it easier for him to get the business at a lower price. You see—'

'Carly, Ricardo has no intention of acquiring the business. In fact, when he telephoned me he made it plain that whilst he had at one stage contemplated doing so, his relationship with you had caused him to change his mind. He also said that you were concerned about Nick's role within the business, specifically when it came to the financial side of things, and that it might be a good idea for me, as Lucy's trustee, to look into it.'

Carly could hardly take in what he was saying.

'But that's not true,' she protested. 'He—'

'I can assure you that it is true. In fact, Ricardo also told me that, because of your concern for Lucy and the business, he wondered if there might be some way that, between us he and I could put together a discreet rescue package, potentially with him using the services of Prêt a Party in connection with his business whilst I deal with the side of things relating to Lucy's trust fund. We agreed that we would both give some thought to our options before making a final decision.

'At that time I rather gained the impression that you and he…' Marcus paused as Carly made a small shocked sound of distress, and then continued, 'However, when he called in to tell me that you were likely to want to see me, he made no mention of your relationship. But he did ask me to give you this.'

Carly was too busy struggling to take in everything Marcus had told her to do anything more than glance vaguely at the small, neatly wrapped box Marcus had handed to her. There was one question she had to ask.

'When...when exactly did Ricardo first telephone you?'

Marcus was frowning.

'Let me have a look in my diary.'

He opened a large leather-bound desk diary and flicked through it.

'Yes, here it is...'

Ricardo had spoken to Marcus *before* she had seen the papers on his desk. He had told Marcus then about her concern and his own decision not to go ahead with any acquisition because of his relationship with her. And she had accused him of lying to her, betraying her.

She was in the taxi Marcus had insisted on calling for her before she remembered the parcel he had given her. Shakily, she took it from her bag and opened it. Inside it was a cardboard box, and inside that was her Cartier watch.

Carly tried to focus on it through the tears blurring her vision, and then realised that beneath it was a note from Ricardo which read; 'You left before I could return this to you.'

Nothing else. Just that. No words of love. But on the card was a handwritten address in London and a telephone number.

Initially he had misjudged her, but that had not stopped her loving him. Then she had misjudged him. Was his love for her strong enough to withstand that?

There was only one way she could find out.

Carly rapped on the glass panel separating her from the taxi driver. When he pulled it open, she told him she had changed her mind and gave him the address on Ricardo's note.

She had paid off the taxi and now she was standing uncertainly in front of the imposing Georgian terraced house, its gold-tipped black railings glinting in the sunshine, and trying to remember the words she had rehearsed in the taxi on her way here. Words that would tell him how much she loved him, how much she wished she had listened to him and trusted him.

Would he allow her to say them?

Trying not to give way to the mixture of anxiety, dread, and longing leavened with hope that was gripping her body, Carly walked up the stone steps to the imposing black gloss-painted door, and rang the bell.

Seconds ticked by with no response. The street was empty. Like the house? Had she let her own feelings allow her to put an interpretation on Ricardo's note he had never intended? Should she ring the bell again? It was a huge house and maybe no one had heard it the first time? Or maybe no one was there to hear it, she told herself. But she pressed the bell a second time and waited, whilst her heart thumped and the hope drained from her.

There was no point in her ringing a third time.

Carly walked back down the steps, oblivious to the fact that the reason she was struggling to see properly was because she was crying, oblivious too to the taxi turning into the street—until it screeched to a halt only feet away from her, causing her to freeze with shock.

'Carly!'

Her shock turned to disbelief as the passenger door opened and Ricardo got out, immediately striding towards her.

The taxi driver was reversing and turning round, but Carly didn't notice. She was in Ricardo's arms and he was kissing her with all the passionate hunger and love she had been longing for since she had left him.

'Come on. Let's go inside,' he told her huskily, keeping his arm round her as he guided her back up the stone steps.

'Ricardo, I'm so sorry I refused to believe you. I—'

'Shush,' he told her tenderly as he unlocked the door and ushered her into the hallway.

Motes of dust danced in the sunlight coming through the fanlight, and an impressive staircase curled upwards from the black and white tiled floor. But Carly was oblivious to the elegance of her surroundings, feasting her gaze instead on Ricardo's face.

How could she ever have thought she could live without him?

'You bought my watch back for me,' she whispered emotionally. 'And you told Marcus you didn't want to acquire the business because of me.'

'I knew you would worry about Lucy if I did, and your happiness and peace of mind are far more important to me than any business acquisition. The reason those papers you found were on the desk was because I'd seen how upset you were about Nick and the cheques, and I know Marcus vaguely, and so I'd decided that maybe it was worth making contact with him, to see if between us we couldn't do something that would set your mind at rest. I reasoned that since he was Lucy's trustee he would want to protect her, just as I wanted to protect you.'

'And then I accused you of trying to use me. I'm surprised you even want to see me again.'

'Well, you shouldn't be. Real love, true love, the kind of love I feel for you and you feel for me, is far stronger than pride—as you have proved by coming here to find me. Now, did Marcus tell you that I'm going to give Prêt a Party some business?'

'What?' said Carly blankly. 'Well, yes…'

'I've got several events in mind I can use them for, but the first and most important of them all is going to be our wedding.'

Carly looked up at him. 'You want us to get married?'

Ricardo nodded his head.

'I want us to get married; I want you to be my wife; I want you to be the mother of my children. You are my soulmate, Carly, and my life is of no value to me without you in it, at my side… But this is not the way or the place in which I had intended to propose to you.'

'It isn't?'

'No. I wanted something far more romantic—something that would make up for all the unhappiness life has brought you and show you how much I love you. A room filled with roses, perhaps, or—'

Carly reached up and placed her finger against his lips.

'I don't need or want that, Ricardo. All I want is you, and your heart filled with love for me.'

'Always,' he told her softly, before bending his head to kiss her.

HER BOSS'S BABY PLAN

HER BOSS'S BABY PLAN

BY

JESSICA HART

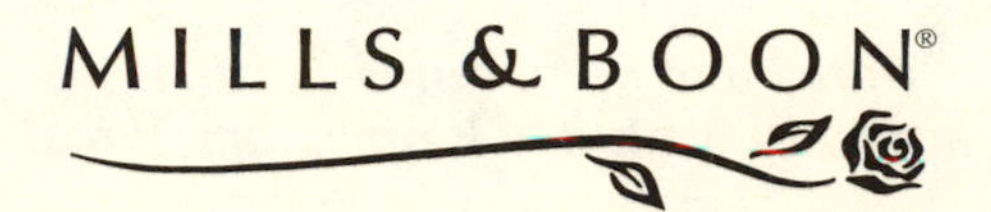

For Dora, with love

All the characters in this book have no existence outside the imagination of the author, and have no relation whatsoever to anyone bearing the same name or names. They are not even distantly inspired by any individual known or unknown to the author, and all the incidents are pure invention.

First published in Great Britain 2003
Large Print edition 2004
Harlequin Mills & Boon Limited,
Eton House, 18-24 Paradise Road,
Richmond, Surrey TW9 1SR

ISBN 0 263 18081 6

Set in Times Roman 16¼ on 17¼ pt.
16-0604-56150

Printed and bound in Great Britain
by Antony Rowe Ltd, Chippenham, Wiltshire

CHAPTER ONE

MARTHA looked at her watch. Twenty to four. How much longer was Lewis Mansfield going to keep her waiting?

His PA had apologised when she had turned up as instructed at three o'clock. Mr Mansfield, she said, was very busy. Which was fine. Martha knew about being busy, and she couldn't afford to make a grand gesture and walk out in a huff. Lewis Mansfield was her best chance—OK, her only chance right now—of getting out to St Bonaventure, so she was just going to have to wait.

Only she wished that he would hurry up. Noah had woken up and was getting restless. Martha hoisted him out of his buggy and carried him over to look at the enlarged black and white photographs that lined the walls.

They were not very interesting. A road stretching out across a desert. A runway. A port. Another road, this one with a tunnel. A bridge. Dramatic in their own way, but personally Martha preferred a bit of life. Including a person in the shot would have given the structures some sense of scale and humanised the pictures. Now, if they had just had a model striding across the tarmac…

'I'm thinking like a fashion editor,' Martha told Noah. 'I'd better stop it, hadn't I? I've got a new career now.'

Could you call being a nanny for six months a career? It certainly wasn't the one she had had in mind when she left university. Martha thought about her exciting job at *Glitz*, and sighed inwardly. Somehow, being a nanny didn't have quite the same ring to it.

Noah, at eight months, was not yet up to much in the way of conversation, but he bumped his forehead affectionately against Martha's jaw in reply and she hugged him back. He was worth more than any dazzling career.

The door to Lewis Mansfield's office opened and Martha turned hopefully as his PA reappeared.

'Lewis will see you now,' she said. 'Sorry you've had to wait so long.' She looked a little doubtfully at Noah. 'Do you want to leave him with me?'

'Thanks, but now he's awake I think I'd better take him with me,' said Martha. 'Could I leave the buggy here, though?'

'Sure.' The PA lowered her voice and nodded her head towards the closed door. 'He's not in the best of moods,' she warned.

Oh, great, thought Martha, but it was too late to turn back now. 'Maybe he'll cheer up when he discovers that I'm the answer to his prayers?' she suggested, but the PA's answering smile was disturbingly sympathetic.

'Good luck,' was all she said.

Behind the closed door Lewis shuffled the papers morosely on his desk and waited for Martha Shaw to appear. To say that he was not in the best of moods was an understatement.

It had been a hellish day so far, kicked off bright and early by Savannah turning up on his doorstep in a terrible state, followed inevitably by reporters ringing the bell, eager to discover the sordid details of the last instalment in the long-running melodrama that was Savannah's relationship with Van Valerian.

He had finally calmed his sister down, fought his way through the pack of paparazzi at the door, and champed in frustration at endless traffic delays, only to get to work and discover one crisis after another, all of which had to be dealt with urgently. Just to make things more interesting, the nanny had turned up at lunchtime saying that her mother had been taken into hospital and dumping Viola with him until the evening.

At least Viola was behaving herself, thought Lewis. So far, anyway. He eyed the carry-cot in the corner dubiously. She was sleeping peacefully, but the way today was going that wouldn't last.

He would have to make the most of the time he had left today. He wished he hadn't agreed to see Martha Shaw, but Gill had been so insistent that her friend was just the person he needed to look after Viola that in the end he had given in just to shut her up. 'Martha will be absolutely perfect for you,' she had insisted.

Lewis wasn't so sure. Gill was a friend of Savannah's and worked on some glossy, glittery magazine. He couldn't imagine her being friends with a nanny at all, let alone the kind of calm, sensible, solid nanny that he wanted.

The door opened. 'Martha Shaw,' said his PA brightly, and ushered in exactly the kind of woman Lewis least wanted to see right then.

He should have known, he thought bitterly, taking in the slightly dishevelled glamour and the brittle smile. She was attractive enough, with a swing of dark straight hair and that generous mouth, but she was far too thin. Lewis preferred women who didn't look as if they would snap in two the moment you touched them.

So much for a calm, solid nanny. Martha Shaw radiated nervous exhaustion. Her huge dark eyes were smudged with tiredness, and she held herself tensely.

And she wasn't just holding herself.

'That,' said Lewis, ignoring her greeting and levelling an accusing stare at her hip, 'is a baby.'

Martha followed his gaze to Noah, who was sucking his thumb and gazing around him with round blue eyes. Nothing wrong with Lewis Mansfield's powers of observation then, even if his manners left something to be desired.

'Good heavens, so it is!' she exclaimed with an exaggerated start of surprise. 'How did that get there?'

Her facetiousness was met with a scowl that made her heart sink. Not only was Lewis sadly lacking on the courtesy front, but he clearly had no sense of humour either. *Not* a good start to her interview.

Time to try charm instead. 'This is Noah,' she said with her best smile.

It was not returned. Somehow she hadn't thought that it would be. Lewis Mansfield was the walking, talking embodiment of dour. He was tall and tough-looking, with an austere, angular face and guarded eyes. It was hard to believe that he could be related in any way to the golden, glamorous Savannah Mansfield, with her famously volatile temper and celebrity lifestyle.

Gill might have warned her, thought Martha with a touch of resentment. Admittedly, Gill had said that Lewis could be a bit gruff. 'But he's a sweetie really,' she had hastened to reassure Martha. 'I'm sure you'll get on very well.'

On the receiving end of his daunting glare, Martha somehow doubted that.

She studied Lewis with a dubious expression as she waited for him to apologise for keeping her waiting, or at least to ask her to sit down. Very dark, very thick brows were drawn together over his commanding nose in what looked suspiciously like a permanent frown, and she searched in vain for any sign of softness or sensitivity in the unfriendly eyes or that stern mouth. He looked grim and grumpy and, yes, definitely gruff, but a *sweetie*? Martha didn't think so.

'He's very good,' she offered, ruffling Noah's hair when it was obvious that no apology would be forthcoming. They could hardly stand here all afternoon glaring at each other, so one of them was going to have to break the silence and it looked as if it was going to have to be her. She hoped Lewis couldn't see her crossed fingers when she thought about all the broken nights. 'He won't be any trouble.'

'Hah!' grunted Lewis, prowling out from behind his desk. 'I've heard *that* before—usually from women who promptly hand over their babies and go off, leaving you to discover for yourself just how *much* trouble they are!'

Oh dear, this wasn't going well at all. Martha sighed inwardly. Gill had given her the impression that Lewis Mansfield was a frazzled engineer, struggling to build up his own company and overwhelmed by the unforeseen responsibility of looking after his sister's baby. She hadn't actually *said* that he was tearing his hair out and desperate for help, but Martha had come fully expecting him to fall on her neck with gratitude for turning up just when he needed her.

Dream on, Martha told herself wryly. One look at Lewis Mansfield and it was obvious that he wasn't the demonstrative type. He didn't look the slightest bit desperate or overwhelmed, and as for feeling grateful…well, there clearly wasn't much point in holding her breath on *that* front!

She thought about St Bonaventure instead and forced a cheerful smile. 'That's why I'm here,' she pointed out, and sat down on one of the plush black leather sofas.

To hell with waiting to be asked, she thought. Noah was heavy and she was tired and her feet hurt. If Lewis Mansfield didn't have the common courtesy to ask her to sit down, she would sit anyway.

She settled Noah beside her, ignoring Lewis's look of alarm. What did he think Noah was going to do to his swish sofa? she wondered, exasperated. Suck it apart? He was only eight months. He didn't have the teeth or the hands for wholesale destruction.

Yet.

'Gill said that you're looking after your sister's baby for a few months,' she persevered. 'I gather you're going out to the Indian Ocean and will take the baby with you, so you need someone to help. Gill suggested I could be the someone who makes sure that she isn't any trouble to you while you're away.'

'It's true that I need a nanny,' said Lewis, as if unwilling to admit even that much. 'Savannah—my sister—is going through a very…stressful…time,' he said carefully, as if Martha wouldn't have read all about his sister's tempestuous affair, wedding and now divorce in the pages of *Hello!*

'She's finding it hard to cope with the baby and everything else that's going on at the moment,' he went on, 'and now she wants to check herself into a clinic to sort herself out.'

Martha knew about that too. *Hello!* was required reading in the *Glitz* offices and it was a hard habit to kick. She didn't blame Lewis Mansfield for the faint distaste in his tone. Savannah Mansfield was ravishingly pretty, but she had always struck Martha as a spoilt brat who was far too prone to tantrums when she didn't get her own way. Her marriage to the brooding rock star Van Valerian, not renowned for the sweetness of his own temper, had been doomed from the moment their engagement was announced with full photo coverage and much flaunting of grotesquely large diamond rings.

Now Savannah was checking herself into a clinic famous for its celebrity clientele, most of whom seemed to Martha to be struggling solely with the pressure of being too rich and too thin. Meanwhile poor little Viola Valerian had been abandoned by both parents and handed over to her grim uncle.

Martha felt sorry for her. Lewis Mansfield might be a responsible figure, but he didn't look as if he would be a very jolly or a very loving one.

Which was a shame. It wasn't that he was an unattractive man. Her dark eyes studied him critically. If he smiled he could probably look quite different, she thought, her gaze lingering on the stern mouth, but when she tried to imagine him smiling or loving a queer feeling prickled down her spine and she looked quickly away.

'Who's looking after Viola at the moment?' she asked, really just for something to say while she shook off that odd sensation.

'Her nanny. She's been with Viola since she was born, but she's getting married next year and she doesn't want to be away from her fiancé for six months.'

It seemed fair enough to Martha, but Lewis sounded impatient, as if Viola's poor nanny was being completely unreasonable in wanting to stay with the man she loved.

'I need someone experienced at caring for babies who's prepared to spend six months in St Bonaventure,' he went on, and Martha straightened her back, pleased that they had at last come to the point.

'I'm your gal!' she told him cheerfully. 'You need someone who knows how to deal with babies. I know how to deal with babies. You want someone who doesn't mind going to St Bonaventure for six months. I want to go there for six months. I'd have said we were made for each other, wouldn't you?'

She should have known better than to be flippant. Lewis regarded her with deep suspicion. 'You don't look much like a nanny to me,' he said finally.

'Well, nannies nowadays don't tend to be buxom and rosy-cheeked old retainers,' Martha pointed out.

'So I'm discovering,' said Lewis glumly. He was obviously hankering after a grey-haired old lady who had been with the family for generations and who would call him Master Lewis.

Come to think of it, why *didn't* the Mansfields have someone like that to call on? Martha wondered. She didn't know much about them, but they had always sounded a famously wealthy family, the kind that threw legendary parties and flirted with scandal and generally amused themselves without ever doing anything useful.

At least, that was how she had thought of them until she met Lewis. Perhaps he was a throwback?

'We may not be very good at tugging our forelocks, but it doesn't mean that modern nannies don't understand babies just as well,' she said, and smiled fondly down at Noah, who had propped himself up on one chubby hand and was patting the leather cushion with a puzzled expression. He hadn't come across anything quite so luxurious before.

'I suppose so.' Lewis sounded unconvinced, and was obviously eyeing Noah's exploration of his sofa askance.

Martha dug around in the capacious bag she always carried with her now and pulled out a rattle to distract Noah. Grabbing it, he shook it energetically and squealed with delight. The sound that it made never failed to amuse him, and the way his round little face split into a smile never failed to squeeze Martha's heart.

He was so adorable. How could anyone resist him?

Glancing back at Lewis, she saw that he was resisting Noah's appeal without any trouble at all. Still, at least he had come to sit on the sofa opposite her. That was something, Martha thought hopefully.

'Is this your current charge?' he asked, as if Noah were some kind of bill.

'He's my permanent charge,' Martha told him, pride creeping into her voice. 'Noah is my son,' she added patiently when it was clear that Lewis was none the wiser.

'Your *son*?' He didn't actually recoil, but he might as well have done. 'Gill didn't mention anything about you having a baby.'

Gill hadn't mentioned anything about him being the human equivalent of the north face of the Eiger either, thought Martha. You could hardly hear yourself think for the sound of illusions being dashed all round.

Not that she really blamed Gill. The other woman had taken over from her as fashion editor at *Glitz*, and she was clearly keen to pack Martha off to the Indian Ocean where she wouldn't be in a position to angle for her old job back. Martha could have told Gill that she was welcome to the job, and she certainly would have done if it had meant that she had been rather better prepared to face Lewis Mansfield.

As it was, things seemed to be going from bad to worse. She would never get to St Bonaventure at this rate.

'I'm sorry,' she said carefully. 'I assumed that Gill would have told you about Noah.'

'She just said that you were experienced with babies, that you were free for six months and that you could leave almost immediately,' said Lewis, as if bedgrudging allowing even that much. 'She also said that you were very keen to go to St Bonaventure.'

Thanks, Gill, said Martha mentally, revising her earlier, less grateful opinion of her successor.

'All that is true,' she told Lewis. 'I'm very—'

She stopped as Noah threw his rattle at Lewis with a yell. 'Shh, darling,' she admonished him, reaching over to retrieve the rattle, but it was too late. The baby sleeping in the carrycot had woken up and was uttering sputtering little cries that signalled a momentous outburst.

Lewis rolled his eyes. 'That's all I need!'

Leaping to her feet before Lewis could get too harassed, Martha went over to pick up Viola and cuddled her against her shoulder until her cries subsided into hiccuping little sobs.

'Now, let's have a look at you,' she said, settling back on the sofa and turning Viola on her knee so that she could examine her. 'Oh, you're very gorgeous, aren't you?'

All babies were adorable as far as Martha was concerned, but Viola was exceptionally beautiful, with her golden curls, pansy-blue eyes and ridiculously long lashes where the tears still shimmered like dewdrops. She looked doubtfully back at Martha, who smiled at her.

'I think you probably know it too, don't you?' she said, and Viola dissolved into an enchanting smile that in anyone older than a baby would have undoubtedly been classified as a simper.

'How old is she?' Martha asked Lewis as she tickled Viola's tummy and made her giggle.

'What?' Lewis sounded distracted.

'She looks about the same age as Noah.'

Annoyed for some reason by the unexpected sweetness of Martha's smile, Lewis pulled himself together with an effort. How old *was* Viola?

'She's about eight months,' he said after a mental calculation.

'Oh, then she is the same as Noah.'

Noah was beginning to look a bit jealous of all the attention Viola was getting, so Martha put them both on the carpet where they could sit and subject each other to their unblinking baby stares. She watched them fondly for a moment.

'They could almost be twins, couldn't they?'

'Apart from the fact that one's blonde and the other is dark?' countered Lewis, determined not to be drawn into any whimsy.

'OK, not identical twins,' said Martha mildly. 'When's Viola's birthday?'

'Er…May ninth, I think.'

'Really?' Forgetting his disagreeable manners, Martha beamed at Lewis in delighted surprise. 'That's Noah's birthday, too! Isn't that a coincidence? You really are twins,' she told the two babies on the floor, who were still eyeing each other rather uncertainly.

She glanced back at Lewis. 'It must be fate,' she said hopefully.

Lewis looked discouraging, not entirely to Martha's surprise. She hadn't really expected him to be the type who set much store by signs and superstitions and intriguing coincidences. No point in bothering to ask him his star sign, she thought resignedly. He was the kind of man who would just look at you in disgust and not only not care what sign he was but not even know.

'You haven't told me why you're so keen to go to St Bonaventure,' he said, disgruntled in a way he couldn't even explain to himself. It was something to do with the way she had held Viola, with the way she had smiled at the two babies on the floor, with the way her face had lit with surprise. He didn't have time to notice things like that, Lewis reminded himself crossly.

'Does one need a reason to want to spend six months on a tropical island?' Martha turned his question back on him. Her voice was light, but Lewis had the feeling she was holding something back and he frowned.

'I'd want to feel that a nanny who came with us knew exactly what she was getting into,' he said repressively. 'St Bonaventure is isolated, in the middle of the Indian Ocean, and whichever direction you turn it's hundreds of miles to the nearest major city. The island is very small, and once you've been round it there's nowhere else to go except for a scattering of even smaller islands with even less to see.'

It was at that point that Viola, after subjecting Noah to a long, considering stare, reached out deliberately and pushed him over. Startled, Noah let out a wail, and Lewis looked irritated.

Oops, maybe putting the babies together wasn't such a good idea after all. Martha scooped them both up and settled them on either side of her, giving Noah his rattle and finding Viola a dog-eared toy which she promptly stuffed in her mouth.

'Sorry about that.' Martha looked back at Lewis. 'You were saying?' she asked him politely.

Lewis watched his niece glaring haughtily over Martha's lap at Noah and looking for a moment so like her mother that he almost laughed. He glanced at Martha with reluctant respect. He had to admit that she seemed surprisingly competent for such an unlikely-looking nanny.

Viola, as her current nanny was always telling him, could be a handful, and if she took after her mother, as she was already bidding fair to do, that would turn out to be a masterly understatement. But Martha seemed to have got her measure straight away, dealing with her with a combination of tenderness and firmness.

Belatedly, Lewis became aware that Martha had asked him a question and was waiting expectantly for the answer. Cross with himself for letting himself get diverted from the issue, he scowled.

'You were telling me about conditions on St Bonaventure,' Martha prompted kindly.

Not that that made Lewis feel any better. He didn't like looking foolish, and he suspected that was *exactly* how he did look right then. Abruptly getting to his feet to get away from that dark stare, he prowled around the room.

'The island was hit by a cyclone last year which wiped out most of the infrastructure. That's why I'm going,' he told her. 'The World Bank is funding a new port and airport with access roads, so it will be a major project.'

'But surely all that will take longer than six months?' said Martha in surprise.

Lewis gave a mirthless laugh. 'It will certainly do that! We're going to be doing the design and overseeing the construction, so there'll be a resident engineer out there for the duration of the project, but I want to be there for the initial stages at least. It's a prestigious project and this is a critical time for the firm. We need it to be a success.'

'So you'll spend six months setting everything up and then come back to London?'

'That's the plan at the moment. I might end up staying longer—it depends how things go. We'll need to do various surveys, which may mean incorporating various changes into the design, and it's important to establish a good working relationship with all the authorities and suppliers. These things take time,' said Lewis, very aware of Martha's eyes on him.

He wished she would stop looking at him with that dark, disturbing gaze, stop sitting there with a baby tucked under either arm, stop being so…*unsettling*.

'In any case, Savannah should be able to look after Viola herself in six months' time,' he concluded brusquely, uncomfortably conscious that he had lost the thread of what he was saying. Martha didn't need to know about the project, or why it was important to him. Anyone would think he *cared* what she thought. 'It would be a strictly short-term contract as far as a nanny is concerned.'

'I understand,' said Martha.

'The point I'm trying to make is that it's not going to be an extended beach holiday,' Lewis persevered. 'St Bonaventure isn't developed as far as tourism goes, and there's a very small expatriate community. I'm going to be extremely busy, and will be out all day and probably a number of evenings too.

'Whoever comes out to look after Viola is going to be in for a very quiet few months. She's going to have to look after herself. Sure, the weather's nice, but once you've been down to the beach there's nowhere else to go and nothing else to do. The capital, Perpetua, is tiny and there are hardly any shops, and where you do find one it's dependent on imports that can be erratic, to say the least. Sometimes the shelves are empty for months, which can make the diet monotonous.'

'I think you've made your point,' said Martha, smiling slightly, as if she knew that he was doing his damnedest to put her off and wasn't having any of it.

Lewis scowled and dug his hands in his pockets. 'All I'm trying to say is that if you're expecting paradise you'd better think again!'

Martha met his gaze directly. 'I'm not looking for paradise in St Bonaventure,' she said.

'What are you looking for, then?'

For a moment, Martha hesitated. She had hoped that it wouldn't be necessary to tell Lewis Mansfield the whole story at this stage, but it was probably better to be open.

'I'm looking for Noah's father,' she said clearly.

If she had expected a sympathetic response from Lewis she was doomed to disappointment. 'Careless of you to lose someone as important as that,' he commented, and then lifted a sardonic eyebrow. 'Or did he lose you?'

Martha flushed slightly. 'It wasn't like that. Rory is a marine biologist. He's doing a PhD on something to do with ocean currents and coral reefs…I'm not sure exactly, but he's doing his fieldwork on some atoll off St Bonaventure.'

'If you know where he is, he's not exactly lost, is he? Why do you need to go all the way out to the Indian Ocean when you could just contact him? If he's a student he's bound to have an email address, if nothing else. It's not hard to track people down nowadays.'

'It's not that easy,' said Martha. 'I need to see him. Rory doesn't know about Noah, and it's not the kind of thing you can drop in a casual email. What would I say? *Oh, by the way, you're a father*?'

'It's what you're going to have to say when you see him, isn't it?' Lewis countered.

Martha bit her lip. 'I think it would be better if Rory could actually see Noah. He won't seem real to him otherwise.'

'You mean you think you're more likely to get money out of him if you turn up with a lovely, cuddly baby?'

The dark eyes flashed at his tone. 'It's not about money,' she said fiercely. 'Rory's a lot younger than me. He's still a student and finds it hard enough to survive on a grant himself, never mind support a baby. I know he can't afford to be financially responsible for Noah, and I'm not asking him to.'

'Then why go at all?'

'Because I think Rory has the right to know that he's a father.'

'Even though presumably he wasn't interested enough to keep in touch with you and find out for himself that you were all right?'

'It wasn't like that,' said Martha a little helplessly. How could she make someone like Lewis understand?

'I met Rory at the beginning of last year. It wasn't just a one-night stand,' she added, hating the idea that he might think there had been anything sordid or casual about the affair. 'I liked Rory a lot and we had a very nice time together but at the same time we both knew that it wasn't a long-term thing.

'We had completely different lives, for a start. He was only in the UK to go to conferences and write up some of his research, and I had a great job in London. It was always clear that he had to go back to St Bonaventure to finish his thesis, and we both treated it as…' she shrugged lightly, searching for the right description '…as a pleasant interlude.'

'So he didn't know you were pregnant?'

'Yes. I found out just before he left, so I told him. I felt I had to.'

'And he left anyway?' Lewis sounded outraged and Martha looked at him curiously.

'We discussed it,' she told him, 'and we agreed that neither of us was ready to start a family. It was obviously out of the question for him, and I was very involved in my own career. I was incredibly busy then too. There was no way I could imagine fitting a baby into my life…'

She trailed off as she remembered how obvious everything had seemed at the time. 'Anyway,' she went on, recollecting herself, 'the upshot was that I told Rory that I was going to be sensible. I said he didn't need to worry, I would take care of everything.'

For a moment the image of Rory's expression of stunned relief as he realised what she was saying was vivid in her mind. 'It didn't feel like a big deal, then,' she remembered. 'I just thought it would be a straightforward operation and that I would be fine.'

Martha looked down at Noah and smoothed his dark, downy hair. Just the thought of how close she had come to never having him made her shudder now.

'So Rory went back to St Bonaventure,' she finished, glancing back at Lewis. 'And I... changed my mind.'

Of course she had changed her mind, thought Lewis with a jaundiced expression. Changing their minds was what women did, and to hell with the consequences for anyone else involved!

'Don't tell me,' he said dourly. 'Your body clock was ticking, everyone else was having babies and playing at being perfect mothers and you wanted to play too?'

Martha was taken aback by the edge of bitterness in his voice. What was his problem? Don't let him wind you up, she reminded yourself. He's your ticket to St Bonaventure.

'You might be right about the body clock,' she admitted honestly. 'I'm thirty-four, and with no sign of another serious relationship on the horizon I had to face the fact that might not have another chance to have a child. It hadn't been an issue before. I had a boyfriend for eight years and we were both thinking about our careers, not about babies. I thought I was fine with that, but once I was pregnant...it's hard to explain, but everything changed after Rory had gone. I just knew I couldn't go through with it and that I wanted to keep the baby.'

Lewis was looking profoundly unmoved by her story. 'Why didn't you tell him that you'd changed your mind?'

'I knew that he wasn't going to be in a position to help, and anyway I felt that it was my decision in any case. I didn't want Rory to feel responsible.'

'And now you've changed your mind about that too?'

Martha eyed him warily. There was a current of hostility in his voice that she didn't understand. She wasn't sure if it was women generally that he disliked or just single mothers, but there was certainly something about her that was rubbing him up the wrong way.

It was a pity, she thought. She had warmed to him while he was telling her about the project. Striding about the office, the austere face lit with enthusiasm, he had seemed warmer and more accessible somehow. More…well, attractive. She had even begun to think that spending six months with him wouldn't be so bad after all.

Now she wasn't so sure.

CHAPTER TWO

MARTHA set her chin. It didn't matter what Lewis Mansfield was like, or whether he liked her or not. The important thing was to convince him to give her the job. She needed to get out to St Bonaventure, and somehow he had to realise how important it was to her.

She glanced down at her small son. He was why she was here now. 'When Noah was born…' she began slowly, only to pause and rethink what she was trying to say. 'Well, it's hard to explain to someone who hasn't had a baby, but my life changed completely. It was as if everything had turned round and the things that had been important before suddenly didn't matter that much any more. The only thing that really mattered was Noah.

'I want to give him the things every child needs,' she went on, picking her words with care. 'Love, security, support…I can do all of that as a mother, but I can't be his father. The bigger Noah gets, the more I've come to realise that he needs a father as well as me. At the very least, he needs to know who his father is.'

She looked back at Lewis, her gaze very direct. 'I don't want Rory to feel that he has to provide any financial support, but I do want to give him the chance to be part of his son's life, even if it's only occasional contact.

'Of course I'm hoping that he'll want more than that, that he'll want to see Noah grow up and share his life as part of the family,' she said, 'but I'm not setting my heart on that because it might not be right for any of us. But I can't know any of that until I can find Rory himself and introduce him to Noah and that's why I need to get to St Bonaventure as soon as I can,' she finished breathlessly.

Lewis didn't respond immediately. Instead he came back to sit opposite her and regard her with an indecipherable expression.

'If it's so important to you, why don't you just buy a ticket, go out there and find this guy?' he asked at last. 'St Bonaventure is a tiny place. It's not going to be too hard to track him down. Why complicate matters by getting involved as a nanny?'

'Because I can't afford to get there any other way,' said Martha frankly. 'You said yourself that St Bonaventure is not a mass market destination for tourists. That means that there are no package deals, and all the flights I've looked into are phenomenally expensive, especially when I don't know how long it would take me to find Rory. I just don't have that kind of money at the moment.'

She had never met anyone who could use his eyebrows to the effect that Lewis did. One was lifting now, expressing disbelief and disdain in a way no words ever could. 'I'm no expert,' he said—and looking at his conventional suit and tie Martha could believe *that*!—'but those look like pretty expensive clothes to me.'

His slate-coloured gaze encompassed her soft suede trousers, the beautifully cut shirt and the stylish boots. There was nothing obvious about the way she dressed, but she still managed to ooze glamour. 'If you can afford to dress like that I'd have thought you could afford a plane ticket.'

'I bought this outfit a long time before I had Noah,' said Martha, acknowledging the point. 'I couldn't afford any of it now and, to be honest, I wouldn't buy it even if I could.' She looked ruefully down at the stains and creases that Lewis obviously couldn't see from where he was sitting. 'It's totally impracticable for looking after a baby!'

'Presumably when you talked about the great career you had, you didn't mean being a nanny then?' he asked sardonically.

'No. I was a fashion editor for *Glitz*. You won't know it,' she told him before he could say anything, 'but it's a glossy magazine for women, and very high profile. I loved my job and I had a good salary, but unfortunately I had a very expensive lifestyle as well.'

Martha sighed a little, remembering how carelessly she had bought shoes and clothes and the latest must-have accessories. The money she had spent on cabs alone would easily have kept her in St Bonaventure for a year.

'I used to eat out a lot, and had wonderful holidays…I suppose I wasn't very sensible,' she admitted, 'but I never thought about saving. It was just the kind of world where you live for the moment and let the future take care of itself.'

'Which is all very well until you get to the future.'

'Exactly,' she said ruefully.

'Couldn't you go back to work if money's that tight?'

'I tried after Noah was born, but it was just too difficult. I was so tired that I couldn't think straight for the first few weeks, and when I missed one meeting too many the editor said that she was sorry but she had to let me go. Which was a nice way of saying that she was sacking me.'

Martha shrugged slightly. 'I could see her point. I was wandering around like a zombie, and fashion shoots cost a lot of money. You can't afford to have models like the ones *Glitz* uses sitting around waiting for the fashion editor to remember what day of the week it is.'

'Perhaps you should have thought of that before you had a baby,' said Lewis astringently.

'I did think about it,' said Martha, keeping her voice even with an effort. 'That's why I didn't have a baby before, but I don't regret having Noah for a moment. I don't want a demanding job that means I have to leave him all day with someone else. I want to be with him while he's small. I've done various bits of freelancing, but it's not very reliable, and it doesn't help that I'd saddled myself with a huge mortgage just before I met Rory.'

Martha winced just thinking about the money she owed the bank. 'It's a fabulous flat—a loft conversion overlooking the river—but I just can't afford to live in it now and, anyway, it's totally unsuitable for a baby. I've got in tenants and they're just covering the mortgage payments, so Noah and I are living in a little studio, but frankly it's a struggle even to pay the rent on that at the moment.'

'You could sell the flat that you own. If it's as smart as you say it is, it ought to realise you some capital.' Lewis was obviously of a practical turn of mind. Not that surprising in an engineer, now Martha came to think of it.

'I probably will,' she said, 'but I don't want to make any decision until I've seen Rory. I can't really think about what to do until I've done that. I just have the feeling that once I know how he's going to react everything else will fall into place, so getting to St Bonaventure is a priority for me.'

She met Lewis's cool gaze steadily. 'That's why, when Gill told me that you were going there and needed a nanny, it seemed so perfect.'

'For you maybe,' he said with a cynical look. 'I'm not sure what's in it for me if you're going to slope off in search of marine biologists the moment you arrive.'

'There'd be no question of *sloping off*, as you call it.' Martha took a deep breath and forced herself to stay calm. 'I assume that you would provide a proper contract for six months, and I would certainly abide by it. That would give me plenty of time to find Rory, introduce him to Noah and get him used to the idea of having a son, and he wouldn't feel rushed into making a decision. If at the end of that time he wanted us to stay, fine. If not, we would just come back with you and Viola. At least I would have done everything I could to make contact between Noah and his father.'

Viola was getting bored. She started to squirm and Martha lifted her on to her knee, distracting her with another toy from her bag. Satisfied, Viola dropped the rabbit that she had been sucking and grabbed the rubber ring instead.

This left the rabbit free to be handed quickly to Noah, whose little mouth was turning ominously down as he watched his mother giving his rival all the attention. He accepted the rabbit, but very much with the air of one who was prepared to be diverted for now, but would be returning to the main point at issue before long.

Lewis watched Martha juggling the two babies and his brows drew together. 'It's just not practicable for you to be a nanny,' he said brusquely. 'You can't manage two at once.'

'Why not? Neither of them are crying, are they?' asked Martha, praying that Viola and Noah would stay quiet a little while longer.

'Not yet,' said Lewis. 'Jiggling them on your knee and giving them toys is all very well for five minutes, but what happens when both of them are screaming and need to be fed?'

'Mothers with twins manage.'

'Maybe they're used to it.'

'I'd get used to it too,' she said defiantly, but Lewis only scowled.

'Look at you,' he said, feeling cross and disgruntled without being sure why. It was something to do with the way she sat there and looked at him with those dark eyes. Something to do with the straightness of her back and the determined tilt of her chin.

'You look as if you haven't slept for a year,' he said roughly. 'I'm surprised you can cope with one baby, let alone think about looking after two.'

She looked as if she could do with six months in the sun, fattening herself up and catching up on sleep, he thought, and then caught himself. Martha Shaw wasn't his responsibility. It wasn't his fault she was tired. She had chosen to have a baby on her own, and it was too late to complain that it was tiring now.

Although she hadn't actually complained at all, had she? Lewis pushed the thought brusquely away. No, it was out of the question.

'I don't want to find myself looking after you and Noah as well as Viola,' he told her.

Martha wasn't ready to give up yet. 'I'm tougher than I look,' she said. 'I've been looking after a baby for the past eight months and I think I've probably got a better idea than you of what's involved,' she added, with just a squeeze of acid in her voice. 'I'm sure I would be able to cope.'

It went against the grain to plead with Lewis Mansfield, but if she had to she would. 'Please take me with you. I'd love Viola and look after her as if she really was Noah's twin.' She hesitated. How could she make him see how perfectly their needs matched? 'I think we're made for each other,' she said.

Wrong thing to say. One of Lewis's eyebrows shot up and, hearing her own words,

Martha could have bitten her tongue out. And then she had to go and make matters worse by actually blushing!

'You know what I mean,' she muttered.

'I know what you mean,' Lewis agreed dryly as he got to his feet again. Really, the man was as restless as a cat. He took another turn around the room, his shoulders hunched in a way that was already oddly familiar.

'I should tell you that I only agreed to see you as a favour to Gill,' he said brusquely at last. 'Oddly enough, she was very insistent that you were just what I needed too.'

'I think I could be,' said Martha, determined not to repeat her mistake and forcing herself to sound suitably cool, as if the idea that they might be made for each other as lovers had never even crossed her mind.

Lewis wasn't so sure. He couldn't help thinking about what it would be like to share a house with her, to spend the next six months with those dark eyes and that mouth. It would be too distracting, too unsettling, too…too *everything*.

And she was totally unsuitable as a nanny anyway, he reminded himself. There was no way he was going to risk it.

'Perhaps I should have told Gill that I was seeing someone else as well,' he said, pushing away the thought of living with Martha for six months. 'The agency that supplied Viola's current nanny sent along someone this morning and I have to say that she seemed very suitable. Eve is a trained nanny, and she is obviously very...'

Dull was the word that leapt to mind. Lewis forced it down.

'...very efficient,' he said instead.

'Babies don't need efficiency,' said Martha before she could help herself. 'They need love and warmth and routine.'

'Eve comes with very good references so I'm sure she understands exactly what babies need,' said Lewis austerely. 'She's...'

Dull, insisted that wayward voice inside him.

'...a sensible girl...'

Dull.

'...and she doesn't have any other commitments...'

Dull.

'...so she can concentrate on Viola in a way that you wouldn't be able to,' he went on with an edge of desperation.

Yes, but she's dull.

'I need to bear in mind too that I'll be sharing a house with Viola's nanny for six months, so it's important to give the job to someone compatible. Eve seems a quiet, level-headed…'

Dull.

'…reliable person, and I'm sure she'll adapt to the routine out there very quickly.'

Yes, and she'll be very, very dull.

But she wouldn't have dark, disturbing eyes and she wouldn't put him on edge just by sitting there the way Martha did. It would be much better that way.

Dull, but better.

'I see.' Martha got to her feet and handed Lewis his niece, who glared at him.

I'm with you, Viola, thought Martha wryly.

'In that case, there doesn't seem much more to say.'

Determined not to let him see how desperately disappointed she was, she bent to retrieve the toys, stuffed them in her bag, and scooped up Noah. 'Thank you for taking the time to see me,' she said in a cool voice.

Lewis held Viola warily. He could feel her small body revving up to protest as Martha turned to go and she realised that she was going to be abandoned.

'I'm sorry,' he said abruptly, as if the words had been forced out of him against his will. 'I just don't think it would have worked out.'

Dispiritedly, Martha scraped up another spoonful of purée and offered it to Noah, who pressed his lips together and shook his head from side to side in a very determined manner.

Rather like Lewis Mansfield, in fact.

'Why,' asked Martha severely, 'are you men all being so difficult at the moment?'

Noah didn't reply, but he didn't open his mouth either. He could be very stubborn when he wanted.

Also like Lewis Mansfield.

With a sigh, Martha put the spoon in her own mouth and returned to her perusal of the small ads. She had reluctantly decided that she was going to have to put St Bonaventure on the back boiler for a while and find herself another job. The trouble with most part-time jobs was that they didn't pay enough to cover the costs of child care, but she was seriously considering going for a post as a housekeeper or a nanny, where she could take Noah with her and save herself the huge cost of renting even this tiny little flat.

Here was a job in Yorkshire...maybe she could apply for that?

Or maybe not, she decided, as she read to the end of the advertisement. That enticing heading should have read: 'Wanted, any idiot to be overworked and underpaid.'

Martha sucked the spoon glumly and was just turning the page when the phone rang. This would be Liz with her daily phone call to cheer her up.

'Hi,' she said, wedging the phone between her shoulder and her ear and not bothering to take the spoon out of her mouth.

'Is that Martha Shaw?'

Martha nearly choked on the spoon, and the phone slipped from her ear. She had no problem identifying that austere voice, although she was damned if she would give Lewis Mansfield the satisfaction of admitting it.

Hastily rescuing the phone before it fell on the floor, she removed the spoon and cleared her throat.

'Yes?' It came out a little croaky, but she didn't think she sounded too bad.

'This is Lewis Mansfield.'

'Yes?' That was much better. Positively cool.

'I was wondering if you were still interested in coming out to St Bonaventure to look after Viola,' he said, and Martha was delighted to hear the reluctance in his voice.

It was obvious that Lewis Mansfield would rather be doing anything than ringing her up, so something must have gone wrong with his oh-so-sensible plans. He must be desperate, in which case there would be no harm in making him grovel a little!

'I thought you already had the perfect candidate…what was her name again?'

'Eve,' said Lewis a little tightly.

'Ah, yes, Eve. Didn't she want the job?'

'She said she did, and I made all the arrangements, but she's just rung me to say that she doesn't want to go after all.'

'Oh dear,' said Martha, enjoying herself. 'That doesn't sound very reliable of her.'

'The point is,' said Lewis through gritted teeth, 'that we were booked to fly out this weekend and I haven't got the time to re-advertise. If you can be ready to leave then, I'll get a ticket for you and your baby.'

Martha settled back into her chair and took another spoonful of Noah's purée. 'But what about how incompatible you think we are?'

'I didn't say that.'

'You implied it.'

'Well, we'll both just have to make an effort.' Lewis was beginning to sound impatient. 'I've got a job to do, and I won't be around very much in any case.'

There was a tiny pause. 'You know, the right answer there was, "Don't be silly, Martha, I don't think we're incompatible at all, I think you're very nice",' said Martha tartly.

Lewis sighed. 'If you come to St Bonaventure we're just going to have to get on,' he said.

'You make it sound as if it's going to be a real chore!' Martha was obscurely hurt. 'What a pity I can be sensible and reliable and...what was it now?...oh, yes, *efficient*, like Eve!'

'The point about Eve was that she didn't have any other commitments,' said Lewis, exasperated. 'I hope that you *will* be sensible and reliable and efficient—and tougher than you look! You're going to need to be.'

'I'm all those things,' she said sniffily. Shame he hadn't given her the chance to prove it when he saw her!

'And, frankly, *I'm* desperate,' he said. 'I'm not going to grovel or pretend that it was you

I wanted all along. I haven't got time to play games. You said you wanted to get out to St Bonaventure,' he went on crisply, 'and now I'm offering you the chance. If you take the job I'll courier round details and tickets to you tomorrow. If you don't want it, just say so and I'll make other arrangements.'

He would too. Martha wasn't prepared to risk it.

'I'll take it,' she said.

Martha sipped her champagne and tried not to be too aware of Lewis sitting at the other end of the row. They had been given the front row in the cabin so that the two babies could sleep in the special cots provided and the other passengers had understandably given them a wide berth, leaving Lewis and Martha with four seats between them.

By tacit consent they had sat at either end of the row, leaving a yawning gap between them. There had been no chance to have a conversation at Heathrow, with all the palaver of checking in double quantities of high chairs and buggies and car seats. Even with most of it in the hold they still had masses of stuff to carry on board and, as both babies were wide awake at the time, they had both been occupied with keeping them happy until it was time to board.

But now Noah and Viola were asleep, the plane was cruising high above the clouds, and there was a low murmur of voices around them as the passengers settled down with a drink and speculated about the meal to come. And Martha was very conscious of the silence pooling between her and Lewis.

She was beginning to feel a bit ridiculous, stuck at one end of the row. They couldn't have a conversation like this, and it was going to be a long flight.

Making up her mind, she shifted one seat along, although it involved so much balancing of her glass and flipping out and putting away of trays in the arm of the seat, not to mention shifting all the baby paraphernalia from one seat to another, that by the time she was halfway through Martha was already regretting her decision and she felt positively hot and bothered by the time she finally collapsed into the seat.

Lewis was looking at her curiously. 'What are you doing?'

'I just thought I should be sociable,' she said, pushing her hair crossly away from her face.

'We can hardly shout at each other all the way to Nairobi.'

'I thought you might appreciate the extra room if you wanted to sleep,' said Lewis, effectively taking the wind out of Martha's sails. She hadn't expected him to have a considerate motive for putting himself as far away from her as possible!

'We haven't even had our meal,' she pointed out. 'I don't want to sleep yet.'

Uncomfortably aware that she sounded defensive, if not downright sulky, she forced a smile. 'This just seems like a good opportunity to get to know each other. We're going to be spending six months together, after all. Besides, it sounds as if the flight from Nairobi is going to be in a much smaller plane than this, so we're probably going to have to sit right next to each other on that. We might as well get used to the idea of being in close proximity!'

'We're certainly not going to get any closer than that,' said Lewis grumpily.

My, he was a charmer, wasn't he? Martha sighed inwardly.

'Look, I'll move back if you feel I'm invading your personal space,' she said huffily, putting her glass down and making to unfasten her seat belt.

'For God's sake, stay where you are,' he said irritably, and then he sighed.

'I'm sorry,' he said in a different voice, pinching the bridge of his nose. 'I've been very…preoccupied recently. Things are hectic in the office, half our projects seem to be in crisis, the negotiations for the St Bonaventure port have stalled, nothing's getting done. And then there's all this business with Savannah…' He blew out his cheeks wearily.

Martha couldn't help but sympathise. She had read in the gossip columns about the tempestuous scenes his sister had been throwing, the latest of which had resulted in the police being called to her house. In the end, Lewis had taken her to the clinic himself, running the gauntlet of the reporters at the gates who'd banged on the car windows and shouted questions about the most intimate details of his sister's life.

No wonder he was tired.

'My temper's short at the best of times,' he admitted, 'and I know I've probably been taking it out on everyone else. My PA couldn't wait to get rid of me yesterday!'

His mouth twisted ironically and he glanced at Martha. 'You're right, we should probably get to know each other better. I should have made more of an effort earlier.'

'You've had a lot on your mind,' said Martha a little uncomfortably.

Damn, just when she had got used to him being grumpy and disagreeable he had to go and throw her off balance by suddenly acting human! How difficult of him.

'Do you think we could start again?' he asked, making things even worse.

What could she say? 'Of course,' said Martha and held out her hand across the empty seat between them. 'I'm Martha Shaw. How do you do?'

The corner of Lewis's mouth quirked. 'Nice to meet you, Martha Shaw,' he said gravely, and reached across to shake her hand.

Martha wished he hadn't done that. The fingers wrapped around hers were warm and comfortingly strong, and the press of his palm sent a disquieting shiver down her spine.

Pulling her hand away, she took a steadying gulp of her champagne. It was too sweet, and she hadn't really wanted it anyway. She had written enough articles about the dehydrating effects of long haul flights and how the best thing to do was just to drink plenty of water, but when Lewis had tersely asked for a bottle of water himself something perverse in her had made her turn to the flight attendant on her side of the plane and accept a glass of free champagne with a brilliant smile.

It had been silly, and it felt even sillier now that Lewis was turning out to be so unexpectedly approachable. Really, he was being quite nice.

So there was no reason why she shouldn't be able to think of something to say, was there?

No reason other than the tingle of her palm. And the fact that, even though she was staring desperately at the tiny plane heading steadily south across the map of the world on the screen above the travel cots, all she could see was his mouth, with its corner turned up in amusement, and its hint of warmth and humour.

No reason at all, then.

'So, what…' Mortified by the squeakiness of her voice, Martha cleared her throat and started again. 'What happened to Eve?'

'Eve?'

'The nanny who fitted your job description so perfectly,' she reminded him. 'You know, the one who was so reliable and sensible and efficient and lacking in commitments?'

'Oh. Yes.' Lewis had forgotten about Eve for a minute there.

He felt a little light-headed for some reason, which wasn't like him. It definitely wasn't anything to do with Martha's smile, or the depth of her eyes, or the sooty sweep of those lashes against her cheek. Obviously not.

Lewis looked at the glass of water in his hand. He couldn't even blame the feeling on alcohol. Must be the cabin pressure, he decided.

'Apparently Eve fell in love,' he said.

Martha shifted round in her seat to stare at him in surprise. 'In love?'

'So she said.' There was a tinge of distaste in Lewis's voice. 'I interviewed her on Monday, she accepted the job on Tuesday, on Wednesday night she met some man in a club and she rang me on Thursday morning to say that she was going to spend the rest of her life with him so she didn't want to come to St Bonaventure after all, thank you very much.'

'Really?' Martha laughed. 'So she turned out to be not so sensible after all?'

'You could say that. Turning down a perfectly good job to invest everything in a man you've only known for a matter of hours…it's a ridiculous thing to do!'

'It won't seem like that if she fell in love with him.'

'How can she be in love with him?' demanded Lewis with a return to his old acerbic tone. 'She doesn't know anything about this man.'

A flight attendant was hovering, offering Martha more champagne, but she shook her head. She wasn't going to compound her mistake. 'Could I have some water?' she asked as she put her empty glass back on the tray. Now who was the sensible one? she thought wryly.

'Ah, so you're not a believer in love at first sight,' she said with an ironic look. 'Now, why does that not surprise me?'

'Are you?'

Martha thanked the flight attendant for her water before turning back to him. 'I used to be,' she told him.

He hadn't expected her to say that. 'What changed your mind?' he asked curiously.

'Falling in love at first sight and discovering that it didn't last,' she said with a sad little smile. Her eyes took on a faraway look as she remembered how it had been. 'When I met Paul it was like every cliché you ever heard. Our eyes met across a crowded room, and I knew—or thought I knew—that he was the only man for me. We were soul mates. I spent the rest of the night with him, and we moved in together a week later. At least we didn't go as far as getting married,' she joked.

Her description of how she had fallen madly in love coincided with a twinge that made Lewis shift a little irritably in his seat. Maybe it wasn't cabin pressure? Maybe he was coming down with something after all?

'So what happened?'

Martha sighed. 'Oh, the usual…day to day living, routine, stressful careers. It's hard to keep up the magic against all that. Paul and I did our best, but the enchantment wore off eventually and, when it did, there was nothing left,' she said sadly.

'We carried on for a while, but it wasn't the same. Splitting up was awful. Somehow the fact that we'd started with such high expectations made the squabbling even worse, and everything ended up feeling much more bitter than if we'd never had those dreams at all.'

For a moment her shoulders slumped as she relived the misery of those last horrible months with Paul, and then she straightened and made a determined effort to push the memories away. 'I decided then that I wasn't going to go through that again. A successful relationship needs to be based on more than infatuation.'

Lewis lifted an eyebrow. 'Meaning what?'

'Meaning that I think it's better to be pragmatic than romantic when it comes to sharing your life with someone. I'm looking for friendship and respect and a shared attitude to the practicalities of life now. They're going to lead to a happier and more lasting relationship than any amount of physical attraction—although that always helps, of course!'

'So is that what you had with Noah's father…what was his name again?…Rory?' Lewis was horrified to hear the faintest tinge of jealousy in his voice.

Fortunately, Martha didn't seem to have noticed. She was shaking her head.

'No.' She smiled ruefully. 'To be honest, I think it was more a case of lust at first sight! I met Rory at a party. It wasn't long after I'd broken up with Paul and my confidence had taken a knock. I was feeling my age too. Suddenly I seemed to be hurtling into middle age with nothing to look forward to.

'And then I saw Rory,' she said, remembering. 'He's quite a bit younger than me and incredibly good-looking. We were all pale and pasty after a London winter and he'd just breezed in from the Indian Ocean, all blond and tanned and gorgeous! When he walked into that party I swear every woman in the room sucked in her breath and her stomach! Rory could have had his pick. There were lots of really pretty girls there, even a few models, but he spent the entire evening with me. I suppose I was flattered.'

Lewis heard the undercurrent of secret amazement and pleasure she had felt that night in her voice, and wondered if she really didn't know how attractive she was. Personally, he wasn't surprised that Rory had singled her out. The intelligence and character in her face more than compensated for the fine lines round her eyes, and that lush mouth was much more tantalising than the perfect body or smooth, untried expression of a twenty-year-old.

'Rory was just what I needed after Paul,' Martha was saying. 'He made me feel desirable again. It wasn't love at first sight, no, but we did get on really well in spite of the difference in our ages. If we'd had longer together, who knows? Maybe we could have built a good long-term relationship but, as it was, he had to go back to St Bonaventure. We both knew that it was never going to be a permanent thing, so we just enjoyed it for what it was—a lot of fun.'

Lewis was getting a bit tired of hearing about Rory, who was so attractive and such fun and no doubt a real stud in bed, too, he thought sourly. 'Did the fun include getting pregnant?' he asked disapprovingly.

'No, that was an accident,' said Martha. 'We'd been to Paris for the weekend—Rory had never been and I used to go to all the fashion shows—so we thought we'd treat ourselves to a great meal on our last night, and I had oysters. *Big* mistake! I was on the pill, but those oysters definitely disagreed with me. I had an upset stomach for a couple of days after we got back and…well, it happens.'

She shrugged. 'A touch of food poisoning isn't the best of reasons to start a family, I know, but I wouldn't change Noah for the world now. Anyway,' she went on with a sideways glance at Lewis, 'you don't need to worry that I'll do an Eve and throw out all your arrangements by deciding I have met the man of my dreams on St Bonaventure. I'm too much of a realist about love now for that, and even if I wasn't quite frankly I'm too tired to fall in love at the moment!'

CHAPTER THREE

LEWIS'S hard gaze encompassed her pale face and the circles under her eyes. 'You look it,' he said roughly.

'Well, I certainly wouldn't recommend being a single mother to anyone who relies on her sleep,' said Martha with a wry smile.

'You must have known it would be hard work.'

She nodded. 'Yes, I did, but it's like everyone always says…you can say that you know looking after a baby will be tiring, but until you're actually doing it you have no conception of what sleep deprivation does to you or of just what "tired" can mean!'

Lewis hunched a shoulder. 'If it's that bad why do women go on and on about how they want to have babies?'

'Because the joy you get from your child is worth every sleepless night,' said Martha, leaning forward to stroke Noah's cheek. 'It's worth every day you get through like a zombie, every hour you spend worrying about whether he's healthy or happy or how you're going to afford to give him everything he needs.'

Lewis's mouth turned down at the corners. 'That sounds all very fine, but in my experience it's a lot more basic than that. I think a lot of women have children to fulfil their own needs. They think about how much they want to be loved or valued, not about how the child will feel.

'Half the time they have a baby just because it's fashionable,' he said contemptuously. 'A baby is the latest designer accessory. You can dress it up in rinky-dinky little outfits and show it off, which is fine until the fashion changes and you've got to keep up, and then it's *Oh, dear, now what am I going to do with the baby?*'

'Give it to my brother to look after?' suggested Martha, unsurprised at the bitterness in his voice if that was what had happened with Savannah.

'Or a nanny or a mother-in-law or anyone else you can find to deal with all that messy, boring stuff as long as it doesn't stop you doing whatever you want to do!'

There was a little silence. Martha had the feeling that she was treading on dangerous ground. 'Why did you agree to look after Viola if you feel that way?' she asked cautiously after a moment.

'What could I do?' Lewis replied, hunching a shoulder. 'I had my sister in hysterics, the baby crying...'

He shuddered, remembering the scene. 'Savannah's out of control at the moment. She's behaving very badly, but she's still in no state to look after a baby properly. Viola's father is in the States at the moment—or he was last time I heard. Half the time he's too out of it to remember that he's got a daughter, let alone to look after her, and Viola certainly can't look after herself.' He sighed. 'I'm the only one who can be responsible for her at the moment. She's just a baby. I couldn't just say that she wasn't my problem.'

Martha studied his profile, oddly moved by his matter-of-fact attitude. He seemed so hard when you first met him, she thought, remembering how off-putting she had found that austere, unsmiling face and the uncompromising air of toughness and self-sufficiency, but underneath it all he was obviously a kind man, and a decent one.

Kindness and decency weren't qualities she had valued much when she was caught up in the frenetic whirl of activity at work and a hectic social life, but it didn't take long to learn how important they were when life became more difficult.

Knowing that Lewis had them made him seem a much nicer man.

And a much more attractive one.

The thought slid unbidden into Martha's mind and she jerked her eyes away from his face.

Don't even *think* about it, she told herself. It's one thing to realise that Lewis might not be quite as unpleasant as you thought, quite another to start thinking of him as attractive. He's your employer and you're going out to find Rory. Don't complicate the issue.

She took a sip of her water. Maybe she should have stuck to the champagne after all.

'You must be very close to your sister if you're the one she turns to for help,' she said after a while.

Lewis grimaced. 'It's partly my own fault Savannah is the way she is,' he said. 'Her mother left when she was only four, so she never had an example of good parenting.

Michaela—her mother—was an heiress. She was very pretty and very spoilt, just like Savannah. After she divorced my father she went off to the States, but she was killed in a road accident a couple of years later. All her money was put in a trust fund for when Savannah was eighteen, and Savannah has been running through her inheritance ever since.'

'I didn't realise that she was your half-sister,' said Martha, wriggling round in her seat so that it was easier to talk.

'She's fourteen years younger than me, so I wasn't around all that much after I went to university. Poor kid, she didn't have much of a childhood, looked after by a succession of nannies and then packed off to boarding school. My father was never much of a hands-on parent at the best of times,' he added dryly, 'and once his business started going downhill he withdrew into himself even more. I think he forgot about Savannah's existence most of the time.

'I tried to do what I could for Savannah in the holidays, and when our father died she made her base with me, but she was sixteen by then and had got in with a crowd of wild friends.' Lewis sighed. 'I was always bailing her out of trouble. I blame myself sometimes.

Maybe if I'd been firmer with her she'd be less spoilt now.'

'It wasn't your fault,' said Martha stoutly. 'It's hard enough for perfect, supportive parents to deal with ordinary adolescents, let alone troubled ones. You can only have been a young man. I don't see how you could have possibly done more than you did.'

Lewis looked a little taken aback by her support. 'Helen was always telling me I should be stricter with Savannah.'

A few tiny bristles went up on the back of Martha's neck. 'Helen?' she asked in a carefully casual voice.

'My girlfriend.'

Girlfriend? Martha was alarmed by the sinking feeling in her stomach. Why should she be so disappointed…? No, no, scrub *disappointed*, she told herself. That wasn't the right word at all.

Surprised, that was better. Why should she be so *surprised* that Lewis had a girlfriend? She guessed he was in his late thirties. He was intelligent, competent, solvent, and even not bad-looking—if you liked the dour, steely type, that was. Apparently straight, and nothing obviously kinky about him. Of *course* he had a girlfriend.

'We were together for years,' Lewis was saying, 'but she used to get very fed up when Savannah turned up drunk when we had friends round, or rang me in the middle of the night.'

Past tense. Phew! Martha relaxed, only to remember that if she hadn't been disappointed there was no reason to feel relieved, was there?

Unaware of Martha's convoluted mental exertions, Lewis was brooding about his sister. 'I'm sure Helen's right,' he said. 'I probably do encourage Savannah to depend on me too much, but in spite of all that money she hasn't had an easy time of things. Yes, she's been spoilt, but she's very insecure and I can't just turn her away when she needs help, can I? She can behave appallingly sometimes, but when it comes down to it she's still my little sister—'

He broke off suddenly. 'Why are you looking at me like that?' he demanded.

'I'm just thinking that it's a shame that you don't have any children,' said Martha, appalled to find herself blushing slightly. She hadn't meant to stare at him like that. 'Not many men have such a strong sense of family. Don't you want a family of your own?'

'No,' he said, his face hardening. 'Savannah's been quite enough family to deal with, thank you.'

'It would be different if you had your own children.'

He shook his head. 'I wouldn't risk it. There's too much grief when things go wrong.'

'And so much happiness when they go right,' countered Martha.

'You said yourself that having a baby is hard work and you spend most of your time exhausted.'

'Yes, but I also said that it was worth it. And I've been trying to manage on my own. It wouldn't be like that for you.'

'That's what Helen used to say. "It won't be like that for us."' Lewis shook his head. 'I didn't see why it should be different for us.'

'You're…um…not together any more, then?' asked Martha.

'No.' He glanced at her and then away. 'Helen and I had what I thought was an ideal relationship. She's a beautiful, smart, very talented lady.'

Oh, good, thought Martha. The ex from hell.

Although what was it to her, after all? Martha scowled down into her glass of water. Water! What was wrong with her? She had been the ultimate party girl once, the queen of champagne sippers.

'We were together a long time,' Lewis was saying. 'I travel a lot, and she was busy training as a barrister.'

Excellent, a barrister! So Helen was not just beautiful and smart but a serious person. Not the kind of woman who stood around sipping champagne, then.

Oblivious to Martha's mental running commentary, Lewis was still telling her about his relationship. 'We both had our own lives, but we enjoyed the time we spent together and everything was perfect until one day she woke up with her hormones in overdrive.'

His mouth turned down at the edges, remembering. 'That's when she started lobbying for a baby. It wasn't about getting married for Helen. She just wanted a child. "This is the right time," she kept saying.'

'Well, maybe it was for her,' said Martha, beginning to feel a twinge of sympathy for Helen. She might have been intimidatingly clever and beautiful, but she obviously hadn't got very far with Lewis.

'It wasn't the right time for her career,' he said astringently. 'She'd worked incredibly hard and had just qualified. She should have been thinking about getting experience, not babies. I couldn't believe that she would even consider chucking it all in.'

Martha thought about her own career, not quite as impressive as Helen's perhaps, but still, it had meant a lot to her. 'It's surprising what women will give up for a baby.'

'Oh, she wasn't going to give up her career,' said Lewis with an edge. 'Oh, no. She was going to have the baby and then go back to work. I didn't see the point in bringing a child into the world just to hand it over to a nanny while Helen made a name for herself at the Bar. Helen told me I was the one being selfish,' he added ironically.

'What happened?'

'She gave me an ultimatum. Try for a baby, or she'd leave me.'

'And?'

'She left.'

'I'm sorry,' said Martha uncomfortably. She bit her lip. 'Do you ever think you made the wrong decision?'

'No,' said Lewis. 'I miss Helen sometimes. Quite a lot, to tell you the truth,' he admitted, swirling his water around in his glass. 'She's a really special person. Strong, ferociously intelligent, interesting…and very beautiful.' He glanced at Martha. 'Yes, I miss her, but I would have missed her anyway if she'd had a baby. She became so obsessive about it that everything changed in any case. God knows what it would have been like if we'd actually had a baby!'

'You might have felt differently if you'd had a child of your own,' Martha suggested.

'And if I hadn't?' he countered. 'It would have been too late then, wouldn't it?'

Martha had dreamed about landing in St Bonaventure. She had been thinking about getting there for so many months now that she was sure that when the moment actually came the scene would unroll exactly as she had imagined it.

The plane would drop slowly down over the ocean, whose deep blue would fade into turquoise lagoons. She would look down out of her window and see tiny boats out beyond the reefs, startling white beaches fringed with palm trees and everywhere the glitter of sun on the water, and the strain of the last few months would evaporate in the dazzling light. She would hold Noah in her lap and think about

Rory and wonder whether by the time she left they would be a family.

Only it wasn't *quite* like that.

Forty minutes before they were due to land, great, dark rain clouds began boiling up around the plane, and it grew darker and darker. Rain streamed against the windows and the turbulence woke both babies, who screamed as the change in pressure hurt their ears.

Martha held Noah and tried to calm him, but Lewis seemed to be doing a much better job with Viola. He looked like a rock sitting there, as if he hadn't even noticed the terrifying way the wind was buffeting the plane around, his great hands holding the baby firmly against him as she snuffled into his shoulder, evidently soothed by the steady beat of his heart.

Lucky Viola, Martha thought involuntarily. She knew that Noah was picking up on her own fear and that was just making him worse, but how could she be calm when the plane was lurching up and down and the fuselage was shuddering and the only thing between them and the ocean was thirty thousand feet of precisely nothing?

Lewis glanced across at her. 'OK?'

'Oh, yes. Fabulous.' Martha caught her breath as the plane dropped into another air pocket and she bit her lip so hard it began to bleed. 'There's nothing like a bit of dicing with death before breakfast, is there?' she said, wiping the blood away and running her tongue over her bottom lip, but her voice was humiliatingly wobbly.

Lewis shifted Viola on to his other shoulder, holding her in place with one hand, and somehow managed to undo his seat belt and shift into the seat next to Martha's without being thrown off balance.

Quite calmly, he refastened the seat belt and settled Viola securely. 'Give me your hand,' he said.

Martha was cuddling a wailing Noah on her lap. She probably *could* spare a hand. It was embarrassing to admit how much she wanted to hold on to Lewis. Only because she was scared, of course.

If she was less scared, Noah might calm down. So it would probably be best for him if she did take Lewis's hand, wouldn't it?

Shifting Noah into the crook of her arm, she stuck out her free hand almost rudely. Lewis folded his fingers around it and rested their clasped hand on the armrest between them.

'You're quite safe,' he said. 'It's often like this in the rainy season. The pilots are used to it. In a little while we'll be dropping down below the clouds and it'll be much quieter.'

'Doesn't that depend on just how fast we'll be dropping?' said Martha edgily, trying not to notice how warm and comforting his hand felt. 'There's dropping and there's falling!'

The corner of Lewis's mouth twitched. 'We'll be making a controlled descent,' he said gravely. 'Does that make you feel better?'

Actually, what was making her feel better was the warmth of his fingers and the calmness of his voice. There was something incredibly reassuring about the way he sat there so relaxed and at ease, in spite of the baby clutching at his shoulder and the hysterical woman clutching his hand.

Martha's heartbeat slowed steadily and, sensing her growing confidence, Noah buried his face in her breast, his wails subsiding to woebegone sobs as he burrowed instinctively into her for comfort.

Martha hugged him close with one arm, thinking how comforting it would be if she could do the same to Lewis. You would really feel safe with that hard body shielding you, and his arm tight around you and…and good God! What was she *thinking*? Martha caught herself up guiltily.

Pull yourself together, woman, she told herself sternly. It's only a bit of turbulence. No need to lose your head completely.

She didn't let go of his hand, though.

'I wish I could cry like a baby sometimes,' she said shakily, by now more perturbed by her own wayward thoughts than the turbulence.

'I know what you mean.'

'You do?' Martha stole a glance at him under her lashes. He wasn't handsome, with that beaky nose and those intimidating brows, but there was a cool competence and a self-sufficiency about him that was appealing all the same. Looking at the firm jaw and the stern mouth, she couldn't imagine him ever crying.

'Babies have a nice life,' he explained. 'You sleep when you want, eat when you want, and you can let people know exactly what you're feeling. You just let it all out. When you're a baby you don't have to pretend to be happy when you're not, or brave when you're really scared,' he said, sliding a half-smile at Martha.

'You don't have to pretend that you like someone when you don't.'

Or that you don't like them when really you do. Martha half opened her mouth to say it, but then closed it again, afraid that Lewis might ask her what she meant.

Later, Martha couldn't remember what Lewis talked about during the long descent to St Bonaventure. She just kept clinging to his hand and let his calm, steady voice flow over her until at last the plane touched down. It was pouring, and the rain was still streaming against the cabin windows, but at least they were on the ground. That was all Martha cared about right then.

Except that there was no longer any reason to hold his hand.

'All right?' asked Lewis, loosening his clasp.

'Yes.' Reluctantly Martha disengaged her fingers. 'Thank you,' she muttered, and put both her arms around Noah to stop her hand sneaking back towards Lewis's. 'I'm not usually that pathetic.'

'Think nothing of it,' he said, putting a protesting Viola back in her cot while he picked up assorted baby equipment beneath their feet.

'It can be frightening the first time you go through turbulence like that.'

The babies were restless and grizzly as they waited in a rudimentary terminal for the bags and assorted baby equipment to be unloaded from the plane. Martha sat numbly on a plastic chair. She felt as if she had been travelling her entire life. She had no idea what time it was in St Bonaventure, or at home, or anywhere else. Her whole body was buzzing with exhaustion, and it was a huge effort to keep her eyes open.

Afraid that she would simply fall asleep if she sat there any longer, Martha got up and walked Viola up and down.

'I can see why they need a new airport,' she said to Lewis, who was eyeing the building assessingly. She hoped he wasn't planning on rebuilding it there and then. 'If our stuff doesn't arrive soon I think I'm going to keel over right here.'

When they made it through customs at last they were met by a smiling man who introduced himself as Elvis.

So this was where he came, thought Martha fuzzily.

'I'm your driver,' he said, beaming. 'Welcome to St Bonaventure.'

Martha looked outside. She had never seen anything like the rain that sleeted down, bouncing off the tarmac and swirling along the deep gutters. So much for paradise.

'Thank you.' She sighed.

The downpour made it hard to see much as Elvis drove them into town. Martha had a confused impression of ramshackle buildings, but it was hard to take in much when Viola, who was thoroughly bored with travelling by now, decided to express her displeasure by throwing a tantrum.

'You know, you're not the only one who's fed up,' Martha told her, as Viola squirmed and screamed and arched her little body in fury. Suddenly Lewis's decision to stay childless seemed much more understandable.

From the front seat, Lewis turned round and frowned at the noise, which was loud enough even to drown out the thunderous drumming of the rain on the car roof. 'Can't you do anything to quieten her down?' he asked, shouting to make himself heard.

Martha's head was aching. She felt like a zombie and all she wanted to do was sleep for a month. 'Well, I could throw her out of the window,' she snapped, 'but I didn't think that was really an option.'

Oh, God, now Noah was starting as well! Martha joggled him on her knee as best she could. 'Are we nearly there?' she asked Elvis in desperation.

'Two minutes,' he promised.

It was possibly the longest two minutes of Martha's life, but at last they drew up outside a wooden house set in a jungly garden. It had a wide verandah running all the way round it and a corrugated iron roof on to which the rain crashed, but that was all Martha had time to notice as they ran for cover. Even the few seconds it took to get from the car to the verandah was enough to leave them drenched.

Gasping, wiping the rain from her face, Martha found herself being introduced to a plump, motherly-looking woman not much older than she was.

'This is Eloise,' said Lewis. 'I've arranged for her to come in during the day and do the cooking and the housework, so all you have to do is look after the children.'

All? Martha shifted the still yelling Viola to her other arm and jiggled Noah's buggy as he set up a wail as well. Life out here was going to be a doddle, then.

But she smiled at Eloise, who held out her arms for Viola. 'Let me say hello,' she said comfortably. 'I like babies.'

Viola looked extremely dubious, but submitted to being transferred and even stopped crying as she stared at the new face smiling at her. Martha flexed her aching arms and stooped to reassure Noah.

'Thanks,' she said gratefully. If Eloise was good with babies it would make things a whole lot easier.

Inside, the house was spacious and simply furnished. It was probably lovely and cool if you wanted to escape from the heat, but right then it seemed to Martha damp, dark and oppressive.

'Does it always rain like this?' she asked Eloise.

Eloise grinned and shook her head. 'Tomorrow it will be sunny,' she promised.

Martha couldn't imagine it.

By the time they had explored the house, set up the travel cots and unpacked the rest of the babies' stuff it was nearly six, according to Martha's watch, which she had set to local time, and the gloom had intensified into dark. Eloise said she was going home.

'I've left you some supper,' she said. 'You just need to heat it up.' Her face split into a wide smile. 'Have a good evening.'

'Evening?' Martha rubbed the back of her neck wearily as she watched Eloise put up a huge umbrella and disappear down the back steps. 'Do you think that means we'll be able to go to bed soon?'

'Not unless we can persuade these two that it's time to sleep first,' said Lewis, nodding to where Viola and Noah were sitting on a rug energetically thumping the floor with an assortment of toys scattered around them. 'They look suspiciously bright-eyed to me.'

Martha followed his gaze. It was true. After whinging most of the afternoon the two babies had suddenly taken on a new lease of life and looked wide awake.

'I'll give them a bath,' she said. 'With any luck that will make them think that it's bedtime.'

Lewis was unpacking papers from his briefcase. 'Do you need a hand?'

She hesitated. The obvious answer was 'no'. She was the nanny, and she had insisted that she could manage both children by herself.

Which she could do, Martha reminded herself. Once they got into a routine.

'It would make things quicker tonight,' she admitted, swallowing her pride.

Lewis dropped the last sheaf of papers on to the table. 'OK,' he said briskly. 'Let's do it.'

He sat on a stool in the tiled bathroom and watched as Martha put the babies in the bath. She was kneeling on the floor, the sleeves of her pale yellow shirt rolled up and her dark hair pushed behind her ears. Her eyes were huge in her pale face and her skin had the taut look of exhaustion, but there was no trace of impatience in her manner as she gently washed first one baby then the other. They were both sitting up, gurgling and squealing as they beat at the water with dimpled hands, clearly not exhausted at all.

It was all right for them, Lewis thought sourly. They had been able to sleep most of the way, while he and Martha had had to endure the long flight to Nairobi, an interminable delay there while they waited for their transfer, and then the cramped conditions of the little plane that had flown them the last leg.

Had Martha found it as uncomfortable as he had? She hadn't complained, but then perhaps she hadn't been bothered by the way their knees had kept touching, or by the constant brush of their arms.

She had been sitting so close that Lewis had been able to smell the fragrance that she wore. It wasn't one that he recognised. Helen's perfume had been more intense. Martha wore a light, refreshing scent that made him think of fresh herbs and long grass, with just a hint of spice, and it bothered him that once he had started noticing it he couldn't get it out of his mind.

And then they had run into those rain clouds. Lewis could still feel Martha's fingers digging into his hand. It had been just as well, really. The sharpness of her nails had kept him focused and distracted him from her warmth and her softness and the sheen of her hair.

'Hey!' As a particularly vigorous splash caught Martha in the eye she sat back on her heels, laughing, and glanced up at him. 'I'm glad some people are enjoying themselves anyway!'

Her brown eyes were alight with laughter and the warmth of her smile banished the tiredness from her face. She looked so different from the brittle woman who had walked into his office and, unprepared, Lewis was conscious of an unfamiliar feeling that stirred disquietingly inside him.

'Is something wrong?' she asked, puzzled by his arrested expression.

'No.' Lewis looked away. 'When do I get to do my bit?'

'Now.' Martha gave him a towel to spread on his knee and lifted Viola out of the bath. 'Can you dry her?'

She laid Noah on a towel on the floor and wrapped it round him so that she could dry him carefully. Lewis did the same for Viola, but his attention kept wandering away to where Martha was dusting her baby with powder, playing with his kicking feet and blowing kisses against his tummy so that he squealed with delight and clutched at her hair.

Lewis thought about that silky hair drifting over *his* stomach and swallowed hard. Damn. The last thing he needed was to start thinking about that kind of thing. He was Martha's employer, and she had agreed to live with him in the expectation that he would treat her with the respect he accorded any other employee.

Why had that stupid girl…what was her name again? Eve, that was it…why had she taken the ridiculous notion that she was in love into her head? She would have been a perfect nanny. She could have been here now and he wouldn't have been sitting here thinking about Martha's hair brushing his skin or feeling jealous of a *baby*, for God's sake!

If Eve hadn't fallen in love he wouldn't even have known that watching someone bath a baby could be such a turn-on. She would have been able to look after Viola on her own and he could have been going through the contract, the way he should be doing now, not sitting here in the bathroom with a baby on his knee.

'Here.' Martha tossed him the powder. 'Play with her a little. She needs a bit of attention.'

Lewis looked down at his niece's solemn face. It seemed to him that Viola had been demanding and getting attention for the past few hours, but if he concentrated on her he might forget about the way Martha was smiling and swinging her hair against a chuckling Noah and lifting him up and covering him with kisses…

Viola. Focus. Experimentally, Lewis tickled her bare tummy with a finger and was gratified to see her break into a beaming smile. He tried it again and she giggled and grabbed at his hand, so he smiled at her and she laughed back.

Maybe this baby business wasn't so difficult after all, he thought, and then made the mistake of glancing up to find Martha watching him with amusement.

'She likes you,' she said. 'You should play with her more often.'

Feeling like a fool for some reason, Lewis tugged his finger out of Viola's clutches. 'The point of paying a nanny was that I didn't have to do any of this hands-on business,' he said brusquely to cover his embarrassment.

'Stop grumbling,' said Martha, refusing to be cowed by his glare. She was getting used to it now, anyway, and suspected it was more of a defence mechanism than a sign of anger. She reached for a clean nappy and deftly fastened it around Noah before snapping him into a Babygro.

'Viola's your own flesh and blood, for heaven's sake,' she went on, 'and I'm only asking you to dry her. Here, let me have her.'

Shuffling across on her knees, she scooped Viola up from Lewis's lap. 'You don't need to panic, I'll deal with her nappy. Could you hold Noah while I'm doing that, or would that be too much to ask?'

'Oh, all right,' said Lewis grouchily, and found a clean, plump, sweet-smelling baby deposited in his lap.

He and Noah eyed each other, and Lewis was convinced he could identify a smug look on the baby's face, as if he knew quite well what the strange man with the big hands had been thinking about his mother. When Noah reached out and twisted his nose, he was sure of it.

'Ouch!' he exclaimed involuntarily as Noah burst into giggles and reached out again to see if he could get the same reaction, but Lewis was ready for him this time and drew his head sharply out of range.

Martha laughed at his expression. 'It's surprising how strong those little fingers are, isn't it?'

'They certainly are.' Lewis rubbed his nose ruefully. 'I think I'll do the nappy next time!'

'I'll remember that when Viola's nappy gets a bit whiffy,' said Martha, hoisting the baby into her arms for a cuddle. 'Come on, you two, it's time for bed.'

CHAPTER FOUR

'IT'S funny, but I don't feel so tired any more,' said Martha, when they had given the babies a bottle and settled them for sleep. She closed the door gently on them and sent up a silent prayer that they would both fall asleep without any fuss.

'A few hours ago I was ready to sleep standing up, but I've woken up again now,' she told Lewis, who averted his eyes as she stretched.

'Do you want something to eat?' he asked gruffly. 'Eloise said she'd left something for us.'

Deciding she might be hungry after all, Martha followed him into the kitchen to inspect what was on offer. It didn't look very inspiring. Some cold rice, a brown, sloppy stew with unidentifiable ingredients, and a bowl of red sauce.

She and Lewis looked at it and then at each other.

'Maybe it will look more appetising when it's heated up,' Martha suggested hopefully.

It didn't, but they carried it through to the dining area anyway and sat down at the table. Martha helped herself to some rice and a little of the stew, and picked up her fork. 'Well… here goes.'

For a couple of minutes they ate in silence, but their forks moved more and more slowly until she looked up and met Lewis's eyes.

'This is…' she said indistinctly, chewing valiantly.

'…absolutely disgusting?' he suggested, and she put down her fork in relief.

'Revolting,' she agreed.

Lewis poked at the stew on his plate. 'What's that slimy stuff?'

'Okra, I think. I can't even guess at what the rest of it is.' She reached for the red sauce. 'Perhaps this'll cheer it up a bit.'

'Be careful,' said Lewis. 'It's probably quite hot.'

What did he think she was going to do? Empty the whole lot on to her plate? 'I'm not an idiot,' she said irritably, and took a tiny speck with another mouthful of stew.

The top of her head promptly blew off. That was what it felt like anyway. Martha had never tasted anything like it. Her eyes bulged and streamed and her sinuses flamed and her throat seized up so she could only gasp helplessly as Lewis got up without a word and brought her back a bottle of water.

'I think I've been poisoned,' she croaked when she had downed half of it.

'I told you to be careful,' he said.

'You didn't tell me it was the culinary equivalent of an atomic bomb!' Martha felt the top of her head cautiously. It seemed to be all there but it was hard to tell.

'I've never had it,' he protested. 'But I've been offered enough chilli sauces in my time to make me very wary when I see such a little dish.'

Bully for him. Martha cast Lewis a resentful look and pushed her plate away as she gulped down more water. 'Spend six months in the Indian Ocean, I thought. It'll be perfect, I thought. Nothing but sunshine and sea and lovely fresh food. Paradise. And what do I get? A deluge and a slimy brown stew with a sauce that's destroyed my tastebuds for life!'

'The weather will improve,' said Lewis consolingly.

'Yes, but will the food? Do you think this is what Eloise cooks all the time?'

'Probably. The office manager recommended her because she lives nearby, but she never claimed to be able to do anything fancy.'

'A good meal doesn't have to be fancy,' said Martha, grateful that none of her friends were there to groan as she climbed on to her favourite hobby horse. 'The simpler the better, in fact. It's so *easy* to cook a good, nourishing meal.'

She gestured vaguely beyond the verandah. 'I mean, you'd think with all that ocean out there it wouldn't be too much to expect some fresh fish. Just grilled with a squeeze of lime, or baked with coconut, or tossed in a little butter…' Her mouth was watering at the very thought of it. 'And a nice salad on the side, and afterwards a big bowl of tropical fruit or—'

She stopped as she saw Lewis looking at her with new interest. 'What?'

'It sounds as if you can cook,' he said carefully.

'Of course I can cook!' said Martha, ruffled. What did he think? That she had spent her life shoving pre-prepared meals in the microwave? 'I love cooking. In fact, if I hadn't got into journalism, I would have— No,' she interrupted herself, belatedly realising where he was heading.

'Why not?'

'In case you've forgotten, I've got two babies to look after! I won't have time to do the cooking as well.'

'You won't have any housework, and Eloise could help you with the kids. You saw how good she was with Viola when we arrived.'

'Yes, but—'

Lewis nodded towards the pot of stew. 'And you don't *really* want to be eating this for the next six months, do you?'

Martha looked at the congealing mess. 'No,' she admitted. 'I can't say I do.'

'Why don't we renegotiate your contract?' said Lewis persuasively, pressing his advantage. 'Eloise looks after the babies while you're cooking, and she helps you feed and bath them. On top of that, you'll have no housework to do for the next six months.'

'I don't know…' Martha prevaricated.

'How about if I provide a car for you to use?'

She looked at him in surprise. 'Boy, you really don't want to eat that stew again, do you?'

'No, I don't,' he said frankly. 'You can name your terms.'

'Well, this could get interesting!' she said, lifting her eyes heavenwards as if pondering the possibilities.

'Come on, Martha. What do you say?'

Martha had already made up her mind, but she pretended to be thinking about it, just so Lewis didn't think he could push her into anything she hadn't decided for herself.

Eloise was lovely, but she clearly wasn't a cook if this meal was anything to go by. Whereas *she* liked to cook, and there was a lot to be said for doing it herself and ensuring that they all got a proper diet. She could go down to the markets and buy fruit and vegetables and fresh fish.

Martha was beginning to get excited. If Eloise would give her a hand with Noah and Viola, it would be perfect. If nothing else, cooking would make a nice change from changing nappies and wiping noses and trying to spoon food into stubborn little baby mouths, which was all her days would consist of otherwise, paradise or no paradise.

'OK,' she relented at last, and was furious at the thrill that ran through her as Lewis smiled. It was the first time she had seen him smile properly, and she was unprepared for what it did to his face. It wasn't that there was anything extraordinary about it, she tried to rationalise, alarmed by the clench of response at the base of her spine. It was just a smile. But the light in the normally opaque slate eyes was hard to resist and he looked so much younger, and so much warmer.

And so much more attractive.

Enough.

Martha pushed her chair back abruptly and stood up. 'I'll get rid of this and see if I can find some fruit,' she said.

Lewis helped her to clear the plates away. A search of the kitchen revealed some bananas, but not much else, so they took the bunch out to the verandah and put them on the table between two wicker chairs.

'Oh, it's stopped raining!' Martha exclaimed as she sat down, suddenly realising. The rain had been so thunderous on the roof that she was astounded that she hadn't noticed the moment it stopped.

Now the lush vegetation planted right up to the verandah rail was bent and dripping. Insects were scraping and chirruping frantically and the air was heavy with the heady scent of damp earth and frangipani.

'Mmm…' Martha breathed it in appreciatively. 'Lovely! Are we near the sea?'

'Everywhere is near the sea on St Bonaventure,' said Lewis dryly. He pointed towards the end of the garden. 'See those palms?'

Martha peered into the darkness. 'Yes.'

'That's the beach there. Listen.'

He held up a finger and Martha concentrated on tuning out the insects and the dripping, until there, very clearly after all, was the murmur of waves breaking on to the sand.

Her face lit up. 'Oh, I *love* that sound!' She turned to smile at Lewis. 'Things are looking up!'

'Yes, they are,' he agreed, without taking his eyes off her face, and for some reason the breath dried in Martha's throat as she looked back at him, imprisoned by something new and unsettling, something that had slipped unnoticed into the atmosphere between them, tightening the air and making her heart slam inexplicably against her ribs.

When Lewis leant forward all her senses jangled and she only just stopped herself gasping, but he only pulled a banana off the bunch on the table and offered it to her.

'Have a banana,' he said softly.

'Thanks,' she croaked.

At first Martha was glad to have something to do with her hands, but she hadn't even finished peeling it before she faltered, suddenly and ridiculously awkward. She liked bananas. She had eaten thousands of them in her time. Why should eating this one seem uncomfortably suggestive?

Don't be so stupid, she told herself. It's just a banana.

But still she hesitated. Sliding a glance from under her lashes at Lewis, she saw that he was leaning forward, elbows on his knees, as he chomped his own banana thoughtfully and stared out into the darkness. *He* wasn't bothered.

Martha opened her mouth to take a bite. Of course, Lewis would choose that exact moment to look at her.

'Don't you like bananas?' he asked as she lowered hers self-consciously.

'Yes,' said Martha, horribly aware of the defensive note in her voice. Who would be *defensive* about eating a banana?

Lewis dropped his peel on to the table and helped himself to another. 'Aren't you hungry? I am. I couldn't force much of that stew down.'

'A bit.'

A *bit*? She was starving! That just made things worse.

Stupidly, Martha could feel herself blushing and was fervently grateful for the dim light that hid her pink cheeks. She hoped.

She really couldn't sit holding a peeled banana like this. Any minute now, Lewis was going to ask her why she wasn't eating if she was hungry, and what was she going to tell him? That eating it in front of him suddenly seemed bizarrely erotic?

That would be an excellent conversational move on her first night alone with her new employer, wouldn't it?

Hastily, she stuffed the banana into her mouth and stared desperately at the raindrops dripping off the palm by the verandah steps as she chewed.

God, what was wrong with her tonight? It wasn't as if she was prudish or inexperienced. She was Martha Shaw, hard-bitten fashion editor. How many editorial conferences had she sat through at *Glitz* where they had all discussed sexuality from pretty much every angle, some of which she would rather not have known about, without turning a hair? Then, it had been merely a question of deciding what would most intrigue their readers, so you'd think she could manage to eat a banana now, wouldn't you?

'Another one?'

'No, thanks,' said Martha indistinctly, her mouth full. Right then she never wanted to see another banana ever again.

Lewis demolished his second. 'That's better,' he said, tossing the skin on to the table. 'I could get pretty sick of bananas, though. Do you think you could go shopping tomorrow and stock up the fridge? I'll send a car to take you.'

'Good idea,' said Martha, pathetically grateful for the change of subject. 'I'll get Eloise to show me the markets.'

Silence fell, but now that Martha had disposed of her banana it was not an awkward one. Gradually, she began to relax.

It was hot, but not oppressively so, and the scent of the night air was very intense in the humidity. Martha listened to the whirr of the insects and the soft shush of the ocean and the steady drip, drip, drip of the leaves, and felt the tension she had hardly been aware of seeping away. The babies were safe and quiet, and Lewis was still and solid beside her, and at last she could let the tiredness she had been keeping at bay trickle through her.

She needed to sleep, but the very thought of standing up was too much to contemplate. It struck Martha that she was feeling at ease for the first time in months, possibly years. There had always been so much to think about before. Her relationship with Paul, her career, coping with pregnancy on her own, adapting to having a baby, worrying about money…yes, it was a long time since she had felt this relaxed, she realised.

Lately, she had been fixated on Noah and on how she was going to get herself to St Bonaventure, but now here she was. Her body was telling her that she could stop for a while.

It was such a wonderful thought that Martha closed her eyes with a smile and stretched luxuriously, her arms above her head as a yawn escaped her. It felt good to be here.

Opening her eyes, she found Lewis looking at her with an indecipherable expression. Pinioned by his cool gaze, she could only stare back at him in mid-stretch, and the lovely relaxed feeling evaporated as her heart began to thump painfully again.

Swallowing, Martha managed to jerk her eyes away and scramble to her feet. 'I…I think I'll have a shower and go to bed,' she said nervously.

'Good idea,' said Lewis, his voice tinder-dry, and he turned back to contemplate the darkness and try not to think about her standing naked under the water. He would be taking a shower too, but his would definitely be a cold one.

When Martha woke late the next morning it took her some time to remember where she was. She blinked up at the ceiling fan lazily slapping the hot air above her. A chink in the wooden blinds let a shaft of sunlight pierce the dimness and cast a thin stripe across her feet.

Beside her, Viola stirred and flung out one chubby arm. Very cautiously, so as not to wake her or Noah, sleeping soundly on her other side, Martha eased herself upright and pushed her dark hair back from her face. It was all coming back to her now.

It had been a very long night. No sooner had she fallen into a deep sleep than it seemed that the babies' body clocks had kicked in. First Noah, then Viola had woken up, and that had set the pattern for the night. Martha would just get one settled when the other would start.

At one point Lewis had knocked quietly and come in to ask if she needed help—or had she dreamed that? Martha's brow wrinkled in an effort of memory. She had a very vivid picture of him, barefoot and bare-chested, wearing only a pair of loose grey pyjama bottoms.

Odd, she thought. The image had the power to disturb her now, but at the time she couldn't remember feeling at all awkward. She was pretty sure she had just shaken her head and said that there was no point in two of them being awake, as if it was quite normal for him to be half-naked in her bedroom in the middle of the night.

Martha grimaced. She *must* have been tired!

She could certainly remember the point when she had simply given up and taken both babies into bed with her. There would be time enough to get them into a routine later, she had told herself. Comforted by the warmth of her body, Noah and Viola had quietened at last and, snuggling into her, they had slept like…well, babies, allowing Martha to sink into blissful oblivion as well.

Viola's eyes suddenly snapped open and she uttered a tiny squeak.

'Oh, so you're awake, are you?' Martha picked her up and cuddled her, enjoying the feel of the small body snuffling into her. 'Shall we go and see if we can find you something to drink?'

She could hear sounds from the direction of the kitchen. Perhaps Lewis was already up? Rather to her shame, Martha found herself checking her reflection in a mirror to make sure that there was no sleep in the corner of her eyes or mascara stains under her lashes. Her hair looked dreadful, but there wasn't much she could do about that until she had a shower.

Noah was still sound asleep. Martha made sure that he was secure, and carried Viola through to the kitchen.

Lewis wasn't there, and she was cross with herself for the pang of disappointment she felt when Eloise looked up and greeted her instead. Last night she had been able to blame that kind of silliness on jet lag, but if it carried on she was going to have to get a grip.

'Have you seen Lewis yet?' she asked, trying to sound casual, as she found Viola a mug and sat her in a high chair.

Eloise nodded and told her that he had gone to the office.

'Already?' Martha looked at her wrist, but she had forgotten to put on her watch. 'What time is it?'

'Nearly eleven.'

'Eleven?' Aghast, she stared at Eloise. 'You should have woken me!'

'Mr Mansfield said to let you sleep,' said Eloise firmly. 'He looked in on you before he left, but you were all sleeping so soundly he didn't want to wake you.'

Hmm. Martha wasn't sure she liked the idea of Lewis inspecting her while she was asleep. What if her mouth had been open, or she'd been snoring?

Still, there was no doubt that she felt better for the rest, and when Eloise offered to keep an eye on Viola while she had a shower, she began to feel almost human again. Noah was awake by then, and by the time both babies had been fed, washed, and changed, and they had been shopping, it was not until after lunch, when they were having a nap, that Martha had a chance to explore properly.

The house looked very different now that the dampness and the darkness had evaporated like a bad dream. Preoccupied with the babies' needs, it wasn't until the car had turned up and Martha had stepped outside that she had realised what a beautiful day it was. The sunshine and the hot wind had sent her spirits soaring, but it was nothing to how she felt when she pushed open the door that led from the living area to the back verandah and walked out to the top of the steps.

'Oh,' she said on a long breath.

This was where she had sat with Lewis the night before, looking out into the tangled, dripping darkness and trying to imagine it as a garden. It was very simple, with an expanse of grass framed by luxuriant palms and exotic-looking bushes with glossy leaves and vibrantly-coloured flowers. A bright pink bougainvillaea scrambled along the verandah roof and at the foot of the steps stood the frangipani tree whose intense scent Martha had smelt last night.

Martha walked slowly down the steps and across the grass towards the coconut palms that clustered at the end of the garden. Their ridged trunks leant at all sorts of angles, and through them she could glimpse an intense blueness and the glitter of sunlight on water.

The grass gave way to coarse sand littered with coconut husks, and then the ground dipped away and Martha found herself on a curve of white sand edging a perfect lagoon.

'Oh,' she breathed again, afraid that if she moved too suddenly or made a noise the scene would simply shimmer and disappear.

Away from the shade of the garden, it was very hot and very still. Martha slipped off her sandals and curled her toes into the soft sand with a shiver of pleasure.

Sandals dangling from one hand, she walked down to where the water was barely rippling against the beach. Shading her eyes with her hand, Martha looked out to sea. As the beach shelved away, the colour of the water intensified. Over her bare feet it was crystal clear, but it deepened imperceptibly to the palest of greens, and then to a true turquoise and at last to the deep, dark blue of the ocean beyond the reef.

Martha thought of the previous day, of how wet and gloomy it had been, and how depressed she had felt when they had arrived. It was as if she had woken up to find herself transported to an entirely different world. Walking slowly along the beach, she felt the sand warm and soft beneath her toes.

OK, she thought. I was wrong. This *is* paradise, after all.

Lewis didn't come back until nearly seven that evening. Eloise had helped Martha to give the babies a bath, but she had been long gone before the sound of a car drawing up outside sent Martha's heart lurching into her throat.

Noah and Viola were propped up against the cushions on the big sofa in the living room. Martha was alternating giving them a last bottle and trying not to wish that Lewis would come home. What could he possibly be doing all this time? she fretted. It wasn't that she was *lonely* exactly, but he really ought to think about spending some time with Viola before she went to bed.

Not that Martha could think of a way of telling Lewis that without making him think that she had missed him, and she wasn't having *that*.

So when the door opened she pretended to be absorbed in burping Noah. 'Hi,' she said over her shoulder, as casually as she could manage. Obviously that was a better option than 'Where have you been all day?' which was what she really wanted to say.

Lewis looked tired. 'I'm sorry I'm a bit late,' he said, putting his briefcase on a side table.

He must be the only person who could look crisp on a tropical island, thought Martha. It wasn't so much what he was wearing—businesslike trousers and a white short-sleeved shirt—as the way that he was wearing it, as if he would really be a lot more comfortable if he had a tie on as well, and probably a buttoned-up jacket while he was at it.

The man that fashion forgot. Martha couldn't help remembering her days at *Glitz* and how sharply the men she had met then had dressed. Most of them had been gay, of course, or serial adulterers, but still. She tried to picture Lewis at a *Glitz* party, but it involved too great a leap of the imagination. He would have been like a creature from another world.

Maybe that was how she seemed in his, thought Martha with a sudden pang, glancing down at her sleeveless top and loose trousers. It had been one of her favourite outfits the summer before last, effortlessly chic in the way only beautiful material and a designer cut could achieve.

But then she noticed the purée stains from lunch on her trousers, the crumpled collar where Viola had clutched at her with clammy little hands, the marks on her shirt where both babies had wiped their noses, and she felt strangely cheered. She wouldn't belong at a *Glitz* party either nowadays.

'It was one of those days,' Lewis said as he slumped on to the sofa next to hers. 'I meant to be home sooner.'

'It doesn't matter.' Martha was carefully unconcerned. 'What time is it, anyway?'

As if she hadn't been looking at her watch every five minutes for the last three hours.

Lewis looked at his watch. 'Six minutes to seven.'

'Couldn't you be a bit more precise?' she asked ironically.

'Sorry. I've been dealing with details all day, and you get into the habit after a while.' Martha just looked at him and, after a moment, Lewis gave in and laughed. 'OK, so I'm precise. What can I say? I'm an engineer.'

'I thought so.' Martha smiled and put Noah down so that she could give Viola the last of her bottle.

Lewis watched her feeding the baby for a while. 'So, how has your day been?' he asked at last.

'Fine,' she said, her eyes on Viola. 'It's a beautiful place, isn't it? I took Viola and Noah down to the beach for a paddle and they loved the water, but it was really too hot for them. I had to bring them back into the shade after a few minutes. And we went shopping, of course. Thanks for sending the car, by the way. It would have been a long way to walk back with all the stuff.'

'That sounds promising,' said Lewis. 'No more okra stew tonight, then?'

'No. Eloise is delighted that she doesn't have to do the cooking.'

'So I gathered,' he said. 'She practically fell on my neck when I suggested the alternative arrangements. Do you think it will work out?'

'I'm sure it will,' said Martha. 'Of course, it'll be better when we get into a routine.' She turned her attention back to Viola. 'We had a very late start this morning, as you probably know.'

Lewis shrugged, wishing he could shrug off the memory of how she had looked when he had quietly opened her door that morning. She had obviously been too hot in the night and was lying half in and half out of the top sheet, wearing what looked like a man's shirt, which exposed rather more of her legs than she had probably realised.

Averting his gaze, Lewis had spotted Noah and Viola tucked on either side of her. All three of them had been sound asleep. Martha's face had been pressed into the pillow, while the ceiling fan gently stirred her dark hair.

His throat was ridiculously dry for some reason, and he cleared it self-consciously. How could you have a dry throat in this humidity? 'You must have been tired,' he said. 'The babies seemed to be awake most of the night.'

She looked up at him abruptly, her brown eyes very clear and direct. 'Did you come in at one point?' she asked.

'I thought you might need some help,' he said, inexplicably defensive. 'I'm sorry, I did knock, but you obviously couldn't hear. Would you rather I didn't in future?'

'No,' said Martha hastily, and to Lewis's surprise she seemed even more awkward than he did. 'I…I just wondered if I had dreamt it or not, that's all.'

'No,' he said. 'You didn't dream it.'

They looked at each other and the silence strummed between them. For Martha, it was as if she were back in the dimly lit room. Lewis was there, with his bare chest and his bare feet, and she was in an old grandad shirt and nothing else. She had taken to sleeping in it since Noah was born. It was very soft fine cotton in a blue that had faded in washing until it was almost white and came a decent way down her thighs if she didn't bend over too far.

Martha's skin prickled as if she could feel its cool softness against her now, and she was suddenly aware of how naked she had been beneath it in a way she hadn't been the night before. It would have been so easy to have touched Lewis, to have rested her palm against his chest or run her hand down his flank, and what would have happened then? The mere thought was enough to dry the breath in her throat.

With an effort, she dragged her mind back to the present. 'I mean, I don't want you to feel that you need to offer to help,' she said awkwardly. 'You're paying me to be the one who gets up in the middle of the night if Viola is crying.'

Yes, and it might be an idea if she remembered that, Martha reminded herself sternly. She was a nanny and Lewis was her employer, and don't forget it.

Lewis was rubbing the back of his neck tiredly. 'That's the trouble with babies,' he said. 'They make everything so…' he trailed off, searching for the right word '…so *intimate*,' he decided at last. 'You think you'll just hire a nanny to look after the baby, and before you know where you are you're sharing the small hours with a stranger and you're both half naked.'

So he had been thinking about how very few clothes they had on between them too. Martha didn't know whether to be glad or sorry about that.

Take it lightly, anyway, she told herself.

'Hopefully they'll settle into a routine soon, and they won't wake up in the night,' she said, really quite pleased with her careless tone. 'And then there won't be any need for either of us to wander around half naked!'

Viola had come to the end of her bottle, so she sat her up and patted her gently on the back. 'She's a gorgeous baby, isn't she?' said Martha, deciding that it was high time they changed the subject. She turned Viola to face her, holding the baby between her hands so that she could admire her fierce blue eyes and rosebud mouth. 'And don't you know it?' she said to her with a smile.

Viola eyed her consideringly for a moment before responding with an almighty belch so at odds with her daintiness that Martha and Lewis couldn't help laughing.

'That's my girl!' said Lewis, and Viola beamed, not understanding how she had banished the simmering tension in the atmosphere but delighted with their reaction. She held out her arms to her uncle in an unmistakable gesture.

'Do you want to take her?' Martha asked, and Lewis instantly looked alarmed.

'To do what?'

'Don't panic, there's no nappy changing required! Just give her a bit of a cuddle.' Martha deposited Viola in his arms before he had time to think up any objections. 'Look, here's a book,' she said, handing him a board book with bright simple images. 'Read that with her.'

Lewis did his best, but the fact was that Viola wasn't the slightest bit interested in the book. It was more fun to explore her uncle's face with inquisitive little fingers, sticking them in his mouth, patting his nose, tugging at his lips and pulling at his hair until he winced.

'Why won't she sit quietly like him?' he complained, casting an envious glance to where Noah was sitting angelically on his mother's lap, responding suitably with coos and gurgles as she turned the pages.

'I can't imagine.' Martha's lips were pressed together in an effort to stop herself laughing at Lewis's struggles to distract his small niece. 'I think you might find there's some very contrary family genes in Viola!'

'More than likely,' said Lewis glumly, thinking of his sister.

'Just wait until she's old enough to answer back!'

He grimaced. At eight months, the strength of Viola's character was already obvious. God only knew what she would be like once she started to talk.

'She's going to need a very firm hand,' said Martha, reading his expression without difficulty.

'That'll be her parents' problem,' said Lewis, removing Viola's finger from his ear. 'It's nothing to do with me.'

Even to himself that had the ring of famous last words.

CHAPTER FIVE

MARTHA took pity on him at last and took a protesting Viola away to bed. 'I think she likes you,' she told Lewis as Viola set up a wail at being separated from her newest plaything.

Rubbing his nose tenderly, where the tiny fingers had pinched, Lewis wasn't sure that he wanted to hear that.

Both babies went down with suspicious ease. 'Quick,' said Martha, closing the door on them. 'Let's eat before they start.'

She had made a fresh salsa to go with some grilled fish, a simple but effective meal that made Lewis eye her with new appreciation. 'I'm beginning to think it was lucky that Eve fell in love after all,' he said.

Was that a subtle way of reminding her that she wasn't his first choice? Martha wondered. 'Thank you…I think!'

But the truth was that she was glad Eve had fallen in love too. If she hadn't, she would be here in this beautiful place, and when Lewis offered to clear up she was even gladder. 'You go and sit down,' he said. 'I'll bring you some coffee.'

There was no doubt that it was nice to be looked after for a change. Martha sat on the verandah and let herself relax. There was a breeze tonight, and she could hear the sea beyond the rustling palms, while from behind her came the sound of Lewis moving around the kitchen. It was oddly comforting to know that he was in there and would be coming out to join her any minute now.

Not that she was waiting for him or anything.

Although, if she wasn't waiting, why did her heart clutch in that disturbing way as Lewis slid open the door on to the verandah and put a mug on the table next to her?

Suppressing it firmly, Martha thanked him with studied nonchalance. It was no big deal. He had only made coffee, and he had just happened to choose to sit on the chair beside hers. That wasn't a big deal either. He could hardly go and sit at the other end of the verandah, could he? That would look rude.

Lewis leant back with a sigh and closed his eyes. He did look tired, thought Martha, conscious of an alarming impulse to smooth the hair back from his forehead. The soft light from the lamps in the living room behind her spilled out through the sliding glass doors and lit the severe profile.

Martha's gaze drifted along the strong line of cheek and jaw to rest at the edge of that stern mouth where it faltered for a moment as she found herself remembering how it changed when he smiled. There was something intriguing about the way a mouth that looked cool could be transformed in an instant into warmth by the mere stretching of the muscles in his cheeks.

If a smile could have such a dramatic effect, what would a kiss do to it? Lewis seemed so reserved and self-contained, it was hard to imagine him as a lover…or maybe not, thought Martha, her eyes still on his mouth, and a queer feeling stirred inside her as a vivid picture sprang to mind of Lewis smiling, reaching for her, pulling her towards him, of how firm his hands would be on her, of how warm and exciting his lips would feel against hers…

Sucking in her breath, Martha wrenched her gaze away, aghast at how clearly she could imagine it, and at the way the mere thought of his mouth had triggered a tiny trembling just beneath her skin. What was she *doing*?

She sipped her coffee with a kind of desperation. *Stop it*, she told herself fiercely. Just be normal.

'Busy day?' she asked, wincing at the way her voice seemed to loop up and down, as if she really had kissed him.

Lewis opened his eyes and turned his head to look at her. 'More frustrating than busy,' he said. 'It always takes longer than you anticipate to get everything sorted out and everyone in the right place at the right time with the right equipment.'

'You don't just mix up your concrete and start pouring then?'

Lewis stared at her as if he couldn't decide whether she was joking or not.

'Do you know what's involved in setting up a fashion shoot?' said Martha with a shade of defiance.

'No.'

'Well, then.'

His expression relaxed slightly. 'OK,' he said, acknowledging the point with a half smile. 'So, no, we're not in a position to start pouring concrete yet. We won't be doing that for another fifteen months or so.'

'Fifteen *months*? That's over a year!'

Excellent, Martha, she thought, cringing inwardly at her own fatuous comment. Nothing like stating the obvious.

But she was terrified of what she might be tempted to do if they just sat in silence, so she had to keep him talking. Anything was better than sitting there and wondering about his mouth and how it would feel…

She cleared her throat. 'Why does it take so long before you can start building?'

'Why this sudden interest in the construction process?' asked Lewis a little suspiciously. He wouldn't have thought Martha was the type to be riveted by the nitty-gritty of civil engineering.

'I was just making conversation,' she said, a little ruffled. 'Besides, we're going to be spending the next six months together, so I might as well understand what you're going to be doing all day.'

Luckily, Lewis seemed to accept that. He started talking about feasibility studies and exploratory surveys, not much of which Martha understood, but she brightened when he mentioned the specialists who would be coming out to do the topographical and hydrological surveys and a detailed economic analysis.

'I may need to do some entertaining when they all arrive,' he said. 'Would you be able to cope with that, or should I ask around about someone who could cater?'

'No, I could do it,' said Martha quickly, thinking that if she was going to feel as self-conscious as this with him every evening, the more people who were around the better. 'I'd like to do it, in fact. I enjoy making special meals, and it would be great to meet some new people.'

She had only been here a day, thought Lewis, a little disgruntled. Wasn't it a bit soon for her to be craving a social life?

'Well…good,' he said, wishing he could sound as enthusiastic as she did at the prospect.

There was a short silence. Martha was suddenly acutely aware of the suck and sigh of the waves breaking on the shore, and the whispering of the palms as they swayed in the warm breeze.

And of Lewis sitting so still and self-contained beside her.

The silence was beginning to stretch uncomfortably. 'Go on with what you were saying about preliminary design,' she said with an edge of desperation.

She wondered if Lewis had been as aware of the silence as she had been. He certainly seemed grateful for the cue, and plunged back into an explanation of what was involved in designing and constructing two major projects simultaneously.

Most of it went over Martha's head, but it was easier to watch him when he was talking and she liked to see the austere face animated. All she needed to do was prompt him every now and then.

'What's an EIA again?' she asked, confused by the plethora of initials and acronyms.

'An Environmental Impact Assessment,' said Lewis, well into his stride by now. He was feeling better. The silence and the darkness and Martha's deep eyes unsettled him. It was easier to concentrate on talking about the project. He knew where he was with that.

'The World Bank require us to complete detailed studies about the impact any construction will have on the local habitat before funding goes ahead. So we'll get in a botanist to look at the airport site, and a marine biologist who's familiar with these waters to survey the port. We're going to have to dig a deep trench for ships and that can have an effect on bigger fish like sharks and—' He stopped, realising that Martha had straightened with new attention. 'What?'

'Did you say you would be needing a marine biologist?' Martha asked, feeling terrible that she had hardly given Rory a thought since she had arrived. The whole purpose of being here was to find him, and it had taken Lewis's casual mention of a marine biologist to remind her about him at all.

'What about it?' said Lewis, but with foreboding. Even as he said the words he knew that she was going to bring up Noah's father. Sure enough, her response came bang on cue.

'Rory's a marine biologist specialising in this part of the ocean.'

Lewis frowned. It had been a long day and he had just been starting to relax after the excellent meal Martha had cooked. He had got used to solitary evenings after Helen had left, and it had been nice to sit on the verandah and talk at the end of the day for a change. For a minute there he had forgotten just what Martha was doing in St Bonaventure, but she clearly hadn't.

'These are important projects,' he said crossly, knowing that he couldn't really justify his bad temper but unable to do anything about it. 'I can't run around dishing out jobs to any old Tom, Dick and Harry because he happens to be my nanny's boyfriend.'

Martha flushed with annoyance. 'It wouldn't occur to me to ask you to give Rory a job,' she snapped. 'I just thought that you might come across someone who would know him because they work in the same field.'

'It's possible,' Lewis allowed, knowing that it was more than likely. There weren't that many marine biologists qualified to do the EIA at the port, and it would be a small and specialised world.

'Well, when you do appoint a biologist, perhaps you could ask them if they know Rory,' she said, her voice cold. She didn't understand why Lewis was suddenly so grumpy.

'If I remember, and if an opportunity comes up,' he said grudgingly, 'but frankly I've got better things to do than track down your boyfriends for you! In any case, I won't be dealing with the marine survey immediately,' he went on while Martha was still struggling to frame a suitably crushing retort. 'There's plenty to do before we get round to finding a marine biologist.'

'In that case I'd better *track Rory down*, as you put it, myself,' said Martha tightly. 'It can't be that hard on an island this size.'

'I imagine not,' said Lewis in a frosty voice. 'It's no business of mine what you choose to do in your free time, but I'd be grateful if you'd remember that you're here primarily to look after my niece. I don't want her abandoned with Eloise while you chase after marine biologists.'

Tight-lipped, Martha got to her feet. How dared he suggest she would ignore Viola? 'Don't worry, I won't forget,' she said between clenched teeth, and headed inside before she really lost her temper and started telling her employer exactly what she thought about him.

Why had she mentioned Rory? They had been having a nice evening until then. A bit tense at times, perhaps, but not in a bad way. More in an intriguing, secretly exciting type of way. The kind of way that made you very aware of the scent of flowers and the sound of the sea and the warm breeze against your skin. That made you think about your employer in a way you really shouldn't be thinking about him.

Martha kicked off the sheet irritably. It was too hot, and she hadn't been sleepy, anyway, but there was nowhere else to go but bed.

Perhaps it was just as well Lewis had been so disagreeable about Rory, she tried to console herself. It had reminded her that at heart he was just as cold and unpleasant as he had seemed that first day she had met him in London.

There had been no need for him to jump down her throat like that. It was outrageous to suggest that she would neglect Viola. And it wasn't as if she hadn't made it very clear why she wanted to come to St Bonaventure. Anyone would think from the way he had carried on that she had demanded that he produce Rory on a plate for her!

Well, he needn't worry, Martha vowed fiercely. She didn't need Lewis's help. She would be the perfect nanny *and* she would find Rory by herself, and that would show him!

Restlessly, she punched her pillow into shape and threw herself back down, only for it to occur to her that wanting to prove her point to Lewis Mansfield was not the best of reasons for wanting to find Rory. She was supposed to be thinking about Noah's need for a father, not about Lewis.

And she *was*, Martha insisted to herself. It was just that she wanted to show Lewis too.

The next morning, she was determinedly cool. At least her early night had got her back into a more normal routine, and by seven she was in the kitchen with both babies installed in high chairs. None of them were dressed, but you couldn't have everything. Barefoot and wearing her old shirt, Martha had put some coffee on and was getting Viola and Noah a drink when Lewis came in.

'Good morning,' she said, frigidly polite and trying not to notice how crisp and cool he looked. It made her very conscious of her crumpled shirt and unwashed face. Surreptitiously, she wiped under her eyes and pushed her tousled hair behind her ears in an effort to disguise the fact that it was going in all directions.

'Would you like some breakfast?' she asked, the perfect servant.

'I'll just make myself some coffee, thanks.' Lewis seemed a bit disconcerted to find her there.

'There's some in the pot there.' Delighted to be able to demonstrate her efficiency, Martha nodded her head in the direction of the stove and, after a moment's hesitation Lewis went over and poured himself a mug.

Leaning against the counter, he watched her give Viola a two-handled mug and screw the top firmly on to Noah's. She was wearing that shirt again, the one that hung cool and loose and left her legs bare. It didn't cling, and it wasn't transparent or seductive in any way, but every time Lewis looked at it he couldn't help thinking about the fact that she was almost certainly naked underneath.

He made himself concentrate on his coffee instead. 'Look, I'm sorry about last night,' he said abruptly.

Martha looked up from Noah's mug. 'Last night?' she echoed cautiously.

'I could have been more understanding about the fact that you want to find Noah's father.'

Lewis had done some thinking after she had stalked off to bed, and he didn't feel good about the way he had behaved. He had tried telling himself that he was just being protective of Viola and afraid that Martha would simply forget about staying six months when she found Rory, but he had a nasty feeling that he had ended up sounding jealous instead.

'You made it clear that's why you were here,' he persevered, determined to get it all off his chest, 'and we came to an agreement on that basis. It'll be difficult for you to find out much in your free time, with so many places closed on a Sunday, so I just wanted you to know that I will ask around for you and let you know if I hear any news of Rory.'

Martha stared at him, thrown and more than a little frustrated. What was he doing apologising and being nice? If he was going to be totally unreasonable, the way he had been last night, it would really be better if he just stayed that way and then she would know where she was. As it was, she had no sooner fired herself up with a determination to prove him wrong than he had to go and deflate her by offering to find Rory himself. Really, it was almost perverse of him. She could hardly refuse to accept his help, though, could she?

'Oh…well…thank you,' she said awkwardly, not knowing what else she could say.

'It might not be immediately,' he warned, 'but I'll find out what I can.'

'No, that's OK, honestly. There's no hurry. I've got six months, after all.'

'Good.' Back to his usual brisk self, Lewis swallowed the last of his coffee in a gulp. 'I'd better go.'

He put his mug in the sink and headed for the door, only to turn at the last moment. 'By the way, nice shirt,' he said, straight-faced, and then he was gone, leaving Martha standing in the middle of the kitchen, still clutching Noah's mug.

Thirsty, and despairing of his mother ever noticing him while she had that funny expression on her face, Noah let out an indignant squawk. It had the desired effect. Martha started and handed him the mug, although with something less than her usual degree of attention. She was looking down at her bare legs instead and remembering the expression in Lewis's eyes as they rested on them.

Nice shirt? she was thinking, and the faintest of smiles curled her lips.

After the first week Martha felt as if she had been on St Bonaventure for ever. It had taken no time at all to fall into a routine and, with Eloise to help the sun-drenched days blended one into another. Her once chic wardrobe was reduced to a sleeveless T-shirt and a sarong, and her frenetic days in the *Glitz* office to a simpler, slower routine of shopping in the market, cooking, chatting to Eloise in the kitchen, and playing with Noah and Viola.

Some days she would put big floppy hats on their heads and take them down to the beach. Noah loved the water and would sit happily splashing in the lagoon for as long as Martha would let him stay in the sun, but Viola—typically—was more fastidious, and protested loudly if her hands got too sticky with sand.

It was often easier to let them both sit on a rug in the shade of the verandah. Martha never got tired of watching the wonder in their faces as they explored each new sensation. Savannah had sent out a ridiculous number of expensive toys for Viola, but she didn't need any of them. A battered saucepan or an empty plastic bottle to bang on the ground provided entertainment enough.

Martha felt calmer and more relaxed than she had in years, she realised, sitting in the tattered shade of the palms with the 'twins', as she had started to call them, asleep on a rug beside her. She had loved the frenetic life at *Glitz*, the gossip and the parties and the tantrums and the adrenalin rush of constant deadlines, but it seemed to belong to a parallel universe now, where a girl who looked just like her had splurged money on shoes and handbags and the latest must-have accessories without a thought for the future.

It was odd to be able to remember it all so clearly and yet feel as if the memories belonged to someone else entirely. She had had a wonderful time, that was for sure, but she didn't miss any of it.

How could she miss anything when she was in paradise? Martha wondered, watching a cat's paw of wind shiver across the lagoon.

Only…if this was paradise, why wasn't she completely happy?

She was getting paid to live in this beautiful place. The babies were gorgeous and blooming. All things considered, she had a pretty easy life.

It was just that sometimes she felt…Martha's brow furrowed as she sought for the right word…felt a little, well, *lonely*. Which was ridiculous when she had Eloise to talk to all day, and the fishermen and market traders to banter with when she went shopping.

And, in the evenings, there was Lewis.

Martha didn't like the way she looked forward to his return every day, or the way the dreamlike state in which she spent her days snapped into something more vivid the moment he walked through the door. It made her feel edgy and unsettled, as if she somehow wasn't quite complete until he was there.

It wasn't even as if Lewis made any particular effort to turn on the charm. Far from it. He was austere and often brusque, and there was an acid edge to his tongue at times. His logical approach to everything drove Martha mad, and they argued hotly at times. At least, *she* argued hotly. Lewis just sat there and infuriated her by being practical and rational and thinking things through before he opened his mouth.

So why did she start listening for his car at six o'clock, and why did a tiny thrill shiver down her spine as soon as he appeared?

She needed to meet more people, Martha decided. Make her life bigger. Wasn't that what the agony aunt at *Glitz* always said to readers? If she made the effort to get out more and develop a social life of her own, she wouldn't be so dependent on Lewis.

She ought to make an effort to find Rory too. And she would…just as soon as she had found her feet.

It was hard to get up the energy to make the effort, though, when the days blended into each other in a haze of sunshine and shushing waves and soft breezes. And when Lewis asked her that morning if she had any plans for the day, Martha could only look at him in surprise.

'Plans? No. Should I have?'

'It's Sunday,' he said. 'Your day off.'

'Oh.' How could you have a day off in paradise? Martha wondered.

'I thought you might like some time to yourself,' said Lewis. 'You could have the car, if you like. Take Noah with you, or leave him with me and Viola. It's up to you.'

'Well…I hadn't really thought,' she said uncertainly. Shouldn't the thought of a day on her own be more appealing? 'The thing is, I wouldn't want to leave Noah, but I don't think it's a good idea to split him and Viola up just when they're getting used to being together all the time.'

It was a pretty lame excuse, but Lewis seemed to fall for it.

'In that case, perhaps you'd like to go out to lunch?' he suggested. 'The office manager was telling me about a restaurant on the other side of the island. I gather it's not much more than a shack, but the fish is supposed to be excellent, and it's right on the beach so the twins aren't likely to be a problem.'

Martha liked the way he had started calling Noah and Viola the 'twins' without thinking about it.

'If nothing else, it would make a change for you if someone else did the cooking,' he said.

The trouble with Lewis was that it was impossible to tell what he was thinking most of the time. Was that austere air a cover for the fact that he really wanted to take her out to lunch, or was he just being polite?

And did it really matter? Martha asked herself. She wanted to go, whatever his reason for asking her, and there was no point in pretending that she didn't.

'That sounds wonderful,' she said. 'Thank you.'

'It's the least I can do after you've saved me from Eloise's okra stew,' he said gruffly. 'Bring a swimming costume. The water is deeper there and I'm told it's better for swimming.'

The office manager hadn't been exaggerating when he had said that the restaurant wasn't much more than a shack. Open on one side, its walls were cobbled together with a mixture of wood and tin, and the menu was scrawled on a bleached piece of driftwood, but the tables were set out under a shade made from woven palm leaves, the beer miraculously cold, and the fish the freshest Martha had ever seen.

'And it comes with built-in babysitters,' she said to Lewis as Viola and Noah were swept off by a group of women sitting at the next table who exclaimed over their fairness and insisted on looking after them. Noah was a bit doubtful at first, but Viola loved the attention, and after a while he succumbed and stopped looking over his shoulder for his mother.

'Your niece is a terrible flirt,' Martha said with mock severity. 'Look at the way she's batting her eyelashes and just revelling in the attention! I wish I had half her technique!'

Lewis looked across the table at Martha. She was smiling as she watched the women with the two babies. She had been careful not to get burnt, but a week in the sun had given her a glow. She had put on some weight, too, and in her sleeveless T-shirt and carelessly tied sarong she looked like another woman entirely from the one who had walked into his office that day.

Lewis's eyes dwelt on her face as he tried to work out where the difference lay. She wasn't classically beautiful, and without make-up he could see the fine lines around her eyes that betrayed her age. Her nose was too big and her mouth too wide for prettiness, but now that the chic, brittle air had vanished she looked relaxed and somehow much more appealing. She had grown familiar to him, too, he realised. It was as if he had always known the exact colour of her eyes, the tilt of her lashes, the way she pushed her hair behind her ears or smiled as she picked up a baby.

'I can't believe your technique ever needed any improvement,' he said without thinking, and Martha glanced at him.

'You'd be surprised,' she said ironically, thinking of some of her more unsatisfactory relationships. 'I certainly never had Viola's ability to twist perfect strangers round her little finger. She's going to be a force to be reckoned with when she grows up. I've never met a baby with so much character!'

Lewis looked at his niece, chortling and gurgling to the accompaniment of much cooing. 'Too much character sometimes,' he said in a dry voice. 'Noah is much more easygoing. I've been hoping his laid-back approach will rub off on Viola.'

'I doubt it,' said Martha, eyeing her small son fondly. 'He's just like his father—laid back and chilled out.'

'Can you really tell who he's like at this stage?' Lewis was unaccountably ruffled by the affection in her voice.

'Well, he's certainly not like me. I can't see any physical resemblance,' she admitted, 'but in temperament Noah is just like Rory. Rory was always incredibly easygoing too. When you're used to dealing with prima donnas all day it's incredibly refreshing to come across someone with such a sweet temper. He never needed anyone to dance attendance upon him or flatter him or tell him he was wonderful. He just lay back and let life wash over him.'

'Isn't that just another way of saying that he was completely passive?' said Lewis in a hard voice.

Martha frowned slightly and thought about it as she drank her beer. 'I don't think he was *passive*, exactly,' she said after a moment. 'I think it was more a sort of laziness. Rory never had to make much of an effort because he was so nice and so good-looking that people came to him. He's never going to make a fortune, but he'll probably have a good time, and there's a lot to be said for that.'

'Yes, it's a great life if you can get everyone else to do your dirty work for you,' Lewis agreed. 'All you've got to do is turn on the charm and let all those boring, sensible people take decisions and be responsible while you just get on with being laid-back and relaxed and at one with yourself.'

The unmistakable bitterness lacing his voice made Martha look at him curiously. 'It sounds like you're thinking of someone in particular,' she said. 'Your sister?'

'Savannah?' Lewis gave a mirthless laugh. 'No, she's certainly irresponsible, but if there's one thing you can't call Savannah it's "laid-back"!'

'Who, then?'

'I was thinking about my mother,' he admitted after a momentary hesitation. 'She's never been one to burden herself with responsibilities.'

'I didn't realise you had a mother,' said Martha without thinking.

'What, did you think I came into this world wearing a suit and tie?' he asked sardonically.

'Of course not,' she said, feeling a fool. 'Though, come to think of it, it's hard to imagine you as a little boy. What were you like?'

'Just the way I am now, I expect, but shorter.'

Martha gave him an old-fashioned look, and picked up her beer once more. 'You've never mentioned your mother before.'

'She's not a big part of my life.' He shrugged. 'She certainly didn't feature much in my childhood. It didn't take her long to get bored of marriage and motherhood, but I suppose she lasted longer than Savannah's mother, at least. I was about six when she left.'

Six? Martha couldn't believe a mother would walk out on a six-year-old. 'Why did she leave?'

'She wanted to "find herself".' Lewis hooked his fingers to add ironic quotation marks around the phrase. 'She's still searching, as far as I know,' he added dryly.

'Is she still alive?'

'Oh, yes. She drifts around the world pleasantly enough, I think. She's the kind of person who thinks it's oppressive to live in a house. She's always in some ashram, or tepee, or tribal longhouse, chanting about peace and love.'

Lewis took a pull of his beer and stared out at the sea glittering beyond the palm shade. 'She's not insincere. I think she probably really believes that if she stands on her head for a month, or only eats seaweed, that the world will change, but of course it doesn't. You'd think she'd get cynical after a while, but she never does.'

'Do you ever see her?'

'Occasionally. It's hard to think of her as a mother, really. She's just an eccentric stranger who turns up every now and then and enthuses about the latest alternative therapy that prevents her facing up to her own responsibilities.'

Martha looked across at the other table, where Noah was being cuddled against an ample bosom, and she shuddered. She couldn't bear the thought of him describing her as an eccentric stranger a few years down the line. But then, she couldn't imagine ever leaving him.

Her heart cracked at the thought of Lewis, aged six, left behind while his mother went off to find something more interesting to do, and her fingers curled in her lap. It wasn't surprising that he had a jaundiced view of women with the example he had been set by the women in his own family.

She glanced at him from under her lashes. He was watching the sea, his mouth set in a grim line, and she sensed that he was revisiting some unhappy memories.

'I always wanted to be laid-back, but I was never very good at it,' she said to lighten the tone. 'I was a terrible swot at school, and very ambitious. I always knew that I wanted to work on a magazine, and I loved my job, but after a while it just took over my life. You're always looking over your shoulder at the others coming behind you, and you know that if you mess up just once you'll be stabbed to death by all the stilettos trampling over you while you're down.'

Lewis had turned to listen to her, and she was glad to see that the bitterness had gone from his face. 'You can't afford to relax when you're under that kind of pressure. You spend your whole life running on adrenalin, because that's the only way you're going to make the next party, the next deadline, the next edition, the next season's looks.'

She shook her head, remembering. 'When I think about it now, I was permanently tense. It's not good to live like that.'

Lewis's eyes rested on her. 'You've changed,' he said.

CHAPTER SIX

MARTHA smiled reluctantly. 'Noah has changed me,' she said. 'I wouldn't have changed by myself, I don't think. I never have had the time to think about what I might want to change into,' she added thoughtfully. 'It's not always a bad thing to slow down, and it's not the same as opting out completely.'

'No, I know.'

'I don't regret it for a moment,' she went on, her eyes on Noah, 'but for a time there after Noah was born it was really scary. I felt as if my entire life was unravelling. One minute I had a great social life, a fantastic job, and lots of money, and the next it seemed as if it had all gone. I hadn't realised how interconnected they all were. When one fell apart, the others did too.'

She grimaced at the memory of how lonely it had been. Most of her friends had worked for *Glitz*, so as soon as she lost her job she had been out of the gossip loop, and that was fatal.

It wasn't that anyone had deliberately dropped her, but the fact was that they were all living the free-wheeling life she had enjoyed for so long, and she just didn't fit into it any more. They worked hard and they played hard, and they didn't have children to go home to. They could afford to go out and enjoy themselves, and had the stamina to stay out all night, just as she had once done.

'It's frightening how quickly everything gets out of control,' she confessed to Lewis. 'Slowing down is fantastic in a place like this—' gesturing at the idyllic beach in front of them '—but when you've slowed right down in an expensive city with no money and all your friends are busy with careers and there's no one to help you with your new baby, it's not so much fun.

'That's why I'm really grateful to you for giving me this job.' Martha turned back to smile at Lewis. 'If I hadn't had this chance to unwind I'm not sure how much longer I could have gone on without snapping. I've only been here a week and already I feel like a completely different person.' She let out a long sigh. 'Thank you,' she said simply.

'There's no need to thank me,' said Lewis gruffly, averting his eyes from her smile. 'You're doing a good job.'

He stared at the bay, wondering how he could look at the water and see only her smile shimmering in front of his eyes.

'I just hope you'll feel the same in six months' time,' he said.

'I think I will,' said Martha.

'Will you? You've talked about the kind of life you used to have, hectic work, frenetic social life, always on the go…you don't think there's a danger that you'll get bored here after a while?'

Not if you're here too. The words hovered on Martha's tongue, springing there so immediately that for an awful moment she thought she had actually said them aloud.

And how would she explain *that*?

She stared out as Lewis had done, beyond the tatty shade to the glare of the white sand and the glittering water. She was suddenly, intensely conscious of the cold beer in her hand, of the press of the rickety wooden chair underneath her thighs, and the smell and sizzle of fish being cooked in the shack behind her. The chatter of the women at the next table had faded to a background murmur, and there was only Lewis, sitting still and solid and somehow, suddenly, sexy as hell.

Uh-oh.

'I…er…I probably do need to make more of an effort to meet people,' she said. 'We've been settling in this week, but now that we've got a routine I can find out if there's anything like a mother and baby group in Perpetua.' Martha tried to sound enthusiastic about the prospect.

'I was thinking more about you needing some adult company,' said Lewis. 'Leave the twins with Eloise one day, and come and have lunch in town. I'll introduce you to some people.'

Martha glanced at him uncertainly. Why was he so keen for her to expand her social life? What if he was afraid that *he* was one who would be bored with just her for company for the next six months? Was that what she had come to? Martha Shaw, social burden?

She cringed at the very thought. Well, Lewis needn't worry if that was the case. It ought to be easy enough to show him that she wasn't the needy type, and had no intention of hanging around the house all day waiting for him to come home.

The way she had been doing all week, in fact.

That was all going to change. 'Would you really?' she said brightly. 'That sounds fantastic! I'd love to meet some new people.'

Lewis looked a bit taken aback by her show of eagerness, but he nodded. 'I'll let you know,' he said.

Reclaiming the two babies from the neighbouring table, they fed them on their laps before their own meals arrived. It was so much easier when there were two of you, Martha thought.

Of course, Eloise was usually there to help, but it was different with Lewis. Martha couldn't quite think of a good reason why it should be so, she just knew that it was.

She looked across the table. Lewis had Noah on his lap, and was giving him a piece of banana that he had just retrieved from his shirt. The strong nose wrinkled fastidiously at the mess Noah had made of it already, but when he glanced up and caught Martha's eye he grinned, and the breath snared in her throat as something shifted dangerously inside her.

'Disgusting, aren't they?' he said, and she managed to tear her eyes away.

'Revolting,' she agreed shakily.

Afterwards, the babies slept in the shade while Martha and Lewis ate lunch. The fish was as delicious as promised, but Martha couldn't concentrate on the meal. She was terribly aware of Lewis, for some reason, and nervous of the silence that fell whenever she looked at him and thought about his hands and his mouth, and wondered what it would feel like if she could reach across and run her fingers along the strong forearm, down over the soft, dark hairs to the broad wrist and the back of his hand, what it would be like to be able to lace her fingers between his and turn his hand over and lift his palm to her mouth…

Gulping, she made herself talk brightly instead, and whenever a pause loomed she asked him another question about the project, and the firm, and how he had set it up with a friend three years ago.

'We've got a very small staff at the moment,' Lewis told her, a bit wary of her almost feverish interest but deciding it was easier to answer than to probe as to why she was suddenly acting so nervous. 'We have resident engineers on each site, but otherwise we employ freelance specialists, and I move between sites just to keep an eye on things or, like now, get the project up and running.'

'It must mean a lot of travelling for you.'

'It makes sense for me to do it. Mike is married and he's got a young family, so he stays in London and runs our head office. I don't have any commitments so I'm much more flexible.'

'Don't you ever get tired of it?' she asked.

'Of travelling?'

Martha turned her head to look straight at him. 'Of not having any commitments to go home to,' she said.

There was a pause. Lewis found himself staring back at her as if riveted by the brown eyes, until he managed to wrench his gaze away.

'I decided a long time ago that I wasn't getting involved with family life,' he said flatly. 'I'm not going to be responsible for putting any more children through what Savannah and I went through.'

'You know, it doesn't have to be that way,' she said quietly. 'Not all mothers walk out on their children.'

'Maybe not, but in my experience it doesn't take them long to get bored, no matter what they say about the joys of being a mother.'

Lewis's expression was hard. 'Did I tell you that I had an email from Helen yesterday?'

Helen. The beautiful girlfriend. The one he missed.

Martha stiffened in spite of herself. 'Oh?'

'She told me she'd had a baby girl, and was ecstatically happy.'

Was he jealous? 'Oh. Well…that's good.'

'Helen's gone back to work already, but she tells me that the nanny is wonderful,' Lewis went on abrasively. 'Apparently I've got no idea how fantastic family life can be.'

'I don't know about that,' said Martha. 'Here you are, sitting over Sunday lunch, with two babies sleeping under a tree. Isn't that what family life is all about?'

Lewis glanced over towards Viola and Noah, sleeping soundly the way only babies could.

'We're not a family,' he said.

'Not officially, but we're two adults and two children, and we're living together. We count as a temporary family, don't we?'

'But that's the thing about families,' he objected. 'They're not temporary. Families should stay together, shouldn't they?'

Martha's smile evaporated as she thought about Noah and what she wanted for him.

Lewis was right. Temporary wasn't good enough.

'Yes,' she said, 'they should.'

'Have you got any plans for today?' Lewis asked one morning later the following week as he swallowed the last of his coffee.

'Just the usual,' said Martha, wiping Viola's face and hands. 'Why?'

'I thought you might like to come into town and I'll take you out to lunch. Eloise will keep an eye on these two, won't she?'

'I'm sure she will.' Martha concentrated on not looking too excited. It was only lunch after all. And it was only Lewis. Not exactly a hot date, then. And no reason for her heart to start skittering around in her chest.

'About twelve-thirty, then?'

'Sure. Fine. Thanks.'

She couldn't wait for him to go so that she could start smiling.

'And don't look at me like that,' she told Noah and Viola, who were staring at her with identically sceptical expressions. 'I'm allowed to go out to lunch, aren't I? I'm not going to do anything stupid.'

Like fall for a man who had made it crystal-clear that he wasn't going to be part of any family. Martha sobered at the thought. It would be too easy to forget, but a family was what Noah needed. Lewis hadn't said anything more about asking around about Rory, and she hadn't liked to nag him about it.

Hadn't thought about it at all, she corrected herself guiltily.

She really should make more of an effort. The days were slipping by, and she hadn't even *tried* to find Rory herself. It was hard to believe now that she had spent all those months in London fixated on the idea of getting out here so that she could introduce Noah to his father. Somehow it didn't seem quite so important now, and Martha felt ashamed of herself. Rory was Noah's father. He was the reason she was here, and it was still important to find him.

Maybe Lewis would introduce her to some people today. She could ask if anyone knew Rory. That was a better reason for wanting to go to lunch than the thought of sitting next to Lewis and hearing his voice and watching the way his eyes creased when he smiled.

She had agreed to meet him at a restaurant in Perpetua's one and only main street.

Martha's plan was to get there early and to be waiting serenely when Lewis arrived but, as so often in life, things didn't quite turn out the way she had imagined them. First Noah needed his nappy changed, and then Viola threw a tantrum which meant that Martha forgot to take her umbrella, which was just asking for the heavens to open, which they duly did, waiting until she just about halfway so she was going to get drenched whichever way she ran.

So serene was the last thing Martha was feeling as she squelched up the restaurant steps nearly twenty minutes late. She paused in the doorway, wiping the rain from her face with the back of her hands, and making a futile attempt to wring the worst of the water from her dress.

She had deliberately chosen a pretty one that Lewis hadn't seen before. She had bought it years earlier, when boho chic was all the rage and, although it was old and faded now, it was still one of her favourites. The soft colours and floaty material always made her feel very feminine.

The effect wasn't the same when it was wet. Glancing down at herself, Martha was aghast to realise that the material was practically transparent. Thank God she had worn a bra!

Grimacing, she looked up with a twist of material still between her hands, and spotted Lewis sitting on the far side of the restaurant. He was with a woman about Martha's own age, and she forgot about her dress for a moment as her eyes narrowed. The tables in between them were full, and she couldn't see much beyond the fact that the other woman was very elegant and very blonde. Very attractive, too, if ice maidens were your thing, Martha supposed sourly.

And it looked as if they might be Lewis's. He wasn't exactly fawning over the woman—this was Lewis Mansfield, after all, and fawning was not his style—but he was sitting forward and listening, nodding occasionally, and his body language said that he was definitely interested.

Martha's heart sank. Had he used lunch with her as an excuse to invite the other woman along, or had he joined her when it looked as if Martha wasn't coming? Either way, it didn't look as if he needed her now. Perhaps she should just slip away?

But she had hesitated too long. Lewis glanced across the room and saw her lurking in the doorway, and for a fleeting instant his face blazed with an expression that was so quickly veiled by his normal, slightly exasperated look that Martha had no chance to interpret it and decided in the end that she must have imagined it. He was beckoning her irritably now. Too late to make her escape.

Martha made her way across the restaurant, leaving a trail of wet footprints on the wooden floor. Her dress was clinging to her, clammy and uncomfortable, and her hair was hanging in rats' tails. She didn't feel pretty and feminine now. She felt like a moron.

Lewis got to his feet as she reached the table. 'Where on earth have you been?' he said by way of a greeting. 'I was beginning to think something had happened to you.'

'Something did happen to me—your niece! I was late by the time I'd sorted her out, and then I was rushing, and of course I forgot my umbrella…'

'So I see.' Lewis's derisive gaze rested on her for a quelling moment before he pulled out a chair between him and the ice maiden. Martha was depressed to note that close up she looked even crisper and more elegant than she had from a distance.

'You'd better sit down,' he said. 'That dress isn't decent.'

He made the introductions. The ice maiden was called Candace Stephens. 'Candace is manager of a new resort that's just been opened along the coast from here,' he told Martha.

'We're hoping to take advantage of the new airport.' Candace smiled prettily, but Martha wasn't fooled. Candace was interested in more than the length of Lewis's runways. She could see it in her eyes.

'Martha is Viola's nanny,' Lewis finished the introductions.

Oh, that was great! How to make her feel completely insignificant in one easy move! Viola's nanny…was that really all she was?

'And cook,' said Martha defiantly. 'Don't forget that.'

'It must be marvellous to have a job where you use your hands,' sighed Candace. 'So much more relaxing than spending all day in boring meetings—oh, I don't mean with *you*!' She laughed across the table at Lewis and put out her hand towards him, although he hadn't fed her any cue and, indeed, had his distant look on.

Martha eyed Candace with dislike. Why not come right out and accuse her of having a mindless job while they were having high-powered meetings about how many jumbo jet-loads of tourists could land at his precious airport?

'Well, it's a nice idea,' she said frostily, 'but you don't get much chance to relax when you're looking after two babies.'

'Two?' Candace lifted perfectly shaped eyebrows, the kind of brows Martha used to have in the days when she had had time to go to a beautician. 'I thought you just had your niece with you?' she said to Lewis.

Oh, so she and Lewis had been exchanging life stories, had they? Martha wiped a trickle of water from her neck and opened the menu with a snap. She didn't know what was worse, that he had told her about Viola, or that he hadn't mentioned Noah.

'Noah is Martha's son,' said Lewis. 'He's the same age as Viola, so they do everything together.'

He was trying not to look at Martha, but it was difficult when she was sitting there with that damned dress clinging to her and her eyes snapping dangerously. Her lashes were spiky with rain, her hair still plastered to her head, and a drop of water was trickling tantalisingly from her clavicle down towards her cleavage.

Lewis wanted to reach out and stop it with his finger, to stop her looking disturbingly sexy. He didn't like the way the other men in the restaurant had followed her with their eyes as she walked across the room.

He wished he hadn't invited her to lunch now. Seeing her on her own like this made it harder to think of her as just Viola's nanny, just an employee. But he'd promised to introduce her to some people, and he'd thought that she and Candace would get on.

Big mistake. They both had that tight-jawed look of people forced to be polite and hating every second of it.

'Oh, you've got a baby?' Candace was saying with an unnecessarily baffled air, as if Noah were a giraffe, or a pet slug.

'That's right,' said Martha tersely, without lifting her eyes from the menu. 'I'm a single mother.'

'How brave of you!'

Martha looked up at that. 'Why do you say that?' she asked with a challenging stare.

'Well, it's a lot to take on, isn't it?' The pitying note in Candace's voice set Martha's teeth on edge. 'It's exhausting enough when you can share the child care with a partner. I can't tell you how many friends I've seen go from bright, go-ahead women to brain-dead zombies who can't talk about anything except breast pumps and sleeping patterns! They all had really promising careers, but they've given it all up—and for what? The torture of no sleep and no stimulation!'

Candace gave an exaggerated shudder. 'It's not for me.'

'No, it doesn't sound as if you would be a very good mother,' said Martha evenly. 'You should have lots in common with Lewis, though. He's not keen on procreating either, are you?'

Lewis frowned but Candace's eyes narrowed with renewed interest. After that, there was no stopping her. She manoeuvred the conversation to business, and kept it firmly there.

Martha wondered what she was supposed to contribute. A bright account of how many nappies she had changed yesterday, perhaps, or a description of Viola's runny nose?

As it was, she ate her lunch and observed Candace's technique sourly. She could practically see the other woman's mind working furiously. There wouldn't be that many eligible men on an island this size, and Martha could just imagine how Candace's eyes must have lit up when Lewis swam into view.

She had probably been disappointed when she discovered that they weren't lunching alone, and it may have seemed on paper as if Viola's nanny, actually sharing a house with him, would be a bit of a threat, but one look at Martha in her bedraggled state must have reassured her. And, of course, knowing that he had no interest in babies either would mean that they had one more thing in common.

Surely, Candace was no doubt thinking, Lewis would be looking for a woman who was as dedicated to her career as he was. That would explain why she was rabbiting on about it, Martha thought, profoundly unimpressed. Candace was only managing a hotel, for God's sake. It didn't take a genius to organise a rota for receptionists or make sure the chambermaids changed the towels, did it? Anyone would think Candace was finding a cure for cancer the way she was carrying on.

It was difficult to tell what Lewis thought of her. Martha studied him from under her lashes. He responded politely enough, and she had to admit that he made an effort to include her in the conversation, but Candace wasn't having any of it. She was bent on pointing up the contrast between her own blonde elegance and efficiency and Martha, left wet and crumpled and with nothing to talk about.

It would have been amusing if Candace hadn't been quite so pretty, Martha thought glumly. She was tall and statuesque, with perfect skin and green eyes, and her platinum blonde hair was drawn back from her face in a neat French twist. She would have been beautiful if she had more warmth and animation.

But maybe Lewis didn't care about that. He was hardly the king of warm and caring himself, was he? Martha sighed as she put down her fork, thinking of how much she had looked forward to her lunch. She should have known. If they could have spoken, even Noah and Viola could probably have told her that it would turn out like this.

She had been living in a dangerous dream world where the fact that Lewis didn't want children and didn't want to be part of a family and wouldn't want her even if he did was conveniently forgotten. Time to wake up and smell the coffee, as they had said at *Glitz*.

'I'd better get back,' she said as soon as she had finished eating. 'It's not fair to leave Eloise too long with the twins. Don't get up,' she added as Lewis made to push back his chair. 'You two stay and finish your meal.'

Lewis looked as if he were about to protest but Candace was smiling prettily. 'I'd love a coffee,' she said, apparently deciding that the leisure industry could survive a few more minutes without her.

'I'll see you later,' Martha said coolly to Lewis. 'Thanks for lunch.'

'You're very quiet,' Lewis said later that night, when the babies were in bed and Martha was serving up supper.

'You know me,' said Martha, banging saucepans around. 'Nothing to talk about except breast pumps and sleeping patterns! I don't want to bore you.'

The odd thing was that he had never felt bored when he was with Martha. Why was that? Lewis wondered, distracted for a moment, but she was obviously in a bad mood and it wasn't hard to guess the reason why.

Sighing, he moved out of her way as she reached for a salad bowl. 'Look, I'm sorry about lunch,' he said. 'I only invited Candace because you said you wanted to meet some new people. I thought you would get on.'

'Really?' said Martha tightly, tearing up lettuce with a kind of savagery. 'What on earth made you think that?'

Lewis shrugged. 'You're both the same sort of age, both single women, both expats…'

'Oh, and that's supposed to make us friends, is it? Forget the fact that we have absolutely nothing else in common!'

'I didn't realise that when I invited her to lunch,' he said, holding on to his temper with difficulty. 'I met her at some meeting and she said she'd just arrived on the island and hadn't had a chance to make many friends. I hardly know her.'

'You surprise me.' Martha took a knife to some tomatoes. 'She seemed to think that she knew *you*. No prizes for guessing whose friend Candace wants to be!'

He looked wary. 'What do you mean?'

'Come on, Lewis, it's obvious she's interested in you! I've never felt such a gooseberry. She didn't want me there, spoiling things and being downtrodden and boring and oppressed by motherhood!'

Lewis sucked in an irritable breath. 'I've told you, I barely know Candace.'

'Well, that can change. You should go for it,' said Martha with a brittle smile as she scraped the tomatoes into the bowl. To hell with presentation. 'Candace's perfect for you. You know she's not going to do a Helen and go all broody on you, so you can have a lovely time comparing your high-powered careers and pitying poor schmucks like me who tie themselves down with children and think happiness and love and security are more important than promotion or winning some contract!'

Lewis's mouth tightened. He didn't understand why she was so cross. So lunch hadn't been a success. It wasn't his fault they hadn't got on, was it? At least he had made an effort to introduce her. There was no need for all this fuss. If anything, she should have been grateful.

He scowled as Martha put the salad on the dining table. He didn't like it when women were irrational like this. He didn't like their baffling leaps of logic. But mostly he didn't like the way he hadn't been able to stop thinking about her in that wet dress.

He had hardly got any work done that afternoon. It was pathetic. Pathetic how disappointed he had been to come home and find her back in loose trousers and a sleeveless shirt, looking cool and chic and utterly different from the way she had looked in the restaurant, all hot and bothered and dripping, with the sodden dress clinging to her skin so that he could see her warm curves—

'What?' He jerked back to attention.

'I said, are you coming to sit down?'

'Yes.' Lewis cleared his throat. 'Yes, of course.'

Viola was fretful all evening and Martha had to get up from the table to her a couple of times. 'I think she might be getting a cold,' she said, feeling the hot little forehead. 'If she's not better in the morning I'll find a doctor.'

In the meantime, there was a whole night to get through. Martha dosed the baby up with what she had, but Viola refused to settle. She would wake up crying, allow herself to be comforted and go back to sleep, only to start again a few minutes later.

Eventually, she woke Noah, who started to grizzle. Martha had Viola in one arm, and was leaning over Noah's cot, trying to comfort him with her other hand, when Lewis appeared.

'It sounds like you need a hand,' he said.

Martha was too tired by then to stand on ceremony. She had no idea what time it was, and her ears were ringing with the combined sound of two crying babies. 'Do you think you could walk Noah round for a bit while I give Viola some water?'

She made up a bottle in the kitchen one-handed, and took it back into the living area to collapse onto the sofa. Cradling Viola in her arms, she offered her the drink and, to her relief, it seemed to be what the baby wanted. She stopped crying, and for a while there was a blissful silence. Martha let her head fall back against the cushions in weary relief.

Lewis was pacing up and down in front of the sliding doors that led out on to the verandah. He was wearing the same loose grey pyjama bottoms that he had worn before, and was holding Noah against his bare chest. Martha watched him languorously from under drooping lashes. He was rubbing the baby's back, the big hands circling in a gentle rhythm, while Noah cuddled into his neck and sucked his thumb, a sure sign that he was comforted.

Lucky Noah. The thought popped treacherously into Martha's head and she straightened abruptly and turned her attention back to Viola.

'How's she doing?' Lewis asked softly.

'Fine.' Martha's voice sounded horribly brittle. 'I think she may sleep after this. I hope so, anyway.'

'This little chap's almost asleep too.'

To her horror, he came to sit next to her on the sofa, and every single one of Martha's senses jerked and jangled with a disturbing awareness. Stretching out his legs in front of him, Lewis let out a long, weary breath. 'It would be nice to get some sleep tonight,' he said.

'Yes,' said Martha huskily, her eyes riveted on his feet because that seemed safer than staring at the rest of him, but even they were distracting. Nice toes, she found herself thinking. Nice everything.

He was so close. Not awkwardly so, but definitely close enough to touch if she wanted to. Which she didn't. Shouldn't, anyway.

But her fingers still itched to reach out and feel the solid warmth of his body. That would be a bad idea, Martha reminded herself. A very bad idea, because…because… She sought frantically for a reason why it would be so bad.

Because of her responsibility to Noah. She seized on the thought. That was right. Noah needed a father, so there was no point in getting involved with a man who didn't want children, didn't want a family, a man with whom she and her son could never share a future.

It wasn't even as if Lewis were that attractive, she told herself with an edge of desperation. His nose was too big, his brows too fierce, his jaw too strong. He was dour and deliberate and infuriatingly logical. He was stern and stubborn, reserved and probably repressed. There was no reason to find him attractive.

No reason to want to touch him, to know whether his mouth was as cool and firm as it looked. No reason to want the feel of his hands on her body. No reason to think about burrowing into him and pressing her lips to his throat and tasting his skin.

No reason at all. Martha drew a shuddering breath and Lewis turned his head to look at her closely.

'You must be tired,' he said.

'Yes…yes, I am tired,' she said huskily

That must be all it was. It was dark and late and the tropical night was heady with perfume and the rasp of insects and the seductive murmur of the ocean beyond the palms, and she was just tired. That was why her heart was thumping in time with the ceiling fan overhead. That was why her blood was beating and booming beneath her skin, and her mind was fuzzy with desire, and her bones had dissolved.

Tiredness. That was all it was.

'Let me see if he'll go down.' Lewis levered himself up and took Noah into the bedroom. Half relieved, half disappointed, Martha remembered Viola and looked down to see her ridiculously long lashes fluttering and the teat of the bottle slipping from her mouth. She was asleep too.

'I'll take her.' Lewis was back. Reaching down, he lifted his niece gently from Martha's arms, and the brush of his hands against her bare skin was enough to make her heart clench with desire.

She should get up and go to bed. Martha knew that, but she couldn't move. She felt boneless and giddy. *I'm just tired*, she said to herself like a mantra. Just tired. *That's all.*

CHAPTER SEVEN

'COME on, time for bed.' Lewis spoke above her, and Martha opened her eyes, huge and dark in the dim light. There was something odd about his voice, but she couldn't pinpoint what it was.

'I'm too tired to move,' she managed. 'I think I'll stay here.'

'You'd be better off in bed.' Lewis held down a hand. 'Here, I'll help you up.'

Martha stared at his hand. She had the oddest feeling that her whole life had come down to this moment, that she had reached the point where her future forked. Taking his hand would lead one way, refusing it another.

She shook her head slightly. This was silly. She was so tired she wasn't thinking straight. Lewis wasn't offering her a life-changing choice. He was offering her a hand to help her upright.

She smiled wearily up at him. 'Sorry, I'm just a bit dopey,' she said, and took his hand.

As soon as she felt his fingers close firmly around hers, Martha knew that she had made a mistake. He drew her up, but it was as if all her bones had liquefied, so that she had to cling to his hand as the only thing holding her upright. Her legs gave way and she would have fallen if Lewis hadn't felt her buckle and clamped her instinctively to him.

Martha gasped at the feel of his body, just as hard and solid as she had imagined. His bare shoulder was only millimetres from her mouth, his skin a breath away from her own. With one detached part of her mind she knew that it should be possible to avoid Lewis's gaze and step past him with a polite apology, but somehow she couldn't do it. Something a lot stronger and more insistent made her lift her eyes instead and look straight into Lewis's face, and what she read there made the breath leak from her lungs.

There was a long, long moment when time seemed to stretch into infinity as they stared at each other. Afterwards, Martha was never sure what had shattered that breathless pause. Did she kiss Lewis, or did he kiss her? It didn't matter, anyway. All that mattered was that in a burst of glorious release from the tension they were kissing, deep, hot, hungry kisses, and it felt wonderful.

Gasping, still kissing, they sank back down on to the sofa, and she wrapped her arms around him, craving the feel of his body, so hard, so sure against hers. Dizzy with the relief of being able to touch him at last, she ran her hands over his bare back, down his flanks, up over his shoulders, revelling in the feel of him, and all the time his mouth was demanding, his hands insistent, exploring, under her knees, over her thighs, easing beneath her shirt until she shuddered and arched towards him.

God, it felt so good! Martha couldn't remember how she had been able to convince herself that it would be a bad idea. It was a great idea. A *fantastic* idea. How could anything that felt this exciting and right not be?

She wound her arms around him and kissed Lewis back as he rolled her beneath him, tipping her head back to let him press kisses down the side of her neck in a way that made her shiver deliciously. Her head was spinning with sheer sensation, and there was nothing but the feel of his body and the touch of his lips and their ragged breathing…

…and dimly, distantly, the sound of a baby crying.

Lewis heard it at the same time and he stilled, dropping his forehead on to her shoulder for a moment before he lifted his head reluctantly and looked down into Martha's face.

She never forgot the way his expression cleared with shock. 'God, what am I doing?' he said blankly.

Martha had never been with a man who had kissed her the way Lewis had, or made her feel the way he had, but she had certainly had kisses that ended with more finesse. As a way of letting her know that he hadn't meant to kiss her at all, and was horrified to realise that he had, it could hardly be bettered. Anyone would think he had picked up a slug in the dark.

Mortified, Martha struggled upright. 'That's Viola,' she managed shakily. 'I'd better go.'

Lewis put his head in his hands with a muttered expletive as she tugged down her shirt, ignoring the fact that it was too late for modesty, and somehow made it on trembling legs to Viola's cot. A few gentle pats and a murmured word were all it took to reassure the baby, who was soon asleep again.

Martha lingered by the cot, envying Viola her ability to relax completely. If only a few pats were enough to comfort *her*! Not that there were likely to be many pats coming her way in the near future. Judging by Lewis's expression as he levered himself off her, he would never touch her again.

Martha's throat closed painfully at the thought. Was it her fault? Had she just grabbed him? she wondered desperately. Oh, God, what if she had? What if he had just been too polite to push her away? A deep flush spread through her as she remembered how wonderful it had felt to kiss him, how eagerly she had responded. She had been all over Lewis, kissing him, touching him. No wonder he had been horrified!

Martha looked down at the sleeping babies and wished she could be sound asleep too. Maybe then she would wake up and find that she hadn't made a complete fool of herself in front of Lewis after all. But her body was still twitching and tingling, and her lips were swollen, and the memories were much, much too vivid to have been a dream.

Which meant that some time she was going to have to stop lurking in here and face him again. And say what? Sorry, Lewis, just got a bit carried away by my hormones there? Was it too late to blame it on jet lag? Except feeling jet lagged didn't normally involve dragging your employer on to a sofa and ravishing him.

Sighing, Martha ran her fingers through her hair in despair.

'Is Viola all right?'

Lewis's voice in the doorway made her heart jerk so violently it was a moment before she could speak.

'She's fine,' she muttered.

He hesitated. 'Are you OK?'

'I'm fine,' said Martha, still without looking at him.

Another pause, and then Lewis turned on his heel. 'I'll leave you to it, then,' he said curtly. A moment later Martha heard the sound of his bedroom door being very firmly closed. He was probably wedging a chair under the handle in case she tried to follow him.

So, that was one problem solved. If Lewis was going to pretend that nothing had happened she would be spared the need to come up with a convincing explanation as to why she had jumped him like that.

Martha was torn between relief and a gathering fury. How dared he pretend nothing had happened? Something most definitely had happened! And, OK, it might have been her that started it, but it took two, and he had been joining in there. If Viola hadn't cried…

Just thinking about what would have happened if Viola hadn't woken up right then made Martha want to bang on Lewis's bedroom door and demand that he finish what he had started. It wasn't fair to set her on fire like that and then decide to *leave her to it.*

It was probably better, though. Martha blew out a long sigh. Lewis was right. The situation was awkward for both of them, but they were grown-ups, so they would just have to deal with it. And the best way to do that was to ignore the fact that they had kissed at all, forget the thrill of his hands and his lips on her body, pretend that she didn't know how it felt to be pressed beneath that hard body, that she couldn't imagine the rocketing excitement, that she had never arched to his touch. That she hadn't wanted it to stop.

If Lewis could do all that, then so could she.

She could try, anyway.

* * *

'I owe you an apology.'

Lewis put his mug down on the counter and looked straight at Martha. They had exchanged strained greetings when she carried Noah into the kitchen early the next day. After her active night, Viola was still sleeping peacefully, and Martha concentrated fiercely on putting Noah in his high chair, finding him a drink, anything other than face the taut silence.

She had hardly slept, and her body was buzzing and thumping in a peculiar combination of exhaustion and frustration. Her only consolation had been the certainty that Lewis wouldn't say anything so that she could pretend that nothing had ever happened at all, and now here he was, raising the subject before she was in any state to discuss anything, let alone that. She wasn't even dressed, and it didn't help that Lewis now knew for sure exactly how little she wore underneath her old shirt.

'There's no need for you to apologise,' she said almost crossly.

'I think there is.'

Lewis set his jaw. He wished she wasn't wearing that shirt. It reminded him too vividly of the night before, when she had been sitting in the half-light, and as she had cradled the baby in her arms one sleeve had slipped slightly off her shoulder to reveal the seductive line of her clavicle. Her hair had been mussed and her eyes dark. She had looked tired and tousled and sexy, and he hadn't been able to keep his eyes off her, or stop thinking about what it would be like to touch her.

He hadn't meant to kiss her. He had thought that he had himself well under control, thought that he had taken on board all the reasons why touching her would be a really bad idea. When he had held down his hand to help her up he had really believed that the best thing would be if they went to their very separate beds.

But then she had fallen against him and he had felt how soft she was, and how warm, and his mind had gone blank, and the next thing he had known they were on the sofa and all his stern resolutions had evaporated in the excitement that rocketed so unexpectedly and so unstoppably. Only a saint would have remembered that he wasn't supposed to kiss her at all.

'I should never have touched you last night,' he said, squaring his shoulders. 'I didn't mean to, and I'm still not quite sure how it happened, but that's no excuse. It was unacceptable to grab you like that and…'

He trailed off into a sizzling pause while they both remembered what had come next.

'Anyway,' said Lewis, regrouping with an effort, 'I'm sorry. You're my employee and you'd be well within your rights to object to the way I behaved last night. I'm paying you to look after Viola, not to…to…' He was getting on to dangerous ground again. He had a nasty feeling he was making things worse, not better. Maybe it would be better not to finish that sentence?

'You should feel safe,' he said instead, 'and not as if you're going to be harassed like that at any time.'

Martha eyed him a little uncertainly. The disjointed apology had banished her crossness with him for raising the matter at all far more effectively than a fluent one would have done. Lewis was a proud man and it must have cost him a lot, she realised. And it really wasn't fair for him to take all of the blame on himself.

'I wouldn't call it harassment,' she said carefully. 'It was just…one of those things. We were both tired, and I think we both got a bit carried away. I don't think either of us really knew what we were doing.'

Lewis was a little daunted by her coolness. *Just one of those things?* She made it sound as if she got kissed on sofas like that all the time. He shook himself mentally. He ought to be grateful that Martha was taking the whole business in her stride, and not storming off back to London or ringing up her solicitor to press charges.

'It's kind of you to look at it that way,' he said formally. No harm in showing her that he could be cool, too. 'But it doesn't change the fact that I'm sorry. I really just wanted to reassure you that it won't happen again.'

Somehow, that wasn't quite what Martha wanted to hear, but she could hardly tell him that.

'I think it would be best if we both forgot all about it,' she said instead.

'Right,' said Lewis. 'Right. Yes. Let's do that.'

Of course, forget it. Why hadn't he suggested that? It should be easy enough. He had plenty of other things to think about. There were the preliminary surveys to be organised, meetings to be had, reports to write, analyses to do. They had run into a legal problem about acquiring land for the airport extension, and there was a looming problem with one of the contracts… No, the last thing he had time to do was brood over a little kiss. He had much more important things on his mind.

And yet, it was funny how hard it was to shift the memory of the heat of her mouth and the softness of her skin and all the warm, vital, responsive warmth of her. As the days passed, Lewis found himself increasingly unsettled. Those memories had an alarming ability to sneak into his mind at odd moments, when he was supposed to be focusing on something else entirely, on something *important*.

Disquieted by his apparent inability to shrug them off, he became even more brusque than usual. The office manager and PA took to treading warily around him at work, and at home things were even worse. In spite—or perhaps because—of the efforts he and Martha made to carry on as normal, the atmosphere between them was horribly constrained.

Everywhere reminded him of Martha. The living room, where the sofa practically pulsated with memories. The verandah, where in easier times they used to sit in the dark and listen to the sea. They never did that any more, and Lewis missed it more than he wanted to admit.

The kitchen, where every morning Martha gave the babies their breakfast barefoot, wearing nothing but that damned shirt, and his fingers itched to catch at it and pull her closer, to tell her it wasn't working, that he couldn't forget.

He wouldn't do it, of course. That would just be asking for trouble, Lewis knew that. Martha was Viola's nanny. Why did he have to keep reminding himself of that fact? What was more, she was good at her job. Even to Lewis's inexperienced eye it was obvious how loving and gentle but firm she was with both babies, and she treated Viola as if she really was Noah's twin.

So he didn't want to lose her as his employee, did he? She was a good cook too. It would be stupid to jeopardise a successful business relationship just because the memory of how warm and responsive she had been kept snagging at his attention.

Very stupid.

And anyway, Martha wasn't really his type, Lewis tried to rationalise it when the employee argument seemed less persuasive. He had always preferred cool, independent women. It made him nervous when they got clingy and needy and started talking about commitment.

Martha hadn't done that yet, but it was obvious what she wanted. She already had a baby and she was looking for a family, with all the mess and complications and emotions that involved. Lewis didn't want any of that, and it would be unfair to pretend that he did, just to get her into bed and satisfy what was clearly only a temporary obsession.

In any case, she had never given the slightest sign that she would want him, Lewis reminded himself. Apart from that night on the sofa, of course, and as she had said that had just been a case of getting a bit carried away. She had been very clear right from the start that her priority was to find Noah's father. Lewis wasn't about to volunteer for that role, not with his experience of family life.

What he needed, Lewis decided, was a distraction. Bumping into Candace Stephens outside the office one day gave him the perfect opportunity, and he invited her out to lunch straight away, almost as if he needed to prove something. Although he wasn't quite sure whether he was proving it to Martha or to himself.

Candace was much more suitable, Lewis told himself, observing her approvingly over lunch.

She was cool and rational and very attractive, and she was insistent about the fact that her career came first. Candace had no time for messy babies or messy emotions. She had her own life, her own job, her own priorities. She wouldn't want to get too involved with anyone. She was perfect for him, in fact.

So what if his skin didn't tingle when he caught sight of her? It didn't matter that Candace didn't have a lush mouth that made his mind go hazy. Lewis told himself that it was a good thing that he could talk to her without being distracted by the sheen of her skin or the silkiness of her hair. Candace was just the distraction he needed.

'I won't be in for supper tomorrow night.' He broke the silence over the meal the next day.

Martha had been toying listlessly with her salad, but she looked up at that. 'Oh?'

'There's some function at the hotel where Candace Stephens is manager.' For some reason Lewis found himself stumbling a little over his explanation. 'She asked if I would like to go along, and I thought—'

Why didn't he just say that he was going out with Candace? Martha wondered crossly. 'You don't need to explain to me,' she interrupted him. 'What you do with your private life is your own business. But thank you for letting me know,' she added with quelling politeness.

Lewis hesitated. 'Will you be all right here on your own all evening?'

'Of course,' she said with a brittle smile. 'I'm quite used to it.'

Which wasn't *quite* true any more. She was used to Lewis being there now. Used to the involuntary jerk of her senses whenever he walked into the room. Used to the way her heart missed a beat at the thought of him.

She was even getting used to lying awake at night and reliving that kiss as it played in an endless loop in her head. And she was learning to accept that when Lewis had said that it wouldn't happen again he had meant it.

Now it looked as if she was going to have to accept that he was going out with Candace, too. That would be nearly as hard, but she could do it. She didn't need Lewis.

'I'm sure Eloise would come over if you wanted.'

Great. Not only was Lewis appalled at the thought of kissing her, he thought she was too pathetic to spend a few hours in a house on her own. What kind of drip did he think she was?

Martha surveyed him coolly. 'You know, I've held down a demanding job and I look after two babies all day, which is even more demanding. I think I can survive an evening on my own! Viola and Noah may need a babysitter, but at thirty-four I think I'm a bit old for one, don't you?'

Lewis scowled. He didn't like it when she was sarcastic. 'I was only trying to think of you,' he said grouchily.

If he were really thinking of her, he wouldn't be going out with Candace, would he? Martha put up her chin.

'You can think of me by asking around at this function tomorrow night and seeing if anyone has heard of Rory,' she told him crisply.

Rory. The toyboy she was so obsessed about. Lewis had almost let himself forget about Rory, and the blunt reminder made the intimidating brows draw together. 'Haven't you found him yet?'

'When do I have a chance to look for him?' countered Martha. 'I'm stuck here all the time!'

'I thought you went out every day?'

'Only to the market, and my Creole's not up to interrogating stallholders yet!'

There were probably lots of other things that she could have done, especially with Eloise to help, but Martha didn't feel like admitting to Lewis that so far she hadn't made any effort at all to find Noah's father. It wasn't that she didn't think about him, she did. Occasionally, anyway, when she looked at Noah. The truth, though, was that recently she had spent a lot more time thinking about Lewis and how he had kissed her than she had about Rory.

Not that she had any intention of admitting *that* to Lewis either!

'I introduced you to Candace,' Lewis pointed out. 'If you had really wanted to get out more you could have followed that acquaintance up.'

'Funnily enough, I didn't see us becoming bosom buddies, her being such a clever career woman and me being a brain-dead zombie with nothing better to do than look after two children!'

'You didn't need to be close friends for her to introduce you to some other people,' said Lewis, pointedly not denying that she was a brain-dead zombie, which Martha thought wouldn't have cost him anything.

'Well, it's not that I didn't appreciate the thought,' she said tartly, 'but maybe next time you could introduce me to someone a little less chilly, and I might make more of an effort.'

Chilly. Lewis couldn't shake the word whenever he looked at Candace the next evening. She was stunning in a silvery sheath dress, but there was something off-putting about her cool beauty. He couldn't help comparing her to Martha, with her dark eyes and her hot mouth and her warm smile, the opposite of chilly.

He didn't like socialising at the best of times, and the evening seemed interminable. Candace was very much on duty, and he was left to make small talk and watch the door, almost as if he were hoping that Martha might miraculously walk in, which was a ridiculous thing to do.

Making his excuses to Candace, he left as early as he could, but Martha had gone to bed anyway by the time he got home. Lewis was furious with himself for being disappointed. He sat on the verandah and scowled at the tropical night and told himself that he was a fool.

Martha was determinedly bright the next morning. 'Did you have a nice time?' she asked, even though Lewis was obviously in a foul mood.

He shrugged. 'It was just one of those parties where you stand around and talk to a load of people you don't know and don't particularly want to.'

'Remind me not to invite you to any of my parties!' said Martha, eyeing him curiously. 'You must have met someone interesting—apart from Candace, of course,' she added snidely. 'I can see how interesting she would be to you!'

Lewis glared at her. 'I didn't meet anyone who knows Rory, if that's what you want to know,' he snapped.

Martha was momentarily taken aback. She had forgotten that she had asked him to see if anyone knew Rory but, now that he had mentioned it, it was an excellent reason for her to be so interested in the party. Nothing to do with wanting to know how he had got on with Candace, for instance.

'Someone must know him,' she said, changing tack. 'It's such a tiny place.'

'Well, if they do they'll be at the reception at the High Commission next week,' said Lewis. 'I accepted an invitation for you, so you can ask around yourself.'

'An invitation?' Startled, Martha paused in the middle of wiping Viola's face and hands. 'For me?'

'They usually invite all the Brits in a place like this.' Lewis drank his coffee, embarrassed to remember that talking about her, even mentioning her name, had been about his only pleasure the night before. 'I told the High Commissioner that you were grumbling about never going anywhere or meeting anyone, and she said we would both get an invitation to the reception. If you don't meet anyone who knows Rory there, you've got the wrong island.'

'Oh.' Martha heard the doubt in her own voice and caught herself up. She ought to be sounding a lot more enthusiastic than that. 'Well…thank you,' she said awkwardly.

What was wrong with her? She ought to be pleased that he had gone to so much effort. Thanks to Lewis, she was a step closer to finding Rory, and she should be grateful, not wondering whether his concern to increase her social life was part of a more complex strategy to get her out of the way.

Perhaps he was really keen on Candace, after all, and afraid that she would hang around casting darkling glances at the sofa and cramping his style? Martha cringed at the very thought. She would just have to show him that, as far as she was concerned, he could do whatever he liked. If it seemed a pity that he should choose a block of ice like Candace Stephens, well, that was none of her business. His mouth was more than capable of melting ice in any case…

Her thoughts were wandering dangerously. Martha pulled herself together. Lewis had made an effort for her, so she could do the same for him. And she could start by being a lot nicer about Candace, otherwise he might suspect that she was jealous of the other woman.

Which was nonsense, of course.

'If you want to return Candace's invitation by having her to dinner here, I'd be happy to cook for you,' she said, lifting first Noah then Viola out of their high chairs and setting them on the floor, where they liked to bang wooden spoons against a saucepan. As entertainment it was cheap and effective, if a bit noisy at times.

'I could make something nice,' she persevered when Lewis didn't respond immediately. 'And you needn't worry about me hanging around. I'd stay in the kitchen.'

'Frankly, I don't think I'd enjoy my meal with the thought of you lurking behind the kitchen door,' said Lewis acerbically. 'There'd be no question of you not *hanging around*, as you put it.'

He hesitated, reluctant to admit even to himself that he didn't really want to spend an evening alone with Candace.

'I tell you what you could do for me, though,' he said. 'I've got a hydrologist, a botanist and an economist arriving tomorrow, to do the preliminary studies for the World Bank. They're just on short-term contracts, so they'll be staying at a hotel—Candace's hotel, in fact—but it would be nice to offer them some home cooking as a change from eating out in restaurants every night. Perhaps I could invite them to supper next week, and invite Candace at the same time?'

Martha brightened. Just because she liked cooking, she told herself. Nothing to do with the fact that Lewis hadn't jumped at the chance of a *tête à tête* with Candace.

'I'll cook something really nice,' she promised.

She planned her menu carefully and was up early on the day of the dinner party to get to the market when everything was really fresh, and give herself plenty of time to prepare everything. She was determined to produce a spectacular meal, to look stunning and be witty and entertaining, just to prove to Candace that having a baby didn't have to be the equivalent of a lobotomy. Everything was going to be perfect.

And it might have been if Eloise's mother hadn't fallen, if Eloise hadn't had to take her to the hospital. If Martha hadn't had to try and shop and cook and clean the house with the twins in tow at all times. If the fishermen had caught the fish she wanted and there hadn't been an inexplicable absence of her key ingredient in the market. If Viola hadn't been in a particularly contrary mood all day, and especially if Noah hadn't been unusually fretful and chosen to throw up all over the sofa just before she put them to bed.

In the resulting rush to check that he wasn't really ill, and clean up the living room, and settle Viola, who always played up the moment she wasn't the centre of attention, Martha forgot all about her pots on the stove and, by the time she had remembered them, her sauce was curdled, the vegetables disintegrating and her precious pudding that she had been so proud of absolutely ruined.

At least Lewis was able to help her put Noah and Viola to bed when he came home, but Martha was still frantically trying to cobble together an alternative meal when the first guests arrived, and there was no time for her to change and be magically transformed into the relaxed, effortlessly stylish superwoman she had planned.

Wiping her hands on a tea towel, she grimaced as she caught sight of herself in a mirror on her way to be introduced. In her limp T-shirt and the stained trousers she had been wearing all day she looked and felt exactly like the zombie Candace had so patronisingly described. Knowing that the other woman would be delighted to have all her expectations confirmed was the icing on the cake of the day from hell, Martha decided.

'My goodness, you *do* look tired!' exclaimed Candace, glowing and immaculate in a white sheath dress, and Martha had to grit her teeth as Candace ladled on the sympathy until everyone was looking at her in a way that made her acutely conscious of her hair hanging limply, and the fact that she didn't have a scrap of make-up on.

Just what her ego needed.

They were all looking so sorry for her by the time Candace had finished that Martha glanced uneasily down at her herself, suddenly struck with the awful suspicion that she had missed some of Noah's sick on her clothes. She had better steer them all out on to the verandah afterwards and make sure they avoided the sofa.

The botanist and the economist turned out to be young men who were both very obviously struck by Candace's cool glamour. As an exhausted, rumpled mum, Martha felt completely invisible to them, but she liked the female hydrologist very much, especially when she heard that she was getting married and hoping to have a family of her own.

After the meal, they moved out to the verandah and, while Candace held court talking business strategies with the three men, Martha and Sarah were able to enjoy a cosy chat about babies.

Martha could feel Lewis glance across at them occasionally, but she turned her shoulder defiantly. Let him and Candace roll their eyes about the dullness of her conversation. She didn't care. Noah was her son, and she wasn't ashamed to find him and Viola more interesting than economic analyses, project management, model systems, post-tender evaluations and all the other jargon they were discussing at the other end of the verandah.

She had a good idea that Sarah did, too, in spite of her professionalism. She had heard Martha referring to Viola and Noah as the 'twins' and confided that she was rather worried about the fact that twins ran in her fiancé's family.

'It's not that I mind the idea of having twins,' she told Martha, 'but it does look like a lot of hard work.'

'It's that all right,' said Martha, thinking of the day she had had. 'I don't know how some mothers manage on their own.'

'Yes, you're lucky to have Lewis.' Sarah looked along the verandah to where Lewis was offering around more coffee. 'I haven't worked with him before, but I've heard about the firm, of course. I guess he's so busy that he doesn't get much of a chance to be a real hands-on father?'

'He's not too bad,' Martha began, thinking of the way Lewis came home and helped her put the babies to bed, and then she stopped, belatedly realising what Sarah had said. 'You don't think…? No, Lewis isn't a father at all, and he's no intention of being one either!'

'Oh.' Sarah looked baffled. 'Then you're not his wife?'

'His wife?' Involuntarily, Martha's gaze went to Lewis. He was setting down the coffee pot, smiling in a restrained kind of way, and she felt something unlock inside her. Almost as if he had heard it, he glanced up and their eyes met for a fleeting instant before Martha jerked hers away.

'No,' she said to Sarah, swallowing the tightness in her throat. 'No, I'm not Lewis's wife. I'm sorry, I thought that was obvious.'

Sarah's sharp gaze flicked between Martha and Lewis and she raised her brows. 'No,' she said slowly. 'It's not at all obvious.'

CHAPTER EIGHT

SARAH'S words fell into a lull in the conversation at the other end of the verandah. 'What's not obvious?' asked Candace, so clearly prepared to be amused at what wasn't obvious to two women who had nothing better to do than talk about babies all night that Martha's fingers tightened painfully around the arm of the wicker chair.

'The fact that Lewis and I aren't married,' she said evenly, and turned back to Sarah before she could see Candace smiling smugly at Lewis. 'I'm just the nanny.'

Lewis frowned. 'I'm sorry, Sarah,' he said, scraping back his chair and bringing the coffee pot over to offer them some more. 'I should have introduced Martha properly when you arrived, but we were having a bit of a crisis in the kitchen then.'

Martha couldn't help warming to that 'we', when the crisis had been all hers. Lewis had just been his normal cucumber self, too cool and competent and self-contained to even know what a crisis meant.

'She's helping me look after my niece for a few months,' he was telling Sarah, who was looking completely confused by now.

'We call Viola and Noah the twins because they have the same birthday, but they're not related at all,' Martha explained.

'I see.' Sarah didn't sound as if she did, really. 'So Noah's father...?'

'Is somewhere here on St Bonaventure,' said Martha brightly for Lewis's benefit. 'In fact, I was wondering if you might have heard of him, since you also work in the watery field. He's a marine biologist, not a hydrologist, though. Rory McMillan? I'm keen to get in touch with him while I'm here.'

Sarah shook her head. 'The name doesn't ring a bell with me, I'm afraid, but, of course I've only just arrived. I'll keep an eye out for you, if you like. What does he look like?'

Martha glanced at Lewis. 'Gorgeous,' she said. 'Tall, tanned, blond, dancing blue eyes, fabulous body...you can't miss him!'

Sarah laughed. 'I can see why you're so keen to get in touch with him!'

Candace had given up the pretence of not listening and had turned her chair round to join them, effectively pinning Lewis against the verandah rail where he was leaning and listening to Martha with a scowl.

'I don't recognise the name either,' she said, shamelessly muscling in on the conversation. 'There are quite a lot of marine projects on the outer islands and we sometimes get scientists in the bar or using the pool when they come back to stock up on supplies or pick up the post. I'll ask around for you, Martha, if you like.'

Martha gritted her teeth. She didn't like. It might be perverse not to welcome any offers to help her find Rory, but she could really do without Candace poking her nose into her private business. It was perfectly obvious Candace just wanted to get her out of the way with Rory so that she would have a free run with Lewis—though why the other woman should feel that she was a threat in her grubby T-shirt and trousers stained with sick was a bit of a mystery. As far as sex goddesses went, she wouldn't even make it to the starting line.

'That's kind of you,' she said with what she hoped was quelling civility, 'but there's no need to bother. I'm going to a reception at the

High Commission next week, so I'll be able to do any asking around myself then.'

'Oh, you're going to that, are you?'

Martha had to hand it to Candace. The tone was absolutely perfect, subtly implying incredulity that the High Commission should bother to invite a dull, dowdy mother smelling of sick without actually saying anything of the kind.

Sighing inwardly, Martha wondered whether Cinderella had felt like this. Still, there were advantages to the Cinderella role, she consoled herself that night as she lay in bed contemplating the ceiling fan—at least Cinderella got her man and a palace thrown in! Maybe a fairy godmother would materialise on the night of the ball—cheese and wine at the High Commission just didn't have the same ring to it—and fix her up with Prince Charming?

She could do with a Prince Charming right now, Martha thought. Rory was charming enough, good-looking enough, and of course he was Noah's father. Surely she should cast him in the lead role when she tried to imagine her own happy ever after? That was the sensible thing to dream about.

It was just that dreaming would be a lot easier if her mind was in a less contrary mood.

She wished it would stop substituting Lewis's austere features for Rory's much more handsome ones. Lewis was all wrong for a hero. He was too dour, too difficult, too determined to avoid family life. Noah needed a father, and if his biological one didn't want the job she would try and find someone else who did. There was no point in wasting time even conjuring up Lewis's face when it came to dreaming about a future.

Unsurprisingly enough, no fairy godmother had appeared by the evening of the reception, but it did seem for once as if the fates were on her side, thought Martha as she got ready to go out. Noah and Viola had been happy all day and had gone to sleep like angels, so she had plenty of time for a shower and to do her hair. Lewis had told her that he would be back in good time to get changed too.

'We might as well go together,' he had said gruffly that morning.

Not perhaps the most romantic of invitations, but in spite of herself Martha's spirits were soaring. Once she would have turned up her nose at the thought of a stuffy diplomatic reception, but it had been so long since she had been anywhere or had a chance to dress up that she felt ridiculously excited at the thought of going out.

She had brought her favourite dress from her days at *Glitz*. Whenever they did a feature on 'My best buy ever' or 'The one piece of my wardrobe I would grab if there was a fire', Martha's dress would make an appearance. It had cost her a ridiculous amount of money, even with the generous discount the designer had given her because she had featured his clothes in *Glitz*, and on the hanger it looked no different from any chainstore dress.

The moment she slipped it on, though…ah, that was a very different matter! The whisper-soft material draped beautifully and never creased, and Martha felt fabulous whenever she wore it. Fashion editors famously wore black, but Martha's dress was a deep, dark gold that warmed her skin and flattered her figure. It was a deceptively simple sleeveless shift that you could wear to the most glamorous of A-list parties with heels and the perfect necklace, or with sandals to a casual bar by the beach.

This was the first time she had worn it since Noah was born, and it had lost none of its effect. Martha smoothed it down over her stomach and wriggled her feet into her kitten heels before twisting one way and another in front of the mirror. She had the strangest sensation that she had come face to face with her old self. With her make-up and her dress and her shoes to die for, she looked like a completely different person, the old Martha who had never cooed over prams or imagined that she would be happy to spend her days in a sarong and flip-flops.

She had been letting herself go, she told herself sternly. No wonder Candace thought she was mumsy.

Well, Candace would see a different Martha tonight! She would show her that she wasn't quite the downtrodden drudge that she imagined.

Lewis was talking to Eloise in the living room, but as Martha's door opened he broke off and turned. He was dressed in a white dinner jacket with a black bow tie, and he looked so austerely attractive that the breath snared in her throat. He seemed equally taken aback at the sight of her. The smile evaporated from his face and for a long moment he just stared in stunned disbelief.

Martha was conscious of a *frisson*, a tiny thrill at succeeding at last in shaking him out of that infuriating self-possession, but it vanished as she saw something oddly like disappointment flicker across his face before the slate eyes shuttered warily and his expression closed.

'You look…very…different,' he said in a voice empty of all expression.

Different? Was that all he could say? He might as well have come right out and said that he didn't like her like this. Obscurely hurt, Martha felt her confidence evaporate before a worse thought struck her.

What if he thought that she had gone to all this trouble for him? If it seemed as if she were angling for a repeat of that kiss? Remembering how horrified he had been when he realised that he was kissing her before, she thought with a sinking heart that it would certainly explain his wary look. He was probably terrified that she was planning to jump him again.

Mortified at the very thought, Martha felt a tide of colour wash up her neck, and the knowledge that she must look as humiliated as she felt only made her feel worse. She still had some pride, though, and gathered its meagre shreds together. Somehow she was just going to have to convince Lewis that kissing him again was the last thing she had in mind.

'Thank you,' she said with a brittle smile. 'I thought I should make an effort. You said all the Brits would be there tonight, so if there's even an outside chance that I might bump into Rory, then I want to make sure I'm looking my best.'

There was a tiny pause. 'Of course,' said Lewis roughly. 'I forgot that you were hoping to come across him.'

'Well, that's why I'm here, isn't it?' Martha managed another over-bright smile. If she said it often enough she might even remember it herself.

How could he have forgotten? How could he have been stupid enough to admit that he had? Lewis castigated himself savagely. It wasn't as if Martha had ever made a secret of why she was here or what she wanted.

He had just been shaken off balance by the way she looked when she came out of the bedroom, and it wasn't a feeling that he liked. He was used to her in a soft T-shirt that left her arms bare, or in her sarong, or in that man's shirt she wore at night, the one that was faded and slipped off her shoulder when she forgot about it. He didn't like her the way she looked now. She was too sophisticated like this, too glamorous, too eager to go out and party.

Lewis preferred her when she was in the kitchen, stirring pots, her face intent as she tasted a sauce, or sitting cross-legged on the floor, laughing as the babies tumbled against her. He liked her as a nanny, not a fashion editor.

But Martha didn't care what he liked, did she?

'We'd better go,' he said brusquely. 'We don't want to be late.'

The High Commission was an imposing colonial building set in immaculate grounds. Tonight was obviously one of the key social events of the year in Perpetua, and the gardens were crowded with people all dressed to the nines.

What if Rory was here after all? Martha viewed the throng with a sudden clutch of panic. What would she say to him? She had made such a fuss about him to Lewis that she couldn't simply ignore his presence. She would just have to hope that the idea of putting on a jacket would discourage Rory from attending the reception even if he had been invited. From what she remembered of him, that would be in character.

'Hello, there!' Candace had obviously been keeping an eye out for Lewis and intercepted him before he had a chance to disappear into the crowds. 'I was wondering when you'd get here.' She smiled at Lewis and laid a familiar hand on his arm. Martha wanted to smack it away.

'Hello,' she said clearly, and saw with satisfaction that Candace did a double take as she glanced at her.

'Martha!' The smug smile was wiped from her face as she took in the transformation, and she took her hand off Lewis, the icy blue eyes narrowing. 'I hardly recognised you.'

'I'm not in nanny mode tonight,' Martha agreed with an equally insincere smile. 'It's my night off.'

'Well…we must make sure you enjoy it, in that case.' Candace had made a quick recovery. 'Let me introduce you to a few people,' she offered in a blatant strategy to separate her from Lewis. Martha could practically see her thinking that while mumsy old Martha wasn't much of a rival, in that dress she might be more of a threat.

Martha could have told her she didn't have any reason to worry. Lewis had hardly said a word to her in the car. He either thought that she looked awful, or was so terrified that she was planning on jumping him again that he couldn't wait to fob her off on someone else. Either way, Martha had no intention of playing gooseberry to the two of them all evening. She put up her chin.

'That's sweet of you, but I've been to one or two parties before, and I think I can probably introduce myself.' She flashed Lewis a glittering smile. 'I'll no doubt see you later.'

Waggling her fingers at them both in her best *Glitz* style, she sashayed off, thanking God for her dress and her heels. She would never have been able to carry it off without them.

After so long as a virtual social recluse it was daunting at first to find herself isolated among complete strangers, but experience of all those parties she had been to in her twenties soon kicked in. Martha turned on the charm and before long was circulating as if she had been an integral part of Perpetua's social scene for years.

It would even have been fun if she hadn't been so aware of Lewis. She kept trying to move to a different part of the party, but wherever she was she seemed to be able to see him out of the corner of her eye, and no matter how hard she tried to ignore him it was as if her senses were fine-tuned to notice whenever he lifted a glass or turned his head.

It wasn't even as if he was making any effort, Martha noted crossly. Clearly not one of nature's party animals, he stood looking forbidding most of the time, and his smiles were perfunctory at best. Martha could almost have felt sorry for Candace, clinging so desperately to his arm. Surely even she could see that he wasn't enjoying himself?

Martha just wished that she wondered why Candace was bothering but, infuriatingly, she could see it all too easily. He made a formidable figure, she thought, watching him covertly as she pretended to listen to a long, involved story about a diving trip. It wasn't just those intimidating brows or that austere look. It was something to do with the steely self-containment, the air of cool competence that set him apart from the crowd.

That and the fact that he was obviously hating this as a waste of time. Why had he come at all? Martha wondered. He could have stayed at home. He could be sitting on the verandah right now, gazing out into the hot darkness and listening to the ocean…

The longing to be there herself grabbed Martha out of nowhere, like a hand gripping her heart, so hard and so unexpected that she actually flinched—and, as if he had heard her sharp, instinctive intake of breath, Lewis looked across the garden and met her eyes.

For Martha, it was as if the ground between them had suddenly opened up, leaving her teetering on the edge of a yawning chasm. She didn't want to be here either, making polite chit-chat with strangers. She wanted to be on the verandah too, and she wanted to be there with him.

'Are you OK?'

Belatedly, Martha realised that the man she was with had broken off his story and was looking at her in some concern. Wrenching her eyes away from Lewis's, she took a gulp of her punch.

'Sorry…yes, I'm fine,' she said, but she didn't feel fine at all. She felt sick and shaken with the enormity of what she had just realised.

She wanted Lewis. There could be no future with him. He wasn't the right father for Noah, and he wasn't the right man for her, but she still wanted him in a way she had never wanted anyone before. She wanted to go over and push Candace away from him, to beg him to take her out to the car and push her up against the door and kiss her as he had kissed her that night. She wanted to drive home through the tropical night, knowing that when they got there she would be able to put her arms around him and burrow into his solid strength.

How much had Lewis seen as she stared at him? Martha felt giddy and disorientated, terrified that naked desire had been written all over her face, but when she risked another glance he was talking to the High Commissioner and looked perfectly normal. At least he didn't look as if his world had fallen apart the way hers had just done, and he wasn't backing out of the party, eyes rolling in search of escape, as he probably would have been doing if he had so much as an inkling of how she felt about him.

There was no use in fooling herself any longer. It was Lewis she wanted, Lewis she was in love with. It wasn't sensible, and it wasn't what she had wanted, but there wasn't anything she could do about it.

All she could do was try not to make a fool of herself and grope for her last shreds of pride. She had to keep remembering his expression when he had realised that he was kissing her, and the wariness that had crept into his eyes when he suspected that she had dressed up for him. The worst possible thing to do would be to tell him how she felt. He would just reject her out of hand, and then she and Noah would have to leave, and she would never see him or Viola again.

No, much better to keep her secret for now. There were months to go before her contract ran out, and a lot could happen in that time. Lewis might change his mind, might get used to having her around, might even think that he would miss her when she had gone.

For now, she just needed time alone to think about how she felt and what she was going to do. Her jaw was beginning to ache with the effort of smiling. She longed to go home but dreaded being alone with him before she had had time to get herself under control. As a result, when Lewis came up to ask if she was ready to go home, Martha produced a brilliant smile.

'The party's hardly started,' she objected, as if she were having a wonderful time. As if her spine hadn't prickled with awareness of him walking up behind her. She hadn't been able to see him, but she had known that he was there.

'I don't want to leave Eloise too long,' said Lewis, who had evidently managed to shake off Candace at last. 'It's not fair on her.'

'I'm sure she wouldn't mind if we stayed a bit longer.'

He scowled. 'I'm not staying any longer. If you want a lift home, you'll have to come now.'

Martha wanted to put her arms around him and kiss the crossness away. How could she love him when he was so difficult? she asked herself in something close to despair, before pushing the feeling firmly away.

'I can always get a taxi,' she pointed out.

'I'll take you home if you like,' offered the man beside her. Martha had been too busy thinking about Lewis to notice him much, but she seemed to remember that he had been introduced as Peter.

His offer didn't go down well with Lewis, but Martha smiled at him. 'Would you really? That would be kind. Thank you *so* much.'

She turned back to Lewis, feeling better now that she didn't have to face the drive home in the dark with him. She wouldn't have to worry about keeping her hands under control, about the urge to touch him in the darkness, to break down and beg him to hold her.

'You go,' she said to Lewis. 'I'll be fine.'

'It's not you I'm worried about,' he said astringently. 'I was thinking more about Eloise. She might want to go home.'

'You're going to be there,' she pointed out, and his mouth tightened.

'It seems to have slipped your mind that I'm not the one employed as a nanny,' he snapped.

Martha hesitated. The only way she was going to get through this was to be as bolshie as possible, and with any luck Lewis wouldn't guess the real reason for her reluctance to go home with him.

'Excuse me,' she said to Peter with a martyred sigh. 'I've just been reminded who pays my wages. It looks as if I'm going to have to go.'

'Spare me the martyr act!' said Lewis, visibly irritated. 'If you're so determined to stay, you'd better stay. Don't mind me.'

'Fine, I won't,' said Martha childishly. It was bizarre how he could make her so cross and make her want to throw herself into his arms and beg him to take her with him at one and the same time.

She should have felt relieved to see Lewis stomp off, but she had to stop herself running after him. Now she just had to face hours of purgatory, pretending to have a great time with Peter. She hadn't registered just how pleased he was at the prospect, or envisaged that he would insist on taking her to Perpetua's only night-club. Once Martha would have been the last person off the dance floor, but now she just wanted to go home, and she couldn't ask after making such a fuss with Lewis.

It was nearly two before Peter drove her back to the house. She was rather dreading it, in case he was expecting to round off the evening with some physical demonstration of her gratitude for possibly the worst four hours of her life, but there was no chance of that when Lewis loomed up on the verandah as the car came to a halt and stood glowering down at them.

'I think I'd better go,' Martha said to Peter, reaching for the door handle with barely concealed relief. 'Thanks for a lovely evening.'

'Where have you been?' Lewis demanded as she climbed the verandah steps wearily and a disconsolate Peter drove off.

'I've been checking out Perpetua's night life.'

'Until two in the morning?'

'That's the thing about night life—it usually happens at night,' Martha confided sarcastically. 'I realise that for you a night out is over at ten o'clock, but for the rest of us things don't get going until after midnight.'

'You could have rung and let me know that you weren't coming back after the reception,' Lewis growled.

'I could have done, but I didn't,' she said, walking past him into the living room. 'A—I thought you'd be in bed, and B—I don't have to account to you for what I do in my free time!'

'I could hardly go to bed until you got home,' he countered furiously. 'I didn't know where you were, or who you were with, or what you were doing. What if I'd needed to get in touch with you?'

Martha perched on an arm of the sofa and eased off her shoes. 'Why would you need to do that?'

'There might have been a problem with Viola or Noah,' said Lewis after a moment.

'Was there?'

'No,' he admitted grudgingly.

'I tell you what,' said Martha, wincing as she rubbed her sore feet. Fab as her shoes were, they weren't made for standing up in for long periods, and certainly not for dancing. 'Next time I go out, I'll check in with you on the hour, every hour. How about that?'

Lewis scowled at her facetiousness. 'What do you mean, *next time*?' he demanded. 'Are you seeing that Peter again?'

Martha flirted with the idea of pretending to have a passionate attraction for the poor, unsuspecting Peter, but decided that she wouldn't be able to carry it off.

'We haven't arranged anything, but I might do,' she said as airily as she could. 'He seemed very nice,' she added provocatively.

Lewis's brows were drawn into one fearsome bridge across his nose. 'I thought you were supposed to be looking for Noah's father?'

'I am, but I didn't meet anybody who knew him tonight.'

'And in the meantime you're keeping an eye out for substitutes, I suppose!' Hunching his shoulders, he prowled restlessly around the room as Martha stared at him furiously.

'What do you mean by that?'

'I saw the way you were chatting up all the men at that reception tonight,' he accused her. 'It looked as if you were working on a fall-back plan in case Rory doesn't appear to sign up for the father thing!'

Martha's eyes flashed dangerously. 'My son deserves better than a fall-back plan! He deserves the best father there is. It might not turn out to be his biological father, but I'm certainly not reduced to trawling round receptions in case I might find someone suitable for the *father thing* as you call it!'

'So what was the point of all that flirting?'

'I wasn't flirting. You and Candace made it very obvious that I was cramping your style, so I left you to your own devices. As far as I was concerned, I was just being pleasant.'

'Pleasant?' Still pacing, Lewis flung the word back at her over his shoulder. 'What does that mean, exactly?'

'Well, I haven't looked it up in a dictionary for a while,' said Martha, holding on to her own temper with difficulty, 'but I think it means smiling and being polite and showing an interest in other people, which was exactly what I was doing. And, frankly, I don't see what it has to do with you in any case!'

There was a pause. Lewis stopped to look at her, and then away. 'I didn't like it,' he said as if the words had been forced out of him. 'I didn't like the idea of you being interested in those other men, and I didn't like them being interested in you. I was jealous,' he added simply. 'I wanted you to be pleasant to *me*.'

It was so unexpected that Martha could only stare at him for a moment, not sure that she had heard him properly. 'Why?' she asked foolishly.

'Why? Look at you!' Lewis turned almost angrily. 'What man wouldn't want you? You look stunning.'

She opened her mouth, then closed it again. 'I didn't think you liked this dress,' was all she could say at last.

'It's not the dress.' He shrugged his shoulders in an odd gesture of defeat. 'The truth is that I didn't like the fact that you wanted to go out. It was childish of me, I know,' he added heavily. 'I wanted you to stay here with me.'

Martha shook her head in incomprehension. 'Why?' she said again, wishing she could think of something perceptive or witty to say instead.

He came over then and took the shoes from her hand, letting them drop on to the wooden floor. 'Why do you think?' he asked, and the look in his eyes set Martha's heart slamming painfully against her ribs.

Her throat was too dry for her to speak. She could only look helplessly up at him, pinioned by the warmth of his gaze, paralysed by the fear that if she moved she would break the moment and that time would rewind, leaving Lewis on the other side of the room, not standing right next to her, watching her with that expression that dissolved her bones and flooded her with warmth.

'I think you know why,' he said softly when she didn't answer. 'I think you know that I haven't been able to stop thinking about how it felt to kiss you, about what it would be like to kiss you again. Every time I see you in that shirt you wear at night I want to take it off you. I want to undo the buttons very slowly and pull it from your shoulders. I want to touch you the way I touched you that night, the way I would have gone on touching you if Viola hadn't cried.'

Martha moistened her lips and found her voice at last. 'But you seemed so horrified, as if you didn't even realise it was me you were kissing.'

'I knew it was you all right,' he said with a twisted smile. 'It wasn't the first time I'd thought about kissing you, but I knew that I shouldn't. You weren't in any position to resist, and I was ashamed of myself for taking advantage of you. I shouldn't have done it.'

'What if I liked being taken advantage of?' said Martha a little shakily. She looked up at him with dark, direct eyes. 'What if I wanted you to take advantage of me?'

'Did you?' Lewis's voice wasn't that steady either. He swallowed. 'Do you?'

She let out a breath, suddenly certain. This wasn't about the future. It was about what she wanted now. She wanted to forget about the future, not for ever, but for now. She didn't want to think about anything but Lewis and the promise in his eyes and how his hands and his mouth and his body would feel against hers.

'Yes,' she said. 'Yes, to both.' And the blaze of expression in his face sent a thrill through her.

He took her hands in his and drew her to her feet. 'Are you sure, Martha?'

Martha's fingers tightened around his and she smiled. 'I'm sure. Are you?'

'Am I sure?' Lewis was shaken by a silent laugh. 'When I've been thinking about this for so long? Yes, I'm sure.'

And then their smiles faded as he bent his head and their lips met at last in a soft kiss that caught and clung and went on and on until they broke apart at last for breath. Lewis's hands slid up to tangle in her silky hair. 'God, yes, I'm sure,' he said raggedly, and then there was no more talking for a very, very long time.

When Martha woke the next morning she was pressed against Lewis's warm, solid back. He was lying with his face buried in the pillow, apparently still asleep, and she kissed the back of his neck where it was irresistibly close to her mouth.

He stirred slightly but didn't move, so she kissed him again, letting her lips drift along his bare shoulder.

Still no response. Piqued, Martha lifted herself up and applied herself to the task more seriously. Starting at the base of his neck, she pressed seductively soft kisses around and up to the lobe of his ear, over the rough prickle of his jaw, and on to linger at the corner of his mouth.

'Are you awake?' she whispered, encouraged by an infinitesimal twitch of his lips.

'No,' said Lewis, barely moving his lips.

'Not even a little bit?'

The dent at the corner of his mouth deepened. 'No,' he said again, and then took her by surprise, rolling over suddenly to pin her beneath him and kiss her. 'But I get the feeling I'm going to be waking up any minute now!'

Martha smiled with satisfaction and stretched beneath his hands. 'What time is it?' she asked lazily.

Lewis raised himself slightly to squint at the clock on the bedside table. 'Too early to get up,' he said, and settled comfortably back on top of her, his face resting in the curve of her throat. 'The babies will still be sound asleep.'

'I'm sorry I woke you in that case,' she said, winding her arms around his back. 'Do you want to go back to sleep?'

There was a pause, just long enough for her to wonder if he had done just that, and then she felt him smile against her skin. 'I don't think I can now,' he said, as his lips drifted downwards. 'How about you? Are you sleepy?'

'No.' Martha caught her breath as his hands traced possessive patterns over her. 'No, not at all.'

CHAPTER NINE

IT WAS the beginning of a golden time for Martha. In some ways nothing had changed. Lewis still went to work every day, she still did the cooking, the babies still needed their nappies changed and their noses wiped and the Indian Ocean still surged against the reef beyond the lagoon.

But in other ways, everything was different. Martha had never felt so fulfilled, so complete, so *alive*. She hadn't known happiness as such a physical sensation before. It tingled at the ends of her fingers and quivered deep inside her, whenever she looked at the two babies, growing browner and bonnier by the day, when she stood on the verandah and caught a glimpse of the sea glittering through the palms, when she woke up every morning next to Lewis and could run her hand luxuriously over his flat stomach and his broad chest, could press her lips against him and smell the scent of his skin and taste his mouth.

He had relaxed in a way she wouldn't have been able to imagine when they first arrived in St Bonaventure. Sometimes Martha would watch him smiling at the babies, and her heart seemed to turn inside out. When he came home he would kiss her unselfconsciously, and scoop up Noah or Viola and toss them in the air until they squealed with delight, and she would feel dizzy with love for him.

Later, when the babies were asleep, they would sit on the verandah and talk, but too often Martha would lose track of the conversation as she thought about the night to come and shivered with delight, knowing that all it would take would be for her to turn her head and smile and Lewis would pull her on to his lap, that she could reach out whenever she wanted and touch him, that when they couldn't wait any longer he would take her to bed and make love to her.

They never talked about the future. If she found herself wondering what would happen at the end of the six months, Martha would push the thought away. She didn't want to think about it. She only wanted to think about now. Lewis seemed so happy too that she let herself hope that he might be coming round to the idea of family life—the *father thing*, as he had called it—after all, but she was afraid to ask when he didn't mention it. At the back of her mind she knew that she still needed to find Rory, that he deserved to know that he had a son, and that Noah would need to know his father, but there was no hurry, was there? All that mattered was now.

So Martha closed her mind to everything but the present. She was happy, Noah was happy. She couldn't ask for more than that.

'How would you feel about having another dinner party?' Lewis asked her one day, kissing the side of her neck as she stirred a pot on the stove and sending a shiver of sheer pleasure down her spine.

Martha smiled at the sensation. 'Who did you want to invite?' she asked, not without some difficulty as his arms were around her waist and his lips were distracting her.

'The resident engineer and his wife, the office manager and a couple of the local contractors. I thought we could ask Candace as well,' he added casually.

'Candace?' Martha bristled in spite of herself. 'Why her?'

'She's got some useful contacts,' he told her. 'She's been very helpful in one way and another.'

Martha had no problem imagining that! Pressing her lips together, she moved out of the circle of Lewis's arms and pretended to be consulting her recipe.

'Martha, you're not jealous of Candace by any chance, are you?' There was an undercurrent of laughter in his voice that sent warmth seeping along her bones.

'No,' she lied, steeling herself against it, but then she met his eyes and relented. 'Well, maybe a bit,' she conceded. 'She's just so perfect.'

Lewis turned her back to face him and held her firmly by the waist. 'She's not perfect for me,' he said. 'You know there's no need for you to be jealous of Candace, really, don't you?'

Martha looked into his face, and what she read there made her heart contract. No man could look at her like that if he had any interest at all in another woman, least of all a man like Lewis. She was being silly.

'Yes,' she said, 'I know.'

It didn't mean that she was looking forward to meeting Candace again, though. At least dinner wasn't the disaster it had been the last time, and she had things much more under control.

There was even time to change before the guests arrived, but Martha was chagrined to find that she was still intimidated by Candace's icy perfection. She could forget about her fashion editor past. Whatever she wore now, and whatever she did, she was tarred with the slightly scruffy, chaotic brush of motherhood and it was impossible to remove.

Oh, well, thought Martha. If she had to choose between being perfect and being a mother, she knew which one she would choose every time. It would just be nice if she could be both occasionally.

Without discussing it, she and Lewis made an effort to behave as if nothing had changed between them. There were certainly no 'darlings' or kisses blown across the table—neither of which would have been Lewis's style, or hers, come to that—but Candace still picked up on the current of awareness between them immediately. Martha saw the glacial blue eyes narrow as she looked from one to the other.

Candace didn't say anything, but the first lull in the conversation gave her the opportunity she had been waiting for, and she leant across her neighbour and asked Martha very clearly whether she had managed to track down Rory yet.

Martha glanced at Lewis, and saw with a sinking heart that the old guarded look had clanged back into place at the mention of Rory. If Candace's object had been to remind him of Martha's original intentions, she had obviously succeeded.

'No, not yet,' she said after a moment.

'It's a very romantic story,' Candace told the other guests. 'Martha lost touch with her baby's father, but she's come out here specifically to find him, so you must all let her know if you come across any marine biologists.'

Which, as a way of suggesting that Martha slept around casually, carelessly got herself pregnant and then pursued Rory across continents, having not bothered to keep in touch with him before, wasn't bad, Martha told herself wryly. Candace was quite an expert. If nothing else, she was obviously determined to get Martha out of Lewis's life as soon and as permanently as possible. If Martha had felt more sure of Lewis it would have been funny. As it was, she had a nasty feeling that some of Candace's needling remarks might be hitting home.

Not receiving any encouragement to pursue the theme of Martha as a feckless mother, Candace sought around for another subject that might discomfit her, settling at last on that old favourite—children. She did it very cleverly too, pretending to admire Martha for her patience while subtly reminding her audience—Lewis—of how messy and demanding babies were, before moving on to ask him delicately if he was expecting to hear from his sister soon.

'I'm sure Savannah must be eager to have her baby back as soon as possible,' she said. 'I must say I think you've been marvellous, Lewis, coping with all that extra responsibility when you've got this big project on.'

'It's Martha who's been coping with Viola,' he said, but Candace seemed oddly oblivious to the curtness in his voice.

'Oh, I know she's a wonderful nanny,' she agreed, putting Martha firmly in her place, 'but it's still been a bit of an imposition, hasn't it? I remember how much I sympathised when you told me how important it was for you to feel that your home was quiet and ordered, and you never get that with a baby around, do you?'

She didn't quite come out and remind him that he would have his perfect life back the moment he got rid of Viola, and therefore any need for Martha and Noah to hang around, but she might as well have done, thought Martha. Lewis was looking withdrawn, and she was afraid that Candace had had exactly the effect she wanted.

A little chill crept into Martha's heart. They had been so happy. Surely Candace couldn't spoil everything that easily?

She dreaded the moment when all the guests would leave, imagining how Lewis would be remembering how his life used to be, but when he had closed the door after the last of them had gone he only sighed with relief.

Martha was gathering up coffee cups and bracing herself for him to tell her that he didn't want to get any more involved, so convinced of what his reaction would be that when he came over to take her hands she was quite unprepared for what he actually said.

'Leave them,' said Lewis. 'We can do that in the morning. Let's go to bed.'

He didn't say anything else, but he made love to her with an urgency that left Martha shaken with a mixture of fulfilment and concern.

'What is it?' she asked softly as they lay together afterwards.

'Nothing,' he said.

He couldn't explain to her how he had felt as Candace's voice went on and on, how much he had wished that she would just shut up. He hadn't wanted to be reminded about Rory, and he certainly hadn't wanted to think about the future, but Candace had forced him to face the prospect of life without Martha and the babies.

For the first time Lewis had questioned what he really wanted. It wasn't that he was in love with Martha—he was too old for all that stuff—but he liked her and he desired her and he felt comfortable with her. That wasn't the same as being ready to settle down, take on responsibility for Noah and spend the rest of his life with her, was it?

No, it wasn't love. It was just that he couldn't imagine how it would be without them. What it would be like to come home at the end of the day to an empty house.

That was how it would be if Savannah did turn up to claim Viola, and he wouldn't put it past her to do just that. Jumping on a plane and demanding her baby back was exactly the kind of thing his sister did on a whim. It wasn't so long ago that Lewis would have welcomed her, but he had a nasty feeling that if she rang him now to say that she was on her way the bottom would fall out of his world.

Of course, that didn't mean that he wanted to look after Viola for ever. It didn't mean that he wanted Martha to stay for ever. It meant that he wanted… The fact was, Lewis didn't *know* what he wanted any more. He just knew that he felt restless and unsettled, and he didn't like it.

Nothing had changed, he tried to reassure himself. Martha would be as reluctant to get too involved as he was. As Candace had reminded him, she had made it very clear that she was in search of a father for Noah, and he wasn't prepared to fulfil that role, so if their six months were up with no sign of Rory, she would say goodbye.

And that would be that.

Without meaning to, his arms tightened around Martha. 'Are you happy?' he asked her almost fiercely.

She eased herself above him so that she could look down into his face, studying him with her dark eyes, her silky hair swinging softly against his cheek. 'Right now?' she said, and bent down to kiss him. 'Yes,' she murmured against his mouth, 'I am.'

And she *was*, Martha told herself later, suppressing the tiny niggle of doubt about the future. Lewis evidently didn't want to think about what would happen then, and neither did she.

So they both carried on not thinking about it, and as the days passed, and then the weeks, it became more and more difficult to broach the subject. It was easier to push the thought aside, to decide that they would deal with the future when it came and not before.

Until the afternoon Candace turned up on the front verandah.

'I was just passing,' she said. 'I thought I'd drop in and say hello.'

Martha couldn't hide her surprise. 'Lewis is still at work,' she said, hoping she was more successful at masking her dislike. 'He won't be back until a bit later.'

Candace waved an airy hand. 'It's you I came to see,' she said.

After that, Martha didn't have much choice but to ask her in for a drink. They made stilted conversation as she made some tea and took it out on to the verandah, where she installed

Viola and Noah in their high chairs and gave them a rusk each to keep them quiet.

'I felt I had to come out and congratulate you,' said Candace, averting her eyes from the way Viola was smearing her soggy biscuit over the tray.

Martha was busy rescuing Noah's as it threatened to fall on to the floor, so she thought she must have misheard.

'Sorry, congratulate who?' she asked when Noah was happily sucking his biscuit once more.

'You.' Candace beamed at her in a way that Martha found oddly chilling. 'You must be thrilled!'

A nasty feeling was beginning to uncurl inside Martha. She didn't know what was coming, but she knew she wasn't going to like it.

'I'm sure I would be if I knew what you were talking about,' she said.

'Why, finding Noah's father, of course!'

There was a frozen pause. 'Rory?' said Martha carefully.

'Yes, Rory McMillan. It is him, isn't it?' Candace settled back in her chair, enjoying the effect her words were having. 'What a coincidence, him turning out to be part of the team that Lewis is using for the environmental study for the port!'

Yes, what a coincidence, thought Martha grimly. 'Where did you meet him?'

'Oh, I haven't actually met him myself,' said Candace with obvious regret. 'I gather there are a group of them over here, and they all came into the bar at the hotel the other day. By the time I'd realised that they were working on a marine project, Rory had left, apparently, but I asked if they knew of him, of course, and that's when they told me he was working for Lewis.'

She glanced slyly at Martha, who was doing her damnedest not to give her the satisfaction of reacting the way she really wanted to react. Beginning with killing Lewis. Or possibly Candace, and then Lewis. The possibilities were endless, when you came to think of it.

'I would have asked them to pass a message on to Rory, asking him to get in touch with you, but I knew that if he was working for Lewis then of course Lewis would know all about him anyway, and tell you.'

'Of course,' said Martha through her teeth.

Except that he hadn't told her, had he?

When Lewis came back that night he could see at once that something was wrong. Martha was holding herself rigidly, and she was as taut as a suspension cable on one of his bridges, but she refused to talk until the babies were safely in bed.

'So, are you going to tell me what's wrong now?' he asked as she shut the bedroom door gently behind her.

'I am indeed,' said Martha, walking into the living room and folding her arms in an effort to keep herself under control. She was so angry that she was afraid she would cry. That or throw something.

She turned to face Lewis from a safe distance. 'I understand that you've taken on some marine biologists to do a study of the environmental effects of building the port?'

Lewis's expression froze. This was the moment that he had been dreading. 'Yes,' he said, still hoping against hope that she didn't know the whole truth.

'And one of them is called Rory McMillan?'

Well, he had known that it was a pretty futile hope. Deep down, he had known from the moment he walked in this evening. 'Yes,' he said.

'The very same Rory McMillan I've been trying to contact ever since I came here?'

She hadn't been trying that hard, Lewis thought with a flare of resentment, but decided that it would be wiser not to say it at this stage. 'Who told you?' he asked instead, which turned out to be just as bad.

Martha's eyes were bright with temper. 'Not the person who should have done, obviously! As it was, I had to hear the good news from your friend Candace. She couldn't wait to get over here and congratulate me on my good fortune.'

'Candace?' Lewis frowned. 'How did she know?'

'I don't think that's the point, is it, Lewis? The real point is that you knew and you didn't tell me.'

Couldn't he *see* that? Couldn't he tell how much that hurt? Martha hugged her arms together and forced back the tears, swallowing the hard, angry lump in her throat. 'How long have you known Rory?'

'I don't really know him,' said Lewis defensively. 'I just talked to the project leader, some guy called Steve. Surveys like the one we need for the port give their projects extra income to fund research, so he was willing to send a couple of his marine biologists along. They just introduced themselves as John and Rory. I didn't know it was him for sure.'

'But you had a good idea?'

'Yes,' he admitted, remembering the sick feeling of recognition as Rory had strolled into the office. *Gorgeous*, Martha had called him. *Tall, tanned, blond, dancing blue eyes*. Lewis didn't know about gorgeous, but the rest of her description had fitted pretty well. Personally, he had disliked Rory on sight. He was too cocky by half.

'How long ago was this?' Martha asked, with the same stony expression.

Lewis sighed. 'About ten days.'

'Ten days?' Unable to stand still, Martha took a turn around the room while she struggled with the urge to have the kind of tantrum Viola indulged in with such effect. 'Why didn't you *tell* me?'

Why *hadn't* he told her? Lewis asked himself. It was hard to explain now his sick, shameful feeling that had been perilously close to panic. The realisation that those weeks with Martha would end after all. The fear that she would take one look at Rory and fall for him all over again.

Lewis was under no illusions about how he would compare to Rory. The other man was young and good-looking, and had the sort of breezy, careless charm that he had never been able to master. On top of which, Rory was Noah's father. What did *he* have to offer compared to that?

Unable to admit just how afraid he was that Martha would simply take Noah and leave him for Rory, Lewis had let himself believe that there was no need for her to know yet. He had planned to tell her when Rory was safely back on his atoll, so that she could contact him when the six months was up.

'I was going to tell you,' he said to Martha, although it was hard to talk to her when she was stalking around like that. 'The time just never seemed right.' That sounded lame, even to his own ears. 'I wanted Rory to concentrate on the study. There's a deadline for that, and it's not as if you needed to contact him urgently.'

'Oh, yes, we mustn't forget the *study*, must we?' She rounded on him. 'I'm *so* glad you thought of that! Forget the fact that you knew Rory was the reason I came here in the first place!'

Lewis could feel himself being driven into a corner. Everything he said just seemed to make things worse. What was it about Martha that made him lose his cool? He was famous for his ability to sort out crises on site, for his relentless control in the most fraught of negotiations. Now look at him, stumbling over explanations like a fool!

'Viola wasn't well,' he tried, 'and you had a lot of things on your mind.'

'Yes, and one of them was finding Noah's father! I think I could have coped with a bit of good news!'

'I didn't know if it *would* be good news,' Lewis was provoked into saying.

At least that got her to stop pacing. She stared at him furiously. 'What do you mean by that?'

'You said you were happy,' he reminded her deliberately, and she turned her face away.

'That was before I knew you were capable of keeping something this important from me.'

Lewis set his jaw. He had made such a mess of it he might as well go on. 'And I'm not sure Rory would be a good father for Noah,' he told her. 'He seems very young to me, and very casual about everything. I couldn't see him changing nappies. From what I can gather, he keeps the bars going when he's here, and spends the rest of his time on the project which is based on a tiny uninhabited island. An atoll isn't a suitable place to bring up a baby.'

'It's not for you to decide who would or wouldn't be a good father for Noah!' Martha eyed him with freezing scorn. 'The fact is that Rory *is* his father, and there's nothing you or I or anyone else can do about it. And frankly,' she swept on, 'you're not exactly in a strong position to criticise when it comes to fatherhood either, are you? The chances are that Rory would make a better father than you. At least he doesn't lie!'

There was a white shade around Lewis's mouth. 'I haven't lied.'

'Oh, so when I asked you if anything interesting had happened during your day, the way I always do when you get home, and you didn't tell me that you had bumped into the father of my baby, the very man I've spent months trying to track down, you didn't think that it was a lie when you said "no"?'

Lewis dropped on to one of the chairs and rested his elbows on his knees, raking his fingers through his hair with a sigh. 'Look, I'm sorry,' he said after a fraught silence, 'but it's not the end of the world, is it? Rory's not going anywhere. You wanted to know how to contact him, and now you do. I don't understand what the problem is.'

He didn't understand? Martha stared at him in disbelief. That made them equal then. It was like trying to talk to someone from a different planet. Maybe there was something in this Venus and Mars stuff after all.

'You make it sound as if I'm making a big fuss about nothing,' she said tightly. 'Can't you imagine what it was like for me to hear about Rory from Candace? She just sat there, *gloating*! She knew you hadn't told me anything. Have you any idea how humiliating that felt?'

In spite of herself, her voice wobbled, and she drew a steadying breath. 'Have you got any idea what it feels like to discover that the man you—' she nearly said 'love' but checked herself just in time '—the man you've been sleeping with, the man you've *trusted*, turns out to be arrogant and deceitful and selfish enough to keep something so important from you, and then *stupid* enough not to understand why you're angry?'

Even in the white-hot flame of her fury Martha held on to the thought that if he would just say that he hadn't told her because he was afraid of losing her it might be all right.

But Lewis didn't say that.

'I didn't want you to forget that you're here on a contract,' he said instead. 'How would I cope with Viola if you were chasing around after Rory McMillan?'

The contract? Was that all he cared about? Hurt tore across Martha's heart and stung her eyes. He had never mentioned love, it was true, but she had thought that she meant more to him than that.

'Don't worry, I'm in no danger of forgetting my contract,' she said tightly. 'But there's nothing in it to say that I can't make contact with Rory before the six months is up.' She stopped as a horn sounded aside. 'Talking of which, that'll be my taxi.'

Taxi? What taxi? Lewis watched Martha cross the room to pick up her bag with a mixture of fear and frustration. 'Where are you going?'

'I'm going to find Rory and talk to him.'

'Now?' he demanded, getting to his feet.

'Yes, now. I wouldn't dream of interrupting while he's working on your precious survey, so the evening is the best time to find him. You said that he spends his spare time in bars, so it shouldn't be too hard to track him down. The town's not that big.'

Lewis could feel himself flailing. 'What about the babies?'

'You can babysit,' she told him. 'I would have thought it's the least you can do, in the circumstances!'

She was walking away; her hand was on the door. Lewis looked at her with a kind of desperation. He wanted to go after her, to push the door back into place, to beg her to stay, but she was too angry. She wouldn't believe anything he said now.

He swallowed. 'When will you be back?' he heard himself ask, as if from a great distance.

'When I've talked to Rory.' Martha turned at the door, and her expression was colder than he had ever seen it. 'Don't wait up.' Then the door had closed behind her, and she was gone.

Rory was in the third bar she tried. He was sitting at a table with several others, all dressed in shorts and casual tops. They were all young, all tanned, all glowing with health and vitality. They looked as if they were waiting to audition for *Baywatch*.

Martha hesitated, watching Rory across the room. It was hard to imagine anyone more different from Lewis. He looked younger even than she had remembered, but the blue-eyed charm was still plainly in evidence as he flirted with a very pretty girl, as blonde as he was, who kept tossing her hair back and laughing just a little too loudly.

Maybe this wasn't a good time? Rory was obviously otherwise occupied and, judging by her body language, the girl wouldn't welcome an interruption either.

But, then, there was never going to be a good time, was there? And her alternative was to go home to Lewis. Deep down, the thought of doing just that was so appealing that Martha wavered, before she stiffened her spine with the memory of the reasons he had given for keeping her in the dark. The environmental study. That contract. How could she go back to him now and admit that she hadn't even talked to Rory?

So Martha took a deep breath, squared her shoulders and walked across the bar to Rory's table. 'Hello, Rory,' she said.

Rory looked up, his blank expression replaced after a couple of seconds by one of ludicrous amazement. *'Martha?'*

'Well, that's good,' said Martha, forcing a smile. 'I wasn't sure if you'd remember me at all.'

'Of course I do!' Rory leapt to his feet, beaming. 'Hey, it's great to see you!' He gave her a big, unselfconscious hug, and then held her away from him, still shaking his head in surprise. 'You're the last person I expected to see here! I just didn't recognise you at first. You look so different!'

'Do I?' said Martha, a little taken aback. 'How?'

But Rory was already reaching for a chair and urging her to sit down, waving at the waitress to bring another beer. 'Move up, everyone,' he said, making room for her beside him, and although the blonde girl masked her disappointment quickly Martha caught a flash of resentment and felt uncomfortable. She hadn't thought about what impact her news would have on anyone else, she realised guiltily.

'Meet Martha, everybody.' Rory ran through the names of the others round the table, although the only one that registered with Martha was the girl, who was called Amy. 'I met Martha when I was in London last year,' he continued proudly. 'She's a fashion editor and has an incredibly glamorous lifestyle.'

Nobody said anything, but the looks of polite disbelief around the table told Martha just how much she had changed since coming to St Bonaventure. She had been so angry that she hadn't stopped to change or put on any make-up, and now she felt horribly conscious of the crow's-feet around her eyes and strands of grey in her dark hair. She always pulled them out when she saw them, but today had been the kind of day that put them all back.

'So, what are you doing here, Martha?' Rory asked, turning to her, his handsome face lit up with a kind of puppyish enthusiasm.

'I'm…working,' she said carefully.

'Bikinis on the beach, all that kind of thing? Cool.'

'Not exactly,' said Martha, as her beer arrived. She didn't want one, but she took a sip anyway. 'Actually, I'm here as a nanny.'

There was a pause, and then Rory burst out laughing. 'You're kidding, right? I can't imagine you with kids!'

Martha kept the smile on her face with difficulty. 'It's true.'

He stared at her. 'I always thought you were so cool,' he said, baffled. 'Why would you give up a great career like that to be a *nanny*?'

Her hands tightened in her lap and she forced herself to relax them. Be fair, she told herself. You used to think that looking after children would be the pits, too.

'Perhaps I fancied a career change,' she said.

Rory shook his head, still struggling with the idea of her change of image. He obviously hadn't entirely given up on the idea that she might be pulling his leg. 'Are you really a nanny?'

'Yes.' Martha took a breath. 'In fact, I think you know who I'm working for—Lewis Mansfield?' It hurt just to say his name.

'Lewis? Yeah, I know him all right.' Rory grinned and rolled his eyes. 'That's one scary guy! Does he ever smile?'

Martha thought about the way he smiled as he pulled her on to his lap. The way he smiled as he carried Noah into the sea, the sunlight reflected from the water rocking over their skins. The way he smiled against her skin.

She swallowed. Crying now would *not* be a good idea. 'Sometimes,' she said.

'He certainly doesn't smile at me,' said Rory, picking up his beer. 'I don't think he likes me.'

'Oh, come on,' said Amy, bang on cue. 'Why on earth wouldn't he like you?'

'Jealous of my legendary charm, perhaps?' Rory joked. 'What do you think, Martha? You must know him quite well.'

'Quite well, yes,' said Martha with a tight feeling in her chest.

'He's not the matiest of blokes, is he? He reminds me of my old maths teacher. Talk about grim!'

'Yeah,' agreed someone else. 'Only in my case it was geography. When he fixes you with that look you feel like you're twelve and he's about to give you a detention for talking at the back of the class!'

They all laughed, and Martha bit her lip.

'It just takes a little while to get to know him, that's all,' she said.

She couldn't bear it. She didn't want to be here in this loud bar, with these young, trendy people, listening to them mock Lewis. They didn't know him. They had no idea what he was like.

She wasn't going to be able to talk to Rory here, anyway. She could hardly announce his fatherhood in front of this audience. Quite apart from anything else, she would have to shout to make herself heard over the music. That wasn't the way she wanted to introduce the idea of Noah to his father.

So she carried on smiling, finished her beer, then said that she had to go. 'But it would be great to catch up with you properly,' she said to Rory as he got to his feet to say goodbye. 'What about lunch tomorrow?'

'Sure,' he said, surprised but pleased. He put his arm round her and gave her a hug. 'You know, it's really good to see you again, Martha. I often think about that time in London. We had a good time, didn't we?'

'Yes.' Martha disengaged herself as unobtrusively as she could. She knew that she ought to be delighted that he seemed so pleased to see her, but right now the thought of him wanting to pick up their previous relationship was downright unnerving. It wasn't that he wasn't attractive. He was.

He just wasn't Lewis.

CHAPTER TEN

MARTHA took Noah with her to lunch the next day, and made sure that they were there early so that they had a quiet table. Rory wasn't unduly surprised to see her with a baby, and gave Noah a careless pat as he sat down.

'So you really are a nanny! Is this your charge?'

'You could say that,' said Martha. 'This is Noah. He's my son.'

'Your *son*?'

She could see him assessing Noah's age and doing some rapid calculations. He was a biologist, after all, and he wasn't stupid. His face changed.

'Yes,' she told him gently, knowing that he had already worked it all out. 'Noah's your son, too.'

At first Rory was too shell-shocked to take much in. He kept staring at Noah as if he couldn't quite believe that he was a real baby, and it took some time for Martha to convince him that she wasn't interested in financial support. 'It's not about money,' she insisted. 'I just want Noah to know who his father is.'

Rory relaxed once the prospect of handing over a share of his grant had been removed, and as he got used to the idea of being a father he became positively enthusiastic.

Once, Martha had found that puppyish enthusiasm endearing, but now it seemed naïve. Unlike Lewis, Rory obviously had no idea what was involved in looking after a baby, but she couldn't discourage him, not after coming this far, and when Rory suggested that she and Noah move in with him for a while she felt trapped.

'The others are going back to the project site tomorrow, but I'm staying on to finish the survey on the port,' he was explaining. 'I'll be here for another month or so, and I'll have the project house to myself. You and Noah could come and live with me and we could get to know each other properly.'

It should have been her dream scenario. Wasn't this exactly what she had wanted when she had first thought about coming out to St Bonaventure?

Martha told herself she ought to be thrilled that everything was working out so well. Rory had come round to the idea of fatherhood far more quickly than she had expected. He was saying all the right things, doing all the right things. He had Noah on his knee now and was making him chuckle. It was all perfect.

Only it didn't feel perfect. Martha didn't want to move in with him straight away. She didn't want to leave Viola.

Or Lewis.

'That would be lovely, Rory,' she said dutifully, 'but we can't come straight away. I've got another baby to look after, and my contract lasts another couple of months.'

'I'll be back on the project then,' objected Rory. 'We just camp out there, so it would be hard with Noah. I'm sure we could work something out about the other baby. Why don't you ask Lewis, anyway?'

Noah's father, anxious to spend time with their son. How could she argue with that?

'All right,' said Martha. 'I'll ask him.'

'So, how was your lunch?' Lewis asked sardonically when he came home that night.

He had given himself a good talking to the night before and, having cursed himself for a fool at first, was now well on the way to persuading himself that this was all for the best. Things had been getting too cosy with Martha and the two babies. If they had gone on much longer he might easily have found himself sucked into the kind of commitment he had been so careful to avoid for so long.

Perhaps it was just as well that Rory had turned up when he did. Now all it needed was for Martha to have calmed down and they could end things in a civilised way.

Which was fine in theory, but less easy in practice, when he had spent the night before and all of that day torturing himself by thinking about Martha and Rory together.

'Lunch was fine,' said Martha. She had calmed down all right. Last night's fury had petered out and she was looking tired and strained. Lewis wanted to gather her into his arms and hold her until the tension drained out of her body.

Not that she would want to be comforted by someone arrogant, selfish and…what was it?…yes, deceitful. She might not be spitting sparks any more, but she wouldn't have forgotten.

Lewis looked away, steeling himself against the urge to go down on his knees and tell her that he was sorry, to beg her to forgive him and ask if they could go back to the way they were before. It was too late for that now.

'Did Rory acknowledge Noah as his son and heir?' he asked instead.

'Yes.' Martha drew a breath. 'He wanted us to spend the next couple of weeks with him, but I explained about Viola and the fact that I hadn't finished my contract yet.'

'Don't worry about it,' said Lewis, and only he knew what that careless shrug cost him. 'I guessed that's what you would want to do, so I've already spoken to Eloise, and she's agreed to look after Viola during the day.'

She swallowed. 'What about the evenings?'

'I'm sure I'll manage,' he said indifferently. 'I'm not completely useless, and it's not as if it's for much longer, anyway.'

'But…what about the contract?' said Martha, stricken. He had gone on and on and *on* about that contract. How could he suddenly pretend that it didn't matter to him? She had been depending on him to insist that she and Noah stayed, and now it was as if he couldn't wait to get rid of her.

'Far be it from me to stand in the way of reuniting a happy family,' said Lewis, looking withdrawn. 'I'm not a monster. You've been very clear about what you wanted, and now that it looks as if things are working out for you I'd be unreasonable to insist on you fulfilling the terms of your contract.'

'Well…perhaps we could treat it as a few days off?' Martha was struggling not to sound desperate, but Lewis didn't seem to care one way or another.

'I'm sure you don't want to commit yourself to anything,' he said, his eyes shuttered. 'There's no telling what might happen. Rory might decide that he likes family life so much that he doesn't want to go back to the project. I'm going to try and contact Savannah tomorrow, too, and if she's ready to have Viola back I won't need you at all.'

That hurt more than anything. He wasn't even going to try and persuade her to stay, Martha realised bleakly.

It looked as if she didn't have much choice. She could hardly insist on remaining with Viola after everything that she had said last night, but saying goodbye to the baby was one of the hardest things she had ever done. She couldn't even explain why she was going. It made Martha realise just how much she had come to love Viola, and how much she was going to miss her.

And her stubborn, difficult uncle.

To the very last minute Martha let herself hope that Lewis would change his mind. Their last morning was bizarrely normal. Viola and Noah were up early, and she was in the kitchen giving them both breakfast as Lewis came in, hesitating only a second before he poured himself a cup of the coffee she had made the way she always did.

Martha closed her eyes and wished that she could rewind time. That when she opened them again they would be back to where they had been before. Lewis would put down his cup and kiss her goodbye, and when he came home he would smile and toss the babies in the air, the way he always did.

But it wasn't going to happen that way. When he came home tonight she wouldn't be here. Martha felt sick at the thought.

No amount of wishing was going to change things now. Nothing could undo the fact that Lewis had lied to her, but if he would only ask her to stay she was sure that they could work something out.

Lewis gulped down his coffee and set down his cup. 'I have to go,' he said brusquely. His face was like a mask, but Martha saw his eyes rest on Noah and for a fleeting moment something flickered in his expression and was gone before he turned to her.

'Thanks for everything,' he said.

That was it? *Thanks for everything?* When Martha thought of the times they had shared, the sunlit mornings and the dark evenings on the verandah and the long, hot tropical nights, she wanted to throw something after him. The surge of anger was oddly comforting, though. It consumed her as she chucked her things into a case and dismantled Noah's cot, and stopped her from thinking about how much she was hurting.

She was furious with Lewis, but far more so with herself. Why had she let herself get so involved? She had known all along what he was like. She had known there would be no happy-ever-after with him. It had always been doomed to end in tears.

It was her own fault for forgetting what was really important. Noah needed a father, and she should have been thinking about finding a family for him, not about Lewis's mouth and

Lewis's hands and how they felt against her skin.

Well, now she had a chance to put that right. Rory was Noah's father, and he seemed keen to bond with his small son. She could build a future with him in a way she would never have been able to do with Lewis. Hadn't she told Lewis that successful relationships were about friendship, not passion? Martha slammed the lid of her case down and snapped the locks. She had believed it before, and she would believe it again. She was a pragmatist, not a romantic. It was time to put this infatuation with Lewis behind her and get on with real life again

But first she had to say goodbye to Viola. Lewis's niece was in a sunny mood and at her most charming. She was irresistible when she was like this, thought Martha, her throat tightening. Viola gurgled up at her, played with her toes, flirted with her lashes…she might almost have known that Martha was thinking about leaving her and doing her damnedest to make it as hard as she could.

And succeeding. Martha set her jaw and concentrated on not crying as she changed Viola's nappy for the last time. She didn't want to upset her, but when the taxi came, and Viola realised that Martha was taking Noah but leaving her behind, her small face crumpled with distress and she started to wail.

It was a struggle for Eloise to hold her. 'You should stay,' she told Martha tearfully. 'You belong here.'

Martha's throat was so tight she could hardly speak. 'I can't,' she whispered in a broken voice, that wonderful, invigorating anger swept away in a tidal wave of misery.

'I don't understand why you're leaving,' said Eloise, shaking her head.

Martha didn't understand either by then. She just knew that Lewis had said that he didn't need her.

The tears were pouring down her face as she tried to kiss Viola goodbye, but the baby twisted her head away and hit out at her furiously. It was all she deserved for making such a mess of things, thought Martha desolately, aware that Noah was getting upset as well.

'I'll come back and see you,' she promised, but Viola couldn't understand.

Eloise was crying too by now. 'Better go quickly,' she said.

Rory couldn't understand why Martha was so upset. 'She'll be fine,' he said heartily when she tried to explain how hard it had been to say goodbye. 'Babies don't know who's looking after them, do they?'

Five minutes as a father and suddenly he was an expert on babies. Martha was too tired and dispirited to correct him, but she tried to whip up some enthusiasm as Rory showed her proudly round the project house.

'What do you think?' he asked.

Martha thought it was horrible. It was a small square house, basically furnished, with a fridge full of beer and not much else. The members of the project seemed to use it as a dump more than a base. The scrubby garden was full of empty bottles and broken diving gear, and the living area was piled high with computer print-outs, sample jars, crisp packets, squeezed cans of drink, and back copies of scientific journals. There was no shade and the air-conditioning rattled monotonously.

Heartsick, Martha hugged Noah as she looked around her. No deep verandah, no slow *thwock* of ceiling fans, no lagoon at the end of the garden. And, worse, no Eloise, no Viola. No Lewis.

But she had a family. Almost. Maybe.

'This is my room.' Rory opened a door into a room so messy that it made the rest of the house look as if it were the object of obsessive housekeeping. Kicking clothes out of the way, he sat down on the bed and patted it invitingly. 'So, shall we take up where we left off?'

He smiled at her and Martha marvelled at herself. He was gorgeous, blond, smiling, a hunk of manhood oozing sex appeal, and he wanted her, with her crow's-feet and her stretch marks. She should be turning handsprings with gratitude, but she felt absolutely nothing.

'I don't think that's a good idea,' she said, staying by the door. 'Not yet, anyway,' she added as his face dropped. Who knew? She might decide that a younger man with warm blue eyes and the body of a god was preferable to an uptight, middle-aged engineer.

'I just think it would be better if we got to know each other again before we sleep together,' she tried to explain.

'We didn't know each other before,' Rory pointed out with just a trace of sullenness.

It was a fair point. Martha sighed a little. 'It was different then,' was all she could say. She wished Rory wasn't reminding her of a sulky little boy who'd just had his lollipop taken away.

'Noah will probably wake up in the night,' she said, aware that she was trying to placate him and exasperated with herself for doing it. 'I think I'd better sleep with him until he's settled. By then we'll be used to each other again and…well, we'll see.'

It was a sensible enough plan, but as a start to a future which would hopefully give Noah the stability of a secure family background it sounded a little lacking in joy. Martha's mind veered dangerously to the long nights she had spent with Lewis—uptight, middle-aged engineer that he was—and then away again. This wasn't about rocketing passion or the slow burn of desire. This was about building a family for Noah. It was *about* being sensible, not joyful.

In the event, her prediction that Noah would be unsettled that night proved to be well-founded. He cried and cried, and Martha, tired and miserable and very close to the edge, wished she could do the same. She missed the house by the lagoon. She missed Viola, and she missed Lewis with a physical ache.

She did her best to comfort Noah and keep him quiet, but the walls were very thin, and they might as well have been sharing a room for all the noise that Rory was spared. He was looking distinctly frazzled by the morning.

'I guess that's what comes with being a father,' he said bravely.

'I'm afraid so,' said Martha, thinking privately that what came with being a father was taking it in turns to get up in the middle of the night. Even Lewis, Mr I'm-never-going-to-be-a-father himself, would get up sometimes to settle Viola or Noah to give her a break…

But she wasn't supposed to be thinking about Lewis, was she?

She smiled brightly. 'Shall I cook something nice for tonight?'

Rory didn't think much of that suggestion. Martha gathered that what little money he had was kept for beer, and that the project members lived off chips and dips while they were in town. A quick look through the kitchen cupboards revealed very little in the way of kitchen equipment, so perhaps that was the only sensible solution.

Bang went her hope of making herself at home in the kitchen. Martha spent the day tidying instead, but that turned out to be a *big* mistake. Rory was horrified when he came home. 'What have you done?' he demanded, looking around him at the immaculate house in dismay. 'We'll never be able to find anything now!'

He recovered his temper in the shower, and apologised to Martha afterwards. 'I'm sorry. I just had a bad day,' he said. 'I don't know what was wrong with that Lewis guy, but he was on my case all day. I couldn't do anything right.' He smiled ruefully at her. 'Let's go out and have a drink.'

Martha had to point out that it was Noah's bedtime, and that they had no babysitter.

'Oh. Right.'

To do him justice, Rory made a quick recovery and spent some time playing with Noah before his bath, but Martha could tell that he was quickly bored. When Noah was in bed they sat in the uncomfortable living area, with its single, harsh overhead light, and made polite conversation over the noise of the air-conditioning.

He's a nice guy, Martha reminded herself. He's intelligent and good-looking and fun and Noah's father. He'd be kind to me and we'd get on, and sex wouldn't be a problem. At least we know that we're compatible in bed. Or we were.

So why do I feel as if I've caught the wrong train and am hurtling in the wrong direction?

She knew why. Rory wasn't Lewis.

Martha could hear Viola crying as she shifted Noah on to her other hip and knocked on the door.

There was a long pause, then Lewis yanked the door open abruptly. 'Yes?' he snapped, before he realised who was standing there, and then he stopped in utter disbelief.

He had Viola, clumsily wrapped in a towel, under one arm. She was still yelling her head off, and he was looking wet and harassed, but to Martha they both looked wonderful. Just seeing them sent a great whoosh of joy and relief through her, depriving her of breath so that all she could do was smile.

Noah, recognising Lewis, and no doubt the sound of Viola's voice, took his thumb out of his mouth and beamed too.

'Martha!' Lewis took an involuntary step towards her and the blaze of expression on his face told Martha all that she needed to know. It was quickly masked, but she had seen. He could pretend all he liked; she wouldn't believe that he wasn't pleased to see her now.

'Shall we swop?' she suggested serenely.

She held out Noah to him, and Lewis was so taken aback that he found himself passing over Viola. The exchange of babies brought them close together, and the scent of her hair made him light-headed. He wanted to clutch her to him to make sure that she was real, but she was already stepping back, murmuring to Viola, who was piggy-eyed with crying and hiccuping disconsolately into Martha's neck, comforted already by her familiar smell.

'Come on, let's get you dried,' Martha said to her, and headed calmly towards the bathroom.

Lost for words, Lewis stared after her for a moment, before he turned his gaze to the stuff that the taxi driver had unloaded on to the verandah, and lastly to Noah. The baby smiled and bumped his forehead against him in greeting and Lewis felt something hard and tight inside him dissolve as he found himself smiling back.

'Welcome back,' he said to Noah. 'It's good to see you again.'

Following Martha to the bathroom, he found her expertly dusting Viola with baby powder.

'Martha, what's going on?' he said in an effort to sound in control. 'What are you doing here?'

'I've come to finish my contract,' she said without looking up from the baby.

Lewis closed his eyes briefly. It was so much what he had wanted to hear that he was afraid he might be imagining things, and that this would all turn out to be a dream, but when he opened them again Martha was still there.

'What about Rory?' he asked, finding his voice at last.

Her hands stilled for a moment, and she glanced at him with one of her clear, direct looks. 'I made a mistake,' she said. 'I'd convinced myself that what Noah needed more than anything was a father, and that the best thing for him would be to grow up in a proper family, but what's the point of a family if it's not a happy one?'

Without waiting for his answer, she turned her attention back to the baby. She fastened the nappy with deft hands and put Viola into a Babygro with an ease that Lewis could only marvel at. When he had tried the two previous nights it had taken him ages as he struggled to keep Viola still and she wriggled and fought and bellowed objections. Martha made it look as if it was the simplest thing in the world.

'I've done a lot of thinking over the last couple of days,' she went on, lifting Viola against her shoulder and cuddling her warm little body, 'and I've changed my mind.'

She turned to face Lewis squarely. 'Now I think that all Noah really needs is for his parents to be happy. It doesn't matter whether we're together or apart, as long as Noah senses that we're doing what we want to do and are with the person we want to be with.

'Rory wouldn't be happy if he's forced into responsibility before he's ready for it,' she said. 'He'll be a better father to Noah for not feeling tied down now. Have you got some milk for her?'

Lewis blinked at the abrupt change of subject, but recovered quickly enough. 'In the kitchen.'

Still gripped by a feeling of unreality, he divided the milk between two bottles and they sat at either end of the sofa with a baby each.

'What did you say to Rory?' he asked Martha when Noah and Viola were guzzling contentedly.

'I told him that it wasn't going to work,' she said, adjusting Noah's bottle slightly as he clutched at it with greedy little hands. 'I told him that nothing would change the fact that he would always be Noah's father, and that I hoped that he would keep in touch so that Noah could get to know him as he's growing up. I said that it would be better for all of us if we didn't try and pretend that we belonged together when we don't, so I was leaving.'

For the first time Lewis felt a twinge of sympathy for Rory. He knew what it was like when Martha said that she was leaving. 'How did he react?'

'I think he was more relieved than anything,' said Martha reflectively. 'He was prepared to have a go, but even after a few days he realized that Noah and I just didn't fit into his life. He's not ready for commitment. He feels that he would be a better father if we weren't together.' She went on with a sideways glance under her lashes at Lewis, 'But he did say that he would come and see Noah when he can.'

Lewis shifted Viola up his arm. 'Where does that leave you?' he asked.

'It leaves me trying to be happy myself.'

'And how are you going to do that?'

'Well,' said Martha, 'I was hoping that you would give me my job back, for a start.'

'Even though that would mean working for someone who's arrogant and selfish and stupid?'

She looked at him with a half-smile. 'You know I don't really think you're stupid, Lewis.'

But arrogant and selfish were still OK, apparently? 'Gee, thanks!' he said ironically.

'I missed Viola,' Martha explained, lifting Noah to rub his back until he burped. 'So did Noah. The days were much too quiet without her. We decided it was worth putting up with you for her, didn't we?' she asked Noah, who gurgled back at her.

She was smiling at her baby and Lewis eyed her, uncertain how much she was joking, until she glanced at him and the gleam of laughter in her brown eyes let him release the breath that he hadn't even been aware that he was holding.

No more was said until Noah's cot had been set up and both babies were settled for sleep, but it was as if everything important had already been said. Martha and Lewis moved easily together, aware that there was no rush, until at last they were able to sit back on the verandah in the dark.

Martha breathed in the scents of night. She could hear the familiar rasp of the insects and the hot wind soughing through the palms, their rustling leaves drowning out the sound of the sea. Beside her, Lewis was solid, real, close enough to touch. She remembered the look on his face when he saw her, and leant back in her chair, closing her eyes with a sigh of pleasure. She had only been away three days, but it felt as if she had been on a long journey and had only just made it home.

'So you came back for Viola?' asked Lewis.

'Partly.' She smiled at his fishing without opening her eyes.

'And?' he prompted her.

Martha lifted her lashes at that, and looked at the bougainvillaea scrambling along the verandah roof. 'And because I was happier here than I've ever been anywhere else,' she said quietly. 'I was never going to be really happy with Rory. He's great, but he's not…' she turned her head to look directly at Lewis '…he's not you.'

There, she had said it. She let out a long breath.

There was a long, long pause. 'You came back for me?' said Lewis in such a peculiar voice that all at once Martha lost her nerve. Had she been wrong about that expression, after all?

'I know it won't be for ever,' she hastened to reassure him. 'I know you don't want a family. That's OK,' she said. 'I just thought that we could have another couple of months together. We had a good time before, didn't we?'

'Yes,' agreed Lewis. 'We did.'

'I'm not asking for any more than that,' said Martha. 'Just two months, being the way we were before. No commitments, no creeping domesticity…just the two of us.'

'And Viola and Noah,' he pointed out. 'They're commitments, aren't they?'

She looked at him, a little confused. 'Of course they are, but I was thinking about the evenings, after they're in bed. It would just be the two of us then. I'm not talking about for ever, Lewis. I'm talking about now.'

'And would that really be enough to make you happy? Two months, and then goodbye?'

Martha swallowed. 'I would be happier than I would be if I wasn't here with you,' she told him.

'Why?' asked Lewis softly, and her mouth dried.

'You know why.'

'I want you to say it.' He held out his hand. 'Come here,' he said, and tugged her gently on to his lap. 'Say it,' he said.

'I love you,' said Martha. It was easier to say than she had thought. She slid her arms around his neck and said it again. 'I love you. I need you. I've missed you.'

Lewis smiled and ran his hand down her spine, sending a delicious shiver of anticipation through her. 'Say it again.'

'I love you. I love you,' she said obediently, punctuating her words with little kisses, a blizzard of them, all along his jaw from his ear to the edge of his mouth. 'I love you.'

His smile deepened, but still he held back tantalisingly. 'Is this love as in companionship and respect?'

'No, it's love as in passion and desire and wanting you more than I've ever wanted anyone before,' Martha murmured. 'I've changed my mind about love.'

'Ah,' said Lewis, pulling her closer. 'You don't think it's about practicality any more?'

'No.' She nestled into him, pressing her face into his throat, breathing in the scent of him, touching her lips to his skin. 'I think it's about not feeling complete without you,' she whispered against his jaw. 'It's about the world being out of kilter when you're not there. It's about that feeling of coming home when you hold me like this.'

'That is a change,' he agreed, and the undercurrent of laughter in his voice warmed her.

'It's about feeling as if the sun's come out whenever you smile. About the way you only have to touch me and I'm on fire. About lying next to you and feeling that my heart is going to burst with loving you.'

'In that case,' said Lewis, 'I think I must love you too.'

Martha straightened abruptly. 'Really?'

'Well, don't sound so surprised!' He pretended to sound offended, and then his smile faded and his face was very serious as he smoothed the hair away from her face and held her between his palms. 'I missed you,' he said softly. 'When you left…' He trailed off. 'I can't tell you how I felt then. It was as if someone had switched off all the lights, and then tonight, when I opened the door and there you were, and suddenly they were all blazing again.'

'That's very poetic for an engineer,' she teased him.

'It's true,' said Lewis. He searched her face with his eyes. 'I do love you, Martha. I love you more than you'll ever know.'

And then, at last, he kissed her. Martha melted into him, giving herself up to the heady pleasure of being able to kiss him back, to touch him and taste him and hold him. She pressed herself against him as they kissed, long, deep, delicious kisses, while the knowledge that he loved her lit a glow deep inside her. It seeped outwards, to her fingertips and the ends of her lashes and out through her pores, until she was incandescent with happiness, radiating it so intensely that she half expected to see her skin luminous in the darkness.

'You know,' murmured Lewis after a while, 'there's still one or two things that we should clear up.'

'Later,' whispered Martha against his mouth. She didn't want to clear anything up. She didn't want to stop, and she didn't want to talk. She just wanted to touch him more, kiss him more, feel him more…

'Later,' Lewis agreed raggedly, and tipped her off his lap to pull her ungently to his room where they fell together on to the bed and forgot about anything but each other.

It was a very long time before they got round to clearing anything up. They lay tangled together, boneless and breathless with delight, still savouring the magic they had created between them.

'Is this you trying to soft-soap me into giving you your job back?' Lewis asked lazily as her hand drifted possessively over his chest.

Martha laughed and turned to press a kiss into his warm shoulder. 'Is it working?'

'Well, I don't know,' he said, pretending to consider. 'There's a bit of a problem.'

'What sort of problem?' She smiled as her hand slid lower.

'Stop that,' said Lewis, but without much conviction. 'The thing is, I'm not sure if I can give you your job back at all—or at least not under the same terms.'

Martha paused. 'You're not serious?'

'I am, I'm afraid. I'm not going to need a nanny any more.'

'Oh.' Taking her hand away, she lay back down beside him. 'Oh, I see.' That was a lie, for a start.

'I talked to Savannah today,' Lewis began to explain. 'She's out of the clinic and raring to start a new life.'

'Well...that's good...' Martha forced herself to sound more enthusiastic. 'Good, I'm pleased.' Another lie. She didn't feel pleased at all. She felt jealous. She'd just got Viola back and she didn't want to lose her again, but how could she say that? Savannah was Viola's mother.

She drew a breath. 'When is she coming to get Viola?'

'She's not.' Under even fewer illusions about his sister, Lewis's voice was very dry. 'She was full of some man she'd met in the clinic. It turns out that he's something in television. He's convinced her that she has a great future as a chat show hostess, of all things, and he wants to take her to the States. Savannah thinks that Viola might complicate things,' he finished.

It was all Martha could do to bite back her opinion of a mother who could think of her baby as a complication, but in the event she might as well not have bothered.

'I know,' said Lewis, exactly as if she had spoken. 'She wanted me to keep Viola for another six months.'

'And you said no?'

'No, I told her that she can't pick up Viola and drop her whenever it suits her. Of course she'll always be Viola's mother, and she can jet in and out as often as she wants, but if Viola stays, she stays permanently. She needs the security of knowing that whatever her mother is doing her home will always be with me.'

'What did Savannah say to that?' asked Martha, knowing how she would have reacted if anyone had proposed bringing up Noah for her.

'She thought it was a wonderful idea,' said Lewis. He looked at her out of the corner of his eye and a smile touched the corners of his mouth. 'She's not like you.'

'But doesn't she know how you feel about families?'

'Ah, but you see I've changed my mind too.' He rolled over to lean up on one elbow and smooth a strand of hair from her face with such tenderness that Martha's heart cracked.

'The trouble is,' he said, 'I've got used to having a family now, and when you and Noah left I realised that I couldn't go back to living on my own, even if I'd wanted to. I'm sure I'd get more work done, but I wouldn't feel so alive, and the house would be empty and I would be all on my own. I don't want that any more.'

Lovingly, his fingers traced the line of her cheek. 'It wasn't a home any more when you were gone. Viola hated it, and so did I. We needed you and Noah to come back, and now that you have everything feels right again.'

Martha smiled and slipped her arms around him. 'I still don't see what the problem is,' she confessed. 'If Viola is going to be a permanent part of your life, then you're going to need a nanny more than ever, aren't you?'

'No.' Lewis shook his head definitely. 'I don't need a nanny. I need you. I need you to make wherever we are a home, and nannies don't do that. I've got to know that you're going to stay for a lot longer than a couple of months.'

'That shouldn't be a problem,' she said. 'How long were you thinking of?'

'A very long time,' he said firmly.

'How long is very long?'

He pretended to consider. 'I'm not sure that I'm prepared to settle for anything less than for ever.'

'I think I could do that,' said Martha.

'Thinking isn't good enough,' he said. 'You've got to be sure.'

'I am sure,' she said. 'I'm surer than I've been about anything else in my life,' she told him, and drew his head down for a long, sweet kiss of promise.

'For ever it is, then,' said Lewis contentedly when he lifted his head at last.

'I hope you're going to make it worth my while,' she teased. 'I'm used to a salary, you know.'

'It's not really economical to keep paying you a salary,' he pointed out, straight-faced, as she stretched luxuriously beneath his hands. 'I was thinking more of marrying you and saving on that particular cost.'

Martha managed a mock pout. 'That's all very well, but what would I get out of it?'

'You'd get me, you'd get Viola.' Lewis ticked off the advantages on his fingers. 'You'd get a family for Noah, and you'd get to be loved and needed by all of us.' His smile faded as he looked down into her dark, shining eyes. 'What do you say?'

'I couldn't ask for anything more,' she said honestly.

'Do I take that as a "yes", then?'

'That really depends on what the question was,' she pointed out, and he drew her closer.

'If the question was "Will you marry me?"...'

Martha heaved a blissful sigh. 'Then my answer would definitely be "yes"!'

MILLS & BOON® PUBLISH EIGHT LARGE PRINT TITLES A MONTH. THESE ARE THE EIGHT TITLES FOR JUNE 2004

SOLD TO THE SHEIKH
Miranda Lee

HIS INHERITED BRIDE
Jacqueline Baird

THE BEDROOM BARTER
Sara Craven

THE SICILIAN SURRENDER
Sandra Marton

PART-TIME FIANCÉ
Leigh Michaels

BRIDE OF CONVENIENCE
Susan Fox

HER BOSS'S BABY PLAN
Jessica Hart

ASSIGNMENT: MARRIAGE
Jodi Dawson

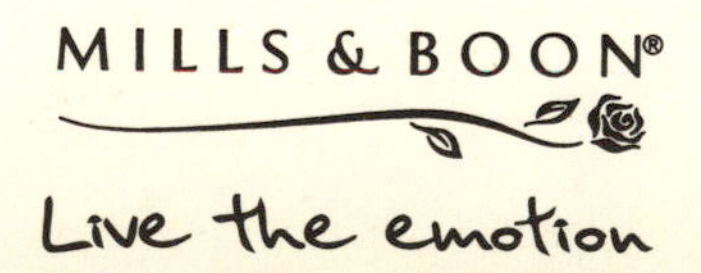

0504 Rom LP

MILLS & BOON® PUBLISH EIGHT LARGE PRINT TITLES A MONTH. THESE ARE THE EIGHT TITLES FOR JULY 2004

THE BANKER'S CONVENIENT WIFE
Lynne Graham

THE RODRIGUES PREGNANCY
Anne Mather

THE DESERT PRINCE'S MISTRESS
Sharon Kendrick

THE UNWILLING MISTRESS
Carole Mortimer

HER BOSS'S MARRIAGE AGENDA
Jessica Steele

RAFAEL'S CONVENIENT PROPOSAL
Rebecca Winters

A FAMILY OF HIS OWN
Liz Fielding

THE TYCOON'S DATING DEAL
Nicola Marsh

THE HONEYMOON CONTRACT

THE HONEYMOON CONTRACT

BY

EMMA DARCY

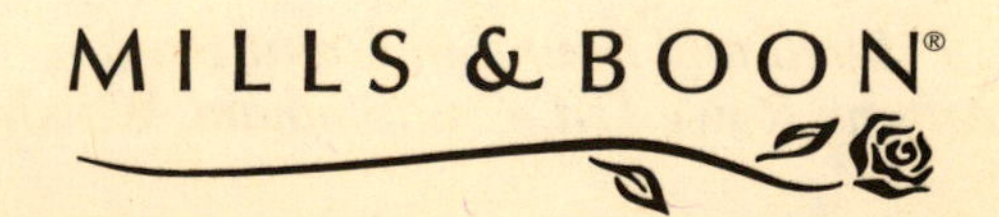

First published in Great Britain 2002
Large Print edition 2002
Harlequin Mills & Boon Limited,
Eton House, 18-24 Paradise Road,
Richmond, Surrey TW9 1SR

ISBN 0 263 17376 3

Set in Times Roman 16¾ on 19 pt.
16-1202-46237

Printed and bound in Great Britain
by Antony Rowe Ltd, Chippenham, Wiltshire

CHAPTER ONE

MATT KING had spent a highly satisfying day, whitewater rafting on the Tully River with his friends. It was good to be single and unattached, free to enjoy fun and games anytime he liked. At thirty, Matt figured he had a few more carefree bachelor years up his sleeve before marriage became a serious item on his agenda and he was not about to fall victim to any plans his grandmother might have to get him wed.

Today's activity had been the perfect excuse not to turn up at the Sunday luncheon she had organized for the purpose of introducing her latest female protégée to the family. Matt knew it was only delaying the inevitable. Sooner or later he would have to meet this Nicole Redman. He could hardly avoid her for the whole six months she was under contract to write the family history, especially as she was staying as *a guest* at King's Castle for the duration. Nevertheless, he was determined not to dance to his grandmother's tune.

The telephone rang just as he was about to settle down and watch a bit of television before going to bed. Feeling at peace with his world, and pleased with the neat little sidestep he'd performed today, Matt even smiled indulgently when he heard his grandmother's voice on the other end of the line.

"Ah! You are safely home, Matteo," she said, letting him know she disapproved of dangerous pursuits that risked life and limb for no good reason.

"Yes, Nonna. I managed not to drown or break any bones," he answered cheerfully.

"More good luck than good management," she muttered darkly before moving to the real point of her call. "Will you be in your bus depot office in the morning?"

No ducking out of this one, Matt thought. Business was business and his grandmother knew his work routine. Midweek he moved around the tropical fruit plantations but Mondays and Fridays were spent with the transport company he'd developed himself, picking up the tourist dollar in a big way.

"Yes," he replied to the lead-in question, waiting for the crunch.

"Good! I'll send Nicole along to you. I want you to give her a gold pass so she can travel freely on any of your bus tours."

"Doesn't she have a car?" Matt asked very dryly, knowing he was about to be outmanoeuvred but putting in a token protest anyway.

"Yes. But the bus tours will give her a general feel of the area she will have to cover in her research and your drivers do give potted histories as they go."

"More gossip than fact, Nonna. The aim is to entertain, not cram with information."

"It adds a certain flavour that is distinctive to far North Queensland, Matteo. Since Nicole is not familiar with Port Douglas or its environs, I don't see it as a waste of time.''

''A pity you didn't employ someone local who wouldn't have to start from scratch,'' he remarked.

''Nicole Redman had the qualifications I wanted for this project,'' came the definitive reply.

''Nothing beats local knowledge,'' he argued, strongly suspecting *the qualifications* had very little to do with writing a family history.

He was awake to his grandmother's matchmaking game. His two older brothers hadn't twigged to it and here they were, neatly married off to brides of their choice, or so they thought. Not that Matt had any quarrel with the women they'd wed. Gina and Hannah were beautiful people. It was just that he now knew they'd been Nonna's choices for Alex and Tony before his brothers had even met them.

Good thing he'd overheard her triumphant conversation with Elizabeth King at Tony's wedding, plus the voiced hope that she would be able to find a suitable wife for her third grandson. Matt had little doubt that Nicole Redman was the selected candidate.

She probably didn't know it, any more than he was supposed to know it, but that didn't change the game. Her arrival on the family scene repeated the previous pattern of his grandmother employing a young woman who ended up married to one of her grandsons. Since *he* was the only one left unmarried…

"Many people can do research and write down a list of facts, Matteo," his grandmother declared in a tone of arch disdain, applying her authority in no uncertain terms. "Having the skill to tell a story well is something else. I do not want an amateurish publication. This is important to me."

It was pure Isabella Valeri King…not to be denied. Even at eighty years of age she was still a formidable character and Matt loved and respected her far too much not to give in…a little.

"Sorry, Nonna. Of course it is," he quickly conceded. "You know best what you want and if a gold bus pass will help the project, I'm only too happy to assist."

It would only take a minute of his time. A brief meeting during business hours—no social obligation attached to it—would serve to satisfy his curiosity about what made Nicole Redman *suitable* for him in his grandmother's eyes.

"I thought you could also supply the road maps she will need when she does venture out by herself. Explain the various areas of particular family interest to her and how best to get there."

Matt could see the minute stretching to half an hour but there was no way he could refuse this reasonable request. "Okay. I'll have them ready for her." With all the plantations marked on them from Cape Tribulation to Innisfail. That would save time and evade the cosy togetherness his grandmother was undoubtedly plotting.

"Thank you, Matteo. When would be most convenient for Nicole to call by?"

Never. He suppressed the telling word and answered, "Oh, let's say ten-thirty."

The call ended on that agreement and for quite some time afterwards, Matt mused on how very clever his grandmother was, keeping strictly to business, no hint of trying to push any personal interest, not even a comment on Nicole Redman as a person, simply pressing a meeting which was reasonably justified.

Could he be wrong about this plot?

No, it still fitted the modus operandi.

His grandmother had produced Gina Terlizzi, a wedding singer, just as Alex was planning his wedding to a woman his grandmother didn't like. With good reason, Matt had to concede. He hadn't liked Michelle Banks, either, and was glad Alex had married Gina instead. Nevertheless, it was definitely his grandmother's guiding hand behind the meetings which had brought the desired result.

Then she had trapped Tony very neatly, choosing Hannah O'Neill to be the new chef on his prized catamaran, *Duchess.* Never mind about her highly questionable qualifications to be a cook. Tony had made the mistake of giving their grandmother the task of interviewing the applicants and making the choice, which had allowed her to present him with a *fait accompli* which sealed his fate. Impossible to ignore Hannah's other qualifications when they were inescapably right in his face. Tony had been down for the count in no time flat.

Two protégées married to his brothers.

Third one coming up.

Nicole Redman had to be aimed at him. The only question was...what ammunition did she have to shoot him into the marriage stakes? It certainly added a piquant interest to tomorrow morning's meeting.

He grinned with easy confidence as he switched on the television.

Didn't matter what it was, he was proofed against it. There was not going to be a honeymoon contract attached to the contract Nicole Redman had with his grandmother. No way was *he* ready to get married!

CHAPTER TWO

NICOLE paused at the head of the steps that led down to Wharf Street and looked back at King's Castle, marvelling that such a place had been built here back in the pioneering days. Tropical North Queensland was a long way from Rome, yet Frederico Stefano Valeri, Isabella's father, had certainly stuck to his Italian heritage when constructing this amazing villa on top of the hill overlooking Port Douglas.

The locals had come to call it a castle because of the tesselated tower that provided the perfect lookout in every direction, but the loggia and the fountain had definitely been inspired by Roman villas. And all of it built with poured concrete, a massive feat in those early times, although no doubt Frederico, having seen the timber buildings of Port Douglas destroyed in the 1911 cyclone, had been intent on having his home stand against anything.

Home and family, Nicole thought, her mind turning to the two great-grandsons she had met yesterday, both of them exuding the kind of strength that would tackle any problem and come out on top. The sense of family heritage and tradition was very much alive in them, nurtured no doubt by their extraordinary grandmother. It would be interesting to see if their younger brother fitted the same mould.

Three brothers—Alessandro, Antonio, Matteo—carrying the past into the future, adding to the levels of enterprise that had been started by Frederico when he had left Italy to start a new life in Australia in 1906. A fascinating family with a fascinating history and an equally fascinating present, Nicole decided, turning away from the castle to continue her walk to the KingTours head office.

It was only ten o'clock in the morning but already the heat was beating through her wide-brimmed straw hat. All too easy to get sunstroke up here in the tropics, she'd been warned, so she kept to the shade of the trees bordering the road on her leisurely stroll down the hill to the main business centre. Given her very fair skin, she had to protect herself against sunburn, as well. It was to be hoped the block-out cream she'd lavished on her arms and legs would do the job.

Being a redhead did have drawbacks in a country devoted to sunshine and outdoor pursuits. It was lucky she had always loved books, reading and writing being her dearest pleasures. Staying indoors had never really been a hardship, plus living with her father for the last few years of his life had left her with the habit of being a night owl—a habit she had to change while working with Isabella Valeri King.

Still, that was no real hardship, either. There was a special brilliancy to the days in Port Douglas; the magic of sunrise over the ocean, the kind of sharp daylight that made colours more vibrant. One never saw green this *green* in Sydney, and the reds and oranges and yellows of the tropical flowers were quite wonderful.

Everything was different; the whole laid-back pace of the town, no sense of hustle and bustle, the heat of the day followed by a downpour of incredibly heavy rain most afternoons. It spurred an awareness of nature and the need to live in harmony with it. She felt a long long way from city life, as though she'd moved to another world that worked within parameters all its own. It was a very attractive world that could easily become addictive.

Here she was, swinging along at a very leisurely pace, flat sandals on her feet, no stockings, wearing a yellow sleeveless button-through dress that loosely skimmed her body, minimal underclothing, a straw hat featuring a big yellow sunflower on her head, and it didn't matter what anyone thought of her. No students to teach, no fellow academics pushing their political agendas at her, no back-biting about the book she'd written on her father's life.

Freedom…

She grinned, happy with the feeling. It was like starting a new life even though she'd be researching old lives for the next six months, writing a history. But it was a history *she* hadn't lived and it was about a family who had endured and survived and was still thriving, the kind of family she didn't have and had never known. Another attraction…finding out first-hand what it was like to actually belong to a place, deep roots and long lines of growth.

She reached Macrossan Street and strolled along it until she found the King building where Alessandro—Alex, as he was called by everyone except his grandmother and Rosita, the very motherly Italian housekeeper at the castle—managed investments and property development, as well as handling all the business attached to the sugarcane plantations.

Further down Wharf Street was the marina where Antonio/Tony operated the Kingtripper line of catamarans, taking tourists out to the Great Barrier Reef. That was his personal enterprise, apart from managing the tea plantations which was his family responsibility. Nicole intended to check out the Kingtripper company office after her meeting with Matteo/Matt.

She turned into Owen Street which led down to the bus depot and the KingTours main office. The transport company was Matt's brainchild and one of the tours he ran was to his exotic fruit farm, an extension of the tropical fruit plantations that came under his umbrella of family responsibility.

It was interesting that none of the three brothers had simply accepted their inheritances and been content to live off them. Which they could have done, given the current prosperity of all the plantations. Of course, diversity was always a healthier situation in any financial sense, but Nicole suspected the pioneering blood ran strongly in these men. Perhaps it was the challenge of going for more that drove them. Or a *male* thing, wanting to conquer new territories.

Certainly Alex and Tony King were different to all the city men she'd known. They were very civilised, very polished in their manners, yet they had a masculinity that was somehow more aggressive. In her mind's eye she could see the two of them going into battle, shoulder to shoulder, emanating the attitude that nothing was going to beat them. Perhaps it was fanciful imagination but that was how they had impressed her.

Would the third brother measure up to the other two?

It was with a very lively anticipation that Nicole stepped into the KingTours main office. A fresh-faced boy, possibly in his late teens, was manning a large L-shaped desk. He looked up from his paperwork, gave her a quick once-over, then a welcoming grin.

''You Miss Redman?''

‘‘Yes.’’

He waved to a door in the back wall to the side of his desk. ‘‘Just step this way to the boss’s office. He’s got all the maps ready for you.’’ His blue eyes twinkled as though that statement reflected some private joke. ‘‘I marked out the main locations of interest myself so you can’t possibly miss them,’’ he added, making Nicole wonder if he’d been told to assume she was the most hopeless navigator in the world.

He already had the door open for her so there was no time to chat with him. ‘‘Miss Redman,’’ he was announcing, even before she thought to remove her hat.

Indeed, the ushering was effected so quickly, Nicole found herself inside Matt King’s office with her hat still on and her wits completely scattered at being confronted by the man himself. Not like Alex. Not like Tony. This brother was wickedly handsome. If the devil was rolling out every sexual temptation he could load into a male body, Matt King had to be his masterpiece.

His hair was very black, very shiny and an absolute riot of tight curls, a tantalising invitation to be touched. It didn't soften the strong masculine cast of his face. Somehow the contrast added a wildly mischievous attraction, as did the long, thick, curly eyelashes to the dark chocolate eyes. And his olive skin had such a smooth sheen, the pads of Nicole's fingers actually prickled with the desire to stroke it. All that on top of a physique that seemed to pulse manpower at her.

He came out from behind his desk, tall, big, dressed in a blue sports shirt and navy chinos, white teeth flashing at her, and Nicole felt as though every bit of oxygen had been punched out of her lungs. Her heart catapulted around a chest that had suddenly become hollow. It was purely a defensive instinct that lifted her hands to grab her hat and bring it down in front of her like a shield against the impact of his approach.

The action startled him into pausing and Nicole's cheeks flamed with embarrassment. Such a clumsy thing to do, no grace at all in this foolish fluster. And she'd probably mussed her hair. He was staring at it. A slight frown drew his brows together as his gaze dropped to hers, his eyes brilliantly sharp now, seemingly as black as his hair and with a penetrating power that felt so invasive it made her toes curl.

She had the weird sense he was searching for some sign of recognition. It forced her to collect her wits and speak, though her tongue moved sluggishly and she had to push the words out. "Your grandmother sent me. I'm Nicole Redman."

"Red..." he said with an ironic twist, then appeared to recover himself. "Forgive me for staring. That shade of hair is not exactly common. It surprised me." He stepped forward and offered his hand. "Matt King."

She unlatched the fingers of her right hand from the hat and gingerly met his grasp. "I'm pleased to meet you,'' she managed stiltedly, absorbing the shock wave of his engulfing touch with as much control as she could muster. A bolt of warm, tingling vitality shot up her arm and caused her heart to pump harder.

His gaze dropped to her mouth, studying it as though it held secrets she was not revealing. Her throat constricted, making further speech impossible.

''Nicole Redman...'' He rolled her name out slowly, as though tasting it for flavour and texture. His gaze flicked back to hers, his eyes having gathered a mocking gleam. ''This meeting is overdue but no doubt we'll soon get acquainted.''

He had to be referring to his absence from the family luncheon yesterday, yet that look in his eyes was implying more. Mental confusion added to her physical tension and it was a blessed relief when he withdrew his hand and turned aside to fetch a chair for her, placing it to face his on the other side of the executive desk.

"Have a seat," he invited, and Nicole was intensely grateful for it.

Her knees felt like jelly. Her thighs were quivering, too. She found the presence of mind to say, "Thank you," and sank onto the chair, fiercely telling herself to construct some composure fast.

It wasn't as though she hadn't been given a hint of what Matt King might be like, having met his brothers yesterday, both very handsome men who carried an aura of power. She had been able to view them objectively. Why not this one? Why did she feel so personally affected by this one?

It was crazy. She was twenty-eight years old and had met hundreds of men. Probably thousands. Not one of them had scrambled her insides like this. Maybe she was suffering sunstroke and just didn't know it. Come to think of it, she did feel slightly dizzy. And very hot. Hot all over. If she just sat quietly for a minute or two, she'd be fine.

She slid her shoulder-bag off and propped it against the leg of the chair, then set her hat on her lap and focused on the sunflower. By the time Matt King reached his chair and settled himself to chat with her, she'd be ready to look at him and act normally.

All she needed from him was the gold pass for the bus tours and the road maps which his assistant had helpfully marked. It shouldn't take hardly any time at all. A bit of polite to-and-fro and she'd be out of here.

Her hands were trembling.

She willed them to be still.

Her heart persisted with hops, skips and jumps, but it had to steady soon. Clearly she had to be more careful in this tropical heat. Drive, not walk. That was the answer. When Matt King spoke to her she would look up and smile and everything would be all right.

CHAPTER THREE

NO MISTAKE, Matt grimly assured himself as he walked slowly around his desk to his chair, his mind working at hyper-speed to reason out what the hell this woman was doing here, supposedly assisting his grandmother on the family history project.

The flaming red hair had instantly jolted his memory, spinning it back ten years to a night in New Orleans, the night before Halloween in that extraordinary city. The delicately featured face, the white porcelain-perfect skin, the big expressive sherry-brown eyes, the full sensual curves of her mobile mouth…all of it like a video clip coming at him in a flash. A tall slender young woman, swathed in a black cloak lined with purple satin, long red hair flowing free, not rolled back at the sides and clipped away from her face as it was today.

He'd seen her lecturing the tour group outside Reverend Zombie's Voodoo Shop. He'd watched her, listened to her, appreciating the theatrical appearance of her as she captivated the group with her opening spiel for the Haunted History Walking Tour. Just to hear her speaking in an Australian accent added to her allure.

He'd even tagged along for a while, fascinated by the look of her and her performance. He would probably have stayed with it but the novelty appeal of the tour soon wore thin for the friends he was with and they'd moved on to one of the colourful bars in the French Quarter.

Nevertheless, he remembered her very clearly…the hair, the face, the pale, pale skin adding its impact to her ghostly tales. Which raised the question…what tale had she spun his grandmother to get this job? Had she faked qualifications…a con-woman getting her hooks in for a six months' free ride? Had his grandmother checked them out? Or hadn't they mattered, given that her prime objective was finding him a bride?

A spurt of anger put an extra edge on the tension this meeting had sparked. His grandmother had struck out badly on this candidate for marital bliss, being fooled by what he could only think of as a fly-by-night operator, though undoubtedly a very clever and convincing one, calling on her experience with *haunted history,* plus a liberal dash of entertainment.

He slung himself into his chair, barely resisting the urge to give it a twirl as a derisive tribute to the marriage merry-go-round his grandmother was intent upon. Highly disgruntled with this absurd situation, he glowered at the woman sitting opposite to him. *Why her?* What did his grandmother see as the special attributes that made *her* suitable as his wife?

Red hair?

It certainly suited the exotic night-life in New Orleans, but here in the tropics? That pale skin would fry in Port Douglas. Utter madness!

Though he had to concede her dramatic colouring and the delicacy of her fine skin and features did have a certain unique beauty. He'd thought so ten years ago and it still held true. But it was perfectly plain she didn't belong in this environment. As to there being any possibility of her spending a lifetime here…that was definitely beyond the pale.

She sat very still, very primly with her knees pressed together, the hat held on her lap, eyes downcast, projecting a modesty that was at ridiculous odds with the role she had played ten years ago. Uncloaked, she had small but neatly rounded breasts. Her arms were neatly rounded, too, slender like the rest of her but not skinny. Interesting that she wore yellow, which wasn't a modest colour.

She was playing some game with him, Matt decided, and the temptation to winkle it out of her overrode his previous intention to send her on her way as quickly as possible. He leaned back in his chair and consciously relaxed, knowing he had the upper hand since there was no chance of her remembering him. He and his friends had been wearing masks that night, part of the wild revelry leading up to Halloween.

"I understand this is your first visit to the far north," he started.

She nodded and slowly raised her gaze to his. "I did fly up a month ago for the interview with Mrs. King."

Her eyes were wary and he instantly sensed her guard was up against him. He wondered why. A need to hide the truth about herself? Did she see him as a danger spot, a threat to her cosy sinecure at the castle?

Curiosity further piqued, he smiled to put her more at ease as he teasingly asked, "Six months at the castle didn't sound like a prison sentence to you?"

The idea seemed to startle her. "Not at all. Why would you think so?"

"Oh, you'll be stuck mostly with my grandmother for company and the novelty of living in a rather romantic old place won't make up for the things you'll miss or the things you'll have to tolerate," he drawled, watching her reaction to his words.

Her head tilted to one side as though she was critically assessing him. "Don't *you* enjoy your grandmother's company?"

"That's not exactly relevant," he dryly countered.

A slight frown. "You didn't come to the family luncheon yesterday."

"True. I don't allow my grandmother to rule my life. I had another activity booked and I saw no reason to cancel it." He paused, wanting to probe her character. "Were you offended that I didn't roll up on command?"

"Me? Of course not."

"Then why do you think I should have come?"

"I don't. I just thought...you said..." She stopped in some confusion.

"I was simply suggesting that six months under the same roof with an eighty-year-old lady might make King's Castle a prison for a young woman used to all the attractions of city life."

A wry little smile. "Actually I find older people more interesting than younger ones. They've lived longer and some of them have had amazing lives. I can't imagine ever being bored in Mrs. King's company."

Her eyes flashed a look that suggested she could very easily be bored in his, which spurred him into derisively commenting, "So you're prepared to bury yourself in the past and let your own life slide by for the duration of this project."

Her chin tilted in challenge. "I've always found history fascinating. I think there's much to be learnt from it. I don't consider any form of learning a waste of my time."

"A very academic view," he pointed out, wondering what she'd *learnt* from ghost stories. "They say history repeats itself, so what really is gleaned from it?'' he challenged right back. ''Human nature doesn't change.''

She didn't reply. For several moments she looked directly at him in a silence loaded with antagonism. She wanted to attack. So did he. But his grandmother stood between them, a force that demanded a stay of any open hostilities.

''Are you against this project, Matt?''

The question was put quietly, calmly, a straight request to know where he stood.

''Not in the slightest. I think such a publication will be of interest to future generations of our family,'' he answered easily. ''I think it's also meaningful to my grandmother to have a record of her life put into print. A last testament, which she richly deserves.''

''Are you against me doing it?''

Right on target! He had to hand it to Nicole Redman. She certainly had balls to lay the cards right out on the table. ''Why should I be?'' he asked, wondering if she'd let anything slip.

"I don't know." Another wry little smile. "You'll need to tell me."

Clever, throwing the question back onto him. "How old are you Nicole?" he tossed at her.

"Twenty-eight."

"Are you coming out of a bad relationship?"

"No."

"Not engaged with one at the moment?"

"No."

"Not looking for one?"

"No."

"Why not?"

"Why should I be?"

"I would have thought it was a normal pastime for a woman of your age."

Hot colour stained her cheeks. Her eyes burned with pride as she replied, "Then I guess I don't fit your idea of normal."

Which neatly left him nothing to say…on the surface of it. He was not about to fire his hidden ammunition until he knew some facts about her more recent circumstances. A lot could happen in ten years. If she was telling the truth about her age, she'd only been eighteen in New Orleans. A wild youth could have been followed by a more sober settling down.

As it was, she had obviously notched up qualifications in his grandmother's wedding plans; single, unattached, of a mature enough age to find marriage an acceptable idea, and certainly physically attractive if one fancied red hair.

Not everybody did.

So why had his grandmother chosen a redhead for him? Why not a blonde or brunette? He'd never even…

The answer suddenly clicked in. Trish at Tony's wedding. Hannah's sister had long auburn hair and he'd been matched with her in the wedding party, bridesmaid and groomsman. Being a professional model, she was tall and slender, too, and they'd had a lot of fun together at the reception. No serious connection, just light happy flirting, enjoyed by both of them. Had his grandmother read more into it, perceiving Trish as his type of woman?

He shook his head and Nicole took the exasperated action as directed at her.

"This is a project I want to do," she stated, her eyes mocking his assertion that looking for a man should be her top priority. "I understand from Mrs. King that you started this tour company because you wanted to do it. You've also developed a market for exotic fruit, which I assume you wanted to do, as well. I'm sure you had your reasons for taking those directions in your life and I bet they had nothing to do with your lack of, or desire for, a relationship with a woman."

She had him there. This was one smart chick. If he so much as suggested it might be different for a woman, he'd be marked as a sexist pig. Besides, he didn't believe it was different. He'd simply been checking what his grandmother had undoubtedly checked before entering Nicole Redman in her matchmaking game.

"Well, I hope you find as much satisfaction in pursuing the past as I've found in setting up a future," he said with a grin designed to disarm.

She returned an overly sweet smile. "You're very fortunate to have a past that can be built upon."

The slip! It was in her eyes, a bleak emptiness that had escaped her guard. His instincts instantly seized upon it and threw up a quick interpretation. She'd come from nothing and had no future direction. She moved on the wings of opportunity, not having any roots to ground her anywhere. Perhaps she even felt like a ghost, having no family to give her any real solidity. Or was he assuming too much from one fleeting expression?

"What about your own family?" he shot out.

"I don't have one," she answered flatly, confirming his impression.

"You're an orphan?"

A momentary gritting of teeth, then a terse dismissal of that description of her. "I'm an adult, responsible for myself, and I've taken the responsibility of seeing this project through with Mrs. King. A six-month contract has been signed to that effect. If you have a problem with my appointment to this job..."

"It's purely my grandmother's business and I have no intention of interfering with it," he assured her, though whether his grandmother would get value for her choice on the history side of things was yet to be seen. Nevertheless, that was not his problem and he wasn't about to make it his problem.

"I don't want to interfere with your business, either." She surged up from her chair with the clear intention of making a brisk departure. "Your assistant said you had road maps already marked for me..."

Damn! He'd torpedoed any reason for keeping her with him. Had to go with the flow now. He killed the stab of frustration and rose to his feet, telling himself he had six months to get to the bottom of this woman, so no sweat about letting her off the hook this morning.

He picked up the bundle of maps stacked on his side of the desk and set them on her side. "Here they are," he said obligingly. "Using these, you should be able to find your way to every point of historical interest."

"Thank you." She scooped her bag from the floor and rested it on the desk to load the maps into it, her face closed to everything but the purpose that had brought her to him.

Matt didn't like the sense of being put out of Nicole Redman's picture. He wasn't ready to let her go...*to let her win.* He snatched up the gold bus pass he'd laid beside the maps and strolled around the desk, intent on forcing another passage of play.

"And this gives you free travel on any of the tours," he said, holding it out to her.

She jerked towards him, a couple of the maps spilling out of her hand. In her quick fumble to catch them, she dropped her hat.

They both bent to pick it up, their heads almost bumping. She reared back, leaving Matt to retrieve it, which he did, straightening up to find her breathing fast and very flustered by the near collision.

Her mouth was slightly open, her eyes wide in alarm, and this close to her, Matt had the weird sensation of being sucked in by the storm of feeling coming straight at him from the highly luminous windows to her soul. He stared back, momentarily transfixed by a connection that threw him completely out of kilter.

He wanted to kiss her, wanted to draw from her mouth all the secrets she was hiding from him, wanted to bind her to him until she gave up everything she was. The need to know pounded through his mind. Adrenaline was rushing through him, making his heart beat faster, tightening his muscles, driving a fierce urge for satisfaction. An intensely *sexual* urge for satisfaction.

"Thank you."

The words whispered from her lips.

They forced a realisation of what he was supposed to be doing. Shock pummelled the madness out of his mind. This was the woman his grandmother had lined up for him. He was *not* going to fall into her trap.

He thrust out the gold pass.

Her hand was trembling as she took it from him. He tried to rein in the wild burst of energy that had escaped from him. Was she aware of it, affected by it? One part of him savagely hoped so, even as another part just as savagely wanted to deny there was any power of attraction in operation here, on her side or his.

He watched her shove the pass and the maps into the bag, lashes lowered, head bowed, the red of her hair so vibrant he had to clench his hands to stop them from reaching out to touch it. They clenched over the straw brim of her hat. He still had the hat. But it was crazy even thinking he could hold her hostage with a hat. Her haste in packing her bag, slinging it over her shoulder, said she wanted to go. And he should let her go. Any other action would put him well and truly in the loser's seat.

She managed a step away, increasing the distance between them as she turned to face him, her gaze flicking up in frazzled appeal. "My hat..."

He could have handed it to her. It was the simplest response. But some perverse aggressive streak goaded him into setting the hat on that taunting hair himself, as though covering up the temptation would make it go away. He stepped forward and did precisely that, fitting the crown of the hat on her head, focusing on the sunflower to position it as she'd had it positioned when she came in, an unknown woman he'd intended to remain unknown to him in any close personal sense.

Except his whole body was suddenly electrically aware of hers, her height against his, the slightness of her figure, the almost fragile femininity of it, the yellow of the sunflower reminding her of her dress—a button-through dress that could be easily opened—and she was standing so still, submissively still.

"Thank you."

A gush of breath. Had she been holding it?

The thought excited him. He'd won something from her. On a heady wave of triumph he stepped back, smiling. "Got to be careful of the heat up here."

Her cheeks were reflecting an inner heat that put him on a high as he moved to open the office door for her exit. She walked forward with the stiff gait of someone willing her legs into action. Her gaze was fixed on the doorway. She gave him a nod of acknowledgment as she passed by.

Matt grinned as he closed the door behind her.

He'd definitely rattled Nicole Redman's cage.

And he certainly felt a zing of interest in opening the door to it.

Not to marry her, he assured himself as he headed back to his desk. Marriage was not on his agenda. But a few hot nights with Miss Exotic New Orleans would not go amiss. Why not…if she fancied a taste of the tropics? Not under the nose of his grandmother, of course, but if Nicole was doing all the bus tours, sooner or later she would take the trip to Kauri King Park where the exotic fruit was grown.

He would make a point of being there that day.

And see how he felt about her then.

CHAPTER FOUR

AS WAS her habit, Isabella Valeri King took afternoon tea in the loggia by the fountain. The sound of flowing water was soothing. There was always a sea-breeze at this time of day to alleviate the heat. She liked being outside with so much of her world to view, its changing colours, changing light, the sense of being part of it, still alive, though not with as much life left to live as the young woman sitting with her.

Nicole Redman…

So different to Gina and Hannah both in looks and nature, yet she shared with them the quality Isabella most admired—the inner strength to make hard life decisions and follow them through. The book about her father had revealed much about herself—a child who had shouldered the responsibility of an adult, seeing the gain, setting aside the loss—a very mature view for one so young.

Though she had suffered loss.

Just as Isabella had.

The past two hours in the library, reliving the years of the Second World War through old photographs and letters, had left her feeling heavy-hearted. She'd lost both her husband and only brother to that dreadful conflict in Europe, and there'd been other troubles, many of the Italian immigrants in far North Queensland interned because they had not taken out Australian citizenship as her parents had.

Her father had done his best to ease that pain in the Italian community, making a deal with the government, offering land he owned as a suitable camp for *his people,* then talking the forestry department into supplying the plants and trees to construct a rainforest park there, arguing the conservation of tropical species as well as keeping the internees occupied by the work. Better than useless imprisonment. Something good would come of it for everyone.

"After the war, you and Edward can build a home up there, Isabella," he'd told her.

But Edward hadn't come back from the war and Kauri King Park, as it came to be known, had never been her home. It was now Matteo's, and Nicole had not yet been there. Which brought Isabella's focus back to the young woman who had been with her for almost three weeks now.

Only the one meeting with Matteo.

A pity she had been unable to observe it.

Perhaps there would have been nothing to observe. The beauty she saw in Nicole may not have appealed to Matteo. He had made no attempt to pursue an acquaintance with her. Nor had Nicole made any comments that would have revealed a personal interest in him.

Isabella silently conceded the undeniable truth that one could not order mutual attraction. Physical chemistry was ordained by nature and no amount of wanting it to happen could *make* it happen. However, it was curious that Nicole had soaked in the background information from many of Matteo's bus tours, yet had not so far chosen to take the one tour which might bring her into contact with him. Since it was also the one tour most closely connected to the family history, why was she putting it off?

To Isabella's mind it smacked of avoidance. Which could mean something about Matteo moved Nicole out of her comfort zone. A negative reaction? Had Matteo offended her in some way?

Her youngest grandson was not normally an abrasive person. He had a happy, fun-loving personality, very agreeable company to most people. He carried his passions lightly although they ran every bit as deeply as his two older brothers'. The lightness was his way of carving a different niche in the family.

Alessandro…the strong pillar of responsibility.

Antonio…the fierce competitor.

Matteo…the nimble dancer between the other two, pretending to skate through life as though it was a game to be played, but he did care about his responsibilities and he was every bit as competitive as Antonio. He just expressed it differently.

Maybe something had happened between Matteo and Nicole that neither of them wanted to acknowledge. An unexpected chemistry could be uncomfortable, disturbing their sense of control over their lives. Matteo liked to stir things along for other people but he was very much in charge of himself. As for Nicole… she sat with an air of tranquility which was probably hard-won, given all she'd been through. A storm of feeling might tear at nerves that craved peace.

Wishful thinking, Isabella chided herself. Whatever the situation, the history project had to stay on track and it was time for Nicole to see what they had just been talking about.

"Tomorrow I must spend on the organisation of a wedding," she stated. "The bride and her mother are coming to decide on all the details for the reception in the ballroom."

Nicole smiled. "I can't imagine a more romantic setting, having a wedding here at the castle."

"In the old days we held dances and showed movies in the ballroom. I did not want it to fall into disuse so I turned it into a function centre many years ago. Weddings are so popular here, it is used for little else now."

"I'm sure it adds very much to the sense of occasion for the couples getting married."

"I think so. The feeling of longevity is good. It makes something solid of the passage of time. As you'll see when you visit Kauri King Park. Tomorrow would be a good day for you to do that tour, Nicole, since I've just been telling you how it came to be."

The tour that would take her to Matteo's home.

There were instant signs of tension—Nicole's shoulders jerking into a straighter line, hands clenching in her lap, chin jutting slightly, and most interesting of all, a tide of heat rushing up her neck and flooding her cheeks. It could not be the prospect of walking through a rainforest park and an exotic fruit plantation causing such a reaction. If it was the prospect of encountering Matteo...well, perhaps more meetings should be planned.

Isabella waited for Nicole's response.

A fine hand had to be played here.

But her heart was already lifting with hope.

"Tomorrow..." Nicole struggled to hold back a protest against the proposed arrangement. None was justifiable. She had delayed the inevitable as long as she could. There simply was no acceptable excuse for getting out of going to Matt King's territory this time, but everything within her recoiled from being near him again. "Yes," she forced herself to say, then clutched at a dubious lifeline. "Though the tour could be all booked up. It's late to be calling.''

''If so, you could drive up and join it at the gate. It's not far. Just above Mossman. A half hour drive at most. You won't miss much of the background chat from the bus driver,'' came the dismissal of any possible objection.

Nicole's stomach contracted. She had to do it. No escape. All she could hope for was Matt King's absence.

''Tomorrow is a good day,'' Mrs. King ran on. ''Matteo is always there on Thursdays. He can help out with anything you'd like to know.''

It was the worst possible day and she'd now been trapped into it. Her own stupid fault for not going before when she could have avoided meeting him. She knew he was in the tour company office on Mondays and Fridays. The problem was, she hadn't felt safe about going on any day.

If Matt King checked the tour bookings—and she'd had an uneasy feeling he would check on what she was up to—he could waylay her on his home ground whenever she went. Why, she wasn't sure, but everything about him put her on edge. And he knew it, played on it, getting under her skin. She didn't like it, didn't want it.

"I wouldn't want to take him away from his work, Mrs. King," she said quickly, trying to quell the panicky sense of being cornered. "I'm sure the tour guide..."

"Matteo can make the time to oblige you with his more intimate family knowledge of the park."

Intimate. A convulsive little shiver ran down Nicole's spine. Matt King literally radiated male sexuality. Even at that one brief meeting in his office she'd been sucked in by it twice, her whole body mesmerised by the attraction of his, wanting the most primitive of intimacies. She'd never felt anything so *physical.* It even messed up her mind, making it impossible to hang on to any logical thought.

"I'll call him tonight and tell him you're coming so he can watch out for you," her employer said decisively, sealing a totally unavoidable meeting.

The only question left was bus or car. Nicole didn't know which was better; trying to cling to a tour group which might diffuse Matt King's impact on her, or having her car handy so she could leave at a time of her choosing. Either way, she couldn't ignore her job which entailed gathering all the historical information she could from this trip. Somehow she would have to keep her focus on that.

"I'll go and call the tour office and see if there's a seat available on the bus," she said, rising from her chair.

Isabella Valeri King smiled her satisfaction as she nodded approval of the move. Apart from that regal nod, she didn't move herself, remaining where she sat with the quiet dignity which Nicole associated with an inner discipline that would never crack.

There was something about the smile that made her look more sharply at her rather aristocratic employer before going. She had an eerie impression of power shimmering from her...a soft but indomitable power that would not be thwarted by time or circumstance.

Again a little shiver ran down her spine.

Dark shiny eyes...almost black...like Matt's.

This family...she'd known from the beginning it wasn't ordinary...but how extraordinary was it...and where did the power come from?

She walked towards the great entrance doors to the castle, knowing she was entering their world, and finally acknowledging that running away from it wasn't really an option she wanted to take. It intrigued her. It fascinated her. Even what frightened her was also compelling.

Matt King...tomorrow.

CHAPTER FIVE

MATT stood on the balustraded roof of the pavilion café, watching the tour passengers emerge from the bus at the other end of the kauri pine avenue. Phase two of the matchmaking plot, he thought in amusement. Little did his grandmother know, when she'd called last night, he'd already been informed that Nicole Redman was booked to be on this bus today. He would have been waiting for her any day she chose to come.

But she hadn't chosen.

Which put a highly interesting twist on this visit. It was almost three weeks since he'd decided to keep tabs on Nicole's bus tours. She'd done almost every one of them but this, and it was clear from his conversation with his grandmother that the resident family historian had been put under pressure to come today—*his* day for this plantation.

It wouldn't have been a command. No, more a subtle manipulation, shaped in a way that undoubtedly made refusal impossible. Matt was alert to his grandmother's little tricks. But was *she* alert to the fact that Nicole Redman was very reluctant to meet him again.

What was she hiding in the cage he'd rattled?

The question had been teasing Matt's mind ever since he realised that her delay in coming here had to be deliberate. Kauri King Park was prime material for the family history. Anyone eager to research the past would have been drawn to this place within days, not weeks. So how good was Nicole Redman at the job she had taken on? How genuine? Was his grandmother being fooled? His very astute grandmother?

Unlikely, Matt decided. She might have been fooled at the beginning, but not after three weeks. Unless she was blinded by her other agenda. Was that possible? Surely she wouldn't want him to marry a con artist. She might have been beguiled by Nicole's looks, but what about character? How good an actress was this woman?

There she was! Same broad-brimmed straw hat with the sunflower. Even at this distance she stood out amongst the other tourists. She was the only woman in a skirt. The others were in shorts or light cotton slacks, teamed with loose T-shirts or skimpy tops, the usual garb for the tropics. Nicole had chosen to wear a long-sleeved blouse, the same forest green as her skirt which swung almost to her ankles.

Protecting her skin, Matt thought, but on her tall, slender figure, the effect of the outfit was very feminine. Elegantly feminine. Magnetically feminine in that crowd, especially with the hat. Others wore caps or fabric hats which were easily packed. The sunflower hat was well out of that category. It hid her hair but somehow it made an equally dramatic statement. It stood out, as everything about Nicole Redman stood out. Not one of the pack.

Matt felt his body tightening with the desire to have her. He'd lain awake many nights, fantasising her naked on his bed, her long pale body subtly inviting him to experience every pleasure it could give him, her silky hair flaming across the pillow, a provocative promise of the fiery passion he was sure would blaze between them.

Her reluctance to meet him again had actually fuelled an urge to pursue her, but he'd restrained it, not wanting to give her any sense of power over him. Besides, there was no need to pursue when a further meeting was guaranteed, given his grandmother's game plan. Patience was the better play.

But he didn't have to be patient any longer.

She was here.

And for all she knew, he was only doing his grandmother's bidding in personally accompanying her on this tour. Which put him very neatly in control of what happened with Nicole Redman today.

Nicole stared up at the amazing kauri pines as the guide spoke about their planting, sixty years ago. They had such huge trunks running straight up to the sky, no branches at all until the very top and even the foliage they supported seemed dwarfed by the towering height of the trees. The giants of the rainforest, the guide said.

She was reminded of the giant redwoods she'd seen in Muir Woods, just outside San Francisco, but these trees were very different, a mottled bark on the trunks, not stringy, and somehow they looked more primitive. Just as majestic but…her gaze travelled slowly up the avenue as she tried to formulate her impression in words…and caught Matt King striding down it, coming straight at her.

She stood like a paralysed bunny, watching him, feeling the primitive power of him attacking her and charging every nerve in her body with a sizzling awareness of it. Her mind tried to argue he was just a man on a family mission that had been requested of him. It made no difference to his impact on her.

Her eyes registered his casual clothes, dark blue jeans and a red sports shirt. Both garments hugged his big male muscular physique, destroying any sense of security in the normality of how he was dressed. He emitted an animal-like force that could not be tamed or turned away. And the really stunning part was Nicole knew it excited her. Something uncontrollable inside her was wildly thrilled by it.

''Good morning,'' he called to her while he was still some metres away.

Even his voice seemed to put an extra thrum in her bloodstream. She took a deep breath as she fiercely willed herself to respond in a natural fashion. The purpose of her visit here was to see and understand what had been achieved with this park, and the exotic fruit plantation beyond it.

"Hello," she said, more awkwardly than she would have liked. "It's good of you to come and greet me but please...if you should be doing something else..."

He grinned, his dark eyes twinkling at her obvious discomfort. "I don't mind obliging my grandmother, adding my bit to the history of this place."

"The tour..."

"Has moved on while you waited for me."

The realisation he spoke the truth brought an instant flush of embarrassment. She hadn't even noticed, hadn't heard the guide directing everyone elsewhere, hadn't been aware she'd been left standing alone. A babble of voices drew her gaze to the left-hand side of the kauri pine avenue. The group had been diverted down a path bordered by electric-blue ferns.

"Shall we follow or...?"

"Yes," she quickly decided, choosing the safety of numbers and hopefully a dilution of the effect Matt King had on her.

She started off after them and he fell into step beside her, making her extremely conscious of how tall he was. She was above average height for a woman but she was only on eye level with his shoulder, and walking side by side, the broad brim of her hat was a barrier to looking directly at him and vice versa, which gave her time to regain some composure.

"So how's it all going for you?" he asked, reminding her of his sceptical view of her staying power at the castle with his grandmother.

"Fine!" she answered lightly.

"Not feeling swamped?"

"By what?"

"By all the information you'll have to fit into a coherent story."

"It's a big story. Big in every sense. But not overwhelming. There's an innate order to it."

"As there is to any life," he dryly commented. "I assume there's a logic to yours."

"Yes, I guess there is. Though I haven't really reflected on it in that light."

"Perhaps you prefer a haphazard pattern."

"I don't think so."

"But you *are* willing to take on new experiences, despite obvious drawbacks. You're committed to being in Port Douglas for six months although the climate here can't be kind to you."

He was digging at her again, just as he had in his office. Why did he want her to admit she'd made a mistake in taking on this project? Was she some kind of thorn in his side?

"I think it's a wonderful climate," she asserted with a sense of perverse satisfaction in flouting his opinion. "No cold," she added pointedly. "I hate the cold."

"You don't find the heat oppressive?"

"It can be if I'm outside in the middle of the day," she conceded.

"Particularly when you have to cover up to protect your fair skin."

"I'm done that all my life. It doesn't bother me."

"Well, you don't need your hat on now. We're in total shade. And I prefer not to talk to a straw brim."

She had a stubborn impulse to deny him her bare face. On the other hand, he might have the gall to lift her hat off himself, just as he'd taken the liberty of putting it on her head in his office. Better to avoid that kind of familiar contact. She was barely hanging on to a semblance of control as it was. Besides which, it was true the rainforest canopy had now blocked out the sun. It was unreasonable and probably offensive to stick to wearing the hat so she reached up and removed it.

"There! Doesn't that feel better?"

She looked up into wickedly teasing eyes and the strong impression thumped into her heart that he would very much enjoy stripping her of all her coverings. It triggered the thought that he was as sexually attracted to her as she was to him. Which completely blew her mind.

Instinctively she sought time out by attaching herself to the tour group and focusing fiercely on the official guide who was naming ferns and vines. It reminded her she should be paying attention, taking notes, keeping an eye out for what might make good photographs to illustrate what had been achieved here. Determined to get on with her job and not let *this thing* with Matt King throw her completely off course, she fumbled in her carry-bag for her notebook and biro…and dropped her hat.

In a trice Matt scooped it up. "I'll carry it for you."

Heat whooshed into her cheeks. She just knew he'd put it back on her head himself when they emerged into sunshine and he'd reduce her to a quivering mess of jangling nerve-ends. "Thanks," she mumbled, wishing she hadn't clipped back her hair, wishing it was veiling her face as she hunted in her bag for the elusive objects. ''I do need my hands free to take notes,'' she added, finally producing the evidence of this intention, taking out her camera, as well, and hanging it around her neck for easy access.

He reached out, slid his hand around the nape of her neck and lifted her hair out from under the camera strap. Nicole stood stock-still, her heart hammering, her face burning. ''Just freeing your hair,'' he excused, but his fingers stroked down its length before he dropped the uninvited contact.

She didn't know what to do. She'd never felt like this before, so super-conscious of touch, of *who* was touching and the shivery intimacy of it, *the wanting* she could feel lingering on her skin and her own physical response so vibrant it swallowed up any possibility of making even a token protest.

She found herself gripping the notebook and biro with knuckle-white intensity and tried to concentrate on hearing what the guide was saying, jotting down snatches of words which would probably never make sense to her later. It simply gave her some purpose beyond being aware of Matt King beside her, Matt King watching her. Her mind shied from thinking about what he was thinking.

Maybe her imagination was running riot anyway. Let him speak, she decided. If he truly was interested in her as a woman, let him spell that out in no uncertain terms so no mistake could be made on her side. If he didn't, she could conclude that attraction was one thing, pursuing it quite another. He might very well think a relationship with her could end up with more problems than pleasure.

The last thing she wanted was to make a fool of herself over her employer's grandson. It would put her in a dreadfully embarrassing position with no easy escape from it. She had to stay at the castle for five more months and in that length of time there would undoubtedly be family occasions involving him. Caution had to be maintained here. Her own pride and self-respect demanded it. Yet the desire for some verbal rapport with him kept her very much on edge, waiting, listening.

To her intense frustration, Matt King said nothing out of the ordinary. He simply adopted the role of casual companion. They strolled along at the tail end of the tour group, stopping when the group stopped, looking at whatever was being pointed out to them. Nicole took photographs when others were taking photographs, regardless of whether they might be usable for the project or not. It used up otherwise idle time—time which might have led into dangerous ground with Matt King.

As it was, he commented on her prolific use of the camera. ''Are these photos for your own private pleasure of do you imagine they'll provide some kind of pictorial history?'' he said with a mocking amusement that needled her into justifying the activity.

''I don't know yet what will best illustrate this place when I come to writing about it. It will be good to have all these shots to choose from.''

One black eyebrow arched quizzically. ''Have you done much writing so far?''

''I'm still taking notes.''

''So I see.''

The dry tone and a flash of scepticism in his eyes implied he doubted she would ever get around to serious writing. It ruffled Nicole's feathers on a professional level. He had no right to judge her ability to produce what was required. Though she had to concede her erratic note-taking today might not have impressed him.

''I think you'll find the photographs in my home of more pertinent interest—historically speaking—than any you've taken today,'' he drawled. ''They show stages of the park from its inception to its completed state.''

''Why didn't you tell me before?''

''Oh, it was interesting observing what you thought was important. Besides which, you could have asked me.'' He slanted her a sardonic smile. ''I didn't really make myself available to you just to carry your hat.''

Nicole could have died on the spot. She'd been so flustered by his physical presence, so caught up in her own response to it, she hadn't *used* him as she should have done as a source of information on this part of the family history.

''I'm sorry. I was so carried away by the park as it is now...'' She shook her head in obvious self-chiding and managed an apologetic grimace. ''You must think I'm some kind of fraud.''

It was a toss-off line, one she expected him to deny, letting her off the hook. Instead, he delivered another blow to her self-esteem.

''Are you?''

She stopped, shocked that he could actually be thinking that. Her gaze whipped up to his and found his dark eyes glittering with a very sharp intensity.

''No, I'm not,'' she stated with considerable heat.

He cocked his head assessingly. ‘‘Then is there some reason you must cling to this public tour?’’

‘‘I...I came with it.’’

‘‘And I’ll see you return to it before it leaves. Failing that, I’ll drive you back to Port Douglas myself.’’

Her heart was catapulting around her chest at the thought of spending the next few hours alone with Matt King. She could feel the force of his will pressing on her, commanding surrender, and once again feeling under attack, she struggled to retain her independence from him.

‘‘We’re heading for the pavilion now,’’ she rushed out. ‘‘I’d like to walk around it.’’

‘‘Of course.’’ A taunting little smile curved his lips as he waved her into trailing after the group again. ‘‘It was built as a recreation centre for the internees. It gives a fine focal point to the kauri pine avenue and it overlooks the tennis courts on the other side. People can sit on the roof of the pavilion and watch tournaments being played.''

''And your great-grandfather designed it all,'' Nicole quickly slipped in to show her mind *was* on family history.

''Yes. No doubt you've already noticed the touch of old Rome in the construction of the building,'' he returned dryly.

The central block was surrounded by colonnades and the balustrade enclosing the flat roof was cast in a Roman style. ''All that's missing is a fountain,'' she commented.

He laughed. ''There's a row of fountains in a long rectangular pond on the other side.'' He grinned at her. ''Nothing was missed. Frederico Stefano Valeri was very thorough in everything he took on.''

Impulse spilled the question, ''Are you?''

His eyes danced teasingly. ''I guess history will be the judge of that.''

''The tour carries on to your exotic fruit plantation after refreshments in the pavilion.''

''Just feeding a curiosity. You can pick up all the information you might need on that from the pamphlets in the pavilion. You won't miss anything important.'' Again he grinned. ''A detour to my home will save you a long walk in the heat.''

There really was no choice but to go with him. Trying to postpone it longer than she already had would only feed his suspicions she was not up to the job she'd been employed to do. She could hardly explain that *he* was the problem.

''I'll even give you a personal sampling of the exotic fruit I grow,'' he added, piling on the pressure. ''Along with any other refreshment you'd like.''

Sheer wickedness in his eyes.

He knew she didn't want to accompany him.

He was playing a game with her—trap Nicole Redman.

But for what purpose?

Was he about to get…very personal…once they were alone together?

Her pulse drummed in her temples. Her whole body was seized with a chaotically wanton urge to experience this man, but she didn't trust it to lead anywhere good. The sexual pull was very strong—very, very strong—yet other instincts were screaming something was wrong about Matt King's game.

And that meant she had to stay alert and somehow keep a safety door open so she could walk out of the trap with her personal integrity intact.

CHAPTER SIX

DESPITE Matt King's unnerving company, Nicole loved his house. He ushered her into a large open living area which was instantly inviting, full of colour and casual comfort. The floor was of blue-green slate, cool underfoot. The room was cool, too, no doubt kept that way by an air-conditioner—blissful relief from the late-morning heat.

At one side, three green leather chesterfields formed a U to face a huge television screen. A long wooden table with eight chairs balanced it on the other side. A kitchen with a big island bench was accessible to both areas, and beyond them a wall of glass led out to a veranda.

Other walls held paintings of the rainforest and scenes of the Great Barrier Reef with its fabulous coral and tropical fish. It was very clear Matt King loved his environment and was very much at home in it. Even the outside of the house was painted green to merge with its surroundings and the approach to it was beautifully landscaped with palms and shrubs exhibiting exotic flowers or foliage.

"I'll get some refreshments," Matt said, heading into the kitchen. "Leave your things on the table and go on out to the veranda. It overhangs a creek so you'll find it cool enough. Nice place to relax with the sound of water adding to the view."

Any place she could relax was a good idea, Nicole thought, following Matt's instructions. At least he had given her back her hat to put on herself, and he wasn't crowding her now as she took it off again and set it on the table with her bag. Maybe it was stupid to feel so tense. Directing her onto his veranda surely indicated he was not about to pounce on her.

A sliding-glass door led onto it and Nicole moved straight over to the railing, drawn by the sound of rushing water. The creek below ran over clumps of boulders in a series of small cascades. It sparkled with a crystal-like clarity and the view was so pretty with the banks covered with ferns, she momentarily forgot all her troubles.

Birds flitted amongst the trees, their calls adding a special music to the scene—soft warbles, sharp staccatos, tinkling trills. She caught glimpses of beautiful plumage; gold, purple, scarlet. This was a magical place and she thought how lucky Matt King was that he could lay claim to it. To live here with all this…the sheer natural beauty of it, the tranquility…absolute Eden.

"Don't move," came the quietly voiced command from behind her. "Butterflies have landed on your hair. Just let them be until I get a flower and move them off."

She stood very still, entranced by the idea of butterflies being drawn to her, not frightened by her foreign presence. There was the sound of a tray being set on a table, Matt's footsteps as he walked to the end of the veranda and returned. Out of the corner of her eye she glimpsed a bright red hibiscus bloom in his hand, a long yellow stamen at its centre. She felt a light brushing on her hair, then suddenly two vivid blue butterflies were fluttering in front of her, poised over the flower which Matt was now holding out over the railing.

"Oh!" she breathed in sheer wonder. "What a brilliant blue they are!"

"Ulysses butterflies. Lots of them around here," Matt murmured. "The bright colour of your hair attracted them."

"Really?" She looked at him in surprise, still captivated by the pleasure of the experience.

He smiled, even with his eyes, and he was standing so close, it was like being bathed in tingling warmth. For a few heart-lifting moments, it seemed they shared the same vision of the marvels of nature, felt the same appreciation. Then the warmth simmered to a far less comfortable level and Nicole could feel herself tensing again.

"Drawn to the flame," he said in a soft musing tone that set her skin prickling. "I wonder how many it has consumed?"

"I beg your pardon?" she said stiffly.

"Moths...men...your hair is a magnet."

"It doesn't consume things."

"It has the allure of a *femme fatale.*'

"I don't see you falling at my feet."

He laughed and teasingly drew the soft petals of the hibiscus flower down her cheek. It was a shockingly sensual action and he enjoyed every second of it while she lost the ability to breathe, let alone speak.

"Life is full of surprises," he said enigmatically. "Let me surprise your tastebuds with many exotic flavours."

He stepped back and gestured to the table where he'd left the tray. It was a table for two, cane with a glass top, and two cane chairs with green cushions on their seats stood waiting for them. The tray held a platter containing an array of sliced fruit, two small plates with knives and forks and two elegant flute glasses filled with what looked like…

"Champagne?" The word slipped out, bringing home to Nicole how far out of control she was.

"The best complement for the fruit," Matt said with an authority that seemed to make protesting the alcoholic drink too mean-spirited to try. He smiled encouragingly. "It's chilled, which I'm sure you'll appreciate."

He was waiting for her to take her chair. Nicole took a deep breath, needing to collect her scattered wits, and pushed her jelly-like legs into action. As she seated herself, Matt unloaded the tray and placed the scarlet hibiscus flower beside her glass of champagne, a taunting reminder of how easily she could lose her head with this man. She vowed to sip the champagne sparingly.

He sat down and grinned at her, anticipation of pleasure dancing in his eyes, making her heart contract with the thought that it was not the prospect of eating fruit exhilarating him.

She was the target and he was lining her up for the kill. Although her mind was hopelessly woolly on what *kill* meant.

"I think we should start with what is commonly regarded as the king and queen of all tropical fruit." He forked two pieces of fruit onto her plate, pointing each one out as he named them. "The king is durian. The queen is mangosteen."

The durian was similar to a custard apple, only much richer in flavour. Nicole preferred the more delicate taste of the sweet-acid segment of mangosteen. "I like the queen better," she declared.

"Perhaps the king is more of an acquired taste. The more you eat it the more addictive it becomes."

Was he subtly promising this about himself?

"Now here we have the black sapote. It's like chocolate pudding."

He watched her taste it, making her acutely conscious of her mouth and the sensual pleasure of the fruit.

"You'll need to clean your palate after that one," he advised, picking up his glass of champagne and nodding to hers.

She followed suit as he sipped, her own gaze drawn to his mouth, wondering what it would taste like if he kissed her.

"Try a longan. It's originally from China and similar to a lychee."

So it went on—exotic names, exotic tastes—but more and more Nicole was thinking erotic, not exotic. There was a very sexy intimacy in sharing this feast of oral sensations, the conscious sorting out of flavours on the tongue, mouths moving in matching action, relishing delicious juices, trying to define interesting textures, watching each other's response, the telling expressions to each different experience…like an exciting journey of discovery…exciting on many levels.

Matt King…he stirred needs and desires in her that wanted answering. He embodied so much of all she had missed out on in her own life and the craving to know if he could fill that emptiness was growing stronger and stronger. It wasn't just that he was the sexiest man she'd ever met. It felt like...he was a complete person...and she wasn't.

Perhaps it had to do with having a firm foundation of family, a sense of roots, a clear continuity. She felt she was still looking for *her place,* both in a physical and spiritual sense. She wished this was her home, wished she could belong here, wished Matt King would invite her into more of his world.

"Would you like some more champagne?"

It jolted her into the realisation that she'd drained her glass without even noticing the fact. "No," she said quickly. "It was lovely, thank you. It's all been lovely...the park, your home, the fruit, sitting out here with this wonderful view..."

"And you haven't even minded my company," he slid in, his eyes telegraphing the certain knowledge of what had been shared in the past half hour.

Nicole shied from acknowledging too much, telling herself she still had to be careful of consequences. "You've been very generous."

"A pleasure." His smile seemed to mock her caution. "Would you like to see the photographs now?"

"Yes, please."

He laughed as he rose from his chair. "You sound like a little girl. Which makes me wonder how full of contradictions you are, Nicole Redman."

"I'm not aware of any," she retorted lightly, standing to accompany him.

"You're very definitely a tantalising mix." He slanted her a mocking look as he ushered her back into the house. "I'd find it interesting to delve into your history, but that's not why you're here, is it?"

"No." What else could she say? This wasn't a *social* visit. But if he really wanted to know more about her...or was he testing her again? Challenging her? Why did he make her feel uneasy about what should be straightforward?

They walked through the living room. At one end of the kitchen he opened a door which led into a very workman-like office. The far wall had a picture window with a spectacular view of the rainforest park. A long L-shaped desk held a computer, printer, fax machine, telephone, photocopier—all the modern equipment necessary for running a home business. File cabinets lined the other wall. Above them was a series of large framed photographs, depicting various stages of the park.

Nicole was instantly fascinated by them. Matt drew her attention to a framed drawing above the printer. ''You should look at this first. It's the original plan, sketched by my great-grandfather. This is what the internees worked from.''

It was amazing…the thought, the detail, the vision of the man. ''Do you have a photocopy of this?''

"Yes, I can give you one. Now if you look over here..." He directed her to the first photograph by the door. "The first thing planted was this fast-growing bamboo, all around the perimeter of the camp to block out the fences which represented emprisonment."

Understanding and caring, Nicole thought, again marvelling at what a remarkable person Frederico Stefano Valeri had been. As they moved from one photograph to the next, with Matt explaining the story behind each stage of the park, giving it all a very human purpose, she couldn't help wondering if goodness was inherited, as well as strength and the will to meet and beat any adversity.

There was no doubting the strength, both physical and mental, in the man beside her, but what was in Matt King's heart? Was it as big as his great-grandfather's? Did it hold kindness, tenderness? What moved him to act? Would he stand up for others?

Most people, Nicole reflected, were little people, wrapped up in their own self-interest.

They didn't stride through life, shaping it in new ways for the benefit of others. Yet from all she'd learnt of the Valeri/King family, they did just that, certainly profiting themselves, but never at the cost of others. They were *big* people, in every sense.

Her gaze was drawn to the muscular arm pointing to the last photograph, tanned skin gleaming over tensile strength. Her own skin looked white next to his, white and soft, unweathered by time or place. Perhaps it was the contrast that made him so compellingly attractive.

His arm dropped.

The deep rich timbre of his voice was no longer thrumming in her ears.

She looked up to find him observing her with heart-squeezing intensity. Having completely lost track of what he'd been saying, she held her tongue rather than make some embarrassing *faux pas.*

"I have the original photos filed if you want to make use of them," he said, but she knew intuitively that wasn't on his mind.

She shook her head. "I'd rather not have the originals. They're precious. If you could have copies made for me..."

"As you like. I'll bring them to the castle when they're done."

"Thank you."

"It *is* too much for you, isn't it?"

"What?"

"It would be fairer to my grandmother if you admit it now."

"I don't know what you mean."

"Do I have to shake it out of you?" His hands closed around her upper arms, giving substance to the threat.

Alarm screeched around her nerves. "I think you've got something terribly wrong here. Please let me go."

He released her, throwing up his hands in a gesture of angry impatience. His eyes blazed with accusation. "You might have been able to swan through God knows what else on your looks and your ability to adopt a role convincingly, but let me tell you your performance on this project today has been too damned shallow for me to swallow.''

``It's your fault!'' she hurled back at him. ``Making me nervous and...''

``And why do you suppose that is, Nicole?'' he savagely mocked. ``Because I recognise you for what you are?''

She stepped back, confused by the violence of feeling coming from him. It was like a body blow, shattering any possible sense of togetherness with him, shrivelling the desire he'd aroused in her.

``What am I...to you?'' she asked, needing some reason for this attack.

His mouth curled sardonically. ``The same bewitching woman I watched in New Orleans ten years ago.''

``New Orleans?'' He was there...when she was there with her father?

``Don't tell me it's some mistake. The image of you is burned on my memory. Indelibly.''

``I don't remember you.''

''You wouldn't. I was masked that night.''

''What night?''

''You must have spent many nights spinning your ghostly tales on the haunted history tour. You were very good at it.''

''Yes, I was.'' Her chin lifted with defiant pride. ''So what? That was ten years ago.'' And she wasn't ashamed of raking in the tourist dollar then, any more than he'd be of doing it now.

A black cynicism glittered in his eyes. ''Still spinning tales, Nicole? Drawing people in? Getting them to shell out money with clever fabrications and exaggerations? Pulling the wool over their eyes? Eyes already dazzled by the striking combination of pearly skin and flame-red hair?''

Shock spilled into outrage at his interpretation of her character. He had no cause at all to think she was some kind of confidence trickster. Even if she had embellished those old tales a bit, it was only to add to the fun of the tour, giving people more for their money.

"I was doing a job," she cried emphatically. "The only job I could get at the time. I followed a script I was given. I certainly didn't fleece anyone. Everyone got good value on the haunted history."

"And now you're fully qualified to research and write a family history." Scepticism laced every word. "Except you haven't quite demonstrated a fine nose for it today."

"You're right!" she snapped, feeling more and more brittle. "I'm much better at it when there's no hostile force muddling my mind."

"Hostile?" he derided. "I gave you every chance to prove you were on top of this job. You even lost track of what I was telling you right here."

"I was thinking."

"Sure you were! And maybe you were thinking what I was thinking..." His eyes raked her from head to foot and up again. "...how well we might go together in bed."

Her skin was burning. Her insides were quivering. She was in a total mess. For a few soul-destroying seconds she stared at him, knowing at least she hadn't been wrong about the mutual sexual attraction but there was nothing to feel good about in that. No way in the world could she stomach any physical intimacy with him now.

"Please excuse me," she said with icy dignity. "I'll go and rejoin the tour."

A fierce pride gave her the power to walk out of his office and cross the living area to the table where she'd left her hat and bag. She was shaking as she picked them up.

"Running away won't resolve anything."

The mocking drawl flicked her on the raw. She turned her head to give him one last blistering look. He was leaning against the doorjamb, the loose-limbed pose denying any tension on his part. An ironic little smile played on his lips.

"Better to face up to the situation and try to make it more workable," he advised. "I could get you some help."

Her jaw clenched at this offer. She managed to unclench it enough to say, ‘‘Provided I satisfy you in bed?’’

That wiped the smile off his face. ‘‘I don’t trade in sexual favours, Nicole.’’

‘‘Neither do I. And I’ve always found prejudice quite impossible for resolving anything. Please check my professional credentials with your grandmother before we have to meet again. I’d prefer not to feel under fire from you in future.’’

She didn’t run, but she swept out of his house as fast as she could at a walking pace. He didn’t come after her, for which she was intensely grateful because she was right on the edge of bursting into tears. Anger, frustration, disappointment…all of them were churning through her, and she hated herself for having given him any reason to think what he did.

She would not be vulnerable to his…his aggressive maleness…ever again.

Just let him come near her.

Just let him.

She would freeze him into eternity!

CHAPTER SEVEN

THREE hours, Matt told himself, as he drove to the Sunday luncheon he couldn't avoid. Four at most. He should easily manage to pass that length of time with his family without putting a foot wrong with Nicole Redman. He could do a show of polite interest in her work, enough to satisfy his grandmother's standard of good manners, and spend the rest of the time chatting to his brothers.

He was not about to make any judgments today. Let Nicole Redman stew in her inadequacies as far as the family history was concerned. He'd brought the photographs and the photocopied plan she'd requested. He'd hand them over to her and that was his bit done. She wasn't about to seek him out for anything more and be damned if he'd chase her for anything, either.

What was it…ten days since he'd called her bluff? The gall of her to blame *him* for *her* lack of professionalism on the project! Sheer amateursville taking all those tourist photos in the park. No theme, no purpose, just click, click, click. And calling him a hostile force…huh! She hadn't thought he was hostile while they shared the fruit platter on the veranda.

A pity he hadn't taken his chance then and there.

It was well and truly gone now.

Though it was better he hadn't got sexually involved with her. She probably cheated on that level, too, promising more than she'd ever deliver. Visual pleasure definitely wasn't everything. And reality rarely lived up to fantasy.

His grandmother could have Nicole Redman all to herself from now on. She would just have to accept that her matchmaking scheme had bombed out and live with the consequences of her choice. It wasn't paramount that the family history be published at the end of Nicole's contract. Another person could be brought in to get it right. This was not a full-scale disaster, more a minor mess they could all sweep under the carpet.

On the marriage front, she had ready consolation for her disappointment with him. This luncheon…Tony's pressure for him to be there…reading between the lines, Tony was bursting to celebrate with the family the fact that he and Hannah were expecting their first baby. Had to be. Hannah wanted a whole pack of children, having come from a big family herself, and Tony had declared himself happy to oblige her. Three months married…time enough for Hannah to get pregnant.

So today was bound to be happy families day for Nonna. She'd have Alex's and Gina's two children to cluck over and Tony and Hannah promising another great-grandchild. Plenty of good stuff for her to focus on. She could count her blessings and forget about him for a while. A *long* while. He'd get married in his own good time to his own choice of wife.

He drove in to the private parking area behind the castle, noting that Alex's Mercedes was already there and Tony's helicopter was sitting on the pad. He was the last to arrive, which was good. Easier to lose Nicole Redman in a crowd, although if his grandmother parked him with her at the dining table… Matt gritted his teeth, knowing he couldn't completely ignore her. He hated being boxed into a corner. Hated it!

Using the back entrance, he strode along to the kitchen where he was bound to find Rosita, who knew everything there was to know about what went on in the castle. She'd not only been the cook and housekeeper here for over twenty years, she was his grandmother's closest confidante, sharing the same Italian heritage and always sympathetic to her plans.

She was at the island bench, tasting a salad with an air of testing its ingredients for the correct balance. Matt grinned at her. Rosita loved food and didn't mind being plump because of it. He and his brothers had been fed many great feasts in this kitchen.

"Have you got it right?" he teased.

"This is Hannah's special salad. An interesting combination...cabbage, noodles, walnuts...but you do not want to know these things." She gestured expansively. "It is good to see you, Matteo!"

"You, too, Rosita." He gave her a quick hug. "How's everything going here?"

"Oh, busy, busy, busy. You will find everyone in the billiard room."

That surprised him. "Why the billiard room?" He couldn't imagine Alex and Tony wanting to play today.

"It is where Nicole has her work on the family history. Your grandmother is showing them what's been done so far."

"Well, that should be interesting," Matt said dryly, wondering how Nicole was managing to convince them that anything had been done.

"She works too hard, that girl." Rosita shook her head disapprovingly. "Up all hours of the night. I make a supper for her but more times than not she forgets to eat."

"Definitely a crime," Matt commented with mock gravity.

"Oh, go on with you!" She shooed him away. "And do not leave it so long again before visiting your grandmother. Over a month."

"Busy, busy, busy," he tossed back as he left the kitchen.

"Young people," he heard her mutter disparagingly. "Rush, rush, rush."

But Matt didn't *rush* to the billiard room. He was considerably bemused by the picture painted of Nicole Redman by Rosita. Hardworking? And why was such a large room being taken up for this project? How did she justify it?

The door was open. The rest of the family didn't even notice his arrival. Their attention was fixed on the billiard table which was still wearing its protective cover. A quick sweeping glance told Matt Nicole Redman was not present, which made his greeting much more relaxed.

''Hi!'' he said, strolling forward. ''What's the big deal here?''

Everyone answered at once, saying hello and urging him into their midst to look at what was fascinating them. The surface of the billiard table held a pictorial history of the family, a massed display of old photographs, arranged in sequential decades, with a typed annotation of who, where and why underneath each one. Some of them Matt had never seen, or if he had, he didn't remember them.

''This is great, Nonna,'' he couldn't help remarking.

''Nicole and I have been sorting them for weeks. These are the best from a store of old albums and boxes.''

Probably more his grandmother's work than Nicole's, Matt decided.

"Have a look at this time line, Matt." Tony waved him over to a whiteboard which he was now studying. "All the big dates lined up—the wars, the mafia interference, the cyclones, the whole progress of the sugar industry, when the other plantations became viable…and on this side of the line, notes on what the family was doing through these critical times. Just the bare bones but it gets the history in perspective, doesn't it?"

It did. In fact, Matt had to concede it was quite an impressive summary. And a very logical method of getting the whole story in order. He was beginning to have a nasty niggly feeling he might have misjudged Nicole Redman. Yet if she really could do this job, why had she been so inept during her visit to Kauri King Park?

Which reminded him of the bag he was carrying. He turned to his grandmother. "I've got more photographs here. Shots of the park being built. Nicole asked me to get copies of the originals and a photocopy of the plan. Where should I put them?''

''On her desk. Thank you, Matteo.''

Following the direction of his grandmother's nod, Matt saw that a large desk had been brought in and positioned under the window at the far end of the room. It held a laptop computer, piles of manila folders, a tape-player and a stack of cassettes which Alex was sorting through, picking up each cassette and reading the label.

''So what's Nicole Redman's taste in music?'' Matt asked as he put the bag next to the computer.

''It's not music. They're interviews with the old families in the Italian community. Nonna said she's off doing another one today.''

''Not joining us for lunch then?'' Matt now had mixed feelings about whether he wanted her there or not. Easier for him if she wasn't, but if he was guilty of prejudice—and the evidence was stacking up against the assumptions he'd made—an apology was due.

''No. She's gone down to the Johnstone Shire. A couple of hours' drive. Won't be back until late afternoon, I should think.''

Free of her.

Except she sat uncomfortably on his conscience.

''She's certainly compiled a lot of material this past month,'' Alex remarked admiringly.

''Yes, but can she write?'' Matt snapped, part of him needing to justify his stance with her.

Alex gave him a startled look. ''Don't you know...?'' He stopped, frowned. ''That's right. You weren't at the lunch when Nonna introduced Nicole to the rest of us. One of the reasons Nonna chose her to do this was the biography she'd written of her father.''

''A biography,'' Matt repeated, stunned by this new information.

''Mmm... It's called *Ollie's Drum.* Her father was a jazz musician.''

Jazz… New Orleans…

"Have *you* read it?" he shot at his oldest brother, whose opinion he'd always respected.

"No." Alex gave him a droll look. "But biographies don't get published unless the author can write, Matt. Besides, Nonna has read it and it satisfied her."

Ollie's Drum. Matt fixed the title in his mind. He needed to get hold of that book, read it for himself. The ferocity of that thought gave him pause to examine it more rationally. What was the point of pursuing more information about her? If he'd blotted his copybook with Nicole Redman, so what? Hadn't he already decided any kind of relationship with her was not on?

Though he didn't like feeling he hadn't been fair.

Injustice of any kind was anathema to him.

On the other hand, she'd given him every reason to think what he had, and accusing him of being a hostile force, making her nervous…absolute hogwash!

"You're right off base if you're thinking Nicole Redman isn't up to this job," Alex remarked, eyeing him curiously.

"I didn't say that."

An eyebrow was cocked, challenging any doubt at all. "She's got a swag of degrees. History, genealogy, literature..."

Degrees could be forged. With today's computers almost anything could be made to look genuine.

"She's taught various courses at a tafe college, too," Alex went on. "Very highly qualified. Nonna was lucky to get her."

Not even a hint of suspicion that Nicole was not as she had presented herself. If Alex was sold on her...and Alex certainly didn't have a matchmaking agenda...then it had to be conceded Nicole did have the ability to do this job.

Which meant he should apologise.

The sooner, the better, in fact. She couldn't be feeling good about a member of the family casting aspersions on her integrity. She might very well have gone out today to avoid the unpleasantness of his presence. And working on a Sunday could be taken as a slap in the face to him for doubting her commitment to the project.

Her absence suddenly felt very personal.

Matt didn't like it one bit. He'd never been painted as a hostile ogre before. He wished he hadn't brought up the sexual angle with her. It made the situation doubly awkward when it came to back-pedalling on the stance he'd taken. Nevertheless, he couldn't just walk away from it. She had another five months left on this project and leaving her under a black cloud where he was concerned, was not right.

This *blot* had to be confronted and dealt with.

Today.

Even if he had to wait hours for her to return to the castle.

CHAPTER EIGHT

NICOLE glanced at her watch as she drove into the castle grounds, heading for the family parking area at the back. Almost five o'clock. Late enough for everyone to have gone home. Not that she would have minded saying hello to Matt King's older brothers and she really liked their wives. Gina was genuinely warm-hearted and Hannah literally bubbled with the joy of life. Probably more so now if she was expecting a baby, as Mrs. King suspected.

No doubt she would hear all the family news over dinner tonight, though it was a shame she had missed out on Hannah's excitement. Nicole instantly argued that Matt King's presence at the luncheon would have dampened it for her anyway. And if he'd been seated next to her at the dining table...she shuddered at the thought. An utterly intolerable situation.

It was reassuring to see that the helipad was empty. Clearly Tony and Hannah had flown back to their home on the tea plantation at Cape Tribulation. Alex's Mercedes was not in the parking lot, but the one car sitting by itself gave Nicole's heart a nasty lurch—a forest-green Saab convertible, a typical choice for a wealthy, sexy bachelor like Matt King.

She brought her own modest little Toyota to a halt beside it and sat, fighting a sickening rise of tension. She couldn't be certain the sporty convertible was his since she'd never seen him driving a vehicle. Nevertheless, any hope that it belonged to someone else didn't feel very feasible.

Best to assume he had stayed behind with his grandmother and stay clear of where they might be. If she could scoot upstairs to the privacy of her bedroom…no, that would mean passing the library. Maybe she could slink into the billiard room without being seen.

Nicole thumped the driving wheel in disgust at these *fugitive* thoughts. Why should she let herself be intimidated by Matt King? It was wrong. *He* was wrong. While she certainly didn't want to meet him again, it was absurd to shrink from doing so when she was absolutely entitled to hold her ground.

Determined on acting normally, she alighted from her car and walked into the castle, intent on heading openly to the billiard room where she would take her briefcase and empty it of the material collected today. This meant passing through the kitchen and predictably Rosita was there. It was a considerable relief to find the motherly housekeeper alone.

"Ah! You are back!" she said in a satisfied tone, as though Nicole was some recalcitrant chick who had finally returned to the nest.

"Yes, I'm back. Is Hannah expecting a baby, Rosita?"

A triumphant clap of the hands. "Two months pregnant! It is very happy news."

"How lovely!"

"And Matteo is still here, talking to his grandmother. If you would like to go on out to the loggia and join them, I will bring some fresh drinks."

"I'd rather let them enjoy each other's company, Rosita," she quickly excused. "I have some work to get into my computer while it's still fresh in my mind."

This announcement earned a disapproving tut but Nicole was off before Rosita could gear up for her argument that there was more to life than work, especially for a young woman who had not yet been fortunate enough to find a husband to take care of her.

As Nicole walked down the hall to the billiard room, she darkly decided that if Rosita was fondly casting her employer's third grandson in that role, she was doomed to disappointment. No way was matrimonial bliss on that horizon!

In fact, the thought of joining Matt King in any sense raised hackles that might have drawn blood had she gone out to the loggia, despite her respect for her employer. She closed the door of the billiard room very firmly behind her, willing her antagonist to keep his distance because she was not prepared to suffer any more slights on her integrity.

And if he had checked out her qualifications today, she hoped he was stewing in guilt over his rotten accusations. Not that it was likely. He was too arrogantly sure of himself to think he might have been mistaken. Just because he'd been right about the sexual attraction... Nicole heaved a big sigh to relieve the mounting anger in her chest as she marched over to her desk.

Enough was enough!

How many nights had she lain awake, seething over their last encounter? It was such a foolish waste of time and energy. The man was not worth thinking about. To let him get under her skin as far as he had was just plain stupid.

She switched on the computer with more force than was needed. Work was the answer to blocking out unpleasant connections from her consciousness. Her gaze fell on a bag that didn't belong on her desk. A long cardboard cylinder protruded from it. Frowning over the Kauri Pine Park logo on the bag, she set her briefcase on the floor, uncomfortably aware that she had asked Matt King for copies of photographs and the original plan of the park. Was this his delivery?

Her hands clenched, not wanting to touch anything he had touched. Had he brought this bag in here himself, invading her private space, spying on what work she'd done? She shot a quick glance around the room, looking for anything out of place. Only the bag. Yet somehow the very air felt charged with his presence.

It was unnerving, inhibiting. She stared at the bag, telling herself its contents were completely harmless. It didn't matter if they were meant to mock her position here at the castle.

She would use them effectively and show Matt King how very professional she was. Even if he never backed down from his insulting judgment of her, she'd know that he had to know he was wrong once the history was published. There could be no refuting that evidence. In the end, she would triumph.

The only problem was…it didn't take away the hurt.

A knock on the door sent wild tremors through her heart. *Not him…please…not him,* her mind begged as she heard the door open.

"Nicole?"

His voice.

She wanted to keep her back turned to him but what good would that do? *He* would have no compunction about walking in and doing whatever he wanted. She could feel his forceful energy hitting her, commanding an acknowledgment of him. If he didn't get it, he would engineer a confrontation one way or another.

"May I come in?"

The polite query cut into the fierce flow of resentment in her mind. It was just a sham of good manners, she swiftly told herself. The predatory nature of the man simply would not accept a negative reply. Nevertheless, pride in her own good manners demanded he be faced and answered.

Instinctively she squared her shoulders, stiffened her spine, armouring herself against his impact. Impossible to calm her heart. She half turned, enough to see him, watch him, while giving him the least possible target to fire at.

"What do you want?" Blunt words, but she didn't care. Why wait for his attack? Better to get it over with quickly.

He closed the door behind him, ensuring privacy. His face wore a grimly determined look, causing Nicole's stomach to contract in apprehension. The sense of his presence was now magnified a hundredfold. She forced her gaze to rake him from head to toe, as he had done to her at their last meeting, but there was no sexual intent behind the action, more a need to reduce him to just a body without the power behind his eyes.

Except it wasn't just a body.

It had power, too.

And it struck her as hopelessly perverse that she could still feel attracted to it, everything that was female in her responding with treacherous excitement to the aggressive masculinity of his perfectly sculpted physique.

"I want to apologise."

The words wafted quietly across the room and slid soothingly into ears that were clogged by the clamouring of her heart. Nicole wondered if she had imagined them. She saw his hands lift in an open gesture of appeal, giving some credibility to what she'd heard. Her gaze lifted to his mouth, waiting for it to move, to say more, to mitigate the deep offence he'd given.

"I'm sorry I suggested you were not what you portrayed yourself to be. In part, I was influenced by a memory which coloured my judgment.''

It was like pressing the trigger on a shotgun loaded with bitter pellets. ''A *memory!*'' she fired at him, her eyes meeting his in a raging blaze of feeling. ''You didn't even stop to ask why I was there in New Orleans, doing what I was doing. You know nothing about me except...'' Her teeth were bared in savage scorn. ''...you happened to see me one night, leading a haunted history tour.''

He winced.

She kept on blasting. ''And for that you decide I'm little better than a whore, pulling tricks, fleecing people, using whatever sex appeal I have to get out of trouble...''

''I didn't say that,'' he whipped back, frowning at the vehemence of her attack.

''You *thought* it. And you had no right to think it, no reason to think it. It was you...you...who took liberties with me. Touching and...and suggesting...'' A tide of heat was rushing up her neck, flooding into her cheeks, making her wish she hadn't brought up any reminder of how he had mused over how well they might go in bed together.

He took a deep breath and calmly said, "I'm sorry if any action of mine made you feel uncomfortable."

"*If...if?*" His calmness incensed her. "You set out to do it. You know you did," she wildly accused. "Even in your office. Why didn't you just hand me back my hat instead of..."

"It wasn't deliberate. It was pure impulse."

"I didn't invite it."

"No, you didn't." His mouth curved ironically. "Except by being an exceptionally attractive woman."

She shook her head not accepting this excuse. "It showed a lack of proper respect for me."

"Oh, come on, Nicole!" he chided, impatience with her argument slipping through the reins of his control. He started walking towards her, gesturing a mocking dismissal of her case against him. ''You can hardly call putting your hat on your head and touching your cheek major violations. You didn't protest. Didn't flinch away. In fact...''

''Well, please take note of my evasive action right now, Matt King,'' she flung at him, marching pointedly to the other side of the billiard table to put it between them. ''I don't want you near me,'' she stated bitingly.

''Fine!'' he snapped, having already halted. Black derision glittered from his eyes. ''I'd have to give you full marks for the drama queen performance.''

''So much for your apology!'' she mocked.

''A pity you weren't gracious enough to accept it,'' he shot back at her.

Her chin tilted in defiant challenge. ''What's it worth when you're still casting me in a false light and not admitting to any fault yourself?''

''I might have cast you in a false light, lady, but you helped me do it, floundering around as you did in the park.''

''And before that? Your *memory* from New Orleans?''

''Yes,'' he admitted.

From no more than a superficial look at her.

While her memories...the sadness of them still gutted her...although she was glad she had them.

''And just what were you doing there ten years ago?'' she asked, still fiercely resenting his interpretation of one brief view of her.

''Seeing some of the world before settling down to family business,'' he answered with a dismissive shrug.

A wild youthful spree. Totally carefree.

The contrast between them could not have been wider.

Emotion welled as she remembered the heavy weight of her responsibility that year. Impossible to keep it out of her voice. She looked directly at Matt King, wanting to nail home how very mistaken he was about her, but even he faded from her mind as she spoke, the memories sharpening, taking over.

"Well, I was *on* family business. My father was dying of cancer and his last wish was to go back to New Orleans. He was a jazz musician and to him it was his soul city. We had very little money but I took him there and got what work I could to help support us. Every night he sat in Preservation Hall, right across the street from Reverend Zombie's Voodoo Shop, where the haunted history tours started and ended. In case you don't know, Preservation Hall is revered by jazz musicians all around the world. It's where…"

"I know," he broke in. "I dropped in there one evening."

She stared at him, wondering if he'd seen or met her father, heard him perform. A lump rose in her throat. She had to swallow hard to make her voice work and even then it came out huskily.

"Some nights when my father wasn't too ill, he'd be invited to play the drums. He was a great jazz drummer."

"*Ollie's Drum,*" he murmured.

"You know? You heard him play?"

He shook his head. "I only know about the book you wrote."

"The book..." Tears blurred her eyes. "He was a genius on the drums. Everybody said so. A legend. There were so many stories..."

"Did he die over there?"

She nodded, trying to blink back the tears, but she could see the jazz bands playing in the streets behind the coffin and the tears kept gathering, building up.

"I'm sorry, Nicole. I really am sorry."

She nodded. The quiet voice sounded sincere. Though somehow it wasn't important anymore.

"Please...go," she choked out, not wanting to cry in front of him.

He hesitated a moment then gruffly said, "Believe me. You do have my respect."

Without pressing anything else he left the room, closing the door quickly to give her the privacy she needed. Her chest was so tight it felt like a dam about to burst. She felt her way around the billiard table, reached the chair in front of her desk and sagged onto it. She didn't see the plastic bag with the Kauri Pine Park logo this time. She wasn't seeing anything.

It was ten years since she had buried her father.

It felt like yesterday.

And the loneliness of not having anyone to love, or anyone to love her, was overwhelming.

CHAPTER NINE

ONCE Matteo had headed off to the billiard room, Isabella Valeri King moved from the loggia to the library. She sat at her desk, her work diary in front of her, giving some semblance of purpose. She'd opened it to the one date she wanted to discuss with Matteo when he came to say goodbye to her, but work was not on her mind.

There was trouble between Matteo and Nicole—a sure sign they had connected on a personal level, but not a good result so far.

Nicole stiffened up every time his name was mentioned. Even more so since her visit to the park. And there had been no need for her to work today. Even her argument that Sundays were best for chatting to the old Italian families held no weight since the current members of the family she was writing about had all been gathered here—an easy opportunity to get their input on any facet of the history.

Nicole's choice—her very determined choice against the much-pressed invitation to stay and join them for the luncheon—spelled out a resolution to avoid Matteo at all costs. Quite clearly he had been just as resolved on forcing a meeting, staying on at the castle as long as he had and acting like a cat on hot bricks when Rosita had informed them of Nicole's return.

Such strong resolution had to have passion behind it, Isabella decided. Indifference did not give rise to such behaviour. The trick was to channel the passion into a positive direction. She hoped whatever was going on in the billiard room right now was getting rid of the negatives.

Pride could play the very devil in trying to get two people together. Isabella suspected that pride was a big factor here. It was a pity she didn't know what had caused a conflict to erupt between them, but neither of them would welcome interference on her part, anyway. Though, of course, she could stage-manage opportunities for them to reach out to each other...if they wanted to.

Desire...

It had to be there.

Matteo had clearly been distracted today, not his usual cheerful self at all. Brooding over Nicole's absence, Isabella had concluded. Not even celebrating Hannah's pregnancy had kept his spirits lifted for long. The jokey chatting with his brothers had seemed forced, and his conversation with her after everyone else had gone, had been peppered with silences. But he'd come very briskly to life at Rosita's further announcement that Nicole had gone to the billiard room to work.

"I'll just check that Ms. Redman has everything she needs from me before I leave," he'd said.

Which could have been done by telephone anytime.

The desire for physical confrontation had been paramount.

Desire…passion…surely it was the right mix.

Isabella was clinging to this hope when Matteo appeared in the doorway to the library. Her mind instantly dictated acute observation.

"I'm off, Nonna. Great luncheon. Happy news about the baby. You must be pleased."

Short staccato sentences, his mouth stretched into a smile but not a twinkle of it in his eyes, tension emanating from him as he quickly crossed the room to drop a goodbye kiss on her cheek.

"Yes, I am. Pleased for Antonio and Hannah, too. It's what they wanted," she replied, wishing Matteo would confide what *he* wanted.

He hadn't won whatever he'd gone to win from Nicole Redman. His kiss had no feeling in it, a quick performance of what was expected of him before he left. His mind was clearly preoccupied, and not with happy thoughts. Isabella spoke quickly to hold him with her long enough to ascertain his mood towards Nicole.

"I was just looking through my diary."

"Mmm..." No interest. Mental and physical withdrawal under way.

"I trust you have marked Gina's premiere night on your calendar."

He halted beside her desk, frowning at the reminder of his sister-in-law's debut on the stage of the Galaxy Theatre in Brisbane. "When is it again?"

"Two weeks from this coming Thursday. I've booked six seats on a flight to Brisbane that afternoon."

"Six? Won't Alex and Gina be down there already?"

"Naturally. In fact, Alex will have the children there, too, during the last week of rehearsals. He doesn't want Gina worrying about them when she has to concentrate on her singing. Such a big role, playing Maria in *West Side Story.*"

''She's got the voice for it,'' Matteo said dismissively. He gave her a hooded look. ''So who are the six seats for? Tony, Hannah, you, me…''

''Rosita and Nicole.''

A pause. Then in a voice stripped of any telltale expression he asked, ''Nicole will be going?''

Not *Ms. Redman* this time, Isabella noted. ''Yes. She's very keen to hear Gina sing. And see Peter Owen's production of the show. Such a charming man, Peter. He flew up last weekend to iron out some production details with Gina and dropped in to visit me. Gave Nicole a personal invitation to the post-premiere party he's throwing and she was very happy to accept.''

Matteo's jaw tightened.

Peter Owen had a very *colourful* reputation as a latter-day Casanova. Alex had once been quite jealous of his professional association with Gina. It had spurred him to declare his love for her very publicly. Isabella reflected that a highly competitive streak ran through each of her grandsons' characters. Perhaps the threat of Peter Owen's winning charm would sort out Matteo's feelings towards Nicole.

"I've also booked hotel accommodation for all of us that night," she went on. "Does that suit you or do you want to make alternative plans?"

His brow was lowered broodingly. His silence went on so long, Isabella was drawn into a terse command. "You can't miss the premiere, Matteo. If only to support Gina, you must go."

His hand sliced the air. "No question, Nonna. Alex would kill me if I didn't turn up."

"Well, what is the problem? You seem…very distracted."

He grimaced. "Sorry. I'll go along with the arrangements you've made. I suppose it will be red carpet at the theatre. Limousines. Formal dress."

"You can count on it. Peter Owen wouldn't have it any other way."

"The ultimate showman. Well, we'll see, won't we?" he muttered darkly and headed for the door, holding up a hand in a last salute. "'Bye, Nonna. Fax a schedule to my company office and I'll toe the line like a good little boy."

He flashed a mocking smile and was gone.

Definitely not a happy man, Isabella thought.

However, she had achieved the setting for the next scene between Matteo and Nicole, and put in a clever little needle by throwing Peter Owen into the ring. Control of the seating in the plane and in the theatre was hers. As long as neither of the antagonists found some rock-solid excuse for not following through on their given word, they'd have to bear each other's company for many hours.

Isabella smiled to herself.

There was nothing like enforced time together to wear down barriers.

CHAPTER TEN

MATT arrived at Cairns Airport twenty minutes before their flight to Brisbane was scheduled to take off. He didn't have to check any luggage through. A suit bag encased the formal clothes he had to wear to the premiere tonight and a small carry-on bag held the rest of his needs.

Tony met him in the entrance hall, handing over his ticket and seat allocation. "The others have gone through to the departure lounge. Ready to join them?"

"Sure! I guess I'll be sitting next to Nicole Redman on the flight," he commented casually, trying to feel relaxed about it as they strolled towards the security barrier.

"No. Nicole took off early this morning. Nonna said she wanted to spend the day in Brisbane, going through newspaper archives."

Anger blazed through him. She was using the excuse of work to avoid him again. Okay the first time. He had cast slurs on her integrity. But he'd gone out of his way to admit he was wrong and apologise for the offence given. It was definitely not okay a second time. This was a deliberate snub.

"What does she hope to find there?" he asked, barely keeping his anger in check. Some show of interest was called for since he'd brought up her name.

"Well, you know Nonna's husband and brother were on the same boat that sailed from Brisbane when they went off to the Second World War. Nicole wanted some background stuff on how it was for them."

Naturally it *sounded* reasonable, using the plane ticket to serve two purposes. Very conscientious, too, saving Nonna the expense of funding an extra research trip to Brisbane. Except saving dollars was not what this family history project was about and Nonna would not have blinked an eye at any expense it incurred anywhere along the line. So there was no doubt in Matt's mind that Nicole Redman had deliberately engineered this arrangement to thumb her nose at him and his apology.

"Tough luck, Matt! You'll have to put up with your own company for the next two hours," Tony tossed at him teasingly.

"No problem." He laid his bags on the roller table and they stepped through the security gate without setting off any bells.

"Got to hand it to Nicole," Tony rambled on. "Not leaving a stone unturned to do a thorough job on our family history."

"Seems that way," Matt answered noncommittally, collecting his bags and glancing around the departure lounge to spot where the others were seated.

"Over there..." Tony pointed, then grinned at him. "You must be losing your touch, Matt. Gorgeous girl more interested in her work than getting acquainted with you."

He shrugged. "I'm probably not her type."

''Can I take it that's mutual? She's not your type?''

Matt rolled his eyes at him. ''Give it a rest, Tony. I know you're a happily married man but I don't need any matches made for me.''

Certainly not with a fiery little number who wasn't reasonable enough to let her rage go. No, she had to keep rubbing in how offensive he'd been, despite his complete backdown and apology. And to think he'd actually bought the book about her father's life and read it to see where she was coming from, just so he could make his peace with her on this trip, even lying awake half of last night, working out what to say…all for nothing!

He greeted his grandmother, Rosita and Hannah just as the boarding call for their flight was announced. No need to make conversation, which suited him very well because he wasn't in the mood for social chitchat. On the plane he had a window seat with no one next to him. The stewardess handed him a newspaper and he used it to close out everyone else.

His eyes skimmed the print but nothing sank into his consciousness. The empty seat beside him was a constant taunting reminder of Nicole Redman's deliberate absence from it. No truce from her. She'd probably arrange for her seat in the theatre tonight to be the furthest from him. And no doubt she'd ride in the limousine transporting his grandmother and Rosita and he'd be directed to ride with Hannah and Tony and Alex.

Which was fine by him.

He didn't care what she did.

She could flirt her head off with Peter Owen at the post-premiere party, too, and he wouldn't turn a hair. In fact, he'd feel utter contempt for it because it would be an act of blatant dishonesty, pretending she fancied Peter Owen. He hadn't been wrong about the sexual attraction she'd felt with him. She could deny it as much as she liked. He knew better.

She would have let him kiss her out on the veranda, after he'd removed the butterflies from her hair. She had not recoiled from his touch one bit. What did she expect a man to do, anyway? Hold back until she gave verbal permission to come close? Ignore the body language that was telling him he was welcome and wanted?

Just let her try that fruit-tasting exercise with Peter Owen and Casanova Pete would be dragging her under the table to take what she was offering. Given the desire she had aroused, Matt figured he'd been a positive gentleman. And what had he got for his restraint? Lies and abuse.

His fault that she hadn't been able to concentrate on the job!

What absolute rot!

She'd had sex on her mind, same as he had, and he hadn't made one suggestive remark to feed her fantasies all the time they'd been walking through the park. It was totally perverse to blame her thoughts on him. She'd made them up all by herself. So why the hell couldn't she admit it instead of scuttling behind a defence of *his fault?*

She might not like wanting him.

He didn't like wanting her.

That didn't change the truth.

Matt seethed over this truth all the way to Brisbane. He was still seething over it when they booked into the hotel, more so when he reached his room and tossed his things on the queen-size bed, which reminded him how open he'd been in laying out what he'd felt to Nicole Redman, stating an obvious desire when wondering out loud how they might be together in bed.

He'd been wrong about her ability to do the job, wrong about her trading on her looks and being unfair to his grandmother, but even with all his wrong assumptions, he'd offered to smooth the situation over by getting whatever extra help she needed. But did she appreciate he'd been bending over backwards to keep her in Port Douglas? To get rid of the deceit and set up a platform of trust so they could move forward into a relationship that he wouldn't feel bad about?

No!

She couldn't even admit he was right about the mutual lust.

He snatched up the bedside telephone, pressed the button for reception and asked for her room number. He glanced at his watch as the information was given to him. Five-thirty. Everyone in their party was to meet in the hotel lobby at seven-fifteen, ready to be transported to the theatre, and be damned if he was going to be snubbed by Nicole Redman again!

He'd sort this out right now.

She had to be in her room. Women always took forever getting ready for a big night out and tonight was *big* for the family. She'd be aware of when his grandmother was arriving at the hotel, aware that she should be on hand to assure her employer that time was not a problem. Work would definitely be over for today. No one of any sensibility would mess with tonight.

No point in trying to talk to her over the telephone. No way would he give her the satisfaction of hanging up on him. This had to be face to face. And there wasn't one bit of guilt she could throw at him this time. With a burning sense of righteousness, Matt left his room and strode towards Nicole Redman's.

Nicole was luxuriating in a bubble bath. Some sensual pampering was precisely what she needed to relax the tension that had made her feel edgy all day. It was impossible to completely avoid Matt King tonight. She simply had to accept that and keep as much distance between them as she could.

Though she still couldn't stop her mind from circling around him, especially knowing she would be seeing him soon. No doubt he would look even more handsome in formal dress. Every man did. It wasn't fair that *he* was so *physically* attractive. It made her feel she might be missing out on some extra-special experience with such a powerhouse of masculinity.

And she wasn't sure she liked the entirely feline instinct that had drawn her into buying a dress she didn't really need. She'd brought one with her that would do for tonight. This afternoon's wild rush of blood to the head had resulted in sheer unnecessary extravagance. She shouldn't have gone into the shopping mall that housed such an alluring range of designer boutiques, courting temptation. The moment she'd seen the black dress, her mind was consumed by one burning thought…

I'll show him.

Show him what? That she could look attractive, too? Or were her claws out, wanting to get under his skin as much as he got under hers. From afar, of course, so he'd sizzle with frustration…if he still fancied a session in bed with her. Justice, she'd told herself, turning the insults he'd handed out into savage regret on his part. After all, he'd savaged her with his outrageously false reading of her character.

Though he had apologised.

Far too late.

Such a late apology couldn't begin to make up for how he'd made her feel for over a week of miserable days and even more miserable nights.

All the same, maybe she shouldn't wear the dress. Maybe she should return it to the boutique and get her money back. Being vengeful wasn't about to result in anything good. It just kept her thinking about him and his response to her.

Was that a knock on her door?

Yes.

Nicole hauled herself out of the bubble bath, thinking it might be Hannah dropping by for a little chat before they had to dress, probably unable to contain her excitement over Gina's premiere, wanting to share it. She had raved to Nicole about Gina's voice, certain that her sister-in-law was going to be a star in tonight's show, but first-night nerves might have got to her.

Nicole gave herself a quick towelling, then wrapped herself in the big white bathrobe supplied by the hotel as she hurried through the bedroom. Another knock urged her into faster action. Without pausing to check the identity of the caller, she opened the door and stood in paralysed shock at being confronted by Matt King.

With him standing right in front of her, barely an arm's length away, she was swamped by how big he was, how male he was, and all of him bristling with aggression, sending an electric charge through every nerve of her body. She was instantly and acutely conscious of her nakedness under the bathrobe, and the blistering force of his glittering dark gaze reminded her that her hair was piled carelessly on top of her head, pinned there to keep it out of the bathwater.

''Let's talk, shall we?'' he said in belligerent challenge, stepping forward, driving her back from the door and the intimidating power of his advancing presence.

She was hopelessly unprepared for this. It didn't even occur to her to try and stop him as he entered her room and closed the door behind him. She was too busy back-pedalling to put some distance between them, checking that the tie-belt was tied, clutching the lapels of the robe together to prevent any gap from opening, catching her breath enough to speak.

"What do you want to talk about?"

He looked at her mouth. Was it quivering? She had no make-up on, no armour at all in place to give her any confidence in maintaining some personal dignity against the raw onslaught of his sexuality.

His gaze dropped to the hollow in her throat. She could feel the dampness there that she hadn't had time to wipe away. He took in the clutching position of her hands on the hotel robe, an obvious pointer to how vulnerable she felt. His eyes missed nothing. He probably saw her toes curling as he looked at her bare feet, and he surely absorbed every curve of her body as his gaze slowly travelled back up to her face, her mussed hair, her eyes.

''Maybe talking isn't what either of us want,'' he said gruffly, his deep voice furred with the desire for a more primitive means of man/woman communication.

Sheer panic galloped through her heart, contracted her stomach, shot tremulous waves down her thighs. ''I don't know what you mean,'' she gabbled, her mind totally seized up with a clash of fear and excitement.

''Yes, you do.'' His eyes mocked her denial as he moved forward and cupped her chin, fingers lightly fanning the line of her cheek. ''You know exactly what I mean, Nicole Redman. The only question is…will you give an honest response?''

He was going to kiss her.

And she just stood there, mesmerised by the blazing purpose in his eyes, mesmerised by the tingling warmth of the feather-light caress on her cheek, allowing his cupping thumb to tilt her chin to a higher angle, a readily kissable angle, and when his mouth covered hers, it wasn't just her lips yearning to know what his kiss would be like. Her whole body was zinging with anticipation, vibrantly alive to whatever sensations this man would impart.

It wasn't a gentle kiss. She hadn't expected it to be. Didn't want it to be. He'd churned her up so much, the need for some outlet for all the pent-up feelings crashed through her, urging answers from him. His mouth was hotly demanding and hers demanded right back, no holds barred as they merged in a rage of passion that craved satisfaction.

An arm clamped around her back, slamming her against him. The hand that had been holding her face to his, raked through her hair, dislodging pins, exulting in freeing the long tresses, and she exulted in it, too. She revelled in being pinned to the hard surging strength of his powerful physique, loved the feel of his hand in her hair, its aggressive need to tangle in the long soft silkiness of it.

Somehow it freed her to touch him as she liked; the muscular breadth of his shoulders, the wiry curls at the back of his neck. Every contact with him was intensely exciting, the squash of her breasts against the firm hot wall of his chest, the pulsating sense of their hearts drumming to the same fierce escalation of desire for each other, thighs rubbing, pressing, wanting flesh against flesh.

She felt the tie-belt on the robe being yanked, pulled apart. Matt wrenched his mouth from hers, dragging in air as he lifted his head back. His eyes glittered an intense challenge as he moved his hands to hook under the collar of the robe, intent on sliding it from her shoulders. He didn't speak. He didn't have to. The words zapped straight into her mind.

Stop me now if you want to stop.

Her mouth throbbed with the passion he'd fired. Her breasts ached to be touched, kissed, taken by him. Her whole body was aroused, screaming for the ultimate intimacy with this man, uncaring of any moment beyond the experience he was holding out to her.

She didn't speak.

As her hands slid down from his shoulders to make the disrobing easy, her eyes told him there'd be no stopping from her and it wasn't a surrender to his will. It was her choice. And it was up to him to prove the choice was worth taking.

He eased back from her to let the robe slither to the floor. He didn't look down at the nakedness revealed. His gaze remained fastened on hers, the challenge still very much in force as he brought her hands up to his chest, resting them beside the buttons on his shirt.

"Don't give me passive," he growled. "Show me. Get rid of my shirt."

He released her hands. He stood there, inviting her touch but not forcing it. She could feel the burning pride behind his stance, the tension of not knowing whether she might refuse, the determination not to leave himself open to any accusation that he'd taken unfair advantage of her, yet the wanting was not in any way diminished. The heat of it was sizzling around her, bringing tingles to her bare skin and the sense of partnership he was demanding acted like a heady intoxicant to the cocktail of excitement already stirred.

Her hands moved with eager purpose. He'd stripped her naked. He had to be naked, too. She wanted him to be, wanted to feast her eyes on all that made him so masculine, wanted to touch, to absorb the power of him, to experience exactly what it was that compelled such a strong sexual response in her, even against her will, against her reason. She didn't want to fight it now. She had to know.

The shirt was open. She slid it from his shoulders. Warm, satin-smooth skin, tightly stretched over firm muscles. His chest was magnificent. She couldn't resist grazing her fingers through the little nest of black curls below his throat, gliding her palms down towards his flat stomach.

It spurred him out of his tense immobility. It was *his* hands that unfastened his trousers, got rid of the rest of his clothes, stripping with a speed that was breath-taking in its effect of instantly revealing more than she had let herself imagine. He was a big man, big all over, and a little shiver ran through her at the thought of mating with him.

Too late to back off now.

Besides, she didn't want to.

Her heart was thundering in her ears. Her whole body was at fever-pitch anticipation. And there was a wanton primitive streak inside her that was wildly elated when his strong hands gripped her waist, lifted her off her feet and swung her onto the bed.

He loomed over her, all dominant male, and there was a fierce elation in his eyes at having won what he wanted. Though she knew it wasn't true. She was the one taking him. And her eyes beamed that straight back at him. No surrender. A searing challenge to complete what had been started, complete it to *her* satisfaction.

It was like a battle of minds…a battle of hearts…intensely exhilarating…all-consuming…concentration totally focused. There was no foreplay…none needed…none wanted…just this apocalyptic coming together…the ultimate revelation of all the uncontrollable feelings they had struck in each other.

Every nerve in her body seemed to be clustered in that one intimate place, highly sensitised, waiting, poised to react to his entry. There was a tantalisingly gentle probing, a teasing test of how welcome he was. Instinctively, needfully, she clasped him with her legs, urging him on. He plunged forward and her whole body arched up in ecstatic pleasure at the sense of him filling her with his power. It was glorious, having him so deeply inside her, then feeling him thrust there over and over again. Her own muscles joyously adjusted to his rhythm, revelling in the exquisite sensations, craving more and more peaks of pleasure.

Her whole being was centred on how it was with him. She'd never felt anything like it in her entire life, hadn't known what was possible. She lost all sense of self. This was fusion on such an intense level there was no room for any other reality and even when she reached the first incredibly sweet climax, it simply set her afloat on a sea of pleasure that kept on rolling with waves that crested even more deliciously.

How he held his climax back for so long she didn't know, but when it came it was wondrous, too, the fast friction, the powerful surge of energy, the explosion of heat spilling deeply inside her...and a feeling of overwhelming love burst through her, tingling right to her scalp, her fingertips, her toes. And she found herself hugging him to her, hugging him with every ounce of strength she had left in her arms and legs.

His arms burrowed under her and hugged her right back, and there was no letting go, even when he rolled onto his side. He carried her with him, as blindly and compulsively intent as she was on holding on to the togetherness. Time had no meaning. Nothing had any meaning but this.

Until the telephone rang.

CHAPTER ELEVEN

THE telephone!

The realisation of where she was and what she was supposed to be doing came like a thunderclap, jerking Nicole up from Matt King's embrace. Eyes wide open with the shock of having lost track of everything, her gaze instantly targeted the radio clock on the bedside table: 18:33. Only forty minutes left to get ready for tonight's premiere and be down in the lobby for the trip to the theatre!

"Look at the time! We've got to move!" she shot at Matt, heaving herself off him and rolling to the side of the bed to pick up the receiver.

"Right!"

The quick agreement helped to get her mind focused on dealing with the situation. First the call, which was probably from her employer to ask about today's research—her employer who was footing the bill for this hotel accommodation which had just been used for…nothing at all to do with the agenda Isabella Valeri King had approved for today and tonight!

It was some relief to feel Matt moving off the other side of the bed, going straight into action. Nicole swung her legs onto the floor, sat up straight, took a deep breath, lifted the receiver to her ear, and spoke in a reasonably even tone.

The caller *was* Mrs. King.

Nicole quickly expressed satisfaction in the information she'd collected from newspaper archives, replied to various other queries about her day, gave assurances that her hotel room was fine and she hadn't forgotten the seven-fifteen deadline in the lobby, lied about having had something to eat, and every second that ticked by increased the tension of losing more time.

She had her back turned to Matt but she could hear him moving around, pulling on clothes. No sound of his exit, though. Which doubled her tension as she managed to conclude the call. Bad enough that she'd had no option but to remain naked while he dressed. What was he waiting for? Didn't he understand there was no acceptable excuse for not being punctual tonight? And it would be dreadfully inappropriate not to be properly dressed and groomed, as well.

Her heart pitter-pattered nervously. What was his reaction now to what had transpired between them? Had it been as world-shaking for him as it had been for her? Suddenly feeling intensely vulnerable, she forced herself to look at him over her shoulder, needing some reassurance that he had been deeply affected, too.

He stood near the short passageway to the door, his gaze trained very intently on her. He was fully dressed, looking every bit as respectable as when he'd entered, ready to meet anything or anyone.

''Don't try skipping out on me tonight, Nicole,'' he fired at her, his eyes blazing a command that promised she would rue any deviation from what was planned. ''You *be* in the hotel lobby at seven-fifteen. We'll take it from there.''

He was gone before Nicole could even catch her breath. He'd brought an electrifying wave of aggression into her room and his exit left her with the same sense of force which would not be denied, no matter what ensued from this moment.

It stunned her into losing a few more moments.

Her mind rallied to examine what he'd said since it had to be a lead to what he was feeling. *Skipping out on him...* Was that how he viewed her choice to take an earlier flight today? Perhaps even further back, a reference to the family luncheon she'd deliberately missed.

He must have taken both absences as very personal slights. Which they were. But this had to mean he'd been thinking about her as much as she'd been thinking about him, and getting highly riled about it. And he wasn't about to walk away from what had just happened.

Be there!

The command of a very determined man to have her with him. He certainly hadn't had enough of her. Which was fine by Nicole. She hadn't had enough of him, either. Which brought a crooked little smile to her face. She'd leapt in at the deep end with Matt King and didn't know if she'd be able to keep her head above these turbulent waters. But she wasn't about to drown yet.

The black taffeta dress.

Yes, she'd be there in the lobby at seven-fifteen, but not as a woman submissive to his will. In fact, she'd do her absolute utmost to knock his eyes out. Teach him not to take anything about her for granted.

* * *

Matt was the first down. He was early. Eight minutes past seven. He hoped to catch his grandmother before Nicole appeared and ensure the *right* seating in the limousines and at the theatre. He didn't care if this raised her eyebrows or gave her satisfaction. Nicole Redman had certainly proved his match in bed but that didn't mean marriage was on the line.

Ten past seven. Matt breathed a sigh of relief as he saw Rosita, Alex and his grandmother emerge from an elevator. Alex, as always, looked impressive and totally in control of himself. Nonna was in royal-blue silk, very regal with her head of white hair held high and all her best jewellery on. Rosita wore burgundy lace and was beaming with excitement. They all smiled at him.

Matt forced a smile he didn't feel, knowing he should be sharing their anticipation of pleasure in the show and a triumphant night for Gina. All he could think of was getting Nicole Redman to himself again. As the others joined him in the middle of the lobby, he directly addressed his grandmother.

"So what's the arrangement, Nonna? You three go in the first limousine, the rest of us to follow?"

She appeared to consider, then slowly answered, "Nicole may want to ride with us."

"Won't look good for the red carpet arrival at the theatre," he argued. "I think Alex should take both your arm and Rosita's for the walk in. Which would make Nicole the odd woman out. Better that she be accompanied by me, stepping out of the second limousine."

"Matt has a point there, Nonna," Alex remarked supportively. "Peter has lined up media coverage. Bound to be cameras on us."

Was that a smug little smile flitting across her lips? Certainly there was a twinkle in her eyes as she answered, "Then we will do it Matteo's way."

Inwardly he bridled against seeming to fall into her matchmaking trap. He didn't pursue the issue of seating at the theatre, deciding he'd hold on to Nicole's arm so that any separation would not occur, unless she made a point of it. Unlikely that she would carry out a public snub in these circumstances.

The problem was Matt didn't feel sure of her, despite the intimacy they had just shared. Giving in to mutual lust behind closed doors didn't guarantee a positive response in other areas. They hadn't talked, hadn't reached any kind of understanding he could feel comfortable with.

Maybe she'd just been satisfying a sexual curiosity, an itch that needed scratching, and she'd back right off him again now. He found his hands clenching and forced himself to relax. She had to stay beside him for the next few hours. At least that much was assured.

Tony and Hannah emerged from another elevator, Hannah looking absolutely fantastic in a beaded green gown, her long crinkly blond hair billowing around her shoulders. Pregnancy not showing yet.

Matt checked the time on his watch again. Thirteen minutes past seven. If Nicole wasn't here in the next two minutes he'd go up to her room and haul her down. No way was he going to let her call in sick or make some other lame excuse for not joining him tonight. If she thought she could take him for sexual pleasure, then turn her back on him… Matt seethed over the possibility, vowing he'd set her straight in no uncertain terms.

He caught his grandmother observing him and tried to adopt a nonchalant air, glancing around the lobby in a pretence of careless patience for their party to be complete. An image of red and black caught his eye, high in his normal field of vision. His gaze jerked up. There, at the top of the staircase, leading down to the lobby from the mezzanine floor.

She stood looking straight at him.

Checking him out?

Matt neither knew nor cared. His heart turned over as he slipped back in time to the night he'd first seen her in New Orleans. Red and black. And her skin glowing pearly white. Stunning. Fascinating. Compelling him to follow, to watch her, listen to her. Not the time nor place to get to know her then, but now…

''Oh, there's Nicole on the mezzanine level,'' he heard his grandmother say. ''She must have pressed the wrong button in the elevator.''

No, Matt thought. It was deliberate.

Her gaze didn't so much as waver from his as she began her descent to the lobby. He wasn't someone in a mask at the back of a crowd of tourists tonight. She knew who he was and was challenging his interest in her, refiring the desire he'd driven to its ultimate expression earlier, desire she'd conceded herself.

He'd called her a *femme fatale.*

Mockingly.

He could feel her flaunting it in his face with every step she took down the staircase. Her black dress was the sexiest he'd ever seen, its heart-shaped neckline cut wide on the shoulders to little cap sleeves that virtually left her slender white arms bare. The décolletage was low enough to show the valley between her breasts and the upper swell of them on either side. More provocative than blatant. The bodice was moulded to her curves and the whole gown hugged her figure to knee-length. He could see a fishtail train slithering down the steps behind her. The shiny fabric added to the whole sensual effect.

Matt belatedly realised he was moving to meet her. She'd drawn him like a magnet. Too late to stop, to deny her that power. Better to make the action seem perfectly natural, her escort doing the polite thing. He waited at the foot of the stairs, ready to offer his arm, which she'd take if he had to forcibly hook hers around it.

Her hair gleamed like liquid fire, a smooth fall forward over one shoulder, brushed back behind the other. That was provocative, too. Her mouth the same colour red. Her lashes were lowered to make it appear her gaze was focused on the steps, but it wasn't. Through the semi-veil, her eyes were simmering with satisfaction at having him waiting on her.

Matt had to quell a wild surge of caveman instincts. His family was watching and be damned if he'd give his grandmother the satisfaction of knowing *her choice* was making him burn more than any other woman he'd ever known. Now was the time for very polished manners and Nicole Redman had better match him in that.

He offered his arm as she took the last step, his own eyes hooded to prevent her from seeing the inner conflagration of rampant desire and angry frustration with the situation he found himself in. Control was needed. He hated not having it. He would not let this woman take it from him.

The tightness in his chest eased as she slid her arm smoothly around his, no hesitation at all. ''Thank you,'' she said huskily.

''My pleasure,'' he replied, darting a sharp look at her, surprised by the furred tone.

Her gaze fluttered away from the quick probe, but he was left with an impression of uncertainty. No triumph. No confidence, either. She wasn't claiming him. In fact, the hand resting on his coat sleeve was actually tremulous. He quickly covered it with his own, holding it in place. If she was having second thoughts about linking herself to him, no way would he allow her to flit off and leave him standing like a fool.

''You look quite superb tonight,'' he said, determined on appearing outwardly calm and collected as he led her towards the family group.

''So do you,'' she muttered, then took a deep breath as though she needed it to steady herself.

Was she regretting having had sex with him? Worried about it? Afraid he might now take some advantage from it she didn't want? Did her appearance have more to do with bravado than deliberate allure?

Alex was ushering his grandmother and Rosita towards the door. Tony and Hannah were hanging back, waiting. Matt waved them on, wanting them to go ahead and give him a few private moments with Nicole.

''We need to do some talking,'' he shot at her.

Red battle flags in her cheeks. ''I thought you'd done all the talking you wanted to do with me.''

What was this? Blaming him for what she'd wanted to do herself? ''Nowhere near,'' he mocked. ''You could say we now have a basis for a beginning.''

''I thought it was an end in itself,'' came her snippy reply.

''Rubbish! If circumstances were different, we'd still be on that bed.''

Her mouth compressed. No reply. She didn't want to admit it and denial would be a lie. He hadn't actually meant sexual communication. Why was she being difficult?

Talking had to be the next step. He tried again.

"We don't have the time now but after the show..."

"There's a party and I intend to go to it." She turned her head to direct a blaze of defiance at him. "With you or without you. Please yourself. I will not be dictated to by you, Matt King."

"I had mutual interests in mind," he grated out.

"Above the sexual level?"

It goaded him into retorting, "Something wrong with the sexual level?"

"No. But there's more to me than that."

"You think I don't know it?"

"You haven't shown it."

Her head snapped forward, pride stamped on her tilted profile.

Matt fumed at her intransigence. "Precisely how was I supposed to show it when you've been avoiding me like the plague?"

"You *were* a plague."

''Well, well, progress,'' he drawled mockingly. ''Thank you for the past tense. Satisfying our mutual lust was of some benefit.''

Her chin tilted higher, emphasising her long graceful neck. Matt wondered how long it would stay extended if he planted a few hot kisses on it. Going to see *West Side Story* had no appeal to him tonight, even with Gina singing. *The Taming of the Shrew* would have suited him much better.

Ahead of them, Alex was stepping into the first limousine after his grandmother and Rosita. Tony and Hannah were outside the lobby, waiting for the second limousine to slide into place. The hotel doors were being kept open for his and Nicole's imminent passage to the pick-up point.

At least Nicole hadn't queried arrangements. Matt figured he'd won that much from her. And she'd accepted him as her escort. No overt attempt to avoid his physical presence. She might be burning over the fact he hadn't left her with honeyed words after their intimacy, but given the way she'd treated him previously, what could she expect?

He'd been entirely reasonable.

So what the hell was her problem?

"Well, I hope *you* enjoy the show tonight," he said with a twist of irony.

She looked at him, obviously confused by his line of thought. "What do you mean by that?" she asked, her tone wary, suspicious.

"It's about star-crossed lovers, ending unhappily. Which is what you seem determined on for us."

The comment sharpened her eyes into a fine glitter. "You're very fast at assumptions."

"You could try giving me more to work on," he retaliated.

"And you could try asking instead of making up your own scenarios and thinking you can force me into them," she flashed back at him.

"Fine! After the show tonight..."

"I'm going to the party," she said stubbornly.

"So am I," he snapped, having run out of time to say any more.

The first limousine had pulled away, Hannah and Tony were climbing into the second, and he and Nicole were now on their heels, poised to follow. A few seconds later they were all settled inside it and the chauffeur was closing the door on them.

Matt sat facing Tony, almost hating his brother for looking so happy. And there was Hannah next to him, holding his hand, glowing as though all her Christmases had just come. In contrast, he filled the space beside the red-haired witch who kept stirring cauldrons of boiling oil to hang him over them.

But he'd get her tonight.

If she thought she could give him the slip at the post-premiere party, she could think again. He'd be there at every turn, making his presence felt. And she'd feel it all right. He wasn't making any wrong assumptions about the sexual spark between them.

Absolute dynamite.

And the fuse was burning.

CHAPTER TWELVE

THEY had a box at the theatre. Nicole was placed next to Matt in the second row of seats behind Alex and Rosita and Mrs. King, but at least she had Hannah on her other side and the arrangement made for easy conversation amongst the family. She wasn't isolated with Matt, which was an enormous relief since she couldn't trust herself to speak civilly with him.

Not that her inner tension eased much. She was hopelessly aware of him. Their physical intimacy had heightened it a hundredfold, making her acutely conscious of her sexuality and his. It played on her mind so much she could barely think of anything else. Back in the hotel lobby, she'd ended up snapping at him out of her own resentment that it could be so overwhelming.

Other things should be more important. Respect, love, trust, understanding…what about them? And he was so arrogant, confident of claiming her whenever he wanted, and the worst part was she was quivering inside, yearning for what he'd given her to be given again. How was she going to handle this? How? What was the best way? Was there a best way?

Star-crossed lovers…ending unhappily.

Those insidious words lingered in her mind as the show started but she was soon caught up in the Romeo and Juliet story being played out on the stage. The production was vibrant and intensely emotional with its continual overtone of tragedy looming, the inevitable outcome of irreversible conflict.

Every time Gina sang there was an almost breathless silence throughout the theatre, the poignant power of her voice and the empathy she drew from the audience made her a wonderful Maria. The rest of the cast put in very good performances but she shone, and at interval the buzz of excitement and pride in the family box put irrepressible smiles on everyone's faces, even Matt's and Nicole's.

The second half of the show was even more heart-wringing. With tears pricking her eyes, Nicole fumbled around her feet for her evening bag, needing tissues. Matt offered a clean white handkerchief. Rather than make any noise, unclicking her bag, she took it, nodding her thanks. It was very handy when Maria's lover was shot and lay dying with Maria kneeling beside him as they sang a last plea of hope for the world to come right—*''Somewhere...''*

Tears gushed.

Nicole mopped frantically, struggling to stop a sob from erupting.

''Hold my hand...'' The words were so terribly moving, and when Matt's hand covered hers, squeezing sympathetically, she gripped it and squeezed back as though it were a lifeline to stop her from falling apart.

The curtain came down.

The only sounds in the theatre were sniffles being smothered and throats being cleared. The applause was slow in coming, a sprinkle of handclaps quickly joined by more, building like a huge wave to a crescendo that urged more and more clapping. Nicole wanted to use her hands but one of them was still entangled with Matt's and she was suddenly acutely conscious of having hung on to it.

His hand.

The warmth and strength of it zinged up her arm. Her heart skipped a beat. She didn't want to let the comforting contact go but was there really any comfort for her in this attraction to Matt King? Embarrassed, she darted him a look of appeal as she wriggled her fingers within his grip. He returned an ironic little smile and released her hand, moving his straight into a long round of applause.

There was an absolute ovation for Gina, many shouts of "Bravo!" She was presented with a huge bouquet of red roses and she smiled directly up at Alex who leaned on the railing of the box and blew a kiss to her. She blew one back to him. Their obvious love for each other gave Nicole a stab of envy.

Why couldn't it… Her head turned to Matt King even before the thought was completed. *…be like that for them?*

He caught her glance and cocked a quizzical eyebrow.

Heat whooshed into her cheeks and she jerked her attention back to the stage. The thought certainly hadn't occurred to him. The expression lingering on his face from having watched the interplay between his brother and sister-in-law was amusement. Did he find real love between a man and a woman a joke? Was sex all he considered?

Or was it all he was considering with *her?*

Nicole found herself pressing her thighs tightly together, a silent, vehement protest against such a limitation, especially when a relationship could be so much more. Surely such strong sexual chemistry had to be linked to some special selective process. It made no sense otherwise.

She was still battling the feelings Matt aroused when Peter Owen, the director of the show, was called on stage to another loud burst of applause. She couldn't help smiling at his air of elated triumph as he took the microphone and made a short speech, thanking the audience for their acclaim, which of course, was richly deserved, and it demonstrated how magnificently perceptive they all were to recognise and acknowledge it.

As always, he was so charmingly over-the-top he drew laughter and more applause, leaving everyone in high spirits as the final curtain came down. *He's still Peter Pan,* Nicole thought fondly, remembering how he'd brought an effervescent lightness to some of her darker hours in the old days, a kindness that felt more like fun than kindness.

Alex stood and spoke to his grandmother. "I'll just slip backstage while the theatre is emptying. I won't be long."

''Take your time, Alessandro. We're in no hurry.'' She turned around to smile at Nicole and comment, ''Peter made it work wonderfully well, didn't he?''

''A brilliant production,'' she agreed. ''I didn't know he had this in him but he really did pull it off.''

The old lady's gaze shifted to Matt. ''The ultimate showman,'' she said with a nod, as though repeating a remark he'd made. Then in a whimsical tone, she added, ''Nicole knew Peter when he was just starting out as a pianist, getting the occasional gig with jazz bands.''

Matt turned a frown on her. ''In the same bands your father played in?''

''Sometimes,'' she answered evenly, vowing to watch her wayward tongue and invite more normal conversation between them. ''He was more a fill-in than a regular. Though I must say I missed him when he dropped out of the Sydney jazz scene. He took a job as a pianist/singer on a cruise ship and sailed out of our lives."

The frown deepened. "You made no mention of him in your book."

He'd read her book?

Her mind scrambled to fit this stunning news into her picture of Matt King. Her heart lifted at the realisation he had to be interested in her as a person to put the time into reading a biography which revealed her background. It couldn't be just sex on his mind!

"You didn't tell me you'd read *Ollie's Drum,* Matteo," his grandmother half queried, one eyebrow arched in surprise.

Nicole stared at him, still processing her own surprise. He sat back, jawline tightening as though he'd just been smacked on the chin. "Since you've contracted Nicole to write our family history, Nonna, it seemed a good idea to see how she'd dealt with her own," he drawled, deliberately eliminating any *personal* interest in the content.

"I trust you were satisfied," Nicole bit out, anger rising at the lengths he'd gone to, checking that she wasn't cheating his grandmother.

"Very much so," he conceded. "The book was very well written and held my interest."

She burned. He'd probably been flipping through it to see if it contained any evidence of her whoring or fleecing people of their money. Her tongue wanted to whip him for thinking so badly of her, but she restrained it, remembering her outburst in the billiard room when he had apologised for misjudging her.

He had apologised.

He'd even said he respected her.

But then he'd bedded her with only the barest pause for her consent. Nothing to make her feel appreciated or valued. Just straight into sex, since her book had proved she was okay and there probably wouldn't be any nasty comebacks. She hated him for it, hated herself for having been a willing party to it, but in this company she had to appear civil.

"Thank you," she aimed at him, then forced a smile at his grandmother. "To get back to the show, I do think the staging was excellent, but Peter obviously knew what he had in Gina and she certainly delivered it for him."

"Oh, yes!" came the ready agreement. "From the time he first heard her sing, he was determined on showcasing her talent."

"Well, he sure did it tonight," Hannah chimed in, giving Nicole the opening to turn to her and chat on until Alex returned.

This was the signal for them to start making their exit from the box. Alex reported on all the excitement backstage as they milled out into the corridor. Inevitably Nicole was coupled with Matt again for the walk down the stairs to the foyer of the theatre.

As reluctant as she was to take his arm, common sense argued the stairs could be tricky in her long gown and high heels, and it would be too impolite if she ignored his offer and used the banister instead. Better to suffer his rock-steady support than risk losing her dignity by wobbling or tripping, though she inwardly bridled at having to be close to him, feeling the whole length of his body next to hers.

They trailed after the others and she wished he would quicken his pace to catch up, but if anything he slowed it, frustrating her wish not to be alone with him, not to be reminded of how he had felt naked, how she had felt…

"How old were you when Peter Owen featured in your life?" he asked, thankfully pouring cold water on her feverish thoughts.

"Ten and eleven," she answered, relieved that he wasn't dwelling on the same hot memories.

"Just a kid then," he muttered dismissively.

It goaded her into adding, "I might have been *just a kid,* but Peter always went out of his way to make me feel welcome in his company."

"Couldn't resist charming even little girls," came the sardonic comment.

"Charm is often in very short supply," she returned tartly. "And I appreciated it very much at the time."

"No doubt you did. Not much charm in waiting around hotels and nightclubs, watching over an alcoholic father and getting him safely home after his gigs."

The soft derision in his voice piqued her into glancing at him. He caught her gaze and his dark eyes were hard and penetrating as he added, "Was he really worth all you gave him of your life, Nicole?"

"You don't understand..."

"No, I don't. He should have been looking after you. What kind of man puts a set of drums and a bottle of whisky ahead of the welfare of a child? You were nine when your mother died. Nine..."

"He was my father," she answered fiercely.

"Yes, and being a father should mean something," he retorted just as fiercely. "Do you imagine that Alex or Tony would ever neglect their responsibility to their children? That they'd let themselves wallow in depression or find oblivion in a bottle, robbing their children of the sense of security they should have?"

"They occupy a different world," she cried defensively.

"They're men."

"All men aren't the same."

"True. But you're a woman now, not a child, and you should see things how they really were. From the story you've written it's obvious your father could charm birds out of trees when he wasn't completely in his cups. But charm doesn't make up for the rest."

"You're making judgments again about things you don't know," she seethed at him.

His eyes glittered a black challenge back at her. "Well, I do know Peter Owen has been married and divorced twice, and I'm sure his ex-wives were thoroughly charmed by him to begin with. You might keep that in mind at the party.''

She sought to explain the difficulties in living with people who were passionately absorbed in creating a unique form of magic. ''It's hard...living with musicians. If you don't understand how important it is to them...''

''So important that your needs always have to take a back seat to their kind of self-expression?'' He cocked a mocking eyebrow at her. ''You've had a long taste of that, Nicole. Was it so sweet?''

It finally dawned on her that he might be jealous of her interest in Peter. Possibly because she'd made such a firm stand about going to the party where she would inevitably meet her old friend again. Now that he knew of their personal connection, was he imagining she wanted to revive it?

She shook her head, dazed at the convoluted way he had used her life with her father to undermine any chance of her being charmed by Peter. The arm holding hers suddenly felt very possessive, as though it wasn't about to let her stray from his side.

They'd reached the foyer and were trailing the rest of the family group out to the street where the limousines were waiting. In a few minutes they'd be on their way back to the hotel where the party was to be held in a private function room. But Matt King wasn't quite finished pressing his point of view.

"You're free now," he went on in a low intense voice. "Free to pursue what *you* want. *Have* what you want. I gave you a choice up in your room, and you chose me. What do you think that says, Nicole? About your needs?"

She didn't know.

She'd been trying to work out what was happening between them and why. It was confusing, disturbing, and she wasn't acting like her normal self at all. There was no time for a reply, which was just as well, because her mind couldn't fasten on one. She followed

Tony and Hannah into their limousine and put on a congenial mask for the ride back to the hotel.

Behind it she silently acknowledged Matt King was right about one thing. She was free to pursue whatever she wanted. No personal attachments. Her only responsibilities applied to whatever work she took on, and she no longer accepted a job that didn't appeal to her.

Free…

Was it a deliberate choice not to tie herself to anyone in all these years since her father's death? At first, she'd felt emptied of anything to give to a relationship. Easier to keep associations superficial. Nothing could be demanded of her. The need to become a whole person, by herself, for herself, had probably been more instinctive than thought out, but Nicole now recognised it was what she'd been doing throughout her years at university.

After that, well maybe she'd got into the habit of being alone. But she had felt lonely and there'd been a few men she'd dated for a while. Until the balance of what they'd enjoyed together got heavier and heavier on their side and she simply didn't want to be the one doing the majority of the giving and the understanding to keep the involvement going.

It was like a line drawn in her mind. This much I'll do. No more. But Matt King blurred all the lines, smashing every perception she'd ever had about men. The Kings, she decided, were a different breed. Their family history was telling her so with everything she learnt about them. Strong compelling men. Family men. Men who held what they had, looked after it and built on it.

Was that what she needed?

Was this why Matt King drew such an instinctive response from her, bypassing any rational thought?

She looked down at the hand he'd held.

Did he mean to keep holding it…if she let him?

Or was she a passing fancy?

CHAPTER THIRTEEN

''NICKY!''

Matt gritted his teeth as Peter Owen headed towards them, arms outstretched.

''You look wonderful!''

His bedroom-blue eyes might just get socked out if they kept gobbling her up.

''Who'd have thought that skinny little red-haired kid would bloom into such a beauty?'' he raved on, grabbing her upper arms and planting a kiss on both cheeks.

She laughed and bantered, ''Who'd have thought Peter Pan would become such a maestro of the theatre?''

Peter Pan was right, Matt thought darkly. The man was forty and still sparkled with the exuberance of a boy who'd never grow up.

''What a premiere! Are you proud of me?'' he preened.

Again she laughed. ''Immensely. You're Superman tonight.''

''That's exactly how I feel. I could leap off tall buildings...''

Pity he didn't do it!

''Well, don't go faster than a speeding bullet,'' she teasingly advised. ''Enjoy the moment.''

''Ah...you always were a sweetheart, Nicky dear. Good to see you! Got to go and mix now but I'll claim a dance from you later.''

Over my dead body!

He shot a grin at Matt. ''Look after her. She's very special.''

I don't need you to tell me that.

Matt forced a smile. ''Great night, Peter! Well done!''

He paused, lifting a hand in salute to the real star. ''Gina sang like the angel she is,'' he said with sincere fervour before moving on to spread himself around.

It made Matt feel mean about his more violent thoughts. He knew there was real affection between Gina and Peter. Even Alex had grown to like the man. Peter was godfather to their baby daughter. But he did have a reputation for being a world-class womaniser.

Matt turned to the woman beside him, taking some encouragement from the fact that she hadn't tried to drift away in the crowd of people at the party. On the other hand, she probably didn't know anyone here, apart from Peter and the King family. Mostly she'd been silent, filling the time by sampling the gourmet finger food being carried around and offered by numerous waiters.

Had his words as they'd left the theatre got through to her?

Her gaze was following Peter's progress through the crowd. Did she want him back in her life? He'd made her laugh. Matt hadn't heard her laugh before. Usually he did share lots of laughter with the women he spent time with. Why was everything so intense with this one?

He was getting obsessed with her, thinking of little else. Having sex with her hadn't given him any relief from it, either. If anything, it had locked him into a deeper pursuit of the woman she was. He wanted to know how her mind worked, what she felt, how she saw things.

"Do you like being called Nicky?"

She shrugged, not looking directly at him as she flatly answered, "It's a name from a different life."

"One you've moved on from," he pressed, wanting it to be so.

"Yes and no." Her gaze slowly lifted to his, the rich brown of her eyes somehow reflecting a depth of feeling that put him instantly on alert. "Do we ever really leave our past behind? Aren't we the sum of all our years?" A wistful smile flitted across her very kissable lips. "Perhaps even more. Look at you..."

"What about me?"

"You have a heritage to live up to, as well. Don't you feel that?"

"No. I am who I am."

"One of the Kings. Like Alex and Tony whom you invoked earlier as examples of what a father should be. And I'm sure you consider yourself in the same mould. The King mould."

He frowned over this assertion. Pride in his own individuality wanted to deny he was like his brothers, yet they did all have the same background, the same upbringing. There were common factors. And they lived by the same principles, principles that had been hammered into them by their grandmother. Their heritage…

A waiter came by with a tray of drinks, diverting Nicole's attention to it. She picked up a glass of champagne and sipped as though she needed the kick of alcohol. Matt swiped a glass, too, before the waiter moved on. He thought about Nicole's heritage as he sipped.

Her mother had been Irish. She'd met and fallen in love with Ollie Redman when he'd been touring Dublin, married him and came to Australia. There'd been no maternal family in Sydney for Nicole to fall back on when her mother had died. No paternal family, either. Ollie Redman had spent most of his young life in an orphanage. He probably hadn't known what a father should be, having had no role model himself.

People were the sum of their lives…

So what did that make Nicole?

"Why did you take on this project?" he asked, a sixth sense telling him the answer would be enlightening.

She slanted him a half-mocking look. "To find out what a different life was like."

The life of a long-rooted family. That he was part of. Shock stiffened his whole body. Was this why she'd had sex with him? An intimate experience with one of the Kings? The only one who wasn't married?

His mind went into a ferment. She might have been thinking about it ever since they'd met in his office. Certainly when she'd come up to the park, she'd been considering it, wanting it. She'd been eyeing him off as he'd shown her the photographs in his home. If he hadn't put her professionalism on the line, stung her pride...

But they were past that now and tonight she'd taken what he'd offered without so much as a hesitation. Taken it and revelled in it every bit as much as he had. So she would want more. One taste wasn't enough. It certainly wasn't enough for him. They'd barely begun to explore...*what it was like.*

Her head was slightly bowed as though she was contemplating the contents of her glass. His gaze drifted down the gleaming flame-red fall of her hair, the fine silk of it caressing the bare white skin of her back above the dip of her gown, a dip that revealed the sensual curve of her spine. Below it, her delectable bottom jutted out, begging to be touched. Matt felt himself getting aroused, thighs tightening, sex stirring. He wanted this woman again. Again and again and again.

She was rubbing her index finger idly around the rim of her glass. The urge to snatch it away, force her to look at him and admit what she wanted was strong. Then they could get out of this party, go to his room or hers, and…

''What you said about charm…'' She lifted her head and there was sadness in her eyes, making a savage mockery of the desire running rampant through him. ''Neither my father nor Peter had family behind them. The charm is a defence against that emptiness, and a reaching out to be liked. A need for everyone to like them, even if it is only on a superficial level.''

She paused, her eyes begging some understanding from him. ''You don't have that need, Matt. You're very secure in the life you were born into. It makes a difference.''

He felt chastened. He *was* more fortunate than others with his family. No denying it. Yet he couldn't imagine himself not making his own way to a life he could be proud of, in every sense. Having to be propped up by others, dependent on what they did for him…no, that was not a situation he'd ever want or accept.

"Maybe it does," he grudgingly conceded. "But in the end, everybody is responsible for what they make of their own lives. There are choices."

And she'd chosen to have sex with him!

She must have read his thought. A tide of heat rushed into her cheeks. He wondered if she cursed her white skin for being such a telltale barometer of her feelings. It gave him a kick, just watching it, though he'd prefer to touch. His hands itched to touch.

"I think choices are shaped by what's gone before," she argued. "People fall into them because…" She stopped, floundering in the face of what she saw in his eyes.

Matt wasn't hiding what he was thinking, what he was wanting. "Because a need pushed them that way?" he finished for her.

"Yes," she whispered.

"And when there's a mutual need, it's even easier to go with it," he pushed, all his energy pumping into drawing her with him. "And why not? Why not see where it leads?"

She stood absolutely still, her gaze fastened on his, her lips slightly parted as though she needed to suck in air, but if she did it was imperceptible. Matt suspected her lungs weren't working at all, seized up with tension, as his were, waiting for the line to be crossed. The fire in her cheeks did not abate. She didn't speak but Matt knew in his bones she wanted what he wanted. An exhilarating recklessness zinged through him.

A waiter approached, offering another tray of fancy canapes. Matt plucked the glass from Nicole's hold, her fingers sliding from it, not clutching. He put both his and her glass on the tray, uncaring that it was carrying food. The action jerked her gaze towards the tray. Matt wasn't about to give her time to regroup. The wave was going his way and ride it he would.

He grabbed her hand, winding his own firmly around it. ''Come with me,'' he commanded and set off, making a path through the partying crowd, pulling her with him.

She didn't try to pull back.

Her acquiescence put a surge of power into his sense of rightness. Nothing was going to stop him. They had to pass by his grandmother and Rosita. He didn't care if they saw or what they thought of him and Nicole leaving together. Let them wonder. It didn't matter.

A phrase from the old *Star Wars* movie clicked into his mind—*The force be with you!* It was with him all right, pounding through his bloodstream, invigorating every muscle in his body, making his skin tingle with electric vitality.

They were finally free of the function room, out in the corridor, heading for the elevators.

There was a tug on his hand, a breathless cry, "Where are you taking me?"

"Where we can be alone together." He paused long enough to release her hand and put his arm around her waist, wanting her clasped close to him, inseparable. He scooped her with him the last few steps to the bank of elevators and pressed the button to give them access to one of them.

"This isn't right," she gasped, still out of breath.

"Oh, yes it is!"

"I think..."

"That's the problem." His eyes blazed his inner certainty at her. "You've been thinking too much since we were interrupted."

Doors slid open.

He swept her into the empty compartment and pressed the button for the floor where his room was situated.

"This is not a grey issue," he stated as the doors slid shut. "It's black and white..." He turned her fully into his embrace, sliding one hand into her glorious hair to hold her head tilted up to his. "…and red," he added with deep satisfaction, loving the feel of her hair and craving the taste of her red mouth.

He kissed her. Her lips felt soft under his, infinitely seductive. Her mouth was far more intoxicating than champagne. It fizzed with passion, exciting all the primitive instincts she stirred in him.

When the elevator doors opened, it triggered the urge to pick her up, keep hold of her. He bent, hooking his arm around her thighs, and sweeping her up against his chest where his heart was beating like a wild tom-tom, drumming him forward.

He was out of the elevator and striding towards his room, his whole being focused on one outcome, when unbelievably, her hand slammed against his shoulder and she began struggling.

"Let me go! Put me down!" Fierce cries, ringing in his ears.

He stopped, looked his puzzlement at her, realised she was in earnest, wanting to be released, so he set her on her feet, still not understanding what the fuss was about.

She wrenched herself out of his hold, whirling to put distance between, then backing towards the elevator, her hands up in a warding-off action, her face blazing with passionate protest.

"I won't let you do this again!"

"Do what?" He was completely perplexed by her reaction. She'd responded to his kiss…

Her breasts heaved as she drew breath to hurl more words at him. "Just taking me when you feel like it."

"Now hold on a minute. You…" He stepped towards her.

"Stop right there!" Her voice cracked out like a whip. "Don't you dare grab me again!"

He stopped, clenching his hands in frustration at this unreasonable outburst. "You came with me, Nicole," he grated out.

"Yes," she snapped. "But I've come to my senses now and I will not come with you any further, Matt King."

"Why not?"

"Because I don't like myself for...for letting your sex appeal...override everything else. I won't let what happened earlier tonight happen again."

"It was good. It was great," he argued vehemently.

"That's all you want from me, isn't it? More sexual satisfaction."

"You get it from me, too," he countered hotly knowing full well she'd not gone short on pleasure with him.

Heat scorched her cheeks. "So we're supposed to service each other, are we?"

He could feel his chin jutting out at this crude description, but pride wouldn't let him back down. "Seems like a good idea to me."

She shook her head. "That's not who I am."

"What do you mean?"

''I mean...'' Her eyes flashed with scornful pride. ''...find someone else to take to your bed. I don't want that kind of relationship.''

She turned and jabbed the button to summon an elevator. Matt had the sinking feeling he'd just dug his own grave with her. But how could that be? The wanting *was* mutual. What was wrong with being honest? She'd kissed him back in the elevator. Her body had clung yearningly to his.

''What *do* you want?'' he shot at her.

She shook her head. ''I'm going back to the party.''

Her gaze was fixed on the arrow indicating an elevator rising to this floor.

''Nicole!''

She wouldn't look at him.

''The least you can do is answer me.''

''Just...leave me alone...please.''

Her voice wobbled. It struck Matt that she was in acute distress, possibly crying. What had he done? Before he could begin to figure out how to fix the situation, an elevator opened and she moved in a frantic flurry, rushing into it and jabbing at the control panel inside the compartment, her head dipped, her hair swishing forward, curtaining her white face. No colour in her cheeks now.

The doors started to slide shut. Matt moved instinctively to block their closure, the urge to fight any closure with Nicole Redman screaming through him.

"Don't! Please, don't! Let me go!" she cried despairingly, flapping her hands at him in wild agitation as she backed up against the rear wall of the small compartment, her eyes swimming with tears, lashes blinking frantically but unable to stop the moist stream from trickling down her cheeks.

"Just tell me what you do want. Whatever it is you think I won't give you," he demanded hoarsely, churned up by her turbulent emotion. "I need an answer."

"*You* need..." Her throat choked up.

She bent her head and wrapped her arms around herself in a protective hug. He could see her swallowing convulsively and wanted to offer comfort, wanted to hold her and soothe her distress away, but her rejection of him made it impossible.

Her head slowly lifted, lifted high, her chin raised in a proud lonely stand, her eyes bleakly haunted by needs that were part of her world, not his.

"I want to be loved," she said in a raw husky voice. "I want someone to care about me. Look after me. My life is empty of that. Empty…"

It was an instantly recognisable truth. No family, no attachments. And from what he'd read in her book, she'd done all the loving and caring and looking after her father. Not much coming back her way.

Her mouth twisted into a mocking grimace as she added, "And sex doesn't fill that space. It never will."

It shamed him, made him realise how blinded he'd been by his own desire for her, blinded every which way from his initial prejudice against her job with his grandmother to her physical response to the sexual attraction between them.

"Please...will you let me go now?"

What could he do?

He stepped back and let her go, watching the doors slide shut, knowing there was nothing he could say that would change her mind about him. No power in the world would force her to see him differently, not at this point. Besides, it was plain she wanted what he was not prepared to give.

Love...marriage...family.

It was not on his agenda.

But he hated leaving her...so empty.

It made him feel empty himself.

CHAPTER FOURTEEN

ISABELLA VALERI KING sighed in contentment and smiled at her long-trusted confidante. ‘‘What a splendid night, Rosita!’’

They were comfortably seated in armchairs in a corner at the back of the function room. The band’s music was not so loud here and it was possible to converse without shouting. On the table in front of them was a selection of sweets—little fruit tarts, cheesecake, apple slices, florentines—which Rosita was sampling one by one, checking out the quality of the catering.

‘‘Everything is good,’’ came the ready agreement. Rosita’s dark eyes twinkled. ‘‘But I’m thinking you’re especially pleased by the absence of people rather than the presence of people.’’

Isabella allowed herself a smug little smile. "Matteo is definitely taking the initiative. He made himself Nicole's escort tonight, and from my observation before they left this room, they are very caught up with each other."

"The history may suffer," Rosita archly remarked. "When Matteo decides on something he does not let the grass grow under his feet. Nicole will be distracted."

"I would rather have a another good milestone in our family to write about, Rosita. The words can be written when all is resolved."

"You are so sure they will be right together?"

"Did you not see the way they looked at each other when Nicole was coming down the stairs to the lobby?"

"I saw that she looked very striking, very beautiful. Any man would admire her."

"No. It was more than that. I am certain of it."

''Then let us hope it is so. She is too much alone, that one. And immersing herself in other people's lives…'' A sad shake of the head. ''She should have a life of her own. A husband. Babies.''

Isabella couldn't agree more. And Nicole was perfect for Matteo, very strong in her own right, but with much love to give and a sense of loyalty that ran very deep, a woman who would always stand by her man through any hardship.

Her gaze skimmed around the crowd, picking out her other two grandsons and their wives—two couples glowing with happiness. A sense of triumph warmed her heart. If Matteo married Nicole…

There she was!

Isabella sat very upright in her armchair, her back stiffening at a most unwelcome sight.

Nicole was alone.

Where was Matteo?

Most of the people who were not seated as she and Rosita were, had drifted towards the dance floor, either standing in groups around it or gyrating on it in their modern way. Nicole had obviously just re-entered the function room and was in open view as her gaze anxiously searched the more crowded area.

Looking for Matteo?

He was not here.

She looked stressed. Her hands were fretting at the small evening bag she held in front of her at waist level. This was not right to Isabella's mind. What had happened to put Nicole in such a state? Where was Matteo?

"Rosita..." Isabella grasped her arm to draw her attention to Nicole. "...things are not going as they should. Quickly now. Pretend you are going to the powder room. As you pass by Nicole, direct her to me."

"It is not good to meddle," she protested.

"Go! Go!" Isabella commanded, out of patience with holding back and not knowing what was wrong.

Rosita heaved herself up and made her rather ponderous way across the room.

Isabella composed herself, hiding her chagrin and making sure an inviting smile was hovering on her lips. Nicole gave Rosita a nervous acknowledgment, too uptight to manage the usual warmth between them. Rosita played her part well, a wave of her arm forcing Nicole to look at Isabella who instantly applied the smile, forcing her wish to talk. As her employee, Nicole would feel bound to oblige, whatever her private inclinations were.

Isabella felt no guilt whatsoever about flexing her power as she watched the young woman tread a slow and reluctant path to pay her respect. It was important to know what was going on now. The tension she had noted between Matteo and Nicole at the theatre should have eased. They had seemed very much together once they'd arrived at the party, clearly attuned to each other.

How long had they been out of the function room? Twenty minutes? Half an hour? Some conflict must have erupted between them. Who was at fault? Could it be fixed? Time for a more propitious encounter was running out tonight and if barriers were set in place again…oh, this was so frustrating!

"Mrs. King…" Nicole greeted her in a flat voice.

Isabella patted the armrest of the vacated chair. "Come sit with me while Rosita's gone," she invited, thinking that time limit shouldn't strain Nicole's nerves too much and any other choice of action would seem impolite.

She moved around the table and sat down without any attempt at small talk. The passive obedience worried Isabella all the more. "I thought Matteo was looking after you tonight," she probed, keeping her tone lightly interested.

Nicole visibly bridled. "He was with me earlier," she said in a corrective tone, glancing around the room again to evade looking directly at Isabella. "I don't know where he is now."

"Didn't I see you leave the party together?"

"We...parted. I went to the powder room."

"How very ungallant of him not to have waited for you! I must speak to that boy."

Red splotches on her cheeks. "It's not his job to look after me, Mrs. King, and I certainly don't want him to feel obliged to do so." A low ferocity underlined those words.

Pride, Isabella thought. She frowned for Nicole's benefit. "You don't like my youngest grandson? Matteo has done something to offend you?"

Instant agitation. "Please don't think that. It was...kind of him to escort me to and from the theatre. Perhaps he wanted an early night. I am perfectly happy by myself, Mrs. King."

Perfectly miserable!

"He should not have deserted you," she pressed.

"He didn't. Really..." Pleading eyes begging her to desist. "...your grandson is free to do whatever he wishes. Just as I am."

Free...

Freedom was highly overrated in Isabella's opinion. There was Matteo going off doing ridiculously dangerous things like whitewater rafting and bungy-jumping because he didn't have the responsibility of a wife and family. As for Nicole, what was she free for? Books and more books?

She wished she could knock their heads together, get some sense into them. It was clear they had come to the parting of the ways, and Isabella was so annoyed by it, she threw discretion to the winds and bored straight into the heart of the matter.

"I do not like this. I have been aware for some time there is friction between you and Matteo. You were unhappy after your visit to Kauri Pine Park and you have made a point of evading his company since."

This observation startled Nicole but she bit her lips, offering no comment.

"This cannot be pleasant for you, given your situation in our family circle," Isabella went on. "I was hoping it would sort itself out tonight. If it hasn't, Nicole, I feel bound to step in and..."

"No! There is nothing..." Her eyes flashed a wild vehemence. "...nothing between us." Realising that statement didn't answer the questions raised, she hastily added, "There were...differences...which we've cleared. Truly...there is no need for you to say anything, Mrs. King. I'm sorry that you've been worried."

"So everything is fine now?"

Nicole hesitated, hunting for words that would paper over the problem. "We both know where we stand. That makes it easier."

"There was a misunderstanding?"

"Yes. But no more. So it's all right. Truly."

She jerked her focus away from Isabella, fastening her gaze on the crowd around the dance floor. The agitated dismissal of all concern made it too unkind to continue probing. Indeed, Isabella was allowed no time for it.

"There's Peter!" Nicole cried, leaping to her feet. She shot a pleading glance at Isabella. "Please excuse me, Mrs. King. He said he'd dance with me and I'd like to spend some time with him."

"Of course." She managed a benevolent smile. "Go and enjoy yourself."

"Thank you." Intense relief.

Isabella shook her head as she watched Nicole make her way to Peter Owen's side. Matteo was a fool to let this woman go. There was Peter welcoming her company, only too happy to draw her onto the dance floor and give her whatever pleasure she sought with him.

Disheartened by the talk which had revealed, at best, that Nicole and Matteo had established a neutral zone; at worst, they were poles apart in what they wanted from each other. But *the wanting* was very real. Nicole would not be so distressed if it wasn't. As for Matteo...where was he? Why was he turning his back on *the wanting* that had pulled Nicole out of this room with him?

Totally exasperated with the situation and wanting to discuss her thoughts on it, Isabella looked to see if Rosita was on her way back from the powder room. Her heart skipped a beat as her gaze found Matteo standing just inside the entrance to the function room, his face tight as though it had just been soundly smacked, his eyes projecting a glowering intensity as they watched the occupants of the dance floor, notably Peter and Nicole, no doubt.

His hands clenched.

But he didn't move to get closer or cut in on Peter.

In two minds about what his next action should be? Isabella wondered.

Rosita appeared behind him. Isabella instantly signalled for her to grab Matteo and bring him over to her. Rosita heaved a reproachful sigh but went ahead and touched his arm to draw his attention. Matteo turned a frown on her, then cleared his face as he saw who it was. They conversed for a few moments. Rosita gestured towards their table and Isabella gave her grandson a bright look of expectation, which sealed his reluctant acquiescence as deftly as she had sealed Nicole's.

He hooked Rosita's arm around his and escorted her back to her chair, acting the gentleman Isabella had trained him to be. "Nonna..." He nodded to her. "...I take it you're still enjoying yourself? Not ready to retire yet?"

"Such wonderful nights do not come very often, Matteo. At my age, who knows how many more I will have?" Which was a fine piece of emotional blackmail. She smiled an appeal. "Do draw up another chair and share a few minutes with me."

A slight wince as he bowed to her pressure, taking a chair from another table and placing it next to hers. He dropped into it with an air of resignation. He aimed a dry smile at Rosita.

''Fine selection of sweets you've got on the table in front of you.''

''Help yourself, Matteo,'' she invited effusively. ''The cheesecake is very good.''

''No, thanks. Not hungry. I'm glad you're enjoying them.''

''And you, Matteo?'' Isabella broke in. ''Have you been enjoying yourself?''

He shrugged. ''The show was great. Certainly a night to celebrate.''

''Perhaps you would like to dance now. Am I keeping you from it?''

''It can wait,'' he answered in a careless tone.

Isabella put the needle in. ''I see Nicole dancing with Peter. It must be nice for her to renew their old acquaintance.''

''No doubt. A shared background is always congenial.''

Was that the problem? He'd read *Ollie's Drum.* Did he think Nicole's background precluded her from making a life up here? Didn't he know that if a love was strong enough, place didn't matter? Her own mother had sailed halfway around the world to be with her father in a very foreign land. She herself would have gone to the Kimberly Outback if her husband had survived the war. Was Matteo nursing some woolly-headed prejudice?

"I do not think those memories are ones Nicole cherishes," she said. "They were hard years for her. She has said many times how much she likes the life around Port Douglas. I think she may stay after she finishes the project."

"Doing what?" came the mocking question. "She's bound to head back to Sydney once her contract is over. There's nothing for her up here."

"What is in Sydney for her?" Isabella countered. "She has no family to draw her back. No permanent home. Nicole plans to take time off and try her hand at writing fiction. One can write anywhere, Matteo."

He frowned and muttered, ''The heat will get to her. Six months in the tropics will be long enough for the novelty to wear off.''

''Many people love the tropical climate. Look at Hannah. She was from Sydney.''

''Hannah doesn't have red hair and white skin,'' he retorted tersely.

Isabella looked at him in astonishment. ''What has that got to do with anything?''

He grimaced and made a sharp, dismissive gesture. ''Nicole will get burnt. Or suffer sunstroke. She's obviously not suited to...''

''You've met the King family from the Kimberly,'' Isabella cut in, exasperated by this superficial judgment. ''Tommy King's wife, Samantha, has carrot-red hair and very fair skin. She was born and bred in the Outback, with heat and sun that's even more blistering than what we get in Port Douglas.''

''That's always been her life,'' he argued.

''And you think Nicole Redman can't manage it?'' Isabella tossed back, barely able to keep the scorn from her voice. ''Didn't you say you'd read her book about her father, Matteo?''

''Yes, I did,'' he snapped, not wanting to be reminded of it.

''Then didn't it occur to you that Nicole is a survivor?'' Isabella bored in, relentless in her mission to pull the wool from her blind grandson's eyes. ''Given some of the worst circumstances a child could face, that girl came through everything with a strength I can only admire. With a grit and determination that would have served some of the leaders in this country well. With amazing and fearless enterprise, she coped with enormous difficulties and...''

''In my opinion, she wasted her young life on a man who didn't deserve what she did for him,'' Matteo flashed at her, a black resentment in his eyes.

''He was her father,'' Isabella retorted, outraged by this view. ''Would you not have rescued your own father if you could have done so?''

"Yes, I would have braved the cyclone that killed him if I'd been anywhere near him, but..."

"A child does not think of the cost to themselves. We are talking blood family here. Sticking to family. It is a quality all too lacking in modern day society. It is a quality I value very highly. I am disappointed that you do not, Matteo."

"Nonna..." Sheer fury looked at her. He jerked his head away, took a deep breath, expelled it slowly, then rose to his feet and looked down at her with hooded eyes. "I really don't wish to discuss Nicole Redman any further," he stated flatly. "I have an early flight in the morning so please excuse me. Goodnight, Nonna... Rosita..."

He strode off with stiff-necked pride, not glancing at the dance floor, intent on denying any interest whatsoever in Nicole Redman. But Isabella was not in any doubt that he had been trying to justify a view which he was using as an excuse not to commit himself to a serious relationship with Nicole. Why he wanted an excuse was beyond her.

Did *freedom* mean so much to him?

"He is very angry," Rosita murmured.

Isabella sighed. "I lost my temper." She turned to her old friend. "But have you ever heard such nonsense, Rosita?"

She made one of her very expressive Italian gestures. "I think he is hurting badly but he doesn't like to say so. Matteo has always been like that. He jokes to make little of things that hurt."

"He wasn't joking tonight."

"Which means it is a very bad hurt."

"They are both hurting." Isabella shook her head worriedly. "The question is...can they get past it? I may have smashed the barriers in Matteo's mind tonight, but is he prepared to smash the barriers he put in Nicole's?" Her eyes flared her deep frustration. "That is beyond my power. Only Matteo can do it, Rosita. Only he...if he wants to enough."

CHAPTER FIFTEEN

PREGNANT!

Oh, God! Oh, God! Oh, God!

What was she to do?

With shaking hands, Nicole piled all the evidence of the pregnancy test into a plastic bag to dispose of somewhere away from the castle when she felt up to a walk. She couldn't leave it lying around for Rosita to find. The motherly Italian housekeeper was very thorough in her cleaning.

Still in shock, Nicole tottered from her en-suite bathroom, stowed the incriminating packaging in her straw carry-bag, then crawled onto her bed and buried her face in a pillow. It was Sunday morning. She was not expected to work on Sundays. It didn't matter if she was late down for breakfast. In fact, Sunday was a good excuse to miss it altogether. Even the thought of food sickened her, especially first thing in the morning.

Now she knew why.

The punishment for her madness with Matt King.

She couldn't even blame him, knowing she'd been equally responsible. Though *irresponsible* was the correct word. Wild stupid recklessness, not even thinking of the possibility of getting pregnant. Only when she'd gone to bed—alone—after the premiere party had she wondered and worried, and decided there was a good chance she was safe. It simply wouldn't be fair to end up paying even more than the intense emotional letdown from that one experience.

A baby.

No more hiding her head in the sand, finding excuses for her period to be late—the heat, stress, anything but the truth. The truth had just stared her in the face. She was undeniably pregnant. And somehow she now had to plan a future with a baby…a child…a child of her own.

She vividly recalled Matt King spouting off about the responsibilities of fatherhood, but did she want him to be connected to her and their child for the rest of their lives? A man who'd only wanted sex with her? A man who raised turbulent feelings every time she saw him?

Only a few days ago he had dropped in at the castle, stopping to join his grandmother for afternoon tea. He'd breezed out to the loggia where Nicole had been sitting with her employer, cheerfully announcing, "I just left a box of exotic fruit with Rosita in the kitchen." Then with a dazzling grin aimed at her, he'd added, "I brought some mangosteen especially for you, Nicole. It was your favourite, wasn't it?"

"Yes. Thank you," she'd managed to get out as she'd tried to quell the flush erupting from his reminder of their fruit-tasting.

Luckily he'd chatted to his grandmother for a while, giving her time to adjust to his presence. Not that it helped much. Her mind kept fretting over why he'd come and the mention of the fruit seemed like an indication that he still wanted sex with her. Was he scouting his chances?

She'd kept her eyes downcast. It was disturbing enough, hearing his voice, feeling his energy swirling around her. When he'd asked about her progress on the family history, forcing her to look at him, she'd had to concentrate very hard on giving appropriate replies. He'd been quite charming about it, not critical at all, no dubious comments, yet his half-hour visit had left her completely drained.

Even if he remained simply polite to her, she didn't want to be near him. It was too much of a strain, fighting his sexual attraction. And she certainly didn't want him to feel honour-bound to offer marriage because of becoming an accidental father. That would be totally humiliating, knowing he hadn't considered her in the light of a possible wife for him.

No love.

At least, by having a baby, her life wouldn't be empty of love anymore. That was one positive to comfort her. Though how she would manage as a single mother…she would have to start thinking about it, planning.

Four hours later, Nicole was feeling considerably better. She'd walked down to the marina, got rid of the pregnancy test in a large waste bin, idled away some time watching activity on the boats, wandered around the market stalls set up in Anzac Park, lingering at those offering baby clothes and toys, finally buying a gift for Hannah's baby, telling herself it was far too soon to start acquiring anything for her own. Better to wait until she was settled somewhere.

Not here in Port Douglas.

She couldn't live anywhere near Matt King.

The rest of his family she liked very much. Alex and Gina had taken an apartment in

Brisbane for the duration of the show, with Alex commuting to Port Douglas as business demanded. Mrs. King missed having them close, especially the children, but today Tony and Hannah had come to lunch at the castle and their company always cheered her.

Usually Nicole enjoyed being with them, too. They were happy people. But today, as they sat around a table near the fountain in the loggia, their happiness made her feel sad. This is how it should be, she kept thinking, a man and a woman loving each other, getting married, having a baby because they both wanted it. Hannah seemed to glow with good health. Nicole wondered if she had suffered morning sickness earlier on in her pregnancy, but she couldn't ask.

"Matt!"

Tony's cry of surprise sent a shock through her heart. Her head dizzied as her gaze jerked to the man coming out of the castle, brandishing cutlery and serviette.

"Knew you'd be here, Tony, so I thought I'd join you," he announced. "Rosita said you were lunching outside so I've come armed for the feast."

"There's such a nice breeze," Hannah explained. "We didn't want to be inside."

"Good thinking," Matt approved. "I'll just move you up a place, Hannah, so I can sit next to Nonna." He smiled at his grandmother. "I trust I'm welcome?"

She returned his smile. "Always, Matteo."

"Nicole..." He nodded to her as he rearranged the seating. "...how are you?"

"Fine, thank you," she managed to reply, though her stomach was now in knots.

He was seating himself almost directly opposite her, which meant she'd be facing him all through lunch, the man who'd fathered a child with her and didn't know it.

Fortunately, Tony claimed his brother's attention, chatting on about the tourist business which was of vital interest to both of them. They were coming out of the wet season, which meant the influx of visitors to Port Douglas was rapidly increasing, people wanting a vacation in the sun and trips to the Great Barrier Reef and other wonders of the tropical far north.

Rosita wheeled out a traymobile loaded with a variety of salads and a huge coral trout that she'd baked with a herb and pinenut crust. She placed the platter containing the fish in front of Tony to carve into servings and the smell of the herbs wafted down the table, instantly making Nicole feel nauseous. Trying to counter the effect, she sipped her iced juice, desperately breathing in the scent of its tropical fruit.

"Only a very small portion for me please, Tony," she requested when he was about to serve her.

"Don't stint yourself because I'm an unexpected guest," Matt quickly threw in, his gaze targeting her with persuasive intent. "There's more than enough to go around."

‘‘I’m not really hungry,’’ she excused, savagely wishing he wouldn’t look directly at her. He was so wickedly handsome, it screwed up her heart, making it hop, skip and jump in a highly erratic fashion.

‘‘But you missed breakfast this morning,’’ Mrs. King remarked, surprised by Nicole’s lack of appetite.

She sought wildly for a reasonable explanation. ‘‘While I was wandering around the market stalls…’’

‘‘You succumbed to the famous prawn sandwich?’’ Matt supplied, his brilliant dark eyes twinkling teasingly.

She nodded, robbed of speech. He was putting out magnetic sex appeal again, reducing her to a quivering mess inside. Thankfully Hannah rescued her.

‘‘And look what she bought the baby at the markets, Matt!’’ She leaned down beside her chair, took the cleverly crafted caterpillar from the plastic bag and demonstrated how the multi-coloured segments could be stretched out and when released, they'd bunch together again. ''Isn't it gorgeous?''

Hannah was beaming pleasure at her brother-in-law and he beamed pleasure right back at her. ''Fantastic! I can see little hands having a fun time with that.''

Tears pricked Nicole's eyes at the thought of her own baby's little hands, reaching out for a father who wasn't there, a father who'd never watch him or her having fun.

''Well bought, Nicole,'' Matt declared with warm approval, turning her to absolute mush.

Why was he doing this?

Why was he here?

Hadn't she made it clear that she would not have an affair with him? She wanted what Tony and Hannah had, not just a physical thing that went nowhere but bed.

Distractedly she helped herself to salads, hoping to smother the herb smell on the plate Tony had passed to her. The result was a heap of food she couldn't possibly eat, which made her feel even worse. She picked up her knife and fork, telling herself she had to get through this, had to act normally and not draw any attention to her state of helpless torment.

"Did you try one of the exotic fruit ices while you were down in Anzac Park?" Matt asked her, forcing further conversation with him.

Nicole gave him a fleeting glance as she answered, "No, I didn't."

"Then you missed out on a treat," he cheerfully persisted. "They're very flavoursome and refreshing. The people who run the stall buy their fruit from me. They do well with it."

Wishing she could ignore him but knowing it would be perceived as impolite by Mrs. King, Nicole forced her gaze up from her plate and managed a quick smile. "I'm sure they do. I did notice they had quite long queues at that stall, people waiting to be served."

Her eyes didn't quite meet his but only he would notice, and hopefully he would get the message that she wasn't interested and would prefer to be left alone. She picked doggedly at the salads she'd chosen, determined on closing him out as much as she could. He chatted to his grandmother, apparently not having noticed anything untoward in Nicole's behaviour. It was as though he wasn't aware of any tension, or was consciously ignoring it, hoping it would go away.

It didn't go away for Nicole. She had the strong sense of Matt King biding his time, waiting to pounce when the opportunity presented itself, planning how to manoeuvre her away from the others. He'd given no notice of his coming and his arrival had coincided with the serving of lunch, which meant she couldn't easily absent herself. She was sure this was planned, not an impulse. Behind it all was a relentless will beating at her, not letting go.

It made her head ache. Her stomach started to revolt against the food she was doing her best to eat. She sipped her juice, desperate to control the waves of nausea. It was no use. The added stress of Matt King's presence was just too much to bear on top of everything else. The casual cheerfulness of his voice, the confident way he was dealing with his meal, the sheer power of the man…it all made her feel weak and miserable.

She set down her cutlery, placed her serviette by her plate and pushed up from her chair. "Please excuse me." She swept an apologetic look around the table, then directly addressed her employer. "I must have walked too long in the heat this morning." She rubbed her forehead which was definitely clammy. "I'm just not well."

Mrs. King frowned in concern. "Go and lie down, my dear. I'll check on you later."

"Thank you."

"If it's an upset stomach, could be the prawn sandwich," Hannah suggested as Nicole made her way around the table. "Take-away food can be tricky."

"Yes," Nicole agreed weakly.

''Or is it sunstroke?'' Matt queried. ''Do you feel feverish, Nicole?''

''Only a headache,'' she answered, wishing they'd just let her go without fuss, fixing her gaze on the double entrance doors to the castle to deflect any further inquiries about her health.

A chair scraped on the cobblestones. Matt spoke, *not letting her go.* ''I'll accompany you up to your room. Make sure you're all right.''

''No!''

She spun to face the man she most wanted to escape, her hand flying out in a warding-off protest. He was on his feet, so big and tall he seemed to tower over her, filling her vision with multiple images. Which was wrong. She was dizzy from having whirled on him so fast, the shock of his action draining the blood from her face.

The next thing she knew was finding herself clamped to Matt King's chest, then being set in his chair, head down between her knees, his arm around her supportively, his voice ringing in her ears as he crouched to her level.

''Deep breaths. Get some oxygen back in your brain.''

Had she fainted?

Embarrassment churned through her. Having so much attention focused on her was dreadful. ''I'm all right,'' she gasped, intensely distressed at having made this spectacle of herself.

''You were blacking out, Nicole. Take your time now,'' Matt advised. He felt her forehead. ''Not overly hot. A bit clammy.''

''Perhaps I should call a doctor,'' Mrs. King said worriedly.

''No!'' Nicole cried, alarmed by what a doctor might tell her employer. She had to keep the pregnancy a secret. ''I just need to lie down for a while. Truly...''

''I'll carry her up to her room, Nonna. Make sure she's okay,'' Matt said.

''You do that, Matteo, and I'll go and speak to Rosita. She has remedies for everything.''

"Oh, please..." Nicole barely got those words out before she was lifted off the chair and cradled across the same broad masculine chest she had struggled against at the Brisbane hotel.

"I'll get the doors open for you," Tony chimed in, already out of his chair and striding ahead of them.

Fighting them all seemed like fighting an unstoppable juggernaut. Nicole felt too weak to do it. She let herself be carried into the castle, hating the enforced awareness of the man who was carrying her, his strength, the sense of once more being enveloped by him. She refused to put her arms around his neck to make the carrying easier. It would bring her into even closer contact with him, possibly encouraging whatever devious plan he had in mind.

Tony didn't follow them in. Mrs. King left them at the staircase, pursuing her own path to the kitchen and Rosita. This left Nicole alone with Matt King as he started up the stairs.

"Put me down. I can walk," she pleaded.

"It's not far. I can manage," he stated firmly, as though she was worrying about being too heavy a burden.

She closed her eyes and took a deep breath, which was a mistake because she breathed in the warm male scent of him and her head swam again. "Why are you doing this?" she hissed, angry at her own vulnerability to an attraction she didn't want to feel.

"You need help."

"I don't want you holding me."

"You surely don't imagine I'm taking you up to your bedroom to seduce you when you're obviously sick."

She was too agitated to think straight.

"Seduction wasn't what we were about anyway," he added dryly. "You know that, Nicole."

"I'm not going to change my mind," she blurted out, desperate for him to understand her position.

"I didn't expect you to."

"Then why are you here?"

"Was I supposed to be banned from the castle?"

She floundered, knowing it was absurd to try to cut him off from his grandmother for the duration of the project. "You know what I mean," she muttered helplessly.

"You wanted enough notice so you could avoid me?"

She bit her lips, knowing to concede that also conceded how deeply he affected her. But he knew it already, she wildly reasoned. Nothing would have happened between them if she hadn't wanted it to.

"You made your point, Nicole," he went on quietly. "I'm not going to push anything else."

He didn't have to, she thought miserably. She was a mess around him anyway. He'd reached the top of the staircase, seemingly without any effort at all, and headed down the corridor towards the guest suites.

"Which door?" he asked.

"Please...put me down now," she begged. "I'll be fine. The dizziness has gone."

"Which door?" he repeated.

"I don't want you coming into my private room," she cried. "It's *private*... to *me!*"

He stopped. His chest rose as he sucked in a deep breath and fell as he expelled it. Slowly, carefully, he set her on her feet, still holding her as he waited to see if she really was steady enough to be safely released.

"I was only trying to look after you, Nicole, not take some...some crass advantage," he said quietly. "I'm sorry I left you thinking so badly of me. Next time we meet..." Another deep sigh. "There's no need for you to feel stressed in my company. Okay?"

"Yes. Thank you. May I go now?" she rushed out, unable to look at him with tears pricking her eyes again.

"As you wish," he murmured, dropping his hands.

She made it to her room in a blind dash, conscious he was waiting, watching. It was an enormous relief to close the door on him. She stood against it, letting the tears roll, swallowing the sobs that threatened to erupt.

Trying to look after her…

I want someone to care about me. Look after me.

Those were the words she'd hurled at him in the elevator. Did he remember them or was he just reacting to her being ill in front of his family? Nothing really personal. Except he wanted to call at the castle without her being stressed. Which was totally impossible now she was pregnant with his child.

Oh, God! Oh, God! Oh, God!

What was she to do?

CHAPTER SIXTEEN

ISABELLA VALERI KING decided this was no time for sensitivities. There was very little time left for anything. If she was wrong, Matteo could soon set her right. However, if the situation was what she suspected it to be, action had to be taken before Nicole drove back to Sydney. Once in her home city, it would be all too easy for an enterprising and determined woman to make herself uncontactable in any direct sense.

The contract to write the family history would not be broken. Isabella had no doubt about Nicole's integrity on that promise. The research had been thorough with everything recorded for easy reference. The argument that the writing could be done anywhere was irrefutable. Nicole Redman was going and Isabella knew in her heart there'd be no coming back to Port Douglas. An irrevocable decision had been made.

Unless Matteo stopped it.

If he had reason to stop it.

With all this churning through her mind, Isabella entered the KingTours main office, intent on a face-to-face confrontation with her youngest grandson.

"Mrs. King!" the boy behind the desk cried in surprise, this being a rare and unheralded visitation by a woman of legendary stature in the community.

"Is my grandson in his office?" she demanded. He ought to be. It was Friday morning. And she didn't want to hear any excuses for not meeting with her.

"Yes," the boy informed, not seeing any reason to check with his employer.

"Good! You need not announce me," she instructed, leaving him staring after her as she marched into Matteo's office and closed the door firmly behind her.

Matteo looked up from the paperwork on his desk with the same air of stunned surprise. ''Nonna! What are you doing here?''

She paused, for the first time wondering if she was about to do him an injustice. Giving herself more time to think, she moved slowly to the vacant chair on this side of his desk and sat down.

''Is something wrong?'' he asked in quick concern, rising from his chair.

She held up a hand to stop him. ''I only wish to talk, Matteo.''

He frowned, sinking back onto his seat. ''What about?''

''It's Friday. I thought perhaps you might intend to visit me this afternoon.''

He nodded, his brow still creased, more in puzzlement now. ''I had planned to drop by. Is there a problem?''

''Nicole is leaving us. She begins the long drive back to Sydney tomorrow.''

His frown deepened again. ''Do you mean she is breaking her contract with you?''

"No. She will write the family history. But she will not remain at the castle to do so."

"Did she give a reason?"

"She says the heat is getting to her. And it is true that she has been unwell all this week."

He grimaced. "I did say..."

"It is nonsense, Matteo," Isabella cut in. "She has been here three months, through the hottest time of the year, with no ill effect whatsoever. Until very recently."

"Last Sunday..."

"Yes. That was the most noticeable."

"Since then?"

"She has not been...herself."

"Maybe the heat has gradually worn her down, Nonna."

"No. It is not logical."

His eyes narrowed. "So what do you think? Why come to me?" he rapped out.

"I may be old but I'm not blind, Matteo. There has been something between you and Nicole. She is tense in your presence and you are certainly not indifferent to her."

"Are you blaming *me* for this choice she's made?" he challenged tersely.

"Are you to blame?" she fired straight at him.

His hands lifted in an impatient gesture. "I have tried to put Nicole more at ease with me. If she cannot accept that..."

"Maybe it is not possible, Matteo," Isabella said sadly. "Rosita says Nicole is pregnant."

"What?"

His shock was patent.

Again Isabella paused, not certain that he was responsible. She sat silently, watching him deal with what was obviously news to him.

He shook his head incredulously. Then his face tightened as though he'd been hit by some truth he recognised. He shot an intense look at her. "How does Rosita know this?"

Isabella shrugged. "I have never known Rosita to be wrong on the matter of pregnancy. She says there is a look about a woman. She told me Hannah was pregnant weeks before Antonio announced it. I don't doubt Rosita's judgment, Matteo. And as much as Nicole tries to hide it, her morning sickness..."

"She's been sick every morning?"

"For over a week now."

"Before last Sunday?"

"Yes."

Clenched fists crashed down on the desk. "She knew." He erupted from his chair. "She knew!" He paced around the desk, his hands flying out in violent agitation. "Why didn't she tell me? She had the chance."

All doubt was now erased. Isabella took a deep breath and said, "Nicole must have felt she had good reason not to tell you, Matteo."

"But..." He sliced the air in angry dismissal. "...I told her how I feel about fatherhood."

"How *you* feel. Perhaps you should consider how Nicole feels."

"It's my child!" he protested. "She can't just ignore that, Nonna."

"If you want any part in your child's life, I advise you to proceed with great care, Matteo. With great care."

She stood with all the dignity at her command, bringing to a halt the wild tempest of energy emanating from her grandson.

"In this matter Nicole has all the rights," she said to sober him. "And if she leaves tomorrow, your child will be gone with her. This is not a time for rash action or anger, Matteo. It is a time for caring, for kindness, for understanding."

She walked to the door. Matteo did not move to open it for her. She looked back at him, saw conflict raging across his face, tension gripping his entire body, the need to act almost explosive.

Was this turbulence they struck in each other the cause of all the problems?

Isabella shook her head.

What more could she do?

‘‘It is not the heat nor the pregnancy that has made Nicole Redman sick to her soul,’’ she said sadly. ‘‘You would do well to think on that today, Matteo. Whatever you decide to do…you will live with this for the rest of your life.’’

She opened the door and left him.

The decisions were his now.

She could only hope he made the right ones.

CHAPTER SEVENTEEN

EVEN at the last moment, Nicole hesitated, the sealed and addressed envelope still clamped between her finger and thumb as it hovered over the slot in the postal box. It had to be done, she told herself. It wasn't right to deny Matt King knowledge of a child he'd fathered. By the time he received the letter she'd be long gone, although once the baby was born, she would notify him again. Then if he wanted contact…their child had the right to know its father.

That was the really important truth.

She could not turn her back on her child's rights.

Whatever happened with Matt King in the future she would learn to cope with it…somehow. This had to be done. Her finger and thumb lifted apart. The envelope dropped.

Nicole hurried back to her car. No turning back on this course now. All week she had fretted over it. A weight seemed to shift from her shoulders as she settled herself in the driver's seat. There was nothing more that had to be done.

It was almost five o'clock. She'd bought a packet of barley sugar to suck on the trip tomorrow in the hope it would keep any sickness at bay, plus bottles of mineral water to stop dehydration. Only one more night at the castle…

She drove around the town one last time, knowing she would miss this place, wanting to remember everything about it. Maybe, sometime in the future, her child would come here for visits, if Matt King wanted that. It was a heart-wrenching thought. Tears pricked her eyes. She blinked them away and drove up to the castle, wanting to catch the sunset from the tower.

Rosita was in the kitchen when Nicole carried in the bottles of water to put in the refrigerator overnight. ‘‘I have made my special lasagna for your dinner,’’ the motherly housekeeper announced.

Nicole didn’t feel like eating anything heavy but she smiled, knowing Rosita wanted to give her a last treat. ‘‘I’m sure I’ll enjoy it.’’

‘‘I will pack a picnic box for you to take in the morning.’’ Her kind eyes searched Nicole’s in hopeful concern. ‘‘Is there anything else I can do for you?’’

‘‘No, thank you, Rosita. You’ve been marvellous to me. I’m just going up to the tower now to watch the sunset.’’

‘‘Ah, yes. It is a fine view from the tower. Take care not to fall on the steps. They are very old and worn.’’

Nicole took away the strong impression that Rosita knew what she’d tried to keep hidden. Or at least suspected it. All the fussing over her, the admonitions to *take care*… but nothing had been said. Sadness dragged on her heart as she climbed the steps to the tower.

She would miss Rosita's motherliness. Having been motherless for so many years, it had been nice to be fussed over, cared about.

There was so much she would miss.

Many times she had come up here to the topmost level of the castle, having finished work for the day and needing a relaxing break before dinner. The view was fantastic to every horizon, the sea, the mountains, the endless sky, all the colours beginning to change as the sun lowered.

She walked around the tessellated wall, taking in the many vistas one last time, stopping finally at her favourite view over Dickenson Inlet where the boats came into the marina, the cane fields on the other side of it stretching out to sea, and beyond them the darkening hills behind which the sun would sink.

It was so calming, peaceful, beautiful. She thought of her employer's mother, Marguerita Valeri, standing here in the old days, watching the ships come in from the sea, watching the cane fields burn at harvest time, watching the sun set, and for the first time it occurred to Nicole that her child—Matt King's child—was part of the same pioneering bloodline that had built this castle and so much else up here in the far north.

She herself might never belong anywhere but her child had deep family roots. A real history. A history she would write so it would always be known. It was something good she could give. And maybe Matt—if he truly felt the responsibilities of fatherhood—would provide their child with a solid sense of belonging.

Matt reached the top of the tower and halted, gathering himself to do what had to be done. Nicole was standing at the far wall, her back turned to him, her gaze seemingly fixed on the view his grandmother liked best. Her tall slender figure was completely still, wrapped in a loneliness he knew he had to break.

The setting sun gave the frame of her fiery hair a glowing aura. The shining of inner strength, he thought, though the rest of her looked fragile. The urge to simply take her in his arms was strong, but he sternly reminded himself that taking was not keeping and Nicole would resist force.

Only the truth would serve him now.

His anger at her keeping everything to herself had dissipated hours ago. His pride was worth nothing in the face of losing this woman and the child she was carrying. If Rosita was right about the pregnancy, he had to win both of them. He had to reach Nicole with the truth, make it speak for him, make it count.

One chance.

He couldn't afford to mess it up.

Matt took a deep, deep breath and called to her.

"Nicole..."

Her heart leapt.

His voice.

She turned with a sense of disbelief, having already relegated him to the past, and the far future. He wasn't supposed to appear in the here and now. Yet he was striding towards her, large as life, the force of his vital energy making her pulse flutter and spreading a buzz of confusion through her entire body.

"What are you doing here?" she cried, her mind struggling to accept a reality she didn't want to face.

He slowed his step, his hands lifting in an appeal, his dark eyes begging her forbearance. "Sorry if I startled you. I came by after work to see my grandmother. She mentioned you were leaving us tomorrow."

"Yes. Yes, I am. I don't need to stay here to do the writing," she gabbled out, belatedly remembering he worked in the KingTours offices on Fridays and cursing herself for not foreseeing the possibility of a casual visit to the castle. Although why he had to come up here, seeking her out…

"Is it because of me?" he asked, coming to a halt at the tessellated wall right beside her, barely an arm's length away, and turned to face her, an urgent intensity in the eyes searching hers.

Her heart thumped wildly. "Why would you think that? I told Mrs. King..."

"There are more kinds of heat than the weather," he said with savage irony, "and I know I'm guilty of subjecting you to them, Nicole."

He was doing it again right now.

She turned her face to the sunset, hoping the red glow in the sky would somehow hide the tide of heat rushing up her neck, scorching her cheeks. Her mind literally could not come up with a dismissive reply. It was drowning in the truth he'd just spoken, a whirlpool of truth that had swept her around in tormenting circles ever since she had met Matt King.

"I've been very wrong about you," he went on quietly. "And I regret, very deeply, making you feel...threatened by me. I wish I could take it all back and we could start again."

Impossible. What was done couldn't be undone. The new life she carried forced her to move on. And regrets didn't change anything. Though at least his admission of being wrong about her might make a rapprochement between them easier in the future.

"I'm glad you don't think badly of me anymore," she said, steeling herself to look directly at him one more time. "Let's leave it at that."

His gaze locked onto hers with compelling strength. "I can't. I don't want you to go, Nicole."

She shook her head, pained by the raw desire in his eyes, in his voice. Her stomach was curling in protest. She placed her hand over it, instinctively protective. "Please…it's no good."

"It can be good," he argued vehemently. "The two of us together…it *was* good. Better than anything I've known with any other woman."

Sex!

She recoiled from him.

"Wait!" His arm lifted in urgent intent to halt her retreat. "I know I've messed up everything. It was stupid, trying to negate the truth of what I felt, trying to sidetrack it. I didn't want to get...*hooked* on you."

"I'm not...not...*bait!*" she cried, horrified at the image his words conjured up.

"I thought my grandmother..." He broke off, venting a sigh that carried a wealth of exasperation.

"What about your grandmother?"

He grimaced. "Nonna is into matchmaking. She found Gina for Alex, inviting her to the castle as a wedding singer. And she hired Hannah as the cook for Tony's prized catamaran, *Duchess,* putting her right under his nose. I know she wants all three of us married, having families. I thought she'd picked you for me."

She stared at him in total disbelief. "That's...that's crazy!"

Another grimace. ‘‘Not as crazy as it sounds.’’

‘‘You don’t think *I* might have a say in whom I marry?’’

‘‘I’m trying to explain…’’ He looked harassed, raking a hand through the tight curls above his ear, frowning, gesturing an appeal for patience. ‘‘I wanted her to be wrong. And when I remembered you from New Orleans…’’

‘‘You concocted a scenario that put me in the light of a totally unsuitable wife,’’ she hotly accused.

‘‘Yes,’’ he admitted fiercely. ‘‘And grabbed at every other reason I could think of, too. Anything to stop me from even thinking of pursuing the attraction I felt. I was pigheadedly determined not to fall into Nonna’s marriage trap, even though…’’ He shook his head self-mockingly. ‘‘…she had nothing to do with the attraction I felt for you ten years ago.’’

"You mean...in New Orleans?" she asked, confused by his previous interpretation of her work there.

"I tagged on to your tour that night, just to watch you, listen to you. If I hadn't been a tourist...if I could have met you in some appropriate way...but my time there was at an end and I told myself it was fantasy."

Amazed at this turnabout in his view of her, she ruefully murmured, "I wouldn't have had time for you anyway."

"Our paths were at cross-purposes, but does it have to be like that now, Nicole?"

Pain washed through her. The cross-purposes couldn't be worse. Pregnancy was the oldest marriage trap in the world. It was too late to simply pursue an attraction to see where it might lead and he'd just made it impossible for her to admit the truth. He didn't want to be *trapped*.

She stared at him, hopelessly torn by the possibility he offered, wishing time could be turned back, wishing it was just the two of them, a man and a woman, free to start out on a promising journey…but it wasn't so. It just wasn't so.

Her silence pressed him into more speech, his eagerness to convince her of his sincerity permeating every word. "When I read your book, I realised what a fool I'd been to even question your integrity and your ability to do anything you set out to do. I hadn't meant to hurt you. I'm sorry I did. Genuinely sorry."

The passion in his voice stormed around her heart, squeezing. She wrenched her gaze from his, afraid of being swayed into clutching at some way to have another chance with him. But the idea of deception was sickening. The truth about her pregnancy would have to come out. No choice at all. And she couldn't bear him to feel bound to her because of their baby. This nerve-tearing impasse had to be ended.

"I forgive you that hurt," she said flatly, staring at the long red streaks in the sky, the bleeding tatters of a dying day. "You don't have to worry about it anymore."

"That night in Brisbane..."

She tensed, instinctively armouring herself against letting that memory invade and undermine her resolution.

"...you wanted me, too, Nicole," he said softly.

"Yes, I did. You have nothing to blame yourself for on that account," she clipped out as coldly as she could.

"Can you forget it?"

It was a biting challenge, determined on getting to her, arousing all the feelings they had shared in the heat of the moment. No cold then. And he wanted to remove the chill now, reminding her...

She closed her eyes, determined on sealing off all vulnerability to him. If she didn't see, didn't feel...

"I can't. I don't think I ever will," he said with skin-prickling conviction. "It was as though we were meant for each other. Perfectly matched. You tapped things in me I've never felt before."

Nicole gritted her teeth. Just sex, she savagely reminded herself. Great sex, admittedly, but still only sex.

''It was like...all of me reaching for all of you...and finding a togetherness which went beyond the merely physical. And because it was so...so incredible...I was impatient to experience it again, not taking the time to...''

''It's okay!'' she choked out, unable to bear his recollections. ''I didn't anticipate what happened, either. We didn't plan it. We didn't...*choose* it.''

In a spurt of almost-frenzied energy she turned on him, desperate to finish it. ''That's the one right we hold unassailable in our lives...to choose for ourselves. You didn't want your grandmother's choice thrust upon you. I understand that. And I don't want a...a fling with you.''

''That's not what I want, either,'' he shot back.

''Then what do you want?'' she cried helplessly, her hands flapping a frantic protest.

“What’s all this about? Why try to stop me from leaving?”

“Because I love you!” he retorted vehemently, stunning her, stunning himself with the force of feeling he’d hurled into the maelstrom of need that was tearing at both of them.

They stared at each other, a mountain of emotion churning between them. He scaled it first, charging ahead with all the pent-up ferocity of a warrior committed to battle.

“I just need the time to give you every reason to love me. I know I haven’t done that yet, but I will. *I will!*”

Still she couldn’t believe her ears. “You…love…me?”

He drew in a deep breath, but his gaze did not waver even slightly from the incredulity in hers. “I do. I love you,” he stated again. “You’re in my mind, night and day. If you’ll just stop pushing me away, I’ll show you I can and will look after you, that I do care about the person you are. Whatever your needs are, I'll answer them. I want to answer them.''

She stared mutely at him, feeling as though her whole world had just shifted on its axis. ''You hardly know me.'' The words spilled from a swirling abyss of doubts.

''Nicole, I've read parts of your book over and over again.'' He stepped forward and gently cupped her cheek, his eyes burning into hers as his tenderly stroking fingers burnt into her skin, seeking every path to the torment in her soul. ''I love the child who had the courage to lead her father away from the darkness he was in danger of falling into. I love the young woman who gave the end of his life as much meaning as she could. You shine through the whole story...''

''It's not about me,'' she protested, her voice reduced to a husky whisper.

''It reveals the heart of you. The kind of heart a man would be a fool not to love.''

''Maybe...'' She swallowed hard, trying to work some moisture into her mouth. ''Maybe you...you think that. But feeling it is something different.''

''How does this feel?''

He tilted her chin and she was too stunned to take any evasive action before his mouth claimed hers, not with blitzing passion but with a tantalisingly seductive sensuality that wooed her into accepting the kiss, testing it for herself, feeling the electric tingle of his restraint, letting it happen because she needed to know *his* truth beyond any niggle of doubt before she could surrender her own.

''I love you,'' he murmured, feathering her lips with the feeling words, then drawing back to look into her eyes with mesmerising fervour. ''I love everything about you.''

He smiled whimsically as his fingers softly nudged her hair behind her ears. ''Your hair is like a brilliant beacon calling to me.''

A moth to a flame, he'd said before.

His hands trailed down to her shoulders. ''I love the way you hold yourself. It shouts—*I am a woman and proud of it.* And so you should be proud of who you are, all you are, Nicole.''

I am, she thought, ashamed of nothing, not even the slip in sensible caution that had made her vulnerable to falling pregnant. Maybe it was meant to be because he was *the man,* she thought dizzily, and as though he could read her mind, his next words melted the armour she'd tried to hold around her heart.

''It excites me simply to look at you. It's like all my instincts immediately start clamouring—*this is the woman…the woman for me.* It happens every time I see you, and it's so powerful I have no control over it. You can call it primitive. I don't care. It's there…and I believe it's there for you, too, Nicole.''

He shook his head at her, negating any denial she might make. ''You wouldn't have let us come together in Brisbane if you didn't feel the same way,'' he pressed on. ''You would have shot me out of your room. It was right for us. It was how it was meant to be between us, and would have been all along if I hadn't put up barriers to keep you at a distance.''

Was that true? If she hadn't sensed antagonism in him at their first meeting, if he hadn't been so cynically challenging, if he'd been welcoming, charming...she probably would have fallen in love with him on the spot, dazzled right out of her mind. As it was, she'd resented his sexual impact on her, hated it. Yet when she'd surrendered to the intense desires he stirred, it had felt right, beautifully wonderfully right. Could it be that way again if...but there was still the baby.

''All I'm asking is that you stay on here,'' he said earnestly. ''Let me show you...''

''I'm pregnant!'' she blurted out, then instantly averted her gaze from his, frightened of the effect of such a stark statement on his plans for whatever relationship he wanted with her. Only a golden rim of the sun was left shimmering above the dark hills. Twilight hovered above it, a purpling sky that signalled the end of this day. The night would come. And then tomorrow...

"I wrote you a letter. It's posted to KingTours. It says we...we made a baby...when we came together," she said in a desperate rush, needing him to understand the emotional dilemma of a future neither of them had planned or even foreseen. "I would have written again when the baby was born. In case...in case you wanted to be a real father. Like you said..."

Silence.

Silence so fraught she couldn't breathe.

The trap, she thought. He's seeing the trap now.

It was no longer a case of winning her over with a promise of love. It wasn't about today or tomorrow or her staying on at the castle for the last three months of the history project. It was about being bonded by a child for the rest of their lives.

CHAPTER EIGHTEEN

"SO IT'S true. You *are* pregnant."

His words fell strangely on Nicole's ears. She had expected shock. The lack of it was mind-jolting.

"I didn't want to believe you'd go without telling me," he went on, hurt gathering momentum. "Without giving me the chance to..."

"You *knew?*" Her own shock spun her around to face him.

He gestured dismissively as though it didn't matter. "Rosita told my grandmother. She thought I should be informed."

"You knew before you came up here and said all those things to me?" Her voice climbed at the shattering of all she'd wanted to believe.

He frowned at her. "How could you do that? Leaving me *a letter?*"

"You don't have to feel responsible. I don't want you spinning me a whole pack of lies to…"

"A letter!" he thundered, cutting her off. "Letting me know so I could stew about it for the next eight months, wondering how you were, worrying if all was well with the baby, while you took care of everything by yourself, shutting me out of both your lives. Was that the plan?"

"Yes!" she snapped. "I couldn't bear you to feel trapped into something you wouldn't have chosen with me."

"You didn't give me the choice. You chose to give me the hell of being shoved aside. Rendered useless. I wasn't to help you through the pregnancy. I wasn't to be at your side when you gave birth to our child. You were going to cheat me of holding our son or our daughter when it came into this world." He threw up his hands, his whole body expressing a towering rage. ''How could you do that? How?''

''It's all about possession to you, isn't it?'' she fired back at him, defying his stand on what he considered his paternal rights. ''Possession, not love. You didn't want to let me go because you knew I had something you wanted.''

''Let you go? Not in a million years.'' Fierce purpose glared at her. ''I'm not taking any more nonsense from you, Nicole Redman. We are going to get married. We're going to get married so fast, it'll put Nonna in a total tailspin getting it arranged in time.''

She backed away from him. ''You can't make me marry you.''

''Give me one good reason why you won't,'' he challenged, his eyes glittering with wild certainty in his cause.

''No one should marry for the sake of a child. It doesn't work,'' she cried vehemently.

''Marrying for love does.''

''You're just saying that.''

"No. Don't speak for me, Nicole."

"You *said* you didn't want to be trapped into marriage."

"I'm walking right into it with my eyes wide open." He stepped towards her. She retreated. He kept coming as he pressed his view. "No trap. This is precisely what I want. My woman. My child. A home we share. A future we make together."

His aggressive confidence came at her like a tidal wave, swallowing up everything in its path, crashing past barriers as though they were nothing. Nicole struggled to hold on to the sense of the decisions she'd made.

"If I hadn't fallen pregnant..."

"You would have stayed at the castle long enough for me to show you we belonged with each other."

"How can I know that?" She stretched out her hands, pleading her uncertainty. "How can I believe anything?"

"Listen to your heart." He was all command now, brushing aside any equivocation.

"You don't want to be alone in this. You want to be with me. I'm the man who'll look after you. I'm the man who'll always be there for you. The provider. The protector. But most of all, the one who loves you."

"Love..." she repeated, her voice wobbling over the tantalising word, her head reeling from the overwhelming force of arguments which were sweeping into all the empty places of her life and setting up unshakable occupation.

She forgot about backing away from him. He kept coming—big, tall, powerfully built, sinfully handsome, intensely sexy, with a mind that saw obstacles as something to beat, nothing to stop him. And the truth was she loved him. She loved everything about him—this king amongst men.

He seized her upper arms. His eyes blazed with an indomitable will to win. "Stop all this destructive resistance, Nicole," he commanded in a voice that drummed through her heart. "Stop and remember what we felt when we came together. When we made our baby… yours and mine…together. It was right. Admit it!''

The intense blast of his passion poured a sizzling sense of rightness through every cell of her body. And wasn't he promising everything she had ever ached for?

Admit it!

She wanted to be Matt King's wife… wanted to become part of his extraordinary family…wanted their child to belong here.

His fingers pressed urgent persuasion. ''Give us a chance, Nicole. Please…just give us a chance.''

CHAPTER NINETEEN

DEAR Elizabeth,

I write this with great joy. Yesterday Nicole gave birth to a beautiful baby boy. He is to be called Stephen, after my father. Nicole insisted on it. She has a very strong sense of family tradition, which is very comforting to me. I know when I am gone, she will be the keeper of all I have tried to set in place. It is meaningful to her.

Every day I leaf through the family history she wrote for us and I can feel her love of it on every page, even to the way she placed the photographs. I hope she will add to it in the years to come, especially the photograph I am enclosing with this letter. Ah, the love and pride on Matteo's face, looking down at his wife and newborn son, and Nicole glowing the same feelings right back at him. It brings happy tears to my eyes.

This was a match truly made in heaven, though God knows they were difficult people to bring together. It was so fortunate they were blessed with a child to make them come to their senses and acknowledge what they were to each other. Well, you saw them at their wedding. Such strong passion between them. There will never be anyone else for those two.

I can rest content now. Alessandro, Antonio, Matteo…they have the right partners. And here I am with four great-grandchildren, two boys, two girls. Antonio and Hannah adore their darling daughter and no doubt she and Stephen will be splendid company for each other, born so closely together.

There is nothing like family. To me it is the keystone of our lives—our past, our present, our future. I know you feel this, too. I enjoy our correspondence very much, and I want to thank you once again for all your wise advice. Each night I lie in bed and I think of our family lines—yours in the Kimberly, mine here in the far north—and I see them thriving for a long, long time, Elizabeth. I go to sleep with a smile.

I am sure it is a smile we share.

With love,
Isabella Valeri King

MILLS & BOON® PUBLISH EIGHT LARGE PRINT TITLES A MONTH. THESE ARE THE EIGHT TITLES FOR DECEMBER 2002

THE HONEYMOON CONTRACT
Emma Darcy

ETHAN'S TEMPTRESS BRIDE
Michelle Reid

HIS CONVENIENT MARRIAGE
Sara Craven

THE ITALIAN'S TROPHY MISTRESS
Diana Hamilton

THE FIANCÉ FIX
Carole Mortimer

BRIDE BY DESIGN
Leigh Michaels

THE WHIRLWIND WEDDING
Day Leclaire

HER MARRIAGE SECRET
Darcy Maguire

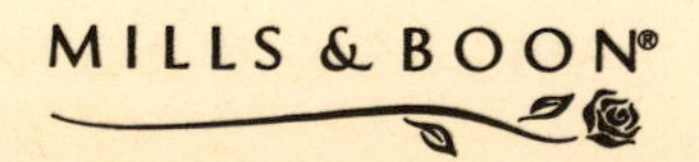

MILLS & BOON® PUBLISH EIGHT LARGE PRINT TITLES A MONTH. THESE ARE THE EIGHT TITLES FOR JANUARY 2003

A PASSIONATE SURRENDER
Helen Bianchin

THE HEIRESS BRIDE
Lynne Graham

HIS VIRGIN MISTRESS
Anne Mather

TO MARRY McALLISTER
Carole Mortimer

MISTAKEN MISTRESS
Margaret Way

THE BEDROOM ASSIGNMENT
Sophie Weston

THE PREGNANCY BOND
Lucy Gordon

A ROYAL PROPOSITION
Marion Lennox

Joe stopped as he came into the waiting room and saw Rachael.

'Uh…hi.' Then he looked at the person by her side. Rachael dropped her arm from around Declan's waist and clenched her hands tightly in an effort to control the feeling of dread which swamped her.

Rachael watched as Joe looked the boy up and down before slowly shaking his head. 'Er…Joe.' She cleared her throat and forced the words out. 'I'd like you to meet Declan. My son.'

'Joe?' Declan asked, and Rachael turned to look up at him. She nodded. '*The* Joe?'

Rachael nodded again.

'My *dad*—Joe?'

Rachael glanced at her son, then Joe. 'Yes.'

Lucy Clark began writing romance in her early teens and immediately knew she'd found her 'calling' in life. After working as a secretary in a busy teaching hospital, she turned her hand to writing medical romance. She currently lives in South Australia with her husband and two children. Lucy largely credits her writing success to the support of her husband, family and friends.

Recent titles by the same author:

THE ENGLISH DOCTOR'S DILEMMA
DIAGNOSIS: AMNESIA
UNDERCOVER DOCTOR

DR CUSACK'S SECRET SON

BY
LUCY CLARK

MILLS & BOON®

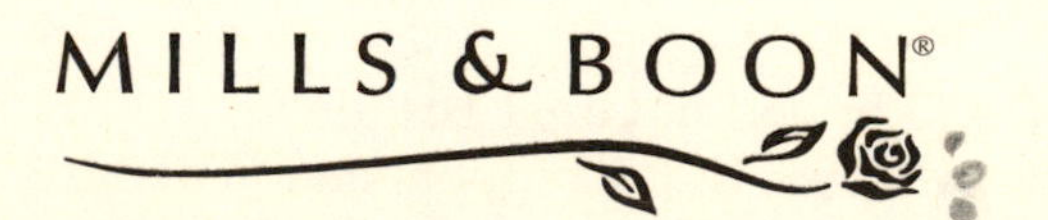

To my sister Claire,
Here is your Joseph. I hope you love him as much as I do.
1 John 1:9

Firs
Lar
Har
Etor
Ricl

ISBN 0 263 18481 1

Set in Times Roman 15¾ on 17½ pt.
17-1005-51441

Printed and bound in Great Britain
by Antony Rowe Ltd, Chippenham, Wiltshire

CHAPTER ONE

'YOU'RE late—*again*!'

Joe grinned at his practice manager. 'Good morning, Helen.' He leaned over the receptionist's counter and gave her a kiss on the cheek. 'What's the good in owning a practice if I can't set my own hours?'

Helen pretended to consider this. 'Hmm, is it because you have patients waiting for you?'

Joe turned and scanned the empty waiting room. 'Are they hiding?'

'No. Mrs Taub called to say she was running late and I bet you've forgotten the other reason I asked you to be early today.'

Joe frowned, thinking hard. 'You're right. I've forgotten.'

'Honestly, Joe. You've a brain like a sieve some days.'

'I'm going to take that as a compliment.' He picked up his patient files and started up the corridor. Helen stopped him.

'The new locum starts today.'

'We have a new locum?'

'Joseph,' she said in that reprimanding voice of hers which never failed to bring a smile to his face. 'You knew Alison was going on maternity leave. Don't tell me you didn't realise the doctor who's worked here for the past two years was pregnant?'

'No.' He headed into his consulting room, Helen hard on his heels. 'Hey, that means I missed her going-away party. Oops.'

'You were on set. It's all right. Alison understands but she's expecting you to visit her once she's had the baby.'

Joe shuddered. 'Do I have to? I'll send a gift but you know how babies make me feel.'

'Just because you don't want to have any children, Joe Silvermark, that's no reason not to be nice to those who do.'

Joe was instantly contrite, remembering Helen had no children of her own…which was where he'd come in. 'You're right. I apologise. When the baby's born, I will visit her. Put it in my diary and bug me until I do it.'

Helen grinned. 'Already done.'

'Good. So, I have a new locum to break in, eh? Male or female?'

'Female.'

'Is she good-looking?'

'She wears a wedding ring so it looks as though you're out of luck there but, yes, she's attractive. She also has brilliant credentials and came highly recommended from a colleague of mine. We were lucky to get her at the last minute, especially as the previous locum I had lined up pulled out without warning.'

'She was probably pregnant as well,' Joe muttered. 'Call the water board and make sure there's nothing in the water,' he joked.

'See, now, I thought she might have pulled out because she'd heard you're hardly here to do any work and would be leaving it all up to her.'

He shrugged. 'So? I own the practice, which means I can employ people to do the work for me. That leaves me free to pursue my own interests in the movie-making business.'

Helen shook her head. 'Whatever am I going to do with you, Dr Hollywood?'

'Nothing.' He grinned again. 'Where's the new recruit?'

'Either in her consulting room or the kitchen.' The bell over the front door jingled. 'Ah, there's my cue. You only have four patients this morning and then you can get back on set.'

'Right.' Both of them walked out of his consulting room—Helen towards the reception area and Joe to the back of the old converted house he'd bought almost five years ago. He checked the other consulting room but found it empty. He breathed in deeply. 'Ah, must be coffee time.' He headed to the kitchen and stopped in the doorway when he saw a woman dressed in a navy skirt and light blue shirt with one long, dark braid hanging down her back standing at the sink, her back to him.

Joe felt an immediate tightening in his gut. It always happened when he saw a woman with hair that colour. Black, as black as the darkest night. Not many women naturally had hair that was jet black but this one did and she instantly reminded him of Rachael—the woman who'd plagued his subconscious for the past fifteen years.

Joe let out a slow breath, waiting for the tightening to disappear, but this time it didn't. He glanced at the woman's legs and shook his head. Her legs were incredible. Rachael's legs had been equally as gorgeous and the sensitive depths of her blue eyes had always been able to bring a response from him. Too bad this woman was married because she appeared to be just his type.

Joe shrugged and pushed all thoughts of Rachael back into the box where they belonged.

He cleared his throat and his new colleague turned.

It was simultaneous.

The colour drained out of both their faces and they each clutched at something for support—Joe the doorframe, Rachael the sink.

Rachael's knees started to buckle and she found it hard to breathe, to concentrate, to do anything. The cup she'd been holding slipped from her hands and shattered at her feet. Thankfully, she hadn't yet filled the cup with anything but her one sugar.

She opened her mouth to speak but found it impossible to form any words. Her heart was pounding fiercely against her ribs, her head was getting lighter by the second due to lack of oxygen, and she felt the dizziness start to claim her.

Her knees gave way and she started to slide down the cupboards. 'No.' She shook her head and finally managed to tear her gaze away from him, her eyes screwed tight. 'No.' She hugged her knees to her chest, trying desperately to get control of her emotions.

This wasn't happening. This wasn't possible. How could she have been so careless? Why, oh, why hadn't she done more research, asked more questions, done her homework before starting work at this particular medical practice? Why had she blindly let her friend and colleague, Lance, set this up for her?

Her next thought was, how could she get out of it? Was it possible to renege on the contract on her first day? She knew it was highly unprofessional but she honestly didn't think she'd be able to work here for the next six months, regardless of how perfect the job had seemed to her.

Feeling her breathing begin to calm, Rachael opened her eyes and was surprised to find no one standing in the doorway. Had she imagined it? She glanced across at the shattered cup beside her. Had she hallucinated? Had she somehow conjured up the image of the man who'd shredded her soul fifteen years ago? The man she'd thought about every day since?

Slowly rising to her feet, Rachael forced herself to concentrate. She found a dustpan and brush and had just finished sweeping the mess up when Helen came into the room.

'Is everything all right?'

Rachael turned to look at her, hoping she was able to keep the look of total panic from her face. 'I broke a cup. Sorry. I'll replace it.'

'Who cares about the cup? You look as though you've seen a ghost...' Helen paused. 'And so does Joe.'

Rachael closed her eyes. 'So it was him.' The words were barely a whisper.

'You two know each other?' Helen's tone was incredulous.

Rachael looked at the other woman. 'You could say that.' Anger...anger she'd thought she'd dealt with years ago began to surface. 'He broke my heart when I was eighteen.'

It was Helen's turn to pale. 'You're *that* Rachael?'

'You know about me?' Now it was Rachael's turn to be surprised.

'I've known Joe since he was a boy and the deal back then was that we didn't keep secrets. He told me about you when he finally returned from America.' Helen shrugged. 'Not all the details but that you'd been married and had had it annulled.'

Rachael swallowed over the hurt at hearing those words. She smoothed a hand down her skirt. 'Look, Helen, I'm sorry but I can't work here with...with...Joe.' She forced herself to say his name out loud. 'I know that means leaving the patients in the lurch and it's highly unprofessional but I just can't.'

When Helen remained silent, Rachael continued. 'I've never done anything like this in my life. I've always been the dependable one. Dependable Rachael, that's me, but right now I don't even think I can depend on myself.'

'Joe's already left.'

'He walked out?' Rachael snorted as anger began to fill her once more. 'Typical. I can see he hasn't changed much in fifteen years.'

'He'll be back in about five minutes. He just needs to get his head around this, just like you do.' Helen pulled out chairs for both of them. 'Sit down a moment.' Rachael did as she was asked. 'Look, I realise this has come as a shock for both of you but perhaps it's for the best. Perhaps this is your opportunity to work through what happened so you can both get closure.'

'I got closure, Helen, when I signed our annulment papers.'

'Really?' Helen raised her eyebrows disbelievingly. 'Then why are you so angry now?' The question hung in the air for a second before she continued. 'Look, Rachael, you were both young and—'

'Stop. I'll stay for today and do the clinic but after that I'm not coming back.'

'You'll be breaking your contract.'

'Feel free to take me to court. I'd rather pay the penalties than stay here.'

'You hate him that much?' Helen asked softly.

Rachael closed her eyes, knowing her emotions for Joe were so jumbled she doubted she could pick just one to describe how she felt. 'It's…complicated, Helen.'

'At least give me until the end of the week to find a replacement. Joe's busy on the set at the moment and he's not scheduled to finish the movie for another two months. Either way, I desperately need someone here to pick up the slack.'

'So now you want me to stay for two months?'

'Your contract is for six months, Rachael,' she pointed out.

'How about two weeks?'

Helen looked at her and Rachael silently hoped the other woman would concede. 'Two weeks.' She nodded. 'Both you and Joe will hardly see each other if that's what you want. I'll schedule different lunchbreaks and, besides, he'll be on set for at least half of every day so he won't even be here.'

'What does that mean? On set?'

'It means,' said a deep voice from the doorway, 'that he's the medical officer at the movie production studio which is a few blocks away.'

'I call him Dr Hollywood,' Helen teased, then quickly wiped the smile off her face when they both glared at her. 'It's a theme park but they also shoot movies there,' Helen added as she stood. 'Some are quite big budget ones, not just the independent films.' She glanced from one to the other, sensing the atmosphere. 'I'll give you some privacy.'

Rachael couldn't look at him. If she did, she thought she might crumble into an unprofessional heap again and that would never do. Joe walked over and pulled out a chair at the other end of the table.

'Are you staying?'

It was amazing. He'd known she would want to leave. She shook her head, bemused by the situation for a moment. Could they still read each other's minds? 'For two weeks until Helen can get someone else.'

'Thank you.'

'Don't patronise me, Joe.'

'I wasn't.' He raised his hands in defence, waited a beat and then said softly, 'You look good, Rach.'

She closed her eyes, desperate to control her heart rate. One nice word from him and she could feel her body turning to mush, although this time it wasn't from shock but from memories of another time when he'd spoken to her in that quiet, caring tone.

Slowly, she forced herself to breathe and opened her eyes again. 'You look good, too, Joe.' Understatement of the year! He looked… incredible. He looked better than her fifteen-year-old memory recalled. Ruggedly handsome with that rebel-without-a-cause attitude which had attracted her to him in the first place. He was also dead sexy.

Instead of the tight denim jeans and leather jacket which had been his standard wardrobe back then, he now wore a crisp cotton shirt, opened to the neck, and a pair of trousers. Still casual but more…grown up. His dark brown hair was more under control than the messy way he'd worn it back then and there was a hint of grey at his temples, which lent him a distinguished air. Joe? Distinguished? She smiled at the thought and shook her head. People didn't change *that* much.

'That's funny?'

'What?'

'That I look good.' He had that teasing tone to his voice and she admitted to herself that she'd missed his humour. He'd always been able to make her laugh.

Her smile started to fade. 'That's not what made me smile. I guess we'd better see to our patients.' She prayed, as she pushed to her feet, that her legs would support her. Thankfully, they did but she didn't let go of the table until she was perfectly sure.

'I'll have Helen bring you in a cup of coffee once you're settled.'

'Thank you.' My, oh, my, weren't they the polite ones?

'Still milk and two sugars?'

'Uh…' Rachael faltered. He remembered how she'd taken her coffee? Was that right? Was he supposed to remember things like that after fifteen years? She cleared her throat, feeling her earlier strength leave her, and reached for the chair to steady herself. 'Uh…no. Actually, I have it black with one sugar.'

Joe clenched his jaw but nodded as she walked from the room. Black with one sugar. That was how he took his coffee and he was the one who'd forced her to try it without milk. Had she changed after that experience? He shook his head as the image of them both wearing matching hotel robes, sitting in the middle of a bed tasting each other's coffee, flooded his mind. Their two days of heaven. Two days of being shut away from the world in a small hotel room in Las Vegas. Two days of wedded bliss where Joe had thought his life had changed for ever because of the love he'd found with Rachael.

'Reality bites.' He shoved the memory away. Now that he'd recovered from the shock of seeing her, here, in the Gold Coast—at his medical practice—Joe began to realise that one memory after another would continue to intrude.

Maybe it was time. Time to face up to what had happened between them all those years ago. She'd agreed to stay for two weeks so maybe, just maybe, he might be able to get some closure. He had regrets and had always secretly hoped for the opportunity to set the record straight, and now he had his chance. He made a mental note to himself not to blow it, not this time.

Joe went to the waiting room, asked Helen to take Rachael a cup of coffee and, seeing that Mrs Taub had arrived, called her through. He'd heard Helen telling Rachael she wouldn't have to see him and, although he knew Rachael would prefer to hightail it out of here as soon as possible, Joe wasn't going to knock this opportunity back. Rachael Cusack was unfinished business as far as he was concerned, and he was determined in the next two weeks to finish that business once and for all.

Rachael looked down at her patient list. Two more to go. Thank goodness. She sat at her desk for a moment and placed her head in her hands, resting her elbows on the desk. She was mentally and physically exhausted. Never had keeping up the pretence of being OK been so hard in her life. Then again, it wasn't every day a woman ran into the man of her dreams.

And that's exactly what Joe Silvermark had been, she told herself sternly. Just a dream. A fantasy that had gone horribly wrong. It had taken her a long time to come to grips with what had happened all those years ago but finally, eventually she'd managed to get on with her life. She'd thought she was over Joe.

Rachael lifted her head and sighed. Who was she trying to kid? After the first initial shock, an amazing surge of desire had spread through her entire body like wildfire. She was not only still attracted to the man but wanted him more than she'd ever wanted anything in her life. After all, she remembered *exactly* how Joe could make her feel.

'This isn't getting your work done,' she told herself as she stood and glanced at the clock. Quarter to four! Declan would be here soon. Her breath caught in her throat. *Declan!*

Rachael's knees started to shake and she quickly sat down again. Declan. She closed her eyes, trying to control her breathing. How was she going to tell him? How was she going to tell Joe? When Declan arrived, she knew that one look at her son would tell Joe the whole story. Ah, but Joe wasn't here this afternoon. Hadn't Helen said as much?

Hoping for a reprieve, she breathed a sigh of relief. She knew she had to tell Joe the truth and she would, but she'd hoped for a little more time to come to terms with everything. Rachael bit her lip. Would Joe want to be a part of Declan's life? She'd never lied to her son, and as he'd grown older they'd openly discussed Joe. She'd always told Declan if he'd wanted to find his father, she'd be there with him every step of the way. Thankfully, though, her son had decided against it and Rachael had been grateful.

'Get through clinic,' she said out loud, and stood again, smoothing a hand down her skirt.

Hopefully, she'd be able to finish with her patients and head home before or even *if* Joe came back to the clinic tonight. Then she would discuss the situation with Declan and together they'd figure how to deal with it.

Rachael headed out to the waiting room. 'Uh, Helen,' she said softly. 'My son's due to finish school soon and as it's just down the road, I've told him to walk here. I was hoping he could just sit in the kitchen and do his homework until I'm done? That's what we did at the last practice I worked at and he won't bother anyone. Sorry, I forgot to mention it before.'

Helen smiled. 'It's understandable with the shock you've had.'

'Thanks.'

'Is he all right to walk here by himself?'

'Sure.'

'He's not too young to be walking along a major road unsupervised?'

Rachael smiled nervously and cleared her throat, hoping Helen wouldn't connect the dots too quickly. 'Oh, he's not little. Taller than me, in fact.'

'Oh. OK. Do you want me to let you know when he arrives?'

'Thanks. I'd appreciate it.' She turned and picked up her next patient's file. 'Mrs Gibson.' Rachael waited while her patient closed the magazine she was reading and levered herself up from the chair.

'Oof. It's getting harder every day to stand up.'

'I remember the feeling. Come this way.' Rachael's patient list had been mainly made up of women requiring their pregnancy or baby checks. She'd had several toddlers in as well and realised that her predecessor, Alison, had obviously taken all the 'family' cases. That didn't surprise her, knowing how Joe had never been interested in children and had declared he never planned to father any. If only he knew. She focused on her patient.

'I overheard you telling Helen you have a son. Was he a big baby?'

'Ten pounds seven ounces and one week early.'

'Ouch. I'm sorry I asked.'

Rachael led Mrs Gibson into her consulting room. 'Why don't you climb up onto the examination bed first to save any unnecessary moving around?' She helped her patient up. 'Is this your first child?'

'Third.'

'Sorry. I haven't had time to look at your notes.'

'That's all right. I'm sure there have been quite a few of us parading through here today. We'd all sit and chat in the waiting room and when Alison finished her day, we'd sometimes meet at the local coffee shop to complain about the frequent trips to the toilet and indigestion.'

Rachael laughed. 'I remember. It was a long time ago but, yes, I remember.'

'Just the one?'

'Yes.' Rachael pulled out the foetal heart monitor and together they listened to the baby's heartbeat. 'Perfect.'

'You didn't want to have any more?'

'I was very young when I had my son, and after he was born I was in medical school and then working.'

'You must have a very understanding husband,' Mrs Gibson said.

'Do you have any pain?' Rachael neatly avoided responding to the other woman's statement. Over the years, she'd found it easier to keep the wedding ring Joe had placed on her finger exactly where it was. Being a single mother had opened her up to all sorts of criticism and speculation from strangers. As Joe had taken care of completely battering her self-confidence, she hadn't needed anyone else's help to make her feel worthless.

Through medical school, after graduating and working extremely long hours at the hospital, she'd found the wedding ring afforded her some space from her colleagues as well as any unwanted attention.

Most importantly, though…she hadn't been able to take it off. Now she was so used to wearing it, she often forgot about it.

'No, no pain.'

'You're currently…' Rachael reached for the file '…thirty-six weeks? Is that right?'

'Well, you know, give or take a week.'

Rachael nodded. 'Have you had a show?'

'No. I didn't with my other two either.'

'OK.' Rachael helped Mrs Gibson to sit up. 'Were your other two early or late?'

'Late. Both of them, and they still are. We're always the last ones to leave places because the boys take so long to get their things together. Always the last to leave school because they just have to have one more go on the slippery-slip.'

Rachael smiled. 'I feel as though I've had a trip down memory lane today. Now I'm used to endless hours of homework and pimple creams in the bathroom.'

'Oh, stop.' Mrs Gibson covered her ears. 'I don't want to know.' The two women laughed.

'Everything looks fine, Mrs Gibson.'

'Wendy, please.'

Rachael nodded and smiled. 'I'll see you next week, if not before.'

'Oh, this one will be late, just like the other two, and, besides, I've got so much to get done before the baby's allowed to come.'

'If you say so, Wendy, but contact me if you have any questions, although I'm sure you know the drill.'

'Well and truly.'

Rachael wrote up the notes after Wendy had left, before going to get her final patient. It was four o'clock on the dot and she thought Declan should have been here by now. Then again, he'd probably stopped at the school library for some books. She forced herself not to worry.

'Bobby Rainer.' There was only one woman with a pram in the waiting room, a screaming baby inside, and Rachael motioned for them to come through.

'Take a seat,' she offered, as she sat behind her desk and checked the name of Bobby's mother. 'Tracy. What can I help you with today?'

'Can't you tell? Isn't it obvious?' The distraught young mother indicated the baby in the pram as she rocked it back and forth. 'Bobby isn't sleeping. It doesn't matter what I do, I can't get him to sleep at all. He just keeps crying.'

'OK.' Rachael stood up and went around to peer in the pram. 'When did you feed him last?'

'Just before we came.'

'He's your first?'

'And last, at this rate.' She sighed. 'That makes me sound like a terrible mother.'

'No.' Rachael smiled. 'It's quite understandable to feel that way, especially when you're probably not getting much sleep yourself. Mind if I pick him up?'

'Be my guest.'

Bobby didn't stop crying immediately when Rachael picked him up and she was silently pleased about that. If he had, it might have made Tracy feel worse. 'OK, OK, calm down, mister. It's all right,' she soothed. 'Does he usually quieten down when you pick him up?'

'Eventually, but I've been doing everything the nurses in hospital told me to do.'

'How old is he now?'

'Four weeks.'

'Feel longer?' Rachael smiled as she asked the question.

'Yes. I'm just so tired and I can't sleep and I'm for ever getting up to him, and my husband's been out of town on business for the past week and it's just got worse.' Tears sprang into her eyes and she took a tissue from a box on Rachael's desk and blew her nose. 'I just can't cope and on top of it all I have my nosy mother-in-law hanging around, telling me what I'm doing wrong and how none of her children ever cried like this. I feel so useless.'

As Tracy began to cry, Bobby began to settle.

Rachael waited a moment before saying, 'I know how you feel.'

'You do?' Tracy looked up in surprise.

'Well, not about the mother-in-law but about being tired and feeling as though you can't cope. I was only eighteen when I had my son. I was at a loss about exactly what I was supposed to do and how to settle him and when to put him down for a sleep and when to feed him.'

Tracy blew her nose. 'I can handle a boardroom full of cantankerous old men, I can prepare documents, write reviews, organise functions, but can I handle my own son? No.' She shook her head. 'It's just that they go through all the steps and what to do so quickly in the hospital, and the nurses are there to help you and then they just send you home and it's as though some maternal gene is supposed to click on and mine hasn't and I don't know what to do,' Tracy wailed, and started to cry again. 'And he cries and he's always hungry and then when he sleeps, I'm trying to get all the things done I need to do but he wakes up and…' she shook her head '…it doesn't work. I'm a failure as a mother.' Another fresh bout of tears followed and little Bobby joined in.

'What sort of help do you have?'

'Help? What help?'

'Friends? Family?'

'My parents are overseas and none of my friends have kids.'

'What about your mother-in-law?'

'I'd hardly call her a help. All she wants to do is criticise me.'

'Will your husband be away for long?'

'He's due back on Friday but I'm at the end, Dr Cusack. I need to do something. I can't take Bobby's screaming any more.' Tracy looked at her imploringly. 'What did you do? Tell me how you coped.'

'I was living at home with my parents. My mum was fantastic. She didn't take over but instead showed me the best way to do things. I honestly wouldn't have coped if it hadn't been for her.'

'You were lucky.'

'Yes.' Bobby had quietened down again, snuffling a little. 'Let's take a look at you, mister.' She carefully placed the baby on the examination couch, one hand holding him as his arms and legs squirmed. The instant he was supine again, he began to scream. She quickly felt his tummy, looked at his eyes, ears, nose and throat, but apart from noticing he was uptight about something, she couldn't see anything wrong. She undid his clothes and checked him for rashes but found nothing.

Rachael picked him up again, this time holding him more upright as she patted his back and soothed him.

'Well? What's wrong with him?'

Rachael walked back towards Tracy as she kept rubbing Bobby's back. His crying had settled again and once more he sniffled. She rubbed her cheek on his soft, downy head, loving the feel. 'Babies cry for many reasons. They're hungry, need a nappy change, have wind, are too hot or too cold, over-stimulated, overtired or even because they're bored.'

'Bored? He's only one month old!'

Rachael smiled reassuringly. 'Yes, bored. He's a male, after all.'

Rachael's sexist comment managed to raise a smile from Tracy. 'True.' She blew her nose and put the tissues in the bin.

'Does he spit up little bits of milk after a feed? When you burp him?'

'Yes, all the time. He sometimes even vomits and then I have to start all over again.'

Rachael nodded. 'Bobby has reflux.'

'What's that?'

'After he's had a feed, when you lie him down on his back, some of the milk mixed with stomach acid comes back up. In essence, it's burning his throat.'

Tracy just stared at her son. 'So something is wrong?'

'Yes.'

'It's not just me?'

'No,' Rachael said softly.

'I'm not a bad mum?'

'No.'

'My poor baby.' A fresh bout of tears misted her eyes. 'Look at me. I can't stop crying.'

'It's quite normal, I'm afraid,' Rachael said with a smile.

'I'm so tired and I'm hardly sleeping and I can feel myself getting angry with him.' Tracy stopped, a guilty look crossing her face.

'You're afraid you're going to hurt him.' Rachael said the words she knew were on the tip of Tracy's tongue.

'I've heard stories about mothers shaking their babies and I used to think it was so cruel and that they should use more self-restraint but…' She shook her head. 'I'm there! I felt like shaking him last night and it scared me to death. That's why I came here today.'

Rachael stopped patting Bobby's back and placed her hand on Tracy's shoulder. 'You did the right thing and I'm proud of you. You're a good mother—and make sure you keep telling yourself that.'

Tracy's smile was heartfelt as she hiccuped a sigh. 'Thanks.'

Bobby had started to settle and was now just making a low groaning noise. Rachael could feel him getting heavier as he rested his head against her shoulder and realised he must be starting to go to sleep. 'Tell me about your day. I know you probably feel as though you're on a merry-go-round but just start somewhere.'

'I feed him, I change him, I burp him—just like the nurses showed me. I try to put him in his cot or on a rug on the floor while I either do the dishes or have something to eat or put the washing on. There's *so* much washing.'

'The washing is *always* there,' Rachael agreed. 'What then? Does he let you leave him?'

'Most of the times he screams and screams, so much that it scares me if I don't pick him up. I check his nappy again, I see if he has wind but he just doesn't settle.'

Rachael could see the anguish in Tracy's face. 'Go on.'

'So I pick him up and end up doing everything one-handed. It takes me for ever to hang up the washing.'

'Have you thought about a sling?'

'A sling?'

'A baby sling. You can put Bobby in the sling, which you wear around you, and then you have both hands free.'

'A sling.' Tracy nodded as though it were the most startling revelation she'd ever heard.

'That only gives you a hands-free option for a while. Keep going. What happens next?'

'It just starts all over again. The feeding, the changing, the burping, the not settling.'

Bobby was now asleep in her arms and Rachael found herself quite content to hold him for a bit longer. Besides, they needed to adjust the pram before he was put back in.

'He cries.'

'Does he seem to be feeding well? Getting enough food? Does he cry for more when he's finished?'

'No. The only time he's quiet is when he's drinking.'

'So you just snatch food whenever you can.'

'Yes. I'm tired and exhausted. I'm up most of the night with him. I'm dead on my feet.'

'You need more sleep.'

'How? I can't wait until Friday when Paul comes home.'

'I'm not suggesting you do. I know this is probably going to drive you crazy, but what about asking your mother-in-law to look after Bobby tomorrow? Just for a few hours so you can get some sleep. Is he her only grandchild?'

'Yes.'

'Then she obviously wants to be involved. Asking her to help in this way may actually serve two purposes. First, it will get her off your back with all her…er…shall we say rather helpful suggestions and, secondly, you get some quality time to sleep.'

'But—'

'Is his cot in your bedroom?'

'No.'

'Bring it in, at least for the next two nights.'

'But all the books say—'

'Let's forget about the books for the moment. Sometimes you need to go with what works. It's not going to be for ever—just a few nights. Your husband isn't home so it would just be you and Bobby. Have the cot by or close to the bed so you don't have to go far to get to him. When you feed him, try and keep him as upright as possible. Use pillows to prop you both up and once you've fed and burped him, give him a bit of antacid.' Rachael named a brand and told Tracy how much to give him. 'I'll give you a medicine syringe so you can measure out the exact dosage. Then you just gently squeeze it into his mouth.'

'And that's it?'

'Try that for the next two nights and see how he settles. You'll need to elevate his cot mattress by putting a pillow underneath it—the same with his pram. Can you raise the back part of the pram so he's sitting more upright rather than lying down?'

Tracy fiddled with the pram for a moment before adjusting it as Rachael had suggested.

'When he's upright, there's less chance of reflux occurring. Giving him the antacid will help soothe the burning he feels, and I wouldn't be at all surprised if you get more sleep tonight.'

'Good. Do I really need to call my mother-in-law?'

Rachael smiled. 'I'd strongly suggest it. If you can get two hours of uninterrupted sleep tomorrow as well as a good sleep tonight, you'll be feeling like a new woman by Wednesday, which is when I want you to come and see me again.'

'Thank you, Dr Cusack. I really mean it. You've made me feel as though I'm a person again.' Tracy laughed. 'That sounds silly.'

'No. It sounds quite logical. I'll walk you out.' Rachael opened the door, still holding little Bobby in her arms. She rubbed her cheek on his head once more and gave him a kiss. 'Thank you for letting me cuddle him.'

Helen cooed and clucked at the sleeping baby as she made another appointment for Tracy. The outside door opened and Declan walked in just as Rachael was settling Bobby into his pram.

'Hi, handsome man.' She turned to Tracy. 'This is what they grow up to be. They continually eat and there's still a lot of washing to do.'

Tracy laughed and Rachael was glad to see a different woman emerge from her consulting room to the one who had gone in. 'See you on Wednesday.'

Declan held the door for Tracy and Rachael was proud of her son's manners and thoughtfulness. Once her patient had gone, he came over and slung his arm about her shoulders. She hugged him close, breathing in his familiar scent, her heart filling with love. 'How was today?'

'OK. You finished yet?'

'Yes. You're a little later than I expected.'

'Stopped by the library.' He jerked a thumb towards his backpack.

'I thought you might. I'll get my things and we can go.' She turned and caught Helen staring at Declan. 'Oh, sorry. I forgot to introduce you. Helen, this is my son, Declan.'

Helen stared in stunned disbelief, her jaw slack.

There was a sound from the back of the house and a door could be heard closing. Muffled footsteps sounded up the carpeted corridor.

'Helen?' Joe was getting closer. 'Did I leave the file on—?' He stopped as he came into the waiting room and saw Rachael. 'Uh…hi.' Then he looked at the person by her side. Rachael dropped her arm from around Declan's waist and clenched her hands tightly in an effort to control the feeling of dread that swamped her.

Rachael watched as Joe looked the boy up and down before slowly shaking his head.

'Er…Joe.' She cleared her throat and forced the words out. 'I'd like you to meet Declan. My son.'

'Joe?' Declan said, and Rachael turned to look up at him. She nodded. '*The* Joe?'

Rachael nodded again.

'My *dad Joe*?'

Rachael glanced at her son, then Helen and finally to Joe. 'Yes.'

CHAPTER TWO

SHE watched as Joe swallowed, once…twice, his gaze never leaving Declan.

Helen was the first to break the silence. 'Well, there's no point in getting a paternity test to confirm this. You're the dead spit of your father when he was your age.'

'You knew him back then?' Declan looked at the woman behind the receptionist's desk.

Helen smiled. 'I've known your father since he was about twelve years old. I may even have a photograph of him somewhere at home.'

'Cool.'

'I'll see if I can find it for you. For now, though, why don't you come through to the kitchen and I'll get you a drink?'

Rachael glanced at Helen, giving her a smile of thanks. Joe barely moved as Helen led Declan past him, but his blue gaze swung to her, pinning her to the spot. It was the exact same look he'd given her the morning they'd signed the annulment papers. Knowing she needed her wits about her, she physically pulled herself up to her full height of five feet eight, and with the added two inches from her shoes, she mentally felt more in control. Smoothing a hand down her skirt to get the perspiration off her hands, she took a breath and indicated to the empty waiting-room chairs.

'Please, sit down, Joe. This can't be easy for you.' Thank goodness her voice sounded natural and calm.

'Don't, Rachael. Don't be the polite, well-bred debutante you were raised to be. It doesn't work in this situation.'

'That's an unfair crack, Joe. I just thought it might be easier to discuss this sitting down.'

'How...civilised. Well, you know me of old, Rach, I'm not a civilised type of guy.'

'What? Going to punch me out?'

'I don't hit women.'

'No, you just break their hearts.'

Joe opened his mouth to say she'd done the same thing to him but stopped. Raking a hand through his hair, he tried to get some sort of control over the shock he'd just received.

'Helen's right. Why bother with a paternity test when the kid looks just like me?'

'Declan. His name is Declan.'

'Declan what? What's his surname, Rach?'

'Cusack.'

'Not Silvermark? Why? Didn't want him following in his father's footsteps?'

'Look, Joe, you made it quite clear you never wanted to have children the day we annulled our marriage. In fact, wasn't that one of the reasons you cited to get the marriage annulled? I wanted children and you didn't, so we were at an impasse?'

'*We* cited.'

'No, Joe. *You.* You were the one who pushed for it.'

'You went along with it.'

'What choice did I have? The man I'd not only fallen head over heels in love with *and* married told me two days later it had all been a joke just to get me into bed. You'd completely humiliated me and broken my heart in the process. You wanted to be rid of me so I let you, but don't go trying to blame our failed relationship on me. At least I was willing to work at it.'

She was right. She had been more than willing to work things out. She'd told him she could do without ever having children but he'd seen in her eyes that she'd been lying. He closed his eyes for a moment, trying to deal with the situation better than he had all those years ago. She'd ended up begging him and she had no idea just how hard it had been for him to walk away. He'd *had* to hurt her, he'd *had* to push her away because back then he'd loved her too much to ruin her life.

'It wouldn't have mattered how much we'd worked at it, Rach, it would have ended in misery.' The words came out dejected and he hated her for hauling all these old emotions back to the surface. Earlier in the day when he'd decided he needed some sort of closure where Rachael was concerned, he hadn't expected the emotions to be so powerful. And now…now…to top everything off, he discovered he had a son.

'Why didn't you tell me about the boy?'

'Would you have listened to me? Believed me? Wanted us back?' He remained silent and she saw the answer right there in his face. 'You'd already said anything between us was doomed to failure. Do you honestly believe that was something I'd do to my son?'

'*Our* son.'

'Oh, so you want one now, do you?'

He ground his teeth together. 'My opinion on children hasn't changed but, regardless of that, I won't deny Declan is mine.'

'How magnanimous of you. Well, for your information, Declan and I are doing just fine and we have for the past fourteen years.'

He deserved that but it was yet another kick in the stomach. 'Is this why you didn't want to stay here at the clinic? Because you were afraid I'd discover the truth about him?'

'No.'

'Wait a minute.' Joe's thoughts began to catch up with him. 'Declan knew my name.'

'Yes.'

'He knows about me?' he asked incredulously.

'I've never lied to him.'

'So he's known about me all along?'

'Yes.'

'Isn't that a bit tough for a young kid to take?'

'I didn't tell him everything the instant he was born, Joe, but neither did I hide the truth. As he's grown older, we've discussed it in more detail. I've always told him that if he ever wanted to find you I would help him, but he decided against it.'

'Probably just as well,' Joe mumbled, but she heard him.

'It's quite clear you don't want either of us in your life, Joe, and that's not a problem. I've agreed to stay here until the end of next week, which gives Helen sufficient time to find another locum to cover the rest of Alison's maternity leave. Once that's over, Declan and I will be out of your life for ever.'

'And if Declan wants to get to know me?'

Rachael frowned, her tone changing. 'I won't have him hurt, Joe. If he does then you have a decision to make. You're either in or you're out because I won't have him messed about.'

'But I'm his father.'

'No.' She hardened her heart against him. She would somehow find a way to cope with the emotions he was evoking within her, but where Declan was concerned she refused point blank to have her son hurt. She'd go head to head with her stubborn ex-husband if she had to. 'You've never been his father, Joe. In fact, you were nothing more than the sperm donor.'

She certainly knew how to cut him to the quick and he tried not to wince at her words. 'Does that mean you were planning to trap me by getting pregnant?'

'Trap you? Trap you with what? Marriage? We were already married, Joe. We didn't have sex until our wedding night. What type of trap are you talking about? Besides, why on earth would I plan to get pregnant at the age of eighteen when I was all set to go to medical school?'

She was right. He wasn't thinking straight. How could he? 'You obviously made it.'

'I was forced to learn at an early age how to survive.' She lifted her chin with a hint of defiance. 'Now, if you'll excuse me, Declan and I have an appointment.'

'Where?'

'It's none of your business, Joe.'

She was right—again. She headed towards him and stopped when there were only inches between them. 'You have a decision to make. You're either willing to get to know him or you're not. Make the choice and let me know your decision. Until then, Declan is off limits.'

'Protecting the young?'

'I'm his mother.' The words were said with pride and confidence. He could tell from the look in her icy-cold blue eyes that she meant business. It was a warning as well as a threat, and Joe nodded sharply, acknowledging her words. He hated it when she was right, and he knew she was. It wasn't fair to the kid. Rachael had always been a straightshooter. She said what she thought and that had been one of the things that had attracted him to her in the first place. OK, the first had been her looks and gorgeous body, but her directness and honesty had been highly important to him, given his past.

Joe couldn't help looking over his shoulder as she stalked down the corridor. Her back was straight, her hips wiggled in that innocent yet provocative way and her skirt, which came to just above the knee, revealed a good portion of those luscious legs he'd coveted all those years ago.

A low, guttural sound of desire rumbled in his throat and he forced himself to look away. He still wanted her. Was that a good sign? Surely it couldn't be a healthy sign! He was looking for closure, not to start anything up with her again.

He headed into his consulting room and shut the door, not wanting to see Rachael and her son—*their* son, he corrected himself as they left. For the first time in fourteen years he wanted a drink. Something smooth and calming—like brandy—to wash away the pain. Or perhaps a few quick shots of tequila to help him forget. But he'd given up drinking after that fateful day on Waikiki beach.

'Where did he go?' Joe heard Declan ask, and held his breath, waiting for his consulting-room door to open. Rachael's muted tones followed and a moment later he heard them leave. He walked around to his desk, knowing Helen would be pouncing on him at any second, and he just wanted another moment's peace to try desperately to get himself together.

There was a brief knock at the door, then Helen entered. 'Mind if I come in?'

'If I say no, will you go away?' he asked rhetorically. 'I'm actually surprised you knocked. Usually you just barge right in.'

'Except when you have patients with you.' He acknowledged her words with a nod while he waited for Helen to seat herself in the chair opposite him. 'Do you think there are any more shocks still to come?' she asked.

'With Rachael? No doubt.'

'Is that a fair statement? Because from everything you've told me about your extremely brief marriage to the woman, it sounds as though she wasn't at fault for any of it. You can hardly blame her for not telling you about the boy.'

'Hey, whose side are you on?'

'Hers.'

'Thanks. I thought you were my friend.'

Helen had the audacity to laugh. She walked around and leant against his desk, placing a maternal hand on his shoulder. 'I couldn't have children, Joe. You've always known that, and for some reason when I met you at the hospital when you were brought in at the age of twelve for your first set of stitches, well for some strange reason I took a liking to you. I thought to myself, Helen, old girl, here is a kid who's good at heart and with a little love and kindness will make a real difference in the world.' She paused and moved her hand to cup his cheek. 'Of course I'm your friend, Joe. I love you like a son and I'm proud of everything you've accomplished. You've pulled yourself up from the depths of the gutter and made a success of your life.'

'Why do I feel there's a "but" coming?'

'Because there is, Declan. I only spent a few minutes with him, Joe, but he's a good kid. A *smart* kid. He's going to that co-ed school down the road.'

'The one for gifted children?'

'Yes. He told me he was successful in getting a place there—and, believe me, they don't accept new candidates lightly. Rachael quit her practice in Cairns to move here for him.'

Joe nodded. 'Sounds like a Rachael thing to do.'

'You told me once that you trusted her. You're not a man to trust easily, Joe, so when you give your trust to someone, it's like a rare and very precious gift.' Helen paused, watching him closely. 'I know you've only spent a brief amount of time with both of them, but do you trust her with Declan?'

'That's a strange question. How should I know?'

'You're looking at it from a worldly angle. I'm asking about your gut instincts, your heart and soul. Do you trust her with Declan?'

Joe thought for a moment, remembering that protective look she'd levelled him with. A mother protecting her chick. 'Yes.'

'Would you trust yourself with him?'

Again Joe thought. He was on Helen's wave-length now and he felt a lot of the emotions he'd fought off as a child beginning to return. 'I never asked to be a father.' The words came out choked. He remembered hearing those same words come out of his own father's mouth when his mother had been pregnant with his baby brother. *I never asked to be a father!* The words had been hurtled abusively, along with a few slaps across his mother's face. Both of them had been drunk but at the time he hadn't realised that. All he'd known at the age of four had been the feeling of total rejection and utter fear. 'I didn't want to be a father.'

'But you are.' Helen's tone was firm.

'I'm no good at this stuff. Caring for people. Playing happy families. It's just not me. I'll stuff it up, just like my old man did.'

'What utter garbage, and I personally resent it. You are nothing like your old man or any of those other jerks your mother hooked up with. You are more than capable of caring for people. Just look at Melina and myself.'

'Melina's my half-sister and you're different.'

'How?'

'You're *you*.' Joe raked a hand through his hair. 'You know what I mean.'

'Yes, I do, and that's my point. I know you care for me, Joe, and you have done for almost twenty years.'

He smiled, trying to lighten the moment. 'Has it been that long?'

'Declan is a part of you.' Helen's words were soft but imploring and Joe's smile disappeared. 'Your blood runs through him. No, you didn't ask for it but it's happened. Accept it and think about his life. You didn't know about him before but you do now and the decisions you make will have long-lasting repercussions.' Helen's gaze softened. 'He seems like a good kid, and he was so excited to finally get to meet you.' She paused.

'Don't mess with him, Joe. At the very least, you owe him that.'

His pager beeped and he glanced at the number. 'They need me back on set.'

Helen nodded and moved away from him. 'Go. Work. Think. I'll lock up.'

Joe waited until she'd left his room before taking a deep breath. He could feel the dark clouds beginning to close in on him once more and he hated that feeling. Move. Move! He needed to keep busy, to get to the studio where he could immerse himself in the intricacies involved in movie-making.

The studio wasn't far and Joe, who felt like just driving his car far out of town until it ran out of petrol, forced himself to slow down and obey the road rules. He tried not to think about Rachael or Declan while he worked, but found it almost impossible. Dark thoughts, distant memories from his childhood kept raising their ugly heads. His father hitting his mother, his father hitting him, his father walking out the door. The losers his mother had hooked up with after that... One by one he recalled their faces, surprised at how the boxes he'd thought firmly locked in his subconscious opened easily with little prompting.

The babies his mother had had. For a while there she'd seemed to be constantly pregnant and always by a different guy. Joe shook his head, almost desperate to get the lids back on those boxes and push them back into the shadows where they belonged. He couldn't be a father. He refused to take responsibility for wrecking Declan's life, as he knew he would. It was genetic. His old man had been a loser and Joe had worked long and hard…struggled and scraped…to get himself to where he was. He'd taken a stand and refused to ruin his life, but when it came to the paternal instinct, he doubted he had one.

After two hours on the set, watching the actors do a fight sequence over and over, Joe checked their limbs for new bruises and any circulatory problems before pronouncing them both fine to go home and rest in a bath full of ice.

With his job done, he was free to head home…but home meant being alone with his thoughts and that was the last thing he wanted right now. Joe walked over to Wong, the stunt coordinator. 'Anyone booked in the training room tonight?' he asked his friend.

'No.' Wong peered closely at him. 'You don't look so good. Lots of anger around your eyes. Bad day, Joe?'

Had it been bad? No, not bad, just mind-tilting. 'I've had worse.'

Wong laughed. 'I'll bet. You want some help in the training room?'

'Yeah. That'd be great.'

'OK. Get changed, I'll meet you there.'

Joe headed to his car and pulled out a bag. It was an old habit he doubted he'd ever get out of as it contained all the essentials—toothbrush, clean clothes, shaver and brush, as well as a pair of sweats for times like these. When a kid lived on the streets, he learned to pack light and pack well. Joe had lived like that for many years, with one bag containing all his major possessions in the world. Then he'd gone to America…and met Rachael. For the first time, he'd experienced a 'possession' he couldn't fit into a bag.

He let Wong strap his hands before fitting the boxing gloves on top. Joe eyed the bag that hung from the low ceiling which was just waiting for his frustrations to be pounded into it. He thought about Rachael, about Declan, about how his world had just completely changed. He tapped the bag, gently testing but also not wanting to think about her when he was pummelling out his anger. She hadn't done anything wrong. He'd been the one who'd pushed her away, who'd wanted her out of his life. He couldn't blame her for not telling him about Declan.

He could, however, blame his mother. His father. His numerous stepfathers. The welfare system. The teachers at school. The kids who had taunted him and his brother. His brother, John. John, who had followed in his big brother's footsteps and become involved with street gangs. Joe had managed to get out of them in the end but John had died and Joe held himself responsible. He began to hit the bag with more effort and soon was pounding out his ghosts, wanting them gone from his life for ever.

He had no idea how long he'd pounded the bag but when Wong told him to slow down or he'd do himself an injury, Joe did as he was told. When they took off the gloves, the strapping around his knuckles was tinged red with blood.

'Maybe I should have stopped you sooner.' Wong undid the strapping and told him to go and shower. 'Come back tomorrow. You still have lots of aggression left.'

Joe nodded and thanked his friend before heading to the showers. He let the water wash over him and although he felt weary and tired, his mind was still active with questions. Questions he wanted…no, *needed* answers to. There was no way he was going to sleep tonight, even after the workout, until he could get his head around what had happened today.

After he'd changed, he headed back to the clinic. Turning the alarm off, he riffled through the filing cabinet, looking for the file on Rachael. He pulled it out and noted her address, surprised to discover she was staying in a hotel. He grabbed his keys, switched off the lights and re-set the alarm before driving to the address.

With determination in every step, he left the hotel lift and strode down the corridor to the room listed in her file at his medical practice. He knocked, and when she opened the door he tried not to gasp. He also tried to control the twisting of desire in his gut, but it was impossible.

Her dark, wet hair was hanging loosely around her shoulders, contrasting with the white hotel robe belted at her waist. He'd seen her looking like that before and his memory was as clear as though it had been only yesterday…only yesterday when he'd removed the robe and taken his sweet time making love to his wife.

'Oh,' she gasped, a blush tinging her cheeks. She looked him up and down, the blush deepening. Nervously, Rachael swallowed. 'Joe. Uh…I was expecting room service.'

Joe forced his mind to clear. 'Look, Rach, I know you told me to decide about Declan but I can't do that without more information.'

He watched as she switched into protective mother mode. 'What sort of information?'

'Can I see him?'

'He's not here.'

Joe hadn't expected that. 'Where is he?'

'He's gone out with my parents to choose a new place for us to live.'

'But it's almost eight o'clock.'

'And?' She waited. 'What's that supposed to mean?'

'Er… I don't know. Doesn't he have homework? Need to be in bed or something?'

She laughed. 'He's almost fifteen, Joe, not five.'

He could feel her softening and took advantage of the situation. 'Can I come in? Please, Rach? Just for a few minutes. My mind is in a spin.'

She glanced down at her robe, then stepped back from the door. 'OK.' When he walked into the room, it seemed to shrink with his overwhelming presence.

'Nice room.' He waved his arm absently around the space, and she caught a glimpse of his hand. The knuckles were red, cut and bruised.

'What have you done?' Without thinking, she crossed to his side and lifted one hand in hers. Joe jerked back instantly. 'What did you do?'

'Nothing. I was working out.' He tried to control himself but her touch had burned him and her fresh, clean, scent was starting to overpower him. She smelt so good.

'On who?'

'Uncalled for, Rach.'

'Yes. Sorry.'

'I was working out on a punching bag.'

'Oh. It's none of my business. I'm sorry. I'll just get dressed.'

'No need to bother on my account.' The words were out before he could stop them.

'Joe!' The blush grew even deeper, her eyes wide and round with surprise.

'Sorry. That was way out of line.'

'Yes. I guess we're even now.' She snatched up a handful of clothes and headed for the bathroom. Joe wondered what she'd do if he followed her and kissed her the way he had in the past.

She'd probably throw him out and again he acknowledged she'd have every right to, but he had to admit that the attraction between the two of them was as potent as ever. He'd never been one to believe in love at first sight. He was too cynical, too wise to the ways of the world yet—bam! It had hit him like a ton of bricks the first time he'd set eyes on Rachael.

A few minutes later she came out the bathroom dressed, a white towel around her shoulders as she rubbed the ends of her hair. He'd seen her do this before and again he had to force the memories not to intrude. He was here with the purpose of getting answers, and that was exactly what he was going to do.

Joe looked out the window at the ocean view. There were other high-rise apartments and hotels to the left and right but she'd scored a great room with a relaxing view of the ocean. If he looked out the window, it meant he didn't have to look at Rachael. She was too distracting.

'So, what do you want to know?'

'Why you didn't tell me?'

'I tried, Joe.' He turned at her words.

'And that means?'

'I tried to find you.' Rachael sighed and hung the towel over the back of a chair. She bit her lip, watching him closely. 'After I returned home from the trip…I wasn't well. At first I thought it was just heartbreak.' She saw him wince. 'You wanted the truth, Joe, and I hope you still believe that with me, that's what you'll always get.'

He nodded but made no other comment.

'I didn't find out until I was four months pregnant. My body was so out of whack, what with travelling and then being so miserable when I returned. After four months my mother forced me to go to the doctor for a check-up, and that's when I found out.'

'That must have impressed your parents.'

She laughed without humour. 'You have no idea. Until then, I hadn't told them about you. They'd known something had been wrong when I'd returned, but thankfully they hadn't pressured me about it. Now, though, there was a grandchild on the way and the whole ball game changed. So I went to Brisbane to find you.'

'Even though you knew how I felt about children?'

'Yes. You had a right to know, Joe.'

'Yet you didn't find me.'

'You obviously didn't want to be found,' she countered. 'I didn't have much to go on and I had morning sickness throughout my entire pregnancy. By the end of the seventh month, I had pre-eclampsia and my doctor put me in hospital until Declan was born. Anyway, I knew you had lived in Brisbane and which suburb you were raised in, but that was all I had to go on. Finding where you lived was like looking for a needle in a haystack, but I eventually found your mother's house.'

Joe was shocked. 'You spoke to my mother?'

'Yes.'

'Did you tell her about the baby?'

'No. I merely told her I was looking for you.'

Joe turned away from her, unable to believe she'd seen the dive where he'd grown up. In the poorest part of Brisbane, the government weatherboard house falling down around itself. The front yard littered with broken toys, bits of cars and general junk. He felt sick thinking she'd seen that side of his life, the side he'd wanted to protect her from.

'How did she react?'

'She said she hadn't heard from you in over six months and that the money you usually sent had stopped coming. Joe, she thought you'd probably died.'

'She said that?' He looked at Rachael once more.

'In a manner of speaking, yes.'

Joe knew she was giving him the 'cleaned up' version of the story. Knowing his mother, she'd have taken one look at Rachael and tried to figure out how much money she could get out of her. Even now, standing barefoot in a hotel room, she looked as though she'd stepped from a glossy magazine. The denim jeans were designer label, the powder blue top was the latest fashion. Her clothes spoke of style and money. They always had, but he also knew that clothes didn't make the woman.

Rachael had always carried herself well. Her walk was determined, sure and purposeful. Even when she'd been eighteen, she'd had such purpose about her, and Joe had coveted it, wanting to have the confidence that exuded from her.

He was watching her again, the way he had when they'd first met. She'd always thought he'd looked at her as though he'd unwrapped a big, shiny package and wasn't quite sure what to do with it. Warmth spread through her and she felt the stirrings of repressed desire beginning to sizzle once more. How could he do that to her with just one look?

He'd always been able to make her go weak at the knees and today he'd done it several times.

He was dressed in his staple outfit of blue denims and a white T-shirt. All that was missing was the well-worn leather jacket, and he'd be a dead ringer for the instant she'd first laid eyes on him. They stared at each other.

Rachael swallowed nervously, her tongue darting out to wet her lips. Joe groaned as he watched the action and closed his eyes tight. His hands were by his side, also clenched tight as he fought the attraction bubbling between them.

'Did you believe her?' The words were ground out as he finally achieved his goal and opened his eyes. Rachael turned away and crossed to the bedside table to pick up a comb. Slowly she began to pull it through her dark locks.

'Hmm?'

'My mother. When she said I was dead. Did you believe her?'

Rachael remembered the scene as though it had been yesterday. Her heart had stopped for one moment before she'd instinctively known it hadn't been true. 'No.'

'Did you give her any money?'

'Joe, I don't think this is—'

'Did you give her money?' he demanded.

'Yes, but it wasn't a lot. About eighty dollars.'

'That would have been enough. Did she ask for it?'

'No, but she kind of implied she needed it for your siblings.'

'*Half*-siblings.'

Rachael shrugged. 'Whatever.'

'She would have used that money to buy alcohol. You know that, don't you?'

'What? No. Surely she wouldn't. Those kids looked hungry.'

'We were always hungry.' Joe turned away once more. He'd been desperate to shield Rachael from his background, from the life of poverty he'd lived. She was too pure, too special, too loving to even have seen the squalor he'd been raised in.

He needed to move this on. His chest was starting to feel tight, and the longer he remained in a room alone with her, the harder it was to control himself. He wanted to grab her, to crush her to him, to press his mouth firmly on hers and see whether the old spark really *was* still there or whether it was just his memory playing tricks on him.

'OK. So you saw my mother and she didn't know where I was, so then what?'

'Then I tried to remember everything we'd talked about and I realised how little you'd told me about yourself. Oh, I knew what made you laugh, what colour you liked…' She lowered her voice a little. '…How you took your coffee.' She shrugged. 'That sort of thing. But when it came to you and what you'd done before you'd met me, I drew a blank. I honestly didn't know where to look, Joe. I put an ad in the Brisbane, Sydney and Melbourne papers for two months but got no response. I tried again a week or so before I had Declan but still no response. I was scared to be by myself, to be bringing a child into the world. I knew my parents were there to help and, believe me, they were incredible, but it wasn't the same.'

Rachael could feel tears beginning to threaten once more and turned away. 'Sorry. I should be over this by now.'

Joe wanted to go to her. To comfort her. To apologise for his callousness. But he knew that if he touched her, it would mean the end of all rational thought.

She wiped her eyes and took a deep breath, pulling herself together. 'Anyway, to answer your original question, I didn't tell you because I couldn't find you. It's as simple as that.'

'Rach.' He couldn't take it any longer. He covered the distance between them and put his hands on her shoulders. She shied away and Joe winced as though she'd slapped him. She turned to look at him.

'Don't, Joe. Don't touch me.'

'Why not?'

His words were barely audible, but even if he hadn't spoken she could read the message clearly in his eyes. He was still attracted to her and she was sure he could see she reciprocated his feelings. He edged closer. 'Why not?'

'Joe.' Her heart was pounding fiercely against her chest, her breath coming out between her parted lips in shallow gasps. She shook her head as he moved even closer. 'Joe.' This time his name came out as a sigh and she realised her mind was quickly losing the battle to her body and she wanted nothing more than to have his arms wrapped firmly around her, their lips pressed hungrily together.

He trailed his fingers down her cheek, revelling in the smoothness of her skin. 'You're still so beautiful, Rach.' He buried his other hand in her hair, unable to believe he was touching her once more.

'Your skin is so soft.' He brushed his thumb across her lips and almost went to pieces when she gasped at the touch. He groaned and hauled her close, wanting to kiss her but at the same time not wanting to ignite something he wasn't sure he could control. He breathed in the scent of her hair. 'Your hair smells amazing.'

Rachael's eyelids fluttered closed and she clung to him, knowing she was passing the point of no return and not caring. She plunged her fingers into his hair, desperate to bring his head closer to her lips, to erase the agony of wanting him, which was gripping her entire body. 'Joe.' She whispered his name and slid her hands down to cup his face as she looked up into his eyes.

Something deep in the recesses of Joe's mind tugged at him. There was still something he needed to address and it was important. He raised one hand to where she touched him and pulled her left hand away from his face. He glanced down and saw the simple gold wedding band.

Helen had mentioned his new locum was married, but with everything else which had happened today, he'd completely forgotten.

'Joe?' Rachael looked at him in bewilderment. 'Joe? What's wrong?'

Joe let his arms drop and took a step back. 'What's wrong? Rachael—you're wearing a wedding ring!'

CHAPTER THREE

JOE turned away from her and stalked towards the door. 'How could you possibly have forgotten you were married?'

A million emotions flooded through Rachael in a matter of thirty seconds. She wanted to pull him back into her arms and tell him the ring was the same one he'd placed on her finger in that small Vegas chapel all those years ago. Another part of her wanted to hurt him as much as he'd hurt her and let him believe she was married to someone else.

But she'd always been an honest person and regardless of how Joe made her feel, whether it be sensually desirable or flaming mad, she'd always been truthful with him. However, if she confessed it was the ring he'd given her, she'd probably be opening herself up for more hurt in the near future. Two weeks. She only had to stay at his practice for two weeks and then she could move on.

Rachael cleared her throat and flipped her hair out of her face, her chin raised with a hint of defiance. He loved it when she looked like that but he forced himself to concentrate. What possible explanation was she going to give for wearing a wedding ring and falling apart in his arms the moment he'd touched her? The attraction was there between them, it was as strong as ever, but surely not so strong that she'd forget about the man she was married to?

'Joe, I'm not married.'

OK. That was the last thing he'd been expecting her to say. 'But the ring?' He pointed to her hand completely bewildered.

Rachael shrugged. 'I didn't like the stigmatism that went with being labelled a single mother. Nowadays it's a common occurrence but even fifteen years ago a woman pushing a pram without wearing a wedding ring was frowned on. Medical school would have been even more of a nightmare if I'd chosen not to wear the ring. Most of my professors were quite old-fashioned.'

He understood that. He'd had quite a few who, when they'd discovered his background, had told him to forget about medical school. He'd been riled by their comments and even more determined to prove their prejudices wrong.

'Thankfully, times have changed,' she continued.

'So why still wear it?'

She shrugged once more. 'I forget it's there most of the time.' There was a knock at the door. 'That'll be room service.'

'You're not eating with your son?'

'My parents wanted to take Declan out to dinner and then look at apartments. It was a special treat for him.'

'And you weren't invited?'

Rachael walked passed him to the door. 'They haven't seen him for six months and wanted some time alone with him.' She opened the door, thankful for the distraction. There was no way she was telling Joe she'd been unable to go out with her family tonight. The shock of the day had been too much for her to cope with and she hadn't been ready to answer her parents' questions about Joe.

She signed for the food and told the waiter she'd take care of setting it up.

'Thank you, Dr Cusack,' he said, before disappearing.

'I'll go and leave you to eat,' Joe muttered.

'You said you had questions and if you don't mind, I'd rather get them out the way before Declan returns. I want your decision, Joe. You're either in or out of his life and I need that information by tomorrow. Declan's already asking questions and getting excited.' She levelled a firm stare at Joe. 'I won't have him hurt.'

'I understand. All right.' He straightened his shoulders as though he was getting ready for battle. 'Why did you move to the Gold Coast?' Helen had told him it was so Declan could go to that fancy school, but he wanted to hear if Rachael had a different reason. Had she known he lived here? Had she specifically chosen his practice to work at, hoping he might get to know his son?

'For Declan. He was accepted to a good school here.' She named the school and Joe nodded, as impressed as he'd been when Helen had told him.

'Wow. That school is almost impossible to get into. Isn't that a school for gifted children?'

'Yes, although I can't stand that label. Declan has a high IQ, and at the beginning of this term he was offered a place. It's all been rather sudden, hence the fact that we don't have anywhere to live. Still, I'd make any sacrifice for him.'

'High IQ, eh?' Joe felt like preening. His boy, *his son* was smart. He shook his head in bemusement.

'You're no dummy yourself, Joe. You just didn't have anyone to support you while you were growing up. If people tell you you're useless, after a while you begin to believe them.'

He hated it that she could read him so easily.

'This term isn't going to be easy for him. For a start, he's beginning in the second term while all the other new kids started at the beginning of the year. Also, a lot of these kids have been there since they started high school. Then there's the downside to being a smart kid.'

'What's that?'

'He suffers from anxiety. It can get quite bad sometimes, and when it does he doesn't eat, he doesn't sleep and, quite frankly, Joe, it's scary to see him going through it. Can't you see why I need an answer from you? I don't want him stressed out. I don't want him getting his hopes up about you, only to have them dashed when, after a few short weeks, you decide you don't want to play father any more.'

'That's a little unfair.'

'It's very unfair, Joe, but I need that decision. If you're in, then you're in for the rest of his life. Up until now you've had the excuse that you didn't know about him, but now you know.'

'You can't just dump this on me, Rachael. It's a lot to take in. This morning I got up, went to work and saw you. That was bad enough, but by this afternoon I'd discovered I was a father! Now you want me to choose? My whole life has been flipped in less than twenty-four hours.'

'You're thirty-four, Joe. I had all this dumped on me when I was eighteen! My husband didn't want me any more and a few months later I found out I was pregnant, so don't go putting this back on me. You're used to adapting, Joe. It's what you're good at. You adapted to the role of traveller when you set out to see the world. You adapted quickly to the role of friend, then boyfriend and finally husband—all within a matter of three weeks. Then you adapted even more quickly to the role of ex-husband and disappeared off the face of the earth. Don't go giving me speeches and platitudes. It doesn't matter whether or not you gel with Declan, it doesn't matter whether or not you can put up with me. You either want him in your life or you don't. Yes, your life has changed in the past twenty-four hours, but there's no going back. Your life has changed for ever. Now act like a grown-up and deal with it.'

The phone rang and she snatched it up. 'Yes?' Rachael turned away from Joe, forcing herself to take a deep breath.

'Dr Cusack? I'm the night manager. We have an emergency downstairs in the restaurant and need your help.' There was urgency and repressed panic in the man's tone.

'I'll be right there. Meet me at the lift.' Rachael hung up the phone and slipped on a pair of shoes. 'Emergency downstairs.' She grabbed the room key-card and headed out, knowing Joe would follow. He was a doctor and this was what doctors did. They put their personal lives on hold when their work required them to.

The instant the lift doors opened in the lobby, the night manager was by their side. 'Over here. We've called the ambulance but this man isn't at all well.' He led them through the dining room and out the back through to the staff corridors. He opened a side door to reveal an elderly woman weeping next to a man who had just been carried through by two young waiters. The room was quite small and the staff had pushed together two armchairs for the man to lie on.

'No!' Joe snapped authoritatively. 'Get him on the floor.' The two waiters did as they were told. 'We'll take it from here,' Joe said. 'Get me the hotel's medical kit, immediately.'

The night manager nodded and ordered one of the waiters to find one. Rachael began to loosen the man's clothes while the night manager ushered everyone out.

'I want to stay,' his wife begged.

'Of course. Come and sit here and hold his hand.' Rachael sat the woman where her husband could see her but where she was out of the way. 'What's his name?'

'Alwyn.'

'And you are?' While Rachael spoke, she continued to loosen Alwyn's clothing. Joe was checking his mouth, making sure there was no food or anything blocking the windpipe before taking a closer look at the pupils.

'Ethel.'

'I'm Rachael and this is Joe.'

'Pulse is weak,' Joe muttered. 'Skin is clammy. Ethel, does your husband have any allergies or heart problems we should know about?'

'He takes Lopresor.'

'What does he take that for?'

'An irregular heartbeat.'

'Has he had a check-up recently?' Rachael asked.

'No. I've been telling him to go to the doctor but—'

'What was he doing before the pain struck?' Joe asked as Rachael took the man's pulse.

'He was eating and then he just…he just clutched his chest and started shaking.' Ethel began to cry again.

'Pulse is gone!' Rachael's words were sharp. Joe immediately began mouth-to-mouth resuscitation and Rachael began cardiac heart massage. They were both aware of Ethel's sobs and when the night manager brought the medical kit to them, but their concentration was on getting Alwyn to breathe once more.

Rachael was counting out loud as they worked together. When Alwyn gave a spluttering gasp, she quickly reached for the medical kit, hauled it open and pulled out a stethoscope, handing it to Joe. With a medical torch, she checked his pupils.

'Equal and reacting to light. Stay with us, Alwyn,' she said encouragingly, watching him closely.

'Check out what's in that kit, Rach. Any adrenaline?'

She had a quick check. 'No.'

He shook his head. 'Guess it was a long shot.'

Alwyn was still spluttering and turning a lovely shade of green. Rachael dug around in the medical kit and found a lined bag. Moments later, he vomited. Rachael soothed him as Joe pumped up the portable sphygmomanometer he'd found in the kit.

'Ethel,' Joe said as he worked, 'Alywn's still not out of the woods. It appears he's had a heart attack and will need to be hospitalised. While we're waiting for the ambulance, did you want to call someone to come and be with you?'

'I'll get you a phone,' the night manager said from the doorway, and quickly hurried away.

'My daughter. I'll call her. She'll know what to do.'

'Good.'

'Is he going to be all right?' Ethel's grip on her husband's hand was almost vice-like, and Rachael didn't blame her.

'We can't answer that,' she said softly. 'Once we have him at the hospital and he's had further tests, we'll know more. I can tell you that the next twenty-four hours are critical.'

'BP is still low.'

'Skin's still clammy.' Rachael checked Alywn's pupils again as Joe deflated the sphygmo cuff and reached for the stethoscope. 'Stay with us, Alwyn. We can't do this by ourselves, we need your help. Pupils still equal and reacting.' She pressed her fingers to his pulse. 'Pulse is stronger than before. That's it, Alwyn. Just stay focused on what you need to do.'

'Heart rate is improving. No, Alwyn, don't close your eyes. Just keep looking at Rachael…which isn't hard to do. You've got a beautiful woman on either side of you—lucky man.' At Joe's words, a faint smile touched Alwyn's lips and Rachael saw him squeeze Ethel's hand.

'That's it, love,' his wife encouraged him, brushing the tears from her eyes with her free hand. 'The ambulance is coming and they'll get you to hospital.'

'How's the pain, Alwyn? Is it going away?' Rachael asked. 'Squeeze Ethel's hand again if it's getting better.' Rachael watched the muscles in his hands clench around his wife's small, frail fingers.

'He squeezed.' Ethel was exuberant.

'Good. Just stay nice and calm.'

The night manager came back with a phone, which he handed to Ethel, and the news that the ambulance had just pulled up. He disappeared as quickly as he'd come but returned a minute later with the paramedics.

'Hey, Joe.'

'Smitty. Come and meet Alwyn and Ethel. Alwyn.' Joe turned his attention to their patient. 'This is my friend Smitty and he's going to take great care of you.'

Smitty placed a non-rebreather mask over Alwyn's mouth and nose to administer oxygen.

'We'll have you feeling better in next to no time, mate,' Smitty said with a smile. He glanced from the patient to Rachael. 'Mick Schmidt.' He held his hand out to her.

'Rachael Cusack.'

'It is a *pleasure* to meet you, Rachael.'

'Focus, people,' Joe growled, which only made Rachael smile. She'd heard him use that tone in the past and it had been when another man had attempted to chat her up. 'Smitty, get him ready to transfer to the stretcher.'

While they worked, Ethel finished her call to her daughter and went back to holding her husband's hand. The love they shared for each other was clearly evident in their gazes. Rachael sighed, hoping, longing and wishing that she, too, could have had that long-lasting love. She sneaked a glance at Joe and looked quickly away when she realised he was watching her, a scowl on his face.

When Alwyn was ready, Smitty and his colleague wheeled the stretcher out to the ambulance parked at the front of the hotel. A small crowd had gathered around, curious to see what was going on.

'I'll go with him to the hospital,' Joe said.

'What about your car?'

'I'll come and get it later.' He stood beside the open ambulance doors and looked down at her. 'We'll finish our discussion tomorrow.'

She nodded. 'I don't think you got the answers you were looking for, Joe, but the ones I gave you were honest. I hope you know that.'

'You've never lied to me, Rachael. I respect that.' His voice was as smooth as silk, his gaze a gentle caress. She found it hard not to sigh with longing and held herself aloof.

'Mum!' A car had pulled up behind them and Rachael quickly turned to face her son. 'Mum?' Declan's eyes were wide with panic.

'I'm all right, darling. I'm all right.' She held out her arms and he quickly hugged her. 'A guest had a heart attack and they called me down to help. That's all.'

Declan nodded. 'Dad!' His blue eyes were now wide with surprise.

'Dad?' Smitty said as he stepped from the back of the ambulance, glancing at Joe in surprise. 'Now the growl makes sense.'

Joe ignored the paramedic and turned to face his son.

'Dad, what are you doing here?'

Dad! Joe couldn't believe the swell of pride that washed over him at having that one word directed at him. 'Uh…I just dropped by.'

'Joe,' Smitty said. 'We're ready to go.'

'OK.' He went to climb into the back of the ambulance.

'Let me know how Alwyn gets on,' Rachael said.

Joe nodded. He glanced at Declan and opened his mouth to speak, but Smitty started the engine and the other paramedic was waiting to close the rear doors. Joe looked at Rachael. 'I'll see you tomorrow.'

The doors were shut and the ambulance drove off with flashing lights and blaring sirens.

'Excitement just seems to follow you around,' Rachael's mother said as she came to stand by her daughter and grandson. 'Your father's just going to park the car and will meet us up in your room,' Elizabeth Cusack said, rubbing her hands up and down her arms. 'It's getting chilly out here.'

Until her mother had mentioned it, Rachael hadn't noticed. With Declan's arm still protectively around her shoulders, they headed inside, the night manager thanking her profusely for her help and saying that her night's account would be taken care of.

When they got back to their room, Declan headed off to have a shower and Rachael went to the mini-bar.

'Need a drink?' Elizabeth asked. 'I'm not surprised. I gather that was Joe?'

'Yes.'

'Hmm. I can see why you fell for him.'

'Mum!' Rachael whirled around and looked at her mother in astonishment.

'What? All I'm saying is he's a good-looking man. He has that…rebel-without-a-cause look to him.'

'Yes. He had it in abundance fifteen years ago, too.' Rachael shut the fridge door and slumped down into a chair. 'Oh, Mum. I don't know what to do.'

'Meaning?'

'Meaning I'm still attracted to the man.'

'Of course you are. It's a natural reaction, especially as you weren't the one to end things. The question is, how does Joe feel?'

'I guess he's attracted to me.' She glanced up at her mother. 'We almost kissed.' The instant the words were out of her mouth, she buried her face in her hands. 'Oh-h,' she wailed. 'What am I going to do? I'm so confused.'

'Look.' Elizabeth came over and placed a hand on her daughter's shoulder. 'When you came home from America, we knew something was wrong the instant you stepped off the plane. By the time we'd driven home, we both knew the trouble was a man. We didn't push you because we just thought it was some holiday romance.'

'And then I was pregnant.'

'Yes. Well, we were stunned, but that was nothing compared to you telling us you'd *married* the man, only to have your marriage annulled two days later.' Elizabeth shook her head. 'It just wasn't like you at all. You'd always been firm in your goals, dependable and trustworthy. Not that marrying Joe didn't make you less those things, it was just so…out of character for you.'

'I know.'

'The thing is, darling, if Joe hadn't insisted on the annulment, do you honestly believe the marriage would have lasted?'

'I would have worked at it.'

'I'm not saying you wouldn't have. You would have worked hard, made bigger sacrifices and probably compromised your goals and ambitions to fit in with a life you hadn't planned, but surely you can see that it wouldn't have stood the test of time. Both of you, and I say this only from the things you've told me about Joe over the years, needed to grow up. It's sad he didn't know about Declan but you've both been able to achieve a lot in the past fifteen years. Now he's back in your life and the emotions have swamped you all over again.'

'They're just so…so…*big*. And there's so many of them.'

Elizabeth laughed. 'You'll work it out, darling. You always do. We're here to help you as we've always been. We trust you, Rachael, and we trust your instincts. You'll do what's right. And if that's letting Joe into Declan's life?'

'Then that's what will happen.'

'But what about letting Joe back into *your* life?'

'I don't know,' Rachael wailed.

'How does Declan feel about Joe?'

'How many times did he mention Joe this evening?'

'Quite a few,' Elizabeth confessed.

'Then you hardly need to ask. Now that Joe's appeared out of the blue, Declan's eager to get to know him, and I can't say I blame him. I mean, he's almost fifteen. He's coming to that time in his life when I can't do much except just be there for him. I know he has Dad and it's wonderful that he's had a male influence throughout his life but…'

'This is his father, not his grandfather. I understand.' Elizabeth pulled her chair closer. 'And Joe? Does he want to get to know Declan?'

'I'm not sure. I'm pressuring him.'

'Is that wise?'

'Probably not. I just don't want Declan hurt. Joe either chooses to be part of his son's life or he doesn't. I won't have Declan stressed out about Joe. Not now. He's just got into this school and the last thing he needs is more stress.'

'He's much better at managing his anxiety now, and he's a bright boy.'

'And that concerns me more. It's because he's so smart that he might pick up on things an ordinary teenage boy would overlook. He's so sensitive.'

'There comes a time when you need to trust Declan to make his own decisions. He may decide that two weeks getting to know his father is all he wants, or all he needs for that matter.'

'I doubt that. Joe is…' Rachael shook her head and smiled absently. 'Joe is…encompassing. He can make you feel alive in a way you'd never thought possible. I don't know how he does it but he sort of taps into your inner soul and helps you to feel free.'

'Sounds amazing.'

'He is.'

'I think you need to let Declan and Joe work it out for themselves. Just promise me one thing, darling.'

'What?'

'That you'll try to live in the present. Don't rehash the past over and over. It's easy to get caught in the cycle but there's still an attraction between you and Joe. Remember to look forwards, not backwards.'

Rachael thought about her mother's words long into the night. When Joe had almost kissed her she'd felt as exhilarated as she had all those years ago. He'd always made her feel…wonderful, special and cherished, and for a brief moment tonight those feelings had been there again.

A spark of hope ignited deep inside her and, clinging to it, she finally drifted off to sleep.

Rachael looked at her list of patients. Five more to go and her second day at Joe's practice was done. Only eight more days and she was finished. She'd dressed in a pair of black trousers, flat-heeled shoes and a casual red knit top. If Joe didn't wear a suit to work, she'd decided that she didn't need to wear one either. Comfortable, professional. That was her wardrobe anyway, but it was nice not to have to worry about a certain level of clothing formality as she'd had to at her previous practice.

So far today she'd seen three pregnant women and several children, two of whom had required immunisations. She'd called the hospital that morning and had spoken to Ethel who told her Alwyn's condition was improving.

'His cardiac specialist is quite impressed with his recovery so far, but said he'll know better tomorrow morning.'

'That's great news. Do you mind if I call tomorrow for another update?'

'You don't need to ask, dear. If it wasn't for you and Dr Silvermark…well, I don't even want to think about it.'

'We were just doing our job.'

'Well, I'm grateful, deary. You take care of him now. He's quite a catch and it's quite clear you have eyes only for each other.'

It was? 'I'll speak to you tomorrow,' Rachael replied, and rang off. Was it clear? Could complete strangers see the attraction she and Joe felt for each other? She hadn't seen him all day and part of her felt slightly bereft while the other part knew it was for the best to keep her distance.

Rachael read through the file on her next patient—a little boy who'd seen Alison a few times about tummy pains. He'd been tried on liquid paraffin to help bowel motions, but the pains were still continuing. Alison had already had a white-cell count done to check for appendicitis, but the tummy pain was generally on the left rather than the right side. Alison had also noted little Anthony Edmunds was a tantrum-thrower and, if he wasn't watched could end up with a hernia. Rachael stood and went to call him through. 'Anthony.'

The little boy looked at her and then buried himself in his mother's lap. 'No.'

Rachael went over. 'Hello, Anthony. I'm Dr Rachael. How old are you?' She sat down beside his mother.

'He's almost four.'

'Wow. You're so big.' When she received no response from him, she glanced at his mother. 'What can I do for you today?'

'Out here?' His mother looked around. Rachael followed her gaze. There were only two other people in the waiting room, and as they were both above the age of ten and had no children in tow, she deduced they were Joe's patients. She guessed he was here after all.

'To start with.'

'He keeps saying his tummy's sore. I brought him to see Alison two weeks ago but things aren't getting better.'

'OK.' Rachael turned her attention to her small patient. 'Anthony, did you see this book?' Rachael pulled the book off the small table. 'It's a story about a funny puppy. Do you like puppies?'

The little boy looked over his shoulder. 'No.'

'Oh.' She appeared disappointed. 'I guess you won't like this story, then. I'll just read it to myself.' Rachael opened the book and began to read out loud, holding it in such a way that Anthony could just see the pictures. Regardless of the other patients in the room and the fact that Helen was watching her closely, Rachael kept reading and slowly Anthony edged over, listening intently to what she was saying. By the end of the story he was actually leaning his elbow on Rachael's leg, pointing to the pictures.

'That was fun. Would you like to choose another story?' Without a word he quickly reached for a book about cars. 'Ah, so you're a car man. You're just like my son.' Being careful not to let him know he'd come out of his mood, she held out her hand. 'Come and sit on my knee and we'll read it together.'

Anthony clambered up onto her knee and sat enthralled as she read the story. She was pleased when he joined in with the *brm-brm* sounds she was making. 'You're good at that.' When they'd finished that book, she asked Anthony to choose another one. He did and held it out to her. 'Let's go and read this one somewhere else.' She held out her hand for the little boy to take.

'What a good idea,' his mother said, and stood.

Anthony hesitated for a fraction of a second before slipping his hand into hers, holding his other hand out for his mother. It was then Rachael realised she'd really had an audience while she'd been focused on Anthony. Both of Joe's patients were still sitting in the waiting room and Joe was leaning casually against the reception desk where Helen was beaming brightly at her.

'Good work,' Joe said softly as they passed him. Rachael felt pride sweep over her at his praise. Why could he still do that to her? It wasn't fair that he should be able to affect her so easily.

Rachael continued with the consultation and after sitting Anthony up on the examination bed and reading the next story to him, she was finally able to get him to lie down so she could check his stomach.

'Has he been going to the toilet regularly?'

'Yes.'

'Bowel motions?'

'He's still having a little trouble.'

Rachael could feel that for herself. Anthony's bowels were quite tight.

'How's his appetite?'

'He hasn't been eating as much as he usually does.'

'And the liquid paraffin? Has that been helping?'

'Alison only said to give it to him when he hadn't had bowel motions for three days. He had one yesterday.'

'It can't have been a big one.' Anthony was still looking at the pictures in the book she'd just read him. Gently, she probed his tummy once more. 'Does this hurt, Anthony?'

'Nope.'

'How about here?' She gradually made her way from the right side to the left.

'Nope.'

'Here?' She pressed and he winced in pain.

'Ow. That weally hurts.' His lower lip came out and Rachael immediately smiled at him.

'Thank you for telling me. What a brave boy you are. Would you like to sit up now?' She helped him up. 'Did you see those great toys over there?'

'I played with them last time.'

'Do you want to play with them again?' She helped him down from the examination table as she spoke. Once he was settled, she gestured that his mother should have a seat.

'Has he been crying more or having tantrums?'

'No more than usual,' his mother answered.

'How many tantrums would you say he has a week?'

'Two.' His mother shrugged. 'He's just like other boys his age.'

Rachael smiled, noting the defensive tone. 'You're right, but in Anthony's case those upsets are affecting his bowels. What about diet? Does he eat a lot of fibre? Fruit, breads, cereals?'

'He doesn't like them. I've tried several different types of cereals but he just doesn't like them. He'll eat sandwiches and I buy the white bread which is supposed to be high in fibre.'

'Good. Fruit or vegetables?'

'No. I've tried everything to get him to eat them but he just doesn't like them.'

'What type of foods does he like?'

'Junk food. He'll eat chips—as in French fries—and, as I've said, sandwiches.'

'Biscuits? You can buy biscuits with wheat in them.'

'Tried that. He doesn't like them.'

'Prunes? Dried fruits?'

'No.'

Rachael wrote some notes. 'What about a fever? Has he been overly hot or had a temperature? Chills?'

'He was very hot last night, that's why I had to bring him back in today.'

'Did you take his temperature?'

'He wouldn't hold the thermometer under his tongue.'

'OK.' Rachael reached for her timpani thermometer and walked over to Anthony. 'I'm just going to put this into your ear.'

'Does it tickle?' he wanted to know, and by the time he'd asked the question, the thermometer had beeped, giving Rachael the readout. 'Hey, dat didn't hurt.'

'No, it didn't. That's because you're a big, brave boy.' She returned to her desk. 'It's just a bit above normal. Did you give him anything to bring the temperature down?'

'Just paracetamol.'

'Good. I've read in Anthony's notes that Alison has done some tests. I'd like to do a few more.'

'Such as?'

Rachael smiled apologetically. 'Nothing he's going to like, I'm afraid. I noticed Alison did a stool sample about a month and a half ago. I'd like another one done, as well as a urine test.'

'What do you think it might be?'

'Alison's ruled out appendicitis but because Anthony's still having trouble it's definitely something to do with his bowels. That could be diverticulosis, diverticulitis or he could be on his way to a hernia. The tantrums he's having may be causing the bowel to twist, but then again he could be having the tantrums because that's the only way he knows to effectively communicate that he's in a lot of pain. The other test I'd like him to have is a barium enema.'

'That doesn't sound good.'

'It's not. It's where they put a liquid paste into the rectum and lower colon so when they X-ray the stomach, the information is more accurate.'

'Won't it hurt him?'

'He'll be given a sedative as they also need him to be still while the X-ray is being performed.'

Rachael watched the look of astonishment on the mother's face. 'I can call Dr Silvermark in if you'd like a second opinion.'

'Yes, please.'

'Good.' Rachael checked which number she was supposed to call to get Joe's consulting room, and in another moment he picked up the phone. 'Joe, have you got a minute? I need a second opinion.'

'On the little boy?'

'Yes.'

'Give me two minutes.'

Rachael hung up the phone. 'He'll be here in a moment.'

'You're not angry?'

'About what?'

'About me questioning you...wanting another opinion.'

'No. Not only would that be highly unprofessional of me, it's also quite natural. I'm new here and I'm not giving you news you're comfortable with, so naturally you'd want my opinion confirmed.' Rachael smiled. 'Besides, if it were my son, I'd be wanting a second opinion. Bowels are a sensitive area and so many things can go wrong, but if caught early we can do something about it. By you bringing Anthony in now, I'm pretty sure he's going to be fine.'

Joe knocked on her door and came in. Anthony was just as hesitant to have another person touching his stomach, and after Joe was finished he began to cry. 'It feels as though there's a little bump on the left and it's very tender,' he said. 'I'm not sure what tests Alison has already done but I'd want a blood test, stool and urine samples and X-ray.' Joe added, 'How does that compare with your diagnosis, Dr Cusack?'

'You're spot on,' Anthony's mother said as she cradled her son. 'Thank you.'

'OK.' Joe smiled. 'I'll leave you in Dr Cusack's capable hands, then.' He excused himself and left the room.

'That man has a potent smile,' she muttered to Rachael. 'I've never really had much to do with him before but my husband's seen him and is quite confident about him.'

'Are you happy for me to go ahead and organise the tests?'

'Yes.' Anthony had started to settle down again and Rachael printed off the necessary pathology and X-ray request forms, explaining the procedure to his mother.

'Come and see me next week when we should have all the test results back and we can go from there.'

'In the meantime?'

'You need to get more fibre into him.' She pulled open a cupboard that contained pamphlets on a multitude of topics and handed over the one on dietary fibre. 'This contains a list of foods high in fibre and also ways to prepare them so children will eat them. Also, put him back on the liquid paraffin.' Rachael wrote down the dosages Anthony's mother was to follow for the next week. 'If you have any questions, don't hesitate to call.'

'Thank you.'

Anthony didn't want to leave but was pacified by Rachael promising to read him a story the next time he came and the lolly she gave him for being such a good boy.

Once they were gone, Rachael went to the kitchen for a much-needed cup of coffee.

'You were brilliant with him,' Joe said as he walked in. Rachael stirred her coffee and took a quick sip, hoping it would give her strength. She certainly needed all she could get when she was around Joe. Today he was dressed in a pair of black jeans and a black T-shirt with a chambray shirt hanging open like a jacket. Why did he have to look so good? She pushed her frustrated libido away, deciding her best course of action was to hightail it out of there.

'Thanks.' She washed the spoon and picked up her coffee. 'I'd better get back to it.'

'Hey, listen, Rach.' He put out a hand to stop her and she quickly moved away, almost spilling her coffee. 'Uh…is Declan coming here after school again today?'

'Yes.'

'When's that?'

She checked her watch. 'In about fifteen minutes. Why?'

'Well…I…er…thought I might take him with me to the studio this afternoon.'

'Weren't you there this morning?'

'Yes, but they have an afternoon shoot—call-back.'

'Call-back?'

'A stunt they did the other day didn't go as planned, so they're taking another crack at it.'

'What sort of movie is it?'

'Action sci-fi.'

'Hmm.' She sipped her drink. 'And you want to take Declan.'

'Yes. I just wanted to clear it with you first. I could show him around, he could see a different side to medicine rather than just clinics and hospitals.'

Rachael knew his words were just a cover. It was Joe's way of saying he wanted to spend time with his son. Why he didn't come right out and say it she wasn't sure, but things weren't always straightforward where Joe was concerned.

'OK, but not for too long.'

'Sure. Tell me what time you want him back at the hotel and I'll drop him off.'

'Actually, I'll come to you and pick him up.'

'Right. Good. I'll clear it with the security guard for you.'

'I'd appreciate it. I'll come once I've finished here.'

'That doesn't give us long.'

'How long do you want, Joe?' she asked pointedly.

'I can't answer that just yet.' He held up his hand when she opened her mouth. 'Don't pressure me, Rach. You'll get your answer, but at least let me spend a bit of one-on-one time with him.'

'How about dinner, then? The three of us?'

He hesitated and Rachael bit her lip. Had she pushed him too far…again? 'If you have other plans, we understand. We're hardly here to cramp your romantic style.'

'What?' He frowned. 'Romantic style?' A slow smile spread across his mouth as he realised she was not so subtly fishing. 'I'm not dating anyone, if that's what you're trying to get at.'

'Well, I should hope not, especially after you almost kissed me last night.'

'Hmm.' The smile deepened and he took a step towards her. She stood her ground but held her coffee cup between them. 'Now that I know you're not married, do you want to pick up where we left off?'

'Do you mean from last night or from fifteen years ago, Joe? Because my life has changed considerably in fifteen years and I'm no longer so naïve that I'll fall for the smooth lines you dish out.'

The uncomfortable twitch of his left eye was the only outward sign that she'd riled him. *'Touché.'* He stepped back. 'In that case, I'll leave you to your work and I'll see you later.'

Rachael sat at her desk a little later and shook her head. She was going to have to figure out how to deal with the way Joe made her feel. If he decided he wanted to be a part of Declan's life, she would be seeing quite a bit of him from now on. How would she cope if some other woman did come into his life—a new stepmother for Declan?

'Whoa!' She cut her thoughts off like a stylus sliding along a vinyl record. She stood up and paced her office. 'Don't go there. Declan will be fine. He's a smart boy, well adjusted. Joe's only taking him to a studio where everything is perfectly safe and he'll be fine. You'll pick him up, the three of you will have dinner and then Joe will tell you his decision. It's OK. Everything is OK.'

She did some deep breathing and almost jumped out of her skin when there was a knock at the door. She called for whoever it was to come in.

'Hi, Mum.' Declan peered around the door.

'It's OK. I don't have a patient here.' He came further into the room and kissed her. 'You're earlier today.'

He shrugged. 'The teacher let us out early.'

'Good. Good. Uh…honey, Joe wants to take you out.'

'Really? He does?'

She tried not to get too concerned about the look of disbelieving pleasure on her son's face. 'Sure, then I'll come and pick you up and the three of us will have dinner.' It did occur to her that Joe hadn't actually agreed to dinner, but tough luck. He was lumbered with the two of them whether he liked it or not.

'Awesome. Can I leave my bag here?'

'Of course. I'll bring it later.'

'You're the greatest, Mum. I'm going to tell Helen.' And with that, he rushed off.

Once more Rachael forced herself to remain under control. It was all right. Declan had gone out with other people plenty of times. He'd gone to lots of different places with his friends back in Cairns. He'd gone out with her parents and had spent time away from her on school camps, so why was she so worried about a few hours with his father?

The answer came hard on the question's heels. Because Joe had the power to hurt him.

Rachael continued to go through the calming exercises she'd been using for years and finally called her next patient through. The sooner she finished here, the sooner she could head out to the studio to see exactly what it was Joe did when he wasn't here.

Her last few patients seemed to want to chat and she finished over an hour later than she was supposed to. She took the patient files out to Helen and was thankful when the other woman didn't keep her talking.

'Go and see how the boys are getting on.'

'Try and stop me,' she muttered, heading out to her car. She followed the directions to the studio Helen had handed her, and was pleased to find there was no problem about her wandering around in the area roped off to tourists. The theme park was a place she wanted to return to, but for now she had other matters on her mind…namely finding her son.

'Excuse me,' she said, stopping a man who wore an official-looking badge on a chain around his neck. 'I'm looking for Joe Silvermark.'

'Ah, Joe. Joe's through here.' The man led her into a large hangar. To Rachael's surprise it contained several sets and equipment.

'Have you finished for the day?'

'We've nailed one scene but the major stunt is after dinner. Mind the cables.' He took her through the building. 'Have you known Joe long?'

'Well…' She glanced at his badge again. 'Er…Wong, it's a long story.'

'You the boy's mother?' Wong nodded, answering his own question. 'Of course. You're very beautiful. I can see why Joe likes you and why he needed to pound his frustrations out on the punching bag.' Wong chuckled to himself. 'They're out here.' They continued to the other side of the hangar and came out the other end. 'Over there.'

Wong pointed to a large crane set up on the back lot. Rachael's eyes took a moment to adjust to being back out in the daylight. 'They'll be down in a minute.' Wong smiled at his own joke, and as he spoke she saw a person jump off the crane.

Her heart leapt into her throat before she realised the person was bungee jumping. Down—then back up, and then down again. It was then she realised Joe was the person doing the human yo-yo impersonation.

'Oh, my gosh. I can't believe he just did that.' She placed her hand on her chest, surprised to find it pounding hard.

'Joe? He's done it thousands of times. He's just trying to give the boy confidence.'

'*Boy?* What *boy*?' Rachael squinted as she peered up to the top of the crane. There was a small platform there, and to her complete horror she realised the figure standing up there, waiting to jump, was her son.

'Declan!' His name came out in a terrified whisper.

CHAPTER FOUR

'JOSEPH MITCHELL SILVERMARK!'

Rachael had waited while Joe had been hoisted back up to the top and had had his bungee cord removed. As Joe had climbed back down the ladder, the anger in her was ready to burst. She stormed over to her ex-husband.

'Rach! You're earlier than we expected.' If it was possible for him to blanch, she was sure he did.

'You get him down from there this instant.'

'He's all right, Rach. He *wants* to do it.'

'He suffers from anxiety and stress, Joe. Didn't I tell you that? He might be freaking out right now and—'

'If he changes his mind, it's fine. He can come down the normal way.'

'I can't believe you've done this. You've been with him for a few hours and you're already putting him in danger.'

'Rachael—'

'No, Joe. Don't you ''Rachael'' me. If he ends up with nightmares tonight, *I'm* the one who'll be looking after him.'

'Nightmares? Rachael, he's almost fifteen.'

'And that just shows how much you know about him. You don't think ahead, Joe. You just go with whatever whim you—'

'Ready,' a bloke called out and Rachael was paralysed to the spot as she heard a cry.

'Three, two, one, *bungee*!'

'I think I'm going to be sick,' she muttered, and felt her knees weaken. Joe's arm came about her shoulders and she leaned into him, not wanting to watch but unable to take her eyes off her son for an instant. Declan hesitated and then jumped off—flying down towards them with his arms out wide.

She was positive the rope wasn't going to stop him. Positive he was going to hit the ground with a thud and break every bone in his body—at the least.

But just as had happened with Joe, the rope caught him like a giant spring and sent him back up again. She didn't even want to contemplate the damage that might be done to his spine, being jerked around like that.

'He's fine, Rach. Breathe. Breathe.' Joe's words penetrated her head and she belatedly sucked air into her lungs. 'See. He's fine.' Joe squeezed her shoulder before running over to where Declan's bounce was practically at an end.

Rachael watched as her son was hoisted back to the top before he was unhooked. Joe had climbed the steps once more to be there for his son. She watched as Declan wrapped his arms around Joe and the almost hesitant way Joe put his arms around his son for the first time.

A lump formed in her throat and she closed her eyes against the tears that were threatening to overflow. When she opened them it was to find them both climbing down the steps, and when her son's feet were safely back on terra firma, Rachael let out a deep sigh.

Declan rushed over and threw his arms about her shoulders. 'Mum! Mum! Wasn't that amazing?' His face was alive with an exuberant delight Rachael had never seen before. He couldn't stand still and reminded her of when he'd been a little boy and had desperately needed to go to the toilet. 'Wow! I can't believe I just did that.' He let out a loud whoop which made her jump. 'So cool.' He turned to face his father.

'That was the best. You were right, Joe. How cool!'

Joe looked at Rachael. 'See? He's fine.'

But are you? Rachael wanted to ask him. She could see a hint of stunned bewilderment in Joe's gaze at the way Declan had embraced him. Would he ever get used to the affectionate ways of their son? She certainly hoped so because if he didn't, it could destroy Declan.

'What's next?' Declan asked, and Joe laughed.

'That's it for tonight, mate. I think your mother's had enough surprises over the last forty-eight hours.' He leaned closer to Declan and said in a lower voice, 'And I'm trying to get back into her good books.'

'Really?' Rachael knew she was supposed to hear the comment and could see the teasing glint in Joe's blue eyes. 'Why would you want to do that, Joe?'

'Ah, trade secret. Right now, though…' he rubbed his hands together in delight '…it's time for dinner. Unfortunately, I need to stay close to the studio as we haven't finished and will probably be going for a few more hours, but if you don't mind eating with the rest of the cast and crew, there's a great feast put on just over there.' He pointed towards another large hangar.

'Cool. Are the actors going to be there?'

Joe nodded.

Declan looked at his mother. 'Can we? *Please?* Joe told me who the lead actor is, and he's the same guy from the movie we watched last night, Mum. And he's just through there.' Declan pointed to the hangar. 'Can we, Mum? *Please?* I promise I'll do my homework the instant we get back to the hotel. *Please?*'

It had been so many years since Declan had pleaded for anything that Rachael was inclined to give in right there and then. She looked at Joe and then back at her son. Both were wearing identical expressions, just like small children who really wanted to open their Christmas presents early. She couldn't help it and burst out laughing, feeling the tension of the past few days ease out of her.

'Does that mean yes?' Declan asked.

'All right, but so long as we're not intruding?'

'Yes!' Declan pumped the air with his fist before leaning over to kiss her cheek. 'You're the greatest.'

Joe leaned over and kissed her other cheek. 'You *are* the greatest.' He looked at his son. 'Let's go eat.'

Declan linked his arm through his mother's on one side and Joe followed suit on the other. Between the two of them, she was almost propelled into the room where there seemed to be hundreds of people sitting at tables, eating and laughing. The noise was so loud she thought she'd need earplugs. Joe found them a table and then took Declan over to meet the lead actors. Rachael watched Joe, his chest puffed out proudly as he introduced his son. She actually saw the words 'my son' form on Joe's lips and sighed with relief. Joe had accepted Declan.

He motioned for her to come over but she felt too self-conscious and shook her head. She liked watching the two of them together and was still astounded at the similarities. Joe had been nineteen when they'd met, and that's how old Declan would be in just over four years' time. They had the same physique, although Declan was still a miniature version, his shoulders not as broad, his height less...but she knew he'd get there. She'd known from the instant she'd first held her son that he was going to be as devastatingly handsome as his father.

Rachael closed her eyes, praying she'd done the right thing by letting Declan get to know Joe. Would Joe hurt him the way he'd hurt her? She had no idea but, whatever happened, both she and Declan would work it out…somehow.

She opened her eyes and discovered they'd gone. She quickly scanned the room and found them at the large buffet, loading food onto their plates, both of them laughing. When had Declan last been this animated? She couldn't remember. For the past few years since he'd started high school, he'd been very serious, very dedicated to his work and sometimes pushing himself way too hard. Sure, they'd joked and laughed but not like this.

They headed over, both carrying trays loaded with food. 'Here's one for you,' Declan said, handing her a plate. 'I wasn't sure whether you liked prawns but Joe told me you did.'

'Well, she *used* to.' His gaze met Rachael's and she felt her heart rate increase with delighted excitement. He was looking at her as though he'd just won the lottery and didn't have a clue what to do with the winnings. Was that look for her? Was it because of Declan? Either way, it was creating havoc with her equilibrium. The smile on his lips was small yet intimate—she remembered it well.

'He's right. I do like them.'

'Oh. Can I try one?'

'Sure.' Rachael was pleasantly surprised that her son was willing to try a new food.

'But if you like it, you can get your own,' Joe added, pinching one off Rachael's plate and showing him how to shell the prawn.

'Delicious. We should have these at least once a week, Mum.' Declan was out of his chair and heading to the buffet again.

Rachael laughed in astonishment. 'Once a week. Oh, sure, son,' she said to his retreating back.

Joe joined in her laughter. 'I guess he doesn't have any idea how much they cost.'

'So?'

'So, what?'

'Joe. You've obviously decided you want to get to know Declan better, but for how long?'

He shrugged. 'I don't know, Rach. He's a great kid.'

'No argument there, and you've only spent a few hours with him.'

Joe stole another prawn off her plate.

'Hey! Get your own.' She slapped playfully at his hand but he was too quick for her. 'I will say that Declan has many moods.' She grinned at him. 'Just like his father.' Joe merely raised his eyebrows and continued peeling the prawn. 'I think it's wise for you to spend time with him but I reiterate what I said yesterday—I won't have him hurt.'

'I agree with you.' He ate the seafood and wiped his fingers on a napkin. 'I hardly slept last night.'

'Join the club.' Declan returned with a huge plateful of food. 'Declan!'

'It's all right, Mum. Ivan—he's the cook up there—said I could take whatever I wanted, especially as I was Joe's son. He said that Joe saved his life a few years ago and he thinks he's the best person in the world.'

They both looked at Joe who seemed highly uncomfortable with the praise. He shrugged. 'It's just the job. Ivan used to be a stuntman and he was in a bad accident and… You know the drill, Rach. As doctors, we do what it takes.'

Rachael nodded but wasn't surprised to find such high praise about the man sitting opposite her. 'So you've been doing this movie work for some time now?'

'Five years. It's not full-time, only when there's a movie being shot here, and that's usually once every six months. It also depends on the number of stunts they do. Sometimes we're here, sometimes we're on location.'

'So you share your time between here and the clinic for six months, and the other six months?'

He smiled. 'I'm full-time at the clinic.'

'So for six months you work like a normal person and for the other six months you get to play around on a movie set, eating copious amounts of food.'

Joe grinned. 'Fringe benefits.' He shrugged nonchalantly. 'There's not much to my life at all. No dramas, no excitement. Boring ol' Joe, that's me.'

She laughed, not believing a word he said. 'Your nonchalance gives you away every time, Joe.' It was one of his defensive weapons but she'd broken through it before. When he was doing something nice for someone and he didn't want anyone to know about it, nonchalance was his best friend. Joe didn't think he warranted praise about Ivan and she understood his comment about just doing his job, but sometimes people went above and beyond the call of duty.

Although, she reflected, he hadn't been nonchalant on the day he'd asked for the annulment. That had been how she'd known he'd been serious. At first she'd thought he'd been joking, then defensive, then pushing her away for some reason, but in the end—as he'd stood firm in his convictions—she'd realised he hadn't really wanted her for anything but sex.

Rachael pushed the thought away. Now was definitely not the time. Looking down at her plate, she realised she'd eaten far more than she'd thought and now felt a little queasy. She glanced across at Declan's plate and was surprised to find him almost finished. 'Where do you put it all?' she asked rhetorically, smiling at her son.

'I'm a growing kid, Mum.'

'Don't go overboard on the prawns. I don't want you getting stomachache.'

'Spoken like a true mother,' Declan teased, and they laughed.

A bell rang, startling her.

'What's that?' Declan asked the question on her lips.

'Five more minutes and we're to be back on set.'

'Can we stay?' Again, her son's imploring blue gaze was settled on her.

'Actually, it might be fun to watch,' Joe said. 'We're filming a stunt.'

'Do the actors do them?' Declan asked.

'Sometimes, but not tonight. This one's too dangerous.'

'But not for the stunt team, right?' His boyish eyes were wide with unrepressed excitement.

Joe smiled. 'That's right. Wong—you met him earlier—is the stunt coordinator and he and his team are going to jump a car between two trucks.'

'Sounds dangerous.' Rachael frowned.

'There's an element of danger in all stunts, Rach. Wong and his team have rehearsed the stunt and calculated everything down to the nth degree.'

'Accidents do happen, though, Joe.'

'Yes, they do, and that's why I'm here. Tonight there will also be the fire brigade and at least one ambulance on set. All precautions are taken and we all know what jobs we need to do.'

'Maybe we'd better not stay.' She watched as Declan's face fell.

'If you think you're going to be in the way, don't. I wouldn't let you stay if I thought that.'

Rachael checked her watch, admitting she was curious as well. Declan once more wore his pleading face. 'OK, but not for long.'

'You're the greatest, Mum.' He smiled at her in that familiar way which she knew would someday have the women melting at his feet—just like his father.

They finished eating and made their way back with the rest of the cast and crew. They headed in the opposite direction from where they had been before, and soon found themselves on a back lot which was a huge piece of tarmac. She was surprised to find how dark it had become while they'd been eating, but the back lot was lit with enormous spotlights, ensuring everyone could see quite clearly what was going on.

Rachael was fascinated as she watched the second unit director and Wong give last-minute instructions to the stunt team. There were people everywhere, manning cameras, rigging explosions, taping down cables, all working together towards one common goal.

Joe took Rachael and Declan over to the medical section and reintroduced them to Smitty and his ambulance colleague.

'A lovely surprise to see you again so soon,' Smitty said to Rachael as he shook her hand, holding it for a fraction of a second longer than was necessary. Joe glared daggers at him.

'Easy, Joe.' Smitty laughed. 'And this is your son, eh? You and Joe?' He raised an interested eyebrow.

'Yes.' Rachael felt no need to explain as it really wasn't any of the paramedic's business.

'The resemblance is as plain as day.'

'That's what everyone says.' Declan smiled proudly.

Rachael turned to Joe. 'So what's going to happen here?'

Joe pointed out to the tarmac where two semi-trailers were parked—a small gap between the rear of one and the front of the other. 'We're going to jump a car through the gap between the trucks.'

'Are the trucks going to be moving?' Declan asked.

'No. They will be in the movie but that part's already been shot. This is just the camera angles of the jump between the trucks.'

'There are cameras in there?'

'They have cameras everywhere. When we're doing a stunt like this, sometimes you only get one crack at it. The more cameras they have rolling, covering the different angles, the easier it is for the directors and producers to choose which ones they need.'

'There's a fire truck over there.' Declan pointed to where two men were dressed in full firefighting gear.

'As I said, all safety angles are covered.'

'But plenty of people have suffered severe injuries as well as being killed during stunts,' Rachael pointed out.

'Surprisingly, not as many as you'd think, and nine times out of ten the people who have died while doing stunts either didn't work out the angles correctly or didn't take the necessary safety precautions. Sometimes producers cut corners to meet their budget constraints, which means not enough money to do the stunt properly. Sometimes the stunt people involved aren't as qualified as they make out. Wong knows every single person on his team and knows exactly what they're capable of. He's highly sought-after for a lot of action films, and at the moment I think he's booked solid for the next four years.'

Rachael was surprised. 'What? One movie after another?'

'That's his job, Rach.' She shook her head, quite bemused.

'The actors are booked for longer than that. The guy who's playing the lead in this movie has his shooting schedule worked out for the next six years.'

'Wow! That's amazing.' Rachael and Declan watched this alien world with continued amazement.

Wong headed over to them. 'Joe, you set?'

'All ready. How's it looking?'

'Good. Almost ready to go.' He looked at Rachael. 'There are going to be loud explosions so cover your ears, OK? You, too.' He pointed to Declan. 'Got to take care of Joe's family.'

Rachael smiled at him, deciding to ignore his last remark. 'Thanks for the warning.' Wong headed back and Joe pulled on a headset so he could listen to what was going on.

'Joe? Where are the explosions?' Rachael asked, peering closely at the vehicles.

Joe pointed to the truck in the rear. 'In there. The truck explodes in the movie.'

'Why?'

'Because someone has just shot a missile at the car and that's why the car is jumping between the trucks, and the missile hits the second truck instead.'

'Oh.' Rachael frowned. 'What about the poor truck driver?'

Joe laughed. 'What truck driver?'

'In the movie. What about the truck driver?'

'The truck driver isn't important to the story.'

'But does he get out in time? Is he hurt?'

Joe smiled. 'I don't know, but if it makes you feel any better, I'll raise your concerns with the director and find out.'

'Thank you.' She couldn't help the tingles that spread through her from his smile. It really was lethal.

'Ready on the set.' The call came and Rachael reached for Declan's hand, giving it an excited squeeze. She watched him for a second and again saw animated delight on his face. She was thankful to Joe for giving him this experience…even if it meant Declan would hardly sleep tonight.

'Quiet on the set,' came the next call, and Declan dropped his mother's hand to watch intently. Rachael shifted out of his way and turned to glance at Joe, only to find him watching her. She hadn't realised just how close they were to each other. Joe took a step closer and she could feel the warmth emanating from his body.

His gaze seemed to devour her and she gasped at the intensity she saw in his blue depths. Her heart rate doubled in an instant and a flood of excitement ripped through her. She tried to swallow but found her mouth dry and licked her lips.

He groaned when her tongue flicked out and he embraced the instant tightening in his gut. His gaze flicked to her lips and the need to have them pressed against his was overwhelming. He wasn't used to these sensations any more and she'd been the only woman who had ever made him feel this way. Her lips were still parted in anticipation—he could almost taste her.

'Rach.' The deep timbre of his voice made her tremble in a way she thought she'd never experience again. 'You drive me crazy.'

'Mmm.' She was incapable of forming rational or even irrational sentences. All that mattered was the way Joe made her feel. She was alive—truly alive for the first time in fifteen years. How would he react when he learned there had been no other? That he was her one and only true love? He'd hurt, humiliated and rejected her, yet for some masochistic reason she'd remained in love with him and knew it was a love which would last for ever.

He shifted ever so slightly, coming to stand behind her. No longer holding her gaze, he looked unseeingly out at what was happening on the set. She did the same, not really seeing a thing but instead focusing on the way he made her feel.

She gasped again and bit her lip as their fingers touched. The slight roughness of his skin tingled against her soft hands as he tenderly refamiliarised himself with that one small part of her. His arm brushed against her body, sending shocks of pleasure through her.

He laced his fingers with hers, squeezed her hand and her desire grew. He was touching her. He wanted her. Her eyelids fluttered closed for a fraction of a second as she worked hard to control her outward expression. He shifted closer, his body brushing her shoulder. She couldn't breathe but it didn't seem to matter. All she needed was him, and right now she had him.

'I can't take it.' The words were whispered for only him to hear.

'I know. You drive me insane. You always have.'

'Joe.'

'I need you.'

'I know.'

The director called 'Action' over a loudspeaker which made her jump, her back pressing into Joe's. He dropped her hand to steady her, his enigmatic scent winding itself around her. Both of them kept their gazes locked straight ahead, looking as though they were focusing on what was happening before them while all the time their bodies were conducting a completely different action sequence.

The car revved its engine then a squeal of tyres was heard, the smell of burning rubber filling the air. The stunt driver picked up speed, heading for the ramp that would help tip the car up on two wheels, not only to make it slim enough to fit between the two trucks but to also help get the car airborne.

A loud explosion shocked them both and they sprang apart like guilty teenagers, severing all contact. Joe was there one minute and gone the next, grabbing his emergency medical kit before he left. Rachael scanned the area wildly, trying to figure out what had happened. She turned to see Smitty and his colleague rushing over after Joe.

The scene played out before them in slow motion as she and Declan stood there, completely stunned as people yelled, people ran, everyone doing what they were supposed to be doing in order to fix whatever had gone wrong.

'Mum?' Declan reached for her and she held his hand. 'What happened?'

'I don't know, darling.'

The firefighters were heading towards where the car had now come to rest on its roof a long way off from where Joe had said it should land.

She scanned the area for Joe but couldn't find him.

'That car's lost a wheel.' Declan pointed to the stunt car. 'Where's the wheel?'

As Declan spoke, Rachael saw Joe crouch down beside someone and rip open his medical kit.

'Over there.' The food she'd eaten earlier churned in her stomach as she saw the wheel not far from where Joe was bending over his patient. He glanced over to where she and Declan were still standing and motioned for her to come over.

'Joe needs me.' She took a deep breath to calm her stomach, straightened her shoulders and put her professional face on. 'Stay here, Declan.'

'But, Mum…'

She thrust her bag at him. 'Call your grand-parents and ask them to come pick you up. I don't know how long I'll be here.'

'Can't I stay and help? I can help someone while I'm waiting, can't I? I can carry things, I can make drinks.'

'I don't know what the protocol is.' It was then she spotted Ivan, who'd served Declan that hefty helping of prawns. 'Excuse me,' she called, and he came over. 'Can you help us?'

'I want to help,' Declan said earnestly.

'I need to get to Joe.'

Ivan looked at the two of them. 'You go,' he said to Rachael. 'Come on, mate. You can help me. I'll take good care of Joe's son, you can be sure of that,' he promised.

Declan handed his mother back her bag. 'You call Grandma and I'll help out till she comes.'

Rachael nodded and quickly made the call, telling her mother to mention Joe's name to the security guard. Then she left her bag at the medical station and headed over to help.

'Declan OK?' Joe asked, as she knelt down beside him and pulled on a pair of gloves.

'He's fine.' Rachael turned her attention to their patient and gasped when she realised Joe's patient was his friend, Wong. 'Status?'

'Unconscious. BP's dropping. Pupils sluggish. Chest sounds tight. Airway's clear. He's bleeding somewhere but I'm not sure where. Check his legs.'

Rachael reached for a pair of heavy-duty scissors from Joe's kit and started cutting away Wong's jeans before beginning her examination. 'Left femur has lacerations, left tib-fib feels fractured. Right is fine.'

'Left femoral artery?'

Rachael took a closer look. 'Doesn't look like it.' Joe was setting up an IV drip as Smitty came over.

'Anything you need?'

'Need to intubate and get him out a.s.a.p.'

'I've called it in. Reinforcements are on their way.' Smitty rifled through Joe's extensively stocked medical kit, handing the equipment to Joe as he needed it.

'Checking abdomen,' Rachael said. She cut away Wong's shirt and both she and Smitty gasped. 'I'd say every rib is broken.'

'Did he get hit by the wheel?' Smitty was astounded as he secured a cervical collar around Wong's neck.

'Yes.' The one word from Joe was clipped yet full of emotion.

'Rino—ah, he's the stunt driver,' Smitty added for Rachael's benefit, 'feels to have fractured both legs. He's conscious, BP is slightly higher but that's to be expected. Collarbone doesn't feel too good either and he's probably got a case of whiplash, but he's had so many I think he's used to it. My partner's just fixing him up now.' Smitty paused for a breath. 'They've checked the car. The axle sheared right off.'

'And that's how the wheel came off?' Rachael asked, as she gently touched Wong's abdomen. 'The bleeding's internal. Smitty, get a bag of plasma going.'

The paramedic headed off and was back with the equipment they needed. He set up the plasma while Joe finished intubating Wong. Rachael took his vital signs again. 'BP still not good. Pupils still sluggish. Stay with us, Wong.'

'Let's get him ready to transfer.' Joe gave the order, firmly in control of the situation. He glanced at Rachael but the look on his face was that of a stranger. She'd received that look from him before—on the day of their annulment—and it was one that still had the ability to freeze her heart.

Her eyes widened in alarm and all the insecurities she'd thought she'd dealt with fifteen years ago came flooding back in that one instant. Why was he looking at her like that? She was here. She was helping. There was no cause for him to treat her this way. Her mind began to search through a list of reasons, the list she'd come up with all those years ago for him treating her the way he had, but at the moment she needed to focus on her job.

She pushed them away and they all went…all except one. The question started repeating itself over and over in her mind. It had refused to be pushed away fifteen years ago and it was refusing to go now.

What had she done wrong?

CHAPTER FIVE

'READY to transfer,' Smitty said.

Rachael found it hard to look at Joe as they did their job. She ripped off her gloves and rolled them up into a ball, glancing around for a bin.

'Over there.' Joe pointed when he realised what she was looking for. 'Smitty, take Wong. I'll get to the hospital as soon as the situation is stabilised here.'

Smitty nodded as he wheeled the patient towards the waiting ambulance. 'What's next?' she asked Joe, as he picked up his medical kit and carried it over to where the stunt driver was lying on the ground not far from the car wreck. They knelt down and pulled on gloves.

'Hi. I'm Rachael,' she said to both the patient and the two men with him. The patient had a blanket over him and when she lifted it, it was to find his shirt had already been cut open. He was wearing shorts and work boots—the costume the real actor would be wearing in the movie, she realised.

'This is Rino,' Joe said. 'What have you broken this time?' He smiled down at his friend as he started to check him out.

'Legs,' Rino said, his eyes still closed. 'How's Wong?'

Rachael knew whenever there was bad news to give, the easiest way was to come right out and say it. 'He's not good.'

Rino clenched his jaw and squeezed his eyes even tighter. 'Should have checked it out more thoroughly. It's my fault.'

'We all should have checked it out more thoroughly,' the other man sitting beside Rino said. 'How were we to know the axle was going to shear? We take every precaution possible, we check and double-check, but still things happen.'

'It's my fault,' Rino said again.

'Nah, mate. It's the manufacturer's fault for not testing the axle properly. There's no way we could have foreseen this happening,' Joe remarked.

Rachael checked Rino's pupils and was pleased to find them equal and reacting to light. She listened to his chest and took his blood pressure, which was slightly elevated—but that was to be expected.

'So you've been in a few accidents?' she remarked, as Joe drew up an injection of pethidine.

He smiled and opened his eyes. 'Yeah. Quite a few. Never had a doc as pretty as you look after me, though. It's nice to have a change from Joe's ugly mug.'

Rachael laughed.

'You're brave, saying such things when I'm holding a needle,' Joe countered.

'Pethidine?' Rachael queried quietly.

'He's allergic to morphine.' He indicated the Medic-Alert chain around Rino's neck and Rachael read it. Joe knew these people and she was glad he'd stayed, even though she knew he'd desperately wanted to go to the hospital to be with Wong.

'This should help until the ambulance arrives,' Joe said. 'Then we'll get you hooked up to an IV and a bag of plasma.'

'I know the drill.' Rino closed his eyes again. 'Every bone has been broken at one time or another.'

'Then I'd say you definitely know the drill.' Rachael and Joe checked his legs. 'Possible fractures to right tibia and fibula. Left doesn't feel as bad, except for the laceration above your knee. Can you wiggle your toes for me?' He could.

'Good. Do your legs feel funny, like they have pins and needles?'

'No. Spine doesn't feel broken.'

'Really?' she raised her eyebrows. 'When was the last time you broke it?'

'Two years ago,' Joe answered for him, a teasing note in his voice. 'He has volumes one and two in casenotes and X-ray packets at the hospital.'

'Everything's well documented, then,' Rachael commented. 'Good. We'll add a few more X-rays to the packet when we get there.'

'Just to be on the safe side,' Joe added.

Rachael continued checking his ribs. 'Right T4 and 5 don't feel good. Left side is good.' She felt her way to his collarbone. 'Clavicle is fractured on the right side.' She felt both shoulder joints, thankful they didn't feel dislocated. She made her way down his arm but couldn't feel anything. 'Wiggle your fingers for me.' He did. 'Squeeze my fingers.' He did. 'Good.'

The sound of the ambulance sirens could be heard. 'Sounds like your ride,' she told him. 'You have a bruise from the safety harness but thank goodness you were wearing it.'

'I'm safety conscious,' he remarked. 'We all are.'

'Joe told me that earlier.'

'Still didn't help,' Rino growled.

'You and I both know these things happen from time to time and it's no one's fault.'

'But Wong—'

'Wong is receiving the best medical attention, just as you will. Leave it for now.' Joe's words were final as he placed a bandage over the large laceration on Rino's left leg. 'It'll need stitches but this will hold you until you get to Accident and Emergency. Rach, do his obs again.'

As the ambulance arrived, Rachael looked over and saw her parents being directed by a security guard onto the back lot. They looked as lost as she'd felt when she'd first arrived. She glanced around for Declan but couldn't see him.

'I'll go to the next patient,' Joe said, also catching sight of her parents. 'Hand over to the paramedics and get Declan sorted out.'

Rachael nodded and did as he asked. She smiled down at Rino as he was loaded into the ambulance. 'Don't give the paramedics too much of a hard time, even though you know the drill.'

He smiled. 'I'll try not to.'

As the ambulance driver shut the doors, Rachael turned and looked around her, not sure where to go or what to do next. She spotted

Declan putting a blanket around someone and headed over.

'How are you holding up?' She put her arm around his waist.

'Yeah, good.' He looked around the lot and gave a satisfied nod. 'I just wish I knew more stuff, then I could help more.' He frowned for a moment before looking at her. 'I want to be a doctor, Mum.'

Rachael's eyes widened in surprise. 'Really?'

'Why so surprised? You're a doctor. Joe's a doctor.' He shrugged in that self-conscious way she recognised so well.

Rachael squeezed him closer. 'That's great, Dec. It's great that you've got a direction…just as long as you're making the decision for the right reasons.'

'I want to help people.'

Rachael nodded seriously. 'OK. We'll check out what the entry requirements are for university and go from there.' She kissed his cheek. 'I'm so proud of you.'

'Mum! Not here.' He shrugged out of her embrace but she wasn't offended. 'Look, Grandma and Grandad are here.'

'I saw.' She looked over to where the security guard was talking to one of the crew. Rachael met her mother's gaze and beckoned them over. The security guard looked hesitant but then the crew member pointed to Declan. The security guard peered at Declan for a moment before nodding knowingly. Rachael smiled.

'I didn't think we'd ever find you,' Elizabeth said, kissing her daughter's cheek. 'Thank goodness Declan looks like Joe, otherwise I'm sure the security guard thought we were trying to gatecrash the film shoot rather than just trying to collect our grandson.'

'Come in handy, do I?' Declan smiled.

'Sounds reasonable,' her father added. 'All right, Declan. Let's get you home.'

'Is my homework in your car, Mum?'

'Yes, but don't worry too much about it tonight, Dec.' Rachael smiled up at him. 'Just try and unwind. OK?'

He shrugged. 'Sure, Mum.'

'Thanks for your help, Dr Declan.' Declan's grin was instantaneous and he even blushed a little.

'I'll just get my bag so I can give you my keys. I'll need to go to the hospital with Joe once we're finished here, so if you can take my car back to your house now, that will help. I'll get Joe to drop me there later.' She also wanted to confront Joe about those looks he'd been giving her.

'When can we expect you?' Elizabeth asked.

'I have no idea. Depends how long things take at the hospital.'

'All right, dear.'

As they left, she looked around for Joe and headed over once she'd spotted him. 'Need any help?' she asked.

'All stable here,' he remarked, not looking up as he finished bandaging a woman's arm. 'Go home and rest,' he told his patient. 'Take paracetamol six-hourly and call me if you have any problems.'

'Are you sure I can't just spend the night in hospital? My husband's going to be watching over me as I sleep. He's such a worry wart.'

Joe laughed. 'It's probably good if you're monitored tonight and I'm sure your husband would do an excellent job, but I'm not expecting any complications from your arm. They're all textbook injuries.'

'Thanks, Joe.'

Just then Ivan came over, his face white. 'Joe. One of the girls has just started twitching and we don't know what's wrong.'

'Where?' Joe had already ripped off his old gloves and repacked his bag. 'Rach.' He nodded to her and, following Ivan, they rushed over, being careful of the cables and debris on the ground. The woman was shaking and twitching around on the ground, the blanket she'd had over her body tangling around her legs. Rachael removed the blanket.

'How long has she been like this?' she asked the people around her as she checked the woman's airway. No one answered. 'How long?' she repeated forcefully.

'O-only a m-minute or so,' someone stammered.

'Call the ambulance. What's her name?'

'Grace,' Joe supplied.

'Right. Loosen her clothing and, Ivan, make sure she doesn't kick anything or hit herself. Don't restrain her completely, just make sure she doesn't do further injury to herself.'

Rachael looked into Joe's bag as he checked Grace's airway.

'Airway's clear.'

'Good. Do you have phenytoin?'

'Yes.'

Rachael found what she needed and drew up an injection. 'Make sure she doesn't swallow her tongue,' she said as Grace's body kept twitching. She administered the drug and almost straightaway Grace stopped convulsing, her muscles still alternating between rigidity and relaxation. She looked at the patient. 'Grace?'

Joe checked her airway again. 'Clear.'

Rachael reached for the medical torch. 'Grace? Can you hear me?'

'Yes…' The word came out squeaky and broken. Grace coughed.

'I'm Rachael. I'm a doctor. I'm just going to check your eyes.' Pupils were equal and reacting to light. 'Good. They're good.' She reached for the stethoscope. 'I'm going to listen to your chest now. Just relax. Can you hear me, Grace?'

'Yes.' The word was stronger this time.

'Good.' Rachael listened to her chest and was pleased to find everything fine. 'Do you know where you are?'

'Back lot at the studio.'

'Good. Cognitive reasoning is clear.'

'Ambulance should be here soon,' someone said over her shoulder.

'What happened?' Grace asked, and Rachael realised the woman was starting to feel self-conscious and embarrassed.

'You had a seizure.' It was Joe who answered, his voice calm yet authoritative. He wrapped the sphygmomanometer cuff around Grace's arm and took her blood pressure. 'What's the ETA on the ambulance? I want minutes, not *soon*,' Joe instructed quietly, and Ivan directed someone to find out. 'We need to get you to hospital, Grace. We don't know why you had a seizure and we need to find out. Have you ever had one before?'

'No.'

'Have you been in an accident recently?'

'No. Not for about three months.'

'That's right. You had that concussion,' Joe said. 'That was when you were in America filming, wasn't it?'

'Yes. Got hit in the head with debris when they were blowing up a building.'

'Right. The price of stunt work. Ever had an EEG? That's where they scan your brain,' he explained.

'Yes. I had one then but everything was all ri—' Grace stopped speaking, her eyes widening as she glanced wildly at Rachael. She gestured for her to come closer.

'What's wrong?' Rachael leaned closer.

'I feel all…wet.' Grace tried to sit up but Rachael stopped her, urging her to stay still.

'If you sit up now, you'll be very dizzy. I'm just going to check your arms and legs. Does it hurt anywhere?'

'No.'

Rachael checked her legs and then realised what Grace had meant by 'wet'. She reached for the blanket and covered her over to save her further embarrassment. She checked her arms, neck and head. 'I can't feel any broken bones, which is a good sign.' She placed her fingers in Grace's palms. 'Can you squeeze my fingers, please?'

Grace was able to do so on both sides.

'Good.'

'Ambulance is pulling into the theme park now,' someone said.

'Good.' Rachael glanced at Joe. 'Is there anyone else who needs attention?'

'Ivan?' Joe called.

'I heard. I'll check around.'

'Thanks.' They stayed with Grace until the paramedics came over. Rachael smiled as she recognised Smitty. 'Back so soon?' She stood up to meet him.

'Can't keep me away.'

'How's Wong?' Joe asked urgently.

'They whisked him to Theatre to try and find the source of the bleeding. What do you need here?'

Rachael had just done Grace's obs and reported her findings. 'Tonic-clonic seizure. She's stable but needs oxygen and an IV line. Glasgow coma scale is 15. Patient has voided and is highly embarrassed by the whole episode.'

'Not surprising.' Smitty nodded.

'I've given her phenytoin, which should see her through until she's at the hospital.'

'Right. Everything settled here now?' Smitty glanced around at the scene in general.

'We're just waiting for Ivan to give us an update. Once it's clear, we'll follow you to the hospital.'

'I'll get Grace into the ambulance,' Smitty replied.

Rachael helped Smitty get Grace ready for transfer as Joe went to speak to Ivan. 'How are you feeling now?' she asked her patient.

'Stupid.' Grace closed her eyes.

'That's natural. Smitty here's going to take good care of you and I'll catch up with you at the hospital. All right?'

'Yes.' Grace closed her eyes as the stretcher was put into the ambulance.

Rachael looked around for Joe who was headed in their direction. 'All clear?'

'All clear,' he acknowledged. 'We'll see you at the hospital,' he told Smitty, before looking at Rachael. 'Let's go.'

She nodded. 'I'll get my bag.' She collected it and said goodbye to Ivan, thanking him for looking after Declan.

'My pleasure. As I said, anything for Joe and his family.'

Rachael was still smiling as she and Joe walked out to the parking lot. 'Where's your car?' he asked.

'My mum drove it to her house.'

Joe's only answer was to raise an enquiring eyebrow. Rachael decided to ignore it. They walked over to a green Jaguar. She glanced at the number plate and this time it was her turn to raise an eyebrow.

'JOE-19.' She smiled. 'I think you're a little older than that, Joe.'

Joe frowned as he unlocked the door and held hers open. 'Nineteen's my lucky number.' He waited until she was seated before heading around to the driver's side.

'That's it? Nineteen's your lucky number?'

He shrugged. 'A lot happened when I was nineteen.'

The smile slid from Rachael's face. 'Yes. Yes, it did.' She wanted to ask him all the questions that had been floating around in her head, she wanted to sort out the past, to try and make sense of it, but her mother's words about focusing on the here and now slipped into her mind and she forced herself to take a deep, relaxing breath.

'Thank you,' she said, after he'd started the engine and pulled out onto the road.

'For?'

'For being nice to Declan.'

He smiled. 'It's not hard.'

'Still, it means a lot to me, Joe.' She twisted her hands together in her lap, amazed to feel her heart rate start to increase. She took another deep breath, trying to steady her mounting nerves. A few minutes of silence passed. 'Joe.'

'Hmm?'

'I know you said you wanted to spend time alone with Declan and I appreciate that. I'm all for it but…' She closed her eyes, unable to look at him as she spoke just in case he turned her down. 'But would you also like to spend time alone with me?'

Joe glanced at her so suddenly the car swerved slightly. 'Er...uh...sure.' He cleared his throat.

'You don't sound too convinced.'

'No. It's not that. It's just...you caught me by surprise.'

'Oh. So you're open to the idea, then?'

He stopped the car at a red light and turned to look at her. Even beneath the artificial lights outside, it was still difficult to see all of his face, but she hoped his gaze was filled with delight at the prospect.

'Yes. Rach, I'm a little astounded that you needed to ask.'

She shrugged, feeling a little foolish. It had been easier when he hadn't been watching her so intently, and she wished for the light to change so she could escape once more into the dark. 'I'm not saying we jump straight into bed if that's what you're thinking.'

His grin was immediate and wolfish. 'Hey, I wouldn't be a red-blooded male if I didn't admit the thought had already crossed my mind, but I understand what you mean.'

The light turned and he resumed driving. 'I know we still have a lot of things to work out, but it would be nice to just spend some time together. The two of us. Grab a cup of coffee or something.'

'Or something.' He nodded.

Rachael sighed with relief and he chuckled at the sound. 'Surely it wasn't that bad, asking me that question.'

'Of course it was. You have been known to turn me down before.'

'Cheap shot,' he said good-naturedly.

'Yes, it was. I apologise.' She was glad to see he'd lost his black mood from the movie set. Perhaps she'd imagined it and had misinterpreted the dark looks he'd given her. 'I'm glad you're the one driving to the hospital. I would have got lost by now.'

Joe smiled as he turned off for the hospital and parked the Jaguar in the doctors' car park. Rachael grabbed her bag and walked quickly beside him into the hospital, bumping into Smitty again.

'What took you so long?' He grinned at both of them and then held up his hands. 'No. On second thought, don't tell me. I don't want to know.'

'Where's Grace?' Joe asked, ignoring Smitty's teasing words.

'Examination cubicle four, and Rino's at X-Ray.'

'Wong?'

'Still in surgery.'

'Thanks.'

'All part of the service. That should be it for me tonight. I'll catch you folks later.'

Joe guided Rachael over to the nurses' station.

'Oh, so you're Joe's partner. He told us you'd be in at some time. I guess you didn't expect to be here so soon.'

'I'll be in EC-4. Come in when you're done.' Joe went to check on Grace.

'I'm not his partner, just the locum working at his private practice,' Rachael corrected the nurse.

'Whatever. You'll need to fill in some forms, but if you wanted to check out the tonic-clonic patient first, she's in EC-4. The paperwork can wait.' The nurse held out her hand for Rachael's bag. 'I'll lock it in the drawer here.'

'Thanks.' She headed for EC-4 and felt strange pulling back the curtain when she really felt like knocking.

'Rachael.' Grace's gaze fell on her with relief. The oxygen mask was still in place and an IV line was in her arm.

'Finished already?' He raised a teasing eyebrow. 'Come in, come in.'

Joe gave Rachael an updated report on Grace's vital signs and she was pleased to hear everything was fine. 'I was just about to order a few tests for Grace. What do you think, Rach?'

'EEG definitely, and compare it with the one she had three months ago. ECG, full blood work-up and urine analysis.' She shrugged. 'For a start.'

'Good.' Joe nodded to the nurse. 'Can you get them organised please, Beatrice?'

'Sure thing, Joe.'

'Good. We'll be back to check on you later, Grace. You rest and take it easy.'

'Yes, Joe.' Grace smiled as she closed her eyes. 'At least I can try, before they start poking and prodding me.'

They both smiled and headed out the cubicle. 'Are you the treating doctor?'

'Studio rules. All patients from the movie set are admitted under my name, even though several specialists may see them.' He walked over to the nurses' station and picked up the phone. A moment later, he asked the switchboard to page the neurology registrar. 'Although Wong is in surgery with all different kinds of specialists looking after him, I'm the one who coordinates everything because I'm the one who has to write reports for the studio's insurers.'

'Sounds like fun.'

'Oh, it really isn't.' He smiled. 'Let's go find Rino.' She followed him to Radiology and was pleased when they found Rino had just finished there.

'Spine's not busted,' he said. 'Told you.'

'Yes, you did.' They chatted with Rino until the first lot of films came back. 'They're looking good. Nice clean break of the clavicle.' Joe accepted the next lot of films. 'Only your left tibia is fractured, but right side has both tib and fib. Due to the lacerations on your left leg, Zac will probably opt to put an external fixator on that one.'

'Zac?' Rachael asked.

'Orthopaedic surgeon,' Rino supplied. 'Open reduction and internal fixation on the right side?'

'Probably,' Joe responded, as he held the films up to the light so they could all see.

'Ever thought of going into medicine, Rino?' Rachael asked. 'You certainly know more than the average bloke.'

'You pick things up when you've been breaking bones all your life,' Joe teased.

'Not *all* my life, mate, but since I got into stunt work—yeah, quite a bit.'

Joe's pager beeped. 'Theatre,' he said, glancing at the extension number.

'Wong?' Rachael asked.

'Yes. I asked them to page me when they had news.' His face grew grim and the pain Rachael saw there, the deep-seated concern he had for his friend, made her heart melt. She reached out and squeezed his hand encouragingly.

'Go and find out.' She waited with Rino, neither of them speaking. She knew everything was all right the instant Joe returned.

'They've managed to stop the bleeding and he's turned the corner, but the general surgeon said it was touch and go for a while.'

Rachael breathed a sigh of relief and smiled at Rino. The look of guilt that had plagued the stunt driver from the instant she'd seen him had now eased.

'He's going to be fine,' Rachael said to Rino.

'Yeah.'

'Come on, Rach. I think it's coffee time.' Joe looked at Rino. 'Want one?'

'Nah, mate. I'm fine with the shot of pethidine I've had.'

'Suit yourself.' They headed back towards A and E, and when they passed the nurses' station, Beatrice grabbed Joe.

'Did you page the neurology registrar?'

'Yes. Oops.'

'How many times do I have to tell you? If you page someone, stay by the phone until they answer or at least tell someone you've done it and why!'

'Sorry.'

'I presumed it was for Grace.'

'Yes.'

'Well, wait here for three minutes and she'll meet you.'

'OK, but I'll just take—'

'No. You'll stay there, Joe Silvermark,' Beatrice commanded.

'Yes. I'll stay here.' He nodded meekly and Rachael couldn't help but laugh. 'Go and sit in the doctors' tearoom. I'll be there soon.'

'I can wait with you.'

'Rachael!' he said in exasperation.

'All right. Have it your own way.' He gave her directions and she found the room without difficulty. She sat down and put her feet up on another chair, tipping her head backwards as she pulled the braid from her hair and ran her fingers through it, untangling knots. She closed her eyes, feeling the tension of the past few hours began to ease.

It had been a long time since she'd been in an emergency situation like that. Not that it bothered her, just that she was out of practice. Once she was more settled here on the Gold Coast, she'd have to sign up for some GP refresher courses.

Sighing, she lifted her head and slowly opened her eyes. She jumped a little when she realised Joe was standing in the doorway, watching her intently.

'Everything organised?' She should probably sit up straight and take her feet off the chair, but she didn't have the energy.

'Yes. We'll have to get you registered here so you have the authority to admit patients if necessary.'

Rachael shrugged. 'Is there much point? I'll only be at your clinic until the end of next week.'

He frowned and went to sit down on the chair where her feet were. She quickly moved them, but after he'd sat down, he picked them up and placed them on his knee. Carefully he removed her shoes and began tenderly massaging her insteps.

Rachael groaned in pleasure and felt herself begin to melt. 'That feels *so* good.'

'I know.'

'You remember?'

'That you like having your feet massaged? Of course. The first time you let me touch you was to massage your feet on the bus trip.'

'Oh, yeah. I'd forgotten that.'

Joe chuckled. 'Most guys get to hold the girl's hand or put their arm around her shoulders, but me? No. I get to massage her very smelly feet.'

'They weren't smelly.'

'They were so.'

'Were not.'

'Were.'

She giggled. 'Yes, they were, yet you still did it.'

His smile was heart-melting and now he'd brought the topic up, she remembered just how quickly she'd melted beneath those megawatt smiles. 'I was trying to impress you.'

'It worked.'

'So it would seem.'

They both fell silent. 'What happened, Joe?'

'Tonight?'

'No.' She paused and looked into his eyes. 'To us.' She shook her head slowly. 'I still don't understand what happened and I've spent the past fifteen years trying to figure it out. As far as I could tell, one minute we were happily married and the next you were rushing me even faster towards the courthouse for the annulment.' Her words were soft yet filled with repressed hurt.

Joe's face became an unreadable mask. 'It wasn't meant to be, Rach.'

She bit her lip and looked down at her hands. They were clasped tightly together as she worked up the courage to ask her next question. Regardless of his answer, she needed to know, and she hoped this time, with fifteen years having passed, she'd get a different reply. 'Joe…' She swallowed nervously. 'Did you really mean it? What you said? That you'd only married me to get me into bed? That it had all been a joke?'

She held her breath, waiting…waiting for the words that would either make or break her.

CHAPTER SIX

JOE recalled the words with perfect clarity.

He recalled saying them to her with all the venom he'd been able to muster, and he'd felt sick to his stomach as he'd stood there and blatantly lied to her. Looking back—which he often had—he wished he'd handled the situation better, but he'd been a confused and idiotic nineteen-year-old who hadn't known any different.

Joe continued to massage her feet, searching for the right words.

'It's all right,' she said, when he didn't reply. 'Forget it.' She had her answer. His silence was her answer, and he was probably trying to find a nicer way of saying exactly what he'd said that morning. Amazingly, she could feel tears beginning to well and realised she needed to get out of there—as soon as possible!

As she went to remove her feet from his hands, he held onto them. 'No, Rach. You misunderstood my silence. I want to answer but I was trying to think of the best way to explain.' He shrugged. 'We were…young…naïve, impulsive.'

'You weren't naïve, Joe.'

He grimaced wryly. 'No, but you were, and I should never have taken advantage of you.'

'Was it true, though?'

'That I only suggested we get married to get you into bed? No. At the risk of sounding conceited, I would have been able to talk you into it if that had been my sole motive.'

She acknowledged his words with a slow nod. 'So you really did want to marry me? It wasn't a joke?'

After all this time, he knew he owed her the truth. 'No, Rachael. It wasn't a joke.'

A shuddering sob escaped her lips as she was swamped with relief. 'You have no idea how that's haunted me all these years. I'd go over everything in my head like a stuck record. What had I said? What had I done? It had to have been something to make you say such horrible things to me.'

'It wasn't you. You didn't do anything wrong.'

'Then why?'

'I needed to hurt you.'

'You succeeded, but *why*? Why, Joe?' This time, when he remained silent, Rachael slowly began to connect the dots. 'I got too close.' A look of dawning realisation crossed her face.

'*Way* too close.' He exhaled harshly and lifted her feet, tenderly placing them on the chair. He needed a bit more distance between them—even now, although this distance was more physical than emotional, he still needed it.

A nurse poked her head into the room. 'Any-one seen Tess Marshall?'

'No,' Joe replied, and the nurse left. 'This isn't the place for this discussion.'

'Then where? Come on, Joe. We can't just leave it at that. I want to get on with my life, to move forward, but it's just so hard to try and do that when the same questions that were buzzing around in my head fifteen years ago are still there—unanswered.'

'Closure.' He said the word with a nod. 'You're right. We do need to discuss this, but you have Declan waiting for you.'

'He's with my parents. He's fine.'

'Is he staying overnight with them?'

Rachael grimaced. 'No. He's had an extremely full day and usually, when that happens, his mind goes into overload. First going out with you, then bungee jumping, then the accident and helping out. It's a lot for his mind to absorb.'

'He's fourteen, Rach. Don't you think you're overreacting?'

Rachael sighed. 'Think back to when you were fourteen, Joe. You never really told me what your childhood was like but, after seeing where you were raised, I can imagine.'

He grimaced. 'I never wanted you to see that.'

'I know, but I did. As I was saying, remember the things you saw when you were Declan's age. I'm sure they were a lot worse than an accident on a movie set but, still, I'll bet when things didn't go the way you planned, all you wanted was for someone to be there for you. I'm not talking about psychoanalysing or anything like that but just having someone there. To feel that you weren't alone, even if you didn't talk. Someone to put their arms around you and just hold you without probing any further beneath the surface. Didn't you want that when you were fourteen, Joe?'

Joe looked down at the floor. How did she do that? Without him even realising, she just climbed right inside his head and read his mind. It hadn't been the first time it had happened and he realised now it wouldn't be the last. He shuffled his feet, then looked up at her. 'This really isn't the place.' He raked a hand through his hair. 'We should go somewhere else to talk, but I want to stay at the hospital.'

'For Wong.' She nodded. 'I understand.'

'You do, don't you? Somehow, by some miracle, you've always been able to understand me.'

'And that scares you?'

He gave a shout of laughter without humour and shook his head. 'Terrifies me, Rach.'

'And that's why you don't open up to me?'

'I find it hard to open up to anyone but you seem to have this imaginary can-opener and without my permission you get inside.'

'You make me sound like a parasite.'

'You know what I mean.'

'That irritates you, doesn't it? That I get in without permission?'

He turned to face her, his expression earnest. 'I'm a private person by nature, Rach. I'm not into deep relationships, but when I met you and you just seemed to...*get* me, I found myself in uncharted waters.'

'Out of your comfort zone.'

Joe nodded. 'Correct, and I'd taken great pains to have that comfort zone, to find a safe place within me.'

'Joe.' Rachael placed her hand on his arm and looked imploringly at him. 'I never wanted to hurt you, but even from the first moment we met you were an enigma to me. I probe because it helps me understand, and I'm one of those annoying people who needs to understand. Once I understand, I can cope.'

'Hence your current dilemma.'

'Yes. I don't understand why you pushed me away, but let me just say that everything I found out about you when we were together I loved.'

He nodded and took her hand in his. 'The way you spoke to me, the discussions we had… You made me feel smart. You made me feel as though I had worth. No one had ever made me feel that way.'

'Made you *feel* smart?' She smiled at him. 'Joe, you *are* smart. Where do you think Declan gets it from!'

'From both of us.' He reached out his free hand and caressed her cheek. 'You're a highly intelligent woman, Rach, and I could never figure out what it was you saw in me. I was just this loser who'd been raised in an abusive environment and who'd managed to scrape together enough money to get out of the country.'

'That's not what I saw.' When Joe raised his eyebrows she continued. 'I saw a man who knew how to let loose and have a good time. You were wild and exciting and the sexiest man I'd ever met.'

'You decided to slum it.'

'Is that what you think?' Rachael was astonished. 'Because you're wrong. Those were my first impressions of you, Joe. *Then* I got to know you and that's when I started falling in love. We may have initially been attracted to the external packages, but I've always believed we touched each other's souls.'

He couldn't help himself any longer and dragged her close to him. She didn't pull back or resist. Instead, he saw she welcomed the contact. Reaching up, she slowly brushed her fingers through his hair and he groaned at the touch.

'You get my blood pumping faster than any bungee jump or any of the other adrenaline rushes I've experienced over the years.'

Gently, she urged his head down and at the same time she rose up on her toes, the length of their bodies brushing firmly together. He breathed in deeply, the scent of wild berries overpowering him.

'You smell the same,' he whispered, his gaze fixed on her mouth. His hands sensually caressed her back in small circles the way he knew she liked. 'You feel the same.'

'Hurry up and kiss me,' she panted, and watched as the sexy smile she remembered tugged at his lips. Her stomach churned with longing and she was glad he was holding her tightly because she doubted her legs would be able to support her.

'You're still impatient, too.'

'Only with you.'

He continued to tease her by eluding her mouth and burying his face in her neck, filling his senses with her scent. He pressed kisses to her neck. 'You taste the same.'

'Joseph.' She growled his name and he chuckled lightly. Not giving him the chance to escape, she dug her hands into his hair, wrenched his head up and brought it down so their lips could meet… The moment they touched, she sighed with relief.

As ever, his mouth was masterful, knowing exactly how to bring a response from her. Her insides twirled with longing as the sensations continued to grow. Testing, teasing and tantalising… He wasn't going to let her get away with a quick, reuniting kiss—not that she'd want him to. It was as though he was taking his time to familiarise himself with the feel of her mouth beneath his, and she was in no mood to contradict him.

They moved in complete synchronicity, as though the past fifteen years hadn't happened. A reunion they'd both needed with the promise of what they knew lay beyond these heart-wrenching kisses.

With a short groan coming from deep in the back of his throat, he pulled back. 'Mmm. Definitely taste the same.'

'Shh,' was all she said as she dragged his mouth back to hers. This time she took control, desire pouring out of her as she led them both towards a journey they'd taken many years ago. They needed to build bridges, to fix the rift that had grown between them due to both life and circumstances, and she knew this was a sure-fire way to get the building process started…as well as being highly enjoyable.

Her mouth on his was eager and slightly desperate, almost willing him to come along for the ride. If he thought he could tease and nibble, he had another think coming. The impatience she'd felt earlier was nothing compared to how she felt now. The moment seemed to slow down, time seemed to stand still. She waited for him to accept and appreciate her efforts.

She didn't have to wait long.

After a heart-splitting second, his mouth was roving over hers in that hot and hungry way she recalled. The passion, the fire, the heat—it was there, and it was as raw and untamed as it had been when they'd been teenagers. How could the need which had lain so dormant in her suddenly spring to life with such fever? A fever she knew was highly infectious to only one other person—and he was showing the same symptoms.

Ever since she'd first seen him again, her heart had acknowledged the inevitability of this moment, even though her head had denied it. They were meant for each other and right now neither one disagreed.

Where there had previously been apprehension and uncertainty between them, they were now both confident to take the frightening natural attraction which still existed to the next level. On and on the fire continued to rage within them as their mouths hungrily explored and remembered.

'Rachael!' He finally pulled back, both of them panting from lack of air. They'd been completely caught up in each other, neither wanting to be the one to break the contact. Breathing had completely slipped their minds until it had been imperative they part. He sucked in a breath and pressed his lips onto hers, knowing with absolute certainty she would respond.

'You're so…captivating,' he whispered brokenly as his mouth still took hungrily from hers.

'So…vibrant and alive, and if I don't stop myself soon, I'm not going to be able to.' He was talking more to himself than her, but didn't mind she was in on his thoughts.

He had the most sexy, desirable and passionate woman he'd ever known right here in his arms, and he was hard-pressed not to scoop her up and find somewhere soft to lay her down. He even glanced around at their surroundings, hoping to find a bed had miraculously appeared—but it hadn't.

He chuckled and gathered her close, pressing kisses to the top of her head. 'Unbelievable.'

'Isn't it?' She sighed and listened as his erratic heart rate slowly began to return to a normal rhythm.

'I can't believe it's still there. So strong, so…'

'Encompassing.'

'Yes.' He pulled back to gaze down into her face and couldn't resist brushing his lips once more across hers. 'How could you think I wouldn't want to spend time alone with you—especially when we have *this* between us?'

Rachael chuckled and accepted another kiss. 'I'm allowed my own insecurities, Joe.'

'Well, not about me wanting you because, believe me, Rach, I do.' His pager beeped and he released her so he could check the number. 'Theatre,' he said, and went to the phone on the wall, quickly dialling the relevant extension.

'It's Joe,' he said a moment later. 'How's Wong?'

'Everything's going fine,' Zac reported. 'The general surgeons have finished and the urology surgeon is with him now. I have his X-rays back if you wanted to come and have a look.'

'We're in the tearoom.'

'We?' Zac asked. 'I certainly hope this "we" you're referring to involves a beautiful woman.'

'It does.'

'Good. I look forward to meeting her.'

Joe disconnected the call, a silly schoolboy grin on his face at the thought he could show 'his girl' to his mate.

'How is he?'

'Who? Zac?'

'Don't be obtuse, Silvermark.' The fact that he was joking meant things were better than he'd expected.

'Oh. Wong.' Joe passed on the details as he crossed back to her side. 'Want to go look at some X-rays?'

'You're such a party animal and always know how to show a girl a good time,' she teased.

'Be quiet and come here.' He pulled her into the circle of his arms once more and pressed his mouth to hers. Rachael made no move to pull away but instead sighed and snuggled closer to him, her arms about his waist, her eyes closed.

'Joe? Don't we need to go?'

His answer was to kiss her again.

'This isn't helping, Joe.'

'Mmm. I don't know about you but I'm feeling quite fine.'

'Come on.' She pressed a kiss to his lips but couldn't bring herself to end the embrace.

'You're right,' he growled, but even though he spoke the words, he still didn't move.

'You first.'

'You don't play fair.'

Rachael chuckled. 'We're doctors. Since when is life fair?' She opened her eyes and pulled back to look at him. Joe immediately brushed his lips against hers once more.

'I can't get enough of you.'

'The feeling is very mutual.' She moved away slightly and reluctantly he let her go. Rachael reached for his hand and turned it over in both of hers before saying softly, 'What's next, Joe?' She glanced up at him, her expression filled with concern.

'For us? Honestly? I don't know.' He laced their fingers together and gave her hand a little squeeze. 'For now, though, let's have a look at Wong's X-rays.'

Rachael nodded and together they headed out of the tearoom. 'Hey, wait a minute. Don't I still need to fill in some paperwork? Can I just go looking at X-rays and giving my opinion—if I'm asked—if I'm not licensed to work here?'

'It's just X-rays, Rachael. Not espionage. You can fill them in any time tonight because they won't be processed until tomorrow morning, but at least the red tape will be covered.'

'OK. Well, perhaps I should get them out of the way now.'

Joe indulged her and they walked over to the nurses' station where Beatrice handed over the forms to register Rachael as a visiting medical officer. Rachael noticed the glances a few of the staff gave them due to the fact that Joe was still holding her hand and realised hospitals around the world were the same—the staff living off rumours and gossip. She felt like grabbing Joe and planting a big, smoochy kiss on his lips just to ensure the rumours could be confirmed.

'What are you thinking, Rach?' Joe asked quietly as he waited for her to complete the forms.

'Why?'

'You have that teasing look in your eyes. That usually means you're up to no good.'

She glanced at him, doing her best 'who me?' look.

'Yes, Miss Sweetness-and-Light. *You*,' he answered, then chuckled. 'You're conscious that people are watching us together and you're thinking about teasing them.'

Rachael fumbled with what she'd been writing before putting the pen down and staring at him in amazement. Joe straightened up from where he'd been leaning against the desk. 'You mean I'm right?'

'I know we used to be able to read each other's minds, Joe, but this is ridiculous.'

Joe preened like a peacock and Rachael rolled her eyes. He edged closer. 'Let's give them something to talk about.'

Before she could say or do anything, he leaned over and placed his mouth on hers. It wasn't a brief kiss, as she'd expected, but a slow, intimate kiss, his lips slightly open with just a hint of tongue. Soft, sensual and simply seductive. When he pulled back, she saw the desire in his eyes.

'That ought to do the trick,' he murmured, and straightened, getting himself under control.

Rachael cleared her throat and glanced around them. As the nurses went about their business, she knew several had witnessed the kiss. One or two glared daggers at her, a few others had dreamy, romantic looks on their faces. She even heard one of them sigh with longing.

'Trying to scare someone off?'

'Rachael.' He placed a hand over his heart. 'I'm highly offended you should think that.'

'I know you too well, Joseph Silvermark.' She completed the forms.

'When did I ever use you to scare other women off, as you put it?'

'Hmm. Let me think. There was Janice and Celeste, not to mention Freya and Samantha.'

'When?'

'On the tour, Joe. You knew they all had the hots for you.'

The peacock returned as he preened. 'Really? All of them?'

Rachael laughed and shook her head. 'I need to go ring my parents to let them know what's happening.'

Joe sobered immediately. 'And to check on Declan.'

'It's a mother's prerogative.'

'OK, Dr Cusack.' He handed her the phone from the nurses' desk. 'Dial zero to get an outside line.'

'Thank you, Dr Silvermark.'

'What?' Beatrice was astounded. 'You're still on a last-name basis after a kiss like that?'

Both of them laughed.

'I'll go get the X-rays and meet you back in the doctors' tearoom,' Joe said, giving her some privacy.

'OK.' Rachael dialled the number, watching Joe hungrily as he walked away. He had such a nice back with those wonderful broad shoulders. Years ago she'd touched every inch of him and had tenderly caressed the scars he had on his arms and back. She had her theory as to how he'd come across them, but even now the urge to kiss every single one better was growing stronger by the minute.

Declan answered the phone, bringing her back to the present. 'Hi, Mum. How's Wong? And how's the stunt guy?'

'Wong's still in Theatre but apparently things are progressing well, and Rino should be waiting to go into surgery.'

'Then everyone's good, eh?'

'Yes.' She heard her son sigh with relief. 'Are you all right?'

'I'm fine, Mum.' His tone was bored.

'OK. We may be a little while longer but not too much.'

'And Joe's going to drive you back here, right?'

'That's right.'

'Can I see him?'

'You might be asleep.'

'Please, Mum.' The pleading tone was back. 'I just want to see the guy. That's all.'

'OK. When we get to Grandma's, I'll ask him to come in to see you.'

'Excellent.'

'So long as you try and get some sleep to start off with. You have school tomorrow.'

'Yes, Mother.' Again his tone was bored. 'So we're going back to the hotel tonight?'

'Yes.'

'OK. I'll have everything ready by the door.'

Rachael rang off, her thoughts on Declan. She'd heard the tension in his voice no matter how much he'd tried to disguise it. There would be hardly any sleep for either of them tonight and she wasn't looking forward to it.

She saw Joe come out of the emergency theatre block with another doctor in scrubs. The man was a similar height and build to Joe, and she surmised it must be his friend Zac. The two men were talking and when Zac gave Joe a playful thump on the shoulder and glanced over her way, she realised she was the topic of their conversation.

Taking a deep breath, she headed over.

'Declan OK?'

'He's fine.'

'Rachael, this is Zac.'

Zac's smile was teasing, his blue eyes twinkling with repressed humour. '*Very* pleased to meet you, Rachael.' They headed for the doctors' tearoom.

'Likewise.' She paused for a moment. 'Is there some joke I'm missing?'

'No,' Joe said.

'Yes,' Zac said in unison, then chuckled. 'Not a joke, really. Just that I told Joe not so long ago that a person's past has a way of catching up with them and…well…here you are.' At Rachael's confused frown, Zac explained. 'The same thing happened to me. The woman I dated in med school came to work here six years ago and we were reunited. We had a lot of stuff to work through, naturally—hence my crack about the past catching up with you, especially if you lock it away and refuse to deal with it—but work through it we did and we've been happily married since.'

Rachael smiled sincerely. 'I'm glad.' Her opinion of Zac grew immensely because if he knew she was part of Joe's past, it meant here was another person Joe trusted.

'Anyway, let's not get into everything now—except I will say that Julia will definitely want to meet you.'

'Your wife?'

'Yes. She's off on maternity leave at the moment.' Zac preened. 'We've just had a baby girl. Four months old and looks just like her mother. We'll have to arrange for you, Joe and your son to come over some time.'

Rachael glanced at Joe, not sure how he felt about all this, but as he wasn't jumping in to say anything, she decided to wing it. 'Thanks.'

'Let's take a look at these X-rays,' was Joe's only comment, and Rachael realised he was distancing himself again…running, protecting himself because he was once more out of his depth. They studied the films and Rachael wasn't surprised to see that Wong's pelvis was fractured in three different places.

'He's busted up his left leg quite badly.' Zac hooked up a new X-ray beside the pelvic one. 'I'll do the Grosse and Kempf intramedullary nailing down his left femur soon, but the tibia and fibula can wait for another twenty-four hours.'

'And the pelvis?'

'I'll monitor it over the next week because the posterior fracture up here…' he pointed to the fracture in the bone '…may actually heal itself and not require surgical intervention. Besides, it also gives his other abdominal injuries time to heal before he's being poked and prodded there again.'

'You'll call me when he's done in Theatre?'

'Yes.' Zac took the films down and slid them back into the X-ray sleeve as his pager beeped. He checked the extension. 'Theatre two. Looks like they're ready for Rino.'

'You're operating on him now?'

'Yes. We'll fix his right tibia and fibula with ORIF and, depending on when I need to go into surgery with Wong, I might put Rino's external fixator on his left tibia tomorrow. I'll see what the time constraints are.'

'He was right.' Rachael nodded, telling Zac that Rino had known exactly how his legs would be fixed. 'What about his clavicle?'

'I'll strap it, which is going to be highly uncomfortable for him but, hey, I guess that's the price he pays for being a stuntman.'

'It's in his blood.' Joe shrugged.

Zac agreed. 'Hey, you guys look exhausted. Get out of here and go see your son. You know what hospitals are like. If you hang around here for too long, an emergency will come in and you'll be stuck here for hours.'

'Get out while the going's good, eh?' Joe smiled for the first time since he'd introduced Zac to Rachael. 'Good thinking. Take care of Rino and—'

'Let you know what happens in Theatre?' Zac grinned at his friend. 'Will do. Oh, and I'll get Jules to give you a call and fix up a date for dinner.'

'No hurry,' Joe replied as he ushered Rachael out the tearoom. Although he was still smiling as he said the words, the smile didn't quite meet his eyes. It spoke volumes to her and she realised Joe was quite a few steps behind her. Where she knew her love for him had never died, he was still floundering in the dark and running as fast as he could every time a new emotion assailed him.

They checked on Grace, who'd been admitted to the neurology department and was stable. She was sleeping so they headed to the nurses' station to talk to the registrar. 'EEG doesn't tell us much,' the neurology registrar said. 'I'll book her in for a MRI and see what that tells me.'

Joe nodded. 'You know she was in an accident three months ago?'

'I read the notes you wrote, Joe.'

'Just checking.'

'Was she involved in the stunt tonight?'

'No. In fact, she was working the clapperboard.'

'The what?'

'The board that marks the scene on the roll of film.'

'Oh. So she wasn't involved with the stunt tonight?'

'No.'

'Well, thanks to the immediate medical attention, Grace has a good chance of recovery. The question is, will she fit again? That's what we need to determine.'

'Good. I'll catch up with you tomorrow when you know more.' Joe and Rachael said goodbye, stopping by the nurses' station to collect her bag.

'I guess we'll be seeing you around,' Beatrice said to Rachael. Rachael merely smiled and followed Joe as they headed for the exit. The cool autumn air hit Rachael as they walked out of the hospital.

'It's getting cold.'

'That's because it's almost midnight.'

She shook her head. 'Now I remember why I went into private practice.'

'Hospital life's not your scene?'

'Not really. Yours?'

Joe shrugged. 'I like it now and then, a bit of action, but every day?' He shook his head, answering his own question.

'So you get your action from the movie shoots.'

'Yes. Gives me variety, otherwise I'd get bored.'

'Mmm-hmm.' She nodded knowingly.

'What?' he asked defensively.

'You're always looking for the next challenge.'

'So?'

'I'm not criticising, Joe. It's actually quite normal for people with higher-than-average IQs to have that urge.'

He rolled his eyes as they walked to his car. 'How many books have you read on this subject?'

'Quite a few. I've had to so I could learn the most effective way to deal with Declan.'

'Have you ever thought he'd be just fine without all the labels being put on him?'

'I've already told you I don't like the labels but the truth is, I've *needed* to learn. Joe, think back to when you were at school and the work was so boring. You could understand what the teacher was getting at before she'd finished writing the question up on the board. You felt they were almost insulting you asking you to sit there and do such pathetic work. I know that happened to you, even though you've never said one word about it to me. Then I'll bet you started playing up in class and getting into trouble. They labelled you, Joe, but not as gifted. No, they labelled you as a troublemaker who couldn't be bothered with hard work.'

She waited for him to unlock the door then climbed in the passenger seat, watching him walk around to the driver's side and get in. She could tell her words were beginning to affect him as his body language became defensive.

'How do you know all this?'

'From reading the books, Joe, and from seeing it happen with Declan. I was called to the principal's office on his first week at school—he was five years old—and was told that my son was a troublemaker. He played up in class, he couldn't be bothered doing the work.'

'Really? What did you do?'

'I tried talking to Declan. He told me things were too easy. That's when I read my first book and realised it was up to me to do something about it. I asked to see the work they were giving him and eventually got the wheels in motion so Declan was challenged. Once he was working at the right level, he stopped misbehaving.' She paused. 'Don't you wish you'd had someone in your corner back when you started school? I know you didn't, and I'm not trying to resurrect old wounds, but I take my responsibilities as a parent seriously, and if other people think I'm an overreacting, neurotic mother, then so be it. It's better than being a mother who neglects her child's intellect.' She was past caring what other people thought of her but for some reason she desperately wanted Joe's approval. Still, as she'd spoken, she'd felt him tense, and when he glanced at her, she could see the shutters were already in place.

'You really get going on the subject, don't you?' His words were light, showing he wanted to keep this conversation on a more superficial level.

Rachael sighed and rubbed her temples. 'I guess.'

Joe started the engine and drove out of the car park and onto the road. 'Where to?'

She gave him her parents' address and he said he knew the area. It was an affluent area and the old feeling of inadequacy swamped him. He shook it away, telling himself circumstances had changed, and if he wanted to buy a house in the same area, he could well afford to.

Neither of them spoke for a few minutes and she began to feel the weight of the day catch up with her. Leaning her head back, she closed her eyes and sighed again, this time forcing her body to relax.

'I don't mean to preach, Joe, and don't worry that I'm going to psychoanalyse you because I'm not. I'm just trying to let you know how it is with Declan.'

'I appreciate it.'

'Really?' She turned her head so she could see him better. 'Why?'

'Why? Because he's my son and I've missed the first fourteen years of his life.'

'Yes.' She could feel the defensiveness start to kick in again. 'But you can hardly blame me for that.'

'I'm not looking to cast blame. I'm merely stating a fact.' He gripped the wheel as he continued to drive. He also didn't like the fact Rachael knew everything about the boy, whereas he'd barely scratched the surface. Declan was his son! He had a son! A son who was so like him in many respects it scared him. Joe wanted to show the kid how to loosen up a bit, to have some fun, smell the roses, and he knew if he voiced those thoughts out loud, Rachael would take it as a criticism, which it wasn't.

It made him think that if he'd been around while Declan had been growing up, perhaps he wouldn't be having nightmares at the age of fourteen. Joe felt it was a kick in the gut to male pride to still be having bad dreams at such an age. That only happened to little kids. He surmised that Rachael called them nightmares because she didn't want to face that Declan was fast becoming a man. During the next few years, that's exactly what would happen, and Joe felt a sense of pride at the thought.

Paternal pride? Where had that come from, and so quickly? He'd only found out about Declan less than forty-eight hours ago and already he was feeling *pride*?

Joe turned into her parents' street and started checking the house numbers. It was then he noticed Rachael's eyes were closed and her face relaxed as she dozed. Something twisted in his gut at seeing her sitting there, so peaceful, so lovely.

Spotting her car sitting in a driveway, he stopped at the kerb outside the large house. He knew it was her car as it had been parked out the back at his private practice. At least…he *thought* it was her car. He'd better check but he took a moment just to sit there and look at her. Eventually he whispered, 'Rachael?'

'Mmm?' She sighed and tried to snuggle into the seat a bit more.

A slow smiled crossed his face, remembering how wonderful it had felt to have her snuggle into him, his arms securely around her as their heart rates had slowly returned to normal. His Rachael. The smile disappeared. That had been so long ago. He may have thought about her almost every day since they'd parted, but that didn't mean a thing. They were two different people now…two very different people…who just happened to have a son in common. He didn't know where his relationship with Declan was going. And Rachael? He was at an even bigger loss.

He wouldn't deny the attraction was still there, as potent and strong as ever, but that didn't mean a thing. Life could change—that was one lesson he'd learned early on. Clearing his throat, he gently put his hand on her shoulder and shook her.

'Rachael. We're here. Wake up.'

'Hmm?' She opened her eyes and, without moving, scanned her surroundings. Next, she jolted upright so quickly the seat belt restrained her.

'Take it easy.' The smile came naturally to his lips. 'We're here. At your parents' house.'

'Oh. Sorry. I must have dozed off.'

'Not surprising.' He took the keys out of the ignition and climbed out of the car. Rachael grabbed her bag and followed.

'This is a big enough place,' Joe said softly. 'Why aren't you staying here?'

'Because I don't want to take my parents for granted.'

'I doubt they'd think that.'

'That's not the point, Joe. They already do far too much for me and my dad's health isn't the best at the moment. I didn't want to add to his stress.'

'Fair enough.'

They walked across the front lawn and the sensor light came on. As Rachael didn't have her keys, she knocked lightly on the door and waited for someone to answer it. A moment later, her mother opened the door and beckoned them in. When Joe hesitated on the doorstep, Rachael turned and reached for his hand. 'Declan wanted to see you.'

'Oh.' Again, that pleasure and pride filled his heart and he almost felt like puffing out his chest.

'Yes. Come on.'

'Hi,' Elizabeth said, belting her robe around her waist and yawning. 'I'm just going to get my slippers,' she said, and disappeared again.

Joe closed the door behind him and they walked quietly through the house. 'Where is he?'

'He said he'd try and wait up but I think he might have given in to sleep. At least, I hope he has.' She pointed to the lounge room. 'This way.'

Sure enough, there was Declan, sprawled out on the couch, the TV still on, headphones on the floor. Rachael headed over to pick them up and turn the set off when she realised Declan was whimpering, his body twitching.

'No!' All the maternal love she had for her son welled to the surface as the twitching became more insistent. She knelt down and placed her hand on his forehead. 'He's sweating. Declan,' she said in her normal voice. 'Wake up.'

'Mum!' His eyes snapped open and he glanced wildly around the room as though he was searching for her. *'No!'* The sound was wrenched from him and he sat up and hugged his knees to his chest. 'It's too much. It's too much. I can't do it.'

'Declan.' Rachael knew she had to keep her cool. 'It's all right. I'm here.' She put her hand on his arm but he flinched. She persisted, focusing all her attention on her son, vaguely registering that her mother had rushed into the room.

'It's too much,' he moaned with anguish.

'I know.' Rachael sat beside him and held him firmly, not letting him push her away this time. 'It's all right, darling. I'm here. Let it out. Don't hold onto it, Dec. Let it out, darling.'

When the gut-wrenching sobs came, Joe felt his own eyes fill with tears as he watched his son. Rachael was holding him, murmuring soothing words, and slowly the tears subsided. Joe swallowed the lump in his throat as he turned away and walked out of the room.

CHAPTER SEVEN

JOE'S whole body was tense with a pain he'd never experienced before. He pressed his fingers to his carotid pulse and was surprised to find it pounding fiercely. He raked his fingers through his hair, unable to get the image of Declan's wild gaze out of his mind. That was his son and his son was hurting. The urge to protect, to take away the pain, to hold his boy was so overwhelming, he thought he'd choke on the emotion.

Rachael had said Declan had nightmares, but what he'd just witnessed—what he could still hear as Declan continued to sob—was a boy going through pure anguish. What caused them? Why hadn't he woken up when Rachael had called his name? Joe roughly pushed the tears away and took out his handkerchief to blow his nose.

'Devastating, isn't it?' Elizabeth spoke softly from behind him and Joe spun to face her. The woman's eyes were wet with unshed tears and he realised she was in the same boat as him—

onlooker and feeling completely helpless to make any difference. 'He doesn't have them as frequently now he's older, so I guess that's a positive.' She held out her hand. 'I'm Elizabeth.'

'I'm—'

'You're Joe.' She nodded. 'It's nice to finally meet you. The sobs have stopped, which means he's settling. Poor child gets awfully embarrassed if anyone sees him like that. We can go back in.' She headed into the room and Joe was left to follow which he did…hesitantly.

Rachael hadn't moved and neither had Declan. 'He's gone back to sleep,' she whispered when she saw them.

'Good. Do you want to stay here for the night?' Elizabeth asked.

Rachael shook her head. 'Thanks, Mum, but Declan wanted to see Joe and then return to the hotel so while it's more hectic to do that, I think we'll stick with the original plan.'

'OK, darling.' She kissed her daughter's head. 'You both look done in. Why don't I make some tea?' Before anyone could answer, Elizabeth had disappeared into the kitchen.

'Can you grab me that cushion over there? My back's starting to ache.'

Joe obliged and put the pillow behind her back so she could lean on the arm of the couch, shifting Declan and herself into a more comfortable position. 'Thanks. You may as well sit down.'

'You're not going to wake him?'

'Not yet. If I can get him back to sleep, he usually doesn't remember them. Do you mind? I'd like to give him another fifteen minutes if possible.'

'Uh…sure. Sure.' Joe sat in the armchair opposite her and raked a hand through his hair. 'So was that a mild one?'

Rachael smiled tiredly at his naivety. 'It's not a seizure, Joe, and they're all about the same intensity. I guess it depends on how long it takes me to get to him.'

'And what if you're not around?'

'I usually am. Tonight was a one-off and I don't think he'd been upset for too long.'

'How do you know?'

'Well, for a start, we would have heard him when we walked in the door and, also, it didn't take me too long to calm him down.'

'So this is the main reason you've opted for private practice?'

'Yes. It meant, as a general rule, that I could work normal hours while he was growing up.'

'You would have made a good surgeon.'

'I would have been bored. At least with general practice I get variety.'

'How many varieties of flu are there?'

Rachael laughed. 'Good point.' She sobered. 'Thanks for hanging around.'

'No problem.'

'Are you all right?'

'Me?' He waved away her concern. 'Don't worry about me.'

'It's scary, Joe. It's scary to watch your child go through any pain.'

'So I'm beginning to realise,' he mumbled, giving in to the fact that Rachael could read him like a book. 'How often does he have them?'

Rachael shrugged slightly. 'Usually when too much has happened. I can't say I'm surprised he's had one, after the past few days. Meeting you, spending time with you, starting a new school, going to the movie set.'

'The bungee jump, being introduced to so many new people, me thinking he needed more fun in his life.' Joe hung his head in shame. 'Rach, I'm so sorry.'

'It's not your fault, Joe. Declan wanted to do the bungee jump and it's good for him to meet new people, and he does need to have more fun.

Maybe not all in one day…' She smiled as she trailed off.

'I didn't realise this would happen.'

'Leave it, Joe. Trust me, there's no point beating yourself up about the past. Unfortunately for Declan, this is something he needs to learn to manage. He has to realise when he's overloaded and pace himself.'

Joe watched as Declan shifted, sprawling out and raising his arm above his head so it fell across Rachael's face. 'Dec!' She laughed and pushed his arm away, then sighed. 'I hate to think what's going to happen when girls come into his life.'

'Oh, yeah!' Joe's eyes widened. 'I hadn't thought of that.'

'It's the time in a boy's life when he needs his father, Joe.'

'You want me to give him advice about girls?'

'No.' Rachael laughed. 'That's not what I meant. I just meant…you know…he'll be needing that male influence and I don't think my dad's up to it.'

'Discussing the birds and the bees?' Joe raked a hand through his hair again and, unable to sit still any longer, stood and walked around the room.

'He knows about the birds and the bees. In fact, we've already had some very interesting discussions about...body changes.'

Joe groaned and shook his head.

'Here's the tea,' Elizabeth said cheerfully as she carried the tray into the dimly lit room. Rachael realised at some point her mother had switched off the television, coiled up the headphones cable and turned on a side lamp.

'Perfect timing,' Joe commented, and Rachael laughed again. She accepted the cup her mother handed her with thanks and watched as Elizabeth fussed over Joe.

'Now, do you prefer to be called Joe or Joseph?'

'Either.'

'Really?' Rachael was surprised and received a glare for her trouble. 'I didn't think you liked Joseph, that's all.'

'I think it's a nice name,' Elizabeth added.

'Then you may call me Joseph,' he said, still wary of Elizabeth but wanting to do whatever he could to help smooth any future contact he might have with her.

'Excellent.' They were all talking quietly but not whispering and Declan stirred a little. 'Oh, he's such a big lad. I can't believe how quickly he's grown.'

'Heavy, too.' Rachael sipped her tea before holding her cup out of the way as one of Declan's hands came towards her again. 'Take this, please, Joe. I think I'll wake him up before he whacks me in the face.' She waited until her hands were empty, then kissed the top of her son's head, glad his temperature had returned to normal. 'Declan? Honey? Wake up.' She touched his face and kissed his head once more. Unlike before, he slowly stretched and this time his hand connected with his mother's face. At the contact, he sat up.

'Mum! Sorry.'

'It's all right. I didn't need that cheekbone,' she joked.

Declan glanced around the room. 'Grandma. Joe!' His eyes widened in surprise. 'What have you all been doing? Watching me sleep?'

'You do it so well,' Rachael murmured, glad to have the blood circulating around her body once more.

'What time is it?'

'Just after midnight.'

'Wow. You were a long time at the hospital.'

'You can say that again.'

'You were a long time at the hospital,' Declan said, smiling at his mother.

Rachael chuckled and glanced at Joe. 'See? He definitely has your warped sense of humour.'

Joe forced a smile. He was still shell-shocked by what had happened to Declan, and now the three other people in the room were behaving as though nothing was out of the ordinary. There was something wrong with his son! He didn't know how to explain the sudden panic that seemed to constrict his chest, and he wasn't sure he could sit and make idle chit-chat. His palms began to sweat and he felt as though the room was closing in on him. He stood up abruptly, almost spilling the cup of tea he'd forgotten he was holding, and quickly put the cup back on the tray. 'I need to go.'

Rachael frowned at his sudden change. 'Joe?'

'Uh…early morning.'

'Are you going to be at the movie set again?' Declan asked eagerly.

'Er…no. I'll take morning clinic so your mother can have a rest.' The words tumbled out of his mouth and he realised he'd do or say anything he had to, to get out of there as soon as possible.

'It's fine, Joe. I'll be at the clinic at the normal time.'

'No.' He smiled again and took a step towards the door. 'You rest. Have a slow morning and come in around ten.'

Rachael stood and faced him, her back to her mother and Declan. 'OK. I'll walk you to the car.'

'Will I see you tomorrow, Joe?' Declan was beside his mother in an instant.

Joe looked at his son and felt a pang of paternal love sweep through him. It was such a foreign emotion but one that felt so right, so instantly right. This time his smile was genuine. 'Sure. We'll arrange something after school.'

'Can we go to the movie set again?'

'Not tomorrow, but we'll think of something.' Something a little less stimulating, he added silently.

'Cool.' Then, to Joe's utter surprise, Declan gave him a hug. It was a male hug where only their torsos touched and he gave a few hearty slaps on Joe's back. 'Thanks, Dad.' The words were said softly but clearly, and for the second time in as many minutes Joe felt tears begin to prick behind his eyes.

Rachael watched them closely, her throat constricting with love. She could see the surprise and struggle Joe was having because the emotions were too new for him to effectively hide them. When Declan released him, she said, 'Get your things together and help Grandma tidy up.'

'OK.' Declan beamed. 'See you tomorrow, Dad.'

Joe headed to the door and sucked in an urgent breath of air once he was outside. 'It's OK, Rach. You don't have to come out. It's getting cold.'

Rachael shut the front door behind her and headed across the grass. 'What happened, Joe?'

'What?' He stopped beside the car and turned to face her. 'Another Spanish Inquisition?'

She smiled. 'It won't work because you're expecting it. Besides, you already know my secret forms of torture.' Joe returned her smile and the weight that had settled on her heart lifted. She reached out and took his hand in hers. 'Parenting isn't an easy thing to do but the only way to learn is by experiencing everything and making the best of it.'

'You don't think I'll stuff him up?'

'Oh, Joe. Is that what's bothering you?' Rachael shook her head and took a step closer. 'I wouldn't let you near Declan if I didn't trust you. Those three weeks we spent together were the happiest of my life. I can't find the words to describe how…magnificent and wondrous it was. We got to know each other on the most intimate of levels and I'm not just talking about our physical relationship.' She brushed her fingers through the hair at his temple. 'We touched souls, Joe. We may not have spilled every detail about our pasts but for who we were right at that moment in time, we bonded… And it's happening all over again.'

'Mmm.' Her touch was making him crazy and he felt as though he was beginning to drown once more, drown in the reality that was Rachael. Her words were true. The bond they shared had already survived so much, and in the back of his mind were the same doubts he'd had all those years ago. Could he make it work? Would he let her down?

He shoved the doubts aside…at least for the moment as he gathered her into his arms.

'You're an incredible man, Joseph Silvermark,' she whispered close to his ear.

'You've changed, Rach. I don't remember you being this forthright before.'

She chuckled and the vibrations from her body passed through to him. 'I'm stronger, Joe. Not necessarily in body, but definitely in mind…and soul.' She pressed a kiss to his neck before pulling back to look into his eyes. 'I'm also more determined to fight for what I want.'

He raised an eyebrow. 'Is that so?'

'I guess you could say I've matured.'

'A word I've always hated.'

'Because you were forced to mature way too fast.' She sighed and hugged him close again, loving the feel of their bodies together. 'Wisdom, Joe.' She pressed kisses to his neck, working her way around to his ear. 'Wisdom and peace come from knowing yourself better, and that's how I feel at the moment.' She nipped at his earlobe with her teeth and was rewarded with a groan. 'Like that, eh?' She did it again, chuckling when he groaned once more. 'I like it when you're at my mercy.'

'And I like being there.' Becoming impatient, he began his own onslaught and after pressing a few kisses to her exposed neck he worked his way around to her mouth. She allowed him one quick kiss before she pulled back and smiled at him.

'I think we can do better than that.'

'Really? I *know* we can.' She laughed, feeling young and free once more as his mouth found hers.

The kiss wasn't hot or hungry, it wasn't sweet and sensual, but more a kiss of…familiarity, and it reminded her just how familiar they'd been with each other in the past. He made her feel safe, comfortable and special. They had affected each other's lives in such dramatic ways and now they had the opportunity to discover new things.

His arms tightened around her as though he sensed her need. She was everything he remembered and more, and he knew he would never get tired of the feel of her mouth against his. They fitted perfectly together—always had—and now…now they were fitting perfectly once more.

He groaned as her mouth responded in complete synchronicity with his. She knew exactly how to get a response from him, both verbally and physically. He could feel the emotions between them spiral…spiral upwards towards the next level. They felt so right together and he couldn't deny it. She gave him hope and that was something he hadn't felt in an extremely long time.

The more he deepened the kiss, the more potent the emotions became. His lips were possessive on hers, staking a claim, and there was no way she would deny him. It felt as though he wanted to mark her, to let the world know she belonged to him, and although she'd always thought of herself as an emancipated woman, she was more than willing to forgo the label if it meant he stayed by her side.

The pressure continued to build, both of them clinging fiercely to each other as they eagerly took and gave in equal amounts. It was the way it had always been between them—equal—and even though she had this new inner strength, he couldn't help but be attracted to it. She was still *his* Rachael.

'Should I get excited about this?' Declan's voice floated over the front lawn towards them.

Rachael broke free and tried to step out of Joe's grasp to face her son, but Joe was taking his sweet time about releasing her.

'Declan.' She cleared her throat. 'Sorry, darling. I didn't hear you come out.'

'I'm not surprised.' He grinned like a Cheshire cat.

'You ready to go, honey?'

'Yes.'

She nodded and smoothed a hand down her trousers. 'OK. I'll be right there.' She turned. 'See you tomorrow, Joe.'

He grinned, obviously enjoying her discomfort. 'Yes, you will, but not before ten or I'll kick you out.'

She smiled. It was just like him to lighten the mood, to help her to feel less self-conscious. 'Are you sure about that? Lots of pregnant women and children are on my list.'

A smile touched his lips and his shrug was also a little self-conscious. 'I'll manage.'

And she knew he would. He always did. 'Thanks.' She squeezed his hand, unsure whether or not to kiss him goodbye. His smile widened and she realised he was once more reading her mind. Thankfully, he took the decision out of her hands by bending to kiss her lips, not once, not twice, but three times.

'Don't start again,' Declan called. 'It's freezing.'

Joe chuckled and released Rachael. ''Night, Declan.'

''Night, Joe.' Declan's grin was wide and teasing as she walked over to him. They both waited for Joe to drive away, waving as he did so.

'Let's get going. I've lost feeling in my toes and my eyelashes are starting freeze.'

'And whose fault is that?' They said goodbye to Elizabeth and drove back to the hotel. 'Are you and my dad getting back together?' Declan asked hopefully.

Rachael sighed and shook her head. 'I don't know, Dec. We're still attracted to each other…'

'That's a good thing, right?'

'But there's so much we need to sort out.'

'Do you still love him?'

'Declan.'

'No. Come on, Mum. Do you?'

'I've always loved Joe.'

'Yeah, but, you know, not in that abstract way but the real way.'

'Although I want to say I do, I'm also very confused. I'm sorry if that's not the answer you're looking for but it's all I can give you. Things have happened so fast but then…' she smiled '…they usually do between Joe and me.'

The phone beside Rachael's bed rang and she woke with a start, glancing at the clock as she picked up the receiver. Three o'clock in the morning usually meant bad news.

'Rach, it's Joe.'

'Joe? What's wrong? Are you all right?'

'I'm fine. Sorry to wake you but I thought you'd like to know. I stopped in at the hospital to check on Wong. His surgery went well and he's finally in ICU, being monitored closely. Everyone's happy with the way the operations went but he still hasn't regained consciousness.'

'To be expected. And Rino?'

'Not a problem with him except his clavicle needed plating, not just strapping as Zac initially thought. The external fixator's on and I think Zac is fixing the right tib-fib fracture later today.'

'Good. Thanks for letting me know. I appreciate it.'

'How's Declan?'

She could hear the hesitancy in his voice. 'Snoring, actually.' She smiled as she listened to her son.

'No more nightmares?'

'No. He's out cold, which is good for him.'

'I'm glad. Well, I'd better let you get to sleep.'

'Is that what you're going to do, Joe? Sleep?'

'Soon.'

'Want to talk for a while?'

'And have you psychoanalyse me?'

She chuckled. 'I could always tell you what I'm wearing.' There was silence, and for a moment she thought he'd hung up. 'Joe?'

'Want to give me heart failure?' Her rich chuckle came down the line again and he groaned.

'Not particularly. I like your heart beating…close to mine.'

'Rachael.' He drawled her name slowly, a warning sign. 'I know which room you're staying in so be careful what you say.'

'I'm wearing…' she began seductively. 'A low-riding pair of…' Again she paused before finishing in her normal voice. 'Flannelette pyjamas.'

'If you think that's going to douse the flames, think again, sweetheart. You've now got me sitting here thinking of all the ways to get you out of those pyjamas.'

'Oh.' It was Rachael's turn to gasp.

'Yes, "*oh*". Don't play with fire, unless you plan to get burnt.' He paused. 'You and I were always hot stuff.'

'Mmm. I have a vivid memory.'

'So do I.' He paused and dragged in a deep breath. 'And now, my sweet Rachael, before this goes any further, I'm going to hang up the phone, go home and take a cold shower.'

'Doesn't sound like a bad idea. These pyjamas have become stifling.'

'Rachael.' Again the warning was there.

She laughed. 'I'll see you in the morning and thanks for the update.'

'Remember, I'll kick you out if you show up at the clinic any time before ten.'

Her smile intensified. 'I wouldn't dream of it.' She paused. 'Thanks, Joe.'

'For what?'

'For being you.'

CHAPTER EIGHT

RACHAEL did exactly as she'd been told the next morning, apart from the leisurely breakfast suggestion. They were up in time to get Declan to school, and afterwards she arranged to meet the estate agent at the apartment Declan and her parents had chosen. She liked what she saw, and as it suited her requirements she started the ball rolling—much to the delight of the estate agent.

She called the hospital and was told by the ICU sister that Wong still hadn't regained consciousness. The sister then transferred Rachael's call through to the coronary care unit so she could speak to Ethel, who was happy to report that Alwyn was being transferred from the unit down to the ward.

'That's wonderful news.'

'Your Dr Silvermark came around early this morning to see him. I wasn't here and Alwyn said it was before eight o'clock, but he said Dr Silvermark was very happy with his progress.'

'I'm glad. You remember to take care of yourself as well. When Alwyn is discharged, you'll need all your strength and patience to cope with him.'

Ethel laughed. 'You're right, dear. I know you are.' They chatted for a few more minutes before Rachael rang off, pleased to hear of Alwyn's progress.

By ten o'clock she'd managed to wander around the shops and buy herself a new pair of boots and was at the practice as promised. Helen smiled as she walked in the door.

'You look chipper.'

Rachael laughed. 'I don't think I've ever been called that before, but thank you.' She smiled politely at the patients in the waiting room and headed through to her office. Helen came in with her list. 'How's Joe this morning?'

Helen grinned. 'Up to his armpits in pregnant women—and I don't mean literally.'

'Thank goodness. Well, it was his idea I start late, but I hope it hasn't disrupted your schedule.'

'No, no. I'm glad you've had a relaxing morning.' Helen hesitated. 'You know, Joe doesn't usually do things like that.'

'What, giving his colleague a morning off?'

'No, I mean taking on a clinic full of expectant mothers and babies. They've never been his style and although he's a fantastic doctor, everyone has their sub-speciality. Family medicine isn't Joe's.'

'Perhaps the fact he's now a father makes a difference.'

Helen smiled again. 'That's exactly what I was thinking—that and the fact I think he's still smitten with you. He'd do anything for you.'

'Not smitten,' Rachael corrected quickly. 'Attracted but never smitten. Anyway, I'm here now so I'd better get my list under way.'

'OK.' Helen crossed to the door then turned. 'I don't want you to think I'm interfering but I've known Joe a long time and I just wanted to say that after his American…holiday, if you can call surfing a holiday. Anyway, when he finally returned, he was different. That's when he started getting real direction in his life and it took him quite a few years before he told me about you. The way he talked about you…' Helen sighed romantically. 'I've never heard him talk about anyone else that way before. You touched him, Rachael, and you touched him deeply. In Joe's world, that's a very rare thing to have happen.'

Rachael nodded. 'I understand. Thank you.' She'd always hoped she'd left a lasting impression on Joe and not just one of lust. Hearing this from Helen, a woman he trusted, made her able to believe what she and Joe had felt for each other back then had indeed been the real thing. Now she had a better understanding of the man, she could see why he had backed away.

It brought a lot of 'what-ifs' to her mind, and as she wasn't the type of person to indulge in what-ifs, she forced herself to concentrate on her work. She contacted the hospital and received a positive update on Grace, glad to hear she hadn't had another seizure during the night and was booked to have further tests later today. The neurology registrar seemed extremely confident and Rachael was glad Grace was being looked after by such a person.

Next, she headed to the waiting room and called her first patient through. Starting work at ten o'clock meant lunchtime came around very quickly, but it was after one o'clock before Rachael ventured into the kitchen to make a cup of coffee.

'Hi.' Joe's voice washed over her as he walked into the room. 'What a morning!'

Rachael smiled. 'How did it go?'

He nodded slowly. 'Not bad, if I do say so myself. I think some of the women were a bit surprised to be seeing me, but I managed.' He paused, then smiled. 'There are some really cute kids in the world.'

Rachael couldn't help but laugh.

'What?'

'Nothing. Hey, any news on Wong? I called the hospital this morning but they said no change.'

Joe shook his head. 'No change.'

'I'm sorry.'

His answer was a heavy shrug.

'Coffee?' It seemed so lame to offer something so mundane when his friend was so sick.

'Thanks.' Then he paused. 'Got any plans for lunch?'

'Actually, I hadn't thought that far.' She glanced pointedly at her watch. 'Besides, my afternoon clinic starts in twenty minutes.'

With that, Joe put her coffee cup on the bench and took her hand, dragging her out of the room.

'Where are we going?'

'Back soon,' he said to Helen as they barrelled out the door and headed down the street to a small café.

'Joe?'

'Lunch, Rach. You need to eat.' He didn't let go of her hand until she was seated at a table with a menu in front of her.

'Is this your idea of a date? If so, your dating skills need brushing up.'

'What do you want? They're pretty fast here, but only if you don't take all day to order.'

'Be still, my beating heart.' She glanced at the menu. 'Club sandwich.'

'Excellent.' The waitress came over. 'Two coffees and two club sandwiches, please.' He smiled at the other woman as she wrote down their orders, and Rachael watched as the waitress melted. She was sure he knew the power of his smile and used it whenever it suited him. He'd probably used it on every one of the women he'd seen this morning and had had them walking out saying how wonderful that sweet Dr Silvermark was.

When the waitress had gone, Joe looked across at Rachael. 'So how was your morning? Did you enjoy a long, leisurely breakfast?'

'No. No time. I did, however,' she quickly continued, 'speak to the real estate agent about the apartment Declan liked.'

He raised his eyebrows. 'So you'll be moving soon?'

'Hopefully some time next week.'

'Terrific.' He paused, then leaned forward a little. 'Tell me what you bought this morning.'

'What makes you think I bought something?'

He laughed. 'When you were eighteen years old, you certainly knew how to shop. Still have your shoe fetish?'

'What woman doesn't?'

'Exactly. So what did you buy?'

Rachael shook her head. 'I shouldn't be amazed you know me so well,' she mumbled, and he chuckled. 'Boots. OK? I bought a pair of boots.'

'Flats or heels?'

'Flats.' She smiled.

'Leather or suede?'

Her smile increased. 'Leather.'

'Black or…' He thought for a moment. 'Red?'

She laughed. 'I love it when you talk shopping. Black, but the red ones looked good, too.'

'I don't even want to ask how much they cost.'

'They'll last me a long time.'

'That means they were expensive.'

'How do you know?'

He raised his eyebrows and grinned like the cat who'd got the cream. 'I know you. Remember?'

'Don't you find it amazing just how much information we've retained about each other?'

He sobered instantly. 'No.'

They sat there looking at each other, absorbing each other. It was as though, for that moment, only the two of them existed. It wasn't the first time it had happened and it wouldn't be the last.

One of the waitresses dropped something, startling Rachael and breaking the bond. She sat up straighter in her chair, feeling a little self-conscious just sitting there staring at Joe in the middle of a coffee shop. Then again, he'd been staring back at her.

'What are you going to do at the end of next week?'

'Hopefully, move into my new apartment.'

'I don't mean that. I mean about work.'

'Oh. Work.' She paused. 'Why?'

'I'm having the papers drawn up to make you a permanent doctor in the clinic.'

'What?'

'I'm offering you a partnership.'

Rachael was speechless. She sat and stared at Joe as though he'd just grown another head. 'What?' she finally managed again. 'Joe, you can't just do that.' She frowned at him. How dared he do this to her? Just when she'd started to relax and feel as though she had some control over her life, he sprang this on her.

'Why not? I own the practice.'

'What about Alison? She leaves to have a baby and you penalise her by giving her job, permanently, to someone else.'

'Alison is more than welcome to come back once she's finished maternity leave. She doesn't want to be a partner in a practice, especially now she's starting her family, and she only wants to work part time so, you see, there is more than enough room for you.'

'And what if I want to have more children and work part time? What then?' She'd meant her words to stun him and she wasn't disappointed. Colour began to drain from his face and he clenched his jaw.

'Is that what you want? I thought you were past all that.'

'Why? Because Declan's a teenager?' Rachael folded her arms across her chest once more.

'There'd be a very large gap in their ages.'

'Obviously, and there's nothing I can do to change that. Still, I believe you at least need to consider that before you offer me a partnership.'

'Do you expect me to put conditions on it?'

'Well, if I were to get pregnant and wanted to work part time, I wouldn't want you to accuse me of not holding up my end of the agreement.' The waitress brought their food and this time Joe had no melting smiles to dish out. Instead, he sat there and glared at Rachael. 'Besides,' she continued as she reached for the sugar, 'partnerships cost money, and I don't think I'm quite ready to invest in one right now.' She smiled politely at him as she stirred her coffee.

'Who are you going to have these children with?'

She took a sip of her drink. 'I beg your pardon? I don't believe you—as my employer—have any right to be discussing my private life.'

'Rachael.' He growled her name and leaned a little closer. 'Declan is my son.'

'Yes, he's mine, too. We established all this a few days ago. Remember?'

'You're being facetious.'

'Yes, I am. My point is, I think you need to give your idea a little more thought.'

'You don't want to work with me,' he stated with a scowl. He glanced at her, then looked away. He was angry but beneath that anger she'd seen the pain.

'I never said that. OK. You tell me why you want me there.'

'You're a good doctor.'

'So is Alison. Come on, Joe, what's your main motivation here? If it's Declan, I won't restrict access to him just because I'm not working with you.'

She waited but all he did was to cross his arms over his chest and scowl at her.

'Joe, I'm not rejecting *you*. I'm saying I don't think you've thought this idea through thoroughly enough. I don't know whether or not I'm going to have more children. I have enough to concentrate on at the moment with Declan, his schooling and moving into an apartment, but I also don't know what the future will bring.' She put her hand on the table, waiting for him to put his into it.

He stirred sugar into his coffee, picked up the cup, took a long sip and glanced down at her hand—rejecting it. Rachael didn't budge.

'Come on. Take my hand and let's be friends.'

'What if I don't want to be friends?'

She couldn't help but laugh.

'What? Now you're laughing at me.' His tone was incredulous.

'No. Oh, Joe. You sounded just like Declan. I'm still getting used to all the similarities and it's strange to hear his pouting, whiny voice from you.'

'I was not pouting neither was I whining.' He slapped his hand into hers as though to prove his point.

She smiled. 'Joe, let's just take things a little slower.'

'Will you at least agree to stay on until the end of the month?' His thumb began to make little circles on her hand, and with each sweeping movement it felt as though a charge was shooting up her arm and exploding throughout her body.

Rachael tried to quash the emotions and think. It was almost impossible. Now that she and Joe had established a rapport, it might be good to stay on for a bit longer. It would give Joe a chance to really cement his relationship with Declan so when she eventually did move to another practice, Joe wouldn't feel too self-conscious about spending time with his son and not having Rachael there as a fall-back plan.

Then again, she had to take her emotions for Joe into account. Sure, it might be in Declan's best interests if she stayed for a bit longer, but what about hers? If she was honest with herself, she'd admit that Joe was far too special to her. History was repeating itself and where history had ended badly last time, it didn't give her much hope for a happy ending this time.

She frowned. 'I need to think about it, Joe.'

'Come on, Rach. Can't you give me an answer? You either will or you won't.'

'It's not that simple.'

'Yes, it is. It's a job.'

'A job that can have a lot of repercussions. I've never been a spontaneous person, Joe.'

'You married me.'

'That was different and you know it. I've never done things on the spur of the moment—apart from that.' And look how it turned out, she wanted to say. Recovering from a broken heart, feeling used and worthless and then discovering you were pregnant was not a good recommendation for her to spend more time with Joe, especially when it appeared she was more than willing to repeat past mistakes.

He let go of her hand. 'How much time? I need to know so I can arrange another locum.' He was all business now, his emotions hidden behind his professional mask.

'You'll have an answer by the end of the day.'

'Thank you.' He turned and motioned to the waitress, who quickly came over. 'We need this to go so would you mind wrapping them up for us, please?' The waitress took their plates. 'Drink your coffee,' he muttered, and followed his own advice.

The atmosphere as they walked back to the practice was the opposite of when they'd walked to the café. Joe's stride was brisk and determined and Rachael didn't even bother to try and keep up. When he realised he was outstripping her, he slowed down a little but only out of politeness, she was sure.

She refused to feel any guilt over his mood. As they walked into the practice, Joe merely nodded at Helen before disappearing into his consulting room.

'Problem?' Helen asked.

'Didn't get his own way.'

'Ah. The partnership. You turned him down?'

'You knew?'

'He asked me to get his solicitor on the line and I guessed.' She opened her mouth to say something else but closed it.

'Go on. What were you going to add?'

'Nothing.'

'Helen.'

The other woman shook her head and the clinic door opened, bringing her first patient for the afternoon. It was Tracy Rainer and her son. This time she didn't have Bobby in the pram but instead she was wearing a sling, Bobby sleeping soundly against her. They could just see the top of his downy head.

'Hi.' Rachael greeted Tracy warmly. 'Come right through, Tracy.' Rachael handed Helen the bag containing the sandwich. 'Would you mind putting that in the fridge for me, please?' Without waiting for an answer, she collected Tracy's file and headed down to her consulting room.

At least today Tracy looked a little more relaxed than she had on Monday, and Bobby appeared more settled.

'How are you feeling?'

'Like a person again.' Tracy smiled. 'This sling is fantastic—once I figured out how to put it on, that is. I can't believe how different I feel.'

'I take it you've managed to get some sleep.'

'Yes. On Monday night I brought the cot into the bedroom, fed him upright and gave him the antacid like you said, and he slept for four hours! I was waking up every hour to check he was all right because it was so unlike him.'

Rachael smiled. 'I can quite understand it. And last night?'

'Again, he slept for four hours after the feed and I did the same.'

'Well done.'

'The antacid has helped him so much and now that I know to keep him upright so he doesn't get reflux, he's more settled.'

Rachael sat at her desk and made a note of these changes in the casenotes. 'And your mother-in-law?'

Tracy grimaced. 'I was reluctant to call her, especially after Bobby had slept on Monday night, but I decided that you knew best and so I did it.'

'Good. And?' Rachael prompted eagerly.

'It wasn't as bad as I'd thought it would be. I think you were right. She wanted to help and I wasn't letting her, so she just criticised me instead. Anyway, she had Bobby for two hours yesterday at my house and then today I dropped him at her place and went shopping.'

'Well done! I am so proud of you.' Rachael beamed. 'I hope you spent some money on yourself.'

'I did...and I bought a few things for Bobby.'

'Naturally.'

'And I bought this.' Tracy reached inside her bag and brought out a little square parcel. She smiled shyly as she held it out to Rachael.

'For me?' Rachael was stunned. 'Thank you.' With great surprise, she unwrapped it to find a lovely photo frame inside. 'Thank you,' she said again. 'It's lovely. I'm moving into a new apartment soon so this will be a lovely addition to our new home.'

'Are you moving in with Dr Silvermark?'

Rachael blinked with astonishment. 'No. Why do you ask?'

'Oh. Sorry.' Tracy shrugged. 'It's just that your son looks just like him and I thought, you know, with you working here and…' Tracy waved her words away. 'Forget it.'

'Joe is Declan's father and…it's a long story.' She stood up and smiled at the sleeping baby. 'I'm reluctant to wake him when he's sleeping so soundly.' She peeked into the sling and brushed a kiss across his head. 'Make an appointment for next week and I'll review his reflux then. Don't change the dosage of antacid as it seems to be working, but if things change and you want me to see him, bring him in earlier.'

'OK.' Tracy smiled and Rachael was glad to have helped her. 'I'll see you next week.'

After they'd left, Rachael wrote up her notes and smiled as she put the photo frame away, still touched by the gesture.

When her last patient had left and she'd written up the notes, she headed into the kitchen, surprised Declan wasn't around. His schoolbag was in the corner so at least she knew he wasn't too far away. 'Probably talking to Joe,' she muttered, as she pulled her sandwich from the refrigerator and turned the kettle on. Sitting at the table, she unwrapped the slightly soggy club sandwich and bit into it gratefully.

Three mouthfuls later, Joe came into the kitchen. 'What! You're just eating lunch now?'

Rachael shrugged. 'You know what it's like, Joe. There was no time before.'

'I found time.'

'Yes, but you eat faster than I do. It's no big deal. Don't freak out.'

'Freak out?'

'Declan's favourite phrase.' She took another bite.

'What's my favourite phrase?' Declan asked, coming into the kitchen.

'Freak out,' Joe said.

'Yeah.' He grinned sheepishly. 'I guess I do say it a bit. Why? Who's freaking out?'

'Your father,' Rachael said, after swallowing her mouthful.

'Your mother's just eating her lunch now.'

'I can see that. Why does that freak you out?'

'Because it's not lunchtime.'

'Oh.' Declan frowned then shrugged. 'Taste good?'

'Terrific,' she said with her mouth half-full.

Declan shrugged again. 'What's the problem? She's a doctor. I thought all doctors ate at odd hours.'

Rachael swallowed her last mouthful. 'That was delicious. Kettle boiled? I'm ready for a cup of coffee.' She threw her rubbish in the bin and washed her hands. 'Dec? You want a drink?'

'No, thanks.'

'Joe?'

He shook his head. 'I'm going to take Declan down to the golf range.'

'Now?' Rachael glanced at her watch. 'It's after five.'

'We're not going to play a round, just have a few practice shots.'

Rachael raised her eyebrows. '*You* play golf?'

'Yeah. So?'

'You. You play golf.'

'Why do you keep saying that? Yes, I play golf. What's the big deal?'

Rachael couldn't help the chuckle that escaped her lips but she quickly squashed it when he frowned. 'Sorry. It…it just doesn't seem like your type of game. You know, being out with nature—trees, grass. Hitting a little white ball around.'

'So what *is* my type of game?'

'I don't know. Ice hockey?'

'Ice hockey?'

'Cool,' Declan said.

'It's a more physical sport, more smash 'em up and stuff.' Rachael made her coffee and took a sip. 'But I guess I'm still thinking of the Joe of the past. So, what time can I expect you back at the hotel?'

'Around seven.' Joe headed for the door. 'In time for dinner. You can wear your new boots!'

He raised his eyebrows teasingly before walking out, but stopped in the corridor when he heard Declan say to Rachael, 'A family dinner. Cool.'

The word *family* caused an icy chill to sweep over his body. Is that what they were becoming? A family? Was that what Declan wanted? A mother and a father? Together? Although he was attracted to Rachael, he wasn't sure he was cut out to play happy families.

'Don't get too excited,' Rachael added. 'It's just dinner.'

'Are you sure that's all? I think he's interested in a lot more than that.'

'Declan!' Rachael could feel her cheeks flush with embarrassment. 'Shh.'

'What? Have you forgotten I caught you two playing tonsil hockey last night? He likes you, Mum.'

'So? There's more to Joe than meets the eye, Dec, and I don't mean that in a bad way. I think he wants to be part of your life and that's great, but happy families just isn't Joe's style.'

'What about you, Mum? Do you want to play happy families with Joe?' Declan wriggled his eyebrows suggestively and Rachael momentarily covered her face. 'You love him, don't you.'

'I gave you my answer last night.'

'I want a different answer.'

Rachael hesitated, unsure whether to confide in her son. What if the truth hurt him? What if she got them both hurt? She dropped her hands and looked at him. He was watching her, his blue gaze intense, and she realised he already knew the answer. She shrugged and spoke with the utmost sincerity.

'I love Joe. I always have and I always will. He's the only man for me, but I've also learned to accept him for who he is, Dec. Spending time with you, getting to know you—if that's all he's capable of, then that's what I accept. You're my first priority and I think you'll soon become his. That's enough for me.'

Declan crossed the room to hug his mother. 'I love you, Mum, even though I think you're lying to yourself.'

Rachael laughed. 'Probably. Get going. Joe's waiting for you. Leave your schoolbag. I'll take it.'

Joe, still standing outside the room, quickly walked down to his consulting room, desperate to pull himself together. Rachael loved him? Was that true? Was she just saying that for Declan's benefit? And what sort of love was it? Was it a friendship love? A compassionate love or the real thing? The emotions he felt for her were increasing every moment he spent with her and they were scaring him senseless…just as they had all those years before.

When Declan appeared in his doorway, Joe shoved the thoughts aside. 'Just let me tidy up here and then we can go.' He shuffled some papers around on his desk, checked his pocket for his car keys and headed to tell Helen they were leaving.

'Have fun, boys,' she called.

'Boys?' Declan asked as they walked to Joe's car.

'She still sees me as a wayward teenager.' Joe's words were light but filled with humour. 'I guess she always will.'

They both climbed into the car and put their seat belts on. 'Were you a wayward teenager?'

Joe tensed. 'Kind of.'

'So what did you do way back then?'

Joe relaxed and smiled. 'You mean when dinosaurs walked the earth?' He started the engine and pulled out onto the street.

'Yeah.'

'Why do you want to know?'

'What do you mean?'

'Why? Has your mum said something?'

'No. I want to know because you're my dad. I know all about Mum because I've lived with her and seen the photo albums and heard Grandma and Grandad talk, but with you...' Declan shrugged. 'I just have blanks.'

'What did your mum tell you about me?'

'While I was growing up?'

'Yeah.' Joe gripped the steering wheel.

'She said my dad was a handsome man who always made her laugh and who she loved very much. She said you needed to find out who you were. I never really understood that but whenever

I asked her if you loved me, she said she was sure you did.'

Joe found it difficult to swallow the lump in his throat. Rachael had had every reason in the world to put him down, to tell her son how badly his father had treated her. The disgust and revulsion he felt about the day they'd had their marriage annulled swamped him.

'Until I met you the other day, Mum and I hadn't talked about you in years.'

Joe nodded slowly, clenching his teeth. 'I didn't know about you. If I had…' He trailed off. What would he have done? Honestly? He didn't have a clue. The fact that the situation had been forced upon him now was different, but if Rachael had managed to find him all those years ago when she'd first discovered she was pregnant, what would he have done?

He'd have walked away.

'We were different people back then. Your mother and I.'

'You were young. I can't believe Mum was only eighteen when she had me. She sometimes says we've grown up together.'

'She's a lot stronger than she used to be. I admire that.'

'What else do you like about her?'

If Joe hadn't overheard the conversation Declan had just had with his mother, he probably wouldn't have been as nervous. 'Lots of things.'

'Like what, specifically?'

Joe pulled into the car park of the golf range and turned the engine off. The silence engulfed them and when he spoke, even he heard the deep emotion in his words. 'I like her hair. Every time I've seen a woman with jet-black hair, it's always reminded me of her.'

'Do you still love her?'

Joe turned and looked at his son and realised that, regardless of what turmoil he was going through, he owed Declan nothing less than the truth. 'I don't know. I think on some level I will always love her. She's one in a million but...'

'But you're not into happy families.' Declan shrugged with feigned nonchalance and it was a mannerism Joe recognised as one of his own. 'It's cool,' the boy said, and pointed to the range. 'Let's go.' He opened the door and climbed out.

As Joe watched him walk away, he realised his son was nowhere near as adept at hiding his true feelings as he himself was...and he envied the kid.

CHAPTER NINE

RACHAEL returned to the hotel where she showered and dressed in a pair of jeans and a pale pink top. She'd just finished drying her hair when the door opened and male voices intruded into her solitude.

'Mum. The driving range was awesome. I was whacking those little white balls everywhere, wasn't I, Dad?' He glanced momentarily at his father before continuing. 'At first I had some trouble but then Dad showed me what I was doing wrong and then I got it on the next try. Didn't I, Dad?'

'You did.'

'I take it you had fun.' Rachael laughed and put her arm around his waist.

'No, it was boring. Whaddya think?' He broke away. 'I'm gonna change.' He grabbed some clothes and headed to the bathroom. Rachael sighed with relief when he'd disappeared. Her son was happy. That was all that mattered in life. 'It stinks all girly in here,' he grumbled through the door, and both she and Joe laughed.

'Thanks, Joe.'

Joe shrugged. 'For what?'

'For making him happy.'

'Hopefully, his mind's not too stimulated and he'll be able to sleep tonight. How does he do it? Survive on such a small amount of sleep?'

'The past few days will catch up with him.'

'When?'

'On the weekend. Trust me. You'll hardly see him on Saturday and Sunday and if you do, it will be after midday before he surfaces. He sleeps and he sleeps and he sleeps, and there's no way I interrupt that.'

'Fair enough.' Joe walked over to the window and looked out. Rachael felt the atmosphere in the room change. She waited, knowing he wanted to say something. It irritated her that she knew him so well, and at the same time she drew comfort from the same fact.

'Rach.'

'Yes.'

'Are you staying on until the end of the month?'

'Yes.'

He turned to face her. 'Really?'

Rachael sighed, knowing she was in for heartache, but whether she stayed or not, the pain would come. 'Yes.'

'Why?'

'Pardon?'

'Why?'

'Because it's good for the patients, good for Declan and gives me time to get my apartment established before looking around for another job.'

'That's it?'

She shrugged. 'What else is there? You asked and I've given you my answer.'

Joe turned back to the window. Why wouldn't she tell him? He'd overheard her telling Declan she loved him.

He stared at his reflection in the window. What had you expected, Silvermark? He shook his head. Did you honestly expect her to come right out and say she's staying on because she loves you? Rachael wasn't the sort of person to let her heart get in the way of her judgement—at least not now. Could he blame her? Fifteen years ago he'd taken the love she'd offered so selflessly and had thrown it back at her. No, he'd trampled on it and *then* rejected it. He'd been scared, confused and had let his defences wreck the best thing that had ever happened to him—receiving an honest love from an honest woman.

Joe shifted so he could see her reflection in the window. She was just standing there, hands in the pockets of her jeans, the pink top making her eyes more vibrant and her black hair shine beautifully as it hung loose around her shoulders.

He turned to face her and she saw the desire in his eyes. She also saw total confusion and her heart went out to him. Joe wasn't the sort of man who was easy with emotions, and although he'd come a long way, he still had much more to experience. If she took a step in faith, if she guided him through the rocky terrain, then maybe…just maybe…there might be a future for all three of them. She stood her ground, knowing this time Joe needed to take the first step. She could help him, she was willing to help him, but he had to be ready to receive the help. She dug her hands further into her pockets.

Joe wished she'd cross the room and put her arms around his neck. Then he'd be back in control because he knew exactly what to do when Rachael's body was pressed against his. She didn't move. Although he saw need and desire in her eyes, he realised she wasn't going to do the chasing. She'd just stand there and wait for him. If he went to her, she'd welcome him with open arms—of that he was certain. If he didn't, she'd stand there, pick up the pieces of her life and move on. The thought terrified him.

'OK.' Declan came out the bathroom and Rachael instantly broke eye contact with Joe and turned to face her son. 'I'm starving.' He threw his school clothes onto her bed and Rachael immediately straightened them out.

'Where do you want to go?'

'Dad and I saw this great Mexican restaurant so we thought we'd go there. It's only a block down the road so we can walk.' Declan shrugged into his jacket.

'Sounds good. Let's go.' Rachael pulled on her new boots.

'Nice.' Joe nodded.

She smiled, thrilled with his comment, and shrugged into her jacket. Joe walked through the door Declan held open. 'Have you got the key-card?' Rachael checked before the door shut behind them.

'Yes, Mum,' Declan declared in a bored tone. 'Here's mine.' Declan waved it in front of her before handing it over. She slid it into her wallet then closed her bag. They rode the lift down and as they walked along the street, Rachael was a little startled to find Joe slipping his hand into hers. Not that she minded—quite the contrary—but it was so unexpected. She smiled up at him and gave his hand a squeeze before continuing her conversation with Declan about his school day.

'You see, Joe,' she said after they'd eaten their fill of the delicious Mexican food and were waiting for their dessert, 'the trick with kids is you have to ask them specific questions. "How was your day?" is only going to get you a general answer like, "Good".'

'What she's trying to say is that she's an expert at being nosy,' Declan added.

Rachael laughed good-naturedly. 'That's a mother's prerogative—nosy and nagging.'

'And you're the best at both, Mum.' Declan grinned at her. 'Every day I get bombarded with questions, especially as I've just started at a new school.'

'Well, what do you expect? I'm still learning all the players.'

'Players?' Joe frowned.

'Other students, teachers, that sort of thing.' Declan shrugged and Joe noticed the nonchalance. Don't get too close, the message said, but Rachael *was* close. She'd worked through

Declan's defences and she knew her son well. It was evident in the way they interacted. Now she was working her way through his defences...and doing a good job of it.

'So...Declan.' Joe took a breath, realising Rachael wasn't just making idle conversation but actually giving him parenting pointers. 'Who do you sit next to in maths?'

Rachael grinned.

'Oh, man. You're gonna start in on this, too?'

'How am I supposed to get to know you?' Joe leaned his elbows on the table. 'You're my son and we have years of catching up to do.' To his surprise, he noticed tears well in Declan's eyes.

'Does this mean you...want to be part of my life?'

Rachael held her breath, waiting anxiously for Joe's answer.

'Yes. In fact, I spoke to my solicitor today. I've had my will adjusted.'

'What?' Rachael and Declan spoke together, staring at him in stunned silence.

'It's my way of saying this is for life. You're my son, Declan. Nothing in the world is going to change that. It's important for me not only to find out about the past fourteen years of your life but to ensure your future is secure as well.'

'Joe.' It was on the tip of Rachael's tongue to tell him she was financially secure. That Declan was well taken care of, not only from herself but from her parents as well, but she closed her mouth, realising the enormity of what Joe had done. He was taking a chance. He was letting Declan in close, and had made it official by changing his will.

'That didn't come out right.' Joe raked a hand through his hair and Rachael's heart went out to him. 'I want to be there for you, son. I want to be your father. I'm just not sure I know how.'

Declan surprised them both by laughing as he brushed a few tears from his eyes. 'Are you kidding? You're the coolest guy I've ever met, and you're my *dad*! It's just so awesome.' He sobered a little. 'Mum's brill and she knows that, but there are…things—you know, guy stuff—and Mum doesn't have a clue. No offence, Mum.'

Rachael smiled. 'None taken. I'm glad you have Joe.'

'Don't get sappy on me, Mum.' Declan ha[illegible] himself under control once more but she knew [illegible] would take ages for the happy, silly grin to [illegible] wiped off his face. As far as Declan was c[illegible]cerned, all his Christmases *had* come at on[illegible]

Rachael still felt Joe watching her closely as she ate as much of her dessert as she could. Halfway through, she passed the rest to Declan who cleaned it up without a problem.

'Hey. How come he gets the leftovers?' Joe demanded.

'Looks as though you've got competition, Dec.'

Their conversation was easy, friendly and jovial as they finished up and walked…or rather *rolled* back to the hotel. 'I can't believe how much I ate.' Rachael patted her stomach. 'Well, here we are.' They stopped outside the entrance to the hotel.

'I'll ride up with you,' was all he said. Outside their door, Joe turned to Declan. 'Would you mind if I spoke to your mum alone for a minute?'

'Nah. I'll go start on my homework.'

'Have a shower first,' Rachael instructed, handing over the key-card.

'Yes, Mum,' he answered in the dull, boyish way he'd done for years. 'Nag, nag, nag.' He nlocked the room and held the door open.

'You may as well come in. Declan will be in shower so we can talk.'

Talk about me?' Declan was all ears.

es. That's what parents do. Now go.'

She waited until the water was running then just as Joe was about to open his mouth, she held up her hand to stop him. Walking quietly over to the bathroom door, she banged loudly on it and received a yell from her son.

'Stop pressing your ear against the door and get in the shower. You're wasting water.'

Joe shook his head in amazement. 'How did you know?'

'He's a teenager and we're going to talk about him. Do you need more deductive reasoning than that?'

'Actually, I wanted to talk about you.' As usual, Joe paced the room then stopped and looked at her. It was his way of getting his thoughts together and she waited.

'OK. What do you want to know?'

'Tell me more about when you tried to find me.'

'OK.' She took a breath. 'Well, I tried when I discovered I was pregnant. When I couldn't track you down, I wondered whether you were dead. For years I didn't know but I forced myself to get on with my life. You'd rejected me and I had to live with that, so I did. Then, when Declan was about nine, you and I were both at the same medical conference.'

'What? Where?'

'It was a GP conference in Sydney.'

'You were there? Why didn't you say something?'

'Our paths didn't cross. I'd missed the first day of the conference because Declan hadn't been well on the flight to Sydney. My parents had flown in to look after him while I was at the conference and had a problem with their hotel reservation. I saw your name on the conference programme and couldn't believe it was really you, so I did some checking. Was there another Joseph Silvermark in the world? Were you associated with the conference? Did the hotel have a contact number for you? No one could give me any personal information as it was against conference and hotel policy, but at least I'd discovered you were not only alive but a doctor! I was stunned to discover you'd gone into medicine and proud at the same time. That probably sounds silly.'

'No. Go on,' he urged.

Rachael laced her fingers together and met his gaze. 'At the end of the second day, I saw you. It was late in the day and you were about to get into a taxi outside the hotel. I was in the lobby. You were with…a woman.'

Joe frowned as he thought back. 'Blonde?'

'Yes. She had her arms around your waist and you had your arm around her shoulders. You were smiling down at her and…' She shrugged. 'I couldn't do it.'

'Do what?'

'Go to you. Talk to you. Walk right up, ask if you even remembered me and then somehow figure out a way to tell you that you had a son! Especially when you had another woman hanging on your arm.'

'How could you think I wouldn't remember you?'

'I don't know.' She threw up her hands in despair. 'It all happened so fast. The two of you got into the taxi and it drove away. I hardly slept that night and was a nervous wreck the next day as I looked for you again.'

'I only stayed for the first two days.'

'So I found out.' She shrugged. 'That's when I started obsessing. Should I find you? Should I leave it? You'd never been keen on children so chances were you might even reject Declan. Still, you had a right to know and so I made some enquiries to see if there was some way I could find you. The Australian GPs' register at least told me where you'd been working, but when I contacted the practice, they told me you'd left for overseas and as you were a locum they had no way of contacting you.'

Joe shook his head in disbelief. 'That's when I started getting into the movie scene as an on-site medic. I was in America for a year then came back here and started up my practice.' He pushed his fingers through his hair. 'Wherever I worked, I always gave them as few personal details as possible. Immediate contact numbers, address, that was it. It stemmed from my childhood of never giving out information that wasn't necessary.'

'It's OK, Joe. In a way it was good for me because at the time I was still clinging to a teenage girl's fantasy that we would one day get back together. Seeing you…' She stopped, unable to believe her voice had choked up.

'Seeing me with that girl? Why should that matter?'

'Why?' She couldn't believe how fast the tears sprang into her eyes. Her throat felt thick but she managed to get the words out. 'Joe, I loved you. You may have treated me like dirt, broken my heart and destroyed my self-worth when you ended our marriage—'

'Care to heap any more guilt on me?'

'I'm just stating the facts. Regardless of what had happened between us, you were Declan's father and the man I loved. I may not have *liked* you very much at times, but I've always loved you.'

'And now?' He took a step closer, trying to ignore the loud pounding of his heart. 'Do you love me now?'

She tilted her head to the side, a small, sincere smile on her lips. 'You know I do.'

Her words were matter-of-fact but he needed more. He needed to dig a little deeper. 'No. I don't mean love me as Declan's father but love *me*, accept *me*…as a man.'

'I know what you mean, Joe.' She took a breath and knew it was now or never. She'd laid herself, her heart, her pride on the line before, and now it was time to do it again. She'd told him she was strong, she'd told him she'd changed, yet right now she felt eighteen years old again. Young, excited, unsure, thrilled. They were now almost toe to toe and he reached out to tenderly caress her cheek.

'Rach?'

She looked up at him, still smiling. A warmth spread through him and he cupped her face in his hands.

'I love you, Joe.' The whispered words were said with meaning and without hesitation. 'I always have and I always will.'

With a smothered groan he pressed his mouth to hers, greedily taking everything she was willing to give. He realised in that second that he'd never be able to get enough of her. She was like a drug and he was totally addicted.

Hot, powerful. Hungry, masterful. He had the ability to take her up so high and he was doing it right now. Lacing her fingers through his hair, she made sure his mouth stayed where it belonged as she continued to declare her love for him through her actions.

'Sweetheart,' he panted, when at last he pulled his mouth from hers. 'You make me crazy.' He pressed feathery-light kisses to her forehead and cheeks. 'No other woman affects me the way you do.'

'Not even the blonde?'

'Blonde? What blonde?'

'At the conference.' It hurt but she needed to know.

Joe leaned back, looking deeply into her eyes. 'Jealous?'

She lifted her chin in that defiant way he loved. 'Yes.' There was no point denying it. The thought of him with any other woman had always driven her insane.

'You have no reason to be. She's my half-sister.'

'Your…your sister?' Her words held a hint of disbelief.

'Half-sister. Her name's Melina, she lives in Sydney and is a bodyguard.'

'A bodyguard?'

'She grew up on the streets, remember. I had to teach her how to protect herself.' He shrugged and then settled his arms about her. 'The rest just followed.'

'Your sister.' Rachael shook her head.

'Yes.'

'She was your sister! I feel so stupid.'

'Rach.' He kissed her. 'Don't beat yourself up. You weren't to know. I didn't know you were there. You tried to find me and couldn't. It's all in the past.'

'Yes. But we need to sort through it, Joe. If we're going to have any hope for a future, we need to sort through the past.'

Any hope for a future… Any hope for a future. The words started repeating in his head and he could feel himself drawing away, distancing himself mentally before he physically released his hold on her. She was still talking and he tried to listen but he couldn't. *Any hope for a future…* Was that what he wanted? A future with Rachael and Declan? He'd made the decision to include Declan in his life but Rachael…he hadn't been able to sort things through yet. He needed time. Space. He took another step back and watched as she stopped speaking, the blue of her eyes changing from warm and inviting to cold and protective.

'Joe?'

He swallowed and was disgusted to find his throat dry, his heart pounding and his hands sweating. He wiped them down his jeans.

Rachael folded her arms over her chest. 'Still pulling away? Still unable to let go of your emotions and follow your heart?'

'Rachael—'

'No. I think it's time for some hard questions, Joe. You've asked me so now I'm going to ask you. Do you love me?'

'Rach.'

'Answer the question, Joe. Do you love me? And I don't mean in an old-friend way or even because I'm Declan's mother. I'm talking about the love shared between a husband and wife, between soul mates. The truest love you could imagine…the love you once made me believe you felt. Is it still there?'

He shrugged, feeling caged, trapped. 'I don't know.'

'Why not?'

'I don't know if I'm capable of love.'

'Do you love Declan?'

'That's different.'

'Do you love Helen?'

'Different.'

'Your sister?'

'Rachael.'

'No, Joe. You are capable of loving. I've seen it. I've *felt* it.'

'I'm not good with emotions.'

'Love isn't an emotion, Joe. Love triggers emotions. Safety, security, happiness. Pain, humiliation, hurt. Frustration, annoyance and anger, Joe. Right now, that's how I'm feeling. You are strong enough to love and your apathy drives me insane. I know you're capable because you loved me. You shared your heart with me, Joe, and for those amazing forty-eight hours you weren't afraid. You weren't on guard. You were alive. For the first time in your life you were alive, and it scared you. You were scared to feel, just as you are now.'

To her utter dismay, Rachael felt tears begin to slide down her cheeks. She sniffed. 'It's all too much,' she said to herself more than to him. 'The past few days have been too emotional. I think we need some time apart. Helen promised I would hardly see you, but you're there every time I turn around.' She pulled a tissue from her pocket as the tears refused to stop.

He started towards her but she held up a hand.

'Just go, Joe.'

'Rachael—' He took another step forward.

'She told you to go.'

Both of them whirled around to see Declan standing outside the bathroom, wrapped in a hotel robe. Rachael gasped, unable to believe she'd forgotten he was around. She hadn't heard the shower stop, neither had she heard him come out. How long had he been there? How much had he heard?

'Declan, I—' Joe began.

Declan walked to his mother's side and put a protective arm about her shoulders. 'Leave us alone.'

Joe took in the determined look on his son's face and realised the boy was serious.

He nodded and without a word, without looking back, he left.

CHAPTER TEN

A WEEK later, Joe was still avoiding Rachael. She'd hardly seen him, just as Helen had initially promised. He was in the clinic for a few hours almost every day but the rest of his time was taken up on set.

Wong had regained consciousness after five days in a coma and was progressing slowly but steadily. Rino was already back on the set, taking over from Wong and making sure the studio lost as little money as possible because of the delays they'd already encountered.

Rachael had spoken to Ethel almost every day and even visited Alwyn once he'd been discharged, and she was glad a lasting friendship seemed to be developing between them. She needed to make new friends.

She'd spoken to Declan about what he'd overheard and after a few days he'd agreed to see Joe. They'd played golf on the weekend and he'd visited the movie set a few more times. Declan seemed to be adjusting to his new life, not only with school but with his father as well.

They moved out of the hotel into their new apartment and finally Rachael started to feel as though she had some sort of control over her life. She had two and a half weeks to go at Joe's practice and then she would need to find somewhere else to work, but the thought of leaving his practice, where she was just starting to get to know her patients, concerned her. She liked it there. Joe wasn't around much, and as the movie still wasn't finished his time at the practice would be minimal. Surely it wouldn't hurt to stay on for her original contract of six months? Declan was getting into a good routine, seeing Joe three times a week after school, and they were planning to play another round of golf this coming weekend.

Rachael resolved to speak to Helen by the end of the day to see if she'd been successful in finding another locum. When she went out to the waiting room, little Anthony Edmunds came running up to her with a book he'd brought from home.

'Read it. Now.' He tugged her to the closest chair and a moment later he'd scrambled up onto her knee and had the book open. Rachael laughed and happily obliged, glad to see Anthony so happy and relaxed. She read it through twice before he'd let her lead him to her consulting room.

'How's everything been this past week?' She flicked through the casenotes, reading the results of the tests.

'He's better and his tantrums have actually decreased,' his mother said.

'That's a positive. The tests show he does have very early diverticulitis but with a healthy diet and regular monitoring, we should be able to treat him without surgical intervention.'

'Oh. You have no idea what a relief that is. I've been trying so hard to get extra fibre into him and yesterday he actually ate what I put in front of him.'

'Good. I'm glad you're being persistent. Keep it up and at the end of next week start introducing a new food. Decrease the amount of liquid paraffin by five mils for the next five days and then decrease by two mils again for seven days. I'll need to review him again then.'

'That's it?'

'Just keep up with those new foods and be persistent. As you've seen, there's been a change in Anthony's attitude and the number of tantrums he's having. His tummy pains are decreasing and that's making him a happier boy.'

His mother smiled. 'You're right.'

'It's a long road.'

'But I'm willing to walk it.'

'That's what I'd hoped to hear.' Rachael took another look at the X-rays and pointed out the area in question to Anthony's mother.

'It all looks like grey and white swirls to me.'

Rachael smiled as she removed the films. 'Keep doing what you're doing and soon you'll find his dietary fibre levels will be excellent.'

She wrote up the notes after Anthony and his mother had left, and headed back out for her next patient.

'Wendy,' she said, delighted to see the expectant mother again. 'How are you feeling today?'

'Horrible. I have so much back pain it hurts to walk. Is there anything you can give me for it?' Wendy waddled down the corridor.

'When did it start?'

'A few hours ago. No contractions or anything just really bad back pain.'

'OK.' Rachael shut her consulting room door. 'Why don't you get up on the examination bed and we'll check what's going on?' She walked over to the sink, washed her hands and pulled on a pair of gloves. When Wendy was ready, Rachael began the examination, her eyes widening in surprise.

A moment later Wendy groaned and closed her eyes. 'The pain is so bad. It's unbearable. I feel sick.'

'That's because you're in labour.'

'What?' Wendy opened her eyes in total disbelief.

'You're fully dilated.'

'That's impossible. I haven't had any contractions, just back pain.'

'Back pain. Contractions.' Rachael shrugged. 'Same difference. Stay where you are.' With her elbow, Rachael pressed the intercom button on her phone. 'Helen, Wendy Gibson's in labour. The baby is coming…' Wendy groaned in pain again and as she did so, the examination bed and surrounding area became wet as her waters broke. '*Now.* Is Joe in?'

'Yes.'

'I'm going to need him and you. Contact the hospital, the ambulance and Wendy's husband.'

'Rachael!' Wendy called, and Rachael rushed to her side.

'I'm here.' She checked again and wasn't surprised this time to see the baby's head crowning. 'Well, you said your other two children were late. This one is simply impatient.'

'Great. Just what I need,' Wendy groaned.

There was a knock at her door and in the next instant Joe was standing there, his face white with shock. 'Helen told me to get in here.'

'Yes. Get the foetal heart monitor on so we can check the heartbeat. Do Wendy's obs and get ready to take over neonate care once the baby's born. You're doing fine, Wendy.'

'I want to push.'

'Then push.' Rachael continued to assist, conscious of Helen coming in and getting everything organised. Joe had the foetal heart monitor on and the beats coming through were strong and steady, no sign of distress.

'How are you feeling, Wendy?' Rachael asked as the contraction eased. 'Still feel sick?'

'Yes.'

'Bucket's at the ready,' Helen soothed, pushing the hair out of the woman's eyes. 'Your hubby's on his way but I think baby might just beat him here.'

'BP's up but nothing out of the ordinary,' Joe reported. He moved around the room, opening cupboards and getting things ready.

'Ow, ow. The pain's coming again.' Wendy shook her head. 'I'm not ready. The baby can come next week. Any time after this weekend, but not now. Aargh.' She pushed again and the head came out just a little bit more.

'You know how kids are,' Rachael soothed. 'They never listen to their parents.'

'Well, why did this one have to start so early?' Wendy complained. 'It's not fair.'

'I know.' Rachael laughed. 'My son was exactly the same except he thought a midnight delivery was more exciting.'

Joe put the monitor on Wendy's stomach again and met Rachael's gaze as they counted the beats together. 'Good.'

Wendy pushed once more and the head was almost out. 'You're doing a brilliant job. Snatch a breath and push again. Squeeze Helen's hand if you want. Turn it purple. Helen won't mind.' Rachael smiled at the other woman.

'Not at all.' Helen put a wet facecloth on Wendy's brow to cool her down. 'I've plenty of experience assisting with births so trouble me for anything you want.'

'I want my husband,' Wendy growled, before relaxing.

'He's coming. He'll be here soon,' Helen promised.

'Two more pushes and the head will be out. You can do it.' She wiped the area and got ready as Wendy began to push again. 'That's it. That's it. Keep it coming.'

Wendy growled, yelled and let her temper show. Joe checked the baby's heartbeat, glad to find it still strong and steady.

'Where is everyone?' came a loud call.

'In here.' Joe headed to the corridor and soon Wendy's husband was by her side, taking over the hand-holding from Helen.

'This is it, Wendy. One big push and the head will be out.' As the contraction hit, Wendy pushed. Rachael found herself holding her breath in sympathy, her teeth clenched as she mentally pushed with her patient. 'That's it. Snatch a breath. Keep going.' She felt Joe come to stand behind her as the head finally came out. 'That's it. Head's out. Now, don't push. I'm just checking the neck while the shoulders rotate.' She ran her fingers around the baby's neck and, sure enough, there was the cord. 'Joe.' She worked to unloop the cord as Joe held the baby's head. 'Don't push, Wendy.'

'I have to. I need to.' Before she'd finished speaking, the contraction came. Rachael frantically pulled the cord free as first one shoulder came out, then the other, and in the next instant the latest edition to the Gibson family entered the world. With one loud gurgling breath, the most beautiful sound in all the world pierced the air around them…the cry of a newborn babe.

Joe held the baby while Rachael found the clamps Helen had laid out and set about getting the cord ready for the baby's dad to cut.

'So what do we have?' Wendy asked impatiently.

Joe held the baby up.

'We have a girl?' Wendy couldn't believe it. Tears overflowed as she gazed with love on her child. Her husband kissed her warmly. Rachael felt the emotions rise within herself and glanced at Joe. He was watching her, and as their gazes held, the feelings between them were raw and real. She saw the love he felt for her in his eyes and she wrapped herself up in that knowledge.

'Ready for the cord?' Helen asked, purposely breaking the fog surrounding Joe and Rachael.

'Uh…yes.' Rachael brought her attention back to the task at hand and soon the new father had cut the cord and Joe took the baby over to Rachael's desk where she realised he'd prepared an area and draped it with soft towels so he could use the small, portable suction machine to clear the baby's mouth and nose. The little girl yelled at him and Rachael laughed.

'You're losing your touch, Joe.'

'Keep quiet,' he grumbled good-naturedly, not bothering to look at her. He couldn't. The one glance they'd just shared had left him naked. Throughout the delivery, he'd been completely aware of Rachael and how she would have gone through this experience without him. He hadn't been there. Wendy's whole attitude had changed when her husband had arrived, and Joe realised just how much he'd really missed of Declan's life. Right now, he would give anything to go back and be able to see his son being born.

'I think I'm getting old,' he said softly to his charge. All she did was wave her arms and legs in the air and cry. 'One-minute Apgar—eight.'

'Excellent.' Rachael and Helen were concentrating on the third stage of labour.

'I've made such a mess,' Wendy said apologetically.

'As if we care about that,' Helen remarked.

Rachael glanced over to where Joe was and couldn't help the way her mouth dropped open to see him carefully wrapping and then cradling the small infant in his arms. It looked so right, so perfect to see him holding the child. How could he possibly think he wouldn't make a great father? She loved him so much and she desperately wanted to show him all he was capable of giving, if only he'd let go and trust her once more.

He looked across at her and they shared another moment before a slow smile spread across his face as he handed the baby to her proud mother.

'Congratulations.'

'Thank you, Dr Silvermark. Oh, she's so perfect.'

'Yes, she is.' Joe was looking at Rachael as he spoke. She was brilliant. She hadn't panicked, she'd done her job, and now there was a healthy baby to show for it. So much could have gone wrong but it hadn't, and the ambulance sirens could be heard in the distance, ready to take the family off to hospital.

Joe quickly cleaned up, setting Rachael's desk back to rights, while he listened to Helen taking charge of the situation.

'I'll ring Patty and she can pick your boys up from school and bring them to the hospital.'

'Thank you,' Wendy replied. 'And to you, Rachael. You were wonderful.'

Rachael smiled and leaned over to brush her finger over the little girl's forehead. 'She's beautiful. Do you have a name?'

'Cynthia.' Wendy kissed her baby. 'Nick and Elliot are going to be so happy they have a sister. They didn't want a brother.'

'Just as well. Welcome to the world, Cynthia.'

Rachael couldn't take her eyes off the beautiful baby who, after her impatience to be born, had now settled down to sleep. Joe watched Rachael watching the baby and felt the old inadequacies surface once more. She'd mentioned she wanted more children and the thought of her having them with anyone but him made him crazy. Declan didn't deserve half-brothers and sisters but siblings who shared the same parents… But he'd vowed *never* to have children. He'd never wanted to risk hurting them as he'd been hurt by his parents.

The sirens had stopped and as both Helen and Rachael were busy, Joe headed out to let the paramedics in. It was his chance to escape, knowing Rachael was more than capable of taking care of things.

He needed to think.

'Where's Joe?' Declan asked when he arrived at the clinic after school.

'Not sure,' Rachael replied. One of her patients had called to cancel at the last minute so it looked as though she could finish early for once. 'Check with Helen.'

Declan disappeared and came back a moment later with a photograph. 'Hey, Mum. Get a load of this.' He held out a photograph. Rachael looked, then frowned.

'I don't remember this being taken. Where was it? You look about eleven.'

'It's not me, it's Joe.'

'Wow!' Rachael took the photo from him and peered at it more closely. 'That's amazing. I couldn't tell the difference.'

'Helen brought it in for me. She said I could keep it.'

'That's very nice of her.'

'She's a nice lady. I like her.'

Rachael smiled. 'I'm glad to hear it.'

'Mum, are you really going to leave here at the end of the month?'

'Funny you should ask that.' She told him her thoughts about staying on and he dragged her out to the front desk so she could discuss it with Helen.

'Of course you can stay, but are you sure you want it just for your locum contract? You don't want to go down the partnership track?'

'I don't want Joe to feel pressured.'

'Rachael, I'm going to stick my nose in again. How do you feel about Joe?' Helen watched her closely.

'She loves him,' Declan answered for her.

Rachael nodded. 'I always have. Joe's it as far as I'm concerned.'

'And he knows this?'

'Yes.'

'Ah. No wonder he's retreated to his cave.'

'Yes.'

'Cave?' Declan frowned at the two women. 'What cave? Why didn't he take me? I'd like to go caving.'

'Not that sort of cave, darling.' Rachael laughed.

'Give him the time he needs,' Helen advised.

'How long's that?'

Helen shrugged. 'Your guess is as good as mine.'

'Things seemed OK during the delivery. He kept smiling at me.'

'I saw.'

'Delivery?' Declan frowned. 'I don't know what you two are on about but if Joe's not here, I guess we're not going to practise our golf swings, so can we go home, Mum?'

Rachael felt Declan's disappointment. 'Sure. Go get your schoolbag.'

'He's new to this father stuff,' Helen defended Joe. 'And his head's all wrapped up in emotions. And, believe me, emotions aren't Joe's strong point.'

'Tell me about it.' Rachael looked at her watch and then back to Helen. 'Want to come over to our new apartment for dinner?'

Helen beamed. 'Are you kidding? That would be wonderful and I'm dying to see the place.'

'Excellent.'

Joe sat on the beach for hours, just watching life go by. His life had gone by pretty quickly and suddenly he'd found himself getting closer to forty. What had Rach said? The older you get, the better you know yourself. She was right. He knew himself better now than he had at nineteen.

He knew he loved her and it was a love that had never died but had lain dormant for years until she'd walked back into his life. He loved the strong, independent woman she'd become—admired her courage. He knew she would go on living her life without him if that was what he wanted but, he finally admitted to himself, it *wasn't* what he wanted.

You're not into happy families.

Declan's words, combined with the pain he'd witnessed in his son's eyes, filtered through his mind. Happy families was what Rachael and Declan wanted…no, needed, and amazingly he realised he needed it, too.

He knew she loved him, she'd told him so and he'd seen it in her eyes when they'd delivered little Cynthia. But what about the future? Did she really want to build one with him? He frowned as another thought came to mind. Knowing there was only one way to get the answer, he stood up, carelessly brushed the sand away and headed to his car.

Five minutes later, he was knocking on Rachael's apartment door. He was surprised when Helen opened it.

'Aha. Didn't expect to see me here, did you? We've just finished dinner. Declan's on the phone with a friend and Rachael's in the kitchen.'

'No, she's not. She's here,' Rachael said from behind Helen as she wiped her hands on a dish towel. 'You OK?'

'Yeah. I wanted to apologise to Declan for not being there this afternoon.'

'He won't be long. Come on in,' she instructed, as they were all standing in the doorway. 'You want the guided tour?'

Joe smiled and shoved his hands deep into his jeans pocket. 'Sure.'

'I'll finish up in the kitchen,' Helen said, and tactfully disappeared.

'Well, this is the living area and over here…' Rachael walked to an archway '…is the hallway, and we have Declan's bedroom down there and mine at the other end.'

'Mmm-hmm.' He followed behind, watching the gentle sway of her hips as she spoke. She'd changed from the clothes she usually wore to work into a denim skirt which came to mid-thigh, revealing her sublime legs. Her T-shirt was big and baggy and looked comfortable. Her hair was loose, her face devoid of make-up and she was barefoot, with painted toenails and a toe ring. He raised his eyebrows and when she realised he was looking down at her feet, she smiled.

'A present from Declan. To keep me young at heart.'

'No piercings? Tattoos?'

'No.'

'Glad to hear it.' He leaned back against the wall in the small hallway. She leant against the opposite wall, facing him.

'Are you here to look at the apartment or me?'

'You.' He took her left hand in his and after a moment gently slid the simple wedding band off her finger. 'Hope you don't mind,' he said. Rachael gasped as her insides churned with longing…but she didn't try to stop him.

He looked at the ring closely, reading the inscription. '"Rach, love Joe".' He nodded slowly. 'Do you wear this because it was the only wedding band you could find to protect yourself from scrutiny, or do you wear it because you couldn't bear to take it off?'

'How important is my answer? I mean, will it alter things?'

'Are you going to be stubborn about this?'

'Are you going to answer my question?'

'Yes, it's important and, no, it won't alter things. I just want to know.'

Her heart was pounding wildly against her chest. 'You put it there, Joe, and I couldn't bring myself to take it off. Call me corny, sappy or whatever else you want, but—'

Her words were cut short as he moved like lightning and pressed his mouth to hers. His body heat warmed her through and through as they hungrily took from each other.

'It's been way too long since you kissed me,' she panted as they broke apart briefly to snatch a breath. He pressed her back against the wall, covering her body with his, needing to get as close as possible to the woman of his dreams.

'Rachael. Rachael,' he panted after a few moments. He pressed kisses around her face, on her neck, before heading home to her mouth again where he forced himself to slow down. The sweet and subtle seduction in his kiss only made her melt even more and finally, when he broke free and gently caressed her cheek with the back of his fingers, he said, 'You were the last person I ever wanted to see again…and you were the only person I ever wanted to see again.'

'I know what you mean. Joe?' She kissed his fingers as they trailed across her lips. 'Can you tell me? About the past?'

'Yes.' He walked back into the living room and shut the door. 'It's time. Have a seat.'

Rachael did as she was asked and waited. He paced the room, glanced unseeingly at pictures on the walls and finally stopped just before her.

'I had no one, Rach. I look at you and the way you are with Declan and I envy that. I had no one until Helen found me, but that's jumping too far ahead.' He took a deep breath. 'I'd learned at an early age not to show my true emotions. From my earliest memory, I was shoved aside if I cried. I was about four years old and my father was yelling at me for something—I can't remember what—and I started to cry and he gave me a backhand right across the face. It was so hard it knocked me off the chair. Then he walked away.'

Rachael watched the controlled emotions as he spoke. She could feel his pain and anguish and her own heart cried out for that little boy who'd been abused.

'It didn't get better. Time and time again he'd hit me. Then he started hitting me just for the fun of it. If I cried, he just hit me harder so I learned not to.' There was an edge to his voice, one she hadn't often heard. 'I'm not telling you this to shock you and I certainly don't want your pity. I want you to know why I pushed you away.'

'I got too close.'

'Yes.'

'All you told me was that you'd been in foster homes and that finally you were old enough to earn some money and escape to travel the world.'

'There's a lot more to it than that.'

'So I figured at the time, but I didn't want to push. When we first met, you were funny and crazy and the most exciting person I'd ever met. You were also one of the smartest.' She smiled. 'Remember how we stayed up late while travelling on the bus, just talking?'

Joe smiled at her. 'From politics to music.'

'We didn't always agree…'

'But, then, who does?' He sat beside her and cupped her face in his hands. 'You were amazing. So caring and accepting. No one had ever treated me like that before. Not in such a personal and romantic way.' He brushed his lips tenderly over hers, drawing those emotions deep into his soul. He looked down into her eyes, still amazed to find her love for him had never died. He could see it reflected in every part of her and it made him feel…special.

Joe knew he had to continue the sordid recount of his past, astonished to find how easy it was to say these things to her. He should have known. This was *Rachael*. The woman who loved him. He brushed one last kiss across her lips before moving away.

Again she waited patiently for him to continue.

'I'd always been put down, even in the foster homes which weren't much better than my real home.'

'Did you live on the streets?'

'Yes. Believe it or not, it was safer.' He shrugged. 'At least in a gang I had people looking out for me. We were all in the same boat, beaten by our parents or foster-parents, and had no one to care for us.'

'So you *cared*—in a very broad sense of the word—for each other.'

'Yes. Getting away from everything, from the streets, from the violence that surrounded me, getting away was all I could think about. It was what kept me going. It was what kept me sane. I dropped out of school and got a job in a junkyard. It was easy money and mindless work. I was still in the gang and although I had several brushes with the law, I was thankfully never convicted.'

'What with?'

'Stealing cars. Sometimes stealing food. At one of the foster places I was in, they wouldn't feed us so we'd sneak down to the kitchen at night and raid the place.'

'Why wouldn't they feed you?'

'The government gave them money to be foster-parents and they just took it all and left us with nothing. They'd put a lock on the food cupboard but I learned how to pick locks at a very young age.'

'What happened?' Rachael was astounded.

'You mean when they found the food gone? I'd get beaten because I was the oldest.'

'You stuck up for the others.'

'They were just kids.'

'And you were? What? Thirteen?'

'Yes.' Joe looked out the dark window, his back rigid. 'One night we ate all the food—even the onions—we were so hungry. I was beaten so badly I ended up in hospital. That's when Helen stepped in.'

'She cared about you.'

Joe turned and looked over his shoulder at Rachael. 'Yes. Took me years to trust her but she saved me from being made a ward of the State and put into a shelter. That's when I started to let myself open up a bit.'

'Did she foster you?'

'Not officially. In those days, you had to be married. She did what she could, though. When I was sixteen, she fixed up a small shack for us to live in, made sure we had food.'

'Who's we?'

'My brother—John.' Joe looked back out the window. 'He was a wild one but I managed to keep him out of the courts. I felt responsible for him.'

'What about Melina? Do you have other… siblings?'

'I had three half-brothers and two half-sisters. Two of my brothers died when they were toddlers.'

'Oh, Joe!' Tears sprang instantly to her eyes and she stood, desperate to go to him. He didn't turn around and she placed her hands on his shoulders, massaging gently.

'Melina's the only one I keep in contact with. I don't know where the others are.'

'And John?'

Joe shook his head and turned, dragging her into his arms. He rested her head on his chest, content to hold her for a moment. 'As I said, I worked for years, slowly getting better jobs until I had enough money to go overseas and lose myself. That trip to America was my freedom trip. It was proof to myself that I could do what I wanted, that I didn't have to follow rules set by anyone else. I could make my own life. My own rules. I planned to do a quick tour, then find somewhere I liked and settle down to work. Didn't know where or what but I was going to be free.' Joe raked his hand through his hair and pulled back to look at her. 'And then I met you.'

'And then you met me.'

'You were so different from the other girls I'd…dated.'

'Meaning I came from a family with money?'

He grimaced but didn't deny it. 'There was that, but that wasn't why I was attracted to you, Rach. In fact, your wealthy background was a turn-off, but for those three weeks we were together, I pushed away the outside world. There was no rich or poor, no right or wrong—just you and me.'

'And then I got too close.'

'You drive me insane, Rachael. My need for you drives me insane, and it scares me that I can't control myself.'

She bit her lip. 'I'm sorry, Joe. I don't mean to get too close.'

'I know. You've got closer than any other woman, and back then I was astounded at how astute you were. I can't believe I actually married you but I couldn't help myself. I wanted you so badly.'

'But as you've said, you could have just talked me into your bed. So why suggest we go down the ''Las Vegas impulsive marriage'' track?'

He grinned. 'Because it seemed like fun. And...' He paused and met her gaze. The smile disappeared from his face as he became serious once more. 'And because I felt you deserved better than to be just a roll in the hay.'

'Deserved better? Hmm. So you married me and then broke my heart.' She nodded. 'I think I would have preferred the hay. At least I wouldn't have built a world on false promises.'

'I deserved that.'

'Yes.'

Joe hung his head and exhaled harshly. It was time to face the past, to tell her the truth, and although he'd taught himself from a very early age to remain numb when anything personal came his way, he knew what he was going to say would hurt her.

'So why *did* you marry me?' She pulled back to really look at him.

'It's simple.' His gaze didn't waver as he spoke. 'I married you...because I loved you. Acknowledging that scared the life out of me but the thought of you with any other guy...' Joe clenched his hands into fists and shook his head. ‘I couldn’t stomach it.’

‘So why end it? If you loved me, if you wanted me with you…*why*? Help me to understand, Joe, because I don’t. I never have. One minute we were happy and the next—*bam*! You were ripping my heart into tiny little pieces and discarding them.’

‘You’re right. You deserve to know.’ He closed his eyes, his voice carefully controlled. ‘You remember that second morning? Of course you do,’ he muttered, answering his own question. ‘On that second morning I got a phone call from Helen.’

‘Helen?’

‘Yes.’ He opened his eyes. ‘She’d been trying for days to track me down through the tour organisers and finally succeeded.’ He paused, his gaze darkening as he remembered. ‘You were in the shower.’

It was all coming back to her now, as though it had happened only yesterday. She’d left their bed and had gone to shower, waiting for Joe to join her as he had every other time she’d left his side. That time he hadn’t. She’d told herself not to be concerned that he hadn’t come into the shower, yet when she’d returned to the bedroom, he'd already got dressed and had been sitting on the edge of the bed with his head in his hands.

'I asked you what was wrong.'

Joe cleared his throat and tried to get his thoughts back in gear. His mind had mentally stalled at the memory of Rachael in the shower, while his body just ached even more to have her with him beneath the spray once more. 'Yes.' He focused. 'You asked what was wrong and I…I turned my pain and my anger on you. I told you I didn't want to be married any more and that I'd only done it as a joke.'

Rachael's throat choked up at hearing those awful words again. 'I'm glad you remember it word for word.'

'Rachael.' Joe placed his hands on her shoulders, his touch almost begging her to understand. 'I'm *so* sorry.' His words were heartfelt and imploring. She could see the pain and anguish in his eyes and knew he finally spoke the truth about that fateful day. 'I knew I'd hurt you, but I had to.'

'Why?'

'Because John had been arrested for armed robbery and had hung himself in gaol.'

'What?' Rachael couldn't believe it. 'Joe. Joe.' She gathered him to her and wrapped her arms about his waist. 'Why didn't you just tell me? I could have been there for you. Helped you. I was your wife!'

Joe hesitated. 'I couldn't tell you *because* you were my wife.'

'What?' She stared up at him. 'That doesn't make any sense.'

'When Helen called and told me about John, it was like a slap in the face. The real world had intruded into our private slice of heaven, and I knew I couldn't drag you back into my real world. It was different from yours and I could never hope to give you the things you needed.'

'All I needed was you, Joe.'

'No. Rachael, we were young and I had no idea what I wanted to do with my life. You'd already been accepted to medical school and had a life planned—a life I would never have fitted into. I felt so worthless…and I knew with such clarity that in time—if we'd stayed together—you would come to realise I *was* worthless.'

'Joe.' She was appalled. 'How could you think that?'

'We were from different worlds. It didn't matter what I *wanted*, it would never happen. John was my brother—my *real* brother. Same mother, same father, and together we'd seen it all. Street fights, gangs, murders, and all by the time I was twelve. We'd been beaten, abused and shoved from one foster family to the next. I did things I'm not proud of and the memories will plague me for the rest of my life, regardless of how sorry I am for ever doing them. I hurt other people because it was the only way I knew to cope.'

Rachael didn't want to hear it but at the same time knew she needed to. She needed to be part of his pain, part of his past if anything was going to happen between them in the future.

'It brought everything home, Rachael. It made me realise I had to push you away. Right then, right there.'

'But we could have worked through things.'

'You would have been hurt worse if we'd tried to make a go of it.'

'I doubt that.'

'It would have been worse.'

'How can you say that?' she pushed.

'Because I know!' Joe ground out, and let her go so he could pace once more. 'Think about it, Rach. What would we have done when we returned to Australia? Where would we have lived? With your parents? In a nice, cushy town house they would have bought you? No. I'm a man who needs to be in control and I wouldn't have been in that situation. Besides, you had six years of medical school ahead of you and the only plan I had was to avoid Australia and become a professional beach bum.'

'And did you?'

Joe exhaled and shook his head. 'I tried to, but four months after John's death my best friend was attacked by a shark. We were surfing at night in Hawaii, and everything happened so fast. I managed to get him back to shore but he died soon after. I didn't know what to do. I didn't know how to save him. If I'd even known CPR, I could have done something. It was then I realised that if I'd been more like you, more dedicated to finding a path for my future, had done a first-aid course, I might have been able to save him or at least get him breathing again until help arrived.'

Her heart went out to him even more and she wanted to comfort the lost boy she saw before her. The number plate on his car now made perfect sense. So many things *had* happened when he was nineteen…life-changing things.

'You can't blame yourself for his death. Depending on how bad he was, he probably would have been in shock and it would have taken a medical professional to be there on the spot to save him.' Rachael paused. 'It wasn't your fault and neither was John's death.'

'It's taken me years to work through that, but you're right. Regardless, after the shark incident, I sat down and did some hard thinking. That's when I decided what to do with my life.'

'To become a doctor?'

'Yes. You'd given me the idea and the surfing trauma and John's senseless death cemented it.'

'I gave you the idea? Joe, I never once suggested you needed to change.'

'No, you didn't. You accepted me for me, just as you've done now. You've put your heart on the line once more, which shows just how much you trust me.'

'Love is nothing without trust, Joe.'

'You're right. You're so right.' Telling her about his past, about John, had lifted an enormous weight from his shoulders.

'Thank you, Joe. Thank you for opening up to me.' She touched the hair at his temple. 'I know how hard it was for you.'

'It was long overdue.'

'Still…thank you.' She wanted him to know she understood the enormity of what he'd revealed. 'But there's just one more thing I need to know.' She held her breath for a second before asking, 'Do you love me? Can you say it? Because I can see it, I can feel it, but I need the words, Joe.'

'I know, sweetheart.' He edged back and looked at her, his blue eyes gazing down into hers. 'I love you, Rachael. I always have and I always will.' He confirmed his words with a bone-melting kiss. When her knees gave way, he held her closer.

'I'm part of a package deal, Joe.'

'I know, and you already know how much I love Declan but I'm going to need help with the parenting thing.'

She smiled. 'My advice to you…just be yourself, Joe. I know how tough that is for you, to open up to someone, but don't shut him out or you'll risk him shutting you out.'

He nodded. 'What about the others?'

'Others?' She frowned and then her eyes widened as his words penetrated the fog beginning to cloud her mind. 'You want to have more children?'

'Only with you. The thought of you with anyone else churns me up. I want to take care of you, to protect you, to help you, to—'

'Smother me?' She laughed. 'Joe, we're a family. We work together to care, protect and help each other.'

'Rach, what I'm trying to say is I *need* you. I need you, I need Declan. I can't go on any more without knowing both of you are going to be there. You were right when you said love creates emotion. It does, and I've been fighting them all my life. I want to stop fighting and start enjoying.'

He took her wedding band from his pocket, and until that moment she'd forgotten he'd taken it off her finger. Then he got down on one knee.

'Joe? What are you doing?' She shook her head but was unable to remove the enormous smile on her face.

'I'm proposing.'

The door to the living room burst open as he spoke.

'You're proposing?' Declan said in a loud voice. Helen came rushing in.

'Did someone mention proposing?'

'Will you both keep quiet and let me do it?' Joe growled.

'Here? In the living room?' Rachael grinned. 'You old romantic, you.'

'Why not? At least it's better than the first time.'

'Where was the first time?' Declan wasn't going anywhere and neither, it seemed, was Helen.

'On a bus with rowdy people all around us. He made a big scene.'

'You loved it.'

She smiled. 'I did. At least we're not being jostled by the bus this time.'

'Are you going to keep quiet?'

'Yes, but only for a second so be quick. I'm already getting excited.'

'Does that mean you'll say yes?'

'Ask the question and find out.'

Joe sobered and took her left hand in his once more. 'Rachael Elizabeth Cusack…' His gaze was intense on hers. There was no one, nothing else—just the two of them. 'I love you, but first I want to ask your forgiveness. I hurt you badly and I never want to do that again. This time it'll be different, I promise. You are my soul mate and I was a fool to let you go. I'm not making the same mistakes again. I'm done running. I want you, I *need* you with me…for ever. Without you, I'm only half a person. Marry me, Rach—make me whole again. Please?'

Rachael closed her eyes for a second, letting go of the pain, hurt and humiliation she'd felt in the past. He'd asked her to forgive him, and she did. They would start their new life together with a clean slate.

She took a breath and looked down at him, her heart reflected in her eyes. 'I love you, Joe, so much it hurts when I'm not with you. Of course I'll marry you.'

Declan and Helen whooped for joy but Rachael and Joe continued to ignore them. Joe slowly placed her wedding ring back on her finger before standing to gather her close. He pressed his mouth to hers and felt the same sense of freedom he'd felt when she'd said yes all those years ago.

'Now, where do you want to get married this time, Dr Cusack?'

'Las Vegas.'

'Again? Are you sure?'

Rachael nodded. 'Declan will love it.'

Joe raised his eyebrows wolfishly. 'He's not the only one.' And bent his head to capture her lips in a kiss which would bind them together, as a family, for ever.

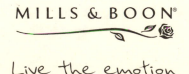

MEDICAL ROMANCE™

Large Print

February

HOLDING OUT FOR A HERO	Caroline Anderson
HIS UNEXPECTED CHILD	Josie Metcalfe
A FAMILY WORTH WAITING FOR	Margaret Barker
WHERE THE HEART IS	Kate Hardy

March

THE ITALIAN SURGEON	Meredith Webber
A NURSE'S SEARCH AND RESCUE	Alison Roberts
THE DOCTOR'S SECRET SON	Laura MacDonald
THE FOREVER ASSIGNMENT	Jennifer Taylor

April

BRIDE BY ACCIDENT	Marion Lennox
COMING HOME TO KATOOMBA	Lucy Clark
THE CONSULTANT'S SPECIAL RESCUE	Joanna Neil
THE HEROIC SURGEON	Olivia Gates

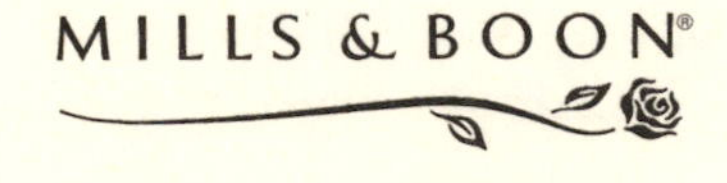

Live the emotion

1005 LP 2P P2 Medical